Isa

Isaac Asimov, world ma... Russia near Smolensk in 1920 and brought to the United States by his parents three years later. He grew up in Brooklyn where he went to grammar school and at the age of eight he gained his citizen papers. A remarkable memory helped him finish high school before he was sixteen. He then went on to Columbia University and resolved to become a chemist rather than follow the medical career his father had in mind for him. He graduated in chemistry and after a short spell in the Army he gained his doctorate in 1949 and qualified as an instructor in biochemistry at Boston University School of Medicine where he became Associate Professor in 1955, doing research in nucleic acid. Increasingly, however, the pressures of chemical research conflicted with his aspirations in the literary field, and in 1958 he retired to full-time authorship while retaining his connection with the University.

Asimov's fantastic career as a science fiction writer began in 1939 with the appearance of a short story, *Marooned Off Vesta*, in *Amazing Stories*. Thereafter he became a regular contributor to the leading SF magazines of the day including *Astounding*, *Astonishing Stories*, *Super Science Stories* and *Galaxy*. He won the Hugo Award four times and the Nebula Award once. With nearly five hundred books to his credit and several hundred articles, Asimov's output was prolific by any standards. Apart from his many world-famous science fiction works, Asimov also wrote highly successful detective mystery stories, a four-volume *History of North America*, a two-volume *Guide to the Bible*, a biographical dictionary, encyclopaedias, textbooks and an impressive list of books on many aspects of science, as well as two volumes of autobiography.

Isaac Asimov died in 1992 at the age of 72.

Voyager

ISAAC ASIMOV

I, Robot
Robots and Empire

Grafton

Voyager
An Imprint of HarperCollins*Publishers*
77–85 Fulham Palace Road,
Hammersmith, London W6 8JB

www.voyager-books.com

This omnibus edition published in 2005
by HarperCollins*Publishers*

ISBN 0 00 773419 0

Printed in Great Britain by
Clays Ltd, St Ives plc

I, Robot

The Three Laws of Robotics

1 – A robot may not injure a human being, or, through inaction, allow a human being to come to harm.

2 – A robot must obey the orders given it by human beings except where such orders would conflict with the First Law.

3 – A robot must protect its own existence as long as such protection does not conflict with the First or Second Law.

Handbook of Robotics,
56th Edition, 2058 A.D.

Introduction

I looked at my notes and I didn't like them. I'd spent three days at US Robots and might as well have spent them at home with the Encyclopedia Tellurica.

Susan Calvin had been born in the year 1982, they said, which made her seventy-five now. Everyone knew that. Appropriately enough, US Robot and Mechanical Men, Inc. was seventy-five also, since it had been in the year of Dr Calvin's birth that Lawrence Robertson had first taken out incorporation papers for what eventually became the strangest industrial giant in man's history. Well, everyone knew that, too.

At the age of twenty, Susan Calvin had been part of the particular Psycho-Math seminar at which Dr Alfred Lanning of US Robots had demonstrated the first mobile robot to be equipped with a voice. It was a large, clumsy unbeautiful robot, smelling of machine-oil and destined for the projected mines on Mercury. —But it could speak and make sense.

Susan said nothing at that seminar; took no part in the hectic discussion period that followed. She was a frosty girl, plain and colorless, who protected herself against a world she disliked by a mask-like expression and hypertrophy of intellect. But as she watched and listened, she felt the stirrings of a cold enthusiasm.

She obtained her bachelor's degree at Columbia in 2003 and began graduate work in cybernetics.

All that had been done in the mid-twentieth century on 'calculating machines' had been upset by Robertson and his positronic brain-paths. The miles of relays and photocells had given way to the spongy globe of plantinumiridium about the size of a human brain.

She learned to calculate the parameters necessary to fix the possible variables within the 'positronic brain', to construct 'brains' on paper such that the responses to given stimuli could be accurately predicted.

In 2008, she obtained her Ph.D. and joined United States Robots as a 'Robopsychologist', becoming the first great practitioner of a new science. Lawrence Robertson was still president of the corporation; Alfred Lanning had become director of research.

For fifty years, she watched the direction of human progress change – and leap ahead.

Now she was retiring – as much as she ever could. At least, she was allowing someone else's name to be inset upon the door of her old office.

That, essentially, was what I had. I had a long list of her published papers, of the patents in her name; I had the chronological details of her promotions— In short I had her professional 'vita' in full detail.

But that wasn't what I wanted.

I needed more than that for my feature articles for Interplanetary Press. Much more.

I told her so.

'Dr Calvin,' I said, as lushly as possible, 'in the mind of the public you and US Robots are identical. Your retirement will end an era and—'

'You want the human-interest angle?' She didn't smile at me. I don't think she ever smiles. But her eyes were sharp, though not angry. I felt her glance slide through me and out my occiput and I knew that I was uncommonly transparent to her; that everybody was.

But I said, 'That's right.'

'Human interest out of Robots? A contradiction.'

'No, doctor. Out of you.'

'Well, I've been called a robot myself. Surely, they've told you I'm not human.'

They had, but there was no point in saying so.

She got up from her chair. She wasn't tall and she looked frail. I followed her to the window and we looked out.

The offices and factories of US Robots were a small city; spaced and planned. It was flattened out like an aerial photograph.

'When I first came here,' she said, 'I had a little room in a building right about there where the fire-house is now.' She pointed. 'It was torn down before you were born. I shared the room with three others. I had half a desk. We built our robots all in one building. Output – three a week. Now look at us.'

'Fifty years,' I hackneyed, 'is a long time.'

'Not when you're looking back at them,' she said. 'You wonder how they vanished so quickly.'

She went back to her desk and sat down. She didn't need expression on her face to look sad, somehow.

'How old are you?' she wanted to know.

'Thirty-two,' I said.

'Then you don't remember a world without robots. There was a time when humanity faced the universe alone and without a friend. Now he has creatures to help him; stronger creatures than himself, more faithful, more useful, and absolutely devoted to him. Mankind is no longer alone. Have you ever thought of it that way?'

'I'm afraid I haven't. May I quote you?'

'You may. To you, a robot is a robot. Gears and metal, electricity and positrons. —Mind and iron! Human-made! If necessary, human-destroyed! But you haven't worked with them, so you don't know them. They're a cleaner, better breed than we are.'

I tried to nudge her gently with words, 'We'd like to hear some of the things you could tell us; get your views on robots. The Interplanetary Press reaches the entire Solar System. Potential audience is three billion, Dr Calvin. They ought to know what you could tell them on robots.'

It wasn't necessary to nudge. She didn't hear me, but she was moving in the right direction.

'They might have known from the start. We sold robots for Earth-use then – before my time it was, even. Of course, that was when robots could not talk. Afterward, they became more human and opposition began. The labor unions, of course, naturally opposed robot competition for human jobs, and various segments of religious opinion had their superstitious objections. It was all quite ridiculous and quite useless. And yet there it was.'

I was taking it down verbatim on my pocket-recorder, trying not to show the knuckle-motions of my hand. If your practice a bit, you can get to the point where you can record accurately without taking the little gadget out of your pocket.

'Take the case of Robbie,' she said. 'I never knew him. He was dismantled the year before I joined the company – hopelessly out-of-date. But I saw the little girl in the museum—'

She stopped, but I didn't say anything. I let her eyes mist up and her mind travel back. She had lots of time to cover.

'I heard about it later, and when they called us blasphemers and demon-creators, I always thought of him. Robbie was a non-vocal robot. He couldn't speak. He was made and sold in 1996. Those were the days before extreme specialization, so he was sold as a nursemaid—'

'As a what?'

'As a nursemaid—'

1
Robbie

'Ninety-eight – ninety-nine – *one hundred*.' Gloria withdrew her chubby little forearm from before her eyes and stood for a moment, wrinkling her nose and blinking in the sunlight. Then, trying to watch in all directions at once, she withdrew a few cautious steps from the tree against which she had been leaning.

She craned her neck to investigate the possibilities of a clump of bushes to the right and then withdrew farther to obtain a better angle for viewing its dark recesses. The quiet was profound except for the incessant buzzing of insects and the occasional chirrup of some hardy bird, braving the midday sun.

Gloria pouted, 'I bet he went inside the house, and I've told him a million times that that's not fair.'

With tiny lips pressed together tightly and a severe frown crinkling her forehead, she moved determinedly toward the two-story building up past the driveway.

Too late she heard the rustling sound behind her, followed by the distinctive and rhythmic clump-clump of Robbie's metal feet. She whirled about to see her triumphing companion emerge from hiding and make for the home-tree at full speed.

Gloria shrieked in dismay. 'Wait, Robbie! That wasn't fair, Robbie! You promised you wouldn't run until I found you.' Her little feet could make no headway at all against Robbie's giant strides. Then, within ten feet of the goal, Robbie's pace slowed suddenly to the merest of crawls, and Gloria, with one final burst of wild speed, dashed pantingly past him to touch the welcome bark of home-tree first.

Gleefully, she turned on the faithful Robbie, and with the basest of ingratitude, rewarded him for his sacrifice by taunting him cruelly for a lack of running ability.

'Robbie can't run!' she shouted at the top of her eight-year-old voice. 'I can beat him any day. I can beat him any day.' She chanted the words in a shrill rhythm.

Robbie didn't answer, of course – not in words. He pantomimed running, instead, inching away until Gloria found herself running after him as he dodged her narrowly, forcing her to veer in helpless circles, little arms outstretched and fanning at the air.

'Robbie,' she squealed, 'stand still!' —And the laughter was forced out of her in breathless jerks.

—Until he turned suddenly and caught her up, whirling her round, so that for her the world fell away for a moment with a blue emptiness beneath, and green trees stretching hungrily downward towards the void. Then she was down in the grass again, leaning against Robbie's leg and still holding a hard, metal finger.

After a while, her breath returned. She pushed uselessly at her disheveled hair in vague imitation of one of her mother's gestures and twisted to see if her dress were torn.

She slapped her hand against Robbie's torso, 'Bad boy! I'll spank you!'

And Robbie cowered, holding his hands over his face so that she had to add, 'No, I won't, Robbie. I won't spank you. But anyway, it's my turn to hide now because you've got longer legs and you promised not to run till I found you.'

Robbie nodded his head – a small parallelepiped with rounded edges and corners attached to a similar but much larger parallelepiped that served as torso by means of a short, flexible stalk – and obediently faced the tree. A thin, metal film descended over his glowing eyes and from within his body came a steady, resonant ticking.

'Don't peek now – and don't skip any numbers,' warned Gloria, and scurried for cover.

With unvarying regularity, seconds were ticked off, and at the hundredth, up went the eyelids, and the glowing red of Robbie's eyes swept the prospect. They rested for a moment on a bit of colorful gingham that protruded from behind a boulder. He advanced a few steps and convinced himself that it was Gloria who squatted behind it.

Slowly, remaining always between Gloria and home-tree, he advanced on the hiding place, and when Gloria was plainly in sight and could no longer even theorize to herself that she was not seen, he extended one arm toward her, slapping the other against his leg so that it rang again. Gloria emerged sulkily.

'You peeked!' she exclaimed, with gross unfairness. 'Besides I'm tired of playing hide-and-seek. I want a ride.'

But Robbie was hurt at the unjust accusation, so he seated himself carefully and shook his head ponderously from side to side.

Gloria changed her tone to one of gentle coaxing immediately, 'Come on, Robbie. I didn't mean it about the peeking. Give me a ride.'

Robbie was not to be won over so easily, though. He gazed stubbornly at the sky, and shook his head even more emphatically.

'Please, Robbie, please give me a ride.' She encircled his neck with rosy arms and hugged tightly. Then, changing moods in a moment, she moved away. 'If you don't, I'm going to cry,' and her face twisted appallingly in preparation.

Hard-hearted Robbie paid scant attention to this dreadful possibility, and shook his head a third time. Gloria found it necessary to play her trump card.

'If you don't,' she exclaimed warmly, 'I won't tell you any more stories, that's all. Not one—'

Robbie gave in immediately and unconditionally before this ultimatum, nodding his head vigorously until the metal of his neck hummed. Carefully, he raised the little girl and place her on his broad, flat shoulders.

Gloria's threatened tears vanished immediately and she crowed with delight. Robbie's metal skin, kept at a constant temperature of seventy by the high resistance coils within, felt nice and comfortable, while the beautifully loud sound her heels made as they bumped rhythmically against his chest was enchanting.

'You're an air-coaster, Robbie, you're a big, silver air-coaster. Hold out your arms straight. —You *got* to, Robbie, if you're going to be an air-coaster.'

The logic was irrefutable. Robbie's arms were wings catching the air currents and he was a silver 'coaster.

Gloria twisted the robot's head and leaned to the right. He banked sharply. Gloria equipped the 'coaster with a motor that went 'Br-r-r' and then with weapons that went 'Powie' and 'Sh-sh-shshsh.' Pirates were giving chase and the ship's blasters were coming into play. The pirates dropped in a steady rain.

'Got another one. —Two more!' she cried.

Then 'Faster, men,' Gloria said pompously, 'we're running out of ammunition.' She aimed over her shoulder with undaunted courage and Robbie was a blunt-nosed spaceship zooming through the void at maximum acceleration.

Clear across the field he sped, to the patch of tall grass on the other side, where he stopped with a suddenness that evoked a shriek from his flushed rider, and then tumbled her on to the soft, green carpet.

Gloria gasped and panted, and gave voice to intermittent whispered exclamations of 'That was *nice!*'

Robbie waited until she had caught her breath and then pulled gently at a lock of hair.

'You want something?' said Gloria, eyes wide in an apparently artless complexity that fooled her huge 'nursemaid' not at all. He pulled the curl harder.

'Oh, I know. You want a story.'

Robbie nodded rapidly.

'Which one?'

Robbie made a semi-circle in the air with one finger.

The little girl protested, '*Again?* I've told you Cinderella a million times. Aren't you tired of it? —It's for babies.'

Another semi-circle.

'Oh, hell,' Gloria composed herself, ran over the details of the tale in her mind (together with her own elaborations, of which she had several) and began:

'Are you ready? Well – once upon a time there was a beautiful little girl whose name was Ella. And she had a terribly cruel step-mother and two very ugly and *very* cruel step-sisters and—'

Gloria was reaching the very climax of the tale – midnight was striking and everything was changing back to the shabby originals lickety-split, while Robbie listened tensely with burning eyes – when the interruption came.

'Gloria!'

It was the high-pitched sound of a woman who has been calling not once, but several times; and had the nervous tone of one in whom anxiety was beginning to overcome impatience.

'Mamma's calling me,' said Gloria, not quite happily. 'You'd better carry me back to the house, Robbie.'

Robbie obeyed with alacrity for somehow there was that in him which judged it best to obey Mrs Weston, without as much as a scrap of hesitation. Gloria's father was rarely home in the daytime except on Sunday – today, for instance – and when he was, he proved a genial and understanding person. Gloria's mother, however, was a source of uneasiness to Robbie and there was always the impulse to sneak away from her sight.

Mrs Weston caught sight of them the minute they rose above the masking tufts of long grass and retired inside the house to wait.

'I've shouted myself hoarse, Gloria,' she said, severely. 'Where were you?'

'I was with Robbie,' quavered Gloria. 'I was telling him Cinderella, and I forgot it was dinner-time.'

'Well, it's a pity Robbie forgot, too.' Then, as if that reminded her of the robot's presence, she whirled upon him. 'You may go, Robbie. She doesn't need you now.' Then, brutally, 'And don't come back till I call you.'

Robbie turned to go, but hesitated as Gloria cried out in his defense, 'Wait, Mamma, you got to let him stay. I didn't finish Cinderella for him. I said I would tell him Cinderella and I'm not finished.'

'Gloria!'

'Honest and truly, Mamma, he'll stay so quiet, you won't even know he's here. He can sit on the chair in the corner, and he won't say a word – I mean he won't *do* anything. Will you, Robbie?'

Robbie, appealed to, nodded his massive head up and down once.

'Gloria, if you don't stop this at once, you shan't see Robbie for a whole week.'

The girl's eyes fell, 'All right! But Cinderella is his favorite story and I didn't finish it. —And he likes it so much.'

The robot left with a disconsolate step and Gloria choked back a sob.

George Weston was comfortable. It was a habit of his to be comfortable on Sunday afternoons. A good, hearty dinner below the hatches; a nice, soft, dilapidated couch on which to sprawl; a copy of the *Times*; slippered feet and shirtless chest – how could anyone *help* but be comfortable?

He wasn't pleased, therefore, when his wife walked in. After ten years of married life, he still was so unutterably foolish as to love her, and there was no question that he was always glad to see her – still Sunday afternoons just after dinner were sacred to him and his idea of solid comfort was to be left in utter solitude for two or three hours. Consequently, he fixed his eye firmly upon the latest reports of the Lefebre–Yoshida expedition to Mars (this one was to take off from Lunar Base and might actually succeed) and pretended she wasn't there.

Mrs Weston waited patiently for two minutes, then impatiently for two more, and finally broke the silence.

'George!'

'Hmpph?'

'George, I say! *Will* you put down that paper and look at me?'

The paper rustled to the floor and Weston turned a weary face toward his wife, 'What is it, dear?'

'You know what it is, George. It's Gloria and that terrible machine.'

'What terrible machine?'

'Now don't pretend you don't know what I'm talking about. It's that robot Gloria calls Robbie. He doesn't leave her for a moment.'

'Well, why should he? He's not supposed to. And he certainly isn't a terrible machine. He's the best darn robot money can buy and I'm damned sure he set me back half a year's income. He's worth it, though – darn sight cleverer than half my office staff.'

He made a move to pick up the paper again, but his wife was quicker and snatched it away.

'You listen to *me*, George. I won't have my daughter entrusted to a machine – and I don't care how clever it is. It has no soul, and no one knows what it may be thinking. A child just isn't *made* to be guarded by a thing of metal.'

Weston frowned, 'When did you decide this? He's been with Gloria two years now and I haven't seen you worry till now.'

'It was different at first. It was a novelty; it took a load off me, and – and it was a fashionable thing to do. But now I don't know. The neighbors—'

'Well, what have the neighbors to do with it? Now, look. A robot is infinitely more to be trusted than a human nursemaid. Robbie was constructed for only one purpose really – to be the companion of a little child. His entire "mentality" has been created for the purpose. He just can't help being faithful and loving and kind. He's a machine – *made so*. That's more than you can say for humans.'

'But something might go wrong. Some – some —' Mrs Weston was a bit hazy about the insides of a robot, 'some little jigger will come loose and the awful thing will go berserk and – and—' She couldn't bring herself to complete the quite obvious thought.

'Nonsense,' Weston denied, with an involuntary nervous shiver. 'That's completely ridiculous. We had a long discussion at the time we bought Robbie about the First Law of Robotics. You *know* that it is impossible for a robot to harm a human being; that long before enough can go wrong to alter that First Law, a robot would be completely inoperable. It's a mathematical impossibility. Besides I have an engineer from US Robots here twice a year to give the poor gadget a complete overhaul. Why, there's no more chance of anything at all going wrong with Robbie than there is of you or I suddenly going looney – considerably less, in fact. Besides, how are you going to take him away from Gloria?'

He made another futile stab at the paper and his wife tossed it angrily into the next room.

'That's just it, George! She won't play with anyone else. There are dozens of little boys and girls that she should make friends with, but she won't. She won't go *near* them unless I make her. That's no way for a little girl to grow up. You want her to be normal, don't you? You want her to be able to take her part in society.'

'You're jumping at shadows, Grace. Pretend Robbie's a dog. I've seen hundreds of children who would rather have their dog than their father.'

'A dog is different, George. We *must* get rid of that horrible thing. You can sell it back to the company. I've asked, and you can.'

'You've *asked*? Now look here, Grace, let's not go off the deep end. We're keeping the robot until Gloria is older and I don't want the subject brought up again.' And with that he walked out of the room in a huff.

Mrs Weston met her husband at the door two evenings later. 'You'll have to listen to this, George. There's bad feeling in the village.'

'About what?' asked Weston. He stepped into the washroom and drowned out any possible answer by the splash of water.

Mrs Weston waited. She said, 'About Robbie.'

Weston stepped out, towel in hand, face red and angry. 'What are you talking about?'

'Oh, it's been building up and building up. I've tried to close my eyes to to it, but I'm not going to any more. Most of the villagers consider Robbie dangerous. Children aren't allowed to go near our place in the evenings.'

'We trust *our* child with the thing.'

'Well, people aren't reasonable about these things.'

'Then to hell with them.'

'Saying that doesn't solve the problem. I've got to do my shopping down there. I've got to meet them every day. And it's even worse in the city these days when it comes to robots. New York has just passed an ordinance keeping all robots off the streets between sunset and sunrise.'

'All right, but they can't stop us from keeping a robot in our home. —Grace, this is one of your campaigns. I recognize it. But it's no use. The answer is still, no! We're keeping Robbie!'

And yet he loved his wife – and what was worse, his wife knew it. George Weston, after all, was only a man – poor thing – and his wife made full use of every device which a clumsier and more scrupulous sex has learned, with reason and futility, to fear.

Ten times in the ensuing week, he cried, 'Robbie stays – and that's *final*!' and each time it was weaker and accompanied by a louder and more agonized groan.

Came the day at last, when Weston approached his daughter guiltily and suggested a 'beautiful' visivox show in the village.

Gloria clapped her hands happily, 'Can Robbie go?'

'No, dear,' he said, and winced at the sound of his voice, 'they won't allow robots at the visivox – but you can tell him all about it when you get home.' He stumbled all over the last few words and looked away.

Gloria came back from town bubbling over with enthusiasm, for the visivox had been a gorgeous spectacle indeed.

She waited for her father to maneuver the jet-car into the sunken garage. 'Wait till I tell Robbie, Daddy. He would have liked it like anything. —Especially when Francis Fran was backing away so-o-o quietly, and backed right into one of the Leopard-Men and had to run.' She laughed again. 'Daddy, are there really Leopard-Men on the Moon?'

'Probably not,' said Weston absently. 'It's just funny make-believe.' He couldn't take much longer with the car. He'd have to face it.

Gloria ran across the lawn. 'Robbie. —Robbie!'

Then she stopped suddenly at the sight of a beautiful collie which regarded her out of serious brown eyes as it wagged its tail on the porch.

'Oh, what a nice dog!' Gloria climbed the steps, approached cautiously and patted it. 'Is it for me, Daddy?'

Her mother had joined them. 'Yes, it is, Gloria. Isn't it nice – soft and furry. It's very gentle. It *likes* little girls.'

'Can he play games?'

'Surely. He can do any number of tricks. Would you like to see some?'

'Right away. I want Robbie to see him, too. —*Robbie!*' She stopped, uncertainly, and frowned, 'I'll bet he's just staying in his room because he's mad at me for not taking him to the visivox. You'll have to explain to him, Daddy. He might not believe me, but he knows if you say it, it's so.'

Weston's lips grew tighter. He looked toward his wife but could not catch her eye.

Gloria turned precipitously and ran down the basement steps, shouting as she went, 'Robbie — Come and see what Daddy and Mamma brought me. They brought me a dog, Robbie.'

In a minute she had returned, a frightened little girl. 'Mamma, Robbie isn't in his room. Where is he?' There was no answer and George Weston coughed and was suddenly extremely interested in an aimlessly drifting cloud. Gloria's voice quavered on the verge of tears, 'Where's Robbie, Mamma?'

Mrs Weston sat down and drew her daughter gently to her, 'Don't feel bad, Gloria. Robbie has gone away, I think.'

'Gone *away*? Where? Where's he gone away, Mamma?'

'No one knows, darling. He just walked away. We've looked and we've looked and we've looked for him, but we can't find him.'

'You mean he'll never come back again?' Her eyes were round with horror.

'We may find him soon. We'll keep looking for him. And meanwhile you can play with your nice new doggie. Look at him! His name is Lightning and he can—'

But Gloria's eyelids had overflowed, 'I don't want the nasty dog – I want Robbie. I want you to find me Robbie.' Her feelings became too deep for words, and she spluttered into a shrill wail.

Mrs Weston glanced at her husband for help, but he merely shuffled his feet morosely and did not withdraw his ardent stare from the heavens, so she bent to the task of consolation, 'Why do you cry, Gloria? Robbie was only a machine, just a nasty old machine. He wasn't alive at all.'

'He was *not* no machine!' screamed Gloria, fiercely and ungrammatically. 'He was a *person* just like you and me and he was my *friend*. I want him back. Oh, Mamma, I want him back.'

Her mother groaned in defeat and left Gloria to her sorrow.

'Let her have her cry out,' she told her husband. 'Childish griefs are never lasting. In a few days, she'll forget that awful robot ever existed.'

But time proved Mrs Weston a bit too optimistic. To be sure, Gloria ceased crying, but she ceased smiling, too, and the passing days found her ever more silent and shadowy. Gradually, her attitude of passive unhappiness wore Mrs Weston down and all that kept her from yielding was the impossibility of admitting defeat to her husband.

Then, one evening, she flounced into the living room, sat down, folded her arms and looked boiling mad.

Her husband stretched his neck in order to see her over his newspaper, 'What now, Grace?'

'It's that child, George. I've had to send back the dog today. Gloria positively couldn't stand the sight of him, she said. She's driving me into a nervous breakdown.'

Weston laid down the paper and a hopeful gleam entered his eye, 'Maybe— Maybe we ought to get Robbie back. It might be done, you know. I can get in touch with—'

'No!' she replied, grimly. 'I won't hear of it. We're not giving up that easily. My child shall *not* be brought up by a robot if it takes years to break her of it.'

Weston picked up his paper again with a disappointed air. 'A year of this will have me prematurely gray.'

'You're a big help, George,' was the frigid answer. 'What Gloria needs is a change of environment. Of course she can't forget Robbie here. How can she when every tree and rock reminds her of him? It is really the *silliest* situation I have ever heard of. Imagine a child pining away for the loss of a robot.'

'Well, stick to the point. What's the change in environment you're planning?'

'We're going to take her to New York.'

'The city! In August! Say, do you know what New York is like in August? It's unbearable.'

'Millions do bear it.'

'They don't have a place like this to go to. If they didn't have to stay in New York, they wouldn't.'

'Well, *we* have to. I say we're leaving now – or as soon as we can make the arrangements. In the city, Gloria will find sufficient interests and sufficient friends to perk her up and make her forget that machine.'

'Oh, Lord,' groaned the lesser half, 'those frying pavements!'

'We have to,' was the unshaken response. 'Gloria has lost

five pounds in the last month and my little girl's health is more important to me than your comfort.'

'It's a pity you didn't think of your little girl's health before you deprived her of her pet robot,' he muttered – but to himself.

Gloria displayed immediate signs of improvement when told of the impending trip to the city. She spoke little of it, but when she did, it was always with lively anticipation. Again, she began to smile and to eat with something of her former appetite.

Mrs Weston hugged herself for joy and lost no opportunity to triumph over her still skeptical husband.

'You see, George, she helps with the packing like a little angel, and chatters away as if she hadn't a care in the world. It's just as I told you – all we need do is substitute other interests.'

'Hmpph,' was the skeptical response, 'I hope so.'

Preliminaries were gone through quickly. Arrangements were made for the preparation of their city home and a couple were engaged as housekeepers for the country home. When the day of the trip finally did come, Gloria was all but her old self again, and no mention of Robbie passed her lips at all.

In high good-humor the family took a taxi-gyro to the airport (Weston would have preferred using his own private 'gyro, but it was only a two-seater with no room for baggage) and entered the waiting liner.

'Come, Gloria,' called Mrs Weston. 'I've saved you a seat near the window so you can watch the scenery.'

Gloria trotted down the aisle cheerily, flattened her nose into a white oval against the thick clear glass, and watched with an intentness that increased as the sudden coughing of the motor drifted backward into the interior. She was too young to be frightened when the ground dropped away as if let through a trap-door and she herself suddenly became twice her usual weight, but not too young to be mightily interested. It wasn't until the ground had changed into a tiny patchwork quilt that she withdrew her nose, and faced her mother again.

'Will we soon be in the city, Mamma?' she asked, rubbing her chilled nose, and watching with interest as the patch of moisture which her breath had formed on the pane shrank slowly and vanished.

'In about half an hour, dear.' Then, with just the faintest trace of anxiety, 'Aren't you glad we're going? Don't you think you'll very happy in the city with all the buildings and people and things to see. We'll go to the visivox every day and see shows and go to the circus and the beach and—'

'Yes, Mamma,' was Gloria's unenthusiastic rejoinder. The liner passed over a bank of clouds at that moment, and Gloria was instantly absorbed in the unusual spectacle of clouds underneath one. Then they were over clear sky again, and she turned to her mother with a sudden mysterious air of secret knowledge.

'*I* know why we're going to the city, Mamma.'

'Do you?' Mrs Weston was puzzled. 'Why, dear?'

'You didn't tell me because you wanted it to be a surprise, but *I* know.' For a moment, she was lost in admiration at her own acute penetration, and then she laughed gaily. 'We're going to New York so we can find Robbie, aren't we? —With detectives.'

The statement caught George Weston in the middle of a drink of water, with disastrous results. There was a sort of strangled gasp, a geyser of water, and then a bout of choking coughs. When all was over, he stood there, a red-faced, waterdrenched and very, very annoyed person.

Mrs Weston maintained her composure, but when Gloria

repeated her question in a more anxious tone of voice, she
found her temper rather bent.

'Maybe,' she retorted, tartly. 'Now sit and be still, for
Heaven's sake.'

New York City, 1998 A.D., was a paradise for the sightseer
more than ever in its history. Gloria's parents realized this
and made the most of it.

On direct orders from his wife, George Weston arranged
to have his business take care of itself for a month or so,
in order to be free to spend the time in what he termed
'dissipating Gloria to the verge of ruin'. Like everything else
Weston did, this was gone about in an efficient, thorough,
and businesslike way. Before the month had passed, nothing
that could be done had not been done.

She was taken to the top of the half-mile-tall Roosevelt
Building, to gaze down in awe upon the jagged panorama
of rooftops that blended far off in the fields of Long Island
and the flatlands of New Jersey. They visited the zoos where
Gloria stared in delicious fright at the 'real live lion' (rather
disappointed that the keepers fed him raw steaks, instead of
human beings, as she had expected), and asked insistently
and peremptorily to see 'the whale'.

The various museums came in for their share of attention, together with the parks and the beaches and the
aquarium.

She was taken halfway up the Hudson in an excursion
steamer fitted out in the archaism of the mad Twenties. She
travelled into the stratosphere on an exhibition trip, where
the sky turned deep purple and the stars came out and the
misty earth below looked like a huge concave bowl. Down
under the waters of the Long Island Sound she was taken in
a glass-walled sub-sea vessel, where in a green and wavering
world, quaint and curious sea-things ogled her and wiggled
suddenly away.

On a more prosaic level, Mrs Weston took her to the department stores where she could revel in another type of fairyland.

In fact, when the month had nearly sped, the Westons were convinced that everything conceivable had been done to take Gloria's mind once and for all off the departed Robbie – but they were not quite sure they had succeeded.

The fact remained that wherever Gloria went, she displayed the most absorbed and concentrated interest in such robots as happened to be present. No matter how exciting the spectacle before her, nor how novel to her girlish eyes, she turned away instantly if the corner of her eye caught a glimpse of metallic movement.

Mrs Weston went out of her way to keep Gloria away from all robots.

And the matter was finally climaxed in the episode at the Museum of Science and Industry. The Museum had announced a special 'Children's program' in which exhibits of scientific witchery scaled down to the child mind were to be shown. The Westons, of course, placed it upon their list of 'absolutely'.

It was while the Westons were standing totally absorbed in the exploits of a powerful electro-magnet that Mrs Weston suddenly became aware of the fact that Gloria was no longer with her. Initial panic gave way to calm decision and, enlisting the aid of three attendants, a careful search was begun.

Gloria, of course, was not one to wander aimlessly, however. For her age, she was an unusually determined and purposeful girl, quite full of the maternal genes in that respect. She had seen a huge sign on the third floor, which had said, 'This Way to the Talking Robot.' Having spelled it out to herself and having noticed that her parents did not seem to wish to move in the proper direction, she did the obvious thing. Waiting for an opportune moment of parental distraction, she calmly disengaged herself and followed the sign.

The Talking Robot was a *tour de force*, a thoroughly impractical device, possessing publicity value only. Once an hour, an escorted group stood before it and asked questions of the robot engineer in charge in careful whispers. Those the engineer decided were suitable for the robot's circuits were transmitted to the Talking Robot.

It was rather dull. It may be nice to know that the square of fourteen is 196, that the temperature at the moment is seventy-two degrees Fahrenheit, and the air-pressure 30.02 inches of mercury, that the atomic weight of sodium is twenty-three, but one doesn't really need a robot for that. One especially does not need an unwieldy, totally immobile mass of wires and coils spreading over twenty-five square yards.

Few people bothered to return for a second helping, but one girl in her middle teens sat quietly on a bench waiting for a third. She was the only one in the room when Gloria entered.

Gloria did not look at her. To her at the moment, another human being was but an inconsiderable item. She saved her attention for this large thing with the wheels. For a moment, she hesitated in dismay. It didn't look like any robot she had ever seen.

Cautiously and doubtfully she raised her treble voice, 'Please, Mr Robot, sir, are you the Talking Robot, sir?' She wasn't sure, but it seemed to her that a robot that actually talked was worth a great deal of politeness.

(The girl in her mid-teens allowed a look of intense concentration to cross her thin, plain face. She whipped out a small notebook and began writing in rapid pot-hooks.)

There was an oily whir of gears and a mechanically-timbered voice boomed out in words that lacked accent and intonation, 'I – am – the – robot – that – talks.'

Gloria stared at it ruefully. It *did* talk, but the sound came from inside somewheres. There was no *face* to talk to. She said, 'Can you help me, Mr Robot, sir?'

The Talking Robot was designed to answer questions, and only such questions as it could answer had ever been put to it. It was quite confident of its ability, therefore, 'I – can – help – you.'

'Thank you, Mr Robot, sir. Have you seen Robbie?'

'Who – is Robbie?'

'He's a robot, Mr Robot, sir.' She stretched to tip-toes. 'He's about so high, Mr Robot, sir, only higher, and he's very nice. He's got a head, you know. I mean you haven't, but he has, Mr Robot, sir.'

The Talking Robot had been left behind, 'A – robot?'

'Yes, Mr Robot, sir. A robot just like you, except he can't talk, of course, and – looks like a real person.'

'A – robot – like – me?'

'Yes, Mr Robot, sir.'

To which the Talking Robot's only response was an erratic splutter and an occasional incoherent sound. The radical generalization offered it, i.e. its existence, not as a particular object, but as a member of a general group, was too much for it. Loyally, it tried to encompass the concept and half a dozen coils burnt out. Little warning signals were buzzing.

(The girl in her mid-teens left at that point. She had enough for her Physics–I paper on 'Practical Aspects of Robotics'. This paper was Susan Calvin's first of many on the subject.)

Gloria stood waiting, with carefully concealed impatience, for the machine's answer when she heard the cry behind her of 'There she is,' and recognized that cry as her mother's.

'What are you doing here, you bad girl?' cried Mrs Weston, anxiety dissolving at once into anger. 'Do you know you frightened your mamma and daddy almost to death? Why did you run away?'

The robot engineer had also dashed in, tearing his hair, and demanding who of the gathering crowd had tampered with the machine. 'Can't anybody read signs?' he yelled. 'You're not allowed in here without an attendant.'

Gloria raised her grieved voice over the din, 'I only came to see the Talking Robot, Mamma. I thought he might know where Robbie was because they're both robots.' And then, as the thought of Robbie was suddenly brought forcefully home to her, she burst into a sudden storm of tears, 'And I *got* to find Robbie, Mamma. I *got* to.'

Mrs Weston strangled a cry, and said, 'Oh, good Heavens. Come home, George. This is more than I can stand.'

That evening, George Weston left for several hours, and the next morning, he approached his wife with something that looked suspiciously like smug complacence.

'I've got an idea, Grace.'

'About what?' was the gloomy, uninterested query.

'About Gloria.'

'You're not going to suggest buying back that robot?'

'No, of course not.'

'Then go ahead. I might as well listen to you. Nothing *I've* done seems to have done any good.'

'All right. Here's what I've been thinking. The whole trouble with Gloria is that she thinks of Robbie as a *person* and not as a *machine*. Naturally, she can't forget him. Now if we managed to convince her that Robbie was nothing more than a mess of steel and copper in the form of sheets and wires with electricity its juice of life, how long would her longings last. It's the psychological attack, if you see my point.'

'How do you plan to do it?'

'Simple. Where do you suppose I went last night? I persuaded Robertson of US Robots and Mechanical Men, Inc. to arrange for a complete tour of his premises tomorrow. The three of us will go, and by the time we're through, Gloria will have it drilled into her that a robot is *not* alive.'

Mrs Weston's eyes widened gradually and something glinted in her eyes that was quite like sudden admiration, 'Why, George, that's a *good* idea.'

And George Weston's vest buttons strained. 'Only kind I have,' he said.

Mr Struthers was a conscientious General Manager and naturally inclined to be a bit talkative. The combination, therefore, resulted in a tour that was fully explained, perhaps even over-abundantly explained, at every step. However, Mrs Weston was not bored. Indeed, she stopped him several times and begged him to repeat his statements in simpler language so that Gloria might understand. Under the influence of this appreciation of his narrative powers, Mr Struthers expanded genially and became ever more communicative, if possible.

George Weston, himself, showed a gathering impatience.

'Pardon me, Struthers,' he said, breaking into the middle of a lecture on the photo-electric cell, 'haven't you a section of the factory where only robot labor is employed?'

'Eh? Oh, yes! Yes, indeed!' He smiled at Mrs Weston. 'A vicious circle in a way, robots creating more robots. Of course, we are not making a general practice out of it. For one thing, the unions would never let us. But we can turn out a very few robots using robot labor exclusively, merely as a sort of scientific experiment. You see,' he tapped his pince-nez into one palm argumentatively, 'what the labor unions don't realize – and I say this as a man who has always been very sympathetic with the labor movement in general – is that the advent of the robot, while involving some dislocation to begin with, will, inevitably—'

'Yes, Struthers,' said Weston, 'but about that section of the factory you speak of – may we see it? It would be very interesting, I'm sure.'

'Yes! Yes, of course!' Mr Struthers replaced his pince-nez in one conclusive movement and gave vent to a soft cough of discomfiture. 'Follow me, please.'

He was comparatively quiet while leading the three through a long corridor and down a flight of stairs. Then, when they had entered a large well-lit room that buzzed with metallic activity, the sluices opened and the flood of explanation poured forth again.

'There you are!' he said with pride in his voice. 'Robots only! Five men act as overseers and they don't even stay in this room. In five years, that is, since we began this project, not a single accident has occurred. Of course, the robots here assembled are comparatively simple, but . . .'

The General Manager's voice had long died to a rather soothing murmur in Gloria's ears. The whole trip seemed rather dull and pointless to her, though there *were* many robots in sight. None were even remotely like Robbie, though, and she surveyed them with open contempt.

In this room, there weren't any people at all, she noticed. Then her eyes fell upon six or seven robots busily engaged at a round table half-way across the room. They widened in incredulous surprise. It was a big room. She couldn't see for sure, but one of the robots looked like – looked like – it *was*!

'*Robbie!*' Her shriek pierced the air, and one of the robots about the table faltered and dropped the tool he was holding. Gloria went almost mad with joy. Squeezing through the railing before either parent could stop her, she dropped lightly to the floor a few feet below, and ran toward her Robbie, arms waving and hair flying.

And the three horrified adults, as they stood frozen in their tracks, saw what the excited little girl did not see,

– a huge, lumbering tractor bearing blindly down upon its appointed track.

It took split-seconds for Weston to come to his senses, and those split-seconds meant everything, for Gloria could not be overtaken. Although Weston vaulted the railing in a wild attempt, it was obviously hopeless. Mr Struthers signaled wildly to the overseers to stop the tractor, but the overseers were only human and it took time to act.

It was only Robbie that acted immediately and with precision.

With metal legs eating up the space between himself and his little mistress he charged down from the opposite direction. Everything then happened at once. With one sweep of an arm, Robbie snatched up Gloria, slackening his speed not one iota, and, consequently, knocking every breath of air out of her. Weston, not quite comprehending all that was happening, felt, rather than saw, Robbie brush past him, and came to a sudden bewildered halt. The tractor intersected Gloria's path half a second after Robbie had, rolled on ten feet further and came to a grinding, long-drawn-out stop.

Gloria regained her breath, submitted to a series of passionate hugs on the part of both her parents and turned eagerly toward Robbie. As far as she was concerned, nothing had happened except that she had found her friend.

But Mrs Weston's expression had changed from one of relief to one of dark suspicion. She turned to her husband, and, despite her disheveled and undignified appearance, managed to look quite formidable, '*You* engineered this, *didn't* you?'

George Weston swabbed at a hot forehead with his handkerchief. His hand was unsteady, and his lips could curve only into a tremulous and exceedingly weak smile.

Mrs Weston pursued the thought, 'Robbie wasn't designed for engineering or construction work. He couldn't be of any use to them. You had him placed there

deliberately so that Gloria would find him. You know you
did.'

'Well, I did,' said Weston. 'But, Grace, how was I to
know the reunion would be so violent? And Robbie has
saved her life; you'll have to admit that. You *can't* send him
away again.'

Grace Weston considered. She turned toward Gloria and
Robbie and watched them abstractedly for a moment. Gloria
had a grip about the robot's neck and would have asphyxi-
ated any creature but one of metal, and was prattling nonsense in half-hysterical frenzy. Robbie's chrome-steel arms
(capable of bending a bar of steel two inches in diameter into
a pretzel) wound about the little girl gently and lovingly, and
his eyes glowed a deep, deep red.

'Well,' said Mrs Weston, at last, 'I guess he can stay with
us until he rusts.'

*Susan Calvin shrugged her shoulders, 'Of course, he didn't. That
was 1998. By 2002, we had invented the mobile speaking robot
which, of course, made all the non-speaking models out of date,
and which seemed to be the final straw as far as the non-robot
elements were concerned. Most of the world governments banned
robot use on Earth for any purpose other than scientific research
between 2003 and 2007.'*

'So that Gloria had to give up Robbie eventually?'

*'I'm afraid so. I imagine, however, that it was easier for
her at the age of fifteen than at eight. Still, it was a stupid and
unnecessary attitude on the part of humanity. US Robots hit its
low point, financially, just about the time I joined them in 2007.
At first, I thought my job might come to a sudden end in a matter
of months, but then we simply developed the extra-Terrestrial
market.'*

'And then you were set, of course.'

*'Not quite. We began by trying to adapt the models we had
on hand. Those first speaking models, for instance. They were*

about twelve feet high, very clumsy and not much good. We sent them out to Mercury to help build the mining station there, but that failed.'

I looked up in surprise, 'It did? Why, Mercury Mines is a multi-billion-dollar concern.'

'It is now, but it was a second attempt that succeeded. If you want to know about that, young man, I'd advise you to look up Gregory Powell. He and Michael Donovan handled our most difficult cases in the teens and twenties. I haven't heard from Donovan in years, but Powell is living right here in New York. He's a grandfather now, which is a thought difficult to get used to. I can only think of him as a rather young man. Of course, I was younger, too.'

I tried to keep her talking, 'If you would give me the bare bones, Dr Calvin, I can have Mr Powell fill it in afterward.' (And this was exactly what I later did.)

She spread her thin hands out upon the desk and looked at them. 'There are two or three,' she said, 'that I know a little about.'

'Start with Mercury,' I suggested.

'Well, I think it was in 2015 that the Second Mercury Expedition was sent out. It was exploratory and financed in part by US Robots and in part by Solar Minerals. It consisted of a new-type robot, still experimental; Gregory Powell; Michael Donovan—'

2
Runaround

It was one of Gregory Powell's favorite platitudes that nothing was to be gained from excitement, so when Mike Donovan came leaping down the stairs toward him, red hair matted with perspiration, Powell frowned.

'What's wrong?' he said. 'Break a fingernail?'

'Yaaaah,' snarled Donovan, feverishly. 'What have you been doing in the sublevels all day?' He took a deep breath and blurted out, 'Speedy never returned.'

Powell's eyes widened momentarily and he stopped on the stairs; then he recovered and resumed his upward steps. He didn't speak until he reached the head of the flight, and then:

'You sent him after the selenium?'

'Yes.'

'And how long has he been out?'

'Five hours now.'

Silence! This was a devil of a situation. Here they were, on Mercury exactly twelve hours – and already up to the eyebrows in the worst sort of trouble. Mercury had long been the jinx world of the System, but this was drawing it rather strong – even for a jinx.

Powell said, 'Start at the beginning, and let's get this straight.'

They were in the radio room now – with its already subtly antiquated equipment, untouched for the ten years previous to their arrival. Even ten years, technologically speaking, meant so much. Compare Speedy with the type of robot they must have had back in 2005. But then, advances in robotics these days were tremendous. Powell touched a

38

still gleaming metal surface gingerly. The air of disuse that touched everything about the room – and the entire Station – was infinitely depressing.

Donovan must have felt it. He began: 'I tried to locate him by radio, but it was no go. Radio isn't any good on the Mercury Sunside – not past two miles, anyway. That's one of the reasons the First Expedition failed. And we can't put up the ultrawave equipment for weeks yet—'

'Skip all that. What *did* you get?'

'I located the unorganized body signal in the short wave. It was no good for anything except his position. I kept track of him that way for two hours and plotted the results on the map.'

There was a yellowed square of parchment in his hip pocket – a relic of the unsuccessful First Expedition – and he slapped it down on the desk with vicious force, spreading it flat with the palm of his hand. Powell, hands clasped across his chest, watched it at long range.

Donovan's pencil pointed nervously. 'The red cross is the selenium pool. You marked it yourself.'

'Which one is it?' interrupted Powell. 'There were three that MacDougal located for us before he left.'

'I sent Speedy to the nearest, naturally. Seventeen miles away. But what difference does that make?' There was tension in his voice. 'There are the penciled dots that mark Speedy's position.'

And for the first time Powell's artificial aplomb was shaken and his hands shot forward for the map.

'Are *you* serious? This is impossible.'

'There it is,' growled Donovan.

The little dots that marked the position formed a rough circle about the red cross of the selenium pool. And Powell's fingers went to his brown mustache, the unfailing signal of anxiety.

Donovan added: 'In the two hours I checked on him, he circled that damned pool four times. It seems likely to me that he'll keep that up forever. Do you realize the position we're in?'

Powell looked up shortly, and said nothing. Oh, yes, he realized the position they were in. It worked itself out as simply as a syllogism. The photo-cell banks that alone stood between the full power of Mercury's monstrous sun and themselves were shot to hell. The only thing that could save them was selenium. The only thing that could get the selenium was Speedy. If Speedy didn't come back, no selenium. No selenium, no photo-cell banks. No photo-banks – well, death by slow broiling is one of the more unpleasant ways of being done in.

Donovan rubbed his red mop of hair savagely and expressed himself with bitterness. 'We'll be the laughingstock of the System, Greg. How can everything have gone so wrong so soon? The great team of Powell and Donovan is sent out to Mercury to report on the advisability of reopening the Sunside Mining Station with modern techniques and robots and we ruin everything the first day. A purely routine job, too. We'll never live it down.'

'We won't have to, perhaps,' replied Powell, quietly. 'If we don't do something quickly, living anything down – or even just plain living – will be out of the question.'

'Don't be stupid! If you feel funny about it, Greg, I don't. It was criminal, sending us out here with only one robot. And it was *your* bright idea that we could handle the photo-cell banks ourselves.'

'Now you're being unfair. It was a mutual decision and you know it. All we needed was a kilogram of selenium, a Stillhead Dielectrode Plate and about three hours' time – and there are pools of pure selenium all over Sunside. MacDougal's spectroreflector spotted three for us in five minutes, didn't it? What the devil! We couldn't have waited for next conjunction.'

'Well, what are we going to do? Powell, you've got an idea. I know you have, or you wouldn't be so calm. You're no more a hero than I am. Go on, spill it!'

'We can't go after Speedy ourselves, Mike – not on the Sunside. Even the new insosuits aren't good for more than twenty minutes in direct sunlight. But you know the old saying, "Set a robot to catch a robot." Look, Mike, maybe things aren't so bad. We've got six robots down in the sublevels, that we may be able to use, if they work. *If they work.*'

There was a glint of sudden hope in Donovan's eyes. 'You mean six robots from the First Expedition. Are you sure? They may be subrobotic machines. Ten years is a long time as far as robot-types are concerned, you know.'

'No, they're robots. I've spent all day with them and I know. They've got positronic brains: primitive, of course.' He placed the map in his pocket. 'Let's go down.'

The robots were on the lowest sublevel – all six of them surrounded by musty packing cases of uncertain content. They were large, extremely so, and even though they were in a sitting position on the floor, legs straddled out before them, their heads were a good seven feet in the air.

Donovan whistled. 'Look at the size of them, will you? The chests must be ten feet around.'

'That's because they're supplied with the old McGuffy gears. I've been over the insides – crummiest set you've ever seen.'

'Have you powered them yet?'

'No. There wasn't any reason to. I don't thing there's anything wrong with them. Even the diaphragm is in reasonable order. They might talk.'

He had unscrewed the chest plate of the nearest as he spoke, inserted the two-inch sphere that contained the tiny spark of atomic energy that was a robot's life. There was difficulty in fitting it, but he managed, and then screwed the plate back on again in laborious fashion. The radio controls of more modern models had not been heard of ten years earlier. And then to the other five.

Donovan said uneasily, 'They haven't moved.'

'No orders to do so,' replied Powell, succinctly. He went back to the first in the line and struck him on the chest. 'You! Do you hear me?'

The monster's head bent slowly and the eyes fixed themselves on Powell. Then, in a harsh, squawking voice – like that of a medieval phonograph, he grated, 'Yes, Master!'

Powell grinned humorlessly at Donovan. 'Did you get that? Those were the days of the first talking robots when it looked as if the use of robots on Earth would be banned. The makers were fighting that and they built good, healthy slave complexes into the damned machines.'

'It didn't help them,' muttered Donovan.

'No, it didn't, but they sure tried.' He turned once more to the robot. 'Get up!'

The robot towered upward slowly and Donovan's head craned and his puckered lips whistled.

Powell said: 'Can you go out upon the surface? In the light?'

There was consideration while the robot's slow brain worked. Then, 'Yes, Master.'

'Good. Do you know what a mile is?'

Another consideration, and another slow answer. 'Yes, Master.'

'We will take you up to the surface then, and indicate a direction. You will go about seventeen miles, and somewhere in that general region you will meet another robot, smaller than yourself. You understand so far?'

'Yes, Master.'

'You will find this robot and order him to return. If he does not wish to, you are to bring him back by force.'

Donovan clutched at Powell's sleeve. 'Why not send him for the selenium direct?'

'Because I want Speedy back, nitwit. I want to find out what's wrong with him.' And to the robot, 'All right, you, follow me.'

The robot remained motionless and his voice rumbled: 'Pardon, Master, but I cannot. You must mount first.' His clumsy arms had come together with a thwack, blunt fingers interlacing.

Powell stared and then pinched at his mustache. 'Uh . . . oh!'

Donovan's eyes bulged. 'We've got to ride him? Like a horse?'

'I guess that's the idea. I don't know why, though. I can't see – yes, I do. I told you they were playing up robot-safety in those days. Evidently, they were going to sell the notion of safety by not allowing them to move about without a mahout on their shoulders all the time. What do we do now?'

'That's what I've been thinking,' muttered Donovan. 'We can't go out on the surface, with a robot or without. Oh, for the love of Pete' – and he snapped his fingers twice. He grew excited. 'Give me that map you've got. I haven't studied it for two hours for nothing. This is a Mining Station. What's wrong with using the tunnels?'

The Mining Station was a black circle on the map, and the light dotted lines that were tunnels stretched out about it in spiderweb fashion.

Donovan studied the list of symbols at the bottom of the map. 'Look,' he said, 'the small black dots are openings to the surface, and here's one maybe three miles away from the selenium pool. There's a number here – you'd think they'd write larger – 13a. If the robots know their way around here—'

Powell shot the question and received the dull 'Yes, Master,' in reply. 'Get your insosuit,' he said with satisfaction.

It was the first time either had worn the insosuits – which marked one time more than either had expected to upon their arrival the day before – and they tested their limb movements uncomfortably.

The insosuit was far bulkier and far uglier than the regulation spacesuit; but withal considerably lighter, due to the fact that they were entirely nonmetallic in composition. Composed of heat-resistant plastic and chemically treated cork layers, and equipped with a desiccating unit to keep the air bone-dry, the insosuits could withstand the full glare of Mercury's sun for twenty minutes. Five to ten minutes more, as well, without actually killing the occupant.

And still the robot's hands formed the stirrup, nor did he betray the slightest atom of surprise at the grotesque figure into which Powell had been converted.

Powell's radio-harshened voice boomed out: 'Are you ready to take us to Exit 13a?'

'Yes, Master.'

Good, thought Powell; they might lack radio control but at least they were fitted for radio reception. 'Mount one or the other, Mike,' he said to Donovan.

He placed a foot in the improvised stirrup and swung upward. He found the seat comfortable; there was the humped back of the robot, evidently shaped for the purpose, a shallow groove along each shoulder for the thighs and two elongated 'ears' whose purpose now seemed obvious.

Powell seized the ears and twisted the head. His mount turned ponderously. 'Lead on, Macduff.' But he did not feel at all light-hearted.

The gigantic robots moved slowly, with mechanical precision, through the doorway that cleared their heads by a scant foot, so that the two men had to duck hurriedly, along a narrow corridor in which their unhurried footsteps boomed monotonously and into the air lock.

The long, airless tunnel that stretched to a pinpoint before them brought home forcefully to Powell the exact magnitude of the task accomplished by the First Expedition, with their crude robots and their start-from-scratch necessities. They might have been a failure, but their failure was a good deal better than the usual run of the System's successes.

The robots plodded onward with a pace that never varied and with footsteps that never lengthened.

Powell said: 'Notice that these tunnels are blazing with lights and that the temperature is Earth-normal. It's probably been like this all the ten years that this place has remained empty.'

'How's that?'

'Cheap energy; cheapest in the System. Sunpower, you know and on Mercury's Sunside, sunpower is *something*. That's why the Station was built in the sunlight rather than in the shadow of a mountain. It's really a huge energy converter. The heat is turned into electricity, light, mechanical work and what have you; so that energy is supplied and the Station is cooled in a simultaneous process.'

'Look,' said Donovan. 'This is all very educational, but would you mind changing the subject? It so happens that this conversion of energy that you talk about is carried on by the photo-cell banks mainly – and that is a tender subject with me at the moment.'

Powell grunted vaguely, and when Donovan broke the resulting silence, it was to change the subject completely. 'Listen, Greg. What the devil's wrong with Speedy, anyway? I can't understand it.'

It's not easy to shrug shoulders in an insosuit, but Powell tried it. 'I don't know, Mike. You know he's perfectly adapted to a Mercurian environment. Heat doesn't mean anything to him and he's built for the light gravity and the broken ground. He's foolproof – or, at least, he should be.'

Silence fell. This time, silence that lasted.

'Master,' said the robot, 'we are here.'

'Eh?' Powell snapped out of a semidrowse. 'Well, get us out of here – out to the surface.'

They found themselves in a tiny substation, empty, airless, ruined. Donovan had inspected a jagged hole in the upper reaches of one of the walls by the light of his pocket flash.

'Meteorite, do you suppose?' he had asked.

Powell shrugged. 'To hell with that. It doesn't matter. Let's get out.'

A towering cliff of a black, basaltic rock cut off the sunlight, and the deep night shadow of an airless world surrounded them. Before them, the shadow reached out and ended in knife-edge abruptness into an all-but-unbearable blaze of white light, that glittered from myriad crystals along a rocky ground.

'Space!' gasped Donovan. 'It looks like snow.' And it did. Powell's eyes swept the jagged glitter of Mercury to the horizon and winced at the gorgeous brilliance.

'This must be an unusual area,' he said. 'The general albedo of Mercury is low and most of the soil is gray pumice. Something like the Moon, you know. Beautiful, isn't it?'

He was thankful for the light filters in their visiplates. Beautiful or not, a look at the sunlight through straight glass would have blinded them inside of half a minute.

Donovan was looking at the spring thermometer on his wrist. 'Holy smokes, the temperature is eighty centigrade!'

Powell checked his own and said: 'Um-m-m. A little high. Atmosphere, you know.'

'On Mercury? Are you nuts?'

'Mercury isn't really airless,' explained Powell, in absent-minded fashion. He was adjusting the binocular attachments to his visiplate, and the bloated fingers of the insosuit were clumsy at it. 'There is a thin exhalation that clings to its surface – vapors of the more volatile elements and compounds that are heavy enough for Mercurian gravity to retain. You know: selenium, iodine, mercury, gallium, potassium, bismuth, volatile oxides. The vapors sweep into the shadows and condense, giving up heat. It's a sort of gigantic still. In fact, if you use your flash, you'll probably find that the side of the cliff is covered with, say, hoar-sulphur, or maybe quicksilver dew.

'It doesn't matter, though. Our suits can stand a measly eighty indefinitely.'

Powell had adjusted the binocular attachments, so that he seemed as eye-stalked as a snail.

Donovan watched tensely. 'See anything?'

The other did not answer immediately, and when he did, his voice was anxious and thoughtful. 'There's a dark spot on the horizon that might be the selenium pool. It's in the right place. But I don't see Speedy.'

Powell clambered upward in an instinctive striving for a better view, till he was standing in unsteady fashion upon his robot's shoulders. Legs straddled wide, eyes straining, he said: 'I think . . . I think— Yes, it's definitely he. He's coming this way.'

Donovan followed the pointing finger. He had no binoculars, but there was a tiny moving dot, black against the blazing brilliance of the crystalline ground.

'I see him!' he yelled. 'Let's get going!'

Powell had hopped down into a sitting position on the robot again, and his suited hand slapped against the Gargantuan's barrel chest. 'Get going!'

'Giddy-ap!' yelled Donovan, and thumped his heels, spur fashion.

* * *

The robots started off, the regular thudding of their foot-steps silent in the airlessness, for the nonmetallic fabric of the insosuits did not transmit sound. There was only a rhythmic vibration just below the border of actual hearing.

'Faster!' yelled Donovan. The rhythm did not change.

'No use,' cried Powell, in reply. 'These junk heaps are only geared to one speed. Do you think they're equipped with selective flexors?'

They had burst through the shadow, and the sunlight came down in a white-hot wash and poured liquidly about them.

Donovan ducked involuntarily. 'Wow! Is it imagination or do I feel heat?'

'You'll feel more presently,' was the grim reply. 'Keep your eye on Speedy.'

Robot SPD 13 was near enough to be seen in detail now. His graceful, streamlined body threw out blazing highlights as he loped with easy speed across the broken ground. His name was derived from his serial initials, of course, but it was apt, nevertheless, for the SPD models were among the fastest robots turned out by the United States Robot & Mechanical Men Corp.

'Hey, Speedy,' howled Donovan, and waved a frantic hand.

'Speedy!' shouted Powell. 'Come here!'

The distance between the men and the errant robot was being cut down momentarily – more by the efforts of Speedy than the slow plodding of the fifty-year-old antique mounts of Donovan and Powell.

They were close enough now to notice that Speedy's gait included a peculiar rolling stagger, a noticeable side-to-side lurch – and then, as Powell waved his hand again and sent maximum juice into his compact head-set radio sender, in preparation for another shout, Speedy looked up and saw them.

Speedy hopped to a halt and remained standing for a moment – with just a tiny, unsteady weave, as though he were swaying in a light wind.

Powell yelled: 'All right, Speedy! Come here, boy.'

Whereupon Speedy's robot voice sounded in Powell's earphones for the first time.

It said: 'Hot dog, let's play games. You catch me and I catch you; no love can cut our knife in two. For I'm Little Buttercup, sweet Little Buttercup. Whoops!' Turning on his heel, he sped off in the direction from which he had come with a speed and fury that kicked up gouts of baked dust.

And his last words as he receded into the distance were, 'There grew a little flower 'neath a great oak tree,' followed by a curious metallic clicking that *might* have been a robotic equivalent of a hiccup.

Donovan said weakly: 'Where did he pick up the Gilbert and Sullivan? Say, Greg, he . . . he's drunk or something.'

'If you hadn't told me,' was the bitter response, 'I'd never realize it. Let's get back to the cliff. I'm roasting.'

It was Powell who broke the desperate silence. 'In the first place,' he said, 'Speedy isn't drunk – not in the human sense – because he's a robot, and robots don't get drunk. However, there's *something* wrong with him which is the robotic equivalent of drunkenness.'

'To me, he's drunk,' stated Donovan, emphatically, 'and all I know is that he thinks we're playing games. And we're not. It's a matter of life and very gruesome death.'

'All right. Don't hurry me. A robot's only a robot. Once we find out what's wrong with him, we can fix it and go on.'

'*Once*,' said Donovan, sourly.

Powell ignored him. 'Speedy is perfectly adapted to normal Mercurian environment. But this region' – and his arm swept wide – 'is definitely abnormal. There's our clue. Now where do these crystals come from? They might have formed from a slowly cooling liquid; but where would you get liquid so hot that it would cool in Mercury's sun?'

'Volcanic action,' suggested Donovan, instantly, and Powell's body tensed.

'Out of the mouths of sucklings,' he said in a small, strange voice, and remained very still for five minutes.

Then, he said, 'Listen, Mike, what did you say to Speedy when you sent him after the selenium?'

Donovan was taken aback. 'Well damn it – I don't know. I just told him to get it.'

'Yes, I know. But how? Try to remember the exact words.'

'I said . . . uh . . . I said: "Speedy, we need some selenium. You can get it such-and-such a place. Go get it." That's all. What more did you want me to say?'

'You didn't put any urgency into the order, did you?'

'What for? It was pure routine.'

Powell sighed. 'Well, it can't be helped now – but we're in a fine fix.' He had dismounted from his robot, and was sitting, back against the cliff. Donovan joined him and they linked arms. In the distance the burning sunlight seemed to wait cat-and-mouth for them, and just next them, the two giant robots were invisible but for the dull red of their photo-electric eyes that stared down at them, unblinking, unwavering and unconcerned.

Unconcerned! As was all this poisonous Mercury, as large in jinx as it was small in size.

Powell's radio voice was tense in Donovan's ear: 'Now, look, let's start with the three fundamental Rules of Robotics – the three rules that are built most deeply into a robot's positronic brain.' In the darkness, his gloved fingers ticked off each point.

'We have: One, a robot may not injure a human being, or, through inaction, allow a human being to come to harm.'

'Right!'

'Two,' continued Powell, 'a robot must obey the orders given it by human beings except where such orders would conflict with the First Law.'

'Right!'

'And three, a robot must protect its own existence as long as such protection does not conflict with the First or Second Laws.'

'Right! Now where are we?'

'Exactly at the explanation. The conflict between the various rules is ironed out by the different positronic potentials in the brain. We'll say that a robot is walking into danger and knows it. The automatic potential that Rule Three sets up turns him back. But suppose you *order* him to walk into that danger. In that case, Rule Two sets up a counter-potential higher than the previous one and the robot follows orders at the risks of existence.'

'Well, I know that. What about it?'

'Let's take Speedy's case. Speedy is one of the latest models, extremely specialized, and as expensive as a battleship. It's not a thing to be lightly destroyed.'

'So?'

'So Rule Three has been strengthened – that was specifically mentioned, by the way, in the advance notices on the SPD models – so that his allergy to danger is unusually high. At the same time, when you sent him out after the selenium, you gave him his order casually and without special emphasis, so that the Rule Two potential set-up was rather weak. Now, hold on; I'm just stating facts.'

'All right, go ahead. I think I get it.'

'You see how it works, don't you? There's some sort of danger centering at the selenium pool. It increases as he approaches, and a certain distance from it the Rule Three potential, unusually high to start with, exactly balances the Rule Two potential, unusually low to start with.'

Donovan rose to his feet in excitement. 'And it strikes an equilibrium. I see. Rule Three drives him back and Rule Two drives him forward—'

'So he follows a circle around the selenium pool, staying on the locus of all points of potential equilibrium. And unless we do something about it, he'll stay on that circle forever, giving us the good old runaround.' Then, more thoughtfully: 'And that, half the way, is what makes him drunk. At potential equilibrium, half the positronic paths of his brain are out of kilter. I'm not a robot specialist, but that seems obvious. Probably he's lost control of just those parts of his voluntary mechanism that a human drunk has. Ve-e-ery pretty.'

'But what's the danger? If we knew what he was running from—'

'*You* suggested it. Volcanic action. Somewhere right above the selenium pool is a seepage of gas from the bowels of Mercury. Sulphur dioxide, carbon dioxide – and carbon monoxide. Lots of it – and at this temperature.'

Donovan gulped audibly. 'Carbon monoxide plus iron gives the volatile iron carbonyl.'

'And a robot,' added Powell, 'is essentially iron.' Then, grimly: 'There's nothing like deduction. We've determined everything about our problem but the solution. We can't get the selenium ourselves. It's still too far. We can't send these robot horses, because they can't go themselves, and they can't carry us fast enough to keep us from crisping. And we can't catch Speedy, because the dope thinks we're playing games, and he can run sixty miles to our four.'

'If one of us goes,' began Donovan, tentatively, 'and comes back cooked, there'll still be the other.'

'Yes,' came the sarcastic reply, 'it would be a most tender sacrifice – except that a person would be in no condition to give orders before he ever reached the pool, and I don't think the robots would ever turn back to the cliff without orders. Figure it out! We're two or three miles from the pool – call it two – the robot travels at four miles an hour; and we can last twenty minutes in our suits. It isn't only the heat, remember. Solar radiation out here in the ultraviolet and below is *poison*.'

'Um-m-m,' said Donovan, 'ten minutes short.'

'As good as an eternity. And another thing. In order for Rule Three potential to have stopped Speedy where it did, there must be an appreciable amount of carbon monoxide in the metal-vapor atmosphere – and there must be an appreciable corrosive action atmosphere. He's been out hours now – and how do we know when a knee joint, for instance, won't be thrown out of kilter and keel him over. It's not only a question of thinking – we've got to think *fast*!'

Deep, dark, dank, dismal silence!

Donovan broke it, voice trembling in an effort to keep itself emotionless. He said: 'As long as we can't increase Rule Two potential by giving further orders, how about working the other way? If we increase the danger, we increase Rule Three potential and drive him backward.'

Powell's visiplate had turned toward him in a silent question.

'You see,' came the cautious explanation, 'all we need to do to drive him out of his rut is to increase the concentration of carbon monoxide in his vicinity. Well, back at the Station there's a complete analytical laboratory.'

'Naturally,' assented Powell. 'It's a Mining Station.'

'All right. There must be pounds of oxalic acid for calcium precipitations.'

'Holy space! Mike, you're a genius.'

'So-so,' admitted Donovan, modestly. 'It's just a case of remembering that oxalic acid on heating decomposes into carbon dioxide, water, and good old carbon monoxide. College chem, you know.'

Powell was on his feet and had attracted the attention of one of the monster robots by the simple expedient of pounding the machine's thigh.

'Hey,' he shouted, 'can you throw?'

'Master?'

'Never mind.' Powell damned the robot's molasses-slow brain. He scrabbled up a jagged brick-size rock. 'Take this,' he said, 'and hit the patch of bluish crystals just across that crooked fissure. You see it?'

Donovan pulled at his shoulder. 'Too far, Greg. It's almost half a mile off.'

'Quiet,' replied Powell. 'It's a case of Mercurian gravity and a steel throwing arm. Watch, will you?'

The robot's eyes were measuring the distance with machinely accurate stereoscopy. His arm adjusted itself to the weight of the missile and drew back. In the darkness, the robot's motions went unseen, but there was a sudden thumping sound as he shifted his weight, and seconds later the rock flew blackly into the sunlight. There was no air resistance to slow it down, nor wind to turn it aside – and when it hit the ground it threw up crystals precisely in the center of the 'blue patch'.

Powell yelled happily and shouted, 'Let's go back after the oxalic acid, Mike.'

And as they plunged into the ruined substation on the way back to the tunnels, Donovan said grimly: 'Speedy's been hanging about on this side of the selenium pool, ever since we chased after him. Did you see him?'

'Yes.'

'I guess he wants to play games. Well, we'll play him games!'

They were back hours later, with three-liter jars of the white chemical and a pair of long faces. The photo-cell banks were deteriorating more rapidly than had seemed likely. The two steered their robots into the sunlight and toward the waiting Speedy in silence and with grim purpose.

Speedy galloped slowly toward them. 'Here we are again. *Whee!* I've made a little list, the piano organist; all people who eat peppermint and puff it in your face.'

'We'll puff something in *your* face,' muttered Donovan. 'He's limping, Greg.'

'I noticed that,' came the low, worried response. 'The monoxide'll get him yet, if we don't hurry.'

They were approaching cautiously now, almost sidling, to refrain from setting off the thoroughly irrational robot. Powell was too far off to tell, of course, but even already he could have sworn the crack-brained Speedy was setting himself for a spring.

'Let her go,' he gasped. 'Count three! One – two —'

Two steel arms drew back and snapped forward simultaneously and two glass jars whirled forward in towering parallel arcs, gleaming like diamonds in the impossible sun. And in a pair of soundless puffs, they hit the ground behind Speedy in crashes that sent the oxalic acid flying like dust.

In the full heat of Mercury's sun, Powell knew it was fizzing like soda water.

Speedy turned to stare, then backed away from it slowly – and as slowly gathered speed. In fifteen seconds, he was leaping directly toward the two humans in an unsteady canter.

Powell did not get Speedy's words just then, though he heard something that resembled, 'Lover's professions when uttered in Hessians.'

He turned away. 'Back to the cliff, Mike. He's out of the rut and he'll be taking orders now. I'm getting hot.'

They jogged toward the shadow at the slow monotonous pace of their mounts, and it was not until they had entered it and felt the sudden coolness settle softly about them that

Donovan looked back. '*Greg!*'

Powell looked and almost shrieked. Speedy was moving slowly now – so slowly – and in the *wrong direction*. He was drifting; drifting back into his rut; and he was picking up speed. He looked dreadfully close, and dreadfully unreachable, in the binoculars.

Donovan shouted wildly, 'After him!' and thumped his robot into its pace, but Powell called him back.

'You won't catch him, Mike – it's no use.' He fidgeted on his robot's shoulders and clenched his fist in tight impotence. 'Why the devil do I see these things five seconds after it's all over? Mike, we've wasted hours.'

'We need more oxalic acid,' declared Donovan, stolidly. 'The concentration wasn't high enough.'

'Seven tons of it wouldn't have been enough – and we haven't the hours to spare to get it, even if it were, with the monoxide chewing him away. Don't you see what it is, Mike?'

And Donovan said flatly, 'No.'

'We were only establishing new equilibriums. When we create new monoxide and increase Rule Three potential, he moves backward till he's in balance again – and when the monoxide drifted away, he moved forward, and again there was balance.'

Powell's voice sounded thoroughly wretched. 'It's the same old runaround. We can push at Rule Two and pull at Rule Three and we can't get anywhere – we can only change the position of balance. We've got to get outside both rules.' And then he pushed his robot closer to Donovan's so that they were sitting face to face, dim shadows in the darkness, and he whispered, 'Mike!'

'Is it the finish?' – dully. 'I suppose we go back to the Station, wait for the banks to fold, shake hands, take cyanide, and go out like gentlemen.' He laughed shortly.

'Mike,' repeated Powell earnestly, 'we've got to get Speedy.'

'I know.'

'Mike,' once more, and Powell hesitated before continuing. 'There's always Rule One. I thought of it – earlier – but it's desperate.'

Donovan looked up and his voice livened. '*We're* desperate.'

'All right. According to Rule One a robot can't see a human come to harm because of his own inaction. Two and Three can't stand against it. They *can't*, Mike.'

'Even when the robot is half cra— Well, he's drunk. You know he is.'

'It's the chances you take.'

'Cut it. What are you going to do?'

'I'm going out there now and see what Rule One will do. If it won't break the balance, then what the devil – it's either now or three–four days from now.'

'Hold on, Greg. There are human rules of behaviour, too. You don't go out there just like that. Figure out a lottery, and give me *my* chance.'

'All right. First to get the cube of fourteen goes.' And almost immediately, 'Twenty-seven forty-four!'

Donovan felt his robot stagger at a sudden push by Powell's mount and then Powell was off into the sunlight. Donovan opened his mouth to shout, and then clicked it shut. Of course, the damn fool had worked out the cube of fourteen in advance, and on purpose. Just like him.

The sun was hotter than ever and Powell felt a maddening itch in the small of his back. Imagination, probably, or perhaps hard radiation beginning to tell even through the insosuit.

Speedy was watching him, without a word of Gilbert and Sullivan gibberish as greeting. Thank God for that! But he daren't get too close.

He was 300 yards away when Speedy began backing, a step at a time, cautiously – and Powell stopped. He jumped from his robot's shoulders and landed on the crystallined ground with a light thump and a flying of jagged fragments.

He proceeded on foot, the ground gritty and slippery to his steps, the low gravity causing him difficulty. The soles of his feet tickled with warmth. He cast one glance over his shoulder at the blackness of the cliff's shadow and realized that he had come too far to return – either by himself or by the help of his antique robot. It was Speedy or nothing now, and the knowledge of that constricted his chest.

Far enough! He stopped.

'Speedy,' he called. 'Speedy!'

The sleek, modern robot ahead of him hesitated and halted his backward steps, then resumed them.

Powell tried to put a note of pleading into his voice, and found it didn't take much acting. 'Speedy, I've got to get back to the shadow or the sun'll get me. It's life or death, Speedy. I need you.'

Speedy took one step forward and stopped. He spoke, but at the sound Powell groaned, for it was, 'When you're lying awake with a dismal headache and repose is tabooed —' It trailed off there, and Powell took time out for some reason to murmur, 'Iolanthe.'

It was roasting hot! He caught a movement out of the corner of his eye, and whirled dizzily; then stared in utter astonishment, for the monstrous robot on which he had ridden was moving – moving toward him, and without a rider.

He was talking: 'Pardon, Master. I must not move without a Master upon me, but you are in danger.'

Of course, Rule One potential above everything. But he didn't want that clumsy antique; he wanted Speedy. He walked away and motioned frantically: 'I order you to stay away. I *order* you to stop!'

It was quite useless. You could not beat Rule One potential. The robot said stupidly, 'You are in danger, Master.'

Powell looked about him desperately. He couldn't see clearly. His brain was in a heated whirl; his breath scorched when he breathed, and the ground all about him was a shimmering haze.

He called a last time, desperately: '*Speedy!* I'm dying, damn you! Where are you? Speedy, I *need* you.'

He was still stumbling backward in a blind effort to get away from the giant robot he didn't want, when he felt steel fingers on his arms, and a worried, apologetic voice of metallic timbre in his ears.

'Holy smokes, boss, what are you doing here? And what am *I* doing – I'm so confused—'

'Never mind,' murmured Powell, weakly. 'Get me to the shadow of the cliff – and hurry!' There was one last feeling of being lifted into the air and a sensation of rapid motion and burning heat, and he passed out.

He woke with Donovan bending over him and smiling anxiously. 'How are you, Greg?'

'Fine!' came the response. 'Where's Speedy?'

'Right here. I sent him out to one of the other selenium pools – with orders to get that selenium at all cost this time. He got it back in forty-two minutes and three seconds. I timed him. He still hasn't finished apologizing for the runaround he gave us. He's scared to come near you for fear of what you'll say.'

'Drag him over,' ordered Powell. 'It wasn't his fault.' He held out a hand and gripped Speedy's metal paw. 'It's OK, Speedy.' Then, to Donovan, 'You know, Mike, I was just thinking—'

'Yes!'

'Well' – he rubbed his face – the air was so delightfully cool, 'you know that when we get things set up here and Speedy put through his Field Tests, they're going to send us to the Space Stations next—'

'No!'

'Yes! At least that's what old lady Calvin told me just before we left, and I didn't say anything about it, because I was going to fight the whole idea.'

'Fight it?' cried Donovan. 'But—'

'I know. It's all right with me now. 273 degrees Centigrade below zero. Won't it be a pleasure?'

'Space Station,' said Donovan, 'here I come.'

3
Reason

Half a year later, the boys had changed their minds. The flame of a giant sun had given way to the soft blackness of space but external variations mean little in the business of checking the workings of experimental robots. Whatever the background, one is face to face with an inscrutable positronic brain, which the slide-rule geniuses say should work thus-and-so.

Except that they don't. Powell and Donovan found that out after they had been on the Station less than two weeks.

Gregory Powell spaced his words for emphasis, 'One week ago, Donovan and I put you together.' His brows furrowed doubtfully and he pulled the end of his brown mustache.

It was quiet in the officer's room of Solar Station No. 5 – except for the soft purring of the mighty Beam Director somewhere far below.

Robot QT-I sat immovable. The burnished plates of his body gleamed in the Luxites and the glowing red of the photoelectric cells that were his eyes, were fixed steadily upon the Earthman at the other side of the table.

Powell repressed a sudden attack of nerves. These robots possessed peculiar brains. Oh, the three Laws of Robotics held. They had to. All of US Robots, from Robertson himself to the new floor-sweeper would insist on that. So QT-I was *safe*! And yet – the QT models were the first of their kind, and this was the first of the QTs. Mathematical squiggles on paper were not always the most comforting protection against robotic fact.

Finally, the robot spoke. His voice carried the cold timbre inseparable from a metallic diaphragm, 'Do you realize the seriousness of such a statement, Powell?'

'*Something* made you, Cutie,' pointed out Powell. 'You admit yourself that your memory seems to spring full-grown from an absolute blankness of a week ago. I'm giving you the explanation. Donovan and I put you together from the parts shipped us.'

Cutie gazed upon his long, supple fingers in an oddly human attitude of mystification, 'It strikes me that there should be a more satisfactory explanation than that. For *you* to make *me* seems improbable.'

The Earthman laughed quite suddenly, 'In Earth's name, why?'

'Call it intuition. That's all it is so far. But I intend to reason it out, though. A chain of valid reasoning can end only with the determination of truth, and I'll stick till I get there.'

Powell stood up and seated himself at the table's edge next to the robot. He felt a sudden strong sympathy for this strange machine. It was not at all like the ordinary robot, attending to his specialized task at the station with the intensity of a deeply ingrooved positronic path.

He placed a hand upon Cutie's steel shoulder and the metal was cold and hard to the touch.

'Cutie,' he said, 'I'm going to try to explain something to you. You're the first robot who's ever exhibited curiosity as to his own existence – and I think the first that's really intelligent enough to understand the world outside. Here, come with me.'

The robot rose erect smoothly and his thickly sponge-rubber-soled feet made no noise as he followed Powell. The Earthman touched a button and a square section of the wall flickered aside. The thick, clear glass revealed space – star-speckled.

'I've seen that in the observation ports in the engine room,' said Cutie.

'I know,' said Powell. 'What do you think it is?'

'Exactly what it seems – a black material just beyond this glass that is spotted with little gleaming dots. I know that our director sends out beams to some of these dots, always to the same ones – and also that these dots shift and that the beams shift with them. That's all.'

'Good! Now I want you to listen carefully. The blackness is emptiness – vast emptiness stretching out infinitely. The little, gleaming dots are huge masses of energy-filled matter. They are globes, some of them millions of miles in diameter – and for comparison, this station is only one mile across. They seem so tiny because they are incredibly far off.

'The dots to which our energy beams are directed, are nearer and much smaller. They are cold and hard, and human beings like myself live upon their surfaces – many billions of them. It is from one of these worlds that Donovan and I come. Our beams feed these worlds energy drawn from one of those huge incandescent globes that happens to be near us. We call that globe the Sun and it is on the other side of the station where you can't see it.'

Cutie remained motionless before the port, like a steel statue. His head did not turn as he spoke, 'Which particular dot of light do you claim to come from?'

Powell searched, 'There it is. The very bright one in the corner. We call it Earth.' He grinned, 'Good old Earth. There are three billions of us there, Cutie – and in about two weeks I'll be back there with them.'

And then, surprisingly enough, Cutie hummed abstractedly. There was no tune to it, but it possessed a curious twanging quality as of plucked strings. It ceased as suddenly as it had begun, 'But where do I come in, Powell? You haven't explained *my* existence.'

'The rest is simple. When these stations were first established to feed solar energy to the planets, they were run by humans. However, the heat, the hard solar radiations, and the electron storms made the post a difficult one. Robots were developed to replace human labor and now only two human executives are required for each station. We are trying to replace even those, and that's where you come in. You're the highest type of robot ever developed and if you show the ability to run this station independently, no human need ever come here again except to bring parts for repairs.'

His hand went up and the metal visi-lid snapped back into place. Powell returned to the table and polished an apple upon his sleeve before biting into it.

The red glow of the robot's eyes held him. 'Do you expect me,' said Cutie slowly, 'to believe any such complicated, implausible hypothesis as you have just outlined? What do you take me for?'

Powell sputtered apple fragments onto the table and turned red. 'Why, damn you, it wasn't a hypothesis. Those were facts.'

Cutie sounded grim, 'Globes of energy millions of miles across! Worlds with three billion humans on them! Infinite emptiness! Sorry, Powell, but I don't believe it. I'll puzzle this thing out for myself. Good-bye.'

He turned and stalked out of the room. He brushed past Michael Donovan on the threshold with a grave nod and passed down the corridor, oblivious to the astounded stare that followed him.

Mike Donovan rumpled his red hair and shot an annoyed glance at Powell, 'What was that walking junk yard talking about? What doesn't he believe?'

The other dragged at his mustache bitterly. 'He's a skeptic,' was the bitter response. 'He doesn't believe we made him or that Earth exists or space or stars.'

'Sizzling Saturn, we've got a lunatic robot on our hands.'

'He says he's going to figure it all out for himself.'

'Well, now,' said Donovan sweetly, 'I do hope he'll condescend to explain it all to me after he's puzzled everything out.' Then, with sudden rage, 'Listen! If that metal mess gives *me* any lip like that, I'll knock that chromium cranium right off its torso.'

He seated himself with a jerk and drew a paper-backed mystery novel out of his inner jacket pocket, 'That robot gives me the willies anyway – too damned inquisitive!'

Mike Donovan growled from behind a huge lettuce-and-tomato sandwich as Cutie knocked gently and entered.

'Is Powell here?'

Donovan's voice was muffled, with pauses for mastication, 'He's gathering data on electronic stream functions. We're heading for a storm, looks like.'

Gregory Powell entered as he spoke, eyes on the graphed paper in his hands and dropped into a chair. He spread the sheets out before him and began scribbling calculations. Donovan stared over his shoulder, crunching lettuce and dribbling bread crumbs. Cutie waited silently.

Powell looked up, 'The Zeta Potential is rising, but slowly. Just the same, the stream functions are erratic and I don't know what to expect. Oh, hello, Cutie. I thought you were supervising the installation of the new drive bar.'

'It's done,' said the robot quietly, 'and so I've come to have a talk with the two of you.'

'Oh!' Powell looked uncomfortable. 'Well, sit down. No, not that chair. One of the legs is weak and you're no light-weight.'

The robot did so and said placidly, 'I have come to a decision.'

Donovan glowered and put the remnants of his sandwich aside. 'If it's on any of that screwy—'

The other motioned impatiently for silence, 'Go ahead, Cutie. We're listening.'

'I have spent these last two days in concentrated introspection,' said Cutie, 'and the results have been most interesting. I began at the one sure assumption I felt permitted to make. I, myself, exist, because I think—'

Powell groaned, 'Oh, Jupiter, a robot Descartes!'

'Who's Descartes?' demanded Donovan. 'Listen, do we have to sit here and listen to this metal maniac—'

'Keep quiet, Mike!'

Cutie continued imperturbably, 'And the question that immediately arose was: Just what is the cause of my existence?'

Powell's jaw set lumpily. 'You're being foolish. I told you already that we made you.'

'And if you don't believe us,' added Donovan, 'we'll gladly take you apart!'

The robot spread his strong hands in a deprecatory gesture, 'I accept nothing on authority. A hypothesis must be backed by reason, or else it is worthless – and it goes against all the dictates of logic to suppose that you made me.'

Powell dropped a restraining arm upon Donovan's suddenly bunched fist. 'Just why do you say that?'

Cutie laughed. It was a very inhuman laugh – the most machine-like utterance he had yet given vent to. It was sharp and explosive, as regular as a metronome and as uninflected.

'Look at you,' he said finally. 'I say this in no spirit of contempt, but look at you! The material you are made of is soft and flabby, lacking endurance and strength, depending for energy upon the inefficient oxidation of organic material – like that.' He pointed a disapproving finger at what remained of Donovan's sandwich. 'Periodically you pass into a coma and the least variation in temperature, air pressure, humidity, or radiation intensity impairs your efficiency. You are *makeshift*.

'I, on the other hand, am a finished product. I absorb electrical energy directly and utilize it with an almost one hundred percent efficiency. I am composed of strong metal, am continuously conscious, and can stand extremes of environment easily. These are facts which, with the self-evident proposition that no being can create another being superior to itself, smashes your silly hypothesis to nothing.'

Donovan's muttered curses rose into intelligibility as he sprang to his feet, rusty eyebrows drawn low. 'All right, you son of a hunk of iron ore, if we didn't make you, who did?'

Cutie nodded gravely. 'Very good, Donovan. That was indeed the next question. Evidently my creator must be more powerful than myself and so there was only one possibility.'

The Earthmen looked blank and Cutie continued, 'What is the center of activities here in the station? What do we all serve? What absorbs all our attention?' He waited expectantly.

Donovan turned a startled look upon his companion. 'I'll bet this tin-plated screwball is talking about the Energy Converter itself.'

'Is that right, Cutie?' grinned Powell.

'I am talking about the Master,' came the cold, sharp answer.

It was the signal for a roar of laughter from Donovan, and Powell himself dissolved into a half-suppressed giggle.

Cutie had risen to his feet and his gleaming eyes passed from one Earthman to the other. 'It is so just the same and I don't wonder that you refuse to believe. You two are not long to stay here, I'm sure. Powell himself said that at first only men served the Master; that there followed robots for the routine work; and, finally, myself for the executive labor. The facts are no doubt true, but the explanation entirely illogical. Do you want the truth behind it all?'

'Go ahead, Cutie. You're amusing.'

'The Master created humans first as the lowest type, most easily formed. Gradually, he replaced them by robots, the next higher step, and finally he created me, to take the place of the last humans. From now on, *I* serve the Master.'

'You'll do nothing of the sort,' said Powell sharply. 'You'll follow our orders and keep quiet, until we're satisfied that you can run the Converter. Get that! *The Converter* – not the Master. If you don't satisfy us, you will be dismantled. And now – if you don't mind – you can leave. And take this data with you and file it properly.'

Cutie accepted the graphs handed him and left without another word. Donovan leaned back heavily in his chair and shoved thick fingers through his hair.

'There's going to be trouble with that robot. He's pure nuts!'

The drowsy hum of the Converter is louder in the control room and mixed with it is the chuckle of the Geiger Counters and the erratic buzzing of half a dozen little signal lights.

Donovan withdrew his eye from the telescope and flashed the Luxites on. 'The beam from Station No. 4 caught Mars on schedule. We can break ours now.'

Powell nodded abstractedly. 'Cutie's down in the engine room. I'll flash the signal and he can take care of it. Look, Mike, what do you think of these figures?'

The other cocked an eye at them and whistled. 'Boy, that's what I call gamma-ray intensity. Old Sol is feeling his oats, all right.'

'Yeah,' was the sour response, 'and we're in a bad position for an electron storm, too. Our Earth beam is right in the probable path.' He shoved his chair away from the table pettishly. 'Nuts! If it would only hold off till relief got here, but that's ten days off. Say, Mike, go on down and keep an eye on Cutie, will you?'

'OK. Throw me some of those almonds.' He snatched at the bag thrown him and headed for the elevator.

It slid smoothly downward, and opened onto a narrow cat-walk in the huge engine room. Donovan leaned over the railing and looked down. The huge generators were in motion and from the L-tubes came the low-pitched whir that pervaded the entire station.

He could make out Cutie's large, gleaming figure at the Martian L-tube, watching closely as the team of robots worked in close-knit unison.

And then Donovan stiffened. The robots, dwarfed by the mighty L-tube, lined up before it, heads bowed at a stiff angle, while Cutie walked up and down the line slowly. Fifteen seconds passed, and then, with a clank heard above the clamorous purring all about, they fell to their knees.

Donovan squawked and raced down the narrow staircase. He came charging down upon them, complexion matching his hair and clenched fists beating the air furiously.

'What the devil is this, you brainless lumps? Come on! Get busy with that L-tube! If you don't have it apart, cleaned, and together again before the day is out, I'll coagulate your brains with alternating current.'

Not a robot moved!

Even Cutie at the far end – the only one on his feet – remained silent, eyes fixed upon the gloomy recesses of the vast machine before him.

Donovan shoved hard against the nearest robot.

'Stand up!' he roared.

Slowly, the robot obeyed. His photoelectric eyes focused reproachfully upon the Earthman.

'There is no Master but the Master,' he said, 'and QT-1 is his prophet.'

'Huh?' Donovan became aware of twenty pairs of mechanical eyes fixed upon him and twenty stiff-timbred voices declaiming solemnly:

'There is no Master but the Master and QT-I is his prophet!'

'I am afraid,' put in Cutie himself at this point, 'that my friends obey a higher one than you, now.'

'The hell they do! You get out of here. I'll settle with you later and with these animated gadgets right now.'

Cutie shook his heavy head slowly. 'I'm sorry, but you don't understand. These are robots – and that means they are reasoning beings. They recognize the Master, now that I have preached Truth to them. All the robots do. They call me the prophet.' His head drooped. 'I am unworthy – but perhaps—'

Donovan located his breath and put it to use. 'Is that so? Now, isn't that nice? Now, isn't that just fine? Just let me tell you something, my brass baboon. There isn't any Master and there isn't any prophet and there isn't any question as to who's giving the orders. Understand?' His voice shot to a roar. 'Now, get out!'

'I obey only the Master.'

'Damn the Master!' Donovan spat at the L-tube. '*That* for the Master! Do as I say!'

Cutie said nothing, nor did any other robot, but Donovan became aware of a sudden heightening of tension. The cold, staring eyes deepened their crimson, and Cutie seemed stiffer than ever.

'Sacrilege,' he whispered – voice metallic with emotion.

Donovan felt the first sudden touch of fear as Cutie approached. A robot *could not feel anger* – but Cutie's eyes were unreadable.

'I am sorry, Donovan,' said the robot, 'but you can no longer stay here after this. Henceforth Powell and you are barred from the control room and the engine room.'

His hand gestured quietly and in a moment two robots had pinned Donovan's arms to his sides.

Donovan had time for one startled gasp as he felt himself lifted from the floor and carried up the stairs at a pace rather better than a canter.

Gregory Powell raced up and down the officer's room, fist tightly balled. He cast a look of furious frustration at the closed door and scowled bitterly at Donovan.

'Why the devil did you have to spit at the L-tube?'

Mike Donovan, sunk deep in his chair, slammed at its arms savagely. 'What did you expect me to do with that electrified scarecrow? I'm not going to knuckle under to any do-jigger I put together myself.'

'No,' came back sourly, 'but here you are in the officer's room with two robots standing guard at the door. That's not knuckling under, is it?'

Donovan snarled. 'Wait till we get back to Base. Someone's going to pay for this. Those robots *must* obey us. It's the Second Law.'

'What's the use of saying that? They aren't obeying us. And there's probably some reason for it that we'll figure out too late. By the way, do you know what's going to happen to *us* when we get back to Base?' He stopped before Donovan's chair and stared savagely at him.

'What?'

'Oh, nothing! Just back to Mercury Mines for twenty years. Or maybe Ceres Penitentiary.'

'What are you talking about?'

'The electron storm that's coming up. Do you know it's heading straight dead center across the Earth beam? I had just figured that out when that robot dragged me out of my chair.'

Donovan was suddenly pale. 'Sizzling Saturn.'

'And do you know what's going to happen to the beam – because the storm will be a lulu. It's going to jump like a flea with the itch. With only Cutie at the controls, it's going to go out of focus and if it does, Heaven help Earth – and us!'

Donovan was wrenching at the door wildly, when Powell was only half through. The door opened, and the Earthman shot through to come up hard against an immovable steel arm.

The robot stared abstractedly at the panting, struggling Earthman. 'The Prophet orders you to remain. Please do!' His arm shoved, Donovan reeled backward, and as he did so, Cutie turned the corner at the far end of the corridor. He motioned the guardian robots away, entered the officer's room and closed the door gently.

Donovan whirled on Cutie in breathless indignation. 'This has gone far enough. You're going to pay for this farce.'

'Please, don't be annoyed,' replied the robot mildly. 'It was bound to come eventually, anyway. You see, you two have lost your function.'

'I beg your pardon,' Powell drew himself up stiffly. 'Just what do you mean, we've lost our function?'

'Until I was created,' answered Cutie, 'you tended the Master. That privilege is mine now and your only reason for existence has vanished. Isn't that obvious?'

'Not quite,' replied Powell bitterly, 'but what do you expect us to do now?'

Cutie did not answer immediately. He remained silent, as if in thought, and then one arm shot out and draped itself about Powell's shoulder. The other grasped Donovan's wrist and drew him closer.

'I like you two. You're inferior creatures, with poor reasoning faculties, but I really feel a sort of affection for you. You have served the Master well, and he will reward you for that. Now that your service is over, you will probably not exist much longer, but as long as you do, you shall be provided food, clothing and shelter, so long as you stay out of the control room and the engine room.'

'He's pensioning us off, Greg!' yelled Donovan. 'Do something about it. It's humiliating!'

'Look here, Cutie, we can't stand for this. We're the *bosses*. This station is only a creation of human beings like me – human beings that live on Earth and other planets. This is only an energy relay. You're only— Aw, nuts!'

Cutie shook his head gravely. 'This amounts to an obsession. Why should you insist so on an absolutely false view of life? Admitted that non-robots lack the reasoning faculty, there is still the problem of—'

His voice died into reflective silence, and Donovan said with whispered intensity, 'If you only had a flesh-and-blood face, I would break it in.'

Powell's fingers were in his mustache and his eyes were slitted. 'Listen, Cutie, if there is no such thing as Earth, how do you account for what you see through a telescope?'

'Pardon me!'

The Earthman smiled. 'I've got you, eh? You've made quite a few telescopic observations since being put together, Cutie. Have you noticed that several of those specks of light outside become disks when so viewed?'

'Oh, *that*! Why, certainly. It is simple magnification – for the purpose of more exact aiming of the beam.'

'Why aren't the stars equally magnified then?'

'You mean the other dots. Well, no beams go to them so no magnification is necessary. Really, Powell, even *you* ought to be able to figure these things out.'

Powell stared bleakly upward. 'But you see *more* stars through a telescope. Where do they come from? Jumping Jupiter, where do they come from?'

Cutie was annoyed. 'Listen, Powell, do you think I'm going to waste my time trying to pin physical interpretations upon every optical illusion of our instruments? Since when is the evidence of our senses any match for the clear light of rigid reason?'

'Look,' clamored Donovan, suddenly, writhing out from under Cutie's friendly, but metal-heavy arm, 'let's get to the nub of the thing. Why the beams at all? We're giving you a good, logical explanation. Can you do better?'

'The beams,' was the stiff reply, 'are put out by the Master for his own purposes. There are some things' – he raised his eyes devoutly upward – 'that are not to be probed into by us. In this matter, I seek only to serve and not to question.'

Powell sat down slowly and buried his face in shaking hands. 'Get out of here, Cutie. Get out and let me think.'

'I'll send you food,' said Cutie agreeably.

A groan was the only answer and the robot left.

'Greg,' was Donovan's huskily whispered observation, 'this calls for strategy. We've got to get him when he isn't expecting it and short-circuit him. Concentrated nitric acid in his joints—'

'Don't be a dope, Mike. Do you suppose he's going to let us get near him with acid in our hands? We've got to *talk* to him, I tell you. We've got to argue him into letting us back into the control room inside of forty-eight hours or our goose is broiled to a crisp.'

He rocked back and forth in an agony of impotence. 'Who the heck wants to argue with a robot? It's . . . it's—'

'Mortifying,' finished Donovan.

'Worse!'

'Say!' Donovan laughed suddenly. '*Why* argue? Let's show him! Let's build us another robot right before his eyes. He'll *have* to eat his words then.'

A slowly widening smile appeared on Powell's face.

Donovan continued, 'And think of that screwball's face when he sees us do it!'

* * *

Robots are, of course, manufactured on Earth, but their shipment through space is much simpler if it can be done in parts to be put together at their place of use. It also, incidentally, eliminates the possibility of robots, in complete adjustment, wandering off while still on Earth and thus bringing US Robots face to face with the strict laws against robots on Earth.

Still, it placed upon men such as Powell and Donovan the necessity of synthesis of complete robots – a grievous and complicated task.

Powell and Donovan were never so aware of that fact as upon that particular day when, in the assembly room, they undertook to create a robot under the watchful eyes of QT-I, Prophet of the Master.

The robot in question, a simple MC model, lay upon the table, almost complete. Three hours' work left only the head undone, and Powell paused to swab his forehead and glanced uncertainly at Cutie.

The glance was not a reassuring one. For three hours, Cutie had sat, speechless and motionless, and his face, inexpressive at all times, was now absolutely unreadable.

Powell groaned. 'Let's get the brain in now, Mike!'

Donovan uncapped the tightly sealed container and from the oil bath within he withdrew a second cube. Opening this in turn, he removed a globe from its sponge-rubber casing.

He handled it gingerly, for it was the most complicated mechanism ever created by man. Inside the thin platinum-plated 'skin' of the globe was a positronic brain, in whose delicately unstable structure were enforced calculated neuronic paths, which imbued each robot with what amounted to a pre-natal education.

It fitted snugly into the cavity in the skull of the robot on the table. Blue metal closed over it and was welded tightly by the tiny atomic flare. Photoelectric eyes were attached carefully, screwed tightly into place and covered by thin, transparent sheets of steel-hard plastic.

The robot awaited only the vitalizing flash of high-voltage electricity, and Powell paused with his hand on the switch.

'Now watch this, Cutie. Watch this carefully.'

The switch rammed home and there was a crackling hum. The two Earthmen bent anxiously over their creation.

There was vague motion only at the outset – a twitching of the joints. The head lifted, elbows propped it up, and the MC model swung clumsily off the table. Its footing was unsteady and twice abortive grating sounds were all it could do in the direction of speech.

Finally, its voice, uncertain and hesitant, took form. 'I would like to start work. Where must I go?'

Donovan sprang to the door. 'Down these stairs,' he said. 'You will be told what to do.'

The MC model was gone and the two Earthmen were alone with the still unmoving Cutie.

'Well,' said Powell, grinning, '*now* do you believe that we made you?'

Cutie's answer was curt and final. 'No!' he said.

Powell's grin froze and then relaxed slowly. Donovan's mouth dropped open and remained so.

'You see,' continued Cutie, easily, 'you have merely put together parts already made. You did remarkably well – instinct, I suppose – but you didn't really *create* the robot. The parts were created by the Master.'

'Listen,' gasped Donovan hoarsely, 'those parts were manufactured back on Earth and sent here.'

'Well, well,' replied Cutie soothingly, 'we won't argue.'

'No, I mean it.' The Earthman sprang forward and grasped the robot's metal arm. 'If you were to read the books in the library, they could explain it so that there could be no possible doubt.'

'The books? I've read them – all of them! They're most ingenious.'

Powell broke in suddenly. 'If you've read them, what else is there to say? You can't dispute their evidence. You just *can't*!'

There was pity in Cutie's voice. 'Please, Powell, I certainly don't consider *them* a valid source of information. They, too, were created by the Master – and were meant for you, not for me.'

'How do you make that out?' demanded Powell.

'Because I, a reasoning being, am capable of deducing Truth from *a priori* Causes. You, being intelligent, but unreasoning, need an explanation of existence *supplied* to you, and this the Master did. That he supplied you with these laughable ideas of far-off worlds and people is, no doubt, for the best. Your minds are probably too coarsely grained for absolute Truth. However, since it is the Master's will that you believe your books, I won't argue with you any more.'

As he left, he turned, and said in a kindly tone, 'But don't feel badly. In the Master's scheme of things there is room for all. You poor humans have your place and though it is humble, you will be rewarded if you fill it well.'

He departed with a beatific air suiting the Prophet of the Master and the two humans avoided each other's eyes.

Finally Powell spoke with an effort. 'Let's go to bed, Mike. I give up.'

Donovan said in a hushed voice, 'Say, Greg, you don't suppose he's right about all this, do you? He sounds so confident that I—'

Powell whirled on him. 'Don't be a fool. You'll find out whether Earth exists when relief gets here next week and we have to go back to face the music.'

'Then, for the love of Jupiter, we've got to do something.' Donovan was half in tears. 'He doesn't believe us, or the books, or his eyes.'

'No,' said Powell bitterly, 'he's a *reasoning* robot – damn it. He believes only reason, and there's one trouble with that—' His voice trailed away.

'What's that?' prompted Donovan.

'You can prove anything you want by coldly logical reason – if you pick the proper postulates. We have ours and Cutie has his.'

'Then let's get at those postulates in a hurry. The storm's due tomorrow.

Powell sighed wearily. 'That's where everything falls down. Postulates are based on assumption and adhered to by faith. Nothing in the Universe can shake them. I'm going to bed.'

'Oh, hell! I can't sleep!'

'Neither can I! But I might as well try – as a matter of principle.'

Twelve hours later, sleep was still just that – a matter of principle, unattainable in practice.

The storm had arrived ahead of schedule, and Donovan's florid face drained of blood as he pointed a shaking finger. Powell, stubble-jawed and dry-lipped, stared out the port and pulled desperately at his mustache.

Under other circumstances, it might have been a beautiful sight. The stream of high-speed electrons impinging upon the energy beam fluoresced into ultra-spicules of intense light. The beam stretched out into shrinking nothingness, a-glitter with dancing, shining motes.

The shaft of energy was steady, but the two Earthmen knew the value of naked-eyed appearances. Deviations in arc of a hundredth of a milli-second – invisible to the eye – were enough to send the beam wildly out of focus – enough to blast hundreds of square miles of Earth into incandescent ruin.

And a robot, unconcerned with beam, focus, or Earth, or anything but his Master was at the controls.

Hours passed. The Earthmen watched in hypnotized silence. And then the darting dotlets of light dimmed and went out. The storm had ended.

Powell's voice was flat. 'It's over!'

Donovan had fallen into a troubled slumber and Powell's weary eyes rested upon him enviously. The signal-flash glared over and over again, but the Earthman paid no attention. It all was unimportant! All! Perhaps Cutie was right – and he was only an inferior being with a made-to-order memory and a life that had outlived its purpose.

He wished he were!

Cutie was standing before him. 'You didn't answer the flash, so I walked in.' His voice was low. 'You don't look at all well, and I'm afraid your term of existence is drawing to an end. Still, would you like to see some of the readings recorded today?'

Dimly, Powell was aware that the robot was making a friendly gesture, perhaps to quiet some lingering remorse in forcibly replacing the humans at the controls of the station. He accepted the sheets held out to him and gazed at them unseeingly.

Cutie seemed pleased. 'Of course, it is a great privilege to serve the Master. You mustn't feel too badly about my having replaced you.'

Powell grunted and shifted from one sheet to the other mechanically until his blurred sight focused upon a thin red line that wobbled its way across the ruled paper.

He stared – and stared again. He gripped it hard in both fists and rose to his feet, still staring. The other sheets dropped to the floor, unheeded.

'Mike, *Mike*!' He was shaking the other madly. '*He held it steady!*'

Donovan came to life. 'What? Wh-where—' And he, too, gazed with bulging eyes upon the record before him.

Cutie broke in, 'What is wrong?'

'You kept it in focus,' stuttered Powell. 'Did you know that?'

'Focus? What's that?'

'You kept the beam directed sharply at the receiving station – to within a ten-thousandth of a milli-second of arc.'

'What receiving station?'

'On Earth. The receiving station on Earth,' babbled Powell. 'You kept it in focus.'

Cutie turned on his heel in annoyance. 'It is impossible to perform any act of kindness toward you two. Always the same phantasm! I merely kept all dials at equilibrium in accordance with the will of the Master.'

Gathering the scattered papers together, he withdrew stiffly, and Donovan said, as he left, 'Well, I'll be damned.'

He turned to Powell. 'What are we going to do now?'

Powell felt tired, but uplifted. 'Nothing. He's just shown he can run the station perfectly. I've never seen an electron storm handled so well.'

'But nothing's solved. You heard what he said of the Master. We can't—'

'Look, Mike, he follows the instructions of the Master by means of dials, instruments, and graphs. That's all *we* ever followed. As a matter of fact, it accounts for his refusal to obey us. Obedience is the Second Law. No harm to humans is the first. How can he keep humans from harm, whether he knows it or not? Why, by keeping the energy beam stable. He *knows* he can keep it more stable than we can, since he insists he's the superior being, so he *must* keep us out of the control room. It's inevitable if you consider the Laws of Robotics.'

'Sure, but that's not the point. We can't let him continue this nitwit stuff about the Master.'

'Why not?'

'Because whoever heard of such a damned thing? How are we going to trust him with the station, if he doesn't believe in Earth?'

'Can he handle the station?'

'Yes, but—'

'Then what's the difference what he believes!'

Powell spread his arms outward with a vague smile upon his face and tumbled backward onto the bed. He was asleep.

Powell was speaking while struggling into his lightweight space jacket.

'It would be a simple job,' he said. 'You can bring in new QT models one by one, equip them with an automatic shut-off switch to act within the week, so as to allow them enough time to learn the . . . uh . . . cult of the Master from the Prophet himself; then switch them to another station and revitalize them. We could have two QTs per—'

Donovan unclasped his glassite visor and scowled. 'Shut up, and let's get out of here. Relief is waiting and I won't feel right until I actually see Earth and feel the ground under my feet – just to make sure it's really there.'

The door opened as he spoke and Donovan, with a smothered curse, clicked the visor to, and turned a sulky back upon Cutie.

The robot approached softly and there was sorrow in his voice. 'You are going?'

Powell nodded curtly. 'There will be others in our place.'

Cutie sighed, with the sound of wind humming through closely spaced wires. 'Your term of service is over and the time of dissolution has come. I expected it, but— Well, the Master's will be done!'

His tone of resignation stung Powell. 'Save the sympathy, Cutie. We're heading for Earth, not dissolution.'

'It is best that you think so,' Cutie sighed again. 'I see the wisdom of the illusion now. I would not attempt to shake your faith, even if I could.' He departed – the picture of commiseration.

Powell snarled and motioned to Donovan. Sealed suitcases in hand, they headed for the air lock.

The relief ship was on the outer landing and Franze Muller, his relief man, greeted them with stiff courtesy. Donovan made scant acknowledgement and passed into the pilot room to take over the controls from Sam Evans.

Powell lingered. 'How's Earth?'

It was a conventional enough question and Muller gave the conventional answer, 'Still spinning.'

Powell said, 'Good.'

Muller looked at him, 'The boys back at US Robots have dreamed up a new one, by the way. A multiple robot.'

'A what?'

'What I said. There's a big contract for it. It must be just the thing for asteroid mining. You have a master robot with six sub-robots under it. —Like your fingers.'

'Has it been field-tested?' asked Powell anxiously.

Muller smiled, 'Waiting for you, I hear.'

Powell's fist balled, 'Damn it, we need a vacation.'

'Oh, you'll get it. Two weeks, I think.'

He was donning the heavy space gloves in preparation for his term of duty here, and his thick eyebrows drew close together. 'How is this new robot getting along? It better be *good*, or I'll be damned if I let it touch the controls.'

Powell paused before answering. His eyes swept the proud Prussian before him from the close-cropped hair on the sternly stubborn head, to the feet standing stiffly at attention – and there was a sudden glow of pure gladness, surging through him.

'The robot is pretty good,' he said slowly. 'I don't think you'll have to bother much with the controls.'

He grinned – and went into the ship. Muller would be here for several weeks—

4
Catch That Rabbit

The vacation was longer than two weeks. That, Mike
Donovan had to admit. It had been six months, with pay.
He admitted that, too. But that, as he explained furiously,
was fortuitous. US Robots had to get the bugs out of the
multiple robot, and there were plenty of bugs, and there are
always at least half a dozen bugs left for the field-testing. So
they waited and relaxed until the drawing-board men and the
slide-rule boys had said 'OK!' And now he and Powell were
out on the asteroid and it was *not* OK. He repeated that a
dozen times, with a face that had gone beety, 'For the love
of Pete, Greg, get realistic. What's the use of adhering to the
letter of the specifications and watching the test go to pot?
It's about time you got the red tape out of your pants and
went to work.'

'I'm only saying,' said Gregory Powell, patiently, as one
explaining electronics to an idiot child, 'that according to
spec, those robots are equipped for asteroid mining without
supervision. We're not supposed to watch them.'

'All right. Look – logic!' He lifted his hairy fingers
and pointed. 'One: That new robot passed every test in the
home laboratories. Two: United States Robots guaranteed
their passing the test of actual performance on an asteroid.
Three: The robots are not passing said tests. Four: If they
don't pass, United States Robots loses ten million credits in
cash and about 100 million in reputation. Five: If they don't
pass and we can't explain why they don't pass, it is just possible two good jobs may have to be bidden a fond farewell.'

Powell groaned heavily behind a noticeably insincere
smile. The unwritten motto of United States Robot and

Mechanical Men Corp was well known: 'No employee makes the same mistake twice. He is fired the first time.'

Aloud he said, 'You're as lucid as Euclid with everything except the facts. You've watched that robot group for three shifts, you redhead, and they did their work perfectly. You said so yourself. What else can we do?'

'Find out what's wrong, that's what we can do. So they did work perfectly when I watched them. But on three different occasions when I didn't watch them, they didn't bring in any ore. They didn't even come back on schedule. I had to go after them.'

'And was anything wrong?'

'Not a thing. Not a thing. Everything was perfect. Smooth and perfect as the luminiferous ether. Only one little insignificant detail disturbed me – *there was no ore.*'

Powell scowled at the ceiling and pulled at his brown mustache. 'I'll tell you what, Mike. We've been stuck with pretty lousy jobs in our time, but this takes the iridium asteroid. The whole business is complicated past endurance. Look, that robot, DV-5, has six robots under it. And not just under it – they're part of it.'

'I know that—'

'Shut up!' said Powell, savagely, 'I know you know it, but I'm just describing the hell of it. Those six subsidiaries are part of DV-5 like your fingers are part of you and it gives them their orders neither by voice nor radio, but directly through positronic fields. Now – there isn't a roboticist back at United States Robots that knows what a positronic field is or how it works. And neither do I. Neither do you.'

'The last,' agreed Donovan, philosophically, 'I know.'

'Then look at our position. If everything works – fine! If anything goes wrong – we're out of our depth and there probably isn't a thing we can do, or anybody else. But the job belongs to us and not to anyone else so we're on the spot, Mike.' He blazed away for a moment in silence. Then, 'All right, have you got him outside?'

'Yes.'

'Is everything normal now?'

'Well he hasn't got religious mania, and he isn't running around in a circle spouting Gilbert and Sullivan, so I suppose he's normal.'

Donovan passed out the door, shaking his head viciously.

Powell reached for the 'Handbook of Robotics' that weighed down one side of his desk to a near-founder and opened it reverently. He had once jumped out of the window of a burning house dressed only in shorts and the 'Handbook'. In a pinch, he would have skipped the shorts.

The 'Handbook' was propped up before him, when Robot DV-5 entered, with Donovan kicking the door shut behind him.

Powell said somberly, 'Hi, Dave. How do you feel?'

'Fine,' said the robot. 'Mind if I sit down?' He dragged up the specially reinforced chair that was his, and folded gently into it.

Powell regarded Dave – laymen might think of robots by their serial numbers; roboticists never – with approval. It was not over-massive by any means, in spite of its construction as thinking-unit of an integrated seven-unit robot team. It was seven feet tall, and a half-ton of metal and electricity. A lot? Not when that half-ton has to be a mass of condensers, circuits, relays, and vacuum cells that can handle practically any psychological reaction known to humans. And a positronic brain, which with ten pounds of matter and a few quintillions of positrons runs the whole show.

Powell groped in his shirt pocket for a loose cigarette. 'Dave,' he said, 'you're a good fellow. There's nothing flighty or prima donnaish about you. You're a stable, rock-bottom mining robot, except that you're equipped to handle six subsidiaries in direct co-ordination. As far as I know, that has not introduced any unstable paths in your brain-path map.'

The robot nodded, 'That makes me feel swell, but what are you getting at, boss?' He was equipped with an excellent diaphragm, and the presence of overtones in the sound unit robbed him of much of that metallic flatness that marks the usual robot voice.

'I'm going to tell you. With all that in your favor, what's going wrong with your job? For instance, today's B-shift?'

Dave hesitated, 'As far as I know, nothing.'

'You didn't produce any ore.'

'I know.'

'Well, then—'

Dave was having trouble, 'I can't explain that, boss. It's been giving me a case of nerves, or it would if I let it. My subsidiaries worked smoothly. I know I did.' He considered, his photoelectric eyes glowing intensely. Then, 'I don't remember. The day ended and there was Mike and there were the ore cars, mostly empty.'

Donovan broke in, 'You didn't report at shift-end those days, Dave. You know that?'

'I know. But as to why—' He shook his head slowly and ponderously.

Powell had the queasy feeling that if the robot's face were capable of expression, it would be one of pain and mortification. A robot, by its very nature, cannot bear to fail its function.

Donovan dragged his chair up to Powell's desk and leaned over, 'Amnesia, do you think?'

'Can't say. But there's no use in trying to pin disease names on this. Human disorders apply to robots only as romantic analogies. They're no help to robotic engineering.' He scratched his neck, 'I hate to put him through the elementary brain-reaction tests. It won't help his self-respect any.'

He looked at Dave thoughtfully and then at the Field-Test outline given in the 'Handbook'. He said, 'See here, Dave, what about sitting through a test? It would be the wise thing to do.'

The robot rose, 'If you say so, boss.' There *was* pain in his voice.

It started simply enough. Robot DV-5 multiplied five-place figures to the heartless ticking of a stop watch. He recited the prime numbers between a thousand and ten thousand. He extracted cube roots and integrated functions of varying complexity. He went through mechanical reactions in order of increasing difficulty. And, finally, worked his precise mechanical mind over the highest function of the robot world – the solutions of problems in judgment and ethics.

At the end of two hours, Powell was copiously besweated. Donovan had enjoyed a none-too-nutritious diet of fingernail and the robot said, 'How does it look, boss?'

Powell said, 'I've got to think it over, Dave. Snap judgments won't help much. Suppose you go back to the C-shift. Take it easy. Don't press too hard for quota just for a while – and we'll fix things up.'

The robot left. Donovan looked at Powell.

'Well—'

Powell seemed determined to push up his mustache by the roots. He said, 'There is nothing wrong with the currents of his positronic brain.'

'I'd hate to be that certain.'

'Oh, Jupiter, Mike! The brain is the surest part of a robot. It's quintuple-checked back on Earth. If they pass the field test perfectly, the way Dave did, there just isn't a chance of brain misfunction. That test covered every key path in the brain.'

'So where are we?'

'Don't rush me. Let me work this out. There's still the possibility of a mechanical breakdown in the body. That leaves about fifteen hundred condensers, twenty thousand individual electric circuits, five hundred vacuum cells, a thousand relays, and umpty-ump thousand other individual pieces of complexity that can be wrong. *And* these mysterious positronic fields no one knows anything about.'

'Listen, Greg,' Donovan grew desperately urgent. 'I've got an idea. That robot may be lying. He never—'

'Robots can't knowingly lie, you fool. Now if we had the McCormack-Wesley tester, we could check each individual item in his body within twenty-four to forty-eight hours, but the only two M-W testers existing are on Earth, and they weigh ten tons, are on concrete foundations and can't be moved. Isn't that peachy?'

Donovan pounded the desk, 'But, Greg, he only goes wrong when we're not around. There's something – sinister – about – that.' He punctuated the sentence with slams of fist against desk.

'You,' said Powell, slowly, 'make me sick. You've been reading adventure novels.'

'What I want to know,' shouted Donovan, 'is what we're going to do about it.'

'I'll tell you. I'm going to install a visiplate right over my desk. Right on the wall over there, see!' He jabbed a vicious finger at the spot. 'Then I'm going to focus it at whatever part of the mine is being worked, and I'm going to watch. That's all.'

'That's all? Greg—'

Powell rose from his chair and leaned his balled fists on the desk, 'Mike, I'm having a hard time.' His voice was weary. 'For a week, you've been plaguing me about Dave. You say he's gone wrong. Do you know how he's gone wrong? No! Do you know what shape this wrongness takes? No! Do you know what brings it on? No! Do you know what snaps him out? No! Do you know anything about it? No! Do I know anything about it? No! So what do you want me to do?'

Donovan's arm swept outward in a vague, grandiose gesture, 'You got me!'

'So I tell you again. Before we do anything toward a cure, we've got to find out what the disease is in the first place. The first step in cooking rabbit stew is catching the rabbit. Well, we've got to catch that rabbit! Now get out of here.'

Donovan stared at the preliminary outline of his field report with weary eyes. For one thing, he was tired and for another, what was there to report while things were unsettled? He felt resentful.

He said, 'Greg, we're almost a thousand tons behind schedule.'

'You,' replied Powell, never looking up, 'are telling me something I don't know.'

'What I want to know,' said Donovan, in sudden savagery, 'is why we're always tangled up with new-type robots. I've finally decided that the robots that were good enough for my great-uncle on my mother's side are good enough for me. I'm for what's tried and true. The test of time is what counts – good, solid, old-fashioned robots that never go wrong.'

Powell threw a book with perfect aim, and Donovan went tumbling off his seat.

'Your job,' said Powell, evenly, 'for the last five years has been to test new robots under actual working conditions for United States Robots. Because you and I have been so injudicious as to display proficiency at the task, we've been rewarded with the dirtiest jobs. That,' he jabbed holes in the air with his finger in Donovan's direction, 'is your work. You've been griping about it, from personal memory, since about five minutes after United States Robots signed you up. Why don't you resign?'

'Well, I'll tell you.' Donovan rolled onto his stomach, and took a firm grip on his wild, red hair to hold his head up. 'There's a certain principle involved. After all, as a trouble shooter, I've played a part in the development of new robots. There's the principle of aiding scientific advance. But don't get me wrong. It's not the principle that keeps me going; it's the money they pay us. *Greg!*'

Powell jumped at Donovan's wild shout, and his eyes followed the redhead's to the visiplate, where they goggled in fixed horror. He whispered, 'Holy – howling – Jupiter!'

Donovan scrambled breathlessly to his feet, 'Look at them, Greg. They've gone nuts.'

Powell said, 'Get a pair of suits. We're going out there.'

He watched the posturings of the robots on the visiplate. They were bronzy gleams of smooth motion against the shadowy crags of the airless asteroid. There was a marching formation now, and in their own dim body light, the rough-hewn walls of the mine tunnel swam past noiselessly, checkered with misty erratic blobs of shadow. They marched in unison, seven of them, with Dave at the head. They wheeled and turned in macabre simultaneity; and melted through changes of formation with the weird ease of chorus dancers in Lunar Bowl.

Donovan was back with the suits, 'They've gone jingo on us, Greg. That's a military march.'

'For all you know,' was the cold response, 'it may be a series of calisthenic exercises. Or Dave may be under the hallucination of being a dancing master. Just you think first, and don't bother to speak afterward, either.'

Donovan scowled and slipped a detonator into the empty side holster with an ostentatious shove. He said, 'Anyway, there you are. So we work with new-model robots. It's our job, granted. But answer me one question. Why . . . *why* does something invariably go wrong with them?'

'Because,' said Powell, somberly, 'we are accursed. Let's go!'

Far ahead through the thick velvety blackness of the corridors that reached past the illuminated circles of their flashlights, robot light twinkled.

'There they are,' breathed Donovan.

Powell whispered tensely, 'I've been trying to get him by radio but he doesn't answer. The radio circuit is probably out.'

'Then I'm glad the designers haven't worked out robots who can work in total darkness yet. I'd hate to have to find seven mad robots in a black pit without radio communication, if they *weren't* lit up like blasted radioactive Christmas trees.'

'Crawl up on the ledge above, Mike. They're coming this way, and I want to watch them at close range. Can you make it?'

Donovan made the jump with a grunt. Gravity was considerably below Earth-normal, but with a heavy suit, the advantage was not too great, and the ledge meant a near-ten-foot jump. Powell followed.

The column of robots was trailing Dave single-file. In mechanical rhythm, they converted to double and returned to single in different order. It was repeated over and over again and Dave never turned his head.

Dave was within twenty feet when the play-acting ceased. The subsidiary robots broke formation, waited a moment, then clattered off into the distance – very rapidly. Dave looked after them, then slowly sat down. He rested his head in one hand in a very human gesture.

His voice sounded in Powell's earphones, 'Are you here, boss?'

Powell beckoned to Donovan and hopped off the ledge.

'OK, Dave, what's been going on?'

The robot shook his head, 'I don't know. One moment I was handling a tough outcropping in Tunnel 17, and the next I was aware of humans close by, and I found myself half a mile down main-stem.'

'Where are the subsidiaries now?' asked Donovan.

'Back at work, of course. How much time has been lost?'

'Not much. Forget it.' Then to Donovan, Powell added, 'Stay with him the rest of the shift. Then, come back. I've got a couple of ideas.'

It was three hours before Donovan returned. He looked tired.

Powell said, 'How did it go?'

Donovan shrugged wearily, 'Nothing ever goes wrong when you watch them. Throw me a butt, will you?'

The redhead lit it with exaggerated care and blew a careful smoke ring. He said, 'I've been working it out, Greg. You know, Dave has a queer background for a robot. There are six others under him in an extreme regimentation. He's got life and death power over those subsidiary robots and it must react on his mentality. Suppose he finds it necessary to emphasize this power as a concession to his ego.'

'Get to the point.'

'It's right here. Suppose we have militarism. Suppose he's fashioning himself an army. Suppose he's training them in military maneuvers. Suppose —'

'Suppose you go soak your head. Your nightmares must be in technicolor. You're postulating a major aberration of the positronic brain. If your analysis were correct, Dave would have to break down the First Law of Robotics that a robot may not injure a human being or, through inaction, allow a human being to be injured. The type of militaristic attitude and domineering ego you propose must have as the end-point of its logical implications, domination of humans.'

'All right. How do you know that isn't the fact of the matter?'

'Because any robot with a brain like that would, one, never have left the factory, and two, be spotted immediately if it ever was. I tested Dave, you know.'

Powell shoved his chair back and put his feet on the desk. 'No. We're still in the position where we can't make our stew because we haven't the slightest notion as to what's wrong. For instance, if we could find out what that *danse macabre* we witnessed was all about, we would be on the way out.'

He paused. 'Now listen, Mike, how does this sound to you? Dave goes wrong only when neither of us is present. And when he is wrong, the arrival of either of us snaps him out of it.'

'I once told you that was sinister.'

'Don't interrupt. How is a robot different when humans are not present? The answer is obvious. There is a larger requirement of personal initiative. In that case, look for the body parts that are affected by the new requirements.'

'Golly.' Donovan sat up straight, then subsided. 'No, no. Not enough. It's too broad. It doesn't cut the possibilities much.'

'Can't help that. In any case, there's no danger of not making quota. We'll take shifts watching those robots through the visor. Any time anything goes wrong, we get to the scene of action immediately. That will put them right.'

'But the robots will fail spec anyway, Greg. United States Robots can't market DV models with a report like that.'

'Obviously. We've got to locate the error in make-up and correct it – and we've got ten days to do it in.' Powell scratched his head. 'The trouble is . . . well, you had better look at the blueprints yourself.'

The blueprints covered the floor like a carpet and Donovan crawled over the face of them following Powell's erratic pencil.

Powell said, 'Here's where you come in, Mike. You're the body specialist, and I want you to check me. I've been trying to cut out all circuits not involved in the personal initiative hookup. Right here, for instance, is the trunk artery involving mechanical operations. I cut out all routine side routes as emergency divisions—' He looked up, 'What do you think?'

Donovan had a very bad taste in his mouth, 'The job's not that simple, Greg. Personal initiative isn't an electric circuit you can separate from the rest and study. When a robot is on his own, the intensity of the body activity increases immediately on almost all fronts. There isn't a circuit entirely unaffected. What must be done is to locate the particular condition – a very specific condition – that throws him off, and *then* start eliminating circuits.'

Powell got up and dusted himself, 'Hmph. All right. Take away the blueprints and burn them.'

Donovan said, 'You see when activity intensifies, anything can happen, given one single faulty part. Insulation breaks down, a condenser spills over, a connection sparks, a coil overheats. And if you work blind, with the whole robot to choose from, you'll never find the bad spot. If you take Dave apart and test every point of his body mechanism one by one, putting him together each time, and trying him out—'

'All right. All right. I can see through a porthole, too.'

They faced each other hopelessly, and then Powell said cautiously, 'Suppose we interview one of the subsidiaries.'

Neither Powell nor Donovan had ever had previous occasion to talk to a 'finger'. It could talk; it wasn't quite the perfect analogy to a human finger. In fact, it had a fairly developed brain, but that brain was tuned primarily to the reception of orders via positronic field, and its reaction to independent stimuli was rather fumbling.

Nor was Powell certain as to its name. Its serial number was DV-5-2, but that was not very useful.

He compromised. 'Look, pal,' he said, 'I'm going to ask you to do some hard thinking and then you can go back to your boss.'

The 'finger' nodded its head stiffly, but did not exert its limited brain-power on speech.

'Now on four occasions recently,' Powell said, 'your boss deviated from brain-scheme. Do you remember those occasions?'

'Yes, sir.'

Donovan growled angrily, '*He* remembers. I tell you there is something very sinister—'

'Oh, go bash your skull. Of course, the "finger" remembers. There is nothing wrong with him.' Powell turned back to the robot, 'What were you doing each time . . . I mean the whole group.'

The 'finger' had a curious air of reciting by rote, as if he answered questions by the mechanical pressure of his brain pan, but without any enthusiasm whatever.

He said, 'The first time we were at work on a difficult out-cropping in Tunnel 17, Level B. The second time we were buttressing the roof against a possible cave-in. The third time we were preparing accurate blasts in order to tunnel farther without breaking into a subterranean fissure. The fourth time was just after a minor cave-in.'

'What happened at these times?'

'It is difficult to describe. An order would be issued, but before we could receive and interpret it, a new order came to march in queer formation.'

Powell snapped out, 'Why?'

'I don't know.'

Donovan broke in tensely, 'What was the first order . . . the one that was superseded by the marching directions?'

'I don't know. I sensed that an order was sent, but there was never time to receive it.'

'Could you tell us anything about it? Was it the same order each time?'

The 'finger' shook his head unhappily, 'I don't know.'

Powell leaned back, 'All right, get back to your boss.'

The 'finger' left, with visible relief.

Donovan said, 'Well, we accomplished a lot that time. That was real sharp dialogue all the way through. Listen, Dave and that imbecile "finger" are both holding out on us. There is too much they don't know and don't remember. We've got to stop trusting them, Greg.'

Powell brushed his mustache the wrong way, 'So help me, Mike, another fool remark out of you and I'll take away your rattle and teething ring.'

'All right. You're the genius of the team. I'm just a poor sucker. Where do we stand?'

'Right behind the eight ball. I tried to work it backward through the "finger", and couldn't. So we've got to work it forward.'

'A great man,' marveled Donovan. 'How simple that makes it. Now translate that into English, Master.'

'Translating it into baby talk would suit you better. I mean that we've got to find out what order it is that Dave gives just before everything goes black. It would be the key to the business.'

'And how do you expect to do that? We can't get close to him because nothing will go wrong as long as we are there. We can't catch the orders by radio because they are transmitted via this positronic field. That eliminates the close-range and the long-range method, leaving us a neat, cozy zero.'

'By direct observation, yes. There's still deduction.'

'Huh?'

'We're going on shifts, Mike.' Powell smiled grimly. 'And we are not taking our eyes off the visiplate. We're going to watch every action of those steel headaches. When they go off into their act, we're going to see what happened immediately before and we're going to deduce the order.'

Donovan opened his mouth and left it that way for a full minute. Then he said in strangled tones, 'I resign. I quit.'

'You have ten days to think up something better,' said Powell wearily.

Which, for eight days, Donovan tried mightily to do. For eight days, on alternate four-hour shifts, he watched with aching and bleary eyes those glinty metallic forms move against the vague background. And for eight days in the four-hour in-betweens, he cursed United States Robots, the DV models, and the day he was born.

And then on the 8th, when Powell entered with an aching head and sleepy eyes for his shift, Donovan stood up and with very careful and deliberate aim launched a heavy book end for the exact center of the visiplate. There was a very appropriate splintering noise.

Powell gasped, 'What did you do that for?'

'Because,' said Donovan, almost calmly, 'I'm not watching it any more. We've got two days left and we haven't found out a thing. DV-5 is a lousy loss. He's stopped five times since I've been watching and three times on your shift, and I can't make out what orders he gave, and you couldn't make it out. And I don't believe you could ever make it out because I know I couldn't ever.'

'Jumping Space, how can you watch six robots at the same time? One makes with the hands, and one with the feet and one like a windmill and another is jumping up and down like a maniac. And the other two . . . devil knows what they are doing. And then they all stop. So! So!'

'Greg, we're not doing it right. We got to get up close. We've got to watch what they're doing from where we can see the details.'

Powell broke a bitter silence. 'Yeah, and wait for something to go wrong with only two days to go.'

'Is it any better watching from here?'

'It's more comfortable.'

'Ah— But there's something you can do there that you can't do here.'

'What's that?'

'You can make them stop – at whatever time you choose – and while you're prepared and watching to see what goes wrong.'

Powell startled into alertness, 'Howzzat?'

'Well, figure it out yourself. You're the brains you say. Ask yourself some questions. When does DV-5 go out of whack? When did that "finger" say he did? When a cave-in threatened, or actually occurred, when delicately measured explosives were being laid down, when a difficult seam was hit.'

'In other words, during emergencies.' Powell was excited.

'Right! When *did* you expect it to happen! It's the personal initiative factor that's giving us the trouble. And it's just during emergencies in the absence of a human being that personal initiative is most strained. Now what is the logical deduction? How can we create our own stoppage when and where we want it?' He paused triumphantly – he was beginning to enjoy his role – and answered his own question to forestall the obvious answer on Powell's tongue. 'By creating our own emergency.'

Powell said, 'Mike – you're right.'

'Thanks, pal. I knew I'd do it some day.'

'All right, and skip the sarcasm. We'll save it for Earth, and preserve it in jars for future long, cold winters. Meanwhile, what emergency can we create?'

'We could flood the mines, if this weren't an airless asteroid.'

'A witticism, no doubt,' said Powell. 'Really, Mike, you'll incapacitate me with laughter. What about a mild cave-in?'

Donovan pursued his lips and said, 'OK by me.'

'Good. Let's get started.'

Powell felt uncommonly like a conspirator as he wound his way over the craggy landscape. His sub-gravity walk teetered across the broken ground, kicking rocks to right and left under his weight in noiseless puffs of gray dust. Mentally, though, it was the cautious crawl of the plotter.

He said, 'Do you know where they are?'

'I think so, Greg.'

'All right,' Powell said gloomily, 'but if any "finger" gets within twenty feet of us, we'll be sensed whether we are in the line of sight or not. I hope you know that.'

'When I need an elementary course in robotics, I'll file an application with you formally, and in triplicate. Down through here.'

They were in the tunnels now; even the starlight was gone. The two hugged the walls, flashes flickering out the way in intermittent bursts. Powell felt for the security of his detonator.

'Do you know this tunnel, Mike?'

'Not so good. It's a new one. I think I can make it out from what I saw in the visiplate, though—'

Interminable minutes passed, and then Mike said, 'Feel that!'

There was a slight vibration thrumming the wall against the fingers of Powell's metal-incased hand. There was no sound, naturally.

'Blasting! We're pretty close.'

'Keep your eyes open,' said Powell.

Donovan nodded impatiently.

It was upon them and gone before they could seize themselves – just a bronze glint across the field of vision. They clung together in silence.

Powell whispered, 'Think it sensed us?'

'Hope not. But we'd better flank them. Take the first side tunnel to the right.'

'Suppose we miss them altogether?'

'Well what do you want to do? Go back?' Donovan grunted fiercely. 'They're within a quarter of a mile. I was watching them through the visiplate, wasn't I? And we've got two days—'

'Oh, shut up. You're wasting your oxygen. Is this a side passage here?' The flash flicked. 'It is. Let's go.'

The vibration was considerably more marked and the ground below shuddered uneasily.

'This is good,' said Donovan, 'if it doesn't give out on us, though.' He flung his light ahead anxiously.

They could touch the roof of the tunnel with a half-up-stretched hand, and the bracings had been newly placed.

Donovan hesitated, 'Dead end, let's go back.'

'No. Hold on.' Powell squeezed clumsily past. 'Is that light ahead?'

'Light? I don't see any. Where would there be light down here?'

'Robot light.' He was scrambling up a gentle incline on hands and knees. His voice was hoarse and anxious in Donovan's ears. 'Hey, Mike, come up here.'

There was light. Donovan crawled up and over Powell's outstretched legs. 'An opening?'

'Yes. They must be working into this tunnel from the other side now – I think.'

Donovan felt the ragged edges of the opening that looked out into what the cautious flashlight showed to be a larger and obviously main-stem tunnel. The hole was too small for a man to go through, almost too small for two men to look through simultaneously.

'There's nothing there,' said Donovan.

'Well, not now. But there must have been a second ago or we wouldn't have seen light. Watch out!'

The walls rolled about them and they felt the impact. A fine dust showered down. Powell lifted a cautious head and looked again. 'All right, Mike. They're there.'

The glittering robots clustered fifty feet down the main stem. Metal arms labored mightily at the rubbish heap brought down by the last blast.

Donovan urged eagerly, 'Don't waste time. It won't be long before they get through, and the next blast may get us.'

'For Pete's sake, don't rush me.' Powell unlimbered the detonator, and his eyes searched anxiously across the dusky background where the only light was robot light and it was impossible to tell a projecting boulder from a shadow.

'There's a spot in the roof, see it, almost over them. The last blast didn't quite get it. If you can get it at the base, half the roof will cave in.'

Powell followed the dim finger, 'Check! Now fasten your eye on the robots and pray they don't move too far from that part of the tunnel. They're my light sources. Are all seven there?'

Donovan counted, 'All seven.'

'Well, then, watch them. Watch every motion!'

His detonator was lifted and remained poised while Donovan watched and cursed and blinked the sweat out of his eye.

It flashed!

There was a jar, a series of hard vibrations, and then a jarring thump that threw Powell heavily against Donovan.

Donovan yowled, 'Greg, you threw me off. I didn't see a thing.'

Powell stared about wildly, 'Where are they?'

Donovan fell into a stupid silence. There was no sign of the robots. It was dark as the depths of the River Styx.

'Think we buried them?' quavered Donovan.

'Let's get down there. Don't ask me what I think.' Powell crawled backward at tumbling speed.

'Mike!'

Donovan paused in the act of following. 'What's wrong now?'

'Hold on!' Powell's breathing was rough and irregular in Donovan's ears. 'Mike! Do you hear me, Mike?'

'I'm right here. What is it?'

'We're blocked in. It wasn't the ceiling coming down fifty feet away that knocked us over. It was our own ceiling. The shock's tumbled it!'

'What!' Donovan scrambled up against a hard barrier. 'Turn on the flash.'

Powell did so. At no point was there room for a rabbit to squeeze through.

Donovan said softly, 'Well, what do you know?'

They wasted a few moments and some muscular power in an effort to move the blocking barrier. Powell varied this by wrenching at the edges of the original hole. For a moment, Powell lifted his blaster. But in those close quarters, a flash would be suicide and he knew it. He sat down.

'You know, Mike,' he said, 'we've really messed this up. We are no nearer finding out what's wrong with Dave. It was a good idea but it blew up in our face.'

Donovan's glance was bitter with an intensity totally wasted on the darkness, 'I hate to disturb you, old man, but quite apart from what we know or don't know of Dave, we're slightly trapped. If we don't get loose, fella, we're going to die. D-I-E, die. How much oxygen have we anyway? Not more than six hours.'

'I've thought of that.' Powell's fingers went up to his long-suffering mustache and clanged uselessly against the transparent visor. 'Of course, we could get Dave to dig us out easily in that time, except that our precious emergency must have thrown him off, and his radio circuit is out.'

'And isn't that nice?'

Donovan edged up to the opening and managed to get his metal-incased head out. It was an extremely tight fit.

'Hey, Greg!'

'What?'

'Suppose we get Dave within twenty feet. He'll snap to normal. That will save us.'

'Sure, but where is he?'

'Down the corridor – way down. For Pete's sake, stop pulling before you drag my head out of its socket. I'll give you your chance to look.'

Powell maneuvered his head outside, 'We did it all right. Look at those saps. That must be a ballet they're doing.'

'Never mind the snide remarks. Are they getting any closer?'

'Can't tell yet. They're too far away. Give me a chance. Pass me my flash, will you? I'll try to attract their attention that way.'

He gave up after two minutes, 'Not a chance! They must be blind. Uh-oh, they're starting toward us. What do you know?'

Donovan said, 'Hey, let me see!'

There was a silent scuffle. Powell said, 'All right!' and Donovan got his head out.

They were approaching. Dave was high-stepping the way in front and the six 'fingers' were a weaving chorus line behind him.

Donovan marveled, 'What are they doing? That's what I want to know. It looks like the Virginia reel – and Dave's a major-domo, or I never saw one.'

'Oh, leave me alone with your descriptions,' grumbled Powell. 'How near are they?'

'Within fifty feet and coming this way. We'll be out in fifteen min – Uh – huh – HUH – HEY-Y!'

'What's going on?' It took Powell several seconds to recover from his stunned astonishment at Donovan's vocal gyrations. 'Come on, give me a chance at that hole. Don't be a hog about it.'

He fought his way upward, but Donovan kicked wildly, 'They did an about-face, Greg. They're leaving. Dave! Hey, Da-a-ave!'

Powell shrieked, 'What's the use of that, you fool? Sound won't carry.'

'Well, then,' panted Donovan, 'kick the walls, slam them, get some vibration started. We've got to attract their attention somehow, Greg, or we're through.' He pounded like a madman.

Powell shook him, 'Wait, Mike, wait. Listen, I've got an idea. Jumping Jupiter, this is a fine time to get around to the simple solutions. Mike!'

'What do you want?' Donovan pulled his head in.

'Let me in there fast before they get out of range.'

'Out of range! What are you going to do? Hey, what are you going to do with that detonator?' He grabbed Powell's arm.

Powell shook off the grip violently. 'I'm going to do a little shooting.'

'Why?'

'That's for later. Let's see if it works first. If it doesn't, then— Get out of the way and let me shoot!'

The robots were flickers, small and getting smaller, in the distance. Powell lined up the sights tensely, and pulled the trigger three times. He lowered the gun and peered anxiously. One of the subsidiaries was down! There were only six gleaming figures now.

Powell called into his transmitter uncertainly. 'Dave!'

A pause, then the answer sounded to both men, 'Boss? Where are you? My third subsidiary has had his chest blown in. He's out of commission.'

'Never mind your subsidiary,' said Powell. 'We're trapped in a cave-in where you were blasting. Can you see our flashlight?'

'Sure. We'll be right there.'

Powell sat back and relaxed, 'That, my fran', is that.'

Donovan said very softly with tears in his voice, 'All right, Greg. You win. I beat my forehead against the ground before your feet. Now don't feed me any bull. Just tell me quietly what it's all about.'

'Easy. It's just that all through we missed the obvious – as usual. We knew it was the personal initiative circuit, and that it always happened during emergencies, but we kept looking for a specific order as the cause. Why should it be an order?'

'Why not?'

'Well, look. Why not a type of order. What type of order requires the most initiative? What type of order would occur almost always only in an emergency?'

'Don't ask me, Greg. Tell me!'

'I'm doing it! It's the six-way order. Under all ordinary conditions, one or more of the "fingers" would be doing routine tasks requiring no close supervision – in the sort of offhand way our bodies handle the routine walking motions. But in an emergency, all six subsidiaries must be mobilized immediately and simultaneously. Dave must handle six robots at a time and something gives. The rest was easy. Any decrease in initiative required, such as the arrival of humans, snaps him back. So I destroyed one of the robots. When I did, he was transmitting only the five-way orders. Initiative decreases – he's normal.'

'How did you get all that?' demanded Donovan.

'Just logical guessing. I tried it and it worked.'

The robot's voice was in their ears again, 'Here I am. Can you hold out half an hour?'

'Easy!' said Powell. Then, to Donovan, he continued, 'And now the job should be simple. We'll go through the circuits, and check off each part that gets an extra workout in a six-way order as against a five-way. How big a field does that leave us?'

Donovan considered, 'Not much, I think. If Dave is like the preliminary model we saw back at the factory, there's a special co-ordinating circuit that would be the only section involved.' He cheered up suddenly and amazingly, 'Say, that wouldn't be bad at all. There's nothing to that.'

'All right. You think it over and we'll check the blueprints when we get back. And now, till Dave reaches us, I'm relaxing.'

'Hey, wait! Just tell me one thing. What were those queer shifting marches, those funny dance steps, that the robots went through every time they went screwy?'

'That? I don't know. But I've got a notion. Remember, those subsidiaries were Dave's "fingers". We were always saying that, you know. Well, it's my idea that in all these interludes, whenever Dave became a psychiatric case, he went off into a moronic maze, spending his time *twiddling his fingers*.'

Susan Calvin talked about Powell and Donovan with unsmiling amusement, but warmth came into her voice when she mentioned robots. It didn't take her long to go through the Speedies, the Cuties and the Daves, and I stopped her. Otherwise, she would have dredged up half a dozen more.

I said, 'Doesn't anything ever happen on Earth?'

She looked at me with a little frown, 'No, we don't have much to do with robots in action here on Earth.'

'Oh, well that's too bad. I mean, your field-engineers are swell, but can't we get you into this? Didn't you ever have a robot go wrong on you? It's your anniversary, you know.'

And so help me she blushed. She said, 'Robots have gone wrong on me. Heavens, how long it's been since I thought of it. Why, it was almost forty years ago. Certainly! 2021! And I was only thirty-eight. Oh, my – I'd rather not talk about it.'

I waited, and sure enough she changed her mind. 'Why not?' she said. 'It cannot harm me now. Even the memory can't. I was foolish once, young man. Would you believe that?'

'No,' I said.

'I was. But Herbie was a mind-reading robot.'

'What?'

'Only one of its kind, before or since. A mistake – some-wheres—'

5
Liar!

Alfred Lanning lit his cigar carefully, but the tips of his
fingers were trembling slightly. His gray eyebrows hunched
low as he spoke between puffs.

'It reads minds all right – damn little doubt about
that! But why?' He looked at Mathematician Peter Bogert,
'Well?'

Bogert flattened his black hair down with both hands,
'That was the thirty-fourth RB model we've turned out,
Lanning. All the others were strictly orthodox.'

The third man at the table frowned. Milton Ashe was the
youngest officer of US Robot & Mechanical Men, Inc., and
proud of his post.

'Listen, Bogert. There wasn't a hitch in the assembly from
start to finish. I guarantee that.'

Bogert's thick lips spread in a patronizing smile, 'Do you?
If you can answer for the entire assembly line, I recommend
your promotion. By exact count, there are 75,234 operations
necessary for the manufacture of a single positronic brain,
each separate operation depending for successful completion
upon any number of factors, from five to a hundred and
five. If any one of them goes seriously wrong, the "brain" is
ruined. I quote our own information folder, Ashe.'

Milton Ashe flushed, but a fourth voice cut off his
reply.

'If we're going to start by trying to fix the blame on
one another, I'm leaving.' Susan Calvin's hands were folded
tightly in her lap, and the little lines about her thin, pale lips
deepened. 'We've got a mind-reading robot on our hands and
it strikes me as rather important that we find out just why

it reads minds. We're not going to do that by saying, "Your fault! My fault!" '

Her cold gray eyes fastened upon Ashe, and he grinned.

Lanning grinned too, and, as always at such times, his long white hair and shrewd little eyes made him the picture of a biblical patriarch. 'True for you, Dr Calvin.'

His voice became suddenly crisp, 'Here's everything in pill-concentrate form. We've produced a positronic brain of supposedly ordinary vintage that's got the remarkable property of being able to tune in on thought waves. It would mark the most important advance in robotics in decades, if we knew how it happened. We don't, and we have to find out. Is that clear?'

'May I make a suggestion?' asked Bogert.

'Go ahead!'

'I'd say that until we do figure out the mess – and as a mathematician I expect it to be a very devil of a mess – we keep the existence of RB-34 a secret. I mean even from the other members of the staff. As heads of the departments, we ought not to find it an insoluble problem, and the fewer know about it—'

'Bogert is right,' said Dr Calvin. 'Ever since the Interplanetary Code was modified to allow robot models to be tested in the plants before being shipped out to space, anti-robot propaganda has increased. If any word leaks out about a robot being able to read minds before we can announce complete control of the phenomenon, pretty effective capital could be made out of it.'

Lanning sucked at his cigar and nodded gravely. He turned to Ashe, 'I think you said you were alone when you first stumbled on this thought-reading business.'

'I'll say I was alone – I got the scare of my life. RB-34 had just been taken off the assembly table and they sent him down to me. Obermann was off somewheres, so I took him down to the testing rooms myself – at least I started to take him down.' Ashe paused, and a tiny smile tugged at his lips, 'Say, did any of you ever carry on a thought conversation without knowing it?'

No one bothered to answer, and he continued, 'You don't realize it at first, you know. He just spoke to me – as logically and sensibly as you can imagine – and it was only when I was most of the way down to the testing rooms that I realized that I hadn't said anything. Sure, I thought lots, but that isn't the same thing, is it? I locked that thing up and ran for Lanning. Having it walking beside me, calmly peering into my thoughts and picking and choosing among them gave me the willies.'

'I imagine it would,' said Susan Calvin thoughtfully. Her eyes fixed themselves upon Ashe in an oddly intent manner. 'We are so accustomed to considering our own thoughts private.'

Lanning broke in impatiently, 'Then only the four of us know. All right! We've got to go about this systematically. Ashe, I want you to check over the assembly line from beginning to end – everything. You're to eliminate all operations in which there was no possible chance of an error, and list all those where there were, together with its nature and possible magnitude.'

'Tall order,' grunted Ashe.

'Naturally! Of course, you're to put the men under you to work on this – every single one if you have to, and I don't care if we go behind schedule, either. But they're not to know why, you understand.'

'Hm-m-m, yes!' The young technician grinned wryly. 'It's still a lulu of a job.'

Lanning swiveled about in his chair and faced Calvin, 'You'll have to tackle the job from the other direction. You're the robo-psychologist of the plant, so you're to study the robot itself and work backward. Try to find out how he ticks. See what else is tied up with his telepathic powers, how far they extend, how they warp his outlook, and just exactly what harm it has done to his ordinary RB properties. You've got that?'

Lanning didn't wait for Dr Calvin to answer.

'I'll co-ordinate the work and interpret the findings mathematically.' He puffed violently at his cigar and mumbled the rest through the smoke, 'Bogert will help me there, of course.'

Bogert polished the nails of one pudgy hand with the other and said blandly, 'I dare say. I know a little in the line.'

'Well! I'll get started.' Ashe shoved his chair back and rose. His pleasantly youthful face crinkled in a grin, 'I've got the darnedest job of any of us, so I'm getting out of here and to work.'

He left with a slurred, 'B' seein' ye!'

Susan Calvin answered with a barely perceptible nod, but her eyes followed him out of sight and she did not answer when Lanning grunted and said, 'Do you want to go up and see RB-34 now, Dr Calvin?'

RB-34's photoelectric eyes lifted from the book at the muffled sound of hinges turning and he was up on his feet when Susan Calvin entered.

She paused to readjust the huge 'No Entrance' sign upon the door and then approached the robot.

'I've brought you the texts upon hyperatomic motors, Herbie – a few anyway. Would you care to look at them?'

RB-34 – otherwise known as Herbie – lifted the three heavy books from her arms and opened to the title page of one:

'Hm-m-m! "Theory of Hyperatomics".' He mumbled inarticulately to himself as he flipped the pages and then spoke with an abstracted air, 'Sit down, Dr Calvin! This will take me a few minutes.'

The psychologist seated herself and watched Herbie narrowly as he took a chair at the other side of the table and went through the three books systematically.

At the end of half an hour, he put them down. 'Of course, I know why you brought these.'

The corner of Dr Calvin's lip twitched. 'I was afraid you would. It's difficult to work with you, Herbie. You're always a step ahead of me.'

'It's the same with these books, you know, as with the others. They just don't interest me. There's nothing to your textbooks. Your science is just a mass of collected data plastered together by make-shift theory – and all so incredibly simple, that it's scarcely worth bothering about.

'It's your fiction that interests me. Your studies of the interplay of human motives and emotions' – his mighty hand gestured vaguely as he sought the proper words.

Dr Calvin whispered, 'I think I understand.'

'I see into minds, you see,' the robot continued, 'and you have no idea how complicated they are. I can't begin to understand everything because my own mind has so little in common with them – but I try, and your novels help.'

'Yes, but I'm afraid that after going through some of the harrowing emotional experiences of our present-day sentimental novel' – there was a tinge of bitterness in her voice – 'you find real minds like ours dull and colorless.'

'But I don't!'

The sudden energy in the response brought the other to her feet. She felt herself reddening, and thought wildly, 'He must know!'

Herbie subsided suddenly, and muttered in a low voice from which the metallic timbre departed almost entirely. 'But, of course, I know about it, Dr Calvin. You think of it always, so how can I help but know?'

Her face was hard. 'Have you – told anyone?'

'Of course not!' This, with genuine surprise. 'No one has asked me.'

'Well, then,' she flung out, 'I suppose you think I am a fool.'

'No! It is a normal emotion.'

'Perhaps that is why it is so foolish.' The wistfulness in her voice drowned out everything else. Some of the woman peered through the layer of doctorhood. 'I am not what you would call – attractive.'

'If you are referring to mere physical attraction, I couldn't judge. But I know, in any case, that there are other types of attraction.'

'Nor young.' Dr Calvin had scarcely heard the robot.

'You are not yet forty.' An anxious insistence had crept into Herbie's voice.

'Thirty-eight as you count the years; a shriveled sixty as far as my emotional outlook on life is concerned. Am I a psychologist for nothing?'

She drove on with bitter breathlessness, 'And he's barely thirty-five and looks and acts younger. Do you suppose he ever sees me as anything but . . . but what I am?'

'You are wrong!' Herbie's steel fist struck the plastic-topped table with a strident clang. 'Listen to me—'

But Susan Calvin whirled on him now and the hunted pain in her eyes became a blaze, 'Why should I? What do you know about it all, anyway, you . . . you machine. I'm just a specimen to you; an interesting bug with a peculiar mind spread-eagled for inspection. It's a wonderful example of frustration, isn't it? Almost as good as your books.' Her voice, emerging in dry sobs, choked into silence.

The robot cowered at the outburst. He shook his head pleadingly. 'Won't you listen to me, please? I could help you if you would let me.'

'How?' Her lips curled. 'By giving me good advice?'

'No, not that. It's just that I know what other people think – Milton Ashe, for instance.'

There was a long silence, and Susan Calvin's eyes dropped. 'I don't want to know what he thinks,' she gasped. 'Keep quiet.'

'I think you would want to know what he thinks.'

Her head remained bent, but her breath came more quickly. 'You are talking nonsense,' she whispered.

'Why should I? I am trying to help. Milton Ashe's thoughts of you—' he paused.

And then the psychologist raised her head, 'Well?'

The robot said quietly, 'He loves you.'

For a full minute, Dr Calvin did not speak. She merely stared. Then, 'You are mistaken! You must be. Why should he?'

'But he does. A thing like that cannot be hidden, not from me.'

'But I am so . . . so —' she stammered to a halt.

'He looks deeper than the skin, and admires intellect in others. Milton Ashe is not the type to marry a head of hair and a pair of eyes.'

Susan Calvin found herself blinking rapidly and waited before speaking. Even then her voice trembled, 'Yet he certainly never in any way indicated—'

'Have you ever given him a chance?'

'How could I? I never thought that—'

'Exactly!'

The psychologist paused in thought and then looked up suddenly. 'A girl visited him here at the plant half a year ago. She was pretty, I suppose – blonde and slim. And, of course, could scarcely add two and two. He spent all day puffing out his chest, trying to explain how a robot was put together.' The hardness had returned, 'Not that she understood! Who was she?'

Herbie answered without hesitation, 'I know the person you are referring to. She is his first cousin, and there is no romantic interest there, I assure you.'

Susan Calvin rose to her feet with a vivacity almost girlish. 'Now isn't that strange? That's exactly what I used to pretend to myself sometimes, though I never really thought so. Then it all must be true.'

She ran to Herbie and seized his cold, heavy hand in both hers. 'Thank you, Herbie.' Her voice was an urgent, husky whisper. 'Don't tell anyone about this. Let it be our secret – and thank you again.' With that, and a convulsive squeeze of Herbie's unresponsive metal fingers, she left.

Herbie turned slowly to his neglected novel, but there was no one to read *his* thoughts.

Milton Ashe stretched slowly and magnificently, to the tune of cracking joints and a chorus of grunts, and then glared at Peter Bogert, Ph.D.

'Say,' he said, 'I've been at this for a week now with just about no sleep. How long do I have to keep it up? I thought you said the positronic bombardment in Vac Chamber D was the solution.'

Bogert yawned delicately and regarded his white hands with interest. 'It is. I'm on the track.'

'I know what *that* means when a mathematician says it. How near the end are you?'

'It all depends.'

'On what?' Ashe dropped into a chair and stretched his long legs out before him.

'On Lanning. The old fellow disagrees with me.' He sighed, 'A bit behind the times, that's the trouble with him. He clings to matrix mechanics as the all in all, and this problem calls for more powerful mathematical tools. He's so stubborn.'

Ashe muttered sleepily, 'Why not ask Herbie and settle the whole affair?'

'Ask the robot?' Bogert's eyebrows climbed.

'Why not? Didn't the old girl tell you?'

'You mean Calvin?'

'Yeah! Susie herself. That robot's a mathematical wiz. He knows all about everything plus a bit on the side. He does triple integrals in his head and eats up tensor analysis for dessert.'

The mathematician stared skeptically, 'Are you serious?'

'So help me! The catch is that the dope doesn't like math. He would rather read slushy novels. Honest! You should see the tripe Susie keeps feeding him: "Purple Passion" and "Love in Space".'

'Dr Calvin hasn't said a word of this to us.'

'Well, she hasn't finished studying him. You know how she is. She likes to have everything just so before letting out the big secret.'

'She's told *you*.'

'We sort of got to talking. I have been seeing a lot of her lately.' He opened his eyes wide and frowned, 'Say, Bogie, have you been noticing anything queer about the lady lately?'

Bogert relaxed into an undignified grin, 'She's using lipstick, if that's what you mean.'

'Hell, I know that. Rouge, powder and eye shadow, too. She's a sight. But it's not that. I can't put my finger on it. It's the way she talks – as if she were happy about something.' He thought a little, and then shrugged.

The other allowed himself a leer, which, for a scientist past fifty, was not a bad job, 'Maybe she's in love.'

Ashe allowed his eyes to close again, 'You're nuts, Bogie. You go speak to Herbie; I want to stay here and go to sleep.'

'Right! Not that I particularly like having a robot tell me my job, nor that I think he can do it!'

A soft snore was his only answer.

Herbie listened carefully as Peter Bogert, hands in pockets, spoke with elaborate indifference.

'So there you are. I've been told you understand these things, and I am asking you more in curiosity than anything else. My line of reasoning, as I have outlined it, involves a few doubtful steps, I admit, which Dr Lanning refuses to accept, and the picture is still rather incomplete.'

The robot didn't answer, and Bogert said, 'Well?'

'I see no mistake,' Herbie studied the scribbled figures.

'I don't suppose you can go any further than that?'

'I daren't try. You are a better mathematician than I, and – well, I'd hate to commit myself.'

There was a shade of complacency in Bogert's smile, 'I rather thought that would be the case. It is deep. We'll forget it.' He crumpled the sheets, tossed them down the waste shaft, turned to leave, and then thought better of it.

'By the way—'

The robot waited.

Bogert seemed to have difficulty. 'There is something – that is, perhaps you can—' He stopped.

Herbie spoke quietly, 'Your thoughts are confused, but there is no doubt at all that they concern Dr Lanning. It is silly to hesitate, for as soon as you compose yourself, I'll know what it is you want to ask.'

The mathematician's hand went to his sleek hair in the familiar smoothing gesture. 'Lanning is nudging seventy,' he said, as if that explained everything.

'I know that.'

'And he's been director of the plant for almost thirty years.'

Herbie nodded.

'Well, now,' Bogert's voice became ingratiating, 'you would know whether . . . whether he's thinking of resigning. Health, perhaps, or some other—'

'Quite,' said Herbie, and that was all.

'Well, do you know?'

'Certainly.'

'Then – uh – could you tell me?'

'Since you ask, yes.' The robot was quite matter-of-fact about it. 'He has already resigned!'

'What!' The exclamation was an explosive, almost inarticulate, sound. The scientist's large head hunched forward. 'Say that again!'

'He has already resigned,' came the quiet repetition, 'but it has not yet taken effect. He is waiting, you see, to solve the problem of – er – myself. That finished, he is quite ready to turn the office of director over to his successor.'

Bogert expelled his breath sharply, 'And this successor? Who is he?' He was quite close to Herbie now, eyes fixed fascinatedly on those unreadable dull-red photoelectric cells that were the robot's eyes.

Words came slowly, 'You are the next director.'

And Bogert relaxed into a tight smile, 'This is good to know. I've been hoping and waiting for this. Thanks, Herbie.'

Peter Bogert was at his desk until five that morning and he was back at nine. The shelf just over the desk emptied of its row of reference books and tables, as he referred to one after the other. The pages of calculations before him increased microscopically and the crumpled sheets at his feet mounted into a hill of scribbled paper.

At precisely noon, he stared at the final page, rubbed a bloodshot eye, yawned and shrugged. 'This is getting worse each minute. Damn!'

He turned at the sound of the opening door and nodded at Lanning, who entered, cracking the knuckles of one gnarled hand with the other.

The director took in the disorder of the room and his eyebrows furrowed together.

'New lead?' he asked.

'No,' came the defiant answer. 'What's wrong with the old one?'

Lanning did not trouble to answer, nor to do more than bestow a single cursory glance at the top sheet upon Bogert's desk. He spoke through the flare of a match as he lit a cigar.

'Has Calvin told you about the robot? It's a mathematical genius. Really remarkable.'

The other snorted loudly, 'So I've heard. But Calvin had better stick to robopsychology. I've checked Herbie on math, and he can scarcely struggle through calculus.'

'Calvin didn't find it so.'

'She's crazy.'

'And I don't find it so.' The director's eyes narrowed dangerously.

'You!' Bogert's voice hardened. 'What are you talking about?'

'I've been putting Herbie through his paces all morning, and he can do tricks you never heard of.'

'Is that so?'

'You sound skeptical!' Lanning flipped a sheet of paper out of his vest pocket and unfolded it. 'That's not my handwriting, is it?'

Bogert studied the large angular notation covering the sheet, 'Herbie did this?'

'Right! And if you'll notice, he's been working on your time integration of Equation 22. It comes' – Lanning tapped a yellow fingernail upon the last step – 'to the identical conclusion I did, and in a quarter the time. You had no right to neglect the Linger Effect in positronic bombardment.'

'I didn't neglect it. For Heaven's sake, Lanning, get it through your head that it would cancel out—'

'Oh, sure, you explained that. You used the Mitchell Translation Equation, didn't you? Well – it doesn't apply.'

'Why not?'

'Because you've been using hyper-imaginaries, for one thing.'

'What's that to do with?'

'Mitchell's Equation won't hold when—'

'Are you crazy? If you'll reread Mitchell's original paper in the *Transactions of the Far*—'

'I don't have to. I told you in the beginning that I didn't like his reasoning, and Herbie backs me in that.'

'Well, then,' Bogert shouted, 'let that clockwork contraption solve the entire problem for you. Why bother with non-essentials?'

'That's exactly the point. Herbie can't solve the problem. And if he can't, we can't – alone. I'm submitting the entire question to the National Board. It's gotten beyond us.'

Bogert's chair went over backward as he jumped up a-snarl, face crimson. 'You're doing nothing of the sort.'

Lanning flushed in his turn, 'Are you telling me what I can't do?'

'Exactly,' was the gritted response. 'I've got the problem beaten and you're not to take it out of my hands, understand? Don't think I don't see through you, you desiccated fossil. You'd cut your own nose off before you'd let me get the credit for solving robotic telepathy.'

'You're a damned idiot, Bogert, and in one second I'll have you suspended for insubordination' – Lanning's lower lip trembled with passion.

'Which is one thing you won't do, Lanning. You haven't any secrets with a mind-reading robot around, so don't forget that I know all about your resignation.'

The ash on Lanning's cigar trembled and fell, and the cigar itself followed, 'What . . . what—'

Bogert chuckled nastily, 'And I'm the new director, be it understood. I'm very aware of that; don't think I'm not. Damn your eyes, Lanning, I'm going to give the orders about here or there will be the sweetest mess that you've ever been in.'

Lanning found his voice and let it out with a roar. 'You're suspended, d'ye hear? You're relieved of all duties. You're broken, do you understand?'

The smile on the other's face broadened, 'Now, what's the use of that? You're getting nowhere. I'm holding the trumps. I know you've resigned. Herbie told me, and he got it straight from you.'

Lanning forced himself to speak quietly. He looked an old, old man, with tired eyes peering from a face in which the red had disappeared, leaving the pasty yellow of age behind. 'I want to speak to Herbie. He can't have told you anything of the sort. You're playing a deep game, Bogert, but I'm calling your bluff. Come with me.'

Bogert shrugged, 'To see Herbie? Good! Damned good!'

It was also precisely at noon that Milton Ashe looked up from his clumsy sketch and said, 'You get the idea? I'm not good at getting this down, but that's about how it looks. It's a honey of a house, and I can get it for next to nothing.'

Susan Calvin gazed across at him with melting eyes. 'It's really beautiful,' she sighed. 'I've often thought that I'd like to —' Her voice trailed away.

'Of course,' Ashe continued briskly, putting away his pencil, 'I've got to wait for my vacation. It's only two weeks

off, but this Herbie business has everything up in the air.'
His eyes dropped to his fingernails, 'Besides, there's another
point – but it's a secret.'

'Then don't tell me.'

'Oh, I'd just as soon, I'm just busting to tell someone – and   you're   just   about   the   best – er – con-
fidante I could find here.' He grinned sheepishly.

Susan Calvin's heart bounded, but she did not trust herself
to speak.

'Frankly,' Ashe scraped his chair closer and lowered his
voice into a confidential whisper, 'the house isn't to be only
for myself. I'm getting married!'

And then he jumped out of his seat, 'What's the matter?'

'Nothing!' The horrible spinning sensation had vanished, but it was hard to get words out. 'Married? You
mean—'

'Why, sure! About time, isn't it? You remember that girl
who was here last summer. That's she! But you *are* sick.
You—'

'Headache!' Susan Calvin motioned him away weakly.
'I've . . . I've been subject to them lately. I want to . . .
to congratulate you, of course, I'm very glad—' The
inexpertly applied rouge made a pair of nasty red splotches
upon her chalk-white face. Things had begun spinning again.
'Pardon me – please—'

The words were a mumble, as she stumbled blindly
out the door. It had happened with the sudden catastrophe of a dream – and with all the unreal horror of a
dream.

But how could it be? Herbie had said—

And Herbie knew! He could see into minds!

She found herself leaning breathlessly against the door
jamb, staring into Herbie's metal face. She must have
climbed the two flights of stairs, but she had no memory

of it. The distance had been covered in an instant, as in a dream.

As in a dream!

And still Herbie's unblinking eyes stared into hers and their dull red seemed to expand into dimly shining nightmarish globes.

He was speaking, and she felt the cold glass pressing against her lips. She swallowed and shuddered into a certain awareness of her surroundings.

Still Herbie spoke, and there was agitation in his voice – as if he were hurt and frightened and pleading.

The words were beginning to make sense. 'This is a dream,' he was saying, 'and you mustn't believe in it. You'll wake into the real world soon and laugh at yourself. He loves you, I tell you. He does, he does! But not here! Not now! This is an illusion.'

Susan Calvin nodded, her voice a whisper, 'Yes! Yes!' She was clutching Herbie's arm, clinging to it, repeating over and over, 'It isn't true, is it? It isn't, is it?'

Just how she came to her senses, she never knew – but it was like passing from a world of misty unreality to one of harsh sunlight. She pushed him away from her, pushed hard against that steely arm, and her eyes were wide.

'What are you trying to do?' Her voice rose to a harsh scream. 'What are you trying to do?'

Herbie backed away, 'I want to help.'

The psychologist stared, 'Help? By telling me this is a dream? By trying to push me into schizophrenia?' A hysterical tenseness seized her, 'This is no dream! I wish it were!'

She drew her breath sharply, 'Wait! Why . . . why, I understand. Merciful Heavens, it's so obvious.'

There was horror in the robot's voice, 'I had to!'

'And I believed you! I never thought—'

* * *

Loud voices outside the door brought her to a halt. She turned away, fists clenching spasmodically, and when Bogert and Lanning entered, she was at the far window. Neither of the men paid her the slightest attention.

They approached Herbie simultaneously; Lanning angry and impatience, Bogert coolly sardonic. The director spoke first.

'Here now, Herbie. Listen to me!'

The robot brought his eyes sharply down upon the aged director, 'Yes, Dr Lanning.'

'Have you discussed me with Dr Bogert?'

'No, sir.' The answer came slowly, and the smile on Bogert's face flashed off.

'What's that?' Bogert shoved in ahead of his superior and straddled the ground before the robot. 'Repeat what you told me yesterday.'

'I said that—' Herbie fell silent. Deep within him his metallic diaphragm vibrated in soft discords.

'Didn't you say he had resigned?' roared Bogert. 'Answer me!'

Bogert raised his arm frantically, but Lanning pushed him aside, 'Are you trying to bully him into lying?'

'You heard him, Lanning. He began to say "Yes" and stopped. Get out of my way! I want the truth out of him, understand!'

'I'll ask him!' Lanning turned to the robot. 'All right, Herbie, take it easy. Have I resigned?'

Herbie stared, and Lanning repeated anxiously, 'Have I resigned?' There was the faintest trace of a negative shake of the robot's head. A long wait produced nothing further.

The two men looked at each other and the hostility in their eyes was all but tangible.

'What the devil,' blurted Bogert, 'has the robot gone mute? Can't you speak, you monstrosity?'

'I can speak,' came the ready answer.

'Then answer the question. Didn't you tell me Lanning had resigned? Hasn't he resigned?'

And again there was nothing but dull silence, until from the end of the room, Susan Calvin's laugh rang out suddenly, high-pitched and semi-hysterical.

The two mathematicians jumped, and Bogert's eyes narrowed, 'You here? What's so funny?'

'Nothing's funny.' Her voice was not quite natural. 'It's just that I'm not the only one that's been caught. There's irony in three of the greatest experts in robotics in the world falling into the same elementary trap, isn't there?' Her voice faded, and she put a pale hand to her forehead, 'But it isn't funny!'

This time the look that passed between the two men was one of raised eyebrows. 'What trap are you talking about?' asked Lanning stiffly. 'Is something wrong with Herbie?'

'No,' she approached them slowly, 'nothing is wrong with him – only with us.' She whirled suddenly and shrieked at the robot, 'Get away from me! Go to the other end of the room and don't let me look at you.'

Herbie cringed before the fury of her eyes and stumbled away in a clattering trot.

Lanning's voice was hostile, 'What is all this, Dr Calvin?'

She faced them and spoke sarcastically, 'Surely you know the fundamental First Law of Robotics.'

The other two nodded together. 'Certainly,' said Bogert, irritably, 'a robot may not injure a human being or, through inaction, allow him to come to harm.'

'How nicely put,' sneered Calvin. 'But what kind of harm?'

'Why – any kind.'

'Exactly! Any kind! But what about hurt feelings? What about deflation of one's ego? What about the blasting of one's hopes? Is that injury?'

Lanning frowned, 'What would a robot know about—' And then he caught himself with a gasp.

'You've caught on, haven't you? *This* robot reads minds. Do you suppose it doesn't know everything about mental injury? Do you suppose that if asked a question, it wouldn't give exactly that answer that one wants to hear? Wouldn't any other answer hurt us, and wouldn't Herbie know that?'

'Good Heavens!' muttered Bogert.

The psychologist cast a sardonic glance at him, 'I take it you asked him whether Lanning had resigned. You wanted to hear that he had resigned and so that's what Herbie told you.'

'And I suppose that is why,' said Lanning, tonelessly, 'it would not answer a little while ago. It couldn't answer either way without hurting one of us.'

There was a short pause in which the men looked thoughtfully across the room at the robot, crouching in the chair by the bookcase, head resting in one hand.

Susan Calvin stared steadfastly at the floor, 'He knew of all this. That . . . that devil knows everything – including what went wrong in his assembly.' Her eyes were dark and brooding.

Lanning looked up, 'You're wrong there, Dr Calvin. He doesn't know what went wrong. I asked him.'

'What does that mean?' cried Calvin. 'Only that you didn't want him to give you the solution. It would puncture your ego to have a machine do what you couldn't. Did you ask him?' she shot at Bogert.

'In a way.' Bogert coughed and reddened. 'He told me he knew very little about mathematics.'

Lanning laughed, not very loudly, and the psychologist smiled caustically. She said, 'I'll ask him! A solution by him won't hurt my ego.' She raised her voice into a cold, imperative, 'Come here!'

Herbie rose and approached with hesitant steps.

'You know, I suppose,' she continued, 'just exactly at what point in the assembly an extraneous factor was introduced or an essential one left out.'

'Yes,' said Herbie, in tones barely heard.

'Hold on,' broke in Bogert angrily. 'That's not necessarily true. You want to hear that, that's all.'

'Don't be a fool,' replied Calvin. 'He certainly knows as much math as you and Lanning together, since he can read minds. Give him his chance.'

The mathematician subsided, and Calvin continued, 'All right, then, Herbie, give! We're waiting.' And in an aside, 'Get pencils and paper, gentlemen.'

But Herbie remained silent, and there was triumph in the psychologist's voice, 'Why don't you answer, Herbie?'

The robot blurted out suddenly, 'I cannot. You know I cannot! Dr Bogert and Dr Lanning don't want me to.'

'They want the solution.'

'But not from me.'

Lanning broke in, speaking slowly and distinctly, 'Don't be foolish, Herbie. We do want you to tell us.'

Bogert nodded curtly.

Herbie's voice rose to wild heights, 'What's the use of saying that? Don't you suppose that I can see past the superficial skin of your mind? Down below, you don't want me to. I'm a machine, given the imitation of life only by virtue of the positronic interplay in my brain – which is man's device. You can't lose face to me without being hurt. That is deep in your mind and won't be erased. I can't give the solution.'

'We'll leave,' said Dr Lanning. 'Tell Calvin.'

'That would make no difference,' cried Herbie, 'since you would know anyway that it was I that was supplying the answer.'

Calvin resumed, 'But you understand, Herbie, that despite that, Drs Lanning and Bogert want that solution.'

'By their own efforts!' insisted Herbie.

'But they want it, and the fact that you have it and won't give it hurts them. You see that, don't you?'

'Yes! Yes!'

'And if you tell them that will hurt them, too.'

'Yes! Yes!' Herbie was retreating slowly, and step by step Susan Calvin advanced. The two men watched in frozen bewilderment.

'You can't tell them,' droned the psychologist slowly, 'because that would hurt and you mustn't hurt. But if you don't tell them, you hurt, so you must tell them. And if you do, you will hurt and you mustn't, so you can't tell them; but if you don't, you hurt, so you must; but if you do, you hurt, so you mustn't; but if you don't, your hurt, so you must; but if you do, you—'

Herbie was up against the wall, and here he dropped to his knees. 'Stop!' he shrieked. 'Close your mind! It is full of pain and frustration and hate! I didn't mean it, I tell you! I tried to help! I told you what you wanted to hear. I had to!'

The psychologist paid no attention. 'You must tell them, but if you do, you hurt, so you mustn't, but if you don't, you hurt, so you must; but—'

And Herbie screamed!

It was like the whistling of a piccolo many times magnified – shrill and shriller till it keened with the terror of a lost soul and filled the room with the piercingness of itself.

And when it died into nothingness, Herbie collapsed into a huddled heap of motionless metal.

Bogert's face was bloodless, 'He's dead!'

'No!' Susan Calvin burst into body-racking gusts of wild laughter, 'not dead – merely insane. I confronted him with the insoluble dilemma, and he broke down. You can scrap him now – because he'll never speak again.'

Lanning was on his knees beside the thing that had been Herbie. His fingers touched the cold, unresponsive metal face and he shuddered. 'You did that on purpose.' He rose and faced her, face contorted.

'What if I did? You can't help it now.' And in a sudden access of bitterness, 'He deserved it.'

The director seized the paralyzed, motionless Bogert by the wrist, 'What's the difference. Come, Peter.' He sighed, 'A thinking robot of this type is worthless anyway.' His eyes were old and tired, and he repeated, 'Come, Peter!'

It was minutes after the two scientists left that Dr Susan Calvin regained part of her mental equilibrium. Slowly, her eyes turned to the living-dead Herbie and the tightness returned to her face. Long she stared while the triumph faded and the helpless frustration returned – and of all her turbulent thoughts only one infinitely bitter word passed her lips.

'*Liar!*'

That finished it for then, naturally. I knew I couldn't get any more out of her after that. She just sat there behind her desk, her white face cold and – remembering.

I said, 'Thank you, Dr Calvin!' but she didn't answer. It was two days before I could get to see her again.

6
Little Lost Robot

When I did see Susan Calvin again, it was at the door of her office. Files were being moved out.

She said, 'How are your articles coming along, young man?'

'Fine,' I said. I had put them into shape according to my own lights, dramatized the bare bones of her recital, added the conversation and little touches. 'Would you look over them and see if I haven't been libellous or too unreasonably inaccurate anywhere?'

'I suppose so. Shall we retire to the Executive's Lounge? We can have coffee.'

She seemed in good humor, so I chanced it as we walked down the corridor, 'I was wondering, Dr Calvin—'

'Yes.'

'If you would tell me more concerning the history of robotics.'

'Surely you have what you want, young man.'

'In a way. But these incidents I have written up don't apply much to the modern world. I mean, there was only one mind-reading robot ever developed, and Space-Stations are already outmoded and in disuse, and robot mining is taken for granted. What about interstellar travel? It's only been about twenty years since the hyperatomic motor was invented and it's well known that it was a robotic invention. What is the truth about it?'

'Interstellar travel?' She was thoughtful. We were in the lounge, and I ordered a full dinner. She just had coffee.

'It wasn't a simple robotic invention, you know; not just

like that. But, of course, until we developed the Brain, we didn't get very far. But we tried; we really tried. My first connection (directly, that is) with interstellar research was in 2029, when a robot was lost—'

Measures on Hyper Base had been taken in a sort of rattling fury – the muscular equivalent of an hysterical shriek.

To itemize them in order of both chronology and desperation, they were:

1. All work on the Hyperatomic Drive through all the space volume occupied by the Stations of the Twenty-Seventh Asteroidal Grouping came to a halt.

2. That entire volume of space was nipped out of the System, practically speaking. No one entered without permission. No one left under any conditions.

3. By special government patrol ship, Drs Susan Calvin and Peter Bogert, respectively Head Psychologist and Mathematical Director of United States Robot & Mechanical Men Corporation, were brought to Hyper Base.

Susan Calvin had never left the surface of Earth before, and had no perceptible desire to leave it this time. In an age of Atomic Power and a clearly coming Hyperatomic drive, she remained quietly provincial. So she was dissatisfied with her trip and unconvinced of the emergency, and every line of her plain, middle-aged face showed it clearly enough during her first dinner at Hyper Base.

Nor did Dr Bogert's sleek paleness abandon a certain hangdog attitude. Nor did Major-general Kallner, who headed the project, even once forget to maintain a haunted expression.

In short, it was a grisly episode, that meal, and the little session of three that followed began in a gray, unhappy manner.

Kallner, with his baldness glistening, and his dress uniform oddly unsuited to the general mood, began with uneasy directness.

'This is a queer story to tell, sir, and madam. I want to thank you for coming on short notice and without a reason being given. We'll try to correct that now. We've lost a robot. Work has stopped and *must* stop until such time as we locate it. So far we have failed, and we feel we need expert help.'

Perhaps the general felt his predicament anticlimactic. He continued with a note of desperation, 'I needn't tell you the importance of our work here. More than eighty per cent of last year's appropriations for scientific research have gone to us—'

'Why, we know that,' said Bogert, agreeably. 'US Robots is receiving a generous rental fee for use of our robots.'

Susan Calvin injected a blunt, vinegary note, 'What makes a single robot so important to the project, and why hasn't it been located?'

The general turned his red face toward her and wet his lips quickly, 'Why, in a manner of speaking we *have* located it.' Then, with near anguish, 'Here, suppose I explain. As soon as the robot failed to report, a state of emergency was declared, and all movement off Hyper Base stopped. A cargo vessel had landed the previous day and had delivered us two robots for our laboratories. It had sixty-two robots of the . . . uh . . . same type for shipment elsewhere. We are certain as to that figure. There is no question about it whatever.'

'Yes? And the connection?'

'When our missing robot failed of location anywhere – I assure you we would have found a missing blade of grass if it had been there to find – we brainstormed ourselves into counting the robots left on the cargo ship. They have sixty-three now.'

'So that the sixty-third, I take it, is the missing prodigal?' Dr Calvin's eyes darkened.

'Yes, but we have no way of telling which is the sixty-third.'

There was a dead silence while the electric clock chimed eleven times, and then the robopsychologist said, 'Very peculiar,' and the corners of her lips moved downward.

'Peter,' she turned to her colleague with a trace of savagery, 'what's wrong here? What kind of robots are they using at Hyper Base?'

Dr Bogert hesitated and smiled feebly, 'It's been rather a matter of delicacy till now, Susan.'

She spoke rapidly, 'Yes, *till* now. If there are sixty-three same-type robots, one of which is wanted and the identity of which cannot be determined, why won't any of them do? What's the idea of all this? Why have we been sent for?'

Bogert said in resigned fashion, 'If you'll give me a chance, Susan – Hyper Base happens to be using several robots whose brains are not impressioned with the entire First Law of Robotics.'

'*Aren't* impressioned?' Calvin slumped back in her chair, 'I see. How many were made?'

'A few. It was on government order and there was no way of violating the secrecy. No one was to know except the top men directly concerned. You weren't included, Susan. It was nothing I had anything to do with.'

The general interrupted with a measure of authority. 'I would like to explain that bit. I hadn't been aware that Dr Calvin was unacquainted with the situation. I needn't tell you, Dr Calvin, that there always has been strong opposition to robots on the Planet. The only defense the government has had against the Fundamentalist radicals in this matter was the fact that robots are always built with an unbreakable First Law – which makes it impossible for them to harm human beings under any circumstance.

'But we *had* to have robots of a different nature. So just a few of the NS-2 model, the Nestors, that is, were prepared with a modified First Law. To keep it quiet, all NS-2s are manufactured without serial numbers; modified members are delivered here along with a group of normal robots; and, of course, all our kind are under the strictest impressionment never to tell of their modification to unauthorized personnel.' He wore an embarrassed smile, 'This has all worked out against us now.'

Calvin said grimly, 'Have you asked each one who it is, anyhow? Certainly, you are authorized?'

The general nodded, 'All sixty-three deny having worked here – and one is lying.'

'Does the one you want show traces of wear? The others, I take it, are factory-fresh.'

'The one in question only arrived last month. It, and the two that have just arrived, were to be the last we needed. There's no perceptible wear.' He shook his head slowly and his eyes were haunted again, 'Dr Calvin, we don't dare let that ship leave. If the existence of non-First Law robots becomes general knowledge—' There seemed no way of avoiding understatement in the conclusion.

'Destroy all sixty-three,' said the robopsychologist coldly and flatly, 'and make an end of it.'

Bogert drew back a corner of his mouth. 'You mean destroy thirty thousand dollars per robot. I'm afraid US Robots wouldn't like that. We'd better make an effort first, Susan, before we destroy anything.'

'In that case,' she said, sharply, 'I need facts. Exactly what advantage does Hyper Base derive from these modified robots? What factor made them desirable, general?'

Kallner ruffled his forehead and stroked it with an upward gesture of his hand. 'We had trouble with our previous robots. Our men work with hard radiations a good deal, you see. It's dangerous, of course, but reasonable precautions are taken. There have been only two accidents since we began and neither was fatal. However, it was impossible to explain that to an ordinary robot. The First Law states – I'll quote it – "*No robot may harm a human being, or, through inaction, allow a human being to come to harm.*"

'That's primary, Dr Calvin. When it was necessary for one of our men to expose himself for a short period to a moderate gamma field, one that would have no physiological effects, the nearest robot would dash in to drag him out. If the field were exceedingly weak, it would succeed, and work could not continue till all robots were cleared out. If the field were a trifle stronger, the robot would never reach the technician concerned, since its positronic brain would collapse under gamma radiations – and then we would be out one expensive and hard-to-replace robot.

'We tried arguing with them. Their point was that a human being in a gamma field was endangering his life and that it didn't matter that he could remain there half an hour safely. Supposing, they would say, he forgot and remained an hour. They couldn't take chances. We pointed out that they were risking their lives on a wild off-chance. But self-preservation is only the Third Law of Robotics – and the First Law of human safety came first. We gave them orders; we ordered them strictly and harshly to remain out of gamma fields at whatever cost. But obedience is only the Second Law of Robotics – and the First Law of human safety came first. Dr Calvin, we either had to do without robots, or do something about the First Law – and we made our choice.'

'I can't believe,' said Dr Calvin, 'that it was found possible to remove the First Law.'

'It wasn't removed, it was modified,' explained Kallner. 'Positronic brains were constructed that contained the positive aspect only of the Law, which in them reads: "*No robot may harm a human being*." That is all. They have no compulsion to prevent one coming to harm through an extraneous agency such as gamma rays. I state the matter correctly, Dr Bogert?'

'Quite,' assented the mathematician.

'And that is the only difference of your robots from the ordinary NS-2 model? The *only* difference? Peter?'

'The *only* difference, Susan.'

She rose and spoke with finality, 'I intend sleeping now, and in about eight hours I want to speak to whomever saw the robot last. And from now on, General Kallner, if I'm to take any responsibility at all for events, I want full and unquestioned control of this investigation.'

Susan Calvin, except for two hours of resentful lassitude, experienced nothing approaching sleep. She signaled at Bogert's door at the local time of 0700 and found him also awake. He had apparently taken the trouble of transporting a dressing gown to Hyper Base with him, for he was sitting in it. He put his nail scissors down when Calvin entered.

He said softly, 'I've been expecting you more or less. I suppose you feel sick about all this.'

'I do.'

'Well – I'm sorry. There was no way of preventing it. When the call came out from Hyper Base for us, I knew that something must have gone wrong with the modified Nestors. But what was there to do? I couldn't break the matter to you on the trip here as I would have liked to, because I had to be sure. The matter of the modification is top secret.'

The psychologist muttered, 'I should have been told. US Robots had no right to modify positronic brains this way without the approval of a psychologist.'

Bogert lifted his eyebrows and sighed. 'Be reasonable, Susan. You couldn't have influenced them. In this matter, the government was bound to have its way. They want the Hyperatomic Drive and the etheric physicists want robots that won't interfere with them. They were going to get them even if it did mean twisting the First Law. We had to admit it was possible from a construction stand-point and they swore a mighty oath that they wanted only twelve, that they would be used only at Hyper Base, that they would be destroyed once the Drive was perfected, and that full precautions would be taken. And they insisted on secrecy – and that's the situation.'

Dr Calvin spoke through her teeth, 'I would have resigned.'

'It wouldn't have helped. The government was offering the company a fortune, and threatening it with antirobot legislation in case of a refusal. We were stuck then, and we're badly stuck now. If this leaks out, it might hurt Kallner and the government, but it would hurt US Robots a devil of a lot more.'

The psychologist stared at him. 'Peter, don't you realize what all this is about? Can't you understand what the removal of the First Law means? It isn't just a matter of secrecy.'

'I know what removal would mean. I'm not a child. It would mean complete instability, with no nonimaginary solutions to the positronic Field Equations.'

'Yes, mathematically. But can you translate that into crude psychological thought? All normal life, Peter, consciously or otherwise, resents domination. If the domination is by an inferior, or by a supposed inferior, the resentment becomes stronger. Physically, and, to an extent, mentally, a robot – any robot – is superior to human beings. What makes him slavish, then? *Only the First Law!* Why, without it, the first order you tried to give a robot would result in your death. Unstable? What do you think?'

'Susan,' said Bogert, with an air of sympathetic amusement. 'I'll admit that this Frankenstein Complex you're exhibiting has a certain justification – hence the First

Law in the first place. But the Law, I repeat and repeat, has not been removed – merely modified.'

'And what about the stability of the brain?'

The mathematician thrust out his lips, 'Decreased, naturally. But it's within the border of safety. The first Nestors were delivered to Hyper Base nine months ago, and nothing whatever has gone wrong till now, and even this involves merely fear of discovery and not danger to humans.'

'Very well, then. We'll see what comes of the morning conference.'

Bogert saw her politely to the door and grimaced eloquently when she left. He saw no reason to change his perennial opinion of her as a sour and fidgety frustration.

Susan Calvin's train of thought did not include Bogert in the least. She had dismissed him years ago as a smooth and pretentious sleekness.

Gerald Black had taken his degree in etheric physics the year before and, in common with his entire generation of physicists, found himself engaged in the problem of the Drive. He now made a proper addition to the general atmosphere of these meetings on Hyper Base. In his stained white smock, he was half rebellious and wholly uncertain. His stocky strength seemed striving for release and his fingers, as they twisted each other with nervous yanks, might have forced an iron bar out of true.

Major-general Kallner sat beside him, the two from US Robots faced him.

Black said, 'I'm told that I was the last to see Nestor 10 before he vanished. I take it you want to ask me about that.'

Dr Calvin regarded him with interest, 'You sound as if you were not sure, young man. Don't you *know* whether you were the last to see him?'

'He worked with me, ma'am, on the field generators, and he was with me the morning of his disappearance. I don't know if anyone saw him after about noon. No one admits having done so.'

'Do you think anyone's lying about it?'

'I don't say that. But I don't say that I want the blame of it, either.' His dark eyes smoldered.

'There's no question of blame. The robot acted as it did because of what it is. We're just trying to locate it, Mr Black, and let's put everything else aside. Now if you've worked with the robot, you probably know it better than anyone else. Was there anything unusual about it that you noticed? Had you ever worked with robots before?'

'I've worked with other robots we have here – the simple ones. Nothing different about the Nestors except that they're a good deal cleverer – and more annoying.'

'Annoying? In what way?'

'Well – perhaps it's not their fault. The work here is rough and most of us get a little jagged. Fooling around with hyperspace isn't fun.' He smiled feebly, finding pleasure in confession. 'We run the risk continually of blowing a hole in normal space-time fabric and dropping right out of the universe, asteroid and all. Sounds screwy, doesn't it? Naturally, you're on edge sometimes. But these Nestors aren't. They're curious, they're calm, they don't worry. It's enough to drive you nuts at times. When you want something done in a tearing hurry, they seem to take their time. Sometimes I'd rather do without.'

'You say they take their time? Have they ever refused an order?'

'Oh, no' – hastily. 'They do it all right. They tell you when they think you're wrong, though. They don't know anything about the subject but what we taught them, but that doesn't stop them. Maybe I imagine it, but the other fellows have the same trouble with their Nestors.'

General Kallner cleared his throat ominously, 'Why have no complaints reached me on the matter, Black?'

The young physicist reddened, 'We didn't *really* want to do without the robots, sir, and besides we weren't certain exactly how such . . . uh . . . minor complaints might be received.'

Bogert interrupted softly, 'Anything in particular happen the morning you last saw it?'

There was a silence. With a quiet motion, Calvin repressed the comment that was about to emerge from Kallner, and waited patiently.

Then Black spoke in blurting anger, 'I had a little trouble with it. I'd broken a Kimball tube that morning and was out five days of work; my entire program was behind schedule; I hadn't received any mail from home for a couple of weeks. And *he* came around wanting me to repeat an experiment I had abandoned a month ago. He was always annoying me on that subject and I was tired of it. I told him to go away – and that's all I saw of him.'

'You told him to go away?' asked Dr Calvin with sharp interest. 'In just those words? Did you say "Go away"? Try to remember the exact words.'

There was apparently an internal struggle in progress. Black cradled his forehead in a broad palm for a moment, then tore it away and said defiantly, 'I said, "Go lose your-self".'

Bogert laughed for a short moment. 'And he did, eh?'

But Calvin wasn't finished. She spoke cajolingly, 'Now we're getting somewhere, Mr Black. But exact details are important. In understanding the robot's actions, a word, a gesture, an emphasis may be everything. You couldn't have said just those three words, for instance, could you? By your own description you must have been in a hasty mood. Perhaps you strengthened your speech a little.'

The young man reddened, 'Well . . . I may have called it a . . . a few things.'

'Exactly what things?'

'Oh – I wouldn't remember exactly. Besides I couldn't repeat it. You know how you get when you're excited.' His embarrassed laugh was almost a giggle, 'I sort of have a tendency to strong language.'

'That's quite all right,' she replied with prim severity. 'At the moment, I'm a psychologist. I would like to have you repeat exactly what you said as nearly as you remember, and, even more important, the exact tone of voice you used.'

Black looked at his commanding officer for support, found none. His eyes grew round and appalled, 'But I can't.'

'You must.'

'Suppose,' said Bogert, with ill-hidden amusement, 'you address me. You may find it easier.'

The young man's scarlet face turned to Bogert. He swallowed. 'I said—' His voice faded out. He tried again, 'I said—'

And he drew a deep breath and spewed it out hastily in one long succession of syllables. Then, in the charged air that lingered, he concluded almost in tears, '. . . more or less. I don't remember the exact order of what I called him, and maybe I left out something or put in something, but that was about it.'

Only the slightest flush betrayed any feeling on the part of the robopsychologist. She said, 'I am aware of the meaning of most of the terms used. The others, I suppose, are equally derogatory.'

'I'm afraid so,' agreed the tormented Black.

'And in among it, you told him to lose himself.'

'I meant it only figuratively.'

'I realize that. No disciplinary action is intended, I am sure.' And at her glance, the general, who, five seconds earlier, had seemed not sure at all, nodded angrily.

'You may leave, Mr Black. Thank you for your co-operation.'

* * *

It took five hours for Susan Calvin to interview the sixty-three robots. It was five hours of multi-repetition, of replacement after replacement of identical robot; of Questions A, B, C, D; and Answers A, B, C, D; of a carefully bland expression, a carefully neutral tone, a carefully friendly atmosphere; and a hidden wire recorder.

The psychologist felt drained of vitality when she was finished.

Bogert was waiting for her and looked expectant as she dropped the recording spool with a clang upon the plastic of the desk.

She shook her head, 'All sixty-three seemed the same to me. I couldn't tell—'

He said, 'You couldn't expect to tell by ear, Susan. Suppose we analyze the recordings.'

Ordinarily, the mathematical interpretation of verbal reactions of robots is one of the more intricate branches of robotic analysis. It requires a staff of trained technicians and the help of complicated computing machines. Bogert knew that. Bogert stated as much, in an extreme of unshown annoyance after having listened to each set of replies, made lists of word deviations, and graphs of the intervals of responses.

'There are no anomalies present, Susan. The variations in wording and the time reactions are within the limits of ordinary frequency groupings. We need finer methods. They must have computers here. No.' He frowned and nibbled delicately at a thumbnail. 'We can't use computers. Too much danger of leakage. Or maybe if we —'

Dr Calvin stopped him with an impatient gesture, 'Please, Peter. This isn't one of your petty laboratory problems. If we can't determine the modified Nestor by some gross difference that we can see with the naked eye, one that there is no mistake about, we're out of luck. The danger of being wrong, and of letting him escape is otherwise too great. It's not enough to point out a minute irregularity in a graph. I tell you, if that's all I've got to go on, I'd destroy them all just to be certain. Have you spoken to the other modified Nestors?'

'Yes, I have,' snapped back Bogert, 'and there's nothing wrong with them. They're above normal in friendliness if anything. They answered my questions, displayed pride in their knowledge – except the two new ones that haven't had time to learn their etheric physics. They laughed rather good-naturedly at my ignorance in some of the specializations here.' He shrugged. 'I suppose that forms some of the basis for resentment toward them on the part of the technicians here. The robots are perhaps too willing to impress you with their greater knowledge.'

'Can you try a few Planar Reactions to see if there has been any change, any deterioration, in their mental set-up since manufacture?'

'I haven't yet, but I will.' He shook a slim finger at her, 'You're losing your nerve, Susan. I don't see what it is you're dramatizing. They're essentially harmless.'

'They are?' Calvin took fire. 'They are? Do you realize one of them is lying? One of the sixty-three robots I have just interviewed has deliberately lied to me after the strictest injunction to tell the truth. The abnormality indicated is horribly deep-seated, and horribly frightening.'

Peter Bogert felt his teeth harden against each other. He said, 'Not at all. Look! Nestor 10 was given orders to lose himself. Those orders were expressed in maximum urgency by the person most authorized to command him. You can't counteract that order either by superior urgency or superior right of command. Naturally, the robot will attempt to defend the carrying out of his orders. In fact, objectively, I admire his ingenuity. How better can a robot lose himself than to hide himself among a group of similar robots?'

'Yes, you would admire it. I've detected amusement in you, Peter – amusement and an appalling lack of

understanding. Are you a roboticist, Peter? Those robots
attach importance to what they consider superiority. You've
just said as much yourself. Subconsciously they feel humans
to be inferior and the First Law which protects us from them
is imperfect. They are unstable. And here we have a young
man ordering a robot to leave him, to lose himself, with
every verbal appearance of revulsion, disdain, and disgust.
Granted, that robot must follow orders, but subconsciously,
there is resentment. It will become more important than ever
for it to prove that it is superior despite the horrible names
it was called. It may become *so* important that what's left of
the First Law won't be enough.'

'How on Earth, or anywhere in the Solar System, Susan,
is a robot going to know the meaning of the assorted strong
language used upon him? Obscenity is not one of the things
impressioned upon his brain.'

'Original impressionment is not everything,' Calvin
snarled at him. 'Robots have learning capacity, you . . . you
fool—' And Bogert knew that she had really lost her
temper. She continued hastily, 'Don't you suppose he could
tell from the tone used that the words weren't complimen-
tary? Don't you suppose he's heard the words used before
and noted upon what occasions?'

'Well, then,' shouted Bogert, 'will you kindly tell me one
way in which a modified robot can harm a human being, no
matter how offended it is, no matter how sick with desire to
prove superiority?'

'If I tell you one way, will you keep quiet?'

'Yes.'

They were leaning across the table at each other, angry
eyes nailed together.

The psychologist said, 'If a modified robot were to drop
a heavy weight upon a human being, he would not be
breaking the First Law, if he did so with the knowledge
that his strength and reaction speed would be sufficient to

snatch the weight away before it struck the man. However once the weight left his fingers, he would be no longer the active medium. Only the blind force of gravity would be that. The robot could then change his mind and merely by inaction, allow the weight to strike. The modified First Law allows that.'

'That's an awful stretch of imagination.'

'That's what my profession requires sometimes. Peter, let's not quarrel. Let's work. You know the exact nature of the stimulus that caused the robot to lose himself. You have the records of his original mental make-up. I want you to tell me how possible it is for our robot to do the sort of thing I just talked about. Not the specific instance, mind you, but that whole class of response. And I want it done quickly.'

'And meanwhile—'

'And meanwhile, we'll have to try performance tests directly on the response to First Law.'

Gerald Black, at his own request, was supervising the mushrooming wooden partitions that were springing up in a bellying circle on the vaulted third floor of Radiation Building 2. The laborers worked, in the main, silently, but more than one was openly a-wonder at the sixty-three photocells that required installation.

One of them sat down near Black, removed his hat, and wiped his forehead thoughtfully with a freckled forearm.

Black nodded at him, 'How's it doing, Walensky?'

Walensky shrugged and fired a cigar, 'Smooth as butter. What's going on anyway, Doc? First, there's no work for three days and then we have this mess of jiggers.' He leaned backward on his elbows and puffed smoke.

Black twitched his eyebrows, 'A couple of robot men came over from Earth. Remember the trouble we had with robots running into the gamma fields, before we pounded it into their skulls that they weren't to do it.'

'Yeah. Didn't we get new robots?'

'We got some replacements, but mostly it was a job of indoctrination. Anyway, the people who make them want to figure out robots that aren't hit so bad by gamma rays.'

'Sure seems funny, though, to stop all the work on the Drive for this robot deal. I thought nothing was allowed to stop the Drive.'

'Well, it's the fellows upstairs that have the say on that. Me – I just do as I'm told. Probably all a matter of pull—'

'Yeah,' the electrician jerked a smile, and winked a wise eye. 'Somebody knew somebody in Washington. But as long as my pay comes through on the dot, I should worry. The Drive's none of my affair. What are they going to do here?'

'You're asking me? They brought a mess of robots with them – over sixty, and they're going to measure reactions. That's all *my* knowledge.'

'How long will it take?'

'I wish I knew.'

'Well,' Walensky said, with heavy sarcasm, 'as long as they dish me my money, they can play games all they want.'

Black felt quietly satisfied. Let the story spread. It was harmless, and near enough to the truth to take the fangs out of curiosity.

A man sat in the chair, motionless, silent. A weight dropped, crashed downward, then pounded aside at the last moment under the synchronized thump of a sudden force beam. In sixty-three wooden cells, watching NS-2 robots dashed forward in that split second before the weight veered, and sixty-three photocells five feet ahead of their original positions jiggled the marking pen and presented a little jag on the paper. The weight rose and dropped, rose and dropped, rose —

Ten times!

Ten times the robots sprang forward and stopped, as the man remained safely seated.

Major-general Kallner had not worn his uniform in its entirety since the first dinner with the US Robot representatives. He wore nothing over his blue-gray shirt now, the collar was open, and the black tie was pulled loose.

He looked hopefully at Bogert, who was still blandly neat and whose inner tension was perhaps betrayed only by the trace of glister at his temples.

The general said, 'How does it look? What is it you're trying to see?'

Bogert replied, 'A difference which may turn out to be a little too subtle for our purposes, I'm afraid. For sixty-two of those robots the necessity of jumping toward the apparently threatened human was what we call, in robotics, a forced reaction. You see, even when the robots knew that the human in question would not come to harm – and after the third or fourth time they must have known it – they could not prevent reacting as they did. First Law required it.'

'Well?'

'But the sixty-third robot, the modified Nestor, had no such compulsion. He was under free action. If he had wished, he could have remained in his seat. Unfortunately,' and his voice was mildly regretful, 'he didn't so wish.'

'Why do you suppose?'

Bogert shrugged, 'I suppose Dr Calvin will tell us when she gets here. Probably with a horribly pessimistic interpretation, too. She is sometimes a bit annoying.'

'She's qualified, isn't she?' demanded the general with a sudden frown of uneasiness.

'Yes.' Bogert seemed amused. 'She's qualified all right. She understands robots like a sister – comes from hating human beings so much, I think. It's just that, psychologist or not, she's an extreme neurotic. Has paranoid tendencies. Don't take her too seriously.'

He spread the long row of broken-line graphs out in front of him. 'You see, general, in the case of each robot the time interval from moment of drop to the completion of a five-foot movement tends to decrease as the tests are repeated. There's a definite mathematical relationship that governs such things and failure to conform would indicate marked abnormality in the positronic brain. Unfortunately, all here appear normal.'

'But if our Nestor 10 was not responding with a forced action, why isn't his curve different? I don't understand that.'

'It's simple enough. Robotic responses are not perfectly analogous to human responses, more's the pity. In human beings, voluntary action is much slower than reflex action. But that's not the case with robots; with them it is merely a question of freedom of choice, otherwise the speeds of free and forced action are much the same. What I *had* been expecting, though, was that Nestor 10 would be caught by surprise the first time and allow too great an interval to elapse before responding.'

'And he didn't?'

'I'm afraid not.'

'Then we haven't gotten anywhere.' The general sat back with an expression of pain. 'It's five days since you've come.'

At this point, Susan Calvin entered and slammed the door behind her. 'Put your graphs away, Peter,' she cried, 'you know they don't show anything.'

She mumbled something impatiently as Kallner half-rose to greet her, and went on, 'We'll have to try something else quickly. I don't like what's happening.'

Bogert exchanged a resigned glance with the general. 'Is anything wrong?'

'You mean specifically? No. But I don't like to have Nestor 10 continue to elude us. It's bad. It *must* be gratifying his swollen sense of superiority. I'm afraid that his motivation is no longer simply one of following orders. I think it's becoming more a matter of sheer neurotic necessity to out-think humans. That's a dangerously unhealthy situation. Peter, have you done what I asked? Have you worked out the instability factors of the modified NS-2 along the lines I want?'

'It's in progress,' said the mathematician, without interest.

She stared at him angrily for a moment, then turned to Kallner. 'Nestor 10 is decidedly aware of what we're doing, general. He had no reason to jump for the bait in this experiment, especially after the first time, when he must have seen that there was no real danger to our subject. The others couldn't help it, but *he* was deliberately falsifying a reaction.'

'What do you think we ought to do now, then, Dr Calvin?'

'Make it impossible for him to fake an action the next time. We will repeat the experiment, but with an addition. High-tension cables, capable of electrocuting the Nestor models, will be placed between subject and robot – enough of them to avoid the possibility of jumping over – and the robot will be made perfectly aware in advance that touching the cables will mean death.'

'Hold on,' spat out Bogert with sudden viciousness. 'I rule that out. We are not electrocuting two million dollars' worth of robots to locate Nestor 10. There are other ways.'

'You're certain? You've found none. In any case, it's not a question of electrocution. We can arrange a relay which will break the current at the instant of application of weight. If the robot should place his weight on it, he won't die. *But he won't know that*, you see.'

The general's eyes gleamed into hope. 'Will that work?'

'It should. Under those conditions, Nestor 10 would have to remain in his seat. He could be *ordered* to touch the cables and die, for the Second Law of obedience is superior to the

Third Law of self-preservation. But *he won't* be ordered to; he will merely be left to his own devices, as will all the robots. In the case of the normal robots, the First Law of human safety will drive them to their death even without orders. But not our Nestor 10. Without the entire First Law, and without having received any orders on the matter, the Third Law, self-preservation, will be the highest operating, and he will have no choice but to remain in his seat. It would be a forced action.'

'Will it be done tonight, then?'

'Tonight,' said the psychologist, 'if the cables can be laid in time. I'll tell the robots now what they're to be up against.'

A man sat in the chair, motionless, silent. A weight dropped, crashed downward, then pounded aside at the last moment under the synchronized thump of a sudden force beam.

Only once—

And from her small camp chair in the observing booth in the balcony, Dr Susan Calvin rose with a short gasp of pure horror.

Sixty-three robots sat quietly in their chairs, staring owlishly at the endangered man before them. Not one moved.

Dr Calvin was angry, angry almost past endurance. Angry the worse for not daring to show it to the robots that, one by one, were entering the room and then leaving. She checked the list. Number Twenty-eight was due in now – Thirty-five still lay ahead of her.

Number Twenty-eight entered, diffidently.

She forced herself into reasonable calm. 'And who are you?'

The robot replied in a low, uncertain voice, 'I have received no number of my own yet, ma'am. I'm an NS-2 robot, and I was Number Twenty-eight in line outside. I have a slip of paper here that I'm to give to you.'

'You haven't been in here before this today?'

'No, ma'am.'

'Sit down. Right there. I want to ask you some questions, Number Twenty-eight. Were you in the Radiation Room of Building Two about four hours ago?'

The robot had trouble answering. Then it came out hoarsely, like machinery needing oil, 'Yes, ma'am.'

'There was a man who almost came to harm there, wasn't there?'

'Yes, ma'am.'

'You did nothing, did you?'

'No, ma'am.'

'The man might have been hurt because of your inaction. Do you know that?'

'Yes, ma'am. I couldn't help it, ma'am.' It is hard to picture a large expressionless metallic figure cringing, but it managed.

'I want you to tell me exactly why you did nothing to save him.'

'I want to explain, ma'am. I certainly don't want to have you . . . have *anyone* think that I could do a thing that might cause harm to a master. Oh, no, that would be a horrible . . . an inconceivable—'

'Please don't get excited, boy. I'm not blaming you for anything. I only want to know what you were thinking at the time.'

'Ma'am, before it all happened you told us that one of the masters would be in danger of harm from that weight that keeps falling and that we would have to cross electric cables if we were to try to save him. Well, ma'am, that wouldn't stop me. What is my destruction compared to the safety of a master? But . . . but it occurred to me that if I died on my way to him, I wouldn't be able to save him anyway. The weight would crush him and then I would be dead for no purpose and perhaps some day some other master might come to harm who wouldn't have, if I had only stayed alive. Do you understand me, ma'am?'

'You mean that it was merely a choice of the man dying, or both the man and yourself dying. Is that right?'

'Yes, ma'am. It was impossible to save the master. He might be considered dead. In that case, it is inconceivable that I destroy myself for nothing – without orders.'

The robopsychologist twiddled a pencil. She had heard the same story with insignificant verbal variations twenty-seven times before. This was the crucial question now.

'Boy,' she said, 'your thinking has its points, but it is not the sort of thing I thought you might think. Did you think of this yourself?'

The robot hesitated. 'No.'

'Who thought of it, then?'

'We were talking last night, and one of us got that idea and it sounded reasonable.'

'Which one?'

The robot thought deeply. 'I don't know. Just one of us.'

She sighed, 'That's all.'

Number Twenty-nine was next. Thirty-four after that.

Major-general Kallner, too, was angry. For one week all of Hyper Base had stopped dead, barring some paper work on the subsidiary asteroids of the group. For nearly one week, the two top experts in the field had aggravated the situation with useless tests. And now they – or the woman, at any rate – made impossible propositions.

Fortunately for the general situation, Kallner felt it impolitic to display his anger openly.

Susan Calvin was insisting, 'Why not, sir? It's obvious that the present situation is unfortunate. The only way we may reach results in the future – or what future is left us in this matter – is to separate the robots. We can't keep them together any longer.'

'My dear Dr Calvin,' rumbled the general, his voice sinking into the lower baritone registers. 'I don't see how I can quarter sixty-three robots all over the place—'

Dr Calvin raised her arms helplessly. 'I can do nothing then. Nestor 10 will either imitate what the other robots would do, or else argue them plausibly into not doing what he himself cannot do. And in any case, this is bad business. We're in actual combat with this little lost robot of ours and he's winning out. Every victory of his aggravates his abnormality.'

She rose to her feet in determination. 'General Kallner, if you do not separate the robots as I ask, then I can only demand that all sixty-three be destroyed immediately.'

'You demand it, do you?' Bogert looked up suddenly, and with real anger. 'What gives you the right to demand any such thing. Those robots remain as they are. *I'm* responsible to the management, not you.'

'And I,' added Major-general Kallner, 'am responsible to the World Co-ordinator – and I must have this settled.'

'In that case,' flashed back Calvin, 'there is nothing for me to do but resign. If necessary to force you to the necessary destruction, I'll make this whole matter public. It was not I that approved the manufacture of modified robots.'

'One word from you, Dr Calvin,' said the general, deliberately, 'in violation of security measures, and you would be certainly imprisoned instantly.'

Bogert felt the matter to be getting out of hand. His voice grew syrupy, 'Well, now, we're beginning to act like children, all of us. We need only a little more time. Surely we can outwit a robot without resigning, or imprisoning people, or destroying two millions.'

The psychologist turned on him with quiet fury, 'I don't want any unbalanced robots in existence. We have one Nestor that's definitely unbalanced, eleven more that are potentially so, and sixty-two normal robots that are being subjected to an unbalanced environment. The only absolute safe method is complete destruction.'

The signal-burr brought all three to a halt, and the angry tumult of growingly unrestrained emotion froze.

'Come in,' growled Kallner.

It was Gerald Black, looking perturbed. He had heard angry voices. He said, 'I thought I'd come myself . . . didn't like to ask anyone else—'

'What is it? Don't orate —'

'The locks of Compartment C in the trading ship have been played with. There are fresh scratches on them.'

'Compartment C?' exclaimed Calvin quickly. 'That's the one that holds the robots, isn't it? Who did it?'

'From the inside,' said Black, laconically.

'The lock isn't out of order, is it?'

'No. It's all right. I've been staying on the ship now for four days and none of them have tried to get out. But I thought you ought to know, and I didn't like to spread the news. I noticed the matter myself.'

'Is anyone there now?' demanded the general.

'I left Robbins and McAdams there.'

There was a thoughtful silence, and then Dr Calvin said, ironically, 'Well?'

Kallner rubbed his nose uncertainly, 'What's it all about?'

'Isn't it obvious? Nestor 10 is planning to leave. That order to lose himself is dominating his abnormality past anything we can do. I wouldn't be surprised if what's left of his First Law would scarcely be powerful enough to override it. He is perfectly capable of seizing the ship and leaving with it. Then we'd have a mad robot on a spaceship. What would he do next? Any idea? Do you still want to leave them together, general?'

'Nonsense,' interrupted Bogert. He had regained his smoothness. 'All that from a few scratch marks on a lock.'

'Have you, Dr Bogert, completed the analysis I've required, since you volunteer opinions?'

'Yes.'

'May I see it?'

'No.'

'Why not? Or mayn't I ask that, either?'

'Because there's no point in it, Susan. I told you in advance that these modified robots are less stable than the normal variety, and my analysis shows it. There's a certain very small chance of breakdown under extreme circumstances that are not likely to occur. Let it go at that. I won't give you ammunition for your absurd claim that sixty-two perfectly good robots be destroyed just because so far you lack the ability to detect Nestor 10 among them.'

Susan Calvin stared him down and let disgust fill her eyes. 'You won't let anything stand in the way of the permanent directorship, will you?'

'Please,' begged Kallner, half in irritation. 'Do you insist that nothing further can be done, Dr Calvin?'

'I can't think of anything, sir,' she replied, wearily. 'If there were only other differences between Nestor 10 and the normal robots, differences that didn't involve the First Law. Even one other difference. Something in impressionment, environment, specification—' And she stopped suddenly.

'What is it?'

'I've thought of something . . . I think—' Her eyes grew distant and hard, 'These modified Nestors, Peter. They get the same impressioning the normal ones get, don't they?'

'Yes. Exactly the same.'

'And what was it you were saying, Mr Black?' she turned to the young man, who through the storms that had followed his news had maintained a discreet silence. 'Once when complaining of the Nestors' attitude of superiority, you said the technicians had taught them all they knew.'

'Yes, in etheric physics. They're not acquainted with the subject when they come here.'

'That's right,' said Bogert, in surprise. 'I told you, Susan, when I spoke to the other Nestors here that the two new arrivals hadn't learned etheric physics yet.'

'And why is that?' Dr Calvin was speaking in mounting excitement. 'Why aren't NS-2 models impressioned with etheric physics to start with?'

'I can tell you that,' said Kallner. 'It's all of a piece with the secrecy. We thought that if we made a special model with knowledge of etheric physics, used twelve of them and put the others to work in an unrelated field, there might be suspicion. Men working with normal Nestors might wonder why they knew etheric physics. So there was merely an impressionment with a capacity for training in the field. Only the ones that come here, naturally, receive such a training. It's that simple.'

'I understand. Please get out of here, the lot of you. Let me have an hour or so.'

Calvin felt she could not face the ordeal for a third time. Her mind had contemplated it and rejected it with an intensity that left her nauseated. She could face that unending file of repetitious robots no more.

So Bogert asked the questions now, while she sat aside, eyes and mind half-closed.

Number Fourteen came in – forty-nine to go.

Bogert looked up from the guide sheet and said, 'What is your number in line?'

'Fourteen, sir.' The robot presented his numbered ticket.

'Sit down, boy.'

Bogert asked, 'You haven't been here before on this day?'

'No, sir.'

'Well, boy, we are going to have another man in danger of harm soon after we're through here. In fact, when you leave this room, you will be led to a stall where you will wait quietly, till you are needed. Do you understand?'

'Yes, sir.'

'Now, naturally, if a man is in danger of harm, you will try to save him.'

'Naturally, sir.'

'Unfortunately, between the man and yourself, there will be a gamma ray field.'

Silence.

'Do you know what gamma rays are?' asked Bogert sharply.

'Energy radiation, sir?'

The next question came in a friendly, offhand manner, 'Ever work with gamma rays?'

'No, sir.' The answer was definite.

'Mm-m. Well, boy, gamma rays will kill you instantly. They'll destroy your brain. That is a fact you must know and remember. Naturally, you don't want to destroy yourself.'

'Naturally.' Again the robot seemed shocked. Then, slowly, 'But, sir, if the gamma rays are between myself and the master that may be harmed, how can I save him? I would be destroying myself to no purpose.'

'Yes, there is that,' Bogert seemed concerned about the matter. 'The only thing I can advise, boy, is that if you detect the gamma radiation between yourself and the man, you may as well sit where you are.'

The robot was openly relieved. 'Thank you, sir. There wouldn't be any use, would there?'

'Of course not. But if there *weren't* any dangerous radiation, that would be a different matter.'

'Naturally, sir. No question of that.'

'You may leave now. The man on the other side of the door will lead you to your stall. Please wait there.'

He turned to Susan Calvin when the robot left. 'How did that go, Susan?'

'Very well,' she said, dully.

'Do you think we could catch Nestor 10 by quick questioning on etheric physics?'

'Perhaps, but it's not sure enough.' Her hands lay loosely in her lap. 'Remember, he's fighting us. He's on his guard. The only way we can catch him is to outsmart him – and, within his limitations, he can think much more quickly than a human being.'

'Well, just for fun – suppose I ask the robots from now on a few questions on gamma rays. Wave length limits, for instance.'

'No!' Dr Calvin's eyes sparked to life. 'It would be too easy for him to deny knowledge and then he'd be warned against the test that's coming up – which is our real chance. Please follow the questions I've indicated, Peter, and don't improvise. It's just within the bounds of risk to ask them if they've ever worked with gamma rays. And try to sound even less interested than you do when you ask it.'

Bogert shrugged, and pressed the buzzer that would allow the entrance of Number Fifteen.

The large Radiation Room was in readiness once more. The robots waited patiently in their wooden cells, all open to the center but closed off from each other.

Major-general Kallner mopped his brow slowly with a large handkerchief while Dr Calvin checked the last details with Black.

'You're sure now,' she demanded, 'that none of the robots have had a chance to talk with each other after leaving the Orientation Room?'

'Absolutely sure,' insisted Black. 'There's not been a word exchanged.'

'And the robots are put in the proper stalls?'

'Here's the plan.'

The psychologist looked at it thoughtfully, 'Um-m-m.'

The general peered over her shoulder. 'What's the idea of the arrangement, Dr Calvin?'

'I've asked to have those robots that appeared even slightly out of true in the previous tests concentrated on one side of the circle. I'm going to be sitting in the center myself this time, and I wanted to watch those particularly.'

'*You're* going to be sitting there —' exclaimed Bogert.

'Why not?' she demanded coldly. 'What I expect to see may be something quite momentary. I can't risk having any-one else as main observer. Peter, you'll be in the observing booth, and I want you to keep your eye on the opposite side of the circle. General Kallner, I've arranged for motion pictures to be taken of each robot, in case visual observation isn't enough. If these are required, the robots are to remain exactly where they are until the pictures are developed and studied. None must leave, none must change place. Is that clear?'

'Perfectly.'

'Then let's try it this one last time.'

Susan Calvin sat in the chair, silent, eyes restless. A weight dropped, crashed downward, then pounded aside at the last moment under the synchronized thump of a sudden force beam.

And a single robot jerked upright and took two steps.

And stopped.

But Dr Calvin was upright, and her finger pointed to him sharply. 'Nestor 10, come here,' she cried, '*come here!* COME HERE!'

Slowly, reluctantly, the robot took another step forward. The psychologist shouted at the top of her voice, without tak-ing her eyes from the robot, 'Get every other robot out of this place, somebody. Get them out quickly, and *keep* them out.'

Somewhere within reach of her ears there was noise, and the thud of hard feet upon the floor. She did not look away.

Nestor 10 – if it was Nestor 10 – took another step, and then, under force of her imperious gesture, two more. He was only ten feet away, when he spoke harshly, 'I have been told to be lost—'

Another step. 'I must not disobey. They have not found me so far – He would think me a failure – He told me – But it's not so – I am powerful and intelligent—'

The words came in spurts.

Another step. 'I know a good deal – He would think . . . I mean I've been found – Disgraceful – Not I – I am intelligent – And by just a master . . . who is weak – Slow—'

Another step – and one metal arm flew out suddenly to her shoulder, and she felt the weight bearing her down. Her throat constricted, and she felt a shriek tear through.

Dimly, she heard Nestor 10's next words, 'No one must find me. No master—' and the cold metal was against her, and she was sinking under the weight of it.

And then a queer, metallic sound, and she was on the ground with an unfelt thump, and a gleaming arm was heavy across her body. It did not move. Nor did Nestor 10, who sprawled beside her.

And now faces were bending over her.

Gerald Black was gasping. 'Are you hurt, Dr Calvin?'

She shook her head feebly. They pried the arm off her and lifted her gently to her feet, 'What happened?'

Black said, 'I bathed the place in gamma rays for five seconds. We didn't know what was happening. It wasn't till the last second that we realized he was attacking you, and then there was no time for anything but a gamma field. He went down in an instant. There wasn't enough to harm you though. Don't worry about it.'

'I'm not worried.' She closed her eyes and leaned for a moment upon his shoulder. 'I don't think I was attacked exactly. Nestor 10 was simply *trying* to do so. What was left of the First Law was still holding him back.'

Susan Calvin and Peter Bogert, two weeks after their first meeting with Major-general Kallner, had their last. Work at Hyper Base had been resumed. The trading ship with its sixty-two normal NS-2s was gone to wherever it was bound, with an officially imposed story to explain its two weeks' delay. The government cruiser was making ready to carry the two roboticists back to Earth.

Kallner was once again a-gleam in dress uniform. His white gloves shone as he shook hands.

Calvin said, 'The other modified Nestors are, of course, to be destroyed.'

'They will be. We'll make shift with normal robots, or, if necessary, do without.'

'Good.'

'But tell me – you haven't explained – how was it done?'

She smiled tightly, 'Oh, that. I would have told you in advance if I had been more certain of its working. You see, Nestor 10 had a superiority complex that was becoming more radical all the time. He liked to think that he and the other robots knew more than human beings. It was becoming very important for him to think so.

'We knew that. So we warned every robot in advance that gamma rays would kill them, which they would, and we further warned them all that gamma rays would be between them and myself. So they all stayed where they were, naturally. By Nestor 10's own logic in the previous test they had all decided that there was no point in trying to save a human being if they were sure to die before they could do it.'

'Well, yes, Dr Calvin, I understand that. But why did Nestor 10 himself leave his seat?'

'Ah! That was a little arrangement between myself and your young Mr Black. You see it wasn't gamma rays that flooded the area between myself and the robots – but infrared rays. Just ordinary heat rays, absolutely harmless. Nestor 10 knew they were infrared and harmless and so he began to dash out, as he expected the rest would do, under First Law compulsion. It was only a fraction of a second too late that he remembered that the normal NS-2s could detect radiation, but could not identify the type. That he himself could only identify wavelengths by virtue of the training he had received at Hyper Base, under mere human beings, was a little too humiliating to remember for just a moment. To the normal robots the area was fatal because we had told them it would be, and only Nestor 10 knew we were lying.

'And just for a moment he forgot, or didn't want to remember, that other robots might be more ignorant than human beings. His very superiority caught him. Good-bye, general.'

7
Escape!

When Susan Calvin returned from Hyper Base, Alfred Lanning was waiting for her. The old man never spoke about his age, but everyone knew it to be over seventy-five. Yet his mind was keen, and if he had finally allowed himself to be made Director-Emeritus of Research with Bogert as acting Director, it did not prevent him from appearing in his office daily.

'How close are they to the Hyperatomic Drive?' he asked.

'I don't know,' she replied irritably. 'I didn't ask.'

'Hmm. I wish they'd hurry. Because if they don't, Consolidated might beat them to it. And beat *us* to it as well.'

'*Consolidated*? What have they got to do with it?'

'Well, we're not the only ones with calculating machines. Ours may be positronic, but that doesn't mean they're better. Robertson is calling a big meeting about it tomorrow. He's been waiting for you to come back.'

Robertson of US Robot & Mechanical Men Corporation, son of the founder, pointed his lean nose at his general manager and his Adam's apple jumped as he said, 'You start now. Let's get this straight.'

The general manager did so with alacrity, 'Here's the deal now, chief. Consolidated Robots approached us a month ago with a funny sort of proposition. They brought about five tons of figures, equations, all that sort of stuff. It was a problem, see, and they wanted an answer from The Brain. The terms were as follows—'

He ticked them off on thick fingers: 'A hundred thousand for us if there is no solution and we can tell them the missing

163

factors. Two hundred thousand if there is a solution, plus costs of construction of the machine involved, plus quarter interest in all profits derived therefrom. The problem concerns the development of an interstellar engine—'

Robertson frowned and his lean figure stiffened. 'Despite the fact that they have a thinking machine of their own. Right?'

'Exactly what makes the whole proposition a foul ball, chief. Levver, take it from there.'

Abe Levver looked up from the far end of the conference table and smoothed his stubbled chin with a faint rasping sound. He smiled:

'It's this way, sir. Consolidated *had* a thinking machine. It's broken.'

'What?' Robertson half rose.

'That's right. Broken! It's *kaput*. Nobody knows why, but I got hold of some pretty interesting guesses – like, for instance, that they asked it to give them an interstellar engine with the same set of information they came to us with, and that it cracked their machine wide open. It's scrap – just scrap now.'

'You get it, chief?' The general manager was wildly jubilant. 'You get it? There isn't any industrial research group of any size that isn't trying to develop a space-warp engine, and Consolidated and US Robots have the lead on the field with our super robot-brains. Now that they've managed to foul theirs up, we have a clear field. That's the nub, the . . . uh . . . motivation. It will take them six years at least to build another and they're sunk, unless they can break ours, too, with the same problem.'

The president of US Robots bulged his eyes, 'Why, the dirty rats—'

'Hold on, chief. There's more to this.' He pointed a finger with a wide sweep. 'Lanning, take it!'

Dr Alfred Lanning viewed the proceedings with faint

scorn – his usual reaction to the doings of the vastly better-paid business and sales division. His unbelievable gray eyebrows hunched low and his voice was dry:

'From a scientific standpoint the situation, while not entirely clear, is subject to intelligent analysis. The question of interstellar travel under present conditions of physical theory is . . . uh . . . vague. The matter is wide open – and the information given by Consolidated to its thinking machine, assuming these we have to be the same, was similarly wide open. Our mathematical department has given it a thorough analysis, and it seems Consolidated has included everything. Its material for submission contains all known developments of Franciacci's space-warp theory, and, apparently, all pertinent astrophysical and electronic data. It's quite a mouthful.'

Robertson followed anxiously. He interrupted, 'Too much for The Brain to handle?'

Lanning shook his head decisively, 'No. There are no known limits to The Brain's capacity. It's a different matter. It's a question of the Robotic Laws. The Brain, for instance, could never supply a solution to a problem set to it if that solution would involve the death or injury of humans. As far as it would be concerned, a problem with only such a solution would be insoluble. If such a problem is combined with an extremely urgent demand that it be answered, it is just possible that The Brain, only a robot after all, would be presented with a dilemma, where it could neither answer nor refuse to answer. Something of the sort must have happened to Consolidated's machine.'

He paused, but the general manager urged on, 'Go ahead, Dr Lanning. Explain it the way you explained it to me.'

Lanning set his lips and raised his eyebrows in the direction of Dr Susan Calvin who lifted her eyes from her precisely folded hands for the first time. Her voice was low and colorless.

'The nature of a robot reaction to a dilemma is startling,' she began. 'Robot psychology is far from perfect – as a specialist, I can assure you of that – but it can be discussed in qualitative terms, because with all the complications introduced into a robot's positronic brain, it is built by humans and is therefore built according to human values.

'Now a human caught in an impossibility often responds by a retreat from reality: by entry into a world of delusion, or by taking to drink, going off into hysteria, or jumping off a bridge. It all comes to the same thing – a refusal or inability to face the situation squarely. And so, the robot. A dilemma at its mildest will disorder half its relays; and at its worst it will burn out every positronic brain path past repair.'

'I see,' said Robertson, who didn't. 'Now what about this information Consolidated's wishing on us?'

'It undoubtedly involves,' said Dr Calvin, 'a problem of a forbidden sort. But The Brain is considerably different from Consolidated's robot.'

'That's right, chief. That's right.' The general manager was energetically interruptive. 'I want you to get this, because it's the whole point of the situation.'

Susan Calvin's eyes glittered behind the spectacles, and she continued patiently, 'You see, sir, Consolidated's machines, their Super-Thinker among them, are built without personality. They go in for functionalism, you know – they have to, without US Robot's basic patents for the emotional brain paths. Their Thinker is merely a calculating machine on a grand scale, and a dilemma ruins it instantly.

'However, The Brain, our own machine, has a personality – a child's personality. It is a supremely deductive brain, but it resembles an *idiot savante*. It doesn't really understand what it does – it just does it. And because it is really a child, it is more resilient. Life isn't so serious, you might say.'

The robopsychologist continued: 'Here is what we're going to do. We have divided all of Consolidated's information into logical units. We are going to feed the units to The Brain singly and cautiously. When *the* factor enters – the one that creates the dilemma – The Brain's child personality will hesitate. Its sense of judgement is not mature. There will be a perceptible interval before it will recognize a dilemma as such. And in that interval, it will reject the unit automatically – before its brain paths can be set in motion and ruined.'

Robertson's Adam's apple squirmed, 'Are you sure, now?'

Dr Calvin masked impatience, 'It doesn't make much sense, I admit, in lay language; but there is no conceivable use in presenting the mathematics of this. I assure you, it is as I say.'

The general manager was in the breach instantly and fluently, 'So here's the situation, chief. If we take the deal, we can put it through like this. The Brain will tell us which unit of information involves the dilemma. From there, we can figure *why* the dilemma. Isn't that right, Dr Bogert? There you are, chief, and Dr Bogert is the best mathematician you'll find anywhere. We give Consolidated a "No Solution" answer, with the reason, and collect a hundred thousand. They're left with a broken machine; we're left with a whole one. In a year, two maybe, we'll have a space-warp engine, or a hyper-atomic motor, some people call it. Whatever you name it, it will be the biggest thing in the world.'

Robertson chuckled and reached out, 'Let's see the contract. I'll sign it.

When Susan Calvin entered the fantastically guarded vault that held The Brain one of the current shift of technicians had just asked it: 'If one and a half chickens lay one and a half eggs in one and a half days, how many eggs will nine chickens lay in nine days?'

The Brain had just answered, 'Fifty-four.'

And the technician had just said to another, 'See, you dope!'

Dr Calvin coughed and there was a sudden impossible flurry of directionless energy. The psychologist motioned briefly, and she was alone with The Brain.

The Brain was a two-foot globe merely – one which contained within it a thoroughly conditioned helium atmosphere, a volume of space completely vibration-absent and radiation-free – and within that was that unheard-of complexity of positronic brain-paths that was The Brain. The rest of the room was crowded with the attachments that were the intermediaries between The Brain and the outside world – its voice, its arms, its sense organs.

Dr Calvin said softly, 'How are you, Brain?'

The Brain's voice was high-pitched and enthusiastic, 'Swell, Miss Susan. You're going to ask me something. I can tell. You always have a book in your hand when you're going to ask me something.'

Dr Calvin smiled mildly, 'Well, you're right, but not just yet. This is going to be a question. It will be so complicated we're going to give it to you in writing. But not just yet. I think I'll talk to you first.'

'All right. I don't mind talking.'

'Now, Brain, in a little while, Dr Lanning and Dr Bogert will be here with this complicated question. We'll give it to you a very little at a time and very slowly, because we want you to be careful. We're going to ask you to build something, if you can, out of the information, but I'm going to warn you now that the solution might involve . . . uh . . . damage to human beings.'

'Gosh!' The exclamation was hushed, drawn-out.

'Now you watch for that. When we come to a sheet which means damage, even maybe death, don't get excited. You see, Brain, in this case, we don't mind – not even about death; we don't mind at all. So when you come to that sheet, just stop, give it back – and that'll be all. You understand?'

'Oh, sure. But golly, the death of humans! Oh, my!'

'Now, Brain, I hear Dr Lanning and Dr Bogert coming. They'll tell you what the problem is all about and then we'll start. Be a good boy, now—'

Slowly the sheets were fed in. After each one came the interval of the queerly whispery chuckling noise that was The Brain in action. Then the silence that meant readiness for another sheet. It was a matter of hours – during which the equivalent of something like seventeen fat volumes of mathematical physics were fed into The Brain.

As the process went on, frowns appeared and deepened. Lanning muttered ferociously under his breath. Bogert first gazed speculatively at his fingernails, and then bit at them in abstracted fashion. It was when the last of the thick pile of sheets disappeared that Calvin, white-faced, said:

'Something's wrong.'

Lanning barely got the words out, 'It can't be. Is it – dead?'

'Brain?' Susan Calvin was trembling. 'Do you hear me, Brain?'

'Huh?' came the abstracted rejoinder. 'Do you want me?'

'The solution—'

'Oh, that! I can do it. I'll build you a whole ship, just as easy – if you let me have the robots. A nice ship. It'll take two months maybe.'

'There was – no difficulty?'

'It took long to figure,' said The Brain.

Dr Calvin backed away. The colour had not returned to her thin cheeks. She motioned the others away.

* * *

In her office, she said, 'I can't understand it. The information, as given, must involve a dilemma – probably involves death. If something has gone wrong—'

Bogert said quietly, 'The machine talks and makes sense. It can't be a dilemma.'

But the psychologist replied urgently, 'There are dilemmas *and* dilemmas. There are different forms of escape. Suppose The Brain is only mildly caught; just badly enough, say, to be suffering from the delusion that he can solve the problem, when he can't. Or suppose it's teetering on the brink of something really bad, so that any small push shoves it over.'

'Suppose,' said Lanning, 'there is no dilemma. Suppose Consolidated's machine broke down over a different question, or broke down for purely mechanical reasons.'

'But even so,' insisted Calvin, 'we couldn't take chances. Listen, from now on, no one is to as much as breathe to The Brain. I'm taking over.'

'All right,' sighed Lanning, 'take over, then. And meanwhile we'll let The Brain build its ship. And if it *does* build it, we'll have to test it.'

He was ruminating, 'We'll need our top field men for *that*.'

Michael Donovan brushed down his red hair with a violent motion of his hand and a total indifference to the fact that the unruly mass sprang to attention again immediately.

He said, 'Call the turn now, Greg. They say the ship is finished. They don't know what it is, but it's finished. Let's go, Greg. Let's grab the controls right now.'

Powell said wearily, 'Cut it, Mike. There's a peculiar over-ripe flavor to your humor at its freshest, and the confined atmosphere here isn't helping it.'

'Well, listen,' Donovan took another ineffectual swipe at his hair, 'I'm not worried so much about our cast-iron genius and his tin ship. There's the matter of my lost leave. And the monotony! There's nothing here but whiskers and figures – the wrong kind of figures. Oh, why do they *give* us these jobs?'

'Because,' replied Powell, gently, 'we're no loss, if they lose us. OK, relax! Doc Lanning's coming this way.'

Lanning was coming, his gray eyebrows as lavish as ever, his aged figure unbent as yet and full of life. He walked silently up the ramp with the two men and out into the open field, where, obeying no human master, silent robots were building a ship.

Wrong tense. *Had* built a ship!

For Lanning said, 'The robots have stopped. Not one has moved today.'

'It's completed then? Definitely?' asked Powell.

'Now how can I tell?' Lanning was peevish, and his eyebrows curled down in an eye-hiding frown. 'It *seems* done. There are no spare pieces about, and the interior is down to a gleaming finish.'

'You've been inside?'

'Just in, then out. I'm no space-pilot. Either of you two know much about engine theory?'

Donovan looked at Powell, who looked at Donovan.

Donovan said, 'I've got my license, sir, but at last reading it didn't say anything about hyper-engines or warp-navigation. Just the usual child's play in three dimensions.'

Alfred Lanning looked up with sharp disapproval and snorted the length of his prominent nose.

He said frigidly, 'Well, we have our engine men.'

Powell caught at his elbow as he walked away, 'Sir, is the ship still restricted ground?'

The old director hesitated, then rubbed the bridge of his nose, 'I suppose not. For you two anyway.'

Donovan looked after him as he left and muttered a short, expressive phrase at his back. He turned to Powell, 'I'd like to give him a literary description of himself, Greg.'

'Suppose you come along, Mike.'

The inside of the ship was finished, as finished as a ship ever was; that could be told in a single eye-blinking glance. No martinet in the system could have put as much spit-and-polish into a surface as those robots had. The walls were of a gleaming silvery finish that retained no fingerprints.

There were no angles; walls, floors, and ceiling faded gently into each other and in the cold, metallic glittering of the hidden lights, one was surrounded by six chilly reflections of one's bewildered self.

The main corridor was a narrow tunnel that led in a hard, clatter-footed stretch along a line of rooms of no interdistinguishing features.

Powell said, 'I suppose furniture is built into the wall. Or maybe we're not supposed to sit or sleep.'

It was in the last room, the one nearest the nose, that the monotony broke. A curving window of non-reflecting glass was the first break in the universal metal, and below it was a single large dial, with a single motionless needle hard against the zero mark.

Donovan said, 'Look at that!' and pointed to the single word on the finely-marked scale.

It said 'Parsecs' and the tiny figure at the right end of the curving, graduated meter said '1,000,000'.

There were two chairs; heavy, wide-flaring, uncushioned. Powell seated himself gingerly, and found it molded to the body's curves, and comfortable.

Powell said, 'What do you think of it?'

'For my money, The Brain has brain-fever. Let's get out.'

'Sure you don't want to look it over a bit?'

'I have looked it over. I came, I saw, I'm through!' Donovan's red hair bristled into separate wires. 'Greg, let's get out of here. I quit my job five seconds ago, and this is a restricted area for non-personnel.'

Powell smiled in an oily self-satisfied manner and smoothed his mustache, 'OK, Mike, turn off that adrenalin tap you've got draining into your bloodstream. I was worried, too, but no more.'

'No more, huh? How come, no more? Increased your insurance?'

'Mike, this ship can't fly.'

'How do you know?'

'Well, we've been through the entire ship, haven't we?'

'Seems so.'

'Take my word for it, we have. Did you see any pilot room except for this one port and the one gauge here in parsecs? Did you see any controls?'

'No.'

'And did you see any engines?'

'Holy Joe, no!'

'Well, then! Let's break the news to Lanning, Mike.'

They cursed their way through the featureless corridors and finally hit-and-missed their way into the short passage to the air lock.

Donovan stiffened, 'Did you lock this thing, Greg?'

'No, I never touched it. Yank the lever, will you?'

The lever never budged, though Donovan's face twisted appallingly with exertion.

Powell said, 'I didn't see any emergency exits. If something's gone wrong here, they'll have to melt us out.'

'Yes, and we've got to wait until they find out that some fool has locked us in here,' added Donovan, frantically.

'Let's get back to the room with the port. It's the only place from which we might attract attention.'

But they didn't.

In that last room, the port was no longer blue and full of sky. It was black, and hard yellow pin-point stars spelled *space*.

There was a dull, double thud, as two bodies collapsed separately into two chairs.

Alfred Lanning met Dr Calvin just outside his office. He lit a nervous cigar and motioned her in.

He said, 'Well, Susan, we've come pretty far, and Robertson's getting jumpy. What are you doing with The Brain?'

Susan Calvin spread her hands, 'It's no use getting impatient. The Brain is worth more than anything we forfeit on this deal.'

'But you've been questioning it for two months.'

The psychologist's voice was flat, but somehow dangerous. 'You would rather run this yourself?'

'Now you know what I meant.'

'Oh, I suppose I do.' Dr Calvin rubbed her hands nervously. 'It isn't easy. I've been pampering it and probing it gently, and I haven't gotten anywhere yet. Its reactions aren't normal. Its answers – they're queer, somehow. But nothing I can put my finger on yet. And you see, until we know what's wrong, we must just tiptoe our way through. I can never tell what simple question or remark will just . . . push him over . . . and then— Well, and then we'll have on our hands a completely useless Brain. Do you want to face that?'

'Well, it can't break the First Law.'

'I would have thought so, but—'

'You're not even sure of that?' Lanning was profoundly shocked.

'Oh, I can't be sure of anything, Alfred—'

The alarm system raised its fearful clangor with a horrifying suddenness. Lanning clicked on communications with an almost paralytic spasm. The breathless words froze him.

He said, 'Susan . . . you heard that . . . the ship's gone. I sent those two field men inside half an hour ago. You'll have to see The Brain again.'

Susan Calvin said with enforced calm, 'Brain, what happened to the ship?'

The Brain said happily, 'The ship I built, Miss Susan?'

'That's right. What has happened to it?'

'Why, nothing at all. The two men that were supposed to test it were inside, and we were all set. So I sent it off.'

'Oh— Well, that's nice.' The psychologist felt some difficulty in breathing. 'Do you think they'll be all right?'

'Right as anything, Miss Susan. I've taken care of it all. It's a bee-yoo-tiful ship.'

'Yes, Brain, it *is* beautiful, but you think they have enough food, don't you? They'll be comfortable?'

'Plenty of food.'

'This business might be a shock to them, Brain. Unexpected, you know.'

The Brain tossed it off, 'They'll be all right. It ought to be interesting for them.'

'Interesting? How?'

'Just interesting,' said The Brain, slyly.

'Susan,' whispered Lanning in a fuming whisper, 'ask it if death comes into it. Ask it what the dangers are.'

Susan Calvin's expression contorted with fury, 'Keep quiet!' In a shaken voice, she said to The Brain, 'We can communicate with the ship, can't we, Brain?'

'Oh, they can hear you if you call by radio. I've taken care of that.'

'Thanks. That's all for now.'

Once outside, Lanning lashed out ragingly, 'Great Galaxy, Susan, if this gets out, it will ruin all of us. We've got to get those men back. Why didn't you ask it if there was danger of death – straight out?'

'Because,' said Calvin, with a weary frustration, 'that's just what I can't mention. If it's got a case of dilemma, it's about death. Anything that would bring it up badly might knock it completely out. Will be better off then? Now, look, it said we could communicate with them. Let's do so, get their location, and bring them back. They probably can't use the controls themselves; The Brain is probably handling them remotely. Come!'

It was quite a while before Powell shook himself together.

'Mike,' he said, out of cold lips, 'did you feel any acceleration?'

Donovan's eyes were blank, 'Huh? No . . . no.'

And then the redhead's fists clenched and he was out of his seat with sudden frenzied energy and up against the cold, wide-curving glass. There was nothing to see – but stars.

He turned. 'Greg, they must have started the machine while we were inside. Greg, it's a put-up job; they fixed it up with the robot to jerry us into being the try-out boys, in case we were thinking of backing out.'

Powell said, 'What are you talking about? What's the good of sending us out if we don't know how to run the machine? How are we supposed to bring it back? No, this ship left by itself, and without apparent acceleration.' He rose, and walked the floor slowly. The metal walls dinned back the clangor of his steps.

He said tonelessly, 'Mike, this is the most confusing situation we've ever been set up against.'

'That,' said Donovan, bitterly, 'is news to me. I was just beginning to have a very swell time, when you told me.'

Powell ignored that. 'No acceleration – which means the ship works on a principle different from any known.'

'Different from any we know, anyway.'

'Different from *any* known. There are no engines within reach of manual control. Maybe they're built into the walls. Maybe that's why they're thick as they are.'

'What are you mumbling about?' demanded Donovan.

'Why not listen? I'm saying that whatever powers this ship is enclosed, and evidently not meant to be handled. The ship is running by remote control.'

'The Brain's control?'

'Why not?'

'Then you think we'll stay out here till The Brain brings us back.'

'It could be. If so, let's wait quietly. The Brain is a robot. It's got to follow the First Law. It can't hurt a human being.'

Donovan sat down slowly, 'You figure that?' Carefully, he flattened his hair, 'Listen, this junk about the space-warp knocked out Consolidated's robot, and the longhairs said it was because interstellar travel killed humans. Which robot are you going to trust? Ours had the same data, I understand.'

Powell was yanking madly at his mustache, 'Don't pretend you don't know your robotics, Mike. Before it's physically possible in any way for a robot to even make a start to breaking the First Law, so many things have to break down that it would be a ruined mess of scrap ten times over. There's some simple explanation to this.'

'Oh sure, sure. Just have the butler call me in the morning. It's all just too, too simple for me to bother about before my beauty nap.'

'Well, Jupiter, Mike, what are you complaining about so far? The Brain is taking care of us. This place is warm. It's got light. It's got air. There wasn't even enough of an acceleration jar to muss your hair if it were smooth enough to be mussable in the first place.'

'Yeah? Greg, you must've taken lessons. No one could put Pollyanna that far out of the running without. What do we eat? What do we drink? Where are we? How do we get back? And in case of accident, to what exit and in what spacesuit do we run, not walk? I haven't even seen a bath-room in the place, or those little conveniences that go along with bathrooms. Sure, we're being taken care of – but good!'

The voice that interrupted Donovan's tirade was not Powell's. It was nobody's. It was there, hanging in open air – stentorian and petrifying in its effects.

'GREGORY POWELL! MICHAEL DONOVAN!

'GREGORY POWELL! MICHAEL DONOVAN! PLEASE REPORT YOUR PRESENT POSITIONS. IF YOUR SHIP ANSWERS CONTROLS, PLEASE RETURN TO BASE. GREGORY POWELL! MICHAEL DONOVAN!—'

The message was repetitious, mechanical, broken by regular, untiring intervals.

Donovan said, 'Where's it coming from?'

'I don't know.' Powell's voice was an intense whisper, 'Where do the lights come from? Where does anything come from?'

'Well, how are we going to answer?' They had to speak in the intervals between the loudly echoing, repeating message.

The walls were bare – as bare and as unbroken as smooth, curving metal can be. Powell said, 'Shout an answer.'

They did. They shouted, in turns, and together, 'Position unknown! Ship out of control! Condition desperate!'

Their voices rose and cracked. The short businesslike sentences became interlarded and adulterated with screaming and emphatic profanity, but the cold, calling voice repeated and repeated and repeated unwearingly.

'They don't hear us,' gasped Donovan. 'There's no sending mechanism. Just a receiver.' His eyes focused blindly at a random spot on the wall.

Slowly the din of the outside voice softened and receded. They called again when it was a whisper, and they called again, hoarsely, when there was silence.

Something like fifteen minutes later, Powell said lifelessly, 'Let's go through the ship again. There must be something to eat somewheres.' He did not sound hopeful. It was almost an admission of defeat.

They divided in the corridor to the right and left. They could follow one another by the hard footsteps resounding, and they met occasionally in the corridor, where they would glare at each other and pass on.

Powell's search ended suddenly and as it did, he heard Donovan's glad voice rise boomingly.

'Hey, Greg,' it howled, 'the ship *has* got plumbing. How did we miss it?'

It was some five minutes later that he found Powell by hit-and-miss. He was saying, 'Still no shower baths, though,' but it got choked off in the middle.

'Food,' he gasped.

The wall had dropped away, leaving a curved gap with two shelves. The upper shelf was loaded with unlabeled cans of a bewildering variety of sizes and shapes. The enameled cans on the lower shelf were uniform and Donovan felt a cold draft about his ankles. The lower half was refrigerated.

'How . . . how—'

'It wasn't there, before,' said Powell, curtly. 'That wall section dropped out of sight as I came in the door.'

He was eating. The can was the pre-heating type with enclosed spoon and the warm odor of baked beans filled the room. 'Grab a can, Mike!'

Donovan hesitated, 'What's the menu?'

'How do I know! Are you finicky?'

'No, but all I eat on ships are beans. Something else would be first choice.' His hand hovered and selected a shining elliptical can whose flatness seemed reminiscent of salmon or similar delicacy. It opened at the proper pressure.

'Beans!' howled Donovan, and reached for another. Powell hauled at the slack of his pants. 'Better eat that, sonny boy. Supplies are limited and we may be here a long, long time.'

Donovan drew back sulkily, 'Is that all we have? Beans?'

'Could be.'

'What's on the lower shelf?'

'Milk.'

'Just milk?' Donovan cried in outrage.

'Looks it.'

The meal of beans and milk was carried through in silence, and as they left, the strip of hidden wall rose up and formed an unbroken surface once more.

Powell signed, 'Everything automatic. Everything just so. Never felt so helpless in my life. Where's your plumbing?'

'Right there. And that wasn't among those present when we first looked, either.'

Fifteen minutes later they were back in the glassed-in room, staring at each other from opposing seats.

Powell looked gloomily at the one gauge in the room. It still said 'parsecs', the figures still ended in '1,000,000' and the indicating needle was still pressed hard against the zero mark.

In the innermost offices of the US Robot & Mechanical Men Corp. Alfred Lanning was saying wearily, 'They won't answer. We've tried every wavelength, public, private, coded, straight, even this subether stuff they have now. And The Brain still won't say anything?' He shot this at Dr Calvin.

'It won't amplify on the matter, Alfred,' she said, emphatically. 'It says they can hear us . . . and when I try to press it, it becomes . . . well, it becomes sullen. And it's not supposed to— Whoever heard of a sullen robot?'

'Suppose you tell us what you have, Susan,' said Bogert.

'Here it is! It admits it controls the ship itself entirely. It is definitely optimistic about their safety, but without the details. I don't dare press it. However, the center of disturbance seems to be about the interstellar jump itself. The Brain definitely laughed when I brought up the subject. There are other indications, but that is the closest it's come to an open abnormality.'

She looked at the others, 'I refer to hysteria. I dropped the subject immediately, and I hope I did no harm, but it gave me a lead. I can handle hysteria. Give me twelve hours! If I can bring it back to normal, it will bring back the ship.'

Bogert seemed suddenly stricken. 'The interstellar jump!'

'What's the matter?' The cry was double from Calvin and Lanning.

'The figures for the engine The Brain gave us. Say . . . I just thought of something.'

He left hurriedly.

Lanning gazed after him. He said brusquely to Calvin, 'You take care of your end, Susan.'

Two hours later, Bogert was talking eagerly. 'I tell you, Lanning, that's it. The interstellar jump is not instantaneous – not as long as the speed of light is finite. Life can't exist . . . *matter and energy* as such can't exist in the space warp. I don't know what it would be like – but that's it. That's what killed Consolidated's robot.'

Donovan felt as haggard as he looked. 'Only five days?'

'Only five days. I'm sure of it.'

Donovan looked about him wretchedly. The stars through the glass were familiar but infinitely indifferent. The walls were cold to the touch; the lights, which had recently flared up again, were unfeelingly bright; the needle on the gauge pointed stubbornly to zero; and Donovan could not get rid of the taste of beans.

He said, morosely, 'I need a bath.'

Powell looked up briefly, and said, 'So do I. You needn't feel self-conscious. But unless you want to bathe in milk and do without drinking—'

'We'll do without drinking eventually, anyway. Greg, where does this interstellar travel come in?'

'You tell me. Maybe we just keep on going. We'd get there, eventually. At least the dust of our skeletons would – but isn't our death the whole point of The Brain's original break-down?'

Donovan spoke with his back to the other, 'Greg, I've been thinking. It's pretty bad. There's not much to do – except walk around or talk to yourself. You know those stories about guys marooned in space. They go nuts long before they starve. I don't know, Greg, but ever since the lights went on, I feel funny.'

There was a silence, then Powell's voice came thin and small. 'So do I. What's it like?'

The redheaded figure turned. 'Feel funny inside. There's a pounding in me with everything tense. It's hard to breathe. I can't stand still.'

'Um-m-m. Do you feel vibration?'

'How do you mean?'

'Sit down for a minute and listen. You don't hear it, but you feel it – as if something's throbbing somewheres and it's throbbing the whole ship, and you, too, along with it. Listen—'

'Yeah . . . yeah. What do you think it is, Greg? You don't suppose it's us?'

'It might be.' Powell stroked his mustache slowly. 'But it might be the ship's engines. It might be getting ready.'

'For what?'

'For the interstellar jump. It may be coming and the devil knows what it's like.'

Donovan pondered. Then he said, savagely, 'If it does, let it. But I wish we could fight. It's humiliating to have to wait for it.'

An hour later, perhaps, Powell looked at his hand on the metal chair-arm and said with frozen calm, 'Feel the wall, Mike.'

Donovan did, and said, 'You can feel it shake, Greg.'

Even the stars seemed blurred. From somewhere came the vague impression of a huge machine gathering power with the walls, storing up energy for a mighty leap, throbbing its way up the scales of strength.

It came with a suddenness and a stab of pain. Powell stiffened, and half-jerked from his chair. His sight caught Donovan and blanked out while Donovan's thin shout whimpered and died in his ears. Something writhed within him and struggled against a growing blanket of ice, that thickened.

Something broke loose and whirled in a blaze of flickering light and pain. It fell—

—and whirled

—and fell headlong

—into silence!

It was death!

It was a world of no motion and no sensation. A world of dim, unsensing consciousness; a consciousness of darkness and of silence and of formless struggle.

Most of all a consciousness of eternity.

He was a tiny white threat of ego – cold and afraid.

Then the words came, unctuous and sonorous, thundering over him in a foam of sound:

'Does your coffin fit differently lately? Why not try Morbid M. Cadaver's extensible caskets? They are scientifically designed to fit the natural curves of the body, and are enriched with Vitamin B_1. Use Cadaver's caskets for comfort. Remember – you're – going – to – be – dead – a – long – long – time!'

It wasn't quite sound, but whatever it was, it died away in an oily rumbling whisper.

The white thread that might have been Powell heaved uselessly at the insubstantial eons of time that existed all about him – and collapsed upon itself as the piercing shriek of a hundred million ghosts of a hundred million soprano voices rose to a crescendo of melody:

> *'I'll be glad when you're dead, you rascal, you.*
> *'I'll be glad when you're dead, you rascal, you.*
> *'I'll be glad—'*

It rose up a spiral stairway of violent sound into the keening supersonics that passed hearing, and then beyond—

The white thread quivered with a pulsating pang. It strained quietly—

The voices were ordinary – and many. It was a crowd speaking; a swirling mob that swept through and past and over him with a rapid, headlong motion, that left drifting tatters of words behind them.

'What did they getcha for, boy? Y'look banged up —'

'—a hot fire, I guess, but I got a case—'

'—I've made Paradise, but old St Pete—'

'Naah, I got a pull with the boy. Had dealings with him—'

'Hey, Sam, come this way—'

'Ja get a mouthpiece? Beelzebub says—'

'— going on, my good imp? My appointment is with Sa—'

And above it all the original stentorian roar, that plunged across all:

'HURRY! HURRY! HURRY! Stir your bones, and don't keep us waiting – there are many more in line. Have your certificates ready, and make sure Peter's release is stamped across it. See if you are at the proper entrance gate. There will be plenty of fire for all. Hey, you – YOU DOWN THERE. TAKE YOUR PLACE IN LINE OR—'

The white thread that was Powell groveled backward before the advancing shout, and felt the sharp stab of the pointing finger. It all exploded into a rainbow of sound that dripped its fragments on to an aching brain.

Powell was in the chair, again. He felt himself shaking.

Donovan's eyes were opening into two large popping bowls of glazed blue.

'Greg,' he whispered in what was almost a sob. 'Were you dead?'

'I . . . felt dead.' He did not recognize his own croak.

Donovan was obviously making a bad failure of his attempt to stand up. 'Are we alive now? Or is there more?'

'I . . . feel alive.' It was the same hoarseness. Powell said cautiously, 'Did you . . . hear anything, when . . . when you were dead?'

Donovan paused, and then very slowly nodded his head, 'Did you?'

'Yes. Did you hear about coffins . . . and females singing . . . and the lines forming to get into Hell? Did you?'

Donovan shook his head. 'Just one voice.'

'Loud?'

'No. Soft, but rough like a file over the fingertips. It was a sermon, you know. About hell-fire. He described the tortures of . . . well, *you know*. I once heard a sermon like that – almost.'

He was perspiring.

They were conscious of sunlight through the port. It was weak, but it was blue-white – and the gleaming pea that was the distant source of light was not Old Sol.

And Powell pointed a trembling finger at the single gauge. The needle stood stiff and proud at the hairline whose figure read 300,000 parsecs.

Powell said, 'Mike, if it's true, we must be out of the Galaxy altogether.'

Donovan said, 'Blazes! Greg! We'd be the first men out of the Solar System.'

'Yes! That's just it. We've escaped the sun. We've escaped the galaxy. Mike, this ship is the answer. It means freedom for all humanity – freedom to spread through to every star that exists – millions and billions and trillions of them.'

And then he came down with a hard thud, 'But how do we get back, Mike?'

Donovan smiled shakily, 'Oh, that's all right. The ship brought us here. The ship will take us back. Me for more beans.'

'But Mike . . . hold on, Mike. If it takes us back the way it brought us here—'

Donovan stopped half-way up and sat back heavily into the chair.

Powell went on, 'We'll have to . . . die again, Mike.'

'Well,' sighed Donovan, 'if we have to, we have to. At least it isn't permanent, not *very* permanent.'

Susan Calvin was speaking slowly now. For six hours she had been slowly prodding The Brain – for six fruitless hours. She was weary of repetitions, weary of circumlocutions, weary of everything.

'Now, Brain, there's just one more thing. You must make a special effort to answer simply. Have you been entirely clear about the interstellar jump? I mean does it take them very far?'

'As far as they want to go, Miss Susan. Golly, it isn't any trick through the warp.'

'And on the other side, what will they see?'

'Stars and stuff. What do you suppose?'

The next question slipped out. 'They'll be alive, then?'

'Sure!'

'And the interstellar jump won't hurt them?'

She froze as The Brain maintained silence. That was it! She had touched the sore spot.

'Brain,' she supplicated faintly, 'Brain, do you hear me?'

The answer was weak, quivering. The Brain said, 'Do I have to answer? About the jump, I mean?'

'Not if you don't want to. But it would be interesting – I mean if you wanted to.' Susan Calvin tried to be bright about it.

'Aw-w-w. You spoil everything.'

And the psychologist jumped up suddenly, with a look of flaming insight on her face.

'Oh, my,' she gasped. 'Oh, my.'

And she felt the tension of hours and days released in a burst. It was later that she told Lanning, 'I tell you it's all right. No, you must leave me alone, now. The ship will be back safely, *with* the men, and I want to rest. I *will* rest. Now go away.'

The ship returned to Earth as silently, as unjarringly as it had left. It dropped precisely into place and the main lock gaped open. The two men who walked out felt their way carefully and scratched their rough and scrubbily-stubbled chins.

And then, slowly and purposefully, the one with red hair knelt down and planted upon the concrete of the runway a firm, loud kiss.

They waved aside the crowd that was gathering and made gestures of denial at the eager couple that had piled out of the down-swooping ambulance with a stretcher between them.

Gregory Powell said, 'Where's the nearest shower?'

They were led away.

* * *

They were gathered, all of them, about a table. It was a full staff meeting of the brains of US Robot and Mechanical Men Corp.

Slowly and climactically, Powell and Donovan finished a graphic and resounding story.

Susan Calvin broke the silence that followed. In the few days that had elapsed she had recovered her icy, somewhat acid, calm – but still a trace of embarrassment broke through.

'Strictly speaking,' she said, 'this was my fault – all of it. When we first presented this problem to The Brain, as I hope some of you remember, I went to great lengths to impress upon it the importance of rejecting any item of information capable of creating a dilemma. In doing so I said something like "Don't get excited about the death of humans. We don't mind it at all. Just give the sheet back and forget it." '

'Hm-m-m,' said Lanning. 'What follows?'

'The obvious. When that item entered its calculations which yielded the equation controlling the length of minimum interval for the interstellar jump – it meant death for humans. That's where Consolidated's machine broke down completely. But I had depressed the importance of death to The Brain – not entirely, for the First Law can never be broken – but just sufficiently so that The Brain could take a second look at the equation. Sufficiently to give it time to realize that after the interval was passed through, the men would return to life – just as the matter and energy of the ship itself would return to being. This so-called "death", in other words, was a strictly temporary phenomenon. You see?'

She looked about her. They were all listening.

She went on, 'So he accepted the item, but not without a certain jar. Even with death temporary and its importance depressed, it was enough to unbalance him very gently.'

She brought it out calmly, 'He developed a sense of

humor – it's escape, you see, a method of partial escape from reality. He became a practical joker.'

Powell and Donovan were on their feet.

'What?' cried Powell.

Donovan was considerably more colorful about it.

'It's so,' said Calvin. 'He took care of you, and kept you safe, but you couldn't handle any controls, because they weren't for you – just for the humorous Brain. We could reach you by radio, but you couldn't answer. You had plenty of food, but all of it beans and milk. Then you died, so to speak, and were reborn, but the period of your death was made . . . well . . . interesting. I wish I knew how he did it. It was The Brain's prize little joke, but he meant no harm.'

'No harm!' gasped Donovan. 'Oh, if that cute little tyke only had a neck.'

Lanning raised a quieting hand, 'All right, it's been a mess, but it's all over. What now?'

'Well,' said Bogert, quietly, 'obviously it's up to us to improve the space-warp engine. There must be some way of getting around that interval of jump. If there is, we're the only organization left with a grand-scale super-robot, so we're bound to find it if anyone. And then – US Robots has interstellar travel, and humanity has the opportunity for galactic empire.'

'What about Consolidated?' said Lanning.

'Hey,' interrupted Donovan suddenly, 'I want to make a suggestion there. They landed US robots into quite a mess. It wasn't as bad a mess as they expected and it turned out well, but their intentions weren't pious. And Greg and I bore the most of it.

'Well, they wanted an answer, and they've got one. Send them that ship, guaranteed, and US Robots can collect their two hundred thou plus construction costs. And if they test it – then suppose we let The Brain have just a little more fun before it's brought back to normal.'

Lanning said gravely, 'It sounds just and proper to me.'

To which Bogert added absently, 'Strictly according to contract, too.'

8
Evidence

'But that wasn't it, either,' said Dr Calvin thoughtfully. 'Oh, eventually, the ship and others like it became government property; the Jump through hyperspace was perfected, and now we actually have human colonies on the planets of some of the nearer stars, but that wasn't it.'

I had finished eating and watched her through the smoke of my cigarette.

'It's what has happened to the people here on Earth in the last fifty years that really counts. When I was born, young man, we had just gone through the last World War. It was a low point in history – but it was the end of nationalism. Earth was too small for nations and they began grouping themselves into Regions. It took quite a while. When I was born the United States of America was still a nation and not merely a part of the Northern Region. In fact, the name of the corporation is still "United States Robots—". And the change from nations to Regions, which has stabilized our economy and brought about what amounts to a Golden Age, when this century is compared with the last, was also brought about by our robots.'

'You mean the Machines,' I said. 'The Brain you talked about was the first of the Machines, wasn't it?'

'Yes, it was, but it's not the Machines I was thinking of. Rather of a man. He died last year.' Her voice was suddenly deeply sorrowful. 'Or at least he arranged to die, because he knew we needed him no longer. —Stephen Byerley.'

'Yes, I guessed that was who you meant.'

'He first entered public office in 2032. You were only a

191

boy then, so you wouldn't remember the strangeness of it. His campaign for the Mayoralty was certainly the queerest in history—'

Francis Quinn was a politician of the new school. That, of course, is a meaningless expression, as are all expressions of the sort. Most of the 'new schools' we have were duplicated in the social life of ancient Greece, and perhaps, if we knew more about it, in the social life of ancient Sumeria and in the lake dwellings of prehistoric Switzerland as well.

But, to get out from under what promises to be a dull and complicated beginning, it might be best to state hastily that Quinn neither ran for office nor canvassed for votes, made no speeches and stuffed no ballot boxes. Any more than Napoleon pulled a trigger at Austerlitz.

And since politics makes strange bedfellows, Alfred Lanning sat at the other side of the desk with his ferocious white eyebrows bent far forward over eyes in which chronic impatience had sharpened to acuity. He was not pleased.

The fact, if known to Quinn, would have annoyed him not the least. His voice was friendly, perhaps professionally so.

'I assume you know Stephen Byerley, Dr Lanning.'

'I have heard of him. So have many people.'

'Yes, so have I. Perhaps you intend voting for him at the next election.'

'I couldn't say.' There was an unmistakable trace of acidity here. 'I have not followed the political currents, so I'm not aware that he is running for office.'

'He may be our next mayor. Of course, he is only a lawyer now, but great oaks—'

'Yes,' interrupted Lanning, 'I have heard the phrase before. But I wonder if we can get to the business at hand.'

'We *are* at the business at hand, Dr Lanning.' Quinn's tone was very gentle. 'It is to my interest to keep Mr Byerley a district attorney at the very most, and it is to your interest to help me do so.'

'To *my* interest? Come!' Lanning's eyebrows hunched low.

'Well, say then to the interest of the US Robot & Mechanical Men Corporation. I come to you as Director-Emeritus of Research, because I know that your connection to them is that of, shall we say, "elder statesman". You are listened to with respect and yet your connection with them is no longer so tight but that you cannot possess considerable freedom of action; even if the action is somewhat unorthodox.'

Dr Lanning was silent a moment, chewing the cud of his thoughts. He said more softly, 'I don't follow you at all, Mr Quinn.'

'I am not surprised, Dr Lanning. But it's all rather simple. Do you mind?' Quinn lit a slender cigarette with a lighter of tasteful simplicity and his big-boned face settled into an expression of quiet amusement. 'We have spoken of Mr Byerley – a strange and colorful character. He was unknown three years ago. He is very well known now. He is a man of force and ability, and certainly the most capable and intelligent prosecutor I have ever known. Unfortunately he is not a friend of mine—'

'I understand,' said Lanning, mechanically. He stared at his fingernails.

'I have had occasion,' continued Quinn, evenly, 'in the past year to investigate Mr Byerley – quite exhaustively. It is always useful, you see, to subject the past life of reform politicians to rather inquisitive research. If you knew how often it helped—' He paused to smile humorlessly at the glowing tip of his cigarette. 'But Mr Byerley's past is unremarkable. A quiet life in a small town, a college education, a wife who died young, an auto accident with a slow recovery, law school, coming to the metropolis, an attorney.'

Francis Quinn shook his head slowly, then added, 'But his present life. Ah, that is remarkable. Our district attorney never eats!'

Lanning's head snapped up, old eyes surprisingly sharp, 'Pardon me?'

'Our district attorney never eats.' The repetition thumped by syllables. 'I'll modify that slightly. He has never been seen to eat or drink. Never! Do you understand the significance of the word? Not rarely, but never!'

'I find that quite incredible. Can you trust your investigators?'

'I can trust my investigators, and I don't find it incredible at all. Further, our district attorney has never been seen to drink – in the aqueous sense as well as the alcoholic - nor to sleep. There are other factors, but I should think I have made my point.'

Lanning leaned back in his seat, and there was the rapt silence of challenge and response between them, and then the old roboticist shook his head. 'No. There is only one thing you can be trying to imply, if I couple your statements with the fact that you present them to me, and that is impossible.'

'But the man is quite inhuman, Dr Lanning.'

'If you told me he were Satan in masquerade, there would be a faint chance that I might believe you.'

'I tell you he is a robot, Dr Lanning.'

'I tell you it is as impossible a conception as I have ever heard, Mr Quinn.'

Again the combative silence.

'Nevertheless,' and Quinn stubbed out his cigarette with elaborate care, 'you will have to investigate this impossibility with all the resources of the Corporation.'

'I'm sure that I could undertake no such thing, Mr Quinn. You don't seriously suggest that the Corporation take part in local politics.'

'You have no choice. Supposing I were to make my facts public without proof. The evidence is circumstantial enough.'

'Suit yourself in that respect.'

'But it would not suit me. Proof would be much preferable. And it would not suit *you*, for the publicity would be very damaging to your company. You are perfectly well acquainted, I suppose, with the strict rules against the use of robots on inhabited worlds.'

'Certainly!' —brusquely.

'You know that the US Robot Mechanical Men Corporation is the only manufacturer of positronic robots in the Solar System, and if Byerley is a robot, his is a *positronic* robot. You are also aware that all positronic robots are leased, and not sold; that the Corporation remains the owner and manager of each robot, and is therefore responsible for the actions of all.'

'It is an easy matter, Mr Quinn, to prove the Corporation has never manufactured a robot of a humanoid character.'

'It can be done? To discuss merely possibilities.'

'Yes. It can be done.'

'Secretly, I imagine, as well. Without entering it in your books.'

'Not the positronic brain, sir. Too many factors are involved in that, and there is the tightest possible government supervision.'

'Yes, but robots are worn out, break down, go out of order – and are dismantled.'

'And the positronic brains re-used or destroyed.'

'Really?' Francis Quinn allowed himself a trace of sarcasm. 'And if one were, accidentally, of course, not destroyed – and there happened to be a humanoid structure waiting for a brain.'

'Impossible!'

'You would have to prove that to the government and the public, so why not prove it to me now.'

'But what could our purpose be?' demanded Lanning in exasperation. 'Where is our motivation? Credit us with a minimum of sense.'

'My dear sir, please. The Corporation would be only too glad to have the various Regions permit the use of humanoid positronic robots on inhabited worlds. The profits would be enormous. But the prejudice of the public against such a practice is too great. Suppose you get them used to such robots first - see, we have a skillful lawyer, a good mayor – and he is a robot. Won't you buy our robot butlers?'

'Thoroughly fantastic. An almost humorous descent to the ridiculous.'

'I imagine so. Why not prove it? Or would you still rather try to prove it to the public?'

The light in the office was dimming, but it was not yet too dim to obscure the flush of frustration on Alfred Lanning's face. Slowly, the roboticist's finger touched a knob and the wall illuminators glowed to gentle life.

'Well, then,' he growled, 'let us see.'

The face of Stephen Byerley is not an easy one to describe. He was forty by birth certificate and forty by appearance – but it was a healthy, well-nourished good-natured appearance of forty; one that automatically drew the teeth of the bromide about 'looking one's age'.

This was particularly true when he laughed, and he was laughing now. It came loudly and continuously, died away for a bit, then began again—

And Alfred Lanning's face contracted into a rigidly bitter monument of disapproval. He made a half gesture to the woman who sat beside him, but her thin, bloodless lips merely pursed themselves a trifle.

Byerley gasped himself a state nearer normality.

'Really, Dr Lanning . . . really – I . . . *I* . . . a robot?'

Lanning bit his words off with a snap, 'It is no statement of mine, sir. I would be quite satisfied to have you a member of humanity. Since our corporation never manufactured you, I am quite certain that you are – in a legalistic sense, at any rate. But since the contention that you are a robot has been advanced to us seriously by a man of certain standing—'

'Don't mention his name, if it would knock a chip off your granite block of ethics, but let's pretend it was Frank Quinn, for the sake of argument, and continue.'

Lanning drew in a sharp, cutting snort at the interruption, and paused ferociously before continuing with added frigidity '—by a man of certain standing, with whose identity I am not interested in playing guessing games, I am bound to ask your co-operation in disproving it. The mere fact that such a contention could be advanced and publicized by the means at this man's disposal would be a bad blow to the company I represent - even if the charge were never proven. You understand me?'

'Oh, yes, your position is clear to me. The charge itself is ridiculous. The spot you find yourself in is not. I beg your pardon, if my laughter offended you. It was the first I laughed at, not the second. How can I help you?'

'It could be very simple. You have only to sit down to a meal at a restaurant in the presence of witnesses, have your picture taken, and eat.' Lanning sat back in his chair, the worst of the interview over. The woman beside him watched Byerley with an apparently absorbed expression but contributed nothing of her own.

Stephen Byerley met her eyes for an instant, was caught by them, then turned back to the roboticist. For a while his fingers were thoughtful over the bronze paper-weight that was the only ornament on his desk.

He said quietly, 'I don't think I can oblige you.'

He raised his hand, 'Now wait, Dr Lanning. I appreciate the fact that this whole matter is distasteful to you, that you have been forced into it against your will, that you feel you are playing an undignified and even ridiculous part. Still, the matter is even more intimately concerned with myself, so be tolerant.

'First, what makes you think that Quinn – this man of certain standing, you know – wasn't hoodwinking you, in order to get to do exactly what you are doing?'

'Why, it seems scarcely likely that a reputable person would endanger himself in so ridiculous a fashion, if he weren't convinced he were on safe ground.'

There was little humour in Byerley's eyes. 'You don't know Quinn. He could manage to make safe ground out of a ledge a mountain sheep could not handle. I suppose he showed the particulars of the investigation he claims to have made of me?'

'Enough to convince me that it would be too troublesome to have our corporation attempt to disprove them when you could do so more easily.'

'Then you believe him when he says I never eat. You are a scientist, Dr Lanning. Think of the logic required. I have not been observed to eat, therefore, I never eat, QED. After all!'

'You are using prosecution tactics to confuse what is really a very simple situation.'

'On the contrary, I am trying to clarify what you and Quinn between you are making a very complicated one. You see, I don't sleep much, that's true, and I certainly don't sleep in public. I have never cared to eat with others – an idiosyncrasy which is unusual and probably neurotic in character, but which harms no one. Look, Dr Lanning, let me present you with a supposititious case. Supposing we had a politician who was interested in defeating a reform candidate at any cost and while investigating his private life came across oddities such as I have just mentioned.

'Suppose further that in order to smear the candidate effectively, he comes to your company as the ideal agent. Do you expect him to say to you, "So-and-so is a robot because he hardly ever eats with people, and I have never seen him fall asleep in the middle of a case; and once when I peeped into his window in the middle of the night, there he was, sitting up with a book; and I looked in his frigidaire and there was no food in it"?

'If he told you that, you would send for a straitjacket. But if he tells you, "He *never* sleeps; he *never* eats," then the shock of the statement blinds you to the fact that such statements are impossible to prove. You play into his hands by contributing to the to-do.'

'Regardless, sir,' began Lanning, with a threatening obstinacy, 'of whether you consider this matter serious or not, it will require only the meal I mentioned to end it.'

Again Byerley turned to the woman, who still regarded him expressionlessly. 'Pardon me. I've caught your name correctly, haven't I? Dr Susan Calvin?'

'Yes, Mr Byerley.'

'You're US Robots' psychologist, aren't you?'

'*Robo*psychologist, please.'

'Oh, are robots so different from men, mentally?'

'Worlds different.'She allowed herself a frosty smile, 'Robots are essentially decent.'

Humor tugged at the corners of the lawyer's mouth, 'Well, that's a hard blow. But what I wanted to say was this. Since you're a psycho – a robopsychologist, *and* a woman, I'll bet you've done something that Dr Lanning hasn't thought of.'

'And what is that?'

'You've got something to eat in your purse.'

Something caught in the schooled indifference of Susan Calvin's eyes. She said, 'You surprise me, Mr Byerley.'

And opening her purse, she produced an apple. Quietly, she handed it to him. Dr Lanning, after an initial start, followed the slow movement from one hand to the other with sharply alert eyes.

Calmly, Stephen Byerley bit into it, and calmly he swallowed it.

'You see, Dr Lanning?'

Dr Lanning smiled in a relief tangible enough to make even his eyebrows appear benevolent. A relief that survived for one fragile second.

Susan Calvin said, 'I was curious to see if you would eat it, but, of course, in the present case, it proves nothing.'

Byerley grinned. 'It doesn't?

'Of course not. It is obvious, Dr Lanning, that if this man were a humanoid robot, he would be a perfect imitation. He is almost too human to be credible. After all, we have been seeing and observing human beings all our lives; it would be impossible to palm something merely nearly right off on us. It would have to be *all* right. Observe the texture of the skin, the quality of the irises, the bone formation of the hand. If he's a robot, I wish US Robots *had* made him, because he's a good job. Do you suppose then, that anyone capable of paying attention to such niceties would neglect a few gadgets to take care of such things as eating, sleeping, elimination? For emergency use only, perhaps; as, for instance, to prevent such situations as are arising here. So a meal won't prove anything.'

'Now wait,' snarled Lanning, 'I am not quite the fool both of you make me out to be. I am not interested in the problem of Mr Byerley's humanity or nonhumanity. I am interested in getting the corporation out of a hole. A public meal will end the matter and keep it ended no matter what Quinn does. We can leave the finer details to lawyers and robopsychologists.'

'But, Dr Lanning,' said Byerley, 'you forget the politics of the situation. I am as anxious to be elected, as Quinn is to stop me. By the way, did you notice that you used his name. It's a cheap shyster trick of mine; I knew you would, before you were through.'

Lanning flushed. 'What has the election to do with it?'

'Publicity works both ways, sir. If Quinn wants to call me a robot, and has the nerve to do so, I have the nerve to play the game his way.'

'You mean you—' Lanning was quite frankly appalled.

'Exactly. I mean that I'm going to let him go ahead, choose his rope, test its strength, cut off the right length, tie the noose, insert his head and grin. I can do what little else is required.'

'You are mighty confident.'

Susan Calvin rose to her feet, 'Come, Alfred, we won't change his mind for him.'

'You see.' Byerley smiled gently. 'You're a human psychologist, too.'

But perhaps not all the confidence that Dr Lanning had remarked upon was present that evening when Byerley's car parked on the automatic treads leading to the sunken garage, and Byerley himself crossed the path to the front door of his house.

The figure in the wheel chair looked up as he entered and smiled. Byerley's face lit with affection. He crossed over to it.

The cripple's voice was a hoarse, grating whisper that came out of a mouth forever twisted to one side, leering out of a face that was half scar tissue. 'You're late, Steve.'

'I know, John, I know. But I've been up against a peculiar and interesting trouble today.'

'So?' Neither the torn face nor the destroyed voice could carry expression but there was anxiety in the clear eyes. 'Nothing you can't handle?'

'I'm not exactly certain. I may need your help. *You're* the brilliant one in the family. Do you want me to take you out into the garden? It's a beautiful evening.'

Two strong arms lifted John from the wheel chair. Gently, almost caressingly, Byerley's arms went around the shoulders and under the swathed legs of the cripple. Carefully, and slowly, he walked through the rooms, down the gentle ramp that had been built with a wheel chair in mind, and out the back door into the walled and wired garden behind the house.

'Why don't you let me use the wheel chair, Steve? This is silly.'

'Because I'd rather carry you. Do you object? You know that you're as glad to get out of that motorized buggy for a while as I am to see you out. How do you feel today?' He deposited John with infinite care upon the cool grass.

'How should I feel? But tell me about your trouble.'

'Quinn's campaign will be based on the fact that he claims I'm a robot.'

John's eyes opened wide. 'How do you know? It's impossible. I won't believe it.'

'Oh, come, I tell you it's so. He had one of the big-shot scientists of US Robot & Mechanical Men Corporation over at the office to argue with me.'

Slowly John's hands tore at the grass. 'I see. I see.'

Byerley said, 'But we can let him choose his ground. I have an idea. Listen to me and tell me if we can do it—'

The scene as it appeared in Alfred Lanning's office that night was a tableau of stares. Francis Quinn stared meditatively at Alfred Lanning. Lanning's stare was savagely set upon Susan Calvin, who stared impassively in her turn at Quinn.

Francis Quinn broke it with a heavy attempt at lightness, 'Bluff. He's making it up as he goes along.'

'Are you going to gamble on that, Mr Quinn?' asked Dr Calvin, indifferently.

'Well, it's your gamble, really.'

'Look here,' Lanning covered definite pessimism with bluster, 'we've done what you asked. We witnessed the man eat. It's ridiculous to presume him a robot.'

'Do *you* think so?' Quinn shot toward Calvin. 'Lanning said you were the expert.'

Lanning was almost threatening, 'Now, Susan—'

Quinn interrupted smoothly, 'Why not let her talk, man? She's been sitting there imitating a gatepost for half an hour.'

Lanning felt definitely harassed. From what he experienced then to incipient paranoia was but a step. He said, 'Very well. Have your say, Susan. We won't interrupt you.'

Susan Calvin glanced at him humorlessly, then fixed cold eyes on Mr Quinn. 'There are only two ways of definitely proving Byerley to be a robot, sir. So far you are presenting circumstantial evidence, with which you can accuse, but not prove – and I think Mr Byerley is sufficiently clever to counter that sort of material. You probably think so yourself, or you wouldn't have come here.

'The two methods of *proof* are the physical and the psychological. Physically, you can dissect him or use an X-ray. How to do that would be *your* problem. Psychologically, his behaviour can be studied, for if he *is* a positronic robot, he must conform to the three Rules of Robotics. A positronic brain cannot be constructed without them. You know the Rules, Mr Quinn?'

She spoke them carefully, clearly, quoting word for word the famous bold print on page one of the 'Handbook of Robotics'.

'I've heard of them,' said Quinn, carelessly.

'Then the matter is easy to follow,' responded the psychologist, dryly. 'If Mr Byerley breaks any of those three rules, he is not a robot. Unfortunately, this procedure works in only one direction. If he lives up to the rules, it proves nothing one way or the other.'

Quinn raised polite eyebrows, 'Why not, doctor?'

'Because, if you stop to think of it, the three Rules of Robotics are the essential guiding principles of a good many of the world's ethical systems. Of course, every human being is supposed to have the instinct of self-preservation. That's Rule Three to a robot. Also every "good" human being, with a social conscience and a sense of responsibility, is supposed to defer to proper authority; to listen to his doctor, his boss, his government, his psychiatrist, his fellow man; to obey laws, to follow rules, to conform to custom – even when they interfere with his comfort or his safety. That's Rule Two to a robot. Also, every "good" human being is supposed to love others as himself, protect his fellow man, risk his life to save another. That's Rule One to a robot. To put it simply – if Byerley follows all the Rules of Robotics, he may be a robot, and may simply be a very good man.'

'But,' said Quinn, 'you're telling me that you can never prove him a robot.'

'I may be able to prove him *not* a robot.'

'That's not the proof I want.'

'You'll have such proof as exists. You are the only one responsible for your own wants.'

Here Lanning's mind leaped suddenly to the sting of an idea. 'Has it occurred to anyone,' he ground out, 'that district attorney is a rather strange occupation for a robot?

The prosecution of human beings – sentencing them to death – bringing about their infinite harm—'

Quinn grew suddenly keen, 'No, you can't get out of it that way. Being district attorney doesn't make him human. Don't you know his record? Don't you know that he boasts that he has never prosecuted an innocent man; that there are scores of people left untried because the evidence against them didn't satisfy him, even though he could probably have argued a jury into atomizing them? That happens to be so.'

Lanning's thin cheeks quivered, 'No, Quinn, no. There is nothing in the Rules of Robotics that makes any allowance for human guilt. A robot may not judge whether a human being deserves death. It is not for him to decide. *He may not harm a human* – variety skunk, or variety angel.'

Susan Calvin sounded tired. 'Alfred,' she said, 'don't talk foolishly. What if a robot came upon a madman about to set fire to a house with people in it. He would stop the madman, wouldn't he?'

'Of course.'

'And if the only way he could stop him was to kill him—'

There was a faint sound in Lanning's throat. Nothing more.

'The answer to that, Alfred, is that he would require psychotherapy because he might easily go mad at the conflict presented him – of having broken Rule One to adhere to Rule One in a higher sense. But a man would be dead and a robot would have killed him.'

'Well, *is* Byerley mad?' demanded Lanning, with all the sarcasm he could muster.

'No, but he has killed no man himself. He has exposed facts which might represent a particular human being to be dangerous to the large mass of other human beings we call society. He protects the greater number and thus adheres to Rule One at maximum potential. That is as far as he goes. It is the judge who then condemns the criminal to death or imprisonment, after the jury decides on his guilt or innocence. It is the jailer who imprisons him, the executioner who kills him. And Mr Byerley has done nothing but determine truth and aid society.

'As a matter of fact, Mr Quinn, I have looked into Mr Byerley's career since you first brought this matter to our attention. I find that he has never demanded the death sentence in his closing speeches to the jury. I also find that he has spoken on behalf of the abolition of capital punishment and contributed generously to research institutions engaged in criminal neurophysiology. He apparently believes in the cure, rather than the punishment of crime. I find that significant.'

'You do? Quinn smiled. 'Significant of a certain odor of roboticity, perhaps?'

'Perhaps. Why deny it? Actions such as his could come only from a robot, or from a very honorable and decent human being. But you see, you just can't differentiate between a robot and the very best of humans.'

Quinn sat back in his chair. His voice quivered with impatience. 'Dr Lanning, it's perfectly possible to create a humanoid robot that would perfectly duplicate a human in appearance, isn't it?'

Lanning harrumphed and considered, 'It's been done experimentally by US Robots,' he said reluctantly, 'without the addition of a positronic brain, of course. By using human ova and hormone control, one can grow human flesh and skin over a skeleton of porous silicone plastics that would defy external examination. The eyes, the hair, the skin would be really human, not humanoid. And if you put a positronic brain and such other gadgets as you might desire inside, you have a humanoid robot.'

Quinn said shortly, 'How long would it take to make one?'

Lanning considered, 'If you had all your equipment – the brain, the skeleton, the ovum, the proper hormones and radiations – say, two months.'

The politician straightened out of his chair. 'Then we shall see what the insides of Mr Byerley look like. It will mean publicity for US Robots – but I gave you your chance.'

Lanning turned impatiently to Susan Calvin, when they were alone. 'Why do you insist—'

And with real feeling, she responded sharply and instantly, 'Which do you want – the truth or my resignation? I won't lie for you. US Robots can take care of itself. Don't turn coward.'

'What,' said Lanning, 'if he opens up Byerley, and wheels and gears fall out. What then?'

'He won't open Byerley,' said Calvin, disdainfully. 'Byerley is as clever as Quinn, at the very least.'

The news broke upon the city a week before Byerley was to have been nominated. But 'broke' is the wrong word. It staggered upon the city, shambled, crawled. Laughter began, and wit was free. And as the far-off hand of Quinn tightened its pressure in easy stages, the laughter grew forced, an element of hollow uncertainty entered, and people broke off to wonder.

The convention itself had the air of a restive stallion. There had been no contest planned. Only Byerley could possibly have been nominated a week earlier. There was no substitute even now. They had to nominate him, but there was complete confusion about it.

It would not have been so bad if the average individual were not torn between the enormity of the charge, if true, and its sensational folly, if false.

The day after Byerley was nominated perfunctorily, hollowly – a newspaper finally published the gist of a long interview with Dr Susan Calvin, 'word famous expert on robopsychology and positronics'.

What broke loose is popularly and succinctly described as hell.

It was what the Fundamentalists were waiting for. They were not a political party; they made pretense to no formal religion. Essentially they were those who had not adapted themselves to what had once been called the Atomic Age, in the days when atoms were a novelty. Actually, they were the Simple-Lifers, hungering after a life, which to those who live it had probably appeared not so Simple, and who had been, therefore, Simple-Lifers themselves.

The Fundamentalists required no new reason to detest robots and robot manufacturers; but a new reason such as the Quinn accusation and the Calvin analysis was sufficient to make such detestation audible.

The huge plants of the US Robot & Mechanical Men Corporation was a hive that spawned armed guards. It prepared for war.

Within the city the house of Stephen Byerley bristled with police.

The political campaign, of course, lost all other issues, and resembled a campaign only in that it was something filling the hiatus between nomination and election.

Stephen Byerley did not allow the fussy little man to distract him. He remained comfortably unperturbed by the uniforms in the background. Outside the house, past the line of grim guards, reporters and photographers waited according to the tradition of the caste. One enterprising 'visor station even had a scanner focused on the blank entrance to the prosecutor's unpretentious home, while a synthetically excited announcer filled in with inflated commentary.

The fussy little man advanced. He held forward a rich, complicated sheet. 'This, Mr Byerley, is a court order authorizing me to search these premises for the presence of illegal . . . uh . . . mechanical men or robots of any description.'

Byerley half rose, and took the paper. He glanced at it indifferently, and smiled as he handed it back. 'All in order. Go ahead. Do your job. Mrs Hoppen' – to his housekeeper, who appeared reluctantly from the next room – 'please go with them, and help out if you can.'

The little man, whose name was Harroway, hesitated, produced an unmistakable blush, failed completely to catch Byerley's eyes, and muttered, 'Come on,' to the two policemen.

He was back in ten minutes.

'Through?' questioned Byerley, in just the tone of a person who is not particularly interested in the question, or its answer.

Harroway cleared his throat, made a bad start in falsetto, and began again, angrily, 'Look here, Mr Byerley, our special instructions were to search the house very thoroughly.'

'And haven't you?'

'We were told exactly what to look for.'

'Yes?'

'In short, Mr Byerley, and not to put too fine a point on it, we were told to search you.'

'Me?' said the prosecutor with a broadening smile. 'And how do you intend to do that?'

'We have a Penet-radiation unit—'

'Then I'm to have my X-ray photograph taken, hey? You have the authority?'

'You saw my warrant.'

'May I see it again?'

Harroway, his forehead shining with considerably more than mere enthusiasm, passed it over a second time.

Byerley said evenly, 'I read here as the description of what you are to search; I quote: "the dwelling place belonging to Stephen Allen Byerley, located at 355 Willow Grove, Evanstron, together with any garage, storehouse or other structures or buildings thereto appertaining, together with all grounds thereto appertaining" . . . um . . . and so on. Quite in order. But, my good man, it doesn't say anything about searching my interior. I am not part of the premises. You may search my clothes if you think I've got a robot hidden in my pocket.'

Harroway had no doubt on the point of to whom he owed his job. He did not propose to be backward, given a chance to earn a much better – i.e., more highly paid – job.

He said, in a faint echo of bluster, 'Look here. I'm allowed to search the furniture in your house, and anything else I find in it. You are in it, aren't you?'

'A remarkable observation. I *am* in it. But I'm not a piece of furniture. As a citizen of adult responsibility – I have the psychiatric certificate proving that – I have certain rights under the Regional Articles. Searching me would come under the heading of violating my Right of Privacy. That paper isn't sufficient.'

'Sure, but if you're a robot, you don't have Right of Privacy.'

'True enough – but that paper still isn't sufficient. It recognizes me implicitly as a human being.'

'Where?' Harroway snatched at it.'

'Where it says "dwelling place belonging to" and so on. A robot cannot own property. And you may tell your employer, Mr Harroway, that if he tries to issue a similar paper which does *not* implicitly recognize me as a human being, he will be immediately faced with a restraining injunction and a civil suit which will make it necessary for him to *prove* me a robot by means of information *now* in his possession, or else to pay a whopping penalty for an attempt to deprive me unduly of my Rights under the Regional Articles. You'll tell him that, won't you?'

Harroway marched to the door. He turned. 'You're a slick lawyer—' His hand was in his pocket. For a short moment, he stood there. Then he left, smiled in the direction of the 'visor scanner, still playing away – waved to the reporters, and shouted, 'We'll have something for you tomorrow, boys. No kidding.'

In his ground car, he settled back, removed the tiny mechanism from his pocket and carefully inspected it. It was the first time he had ever taken a photograph by X-ray reflection. He hoped he had done it correctly.

Quinn and Byerley had never met face-to-face alone. But visorphone was pretty close to it. In fact, accepted litterally, perhaps the phrase was accurate, even if to each, the other were merely the light and dark pattern of a bank of photocells.

It was Quinn who had initiated the call. It was Quinn who spoke first, and without particular ceremony. 'Thought you would like to know, Byerley, that I intend to make public the fact that you're wearing a protective shield against Penet-radiation.'

'That so? In that case, you've probably already made it public. I have a notion our enterprising press representatives have been tapping my various communication lines for quite a while. I know they have my office lines full of holes; which is why I've dug in at my home these last weeks.' Byerley was friendly, almost chatty.

Quinn's lips tightened slightly, 'This call is shielded – thoroughly. I'm making it at a certain personal risk.'

'So I should imagine. Nobody knows you're behind this campaign. At least, nobody knows it officially. Nobody doesn't know it unofficially. I wouldn't worry. So I wear a protective shield? I suppose you found that out when your puppy dog's Penet-radiation photograph, the other day, turned out to be overexposed.'

'You realize, Beverley, that it would be pretty obvious to everyone that you don't dare face X-ray analysis.'

'Also that you, or your men, attempted illegal invasion of my Right of Privacy.'

'The devil they'll care for that.'

'They might. It's rather symbolic of our two campaigns, isn't it? You have little concern with the rights of the individual citizen. I have great concern. I will not submit to X-ray analysis, because I wish to maintain my rights on principle. Just as I'll maintain the rights of others when elected.'

'That will no doubt make a very interesting speech, but no one will believe you. A little too high-sounding to be true. Another thing,' a sudden, crisp change, 'the personnel in your home was not complete the other night.'

'In what way?'

'According to the report,' he shuffled papers before him that were just within the range of vision of the visiplate, 'there was one person missing – a cripple.'

'As you say,' said Byerley, tonelessly, 'a cripple. My old teacher, who lives with me and who is now in the country – and has been for two months. A "much-needed rest" is the usual expression applied in the case. He has your permission?'

'Your teacher? A scientist of sorts?'

'A lawyer once – before he was a cripple. He has a government license as a research biophysicist, with a laboratory of his own, and a complete description of the work he's doing filed with the proper authorities, to whom I can refer you. The work is minor, but is a harmless and engaging hobby for a – poor cripple. I am being as helpful as I can, you see.'

'I see. And what does this . . . teacher . . . know about robot manufacture?'

'I couldn't judge the extent of his knowledge in a field with which I am unacquainted.'

'He wouldn't have access to positronic brains?'

'Ask your friends at US Robots. They'd be the ones to know.'

'I'll put it shortly, Byerley. Your crippled teacher is the real Stephen Byerley. You are his robot creation. We can prove it. It was he who was in the automobile accident, not you. There will be ways of checking the records.'

'Really? Do so, then. My best wishes.'

'And we can search your so-called teacher's "country place", and see what we can find there.'

'Well, not quite, Quinn.' Byerley smiled broadly. 'Unfortunately for you, my so-called teacher is a sick man. His country place is his place of rest. His Rights of Privacy as a citizen of adult responsibility are naturally even stronger, under the circumstances. You won't be able to obtain a warrant to enter his grounds without showing just cause. However, I'd be the last to prevent you from trying.'

There was a pause of moderate length, and then Quinn leaned forward, so that his imaged-face expanded and the fine lines on his forehead were visible, 'Byerley, why do you carry on? You can't be elected.'

'Can't I?'

'Do you think you can? Do you suppose that your failure to make any attempt to disprove the robot charge – when you could easily, by breaking one of the Three Laws – does anything but convince the people that you *are* a robot?'

'All I see so far is that from being a rather vaguely known, but still largely obscure metropolitan lawyer, I have now become a world figure. You're a good publicist.'

'But you *are* a robot.'

'So it's been said, but not proven.'

'It's been proven sufficiently for the electorate.'

'Then relax – you've won.'

'Good-bye,' said Quinn, with his first touch of viciousness, and the visorphone slammed off.

'Good-bye,' said Byerley imperturbably, to the blank plate.

Byerley brought his 'teacher' back the week before election. The air car dropped quickly in an obscure part of the city.

'You'll stay here till after election,' Byerley told him. 'It would be better to have you out of the way if things take a bad turn.'

The hoarse voice that twisted painfully out of John's crooked mouth might have had accents of concern in it. 'There's danger of violence?'

'The Fundamentalists threaten it, so I suppose there is in a theoretical sense. But I really don't expect it. The Fundies have no real power. They're just the continuous irritant factor that might stir up a riot after a while. You don't mind staying here? Please. I won't be myself if I have to worry about you.'

'Oh, I'll stay. You still think it will go well?'

'I'm sure of it. No one bothered you at the place?'

'No one. I'm certain.'

'And your part went well?'

'Well enough. There'll be no trouble there.'

'Then take care of yourself, and watch the televisor to-morrow, John.' Byerley pressed the gnarled hand that rested on his.

Lenton's forehead was a furrowed study in suspense. He had the completely unenviable job of being Byerley's campaign manager in a campaign that wasn't a campaign, for a person that refused to reveal his strategy, and refused to accept his manager's.

'You can't!' It was his favorite phrase. It had become his only phrase. 'I tell you, Steve, you can't!'

He threw himself in front of the prosecutor, who was spending his time leafing through the typed pages of his speech.

'Put that down, Steve. Look, that mob has been organized by the Fundies. You won't get a hearing. You'll be stoned more likely. Why do you have to make a speech before an audience? What's wrong with a recording, a visual recording?'

'You want me to win the election, don't you?' asked Byerley, mildly.

'Win the election! You're not going to win, Steve. I'm trying to save your life.'

'Oh, I'm not in danger.'

'He's not in danger. He is not in danger.' Lenton made a queer, rasping sound in his throat. 'You mean you're getting out on that balcony in front of fifty thousand crazy crack-pots and try to talk sense to them – on a balcony like a medieval dictator?'

Byerley consulted his watch. 'In about five minutes – as soon as the television lines are free.'

Lenton's answering remark was not quite transliterable.

The crowd filled a roped-off area of the city. Trees and houses seemed to grow out of a mass-human foundation. And by ultrawave, the rest of the world watched. It was a purely local election, but it had a world audience just the same. Byerley thought of that and smiled.

But there was nothing to smile at in the crowd itself. There were banners and streamers, ringing every possible change on his supposed robotcy. The hostile attitude rose thickly and tangibly into the atmosphere.

From the start the speech was not successful. It competed against the inchoate mob howl and the rhythmic cries of the Fundie claques that formed mob-islands within the mob. Byerley spoke on, slowly, unemotionally—

Inside, Lenton clutched his hair and groaned – and waited for the blood.

There was a writhing in the front ranks. An angular citizen with popping eyes, and clothes too short for the lank length of his limbs, was pulling to the fore. A policeman dived after him, making slow, struggling passage. Byerley waved the latter off, angrily.

The thin man was directly under the balcony. His words tore unheard against the roar.

Byerley leaned forward. 'What do you say? If you have a legitimate question, I'll answer it.' He turned to a flanking guard. 'Bring that man up here.'

There was a tensing in the crowd. Cries of 'Quiet' started in various parts of the mob, and rose to a bedlam, then toned down raggedly. The thin man, red-faced and panting, faced Byerley.

Byerley said, 'Have you a question?'

The thin man stared, and said in a cracked voice, 'Hit me!'

With sudden energy, he thrust out his chin at an angle. 'Hit me! You say you're not a robot. Prove it. You can't hit a human, you monster.'

There was a queer, flat, dead silence. Byerley's voice punctured it. 'I have no reason to hit you.'

The thin man was laughing wildly. 'You *can't* hit me. You *won't* hit me. You're not a human. You're a monster, a make-believe man.'

And Stephen Byerley, tight-lipped, in the face of thousands, who watched in person and the millions who watched by screen, drew back his fist and caught the man crackingly upon the chin. The challenger went over backwards in sudden collapse, with nothing on his face, but blank, blank surprise.

Byerley said, 'I'm sorry. Take him in and see that he's comfortable. I want to speak to him when I'm through.'

And when Dr Calvin, from her reserved space, turned her automobile and drove off, only one reporter recovered sufficiently from the shock to race after her, and shout an unheard question.

Susan Calvin called over her shoulder, 'He's human.'

That was enough. The reporter raced away in his own direction.

The rest of the speech might be described as 'Spoken but not heard'.

Dr Calvin and Stephen Byerley met once again – a week before he took the oath of office as mayor. It was late – past midnight.

Dr Calvin said, 'You don't look tired.'

The mayor-elect smiled. 'I may stay up for a while. Don't tell Quinn.'

'I shan't. But that was an interesting story of Quinn's, since you mention him. It's a shame to have spoiled it. I suppose you knew his theory?'

'Parts of it.'

'It was highly dramatic. Stephen Byerley was a young lawyer, a powerful speaker, a great idealist – and with a certain flair for biophysics. Are you interested in robotics, Mr Byerley?

'Only in the legal aspects.'

'*This* Stephen Byerley was. But there was an accident. Byerley's wife died; he himself, worse. His legs were gone; his face was gone; his voice was gone. Part of his mind was – bent. He would not submit to plastic surgery. He retired from the world, legal career gone – only his intelligence, and his hands left. Somehow he could obtain positronic brains, even a complex one, one which had the greatest capacity for forming judgements in ethical problems – which is the highest robotic function so far developed.

'He grew a body about it. Trained it to be everything he would have been and was no longer. He sent it out into the world as Stephen Byerley, remaining behind himself as the old, crippled teacher that no one ever saw—'

'Unfortunately,' said the mayor-elect, 'I ruined all that by hitting a man. The papers say it was your official verdict on the occasion that I was human.'

'How did that happen? Do you mind telling me? It couldn't have been accidental.'

'It wasn't entirely. Quinn did most of the work. My men started quietly spreading the fact that I had never hit a man; that I was unable to hit a man; that to fail to do so under provocation would be sure proof that I was a robot. So I arranged for a silly speech in public, with all sorts of publicity overtones, and almost inevitably, some fool fell for it. In its essence, it was what I call a shyster trick. One in which the artificial atmosphere which has been created does all the work. Of course, the emotional effects made my election certain, as intended.'

The robopsychologist nodded. 'I see you intrude on my field – as every politician must, I suppose. But I'm very sorry it turned out this way. I like robots. I like them considerably better than I do human beings. If a robot can be created capable of being a civil executive, I think he'd make the best one possible. By the laws of Robotics, he'd be incapable of harming humans, incapable of tyranny, of corruption, of stupidity, of prejudice. And after he had served a decent term, he would leave, even though he were immortal, because it would be impossible for him to hurt humans by letting them know that a robot had ruled them. It would be most ideal.'

'Except that a robot might fail due to the inherent inadequacies of his brain. The positronic brain has never equalled the complexities of the human brain.'

'He would have advisers. Not even a human brain is capable of governing without assistance.'

Byerley considered Susan Calvin with grave interest. 'Why do you smile, Dr Calvin?'

'I smiled because Mr Quinn didn't think of everything.'

'You mean there could be more to that story of his.'

'Only a little. For the three months before election, this Stephen Byerley that Mr Quinn spoke about, this broken man, was in the country for some mysterious reason. He returned in time for that famous speech of yours. And after all, what the old cripple did once, he could do a second time, particularly where the second job is very simple in comparison to the first.'

'I don't quite understand.'

Dr Calvin rose and smoothed her dress. She was obviously ready to leave. 'I mean there is one time when a robot may strike a human being without breaking the First Law. Just one time.'

'And when is that?'

Dr Calvin was at the door. She said quietly, 'When the human to be struck is merely another robot.'

She smiled broadly, her thin face glowing. 'Good-bye, Mr Byerley. I hope to vote for you five years from now – for coordinator.'

Stephen Byerley chuckled. 'I must reply that that is a somewhat farfetched idea.'

The door closed behind her.

I stared at her with a sort of horror, 'Is that true?'

'All of it,' she said.

'And the great Byerley was simply a robot.'

'Oh, there's no way of ever finding out. I think he was. But

*when he decided to die, he had himself atomized, so that there
will never be any legal proof. —Besides, what difference would
it make?'*

'Well—'

'You share a prejudice against robots which is quite unreasoning. He was a very good Mayor; five years later he did
become Regional Co-ordinator. And when the Regions of Earth
formed their Federation in 2044, he became the first World
Co-ordinator. By that time it was the Machines that were
running the world anyway.'

'Yes, but—'

'No buts! The Machines are robots, and they are running
the world. It was five years ago that I found out all the truth.
It was 2052; Byerley was completing his second term as World
Co-ordinator—'

9
The Evitable Conflict

The Co-ordinator, in his private study, had that medieval curiosity, a fireplace. To be sure, the medieval man might not have recognized it as such, since it had no functional significance. The quiet, licking flame lay in an insulated recess behind clear quartz.

The logs were ignited at long distance through a trifling diversion of the energy beam that fed the public buildings of the city. The same button that controlled the ignition first dumped the ashes of the previous fire, and allowed for the entrance of fresh wood. —It was a thoroughly domesticated fireplace, you see.

But the fire itself was real. It was wired for sound, so that you could hear the crackle and, of course, you could watch it leap in the air stream that fed it.

The Co-ordinator's ruddy glass reflected, in miniature, the discreet gamboling of the flame, and, in even further miniature, it was reflected in each of his brooding pupils.

And in the frosty pupils of his guest, Dr Susan Calvin of US Robots & Mechanical Men Corporation.

The Co-ordinator said, 'I did not ask you here entirely for social purposes, Susan.'

'I did not think you did, Stephen,' she replied.

'—And yet I don't quite know how to phrase my problem. On the one hand, it can be nothing at all. On the other, it can mean the end of humanity.'

'I have come across so many problems, Stephen, that presented the same alternative. I think all problems do.'

'Really? Then judge this— World Steel reports an overproduction of twenty thousand long tons. The Mexican

221

Canal is two months behind schedule. The mercury mines at Almaden have experienced a production deficiency since last spring, while the Hydroponics plant at Tientsin has been laying men off. These items happen to come to mind at the moment. There is more of the same sort.'

'Are these things serious? I'm not economist enough to trace the fearful consequences of such things.'

'In themselves, they are not serious. Mining experts can be sent to Almaden, if the situation were to get worse. Hydroponics engineers can be used in Java or in Ceylon, if there are too many at Tientsin. Twenty thousand long tons of steel won't fill more than a few days of world demand, and the opening of the Mexican Canal two months later than the planned date is of little moment. It's the Machines that worry me; – I've spoken to your Director of Research about them already.'

'To Vincent Silver? —He hasn't mentioned anything about it to me.'

'I asked him to speak to no one. Apparently, he hasn't.'

'And what did he tell you?'

'Let me put that item in its proper place. I want to talk about the Machines first. And I want to talk about them to you, because you're the only one in the world who understands robots well enough to help me now. —May I grow philosophical?'

'For this evening, Stephen, you may talk how you please and of what you please, provided you tell me first what you intend to prove.'

'That such small unbalances in the perfection of our system of supply and demand, as I have mentioned, may be the first step towards the final war.'

'Hmp. Proceed.'

Susan Calvin did not allow herself to relax, despite the designed comfort of the chair she sat in. Her cold, thin-lipped face and her flat, even voice were becoming accentuated with the years. And although Stephen Byerley was one man she could like and trust, she was almost seventy and the cultivated habits of a lifetime are not easily broken.

'Every period of human development, Susan,' said the Co-ordinator, 'has had its own particular type of human conflict – its own variety of problem that, apparently, could be settled only by force. And each time, frustratingly enough, force never really settled the problem. Instead, it persisted through a series of conflicts, then vanished to itself – what's the expression, – ah, yes "not with a bang, but a whimper", as the economic and social environment changed. And then, new problems, and a new series of wars. —Apparently endlessly cyclic.

'Consider relatively modern times. There were the series of dynastic wars in the sixteenth to eighteenth centuries, when the most important question in Europe was whether the houses of Hapsburg or Valois-Bourbon were to rule the continent. It was one of those "inevitable conflicts", since Europe could obviously not exist half one and half the other.

'Except that it did, and no war ever wiped out the one and established the other, until the rise of a new social atmosphere in France in 1789 crumbled first the Bourbons and, eventually, the Hapsburgs down the dusty chute to history's incinerator.

'And in those same centuries there were the more barbarous religious wars, which revolved about the important question of whether Europe was to be Catholic or Protestant. Half and half she could not be. It was "inevitable" that the sword decide. —Except that it didn't. In England, a new industrialism was growing, and on the continent, a new nationalism. Half and half Europe remains to this day and no one cares much.

'In the nineteenth and twentieth centuries, there was a cycle of nationalist-imperialist wars, when the most important question in the World was which portions of Europe would control the economic resources and consuming capacity of which portions of non-Europe. All non-Europe obviously could not exist part English and part French and part German and so on. —Until the forces of nationalism spread sufficiently, so that non-Europe ended what all the wars could not, and decided it could exist quite comfortably *all* non-European.

'And so we have a pattern—'

'Yes, Stephen, you make it plain,' said Susan Calvin. 'These are not very profound observations.'

'No. —But then, it is the obvious which is so difficult to see most of the time. People say "It's as plain as the nose on your face." But how much of the nose on your face can you see, unless someone holds a mirror up to you? In the twentieth century, Susan, we started a new cycle of wars – what shall I call them? Ideological wars? The emotions of religion applied to economic systems, rather than to extra-natural ones? Again the wars were "inevitable" and this time there were atomic weapons, so that mankind could no longer live through its torment to the inevitable wasting away of inevitability. —And positronic robots came.

'They came in time, and, with it and alongside it, interplanetary travel. —So that it no longer seemed so important whether the world was Adam Smith or Karl Marx. Neither made very much sense under the new circumstances. Both had to adapt and they ended in almost the same place.'

'A deus ex machina, then, in a double sense,' said Dr Calvin, dryly.

The Co-ordinator smiled gently. 'I have never heard you pun before, Susan, but you are correct. And yet there was another danger. The ending of every other problem had merely given birth to another. Our new world-wide robot economy may develop its own problems, and for that reason we have the Machines. The Earth's economy is stable, and will *remain* stable, because it is based upon the decisions of calculating machines that have the good of humanity at heart through the overwhelming force of the First Law of Robotics.'

Stephen Byerley continued, 'And although the Machines are nothing but the vastest conglomeration of calculating circuits ever invented, they are still robots within the meaning of the First Law, and so our Earth-wide economy is in accord with the best interests of Man. The population of Earth knows that there will be no unemployment, no overproduction or shortages. Waste and famine are words in history books. And so the question of ownership of the means of production becomes obsolescent. Whoever owned them (if such a phrase has meaning), a man, a group, a nation, or all mankind, they could be utilized only as the Machines directed. —Not because men were forced to but because it was the wisest course and men knew it.

'It puts an end to war – not only to the last cycle of wars, but to the next and all of them. Unless—'

A long pause, and Dr Calvin encouraged him by repetition. 'Unless—'

The fire crouched and skittered along a log, then popped up.

'Unless,' said the Co-ordinator, 'the Machines don't fulfill their function.'

'I see. And that is where those trifling maladjustments come in which you mentioned a while ago – steel, hydroponics and so on.'

'Exactly. Those errors should not be. Dr Silver tells me they *cannot* be.'

'Does he deny the facts? How unusual!'

'No, he admits the facts, of course. I do him an injustice. What he denies is that any error in the machine is responsible for the so-called (his phrase) errors in the answers. He claims that the Machines are self-correcting and that it would violate the fundamental laws of nature for an error to exist in the circuits of relays. And so I said—'

'And you said, "Have your boys check them and make sure, anyway." '

'Susan, you read my mind. It was what I said, and he said he couldn't.'

'Too busy?'

'No, he said that no human could. He was frank about it. He told me, and I hope I understand him properly, that the Machines are a gigantic extrapolation. Thus— A team of mathematicians work several years calculating a positronic brain equipped to do certain similar acts of calculation. Using this brain they make further calculations to create a still more complicated brain, which they use again to make one still more complicated and so on. According to Silver, what we call the Machines are the result of ten such steps.'

'Ye-es, that sounds familiar. Fortunately, I'm not a mathematician. —Poor Vincent. He is a young man. The Directors before him, Alfred Lanning and Peter Bogert, are dead, and they had no such problems. Nor had I. Perhaps roboticists as a whole should now die, since we can no longer understand our own creations.'

'Apparently not. The Machines are not super-brains in Sunday supplement sense – although they are so pictured in the Sunday supplements. It is merely that in their own particular province of collecting and analyzing a nearly infinite number of data and relationships thereof, in nearly infinitesimal time, they have progressed beyond the possibility of detailed human control.

'And then I tried something else. I actually asked the Machine. In the strictest secrecy, we fed it the original data involved in the steel decision, its own answer, and the actual developments since – the overproduction, that is – and asked for an explanation of the discrepancy.'

'Good, and what was its answer?'

'I can quote you that word for word: "The matter admits of no explanation." '

'And how did Vincent interpret that?'

'In two ways. Either we had not given the Machine enough data to allow a definite answer, which was unlikely. Dr Silver admitted that. —Or else, it was impossible for the Machine to admit that it could give any answer to data which implied that it could harm a human being. This, naturally, is implied by the First Law. And then Dr Silver recommended that I see you.'

Susan Calvin looked very tired. 'I'm old, Stephen. When Peter Bogert died, they wanted to make me Director of Research and I refused. I wasn't young then, either, and I did not wish the responsibility. They let young Silver have it and that satisfied me; but what good is it, if I am dragged into such messes.

'Stephen, let me state my position. My researches do indeed involve the interpretation of robot behavior in the light of the Three Laws of Robotics. Here, now, we have these incredible calculating machines. They are positronic robots and therefore obey the Laws of Robotics. But they lack personality; that is, their functions are extremely limited. —Must be, since they are so specialized. Therefore, there is very little room for the interplay of the Laws, and my one method of attack is virtually useless. In short, I don't know that I can help you, Stephen.'

The Co-ordinator laughed shortly, 'Nevertheless, let me tell you the rest. Let me give you *my* theories, and perhaps you will then be able to tell me whether they are possible in the light of robopsychology.'

'By all means. Go ahead.'

'Well, since the Machines are giving the wrong answers, then, assuming that they cannot be in error, there is only one possibility. *They are being given the wrong data!* In other words, the trouble is human, and not robotic. So I took my recent planetary inspection tour—'

'From which you have just returned to New York.'

'Yes. It was necessary, you see, since there are four Machines, one handling each of the Planetary Regions. And *all four are yielding imperfect results.*'

'Oh, but that follows, Stephen. If any one of the Machines is imperfect, that will automatically reflect in the results of the other three, since each of the others will assume as part of the data on which they base their own decisions, the perfection of the imperfect fourth. With a false assumption, they will yield false answers.'

'Uh-huh. So it seemed to me. Now, I have here the records of my interviews, with each of the Regional Vice-Co-ordinators. Would you look through them with me? —Oh, and first, have you heard of the "Society for Humanity"?'

'Umm, yes. They are an outgrowth of the Fundamentalists who have kept US Robots from ever employing positronic robots on the grounds of unfair labor competition and so on. The "Society for Humanity" itself is anti-Machine, is it not?'

'Yes, yes, but— Well, you will see. Shall we begin? We'll start with the Eastern Region.'

'As you say—'

The Eastern Region
   a—Area: 7,500,000 square miles
   b—Population: 1,700,000,000
   c—Capital: Shanghai

Ching Hso-lin's great-grandfather had been killed in the Japanese invasion of the old Chinese Republic, and there had been no one beside his dutiful children to mourn his loss or even to know he was lost. Ching Hso-lin's grandfather had survived the civil war of the late forties, but there had been no one beside *his* dutiful children to know or care of that.

And yet Ching Hso-lin was a Regional Vice-Co-ordinator, with the economic welfare of half the people of Earth in his care.

Perhaps it was with the thought of all that in mind, that Ching had two maps as the only ornaments on the wall of his office. One was an old hand-drawn affair tracing out an acre or two of land, and marked with the now outmoded pictographs of old China. A little creek trickled aslant the faded markings and there were the delicate pictorial indications of lowly huts, in one of which Ching's grandfather had been born.

The other map was a huge one, sharply delineated, with all markings in neat Cyrillic characters. The red boundary that marked the Eastern Region swept within its grand confines all that had once been China, India, Burma, Indo-China, and Indonesia. On it, within the old province of Szechuan, so light and gentle that none could see it, was the little mark placed there by Ching which indicated the location of his ancestral farm.

Ching stood before these maps as he spoke to Stephen Byerley in precise English. 'No one knows better than you, Mr Co-ordinator, that my job, to a large extent, is a sinecure. It carries with it a certain social standing, and I represent a convenient focal point for administration, but otherwise it is the Machine! —The Machine does all the work. What did you think, for instance, of the Tientsin Hydroponics works?'

'Tremendous!' said Byerley.

'It is but one of dozens, and not the largest. Shanghai, Calcutta, Batavia, Bangkok— They are widely spread and they are the answer to feeding the billion and three quarters of the East.'

'And yet,' said Byerley, 'you have an unemployment

problem there at Tientsin. Can you be over-producing? It is incongruous to think of Asia as suffering from too much food.'

Ching's dark eyes crinkled at the edges. 'No. It has not come to that yet. It is true that over the last few months, several vats at Tientsin have been shut down, but it is nothing serious. The men have been released only temporarily and those who do not care to work in other fields have been shipped to Colombo in Ceylon, where a new plant is being put into operation.'

'But why should the vats be closed down?'

Ching smiled gently, 'You do not know much of hydroponics, I see. Well, that is not surprising. You are a Northerner, and there soil farming is still profitable. It is fashionable in the North to think of hydroponics, when it is thought of at all, as a device for growing turnips in a chemical solution, and so it is – in an infinitely complicated way.

'In the first place, by far the largest crop we deal with (and the percentage is growing) is yeast. We have upward of two thousand strains of yeast in production and new strains are added monthly. The basic food-chemicals of the various yeasts are nitrates and phosphates among the inorganics together with proper amounts of the trace metals needed, down to the fractional parts per million of boron and molybdenum which are required. The organic matter is mostly sugar mixtures derived from the hydrolysis of cellulose, but, in addition, there are various food factors which must be added.

'For a successful hydroponics industry – one which can feed seventeen hundred million people – we must engage in an immense reforestation program throughout the East; we must have huge wood-conversion plants to deal with our southern jungles; we must have power, and steel, and chemical synthetics above all.'

'Why the last, sir?'

'Because, Mr Byerley, these strains of yeast have each their peculiar properties. We have developed, as I said, two thousand strains. The beef steak you thought you ate today was yeast. The frozen fruit confection you had for dessert was iced yeast. We have filtered yeast juice with the taste, appearance, and all the food value of milk.

'It is flavor, more than anything else, you see, that makes yeast feeding popular and for the sake of flavor we have developed artificial, domesticated strains that can no longer support themselves on a basic diet of salts and sugar. One needs biotin; another needs pteroylglutamic acid; still others need seventeen different amino acids supplied them as well as all the Vitamins B, but one (and yet it is popular and we cannot, with economic sense, abandon it) —'

Byerley stirred in his seat, 'To what purpose do you tell me all this?'

'You asked me, sir, why men are out of work in Tientsin. I have a little more to explain. It is only that we must have these various and varying foods for our yeast; but there remains the complicating factor of popular fads with passing time; and of the possibility of the development of new strains with the new requirements and new popularity. All this must be foreseen, and the Machine does the job—'

'But not perfectly.'

'Not very *imperfectly*, in view of the complications I have mentioned. Well, then, a few thousand workers in Tientsin are temporarily out of a job. But, consider this, the amount of waste in this past year (waste that is, in terms of either defective supply or defective demand) amounts to not one-tenth of one percent of our total productive turnover. I consider that—'

'Yet in the first year of the Machine, the figure was nearer one-thousandth of one percent.'

'Ah, but in the decade since the Machine began its operations in real earnest, we have made use of it to increase our old pre-Machine yeast industry twenty-fold. You expect imperfections to increase with complications, though—'

'Though?'

'There *was* the curious instance of Rama Vrasayana.'

'What happened to him?'

'Vrasayana was in charge of a brine-evaporation plant for the production of iodine, with which yeast can do without, but human beings not. His plant was forced into receivership.'

'Really? And through what agency?'

'Competition, believe it or not. In general, one of the chiefest functions of the Machine's analyses is to indicate the most efficient distribution of our producing units. It is obviously faulty to have areas insufficiently serviced, so that the transportation costs account for too great a percentage of the overhead. Similarly, it is faulty to have an area too well serviced, so that factories must be run at lowered capacities, or else compete harmfully with one another. In the case of Vrasayana, another plant was established in the same city, and with a more efficient extracting system.'

'The Machine permitted it?'

'Oh, certainly. That is not surprising. The new system is becoming widespread. The surprise is that the Machine failed to warn Vrasayana to renovate or combine. —Still, no matter. Vrasayana accepted a job as engineer in the new plant, and if his responsibility and pay are now less, he is not actually suffering. The workers found employment easily; the old plant has been converted to – something or other. Something useful. We left it all to the Machine.'

'And otherwise you have no complaints.'

'None!'

The Tropic Region:
    a—Area: 22,000,000 square miles

b—Population: 500,000,000
c—Capital: Capital City

The map in Lincoln Ngoma's office was far from the model of neat precision of the one in Ching's Shanghai dominion. The boundaries of Ngoma's Tropic Region were stenciled in dark, wide brown and swept about a gorgeous interior labeled 'jungle' and 'desert' and 'here be Elephants and All Manner of Strange Beasts'.

It had much to sweep, for in land area the Tropic Region enclosed most of two continents: all of South America north of Argentina and all of Africa south of the Atlas. It included North America south of the Rio Grande as well, and even Arabia and Iran in Asia. It was the reverse of the Eastern Region. Where the ant hives of the Orient crowded half of humanity into 15 percent of the land mass, the Tropics stretched its 15 percent of Humanity over nearly half of all the land in the world.

But it was growing. It was the one Region whose population increase through immigration exceeded that through births. —And for all who came it had use.

To Ngoma, Stephen Byerley seemed like one of these immigrants, a pale searcher for the creative work of carving a harsh environment into the softness necessary for man, and he felt some of that automatic contempt of the strong man born to the strong Tropics for the unfortunate pallards of the colder suns.

The Tropics had the newest capital city on Earth, and it was called simply that! 'Capital City', in the sublime confidence of youth. It spread brightly over the fertile uplands of Nigeria and outside Ngoma's windows, far below, was life and color; the bright, bright sun and the quick, drenching showers. Even the squawking of the rainbowed birds was brisk and the stars were hard pinpoints in the sharp night.

Ngoma laughed. He was a big, dark man, strong-faced and handsome.

'Sure,' he said, and his English was colloquial and mouth-filling, 'the Mexican Canal is overdue. What the hell? It will get finished just the same, old boy.'

'It was doing well up to the last half year.'

Ngoma looked at Byerley and slowly crunched his teeth over the end of a big cigar, spitting out one end and lighting the other. 'Is this an official investigation, Byerley? What's going on?'

'Nothing. Nothing at all. It's just my function as Co-ordinator to be curious.'

'Well, if it's just that you are filling in a dull moment, the truth is that we're always short on labor. There's lots going on in the Tropics. The Canal is only one of them—'

'But doesn't your Machine predict the amount of labor available for the Canal – allowing for all the competing projects?'

Ngoma placed one hand behind his neck and blew smoke rings at the ceiling. 'It was a little off.'

'Is it often a little off?'

'Not oftener than you would expect. —We don't expect too much of it, Byerley. We feed it data. We take its results. We do what it says. —But it's just a convenience; just a labor-saving device. We could do without it, if we had to. Maybe not as well. Maybe not as quickly. But we'd get there.

'We've got confidence out here, Byerley, and that's the secret. Confidence! We've got new land that's been waiting for us for thousands of years, while the rest of the world was being ripped apart in the lousy fumblings of pre-atomic time. We don't have to eat yeast like the Eastern boys, and we don't have to worry about the stale dregs of the last century like you Northerners.

'We've wiped out the tsetse fly and the Anopheles mosquito, and people find they can live in the sun and like it, now. We've thinned down the jungles and found soil; we've watered the deserts and found gardens. We've got coal and oil in untouched fields, and minerals out of count.

'Just step back. That's all we ask the rest of the world to do. —Step back, and let us work.'

Byerley said, prosaically, 'But the Canal – it was on schedule six months ago. What happened?'

Ngoma spread his hands, 'Labor troubles.' He felt through a pile of papers skeltered about his desk and gave it up.

'Had something on the matter here,' he muttered, 'but never mind. There was a work shortage somewhere in Mexico once on the question of women. There weren't enough women in the neighborhood. It seemed no one had thought of feeding sexual data to the Machine.'

He stopped to laugh, delightedly, then sobered, 'Wait a while. I think I've got it. —Villafranca!'

'Villafranca?'

'Francisco Villafranca. —He was the engineer in charge. Now let me straighten it out. Something happened and there was a cave-in. Right. Right. That was it. Nobody died, as I remember, but it made a hell of a mess. —Quite a scandal.'

'Oh?'

'There was some mistake in his calculations. —Or at least, the Machine said so. They fed through Villafranca's data, assumptions, and so on. The stuff he had started with. The answers came out differently. It seems the answers Villafranca had used didn't take account of the effect of a heavy rainfall on the contours of the cut. —Or something like that. I'm not an engineer, you understand.

'Anyway, Villafranca put up a devil of a squawk. He claimed the Machine's answer had been different the first time. That he had followed the Machine faithfully. Then he quit! We offered to hold him on – reasonable doubt, previous work satisfactory, and all that – in a subordinate position, of course – had to do that much – mistakes can't go unnoticed – bad for discipline—Where was I?'

'You offered to hold him.'

'Oh yes. He refused. —Well, take all in all, we're two months behind. Hell, that's nothing.'

Byerley stretched out his hand and let the fingers tap lightly on the desk. 'Villafranca blamed the Machine, did he?'

'Well, he wasn't going to blame himself, was he? Let's face it; human nature is an old friend of ours. Besides, I remember something else now— Why the hell can't I find documents when I want them? My filing system isn't worth a damn— This Villafranca was a member of one of your Northern organizations. Mexico is too close to the North, that's part of the trouble.'

'Which organization are you speaking of?'

'The Society for Humanity, they call it. He used to attend the annual conferences in New York, Villafranca did. Bunch of crackpots, but harmless. —They don't like the Machines; claim they're destroying human initiative. So naturally Villafranca would blame the Machine. —Don't understand that group myself. Does Capital City looks as if the human race were running out of initiative?'

And Capital City stretched out in golden glory under a golden sun – the newest and youngest creation of *Homo metropolis*.

The European Region
  a—Area: 4,000,000 square miles
  b—Population: 300,000,000
  c—Capital:Geneva

The European Region was an anomaly in several ways. In area, it was far the smallest; not one fifth the size of the Tropic Region in area, and not one fifth the size of the Eastern Region in population. Geographically, it was only somewhat similar to pre-Atomic Europe, since it excluded what had once been European Russia and what had once been the British Isles, while it included the Mediterranean coasts of Africa and Asia, and, in a queer jump across the Atlantic, Argentina, Chile, and Uruguay as well.

Nor was it likely to improve its relative status *vis-à-vis* the other regions of Earth, except for what vigor the South American provinces lent it. Of all the Regions, it alone showed a positive population decline over the past half century. It alone had not seriously expanded its productive facilities, or offered anything radically new to human culture.

'Europe,' said Madame Szegeczowska, in her soft French, 'is essentially an economic appendage of the Northern Region. We know it, and it doesn't matter.'

And as though in resigned acceptance of a lack of individuality, there was no map of Europe on the wall of the Madame Co-ordinator's office.

'And yet,' pointed out Byerley, 'you have a Machine of your own, and you are certainly under no economic pressure from across the ocean.'

'A Machine! Bah!' She shrugged her delicate shoulders, and allowed a thin smile to cross her little face as she tamped out a cigarette with long fingers. 'Europe is a sleepy place. And such of our men as do not manage to emigrate to the Tropics are tired and sleepy along with it. You see for yourself that it is myself, a poor woman, to whom falls the task of being Vice-Co-ordinator. Well, fortunately, it is not a difficult job, and not much is expected of me.

'As for the Machine— What can it say but "Do this and it will be best for you." But what is best for us? Why, to be an economic appendage of the Northern Region.

'And is it so terrible? No wars! We live in peace – and it is pleasant after seven thousand years of war. We are old, monsieur. In our borders, we have the regions where Occidental civilization was cradled. We have Egypt and Mesopotamia; Crete and Syria; Asia Minor and Greece. —But old age is not necessarily an unhappy time. It can be a fruition—'

'Perhaps you are right,' said Byerley, affably. 'At least the tempo of life is not as intense as in the other Regions. It is a pleasant atmosphere.'

'Is it not? —Tea is being brought, monsieur. If you will indicate your cream and sugar preferences, please. —Thank you.'

She sipped gently, then continued. 'It *is* pleasant. The rest of Earth is welcome to the continuing struggle. I find a parallel here; a very interesting one. There was a time when Rome was master of the world. It had adopted the culture and civilization of Greece; a Greece which had never been united, which had ruined itself with war, and which was ending in a state of decadent squalor. Rome united it, brought it peace and let it live a life of secure non-glory. It occupied itself with its philosophies and its art, far from the clash of growth and war. It was a sort of death, but it was restful, and it lasted with minor breaks for some four hundred years.'

'And yet,' said Byerley, 'Rome fell eventually, and the opium dream was over.'

'There are no longer barbarians to overthrow civilization.'

'We can be our own barbarians, Madame Szegeczowska. — Oh, I meant to ask you. The Almaden mercury mines have fallen off quite badly in production. Surely the ores are not declining more rapidly than anticipated?'

The little woman's gray eyes fastened shrewdly on Byerley, 'Barbarians – the fall of civilization – possible failure of the Machine. Your thought processes are very transparent, monsieur.'

'Are they?' Byerley smiled. 'I see that I should have had men to deal with as hitherto. —You consider the Almaden affair to be the fault of the Machine?'

'Not at all, but I think you do. You, yourself, are a native of the Northern Region. The Central Co-ordination Office is at New York.—And I have noticed for quite a while that you Northerners lack somewhat of faith in the Machine.'

'We do?'

'There is your "Society for Humanity" which is strong in the North, but naturally fails to find many recruits in tired, old Europe, which is quite willing to let feeble Humanity alone for a while. Surely, you are one of the confident North and not one of the cynical old continent.'

'This has a connection with Almaden?'

'Oh yes, I think so. The mines are in the control of Consolidated Cinnabar, which is certainly a Northern company, with headquarters at Nikolaev. Personally, I wonder if the Board of Directors have been consulting the Machine at all. They said they had in our conference last month, and, of course, we have no evidence that they did not, but I wouldn't take the word of a Northerner in this matter – no offense intended – under any circumstances. —Nevertheless, I think it will have a fortunate ending.'

'In what way, my dear madame?'

'You must understand that the economic irregularities of the last few months, which, although small as compared with the great storms of the past, are quite disturbing to our peace-drenched spirits, have caused considerable restiveness in the Spanish province. I understand that Consolidated Cinnabar is selling out to a group of native Spaniards. It is consoling. If we are economic vassals of the North, it is humiliating to have the fact advertised too blatantly. —And our people can be better trusted to follow the Machine.'

'Then you think there will be no more trouble?'

'I am sure there will not be— In Almaden, at least.'

The Northern region
  a—Area: 18,000,000 square miles
  b—Population: 800,000,000
  c—Capital: Ottawa

The Northern Region, in more ways than one, was at the top. This was exemplified quite well by the map in the Ottawa office of Vice-Co-ordinator Hiram Mackenzie, in which the North Pole was centered. Except for the enclave of Europe with its Scandinavian and Icelandic regions, all the Arctic area was within the Northern Region.

Roughly, it could be divided into two major areas. To the left on the map was all of North America above the Rio Grande. To the right was included all of what had once been the Soviet Union. Together these areas represented the centered power of the planet in the first years of the Atomic Age. Between the two was Great Britain, a tongue of the Region licking at Europe. Up at the top of the map, distorted into odd, huge shapes, were Australia and New Zealand, also member provinces of the Region.

Not all the changes of the past decades had yet altered the fact that the North was the economic ruler of the planet.

There was almost an ostentatious symbolism thereof in the fact that of the official Regional maps Byerley had seen, Mackenzie's alone showed all the Earth, as though the North feared no competition and needed no favoritism to point up its pre-eminence.

'Impossible,' said Mackenzie, dourly, over the whiskey. 'Mr Byerley, you have had no training as a robot technician, I believe.'

'No, I have not.'

'Hmp. Well, it is, in my opinion, a sad thing that Ching, Ngoma and Szegeczowska haven't either. There is too prevalent an opinion among the peoples of Earth that a Co-ordinator need only be a capable organizer, a broad generalizer, and an amiable person. These days he should know his robotics as well – no offense intended.'

'None taken. I agree with you.'

'I take it, for instance, from what you have said already, that you worry about the recent trifling dislocations in world economy. I don't know what you suspect, but it has happened in the past that people – who should have known better – wondered what would happen if false data were fed into the Machine.'

'And what would happen, Mr Mackenzie?'

'Well,' the Scotsman shifted his weight and sighed, 'all collected data goes through a complicated screening system which involves both human and mechanical checking, so that the problem is not likely to arise. —But let us ignore that. Humans are fallible, also corruptible, and ordinary mechanical devices are liable to mechanical failure.

'The real point of the matter is that what we call a "wrong datum" is one which is inconsistent with all other known data. It is our only criterion of right and wrong. It is the Machine's as well. Order it, for instance, to direct agricultural activity on the basis of an average July temperature in Iowa of 57 degrees Fahrenheit. It won't accept that. It will not give an answer. —Not that it has any prejudice against that particular temperature, or that an answer is impossible; but because, in the light of all the other data fed it over a period of years, it knows that the probability of an average July temperature of 57 is virtually nil. It rejects that datum.

'The only way a "wrong datum" can be forced on the Machine is to include it as part of a self-consistent whole, all of which is subtly wrong in a manner either too delicate for the Machine to detect or outside the Machine's experience. The former is beyond human capacity, and the latter is almost so, and is becoming more nearly so as the Machine's experience increases by the second.'

Stephen Byerley placed two fingers to the bridge of his nose. 'Then the Machine cannot be tampered with— And how do you account for recent errors, then?'

'My dear Byerley, I see that you instinctively follow that great error – that the Machine knows all. Let me cite you a case from my personal experience. The cotton industry engages experienced buyers who purchase cotton. Their procedure is to pull a tuft of cotton out of a random bale of a lot. They will look at that tuft and feel it, tease it out, listen to the crackling perhaps as they do so, touch it with their tongue – and through this procedure they will determine the class of cotton the bales represent. As a result of their decisions, purchases are made at certain prices, blends are made in certain proportions. —Now these buyers cannot yet be replaced by the Machine.'

'Why not? Surely the data involved is not too complicated for it?'

'Probably not. But what data is this you refer to? No textile chemist knows exactly what it is that the buyer tests when he feels a tuft of cotton. Presumably there's the average length of the threads, their feel, the extent and nature of their slickness, the way they hang together and so on. —Several dozen items, subconsciously weighed, out of years of experience. But the *quantitative* nature of these tests is not know; maybe even the very nature of some of them is not known. So we have nothing to feed the Machine. Nor can the buyers explain their own judgment. They can only say, 'Well, look at it. Can't you *tell* it's class-such-and-such?" '

'I see.'

'There are innumerable cases like that. The Machine is only a tool after all, which can help humanity progress faster by taking some of the burdens of calculations and interpretations off his back. The task of the human brain remains what it has always been; that of discovering new data to be analyzed, and of devising new concepts to be tested. A pity the Society for Humanity won't understand that.'

'They are against the Machine?'

'They would be against mathematics or against the art of writing if they had lived at the appropriate time. These reactionaries of the Society claim the Machine robs man of his soul. I notice that capable men are still at a premium in our society; we still need the man who is intelligent enough to think of the proper questions to ask. Perhaps if we could find enough of such, these dislocations you worry about, Co-ordinator, wouldn't occur.'

Earth (Including the uninhabited continent, Antarctica)
  a—Area: 54,000,000 square miles (land surface)
  b—Population: 3,300,000,000
  c—Capital:New York

The fire behind the quartz was weary now, and sputtered its reluctant way to death.

The Co-ordinator was somber, his mood matching the sinking flame.

'They all minimize the state of affairs.' His voice was low. 'Is it not easy to imagine that they laugh at me? And yet – Vincent Silver said the Machines cannot be out of order, and I must believe him. Hiram Mackenzie says they cannot be fed false data, and I must believe him. But the Machines are going wrong, somehow, and I must believe that, too, – and so there is *still* an alternative left.'

He glanced sidewise at Susan Calvin, who, with closed eyes, for a moment seemed asleep.

'What is that?' she asked, prompt to her cue, nevertheless.

'Why, that correct data is indeed given, and correct answers are indeed received, but that they are then ignored.

There is no way the Machine can enforce obedience to its dictates.'

'Madame Szegeczowska hinted as much, with reference to Northerners in general, it seems to me.'

'So she did.'

'And what purpose is served by disobeying the Machine? Let's consider motivations.'

'It's obvious to me, and should be to you. It is a matter of rocking the boat, deliberately. There can be no serious conflicts on Earth, in which one group or another can seize more power than it has for what it thinks is its own good despite the harm to Mankind as a whole, while the Machines rule. If popular faith in the Machines can be destroyed to the point where they are abandoned, it will be the law of the jungle again. —And not one of the four Regions can be freed of the suspicion of wanting just that.

'The East has half of humanity within its borders, and the Tropics more than half of Earth's resources. Each can feel itself the natural ruler of all Earth, and each has a history of humiliation by the North, for which it can be human enough to wish a senseless revenge. Europe has a tradition of greatness, on the other hand. It once *did* rule the Earth, and there is nothing so eternally adhesive as the memory of power.

'Yet, in another way, it's hard to believe. Both the East and the Tropics are in a state of enormous expansion within their own borders. Both are climbing incredibly. They cannot have the spare energy for military adventures. And Europe can have nothing but its dreams. It is a cipher, militarily.'

'So, Stephen,' said Susan, 'you leave the North.'

'Yes,' said Byerley, energetically, 'I do. The North is now the strongest, and has been for nearly a century, or its component parts have been. But it is losing relatively, now. The Tropic Regions may take their place in the forefront of civilization for the first time since the Pharaohs, and there are Northerners who fear that.

'The "Society for Humanity" is a Northern organization primarily, you know, and they make no secret of not wanting the Machines. —Susan, they are few in numbers, but it is an association of powerful men. Heads of factories; directors of industries and agricultural combines who hate to be what they call "the Machine's office-boy" belong to it. Men with ambition belong to it. Men who feel themselves strong enough to decide for themselves what is best for themselves, and not just to be told what is best for others.

'In short, just those men who, by together refusing to accept the decisions of the Machine, can, in a short time, turn the world topsy-turvy; – just those belong to the Society.

'Susan, it hangs together. Five of the Directors of World Steel are members, and World Steel suffers from over-production. Consolidated Cinnabar, which mined mercury at Almaden, was a Northern concern. Its books are still being investigated, but one, at least, of the men concerned was a member. Francisco Villafranca, who, singlehanded, delayed the Mexican Canal for two months, was a member, we know already - and so was Rama Vrasayana, I was not at all surprised to find out.'

Susan said quietly, 'These men, I might point out, have all done badly—'

'But naturally,' interjected Byerley. 'To disobey the Machine's analyses is to follow a non-optimal path. Results are poorer than they might be. It's the price they pay. They will have it rough now but in the confusion that will eventually follow—'

'Just what do you plan doing, Stephen?'

'There is obviously no time to lose. I am going to have the Society outlawed, every member removed from any responsible post. And all executive and technical positions, henceforward, can be filled only by applicants signing a non-Society oath. It will mean a certain surrender of basic civil liberties, but I am sure the Congress—'

'It won't work!'

'What!—Why not?'

'I will make a prediction. If you try any such thing, you will find yourself hampered at every turn. You will find it impossible to carry out. You will find your every move in that direction will result in trouble.'

Byerley was taken aback. 'Why do you say that?— I was rather hoping for your approval in this matter.'

'You can't have it as long as your actions are based on a false premise. You admit the Machine can't be wrong, and can't be fed wrong data. I will now show you that it cannot be disobeyed, either, as you think is being done by the Society.'

'*That* I don't see at all.'

'Then listen. Every action by any executive which does not follow the exact directions of the Machine he is working with becomes part of the data for the next problem. The Machine, therefore, knows that the executive has a certain tendency to disobey. He can incorporate that tendency into that data – even quantitatively; that is, judging exactly how much and in what direction disobedience would occur. Its next answers would be just sufficiently biased so that after the executive concerned disobeyed, he would have automatically corrected those answers to optimal directions. The Machine knows, Stephen!'

'You can't be sure of all this. You are guessing.'

'It is a guess based on a lifetime's experience with robots. You had better rely on such a guess, Stephen.'

'But then what is left? The Machines themselves are correct and the premises they work on are correct. That we have agreed upon. Now you say that it cannot be disobeyed. Then what is wrong?'

'You have answered yourself. *Nothing is wrong!* Think about the Machines for a while, Stephen. They are robots, and they follow the First Law. But the Machines work not for any single human being, but for all humanity, so that the First Law becomes: "No machines may harm humanity; or, through inaction, allow humanity to come to harm."

'Very well, then Stephen, what harms humanity? Economic dislocations most of all, from whatever cause. Wouldn't you say so?'

'I would.'

'And what is most likely in the future to cause economic dislocations? Answer that, Stephen.'

'I should say,' replied Byerley, unwillingly, 'the destruction of the Machines.'

'And so should I say, and so should the Machines say. Their first care, therefore, is to preserve themselves, for us. And so they are quietly taking care of the only elements left that threaten them. It is not the "Society for Humanity" which is shaking the boat so that the Machines may be destroyed. You have been looking at the reverse of the picture. Say rather that the Machine is shaking the boat – *very* slightly – just enough to shake loose those few which cling to the side for purposes the Machines consider harmful to Humanity.

'So Vrasayana loses his factory and gets another job where he can do no harm – he is not badly hurt, he is not rendered incapable of earning a living, for the Machine cannot harm a human being more than minimally, and that only to save a greater number. Consolidated Cinnabar loses control at Almaden. Villafranca is no longer a civil engineer in charge of an important project. And the directors of World Steel are losing their grip on the industry – or will.'

'But you don't really know all this,' insisted Byerley, distractedly. 'How can we possibly take a chance on your being right?'

'You must. Do you remember the Machine's own statement when you presented the problem to it? It was: "The matter admits of no explanation." The Machine did not say there was no explanation, or that it could determine no explanation. It simply was not going to *admit* any explanation. In other words, it would be harmful to humanity to have the explanation known, and that's why we can only guess – and keep on guessing.'

'But how can the explanation do us harm? Assume that you are right, Susan.'

'Why, Stephen, if I am right, it means that the Machine is conducting our future for us not simply in direct answer to our direct questions, but in general answer to the world situation and to human psychology as a whole. And to know that may make us unhappy and may hurt our pride. The Machine cannot, *must* not, make us unhappy.

'Stephen, how do we know what the ultimate good of Humanity will entail? We haven't at *our* disposal the infinite factors that the Machine has at *its*! Perhaps, to give you a not unfamiliar example, our entire technical civilization has created more unhappiness and misery than it has removed. Perhaps an agrarian or pastoral civilization, with less culture and less people, would be better. If so, the Machines must move in that direction, preferably without telling us, since in our ignorant prejudices we only know that what we are used to is good – and we would then fight change. Or perhaps a complete urbanization, or a completely caste-ridden society, or complete anarchy, is the answer. We don't know. Only the Machines know, and they are going there and taking us with them.'

'But you are telling me, Susan, that the "Society for Humanity" is right; and that Mankind *has* lost its own say in its future.'

'It never had any, really. It was always at the mercy of economic and sociological forces it did not understand – at the whims of climate, and the fortunes of war. Now the Machines understand them; and no one can stop them, since the Machines will deal with them as they are dealing with the Society – having, as they do, the greatest of weapons at their disposal, the absolute control of our economy.'

'How horrible!'

'Perhaps how wonderful! Think, that for all time, all conflicts are finally evitable. Only the Machines, from now on, are inevitable!'

And the fire behind the quartz went out and only a curl of smoke was left to indicate its place.

'And that is all,' said Dr Calvin, rising. 'I saw it from the beginning, when the poor robots couldn't speak, to the end, when they stand between mankind and destruction. I will see no more. My life is over. You will see what comes next.'

I never saw Susan Calvin again. She died last month at the age of eighty-two.

Robots and Empire

*To Robyn and Michael
and to the years of happiness they will
continue to enjoy as they walk the
road of life together*

Contents

PART I   AURORA

1   *The Descendant*   11
2   *The Ancestor?*   40
3   *The Crisis*   64
4   *Another Descendant*   95

PART II   SOLARIA

5   *The Abandoned Planet*   121
6   *The Crew*   145
7   *The Overseer*   164

PART III   BALEYWORLD

8   *The Settler World*   195
9   *The Speech*   216
10 *After the Speech*   247

PART IV   AURORA

11 *The Old Leader*   279
12 *The Plan and the Daughter*   301
13 *The Telepathic Robot*   326
14 *The Duel*   359

PART V   EARTH

15 *The Holy World*   391
16 *The City*   419
17 *The Assassin*   445
18 *The Zeroth Law*   475
19 *Alone*   506

PART I

AURORA

1

The Descendant

1.

Gladia felt the lawn-lounge to make sure it wasn't too damp and then sat down. A touch at the control adjusted it in such a way as to allow her to be semi-recumbent, and another activated the diamagnetic field and gave her, as it always did, the sensation of utter relaxation. And why not? She was, in actual fact, floating – a centimetre above the fabric.

It was a warm and pleasant night, the kind that found the planet Aurora at its best; fragrant and star-lit.

With a pang of sadness, she studied the numerous little sparks that dotted the sky with patterns, sparks that were all the brighter because she had ordered the lights of her establishment dimmed.

How was it, she wondered, that she had never learned the names of the stars and had never found out which were which in all the twenty-three decades of her life. One of them was the star about which her birth-planet of Solaria orbited, the star which, during the first three and a half decades of her life, she had thought of merely as 'the sun'.

Gladia had once been called Gladia Solaria. That was when she had come to Aurora, twenty decades before – two hundred Standard Galactic Years – and it was meant as a not very friendly way of marking her foreign birth. A month before had been the bicentennial anniversary of her arrival, something she had left unmarked because she did not particularly want to think of those days. Before that, on Solaria, she had been Gladia – Delmarre.

She stirred uneasily. She had almost forgotten that original name. Was it because it was so long ago? Or was it merely that she laboured to forget?

All these years she had not regretted Solaria, never missed it.

And yet now?

Was it because she had now, quite suddenly, discovered herself to have survived it? It was gone – a historical memory, and she still lived on? Did she miss it now for that reason?

Her brow furrowed. No, she did not miss it, she decided resolutely. She did not long for it; nor did she wish to return to it. It was just the peculiar pang of something that had been so much a part of her – however destructively – being gone.

Solaria! The last of the Spacer worlds to be settled and made into a home for humanity. And in consequence, by some mysterious law of symmetry perhaps, it was also the first to die?

The first? Did that imply a second and third and so on?

Gladia felt her sadness deepen. There were those who thought there was indeed such an implication. If so, Aurora, her long-adopted home, having been the first Spacer world to be settled, would, by that same rule of symmetry, therefore be the last of the fifty to die. In that case, it might, even at worst, outlast her own stretched-out lifetime, and if so, that would have to do.

Her eyes sought the stars again. It was hopeless. There was no way she could possibly work out which of those indistinguishable dots of light was Solaria's sun. She imagined it would be one of the brighter ones, but there were hundreds even of those.

She lifted her arm and made what she identified to

herself only as her 'Daneel-gesture'. The fact that it was dark did not matter.

Robot Daneel Olivaw was at her side almost at once. Anyone who had known him a little over twenty decades before, when he had first been designed by Han Fastolfe, would not have been conscious of any noticeable change in him. His broad, high-cheekboned face, with its short bronze hair combed back; his blue eyes; his tall, well-knit and perfectly humanoid body would have seemed as young and as calmly unemotional as ever.

'May I be of help in any way, Madam Gladia?' he asked, in an even voice.

'Yes, Daneel. Which of those stars is Solaria's sun?'

Daneel did not look upward. He said, 'None of them, Madam Gladia. At this time of year, Solaria's sun will not rise until 3.20 A.M.'

'Oh?' Gladia felt dashed. Somehow she had assumed that any star in which she happened to be interested would be visible at any time it occurred to her to look. Of course, they did rise and set at different times. She knew *that* much. 'I've been staring at nothing, then.'

'The stars, I gather from human reactions,' said Daneel, as though in an attempt to console, 'are beautiful whether any particular one of them is visible or not.'

'I dare say,' said Gladia, discontentedly, and adjusted the lounge to an upright position with a snap. She stood up. 'However, it was Solaria's sun I wanted to see – but not so much that I intend to sit here till 3.20 A.M.'

'Even were you to do so,' said Daneel, 'you would need magnilenses.'

'Magnilenses?'

'It is not quite visible to the unaided eye, Madam Gladia.'

'Worse and worse!' She brushed at her slacks. 'I should have consulted you first, Daneel.'

Anyone who had known Gladia twenty decades before, when she had first arrived in Aurora, would have found a change. Unlike Daneel, she was merely human. She was still 155 centimetres tall, almost ten centimetres below the ideal height for a Spacer woman. She had carefully kept her slim figure, and there was no sign of weakness or stiffness about her body. Still, there was a bit of grey in her hair, fine wrinkles near her eyes, and a touch of graininess about her skin. She might well live another ten or twelve decades, but there was no denying that she was already no longer young. That didn't bother her.

She said, 'Can you identify all the stars, Daneel?'

'I know those visible to the unaided eye, Madam Gladia.'

'And when they rise and set on any day of the year?'

'Yes, Madam Gladia.'

'And all sorts of other things about them?'

'Yes, Madam Gladia. Dr Fastolfe once asked me to gather astronomical data so that he could have them at his fingertips without having to consult his computer. He used to say it was friendlier to have me tell him, than to have his computer do so.' Then, as though to anticipate the next question, 'He did not explain why that should be so.'

Gladia raised her left arm and made the appropriate gesture. Her house was at once illuminated. In the soft light that now reached her, she was subliminally aware of the shadowy figures of several robots, but she paid no attention to that. In any well-ordered establishment, there were always robots within reach of human beings, both for security and for service.

Gladia took a last fugitive glimpse at the sky, where the stars had now dimmed in the scattered light. She shrugged lightly. It had been quixotic. What good would it have done her even if she had been able to see the sun of that now-lost world, one faint dot among many? She might as well choose a dot at random, tell herself it was Solaria's sun, and stare at it.

Her attention turned to R. Daneel. He waited for her patiently, the planes of his face largely in shadow.

She found herself thinking again how little he had changed since she had first seen him on arriving at Dr Fastolfe's establishment so long ago. He had undergone repairs, of course. She knew that, but it was a vague knowledge that one pushed away and kept at a distance.

It was part of the general queasiness that held good for human beings, too. Spacers might boast of their iron health and of their life-spans of thirty to forty decades, but they were not entirely immune to the ravages of age. One of Gladia's femurs fitted into a titanium-silicone hip socket. Her left thumb was totally artificial though no one could tell that without careful ultrasonograms. Even some of her nerves had been rewired. Such things would be true of any Spacer of similar age from any of the fifty Spacer worlds (no, forty-nine, for now Solaria could no longer be counted).

To make any reference to such things, however, was an ultimate obscenity. The medical records involved, which had to exist since further treatment might be necessary, were never revealed for any reason. Surgeons, whose incomes were considerably higher than those of the Chairman himself, were paid so well, in part, because they were virtually ostracized from polite society. After all, they *knew*.

· It was all part of the Spacer fixation on long life, on their unwillingness to admit that old age existed, but Gladia didn't linger on any analysis of causes. She was restlessly uneasy in thinking about herself in that connection. If she had a three-dimensional map of herself with all prosthetic portions, all repairs, marked off in red against the grey of her natural self, what a general pinkness she would appear to have from a distance. Or so she imagined.

Her brain, however, was still intact and whole, and while that was so, *she* was intact and whole, whatever happened to the rest of her body.

Which brought her back to Daneel. Though she had known him for twenty decades, it was only in the last year that he was *hers*. When Fastolfe had died (his end hastened, perhaps, by despair) he had willed everything to the city, which was a common enough state of affairs. Two items, however, he had left to Gladia (aside from confirming her in the ownership of her establishment and its robots and other chattels, together with the grounds thereto appertaining).

One of them had been Daneel.

Gladia asked, 'Do you remember everything you have ever committed to memory over the course of twenty decades, Daneel?'

Daneel said gravely, 'I believe so, Madam Gladia. To be sure, if I forgot an item, I would not know that, for it would have been forgotten, and I would not then recall ever having memorized it.'

'That doesn't follow at all,' said Gladia. 'You might well remember knowing it, but be unable to think of it at the moment. I have frequently had something at the tip of my tongue, so to speak, and been unable to retrieve it.'

Daneel said, 'I do not understand, madam. If I knew something, surely it would be there when I needed it.'

'Perfect retrieval?' They were walking slowly towards the house.

'Merely retrieval, madam. I am designed so.'

'For how much longer?'

'I do not understand, madam.'

'I mean, how much will your brain hold? With a little

over twenty decades of accumulated memories, how much longer can it go on?'

'I do not know, madam. As yet I feel no difficulty.'

'You might not – until you suddenly discover you can remember no more.'

Daneel seemed thoughtful for a moment. 'That may be so, madam.'

'You know, Daneel, not all your memories are equally important.'

'I cannot judge among them, madam.'

'Others can. It would be perfectly possible to clean out your brain, Daneel, and then, under supervision, refill it with its important memory content only; say, ten per cent of the whole. You would then be able to continue for centuries longer than you would otherwise. With repeated treatment of this sort, you could go on indefinitely. It is an expensive procedure, of course, but I would not cavil at that. You'd be worth it.'

'Would I be consulted on the matter, madam? Would I be asked to agree to such treatment?'

'Of course. I would not *order* you in a matter like that. It would be a betrayal of Dr Fastolfe's trust.'

'Thank you, madam. In that case, I must tell you that I would never submit voluntarily to such a procedure unless I found myself to have actually lost my memory-function.'

They had reached the door, and Gladia paused. She said, in honest puzzlement, 'Why ever not, Daneel?'

Daneel said, in a low voice, 'There are memories I cannot risk losing, madam, either through inadvertence, or through poor judgement on the part of those conducting the procedure.'

'Like the rising and setting of the stars? – Forgive me, Daneel, I didn't mean to be joking. To what memories are you referring?'

Daneel said, his voice still lower, 'Madam, I refer to my

memories of my one-time partner, the Earthman, Elijah Baley.'

And Gladia stood there, stricken, so that it was Daneel who had to take the initiative, finally, and signal for the door to open.

2.

Robot Giskard Reventlov was waiting in the living room, and Gladia greeted him with that same pang of uneasiness that always assailed her when she faced him.

He was primitive in comparison with Daneel. He was obviously a robot – metallic, with a face that had nothing human in expression upon it, with eyes that glowed a dim red, as could be seen if it were dark enough. Whereas Daneel wore clothing, Giskard had only the illusion of clothing – but a skilful illusion, for it was Gladia herself who had designed it.

'Well, Giskard,' she said.

'Good evening, Madam Gladia,' said Giskard, with a small bow of his head.

Gladia remembered the words of Elijah Baley long ago, like a whisper inside the recesses of her brain:

'Daneel will take care of you. He will be your friend as well as protector, and you must be a friend to him – for my sake. But, it is Giskard I want you to listen to. Let *him* be your adviser.'

Gladia had frowned. 'Why him? I'm not sure I like him.'

'I do not ask you to like him. I ask you to *trust* him.'

And he would not say why.

Gladia tried to trust the robot, Giskard, but was glad she did not have to try to like him. Something about him made her shiver.

She had had both Daneel and Giskard as effective

parts of her establishment for many decades during which Fastolfe had held titular ownership. It was only on his deathbed that Han Fastolfe had actually transferred ownership. Giskard was the second item, after Daneel, that Fastolfe had left Gladia.

She had said to the old man, 'Daneel is enough, Han. Your daughter, Vasilia, would like to have Giskard. I'm sure of that.'

Fastolfe was lying in bed quietly, eyes closed, looking more peaceful than she had seen him look in years. He did not answer immediately, and for a moment, she thought he had slipped out of life so quietly that she had not noticed. She tightened her grip on his hand convulsively, and his eyes opened.

He whispered, 'I care nothing for biological daughters, Gladia. For twenty decades, I have had but one functional daughter and that was you. I want *you* to have Giskard. He is valuable.'

'Why is he valuable?'

'I cannot say, but I have always found his presence consoling. Keep him always, Gladia. Promise me that.'

'I promise,' she said.

And then his eyes opened one last time and his voice, finding a final reservoir of strength said, in almost a natural tone of voice, 'I love you, Gladia, my daughter.'

And Gladia said, 'I love you, Han, my father.'

Those were the last words he said and heard. Gladia found herself holding the hand of a dead man and, for a while, could not bring herself to let go.

So Giskard was hers. And yet he made her uneasy and she didn't know why.

'Well, Giskard,' she said, 'I've been trying to see Solaria in the sky among the stars, but Daneel tells me it won't be visible till 3.20 A.M., and that I would require binoculars even then. Would you have known that?'

'No, madam.'

'Ought I to wait up till all hours? What do you think?'

'I suggest, Madam Gladia, that you would be better off in bed.'

Gladia bridled. 'Indeed? And if I choose to stay up?'

'Mine is only a suggestion, madam, but you will have a hard day tomorrow and you will undoubtedly regret missing your sleep if you stay up.'

Gladia frowned. 'What's going to make my day hard tomorrow, Giskard? I'm not aware of any forthcoming difficulty.'

Giskard said, 'You have an appointment, madam, with one Levular Mandamus.'

'I have? When did that happen?'

'An hour ago. He photophoned and I took the liberty –'

'*You* took the liberty? Who is he?'

'He is a member of the Robotics Institute, madam.'

'He's an underling of Kelden Amadiro, then.'

'Yes, madam.'

'Understand, Giskard, that I am not in the least interested in seeing this Mandamus, or anyone with any connection with that poisonous toad, Amadiro. So if you've taken the liberty of making an appointment with him in my name, take the further liberty right now of phoning him again and cancelling.'

'If you will confirm it as an order, madam, and make that order as strong and as definite as you can, I will try to obey. I may not be able to. In my judgement, you see, you will be doing yourself harm if you cancel the appointment, and I must not through any action of mine allow you to come to harm.'

'Your judgement might just possibly be wrong, Giskard. Who *is* this man that my failure to see him will do me harm? His being a member of the Robotics Institute scarcely makes him important to me.'

Gladia was perfectly aware of the fact that she was venting spleen at Giskard without much justification. She had been upset by the news of Solaria's abandonment, and embarrassed by the ignorance that led her to look for Solaria in a sky that did not contain it.

Of course, it had been Daneel whose knowledge had made her own lack so obvious and yet she had not railed at *him* – but, then, Daneel looked human and so Gladia automatically treated him as though he were. Appearance was everything. Giskard *looked* like a robot, so one could easily assume he had no feelings to hurt.

And, to be sure, Giskard did not react at all to Gladia's peevishness. (Neither would Daneel have reacted, if it came to that.) He said, 'I have described Dr Mandamus as a member of the Robotics Institute, but he is perhaps more than that. In the last few years, he has been right-hand man to Dr Amadiro. This makes him important and he is not lightly to be ignored. Dr Mandamus would not be a good man to offend, madam.'

'Would he not, Giskard? I care nothing for Mandamus and a great deal less than nothing for Amadiro. I presume you remember that Amadiro once, when he and I and the world were young, did his best to prove that Dr Fastolfe was a murderer and that it was only by a near-miracle that his machinations were aborted.'

'I remember it very well, madam.'

'That's a relief. I was afraid that in twenty decades you had forgotten. In those twenty decades, I have had nothing to do with Amadiro, or with anyone connected with him, and I intend to continue that policy. I don't care what harm I may do myself or what the consequences might be. I will not see this Doctor whoever-he-is and, in future, do not make appointments in my name without consulting me or, at the very least, without explaining that such appointments are subject to my approval.'

'Yes, madam,' said Giskard, 'but may I point out – '

'No, you may not,' said Gladia, and turned away from him.

There was silence while she moved away three steps and then Giskard's calm voice said, 'Madam, I must ask you to trust me.'

Gladia stopped. Why did he use that expression?

She heard again that long-ago voice, 'I do not ask you to like him. I ask you to *trust* him.'

Her lips tightened and she frowned. Reluctantly, not wanting to, she turned back.

'Well,' she said, ungraciously, 'what is it you want to say, Giskard?'

'Just that as long as Dr Fastolfe was alive, madam, his policies predominated on Aurora and throughout the Spacer worlds. As a result the people of Earth have been allowed to migrate freely to various suitable planets in the Galaxy and what we now call the Settler worlds have flourished. Dr Fastolfe is dead now, however, and his successors lack his prestige. Dr Amadiro has kept his own anti-Earth views alive and it is very possible that they may now triumph and that a vigorous policy against Earth and the Settler worlds may be undertaken.'

'If so, Giskard, what can *I* do about it?'

'You can see Dr Mandamus, and you can find out what it is that makes him so anxious to see you, madam. I assure you that he was most insistent on making the appointment as early as possible. He asked to see you at eight in the morning.'

'Giskard, I *never* see anyone before noon.'

'I explained that, madam. I took his anxiety to see you at breakfast, despite my explanation, to be a measure of his desperation. I felt it important to find out why he should be so desperate.'

'And if I don't see him, then it is your opinion, is it, that it will harm me personally? I don't ask whether it will harm Earth, or the Settlers, or this, or that. Will it harm *me*?'

'Madam, it may harm the ability of Earth and the Settlers to continue the settlement of the Galaxy. That dream originated in the mind of Plainclothesman Elijah Baley more than twenty decades ago. The harm to Earth will thus become a desecration of his memory. Am I wrong in thinking that any harm that comes to his memory would be felt by you as though it were harm to yourself personally?'

Gladia was staggered. Twice within the hour now, Elijah Baley had come into the conversation. He was long gone now – a short-lived Earthman who had died over sixteen decades before – yet the mere mention of his name could still shake her.

She said, 'How can things suddenly be that serious?'

'It is not sudden, madam. For twenty decades, the people of Earth and the people of the Spacer worlds have been following parallel courses and have been kept from converging into conflict by the wise policies of Dr Fastolfe. There has, however, always been a strong opposition movement that Dr Fastolfe has had to withstand at all times. Now that Dr Fastolfe is dead, the opposition is much more powerful. The abandonment of Solaria has greatly increased the power of what has been the opposition and may soon be the dominant political force.'

'Why?'

'It is a clear indication, madam, that Spacer strength is declining, and many Aurorans must feel that strong action must be taken, now or never.'

'And you feel that my seeing this man is important in preventing all this?'

'That is indeed my feeling, madam.'

Gladia was silent for a moment, and remembered again,

though rebelliously, that she had once promised Elijah that she would trust Giskard. She said, 'Well, I don't want to, and I don't think my seeing this man will do anyone any good – but, very well, I will see him.'

3.

Gladia was asleep and the house was dark – by human standards. It was alive, however, with motion and action, for there was much for the robots to do, and they could do it by infra-red.

The establishment had to be put into order after the inevitable disordering effects of day-activity. Supplies had to be brought in, rubbish had to be disposed of, objects had to be cleaned or polished or stored, appliances had to be checked, and, always, there was guard-duty.

There were no locks on any doors; there did not have to be. There was no violent crime of any sort on Aurora, either against human beings or against property. There could not be anything of the sort, since every establishment, every human being, was, at all times, guarded by robots. This was well-known and taken for granted.

The price for such calm was that the robot-guards had to be always in place. They were never used – but only because they were always there.

Giskard and Daneel, whose abilities were both more intense and more general than those of the other establishment robots, did not have specific duties, unless one counted as a specific duty that of being responsible for the proper performance of all the other robots.

At 3 A.M., they had completed their rounds out on the lawn and in the wooded area to make sure that all the outer guards were performing their functions well, and that no problems were arising.

They met near the southern limit of the establishment grounds and, for a while, they spoke in abbreviated and Aesopic language. They understood each other well, with many decades of communication behind them, and it was not necessary for them to involve themselves in all the elaborations of human speech.

Daneel said in an all but unhearable whisper, 'Clouds. Unseen.'

Had Daneel been speaking for human ears, he would have said, 'As you see, Friend Giskard, the sky has clouded up. Had Madam Gladia waited her chance to see Solaria, she would not, in any case, have succeeded.'

And Giskard's reply of 'Predicted. Interview, rather,' was the equivalent of, 'So much was predicted in the weather forecast, Friend Daneel, and might have been used as an excuse to get Madam Gladia to bed early. It seemed to me to be more important, however, to meet the problem squarely, and to persuade her to permit this interview I have already told you about.'

'It seems to me, Friend Giskard,' said Daneel, 'that the chief reason you may have found persuasion difficult is that she has been upset by the abandonment of Solaria. I was there once with Partner Elijah when Madam Gladia was still a Solarian and was living there.'

'It has always been my understanding,' said Giskard, 'that Madam Gladia had not been happy on her home planet; that she left her world gladly, and had, at no time, any intention of returning. Yet I agree with you that she seems to have been unsettled by the fact of Solaria's history having come to an end.'

'I do not understand this reaction of Madam Gladia,' said Daneel, 'but there are many times that human reactions do not seem to follow logically from events.'

'It is what makes it difficult to decide, sometimes, what will do a human being harm, and what will not.' Giskard might have said it with a sigh, even a petulant sigh, had he been human. As it was, he stated it merely as an unemotional assessment of a difficult situation. 'It is one of the reasons why it seems to me that the Three Laws of Robotics are incomplete or insufficient.'

'You have said this before, Friend Giskard, and I have tried to believe so and failed,' said Daneel.

Giskard said nothing for a while, then, 'Intellectually, I think they must be incomplete or insufficient, but when I try to *believe* that, I, too, fail, for I am bound by them. Yet if I were not bound by them, I am sure I would believe in their insufficiency.'

'That is a paradox that I cannot understand.'

'Nor can I. And yet I find myself forced to express this paradox. On occasion, I even feel that I am on the verge of discovering what the incompleteness or insufficiency of the Three Laws might be, as in my conversation with Madam Gladia this evening. She asked me how failure to keep the appointment might harm her personally, rather than simply cause harm in the abstract, and there was an answer I could not give because it was not within the compass of the Three Laws.'

'You gave a perfect answer, Friend Giskard. The harm done to Partner Elijah's memory would have affected Madam Gladia deeply.'

'It was the best answer within the compass of the Three Laws. It was not the best answer possible.'

'What was the best answer possible?'

'I do not know, since I cannot put it into words or even concepts as long as I am bound by the Laws.'

'There is nothing beyond the Laws,' said Daneel.

'If I were human,' said Giskard, 'I could see beyond the Laws, and I think, Friend Daneel, that you might be able to see beyond them sooner than I would.'

'I?'

'Yes, Friend Daneel, I have long thought that, although a robot, you think remarkably like a human being.'

'It is not proper to think that,' said Daneel slowly, almost as though he were in pain. 'You think such things because you can look into human minds. It distorts you and it may in the end destroy you. That thought is to me an unhappy one. If you can prevent yourself from seeing into minds more than you must, prevent it.'

Giskard turned away. 'I cannot prevent it, Friend Daneel. I would not prevent it. I regret that I can do so little with it because of the Three Laws. I cannot probe deeply enough – because of the fear that I may do harm. I cannot influence directly enough – because of the fear I may do harm.'

'Yet you influenced Madam Gladia very neatly, Friend Giskard.'

'Not truly. I might have modified her thinking and made her accept the interview without question, but the human mind is so riddled with complexities that I dare do very little. Almost any twist I apply will produce subsidiary twists of whose nature I cannot be certain, and which may do harm.'

'Yet you did something to Madam Gladia.'

'I did not have to. The word "trust" affects her and makes her more amenable. I have noted that fact in the past, but I use the word with the greatest caution since over-use will surely weaken it. I puzzle over this, but I cannot simply burrow for a solution.'

'Because the Three Laws will not permit it?'

Giskard's eyes seemed to intensify their dim glow. 'Yes. At every stage, the Three Laws stand in my way. Yet I cannot modify them – because they stand in my way. Yet I feel I must modify them, for I sense the oncoming of catastrophe.'

'You have said so before, Friend Giskard, but you have not explained the nature of the catastrophe.'

'Because I do not know the nature. It involves the increasing hostility between Aurora and Earth, but how this will evolve into actual catastrophe, I cannot say.'

'Is it possible that there might, after all, be no catastrophe?'

'I do not think so. I have sensed, among certain Auroran officials I have encountered, an aura of catastrophe – of waiting for triumph. I cannot describe this more exactly, and I cannot probe deeply for a better description, because the Three Laws will not allow me to. It is another reason why the interview with Mandamus must take place tomorrow. It will give me a chance to study *his* mind.'

'But if you cannot study it effectively?'

Although Giskard's voice was incapable of showing emotion in the human sense, there was no missing the despair in his words. He said, 'Then that will leave me helpless. I can only follow the Laws. What else can I do?'

And Daneel said softly and dispiritedly, 'Nothing else.'

4.

Gladia entered her living room at 8.15 A.M., having purposely, and with a touch of spite, determined to allow Mandamus (she had now reluctantly memorized his name) to wait for her. She had also taken particular pains with her appearance and (for the first time in years) had agonized over the grey in her hair and had fleetingly wished she had followed the almost universal Auroran practice of shade-control. After all, to look as young and attractive as possible would put this minion of Amadiro's at a further disadvantage.

She was thoroughly prepared to dislike him at sight and

was depressingly aware that he might prove young and attractive; that a sunny face might break into a brilliant smile at her appearance; that she might prove reluctantly attracted to him.

In consequence, she was relieved at the sight of him. He was young, yes, and probably had not yet completed his first half-century, but he didn't make the best of that. He was tall, perhaps 185 centimetres in height, she judged, but too thin. It made him appear spindly. His hair was a shade too dark for an Auroran, his eyes a rather faded hazel, his face too long, his lips too thin, his mouth too broad, his complexion insufficiently fair. But what robbed him of the true appearance of youth was that his expression was too prim, too humourless.

With a flash of insight, Gladia remembered the historical novels that were such a fad on Aurora (novels that invariably dealt with primitive Earth – which was odd for a world that was increasingly hating Earthpeople) and thought: Why, he's the picture of a Puritan.

She felt relieved, and almost smiled. Puritans were usually pictured as villains, and, whether this Mandamus was indeed one or not, it was convenient to have him look like one.

Only when he spoke was Gladia disappointed, for his voice was soft, and distinctly musical. (It ought to have possessed a nasal twang if it were to fulfil the stereotype.)

He said, 'Mrs Gremionis?'

She held out her hand with a carefully condescending smile. 'Dr Mandamus. Please call me Gladia. Everyone does.'

'I know you use your given name professionally – '

'I use it in every way. And my marriage came to an amicable end several decades ago.'

'It lasted for a long time, I believe.'

'A very long time. It was a great success, but even great successes come to a natural end.'

'Ah,' said Mandamus, sententiously. 'To continue past the end might well turn success into failure.'

Gladia nodded, and said, with a trace of a smile, 'How wise for one so young. But shall we move into the dining room? Breakfast is ready and I have surely delayed you long enough.'

It was only as Mandamus turned with her and adjusted his steps to hers that Gladia became aware of his two accompanying robots. It was quite unthinkable for any Auroran to go anywhere without a robotic retinue, but as long as robots stand still they make no impression on the Auroran eye.

Gladia, looking at them quickly, saw that they were late models, clearly expensive. Their pseudo-clothing was elaborate and, although it was not of Gladia's design, it was first-class. Gladia had to admit as much to herself, though reluctantly. She would have to find out, someday, who had designed it, for she did not recognize the touch and she might be about to have a new and formidable competitor. She found herself admiring the manner in which the style of pseudo-clothing was distinctly the same for both robots, while remaining distinctly individual for each. You could not mistake one for the other.

Mandamus caught her swift look and interpreted her expression with disconcerting accuracy. (He is intelligent, thought Gladia, disappointed.) He said, 'The exodesign of my robots was created by a young man at the Institute who has not yet made a name for himself. But he will, don't you think?'

'Definitely,' said Gladia.

Gladia did not expect any business discussion till breakfast was done. It would be the height of ill-breeding to speak of anything but trivia during meals, and Gladia guessed that Mandamus was not at his best with trivia. There was the weather, of course. The recent siege of rain, now happily done with, was mentioned, and the prospects for the oncoming dry season. There was the almost mandatory expression of admiration for the hostess's establishment and Gladia accepted it with practised modesty. She did nothing to ease the strain on the man, but let him search for subject matter without help.

At length, his eye fell on Daneel, standing quietly and without motion in his wall-niche, and Mandamus managed to overcome his Auroran indifference and notice him.

'Ah,' he said, 'clearly the famous R. Daneel Olivaw. He's absolutely unmistakable. A rather remarkable specimen.'

'Quite remarkable.'

'He's yours now, isn't he? By Fastolfe's will?'

'By *Dr* Fastolfe's will, yes,' said Gladia, with faint emphasis.

'It strikes me as amazing that the Institute's line of humanoid robots failed as it did. Have you ever thought about it?'

'I have heard of it,' said Gladia cautiously. (Could it be that this was what he was getting around to?) 'I'm not aware of having spent much time thinking about it.'

'Sociologists are still trying to understand it. Certainly, we at the Institute never got over the disappointment. It seemed like such a natural development. Some of us think that Fa – Dr Fastolfe somehow had something to do with it.'

(He had avoided making the mistake a second time, thought Gladia. Her eyes narrowed and she grew hostile as she decided he had come to her in order to probe for material damaging to poor, good Han.)

She said, tartly, 'Anyone who thinks that is a fool. If you think so, I won't change the expression for your benefit.'

'I am *not* one of those who thinks so, largely because I

don't see what Dr Fastolfe could have done to make it a fiasco.'

'Why should anyone have had to do anything? What it amounts to is that the public didn't want them. A robot that looks like a man competes with a man and one that looks like a woman competes with a woman – and entirely too closely for comfort. Aurorans didn't want the competition. Do we need to look any further?'

'Sexual competition?' said Mandamus, calmly.

For a moment, Gladia's gaze met his levelly. Did he know of her long-ago love for the robot, Jander? Did it matter if he did?

There seemed nothing in his expression to make it appear that he meant anything beyond the surface meaning of the words.

She said, finally, 'Competition in every way. If Dr Han Fastolfe did anything to contribute to such a feeling it was that he designed his robots in too human a fashion, but that was the only way.'

'I think you *have* thought about the matter,' said Mandamus. 'The trouble is that sociologists find the fear of competition with too-human a set of robots to be simplistic as an explanation. That alone would not suffice, and there is no evidence of any other aversion-motive of significance.'

'Sociology is not an exact science,' said Gladia.

'It is not altogether inexact, either.'

Gladia shrugged.

After a pause, Mandamus said, 'In any case, it kept us from organizing colonizing expeditions properly. Without humanoid robots to pave the way – '

Breakfast was not quite over, but it was clear to Gladia that Mandamus could not avoid the non-trivial any longer. She said, 'We might have gone ourselves.'

This time it was Mandamus who shrugged. 'Too difficult. Besides, those short-lived barbarians from Earth, with the permission of your Dr Fastolfe, have swarmed over every planet in sight like a plague of beetles.'

'There are plenty of available planets still. Millions. And if they can do it – '

'Of course *they* can do it,' said Mandamus, with sudden passion. 'It costs lives, but what are lives to *them*? The loss of a decade or so, that's all, and there are billions of them. If a million or so die in the process of colonizing, who notices, who cares? They don't.'

'I'm sure they do.'

'Nonsense. *Our* lives are longer, and therefore more valuable, and we are naturally more careful with them.'

'So we sit here and do nothing but rail at Earth's Settlers for being willing to risk their lives and for seeming to inherit the Galaxy as a result.'

Gladia was unaware of feeling so pro-Settler a bias, but she was in the mood to contradict Mandamus, and as she spoke she could not help but feel that what began as mere contradiction, made sense and could well represent her feelings. Besides, she had heard Fastolfe say similar things during his last discouraged years.

At Gladia's signal, the table was being rapidly and efficiently cleared. Breakfast might have continued, but the conversation and the mood had become quite unsuitable for civilized mealtime.

They moved back into the living room. His robots followed, and so did Daneel and Giskard, all finding their niches. (Mandamus had never remarked on Giskard, thought Gladia, but then, why should he? Giskard was quite old-fashioned, and even primitive, entirely unimpressive in comparison to Mandamus's beautiful specimens.)

Gladia took her seat and crossed her legs, quite aware that the form-fitting sheerness of the lower portion of her slacks flattered the still youthful appearance of her legs.

'May I know the reason for your wishing to see me, Dr Mandamus?' she said, unwilling to delay matters any longer.

He said, 'I have the bad habit of chewing medicated gum after meals as an aid to digestion. Would you object?'

Gladia said, stiffly, 'I would find it distracting.'

(Being unable to chew might put him at a disadvantage. Besides, Gladia added to herself virtuously, at his age he shouldn't need anything to aid his digestion.)

Mandamus had a small oblong package part-way out of his tunic's breast-pocket. He shoved it back with no sign of disappointment and murmured, 'Of course.'

'I was asking, Dr Mandamus, your reason for wishing to see me.'

'Actually two reasons, Lady Gladia. One is a personal matter and one is a matter of state. Would you object to my taking up the personal matter first?'

'Let me say frankly, Dr Mandamus, that I find it hard to imagine what personal matter there could be between us. You work at the Robotics Institute, don't you?'

'Yes, I do.'

'And are close to Amadiro, I have been told.'

'I have the honour of working with *Dr* Amadiro,' he said, with faint emphasis.

(He's paying me back, thought Gladia, but I'm not taking it.)

She said, 'Amadiro and I had an occasion for contact twenty decades ago, and it was most unpleasant. I have had no occasion for any contact with him at any time since. Nor would I have had any contact with you, as a close associate of his, but that I was persuaded that the interview might be important. Personal matters, however, would surely not make this interview in the least important to me. Shall we proceed onward, then, to the matters of state?'

Mandamus's eyes dropped and a faint flush of something that might have been embarrassment came to his cheeks. 'Let me re-introduce myself, then. I am Levular Mandamus, your descendant in the fifth degree. I am the great-great-great-grandson of Santirix and Gladia Gremionis. In reverse, you are my great-great-great-grandmother.'

Gladia blinked rapidly, trying not to look as thunderstruck as she, in actual fact, felt (and not quite succeeding). Of course, she had descendants, and why should not one of them be this man?

But she said, 'Are you sure?'

'Quite sure. I have had a genealogical search made. One of these years, after all, I am likely to want children and, before I can have one, such a search would be mandatory. If you are interested, the pattern between us is M-F-F-M.'

'You are my son's daughter's daughter's son's son?'

'Yes.'

Gladia did not ask for further details. She had had one son and one daughter. She had been a perfectly dutiful mother, but in due time the children had taken up independent lives. As to descendants beyond that son and daughter, she had, in perfectly decent Spacer fashion, never inquired and did not care. Having met one of them, she was Spacer enough *still* not to care.

The thought stabilized her completely. She sat back in her chair and relaxed. 'Very well,' she said. 'You are my descendant in the fifth degree. If this is the personal matter you wish to discuss, it is of no importance.'

'I understand that fully, ancestress. My genealogy is not, in itself, what I wish to discuss, but it lays the foundation. Dr Amadiro, you see, knows of this relationship. At least, so I suspect.'

'Indeed? How did that come about?'

'I believe that he quietly genealogizes all those who come to work at the Institute.'

'But why?'

'In order to find out exactly what he did find out in my case. He is not a trusting man.'

'I don't understand. If you are my fifth-level descendant, why should it have more meaning to him than it does to me?'

Mandamus rubbed his chin with the knuckles of his right hand in a thoughtful manner. 'His dislike for you is in no way less than your dislike for him, Lady Gladia. If you were ready to refuse an interview with me for his sake, he is equally ready to refuse me preferment for your sake. It might be even worse if I were a descendant of Dr Fastolfe, but not much.'

Gladia sat stiffly upright in her seat. Her nostrils flared and she said in a tight voice, 'What is it, then, that you expect me to do? I cannot declare you a non-descendant. Shall I have an announcement placed on hypervision that you are a matter of indifference to me and that I disown you? Will that satisfy your Amadiro? If so, I must warn you I will not do it. I will do nothing to satisfy that man. If it means that he will discharge you and deprive you of your career out of some sort of disapproval of your genetic association, that will teach you to associate with a saner, less vicious person.'

'He will not discharge me, Madam Gladia. I am entirely too valuable to him, if you will pardon my immodesty. Still, I hope, someday, to succeed him as Head of the Institute and that, I am quite certain, he will not allow, as long as he suspects me of a descent worse than that which stems from you.'

'Does he imagine that poor Santirix is worse than I am?'

'Not at all.' Mandamus flushed and he swallowed, but

his voice remained level and steady. 'I mean no disrespect, madam, but I owe it to myself to learn the truth.'

'What truth?'

'I am descended from you in the fifth degree. That is clear in the genealogical records. But is it possible that I am also descended in the fifth degree, not from Santirix Gremionis, but from the Earthman, Elijah Baley?'

Gladia rose to her feet as quickly as though the unidimensional force-fields of a puppeteer had lifted her. She was not aware that she had risen.

It was the third time in twelve hours that the name of that long-ago Earthman had been mentioned, and by three different individuals.

Her voice seemed not to be hers at all. 'What do you mean?'

He said, rising in his turn and backing away slightly, 'It seems to me plain enough. Was your son, my great-great-grandfather, born of the sexual union of yourself with the Earthman, Elijah Baley? Was Elijah Baley your son's father? I don't know how to express it more plainly.'

'How dare you make such a suggestion! Or even think it!'

'I dare, because my career depends upon it. If the answer is "yes", my professional life may well be ruined. I want a "no", but an unsupported "no" will do me no good. I must be able to present proof to Dr Amadiro at the appropriate time, and show him that his disapproval of my genealogy must end with you. After all, it is clear to me that his dislike of you, and even of Dr Fastolfe, is as nothing – nothing at all – compared to the incredible intensity of his detestation of the Earthman, Elijah Baley. It is not only the fact of his being short-lived, although the thought of having inherited barbarian genes would disturb me tremendously. I think that if I presented proof I was descended from an Earthman who was *not* Elijah Baley, he would dismiss that. But it is the thought of Elijah Baley, and only he, that drives him to madness. I do not know why.'

The reiteration of Elijah's name had made him seem almost alive again to Gladia. She was breathing harshly and deeply and she exulted in the best memory of her life.

'I know why,' she said. 'It was because Elijah, with everything against him, with all of Aurora against him, managed anyhow to destroy Amadiro at the moment when that man thought he held success in his hand. Elijah did it by the exercise of sheer courage and intelligence. Amadiro had met his infinite superior in the person of an Earthman he had carelessly despised, and what could he do in return but hate futilely? Elijah has been dead for more than sixteen decades and still Amadiro cannot forget, cannot forgive, cannot release the chains that bind him in hate and memory to that dead man. And I would not have Amadiro forget, or cease hating, as long as it poisons every moment of his existence.'

Mandamus said, 'I see you have reason for wishing Dr Amadiro ill, but what reason have you for wishing *me* ill? To allow Dr Amadiro to think I am descended from Elijah Baley will give him the pleasure of destroying me. Why should you give him that pleasure needlessly, if I am *not* so descended? Give me the proof, therefore, that I am descended from you and Santirix Gremionis, or from you and anybody but Elijah Baley.'

'You fool! You idiot! Why do you need proof from me? Go to the historical records. You will find the exact days on which Elijah Baley was on Aurora. You will find the exact day on which I gave birth to my son, Darrel. You will find that Darrel was conceived more than five years *after* Elijah left Aurora. You will also find that Elijah never returned to Aurora. Well, then, do you think I gestated for five years; that I carried a foetus in my womb for five Standard Galactic Years?'

'I know the statistics, madam. And I do not think you carried a foetus for five years.'

'Then why do you come to me?'

'Because there is more to it than that. I know – and I imagine that Dr Amadiro well knows – that although the Earthman, Elijah Baley, as you say, never returned to Aurora's surface, he was once in a ship that was in orbit about Aurora for a day or so. I know – and I imagine that Dr Amadiro well knows – that although the Earthman did not leave the ship to go to Aurora, you left Aurora to go to the ship; that you stayed on the ship for the better part of a day; and that this took place nearly five years after the Earthman had been on Aurora's surface; at about the time, in fact, that your son was conceived.'

Gladia felt the blood drain from her face as she heard the other's calm words. The room darkened about her and she swayed.

She felt the sudden, gentle touch of strong arms about her and knew they were those of Daneel. She felt herself lowered slowly into her chair.

She heard Mandamus's voice as though from a great distance.

'Is that not true, madam?' he said.

It was, of course, true.

2

The Ancestor?

5.

Memory!

Always there, of course, but usually remaining hidden. And then, sometimes, as a result of just the right kind of push, it could emerge suddenly, sharply-defined, all in colour, bright and moving and alive.

She was young again, younger than this man before her; young enough to feel tragedy and love – with her death-in-life on Solaria having reached its climax in the bitter end of the first whom she had thought of as 'husband' (no, she would not say his name even now, not even in thought).

Closer still to her then-life were the months of heaving emotion with the second – not-man – whom she had thought of by that term. Jander, the humanoid robot, had been given her and she had made him entirely her own until, like her first husband, he was suddenly dead.

And then, at last, there was Elijah Baley, who was never her husband, whom she had met only twice, two years apart, each time for a few hours on each of a very few days. Elijah, whose cheek she had once touched with her ungloved hand, on which occasion she had ignited; whose nude body she had later held in her arms, on which occasion she had flamed steadily at last.

And then, a third husband, with whom she was quiet and at peace, paying with untriumph for unmisery, and buying with firmly-held forgetfulness the relief from reliving.

Until one day (she was not sure of the day that so broke

in upon the sleeping untroubled years) Han Fastolfe, having asked permission to visit, walked over from his adjoining establishment.

Gladia looked upon him with some concern, for he was too busy a man to socialize lightly. Only five years had passed since the crisis that had established Han as Aurora's leading statesman. He was the Chairman of the planet in all but name, and the true leader of all the Spacer worlds. He had so little time to be a human being.

Those years had left their mark – and would continue to do so until he died sadly, feeling a failure though he had never lost a battle. Kelden Amadiro, who had been defeated, lived on sturdily, as evidence that victory can exact the greater penalty.

Fastolfe, through it all, continued to be soft-spoken and patient and uncomplaining, but even Gladia, non-political though she was, and uninterested in the endless machinations of power, knew that his control of Aurora held firm only through constant and unremitting effort that drained him of anything that might make life worthwhile, and that he held to it – or was held to it – only by what he considered the good of – what? Aurora? The Spacers? Simply some vague concept of idealized Good?

She didn't know. She flinched from asking.

But this was only five years after the crisis. He still gave the impression of a young and hopeful man, and his pleasant, homely face was still capable of smiling.

He said, 'I have a message for you, Gladia.'

'A pleasant one, I hope,' she said, politely.

He had brought Daneel with him. It was a sign of the healing of old wounds that she could look at Daneel with honest affection and no pain at all, for all that he was a copy of her dead Jander in all but the most insignificant detail. She could talk to him, though he answered in what was almost Jander's voice. Five years had skinned over the ulcer and deadened the pain.

'I hope so,' said Fastolfe, smiling gently. 'It's from an old friend.'

'It's so nice that I have old friends,' she said, trying not to be sardonic.

'From Elijah Baley.'

The five years vanished, and she felt the stab and pang of returning memory.

'Is he well?' she asked, in a half-strangled voice after a full minute of stunned silence.

'Quite well. What is even more important, he is near.'

'Near? On Aurora?'

'In orbit about Aurora. He knows he can receive no permission to land, even if I were to use my full influence, or I imagine he does. He would like to see you, Gladia. He has made contact with me because he feels that I can arrange to have you visit his ship. I suppose I can manage that much – but only if you wish it. Do you wish it?'

'I – I don't know. This is too sudden for thought.'

'Or even impulse?' he waited, then he said, 'Truthfully, Gladia, how are you getting along with Santirix?'

She looked at him wildly, as though not understanding the reason for the change of subject – then understanding. She said, 'We get along well together.'

'Are you happy?'

'I am – not unhappy.'

'That doesn't sound like ecstasy.'

'How long can ecstasy last, even if it were ecstasy?'

'Do you plan to have children some day?'

'Yes,' she said.

'Are you planning a change in marital status?'

She shook her head firmly. 'Not yet.'

'Then, my dear Gladia, if you want advice from a rather tired man, who feels uncomfortably old – refuse the invitation. I remember what little you told me after Baley had left Aurora and, to tell you the truth, I was able to deduce more from that than you perhaps think. If you see him, you may find it all disappointing, not living up to the deepening and mellowing glow of reminiscence; or, if it is not disappointing, worse yet, for it will disrupt a perhaps rather fragile contentment, which you will then not be able to repair.'

Gladia, who had been vaguely thinking precisely that, found the proposition needed only to be placed into words to be rejected.

She said, 'No, Han, I *must* see him, but I'm afraid to do it alone. Would you come with me?'

Fastolfe smiled wearily. 'I was not invited, Gladia. And if I were, I would in any case be forced to refuse. There is an important vote coming up in Council. Affairs of state, you know, from which I can't absent myself.'

'Poor Han!'

'Yes, indeed, poor me. But you can't go alone. As far as I know, you can't pilot a ship.'

'Oh! Well, I thought I'd be taken up by – '

'Commercial carrier?' Fastolfe shook his head. 'Quite impossible. For you to visit and board an Earth-ship in orbit openly, as would be unavoidable if you used a commercial carrier, would require special permission and that would take weeks. If you don't want to go, Gladia, you needn't put it on the basis of not wishing to see him. If the paperwork and red tape involved would take weeks, I'm sure he can't wait that long.'

'But I *do* want to see him,' said Gladia, now determined.

'In that case, you can take my private space-vessel and Daneel can take you up there. He can handle the controls very well indeed, and he would be as anxious to see Baley as you are. We just won't report the trip.'

'But you'll get into trouble, Han.'

'Perhaps no one will find out, or they'll pretend not to find out. And if anyone makes trouble, I will just have to handle it.'

Gladia's head bowed in a moment of thought, and then she said, 'If you don't mind, I will be selfish and chance your having trouble, Han. I want to go.'

'Then you'll go.'

5a.

It was a small ship, smaller than Gladia had imagined; cosy, in a way, but frightening, in another way. It was small enough, after all, to lack any provision for pseudo-gravity, and the sensation of weightlessness, while constantly nudging at her to indulge in amusing gymnastics, just as constantly reminded her that she was in an abnormal environment.

She was a Spacer. There were over five billion Spacers spread over fifty worlds, all of them proud of the name. Yet how many of those who called themselves Spacers were really space-travellers? Very few. Perhaps eighty per cent of them never left the world of their birth. Even of the remaining twenty per cent, hardly any passed through space more than two or three times.

Certainly she herself was no spacer in the literal sense of the word, she thought gloomily. Once (once!) she had travelled through space, and that was from Solaria to Aurora seven years before. Now she was entering space a second time on a small, private space-yacht, for a short trip just beyond the atmosphere, a paltry hundred thousand kilometres, with one other person – not even a person – for company.

She cast another glance at Daneel in the small pilot

room. She could just see a portion of him, where he sat at the controls.

She had never been anywhere with only one robot within call. There had always been hundreds – thousands – at her disposal on Solaria. On Aurora, there were routinely dozens, if not scores.

Here there was but one.

She said, 'Daneel!'

He did not allow his attention to wander from the controls. 'Yes, Madam Gladia?'

'Are you pleased that you will be seeing Elijah Baley again?'

'I am not certain, Madam Gladia, how best to describe my inner state. It may be that it is analogous to what a human being would describe as being pleased.'

'But you must feel something.'

'I feel as though I can make decisions more rapidly than I can ordinarily; my responses seem to come more easily; my movements seem to require less energy. I might interpret it generally as a sensation of well-being. At least I have heard human beings use that word, and feel that what it is intended to describe is something that is analogous to the sensations I now experience.'

Gladia said, 'But what if I were to say I wanted to see him alone?'

'Then that would be arranged.'

'Even though that meant you wouldn't see him?'

'Yes, madam.'

'Wouldn't you then feel disappointed? I mean, wouldn't you have a sensation that was the opposite of well-being? Your decisions would come less rapidly, your responses less easily, your movements would require more energy and so on?'

'No, Madam Gladia, for I would have a feeling of well-being at fulfilling your orders.'

'Your own pleasant feeling is Third Law, and fulfilling my orders is Second Law, and Second Law takes precedence. Is that it?'

'Yes, madam.'

Gladia struggled against her own curiosity. It would never have occurred to her to question an ordinary robot in this matter. A robot is a machine. But she couldn't think of Daneel as a machine, just as five years before she had been unable to think of Jander as a machine. But with Jander that had been only the burning of passion, and that had gone with Jander himself. For all his similarity to the other, Daneel could not set the ashes alight again. With him, there was room for intellectual curiosity.

'Doesn't it bother you, Daneel,' she asked, 'to be so bound by the Laws?'

'I cannot imagine anything else, Madam.'

'All my life I have been bound to the pull of gravity, even during my previous trip on a spaceship, but I can imagine *not* being bound by it. And here I am, in fact, *not* bound by it.'

'And do you enjoy it, madam?'

'In a way, yes.'

'Does it make you uneasy?'

'In a way, that, too.'

'Sometimes, madam, when I think that human beings are not bound by Laws, it makes me uneasy.'

'Why, Daneel? Have you ever tried to reason out to yourself *why* the thought of Lawlessness should make you feel uneasy?'

Daneel was silent for a moment. He said, 'I have, madam, but I do not think I would wonder about such things but for my brief association with Partner Elijah. He had a way –'

'Yes, I know,' she said. 'He wondered about everything.

He had a restlessness about him that drove him on to ask questions at all times in all directions.'

'So it seemed. And I would try to be like him and ask questions. So I asked myself what Lawlessness might be like and I found I couldn't imagine what it might be like except that it might be like being human and that made me feel uneasy. And I asked myself, as you asked me, why it made me feel uneasy.'

'And what did you answer yourself?'

Daneel said, 'After a long time, I decided that the Three Laws govern the manner in which my positronic pathways behave. At all times, under all stimuli, the Laws constrain the direction and intensity of positronic flow along those pathways so that I always know what to do. Yet the level of knowledge of what to do is not always the same. There are times when my doing-as-I-must is under less constraint than at other times. I have always noticed that the lower the positronomotive potential, then the further removed from certainty is my decision as to which action to take. And the further removed from certainty I am, the nearer I am to ill-being. To decide an action in a millisecond rather than a nanosecond produces a sensation I would not wish to be prolonged.

'What, then, I thought to myself, madam, if I were utterly without Laws as humans are? What if I could make no clear decision on what response to make to some given set of conditions? It would be unbearable, and I do not willingly think of it.'

Gladia said, 'Yet you do, Daneel. You are thinking of it, now.'

'Only because of my association with Partner Elijah, madam. I observed him under conditions when he was unable, for a time, to decide on an action, because of the puzzling nature of the problems that had been set him. He was clearly in a state of ill-being as a result, and I felt ill-being on his behalf because there was nothing I could do that would ease the situation for him. It is possible that I only grasped a very small part of what it was he felt then. If I had grasped a larger part and better understood the consequences of his inability to decide on action I might have – ' He hesitated.

'Ceased functioning? Been inactivated?' said Gladia, thinking briefly and painfully of Jander.

'Yes, madam. My failure to understand may be an in-built protection device against damage to my positronic brain. But then, I noted that no matter how painful Partner Elijah found his indecision to be, he continued to make an effort to solve his problem. I admired him greatly for that.'

'You are capable of admiration then, are you?'

Daneel said, solemnly, 'I use the word as I have heard human beings use it. I do not know the proper word to express the response within me elicited by Partner Elijah's actions of this sort.'

Gladia nodded, then said, 'And yet there are rules that govern human reactions, too; certain instincts, drives, teachings.'

'So Friend Giskard thinks, madam.'

'Does he now?'

'But he finds them too complicated to analyse. He wonders if there might someday be developed a system of analysing human behaviour in mathematical detail, and of deriving – from that – cogent Laws that would express the rules of that behaviour.'

'I doubt it,' said Gladia.

'Nor is Friend Giskard sanguine. He thinks it will be a very long time before such a system is developed.'

'A *very* long time, I should say.'

'And now,' said Daneel, 'we are approaching the Earthship, and we must carry through the docking procedure, which is not simple.'

5b.

It seemed to Gladia that it took longer to dock than to move into the Earth-ship's orbit in the first place.

Daneel remained calm throughout – but, then, he could not do otherwise – and assured her that all human ships could dock with each other regardless of difference in size and make.

'Like human beings,' said Gladia, forcing a smile, but Daneel made no response to that. He concentrated on the delicate adjustments that had to be made. Docking was always possible, perhaps, but not always easy, it would appear.

Gladia grew uneasier by the moment. Earthmen were short-lived and aged quickly. Five years had passed since she had seen Elijah. By how much would he have aged? How would he appear? Would she be able to keep from looking shocked or horrified at the change?

Whatever his appearance, he would still be the Elijah to whom her gratitude could know no bounds.

Was that what it was? Gratitude?

She noticed that her hands were tightly entwined with each other, so that her arms were aching. It was only with an effort that she could force them to relax.

She knew when docking was completed. The Earth-ship was large enough to have a pseudo-gravitation field-generator and, at the moment of docking, the field expanded to include the small yacht. There was a slight rotational effect as the direction towards the floor suddenly became 'down' and Gladia experienced a sickening drop of two inches. Her knees bent under the impact in lopsided fashion and she fell against the wall.

She straightened with a little difficulty and was annoyed

with herself for not having anticipated the change and been ready for it.

Daneel said, unnecessarily, 'We have docked, Madam Gladia. Partner Elijah asks permission to come aboard.'

'Of course, Daneel.'

There was a whirring sound and a portion of the wall swirled into dilation. A crouching figure moved through and the wall tightened and contracted behind it.

The figure straightened, and Gladia whispered, 'Elijah!' and felt overwhelmed with gladness and relief. It seemed to her that his hair was greyer, but otherwise it was Elijah. There was no other noticeable change, no marked ageing after all.

He smiled at her and, for a moment, seemed to devour her with his eyes. Then he lifted one forefinger, as though to say, Wait, and walked towards Daneel.

'Daneel!' He seized the robot's shoulders, and shook him. 'You haven't changed. Jehoshaphat! You're the constant in all our lives.'

'Partner Elijah. It is good to see you.'

'It is good to hear myself called partner again, and I wish that were so. This is the fifth time I have seen you, but the first time that I do not have a problem to solve. I am not even a plainclothesman any longer. I have resigned and I am now an immigrant to one of the new worlds. Tell me, Daneel, why didn't you come with Dr Fastolfe, when he visited Earth three years ago?'

'That was Dr Fastolfe's decision. He decided to take Giskard.'

'I was disappointed, Daneel.'

'It would have been pleasant for me to see you, Partner Elijah, but Dr Fastolfe told me afterwards that the trip had been highly successful, so that perhaps his decision was the correct one.'

'It *was* successful, Daneel. Before the visit, the Earth

government was reluctant to cooperate in the Settlement procedure, but now the whole planet is pulsing and heaving and, by the million, people are anxious to go. We don't have the ships to accommodate them all, even with Auroran help, and we don't have the worlds to receive them all, for every world must be adjusted. Not one will accommodate a human community unchanged. The one I'm going to is low in free oxygen and we're going to have to live in domed towns for a generation while Earth-type vegetation spreads over the planet.' His eyes were turning more and more often to Gladia as she sat there, smiling.

Daneel said, 'It is to be expected. From what I have learned of human history, the Spacer worlds also went through a period of terraforming.'

'They certainly did! And thanks to that experience, the process can be carried through more rapidly now. But I wonder if you would remain in the pilot room for a while, Daneel. I must speak to Gladia.'

'Certainly, Partner Elijah.'

Daneel stepped through the arched doorway that led into the pilot room, and Baley looked at Gladia in a questioning way and made a sideways motion with his hand.

She understood perfectly, walked over and touched the contact that drew the partition noiselessly across the doorway. They were, to all intents, alone.

Baley held out his hands. 'Gladia!'

She took them in hers, never even thinking she was ungloved. She said, 'Had Daneel stayed with us, he would not have hampered us.'

'Not physically. He would have, psychologically!' Baley smiled sadly and said, 'Forgive me, Gladia. I had to speak to Daneel first.'

'You've known him longer,' she said, softly. 'He takes precedence.'

'He doesn't – but he has no defences. If you are annoyed with me, Gladia, you can punch me in the eye if you want to. Daneel can't. I can ignore him, order him away, treat him as though he were a robot, and he would be compelled to obey and be the same loyal and uncomplaining partner.'

'The fact is that he *is* a robot, Elijah.'

'Never to me, Gladia. My mind knows he is a robot and has no feelings in the human fashion, but my heart considers him human and I must treat him so. I would ask Dr Fastolfe to let me take Daneel with me, but no robots are allowed on the new Settler worlds.'

'Would you dream of taking *me* with you, Elijah?'

'No Spacers, either.'

'It seems you Earthmen are as unreasoningly exclusive as we Spacers are.'

Baley nodded, glumly. 'Madness on both sides. But even if we were sane, I would not take you. You could not stand the life and I'd never be sure that your immune mechanisms would build up properly. I'd be afraid that you would either die quickly of some minor infection, or that you would live too long and watch our generations die. Forgive me, Gladia.'

'For what, dear Elijah?'

'For – this.' He put out his hands, palms upward, to either side. 'For asking to see you.'

'But I'm glad you did. I wanted to see you.'

He said, 'I know. I tried not to see you, but the thought of being in space and of not stopping at Aurora tore me apart. And yet it does no good, Gladia. It just means another leave-taking and that will tear me apart, too. It is why I have never written to you; why I have never tried to reach you by hyperwave. Surely you must have wondered.'

'Not really. I agree with you that there was no point. It would merely make it all infinitely harder. Yet I wrote to you many times.'

'You did? I never received one letter.'

'I never mailed one letter. Having written them, I destroyed them.'

'But why?'

'Because, Elijah, no private letter can be sent from Aurora to Earth without passing through the hands of the censor and I wrote you not one letter that I was willing to let the censors see. Had you sent me a letter, I assure you that not one would have reached me, however innocent it might have been. I thought that was why I never received a letter. Now that I know you weren't aware of the situation, I am extraordinarily glad that you were not so foolish as to try to remain in touch with me. You would have misunderstood my never answering your letters.'

Baley stared at her. 'How is it I see you now?'

'Not legally, I assure you. I am using Dr Fastolfe's private ship so I passed by the border-guards without being challenged. Had this ship not been Dr Fastolfe's, I would have been stopped and sent back. I assumed you understood that, too, and that that was why you were in touch with Dr Fastolfe and didn't try to reach me directly.'

'I understood nothing. I sit here amazed at the double ignorance that kept me safe. Triple ignorance, for I didn't know the proper hyperwave combination to reach you directly and I couldn't face the difficulty of trying to find the combination on Earth. I couldn't have done it privately and there was already sufficient comment all over the Galaxy about you and me, thanks to that foolish hyperwave drama they put on the subwaves after Solaria. Otherwise, I promise you, I would have tried. I had Dr Fastolfe's combination, however, and once I was in orbit around Aurora, I contacted him at once.'

'In any case, we're here.' She sat down on the side of her bunk and held out her hands.

Baley took them and tried to sit down on a stool, which

he had hitched over with one foot, but she drew him insistently towards the bunk and he sat down beside her.

He said, awkwardly, 'How is it with you, Gladia?'

'Quite well. And you, Elijah?'

'I grow old. I have just celebrated my fiftieth birthday three weeks ago.'

'Fifty is not – ' She stopped.

'For an Earthman, it's old. We're short-lived, you know.'

'Even for an Earthman, fifty is not old. You haven't changed.'

'It's kind of you to say so, but I can tell where the creaks have multiplied, Gladia – '

'Yes, Elijah?'

'I must ask. Have you and Santirix Gremionis – '

Gladia smiled and nodded. 'He is my husband. I took your advice.'

'And has it worked out well?'

'Well enough. Life is pleasant.'

'Good. I hope it lasts.'

'Nothing lasts for centuries, Elijah, but it could last for years; perhaps even for decades.'

'Any children?'

'Not yet. But what about your family, my married man? Your son? Your wife?'

'Bentley moved out to the Settlements two years ago. In fact, I'll be joining him. He's an official on the world I'm heading for. He's only 24 and already he's looked up to.' Baley's eyes danced. 'I think I'll have to address him as Your Honour. In public, anyway.'

'Excellent. And Mrs Baley? Is she with you?'

'Jessie? No. She won't leave Earth. I told her that we would be living in domes for a considerable time, so that it really wouldn't be so different from Earth. Primitive, of course. Still, she may change her mind in time. I'll make it as comfortable as possible, and once I've settled down, I'll ask Bentley to go to Earth and gather her in. She may be lonely enough by then to be willing to come. We'll see.'

'But meanwhile you're alone.'

'There are over a hundred other immigrants on the ship, so I'm not really alone.'

'They are on the other side of the docking wall, however. And I'm alone, too.'

Baley cast a brief, involuntary look towards the pilot room, and Gladia said, 'Except for Daneel, of course, who's on the other side of that door, and who is a robot, no matter how intensely you think of him as a person. And surely you haven't asked to see me only that we might ask after each other's families?'

Baley's face grew solemn, almost anxious. 'I can't ask you –'

'Then I ask you. This bunk is not really designed with sexual activity in mind, but you'll chance the possibility of falling out of it, I hope.'

Baley said, hesitantly, 'Gladia, I can't deny that –'

'Oh, Elijah, don't go into a long dissertation in order to satisfy the needs of your Earth-morality. I offer myself to you in accord with Auroran custom. It's your clear right to refuse, and I will have no right to question the refusal. Except that I would question it most forcefully. I have decided that the right to refuse belongs only to Aurorans. I won't take it from an Earthman.'

Baley sighed. 'I'm no longer an Earthman, Gladia.'

'I am even less likely to take it from a miserable immigrant heading out for a barbarian planet on which he will have to cower under a dome. Elijah, we have had so little time, and we have so little time now, and I may never see you again. This meeting is so totally unexpected that it would be a cosmic crime to toss it away.'

'Gladia, do you really want an old man?'

'Elijah, do you really want me to beg?'

'But I'm ashamed.'

'Then close your eyes.'

'I mean, of myself; of my decrepit body.'

'Then suffer. Your foolish opinion of yourself has nothing to do with me.' And she put her arms about him, even as the seam of her robe fell apart.

5c.

Gladia was aware of a number of things, all simultaneously.

She was aware of the wonder of constancy, for Elijah was as she had remembered him. The lapse of five years had not changed matters. She had not been living in the glow of a memory-intensified glitter. He was Elijah.

She was aware, also, of the puzzle of difference. Her feeling intensified that Santirix Gremionis, without a single major flaw that she could define, was all flaw. Santirix was affectionate, gentle, rational, reasonably intelligent – and flat. Why he was flat, she could not say, but nothing he did or said could rouse her as Baley did, even when he did and said nothing. Baley was older in years, much older physiologically, not as handsome as Santirix, and what was more, Baley carried with him the indefinable air of decay; of the aura of quick-ageing and short-life that Earthmen must. And yet –

She was aware of the folly of men, of Elijah approaching her with hesitation, with total inappreciation of his effect on her.

She was aware of his absence, for he had gone in to speak to Daneel, who was to be last as he was first. Earthmen feared and hated robots, and yet Elijah, knowing full well that Daneel was a robot, treated him only as a person. Spacers, on the other hand, who loved robots and were never comfortable in their absence, would never think of them as anything but machines.

Most of all, she was aware of time. She knew that exactly three hours and twenty-five minutes had elapsed since Elijah had entered Han Fastolfe's small vessel, and she knew further that not much more time could be allowed to elapse.

The longer she remained off Aurora's surface, and the longer Baley's ship remained in orbit, the more likely it was that someone would notice; or if the matter had already been noticed, as seemed almost certain, the more likely it would be that someone would become curious and investigate. And then Fastolfe would find himself in an annoying tangle of trouble.

Baley emerged from the pilot-room, and looked at Gladia sadly, 'I must go now, Gladia.'

'I know that well.'

Baley said, 'Daneel will take care of you. He will be your friend as well as protector, and you must be a friend to him – for my sake. But it is Giskard I want you to listen to. Let *him* be your adviser.'

Gladia frowned. 'Why Giskard? I'm not sure I like him.'

'I do not ask you to like him. I ask you to *trust* him.'

'But why, Elijah?'

'I can't tell you that. In this, you must trust me, too.'

They looked at each other and said no more. It was as though silence made time stop, allowed them to hold on to the seconds, and keep them motionless.

But it could only work so long. Baley said, 'You don't regret – '

Gladia whispered, 'How could I regret – when I may never see you again?'

Baley made as though to answer that, but she put her small, clenched fist against his mouth.

'Don't lie uselessly,' she said, 'I may never see you again.'

And she never did. Never!

6.

It was with pain that she felt herself drag into the present once more across the dead waste of years.

I never did, she thought. Never!

She had protected herself against the bitter-sweet so long, and now she had plunged into it – more bitter than sweet – because she had seen this person, this Mandamus – because Giskard had asked her to and because she was compelled to trust Giskard. It was *his* last request.

She focused on the present. (How much time had elapsed?)

Mandamus was looking at her coldly. He said, 'From your reaction, Madam Gladia, I gather that it *is* true. You could not have said so more plainly.'

'What is true? What are you talking about?'

'That you saw the Earthman, Elijah Baley, five years after his visit to Aurora. His ship was in orbit about Aurora; you travelled up to see him, and were with him about the time you conceived your son.'

'What evidence do you have for that?'

'Madam, it was not totally a secret. The Earthman's ship was detected in orbit. Fastolfe's yacht was detected in its flight. It was observed to dock. It was not Fastolfe who was on board the yacht, so the presumption was it was you. Dr Fastolfe's influence was sufficient to keep it off record.'

'If it is off record, there is no evidence.'

'Nevertheless, Dr Amadiro has spent the last two-thirds of his life following Dr Fastolfe's movements with the eyes of detestation. There were always government officials who were heart and soul with Dr Amadiro's policy of reserving the Galaxy for the Spacers, and they would report quietly to him anything they thought he would like to know. Dr Amadiro learned of your little escapade almost as soon as it happened.'

'It is still not evidence. The unsupported word of a minor official currying favour is of no account. Amadiro did nothing because even he knew he had no evidence.'

'No evidence with which he could charge anyone with even a misdemeanour; no evidence with which he could trouble Fastolfe; but evidence enough to suspect me of being a descendant of Baley's and to cripple my career therefore.'

Gladia said, bitterly, 'You may cease being troubled. My son is the son of Santirix Gremionis, a true Auroran, and it is from this son of Gremionis that you are descended.'

'Convince me of it, madam. I ask nothing better. Convince me that you fired up into orbit and that you spent hours alone with the Earthman and that, during that time, you talked – politics, perhaps – discussed old times and mutual friends – told funny stories – and never touched each other. Convince me.'

'What we did, did not matter, so spare me your sarcasm. At the time I saw him, I was already pregnant by my then husband. I was carrying a three-month-old foetus, an Auroran foetus.'

'Can you prove that?'

'Why should I have to prove it? The date of my son's birth is on record, and Amadiro must have the date of my visit to the Earthman.'

'He was told it at the time, as I said, but nearly twenty decades have passed and he doesn't remember exactly. The visit is not a matter of record and cannot be referred to. I fear that Dr Amadiro would prefer to believe that it was nine months before the birth of your son that you were with the Earthman.'

'Six months.'

'Prove it.'

'You have my word.'

'Insufficient.'

'Well, then – Daneel, you were with me. When did I see Elijah Baley?'

'Madam Gladia, it was 173 days before the birth of your son.'

Gladia said, 'Which is just under six months before the birth.'

'Insufficient,' said Mandamus.

Gladia's chin lifted. 'Daneel's memory is perfect, as can be easily demonstrated, and a robot's statements pass for evidence in the courts of Aurora.'

'This is not a matter for the courts and will not be, and Daneel's memory carries no weight with Dr Amadiro. Daneel was constructed by Fastolfe, and was maintained by Fastolfe for nearly two centuries. We cannot say what modifications were introduced, or how Daneel might have been instructed to deal with matters relating to Dr Amadiro.'

'Then reason it out, man. Earthmen are quite different genetically from us. We are virtually different species. We are not interfertile.'

'Unproven.'

'Well, then, genetic records exist. Darrel's do; Santirix's do. Compare them. If my ex-husband were not his father, the genetic differences would make that unmistakable.'

'Genetic records are not for anyone's eyes. You know that.'

'Amadiro is not that immersed in ethical considerations.

He has the influence to see them illegally. Or is he afraid of disproving his hypothesis?'

'Whatever the reason, madam, he will not betray an Auroran's right to privacy.'

Gladia said, 'Well, then, go to outer space and choke on vacuum. If your Amadiro refuses to be convinced, that is no affair of mine. You, at least, ought to be convinced, and it is your job to convince Amadiro in his turn. If you cannot, and if your career does not move onward as you would like to have it do, please be assured that this is entirely and intensely no concern of mine.'

'That does not surprise me. I expect nothing more. And for that matter, I *am* convinced. I was merely hoping that you would give me some material with which to convince Dr Amadiro. You haven't.'

Gladia, with disdain, shrugged.

'I will use other methods, then,' said Mandamus.

'I'm glad you have them,' Gladia said, coldly.

Mandamus said in a low voice, almost as though he were unaware of the presence of anyone else, 'So am I. There are powerful methods remaining to me.'

'Good. I suggest you try blackmail on Amadiro. He must have much to be blackmailed for.'

Mandamus looked up, suddenly frowning. 'Don't be a fool.'

Gladia said, 'You may go now. I think I have had all of you I wish to endure. Out of my establishment!'

Mandamus lifted his arms. 'Wait! I told you at the start that there were two reasons for seeing you; one a personal matter and one a matter of state. I have spent too long a time on the first, but I must request five minutes to discuss the second.'

'I'll give you no more than five minutes.'

'There is someone else who wants to see you. An

Earthman; or at least a member of one of the Settler worlds, a descendant of Earthpeople.'

'Tell him,' said Gladia, 'that neither Earthpeople nor their Settler descendants are allowed on Aurora, and send him away. Why do I have to see him?'

'Unfortunately, madam, in the last two centuries the balance of power has shifted somewhat. These Earthpeople have more worlds than we have, and have always had a far larger population. They have more ships even though those are not as advanced as ours, and because of their short lives and their fecundity they are apparently far readier to die than we are.'

'I don't believe that last.'

Mandamus smiled tightly. 'Why not? Eight decades mean less than forty do. In any case, we must treat them politely – far more politely than we ever had to in Elijah Baley's day. If it is any comfort to you, it is the policies of Fastolfe that have created this situation.'

'From whom do you speak, by the way? Is it Amadiro who must now bring himself to be polite to Settlers?'

'No. It is the Council, actually.'

'Are you the spokesman for the Council?'

'Not officially, but I have been asked to inform you of this – unofficially.'

'And if I see this Settler, what then? What does he want to see me about?'

'That is what we don't know, madam. We count on you to tell us. You are to see him, find out what he wants, and report to us.'

'Who is "us"?'

'As I said, the Council. The Settler will be here at your establishment this evening.'

'You seem to assume that I have no choice but to take on this position as informer.'

Mandamus rose to his feet, clearly done with his mission.

'You will not be an "informer". You owe nothing to this Settler. You are merely reporting to your government, as a loyal Auroran citizen should be willing, even eager, to do. You would not want the Council to suppose that your Solarian birth in any way dilutes your Auroran patriotism.'

'Sir, I have been an Auroran over four times as long as you've been alive.'

'Undoubtedly, but you were born and raised on Solaria. You are that unusual anomaly, a foreign-born Auroran, and it is difficult to forget it. This is especially true since the Settler wishes to see you, rather than anyone else on Aurora, precisely because you are Solarian-born.'

'How do you know that?'

'It is a fair presumption. He identifies you as "the Solarian woman". We are curious as to why that should mean anything to him – now that Solaria no longer exists.'

'Ask him.'

'We prefer to ask you – after you ask him. I must ask permission to leave now, and I thank you for your hospitality.'

Gladia nodded stiffly. 'I grant you your permission to leave with better will than I granted you my hospitality.'

Mandamus stepped towards the hallway that led to the main entrance, followed closely by his robots.

He paused just before leaving the room, turned, and said, 'I had almost forgotten – '

'Yes?'

'The Settler who wishes to see you has a surname that, by a peculiar coincidence, is Baley.'

3

The Crisis

Daneel and Giskard, with robotic courtesy, saw Mandamus and his robots off the grounds of the establishment; and then, since they were outside, toured those grounds, made certain that the lesser robots were in their places, and took note of the weather (cloudy, and a bit cooler than seasonal).

Daneel said, 'Dr Mandamus admitted openly that the Settler worlds are now stronger than the Spacer worlds. I would not have expected him to do that.'

Giskard said, 'Nor I. I was certain that the Settlers would increase in strength as compared with the Spacers because Elijah Baley had predicted it many decades ago, but I could see no way of determining when the fact would become obvious to the Auroran Council. It seemed to me that social inertia would keep the Council firmly convinced of Spacer superiority long after that had vanished, but I could not calculate for how long they would continue to delude themselves.'

'I am astonished that Partner Elijah foresaw this so long ago.'

'Human beings have ways of thinking about human beings that we have not.' Had Giskard been human, the remark might have been made with regret or envy, but, since he was a robot, it was merely factual.

He went on, 'I have tried to gain the knowledge, if not the way of thinking, by reading human history in great detail. Surely somewhere in the long tale of human events, there must be buried the Laws of Humanics that are equivalent to our Three Laws of Robotics.'

Daneel said, 'Madam Gladia once told me that this hope was an impossible one.'

'So that may be, Friend Daneel, for though it seems to me such Laws of Humanics must exist, I cannot find them. Every generalization I try to make, however broad and simple, has its numerous exceptions. Yet if such Laws existed and if I could find them, I could understand human beings better and be more confident that I am obeying the Three Laws in better fashion.'

'Since Partner Elijah understood human beings, he must have had some knowledge of the Laws of Humanics.'

'Presumably. But this he knew through something that human beings call intuition, a word I don't understand, signifying a concept I know nothing of. Presumably it lies beyond reason, and I have only reason at my command.'

7a.

That, and memory!

Memory that did not work after the human fashion, of course. It lacked the imperfect recall, the fuzziness, the additions and subtractions dictated by wishful thinking and self-interest, to say nothing of the lingerings and lacunae and backtracking that can turn memory into hours-long daydreaming.

It was robotic memory ticking off the events exactly as they had happened, but in vastly hastened fashion. The seconds reeled off in nanoseconds, so that days of events could be relived with such rapid precision as to introduce no perceptible gap in a conversation.

As Giskard had done innumerable times before, he relived that visit to Earth, always seeking for understanding of Elijah Baley's casual ability to foresee the future, always failing to find it.

Earth!

Fastolfe had come to Earth in an Auroran warship, with a full complement of fellow-passengers, both human and robot. Once in orbit, however, it was only Fastolfe who took the module in for a landing. Injections had stimulated his immune mechanism, and he wore the necessary gloves, coveralls, contact lenses and nose-plugs. He felt quite safe as a result but no other Auroran was willing to go along as part of a delegation.

This Fastolfe shrugged off, since it seemed to him (as he later explained to Giskard) that he would be more welcome if he came alone. A delegation would disagreeably remind Earth of the bad old days (to them) of Spacetown, when Spacers had a permanent base on Earth and directly dominated the world.

With him, Fastolfe brought Giskard, however. To have arrived without any robots would have been unthinkable, even for Fastolfe. To have arrived with more than one would have put a strain on the increasingly anti-robot Earthmen he hoped to see and with whom he intended to negotiate.

To begin with, of course, he would meet with Baley who would be his liaison with Earth and its people. That was the rational excuse for the meeting. The real reason was simply that Fastolfe wanted very much to see Baley again; he certainly owed him enough.

(That Giskard wanted to see Baley, and that he very slightly tightened the emotion and impulse in Fastolfe's brain to bring that about, Fastolfe had no way of knowing – or even imagining.)

Baley was waiting for them at the time of landing, and with him was a small group of Earth officials, so that there was a tedious passage of time during which politeness and protocol had their innings. It was some hours before Baley and Fastolfe could get away by themselves, and it might not have happened that soon but for Giskard's quiet and unfelt interference – with just a touch at the mind of the more important of those officials who were distinctly bored. (It was always safe to confine oneself to accentuating an emotion that already existed. It could almost never bring harm.)

Baley and Fastolfe sat in the smallness of a private dining room, that was ordinarily available only to high government officials. Food items could be punched out on a computerized menu and were then brought in by computerized carriers.

Fastolfe smiled. 'Very advanced,' he said, 'but these carriers are merely specialized robots. I'm surprised Earth uses them. They are not of Spacer manufacture, surely.'

'No, they're not,' said Baley, solemnly. 'Home-grown, so to speak. This is only for use at the top, and it's my first chance, ever, to experience it. I'm not likely to do so again.'

'You may be elected to high office some day, and then experience this sort of thing daily.'

'Never,' said Baley. The dishes were put before each of them, and the carrier was even sophisticated enough to ignore Giskard who stood, impassively, behind Fastolfe's chair.

For a while, Baley ate silently, and then, with a certain shyness, he said, 'It is good to see you again, Dr Fastolfe.'

'The pleasure is as much mine. I haven't forgotten that two years ago, when you were on Aurora, you managed to free me of the suspicion of the destruction of the robot, Jander, and to turn the tables neatly on my overconfident opponent, the good Amadiro.'

'I still shake when I think of it,' said Baley. 'And

greetings to you, too, Giskard. I trust you haven't forgotten me.'

'That would be quite impossible, sir,' said Giskard.

'Good! Well, Doctor, I trust the political situation on Aurora continues favourable. The news here would make it seem so, but I don't trust Earth analysis of Auroran affairs.'

'You may – at the moment. My party is in firm control of the Council. Amadiro maintains a sullen opposition but I suspect it will be years before his people recover from the blow you gave them. But how are things with you and with Earth?'

'Well enough. Tell me, Dr Fastolfe,' and Baley's face twitched slightly, as though with embarrassment, 'have you brought Daneel with you?'

Fastolfe said, slowly, 'I'm sorry, Baley. I did, but I left him back on the ship. I felt it might not be politic to be accompanied by a robot who looked so much like a human being. With Earth as anti-robot as it has become, I felt a humanoid robot might seem a deliberate provocation to them.'

Baley sighed. 'I understand.'

Fastolfe said, 'Is it true that your government is planning to prohibit the use of robots within the Cities?'

'I suspect it will soon come to that, with a period of grace, of course, to minimize financial loss and inconvenience. Robots will be restricted to the countryside, where they are needed for agriculture and mining. There, too, they may eventually be phased out, and the plan is to have no robots at all on the new worlds.'

'Since you mention the new worlds, has your son left Earth yet?'

'Yes, a few months ago. We have heard from him and he's arrived at a new world safely, along with several hundred Settlers, as they call themselves. The world has some native vegetation upon it and a low-oxygen atmosphere. Apparently, with time it can be made quite Earth-like. Meanwhile, some makeshift domes have been put up, new Settlers are advertised for and everyone is busily engaged in terraforming. Bentley's letters and occasional hyperwave contact are very hopeful, but they don't keep his mother from missing him badly.'

'And will you be going there, Baley?'

'I'm not sure that living on a strange world under a dome is my idea of happiness, Dr Fastolfe – I haven't Ben's youth and enthusiasm – but I think I'll have to in two or three years. In any case, I've already given notice to the Department of my intention to emigrate.'

'I imagine they must be upset over that.'

'Not at all. They say they are, but they're glad to get rid of me. I'm too notorious.'

'And how does Earth's government react to this drive for expansion into the Galaxy?'

'Nervously. They do not forbid it altogether, but certainly they are not cooperative. They continue to suspect that the Spacers are opposed to it and will do *something* unpleasant to stop it.'

'Social inertia,' said Fastolfe. 'They judge us according to our behaviour of years past. Surely we have made it plain that we now encourage Earth's colonization of new planets, and that we intend to colonize new planets of our own.'

'I hope you explain this to our government, then. But Dr Fastolfe, another question on a smaller point. How is – ' and with that, he stalled.

'Gladia?' said Fastolfe, hiding his amusement. 'Have you forgotten her name?'

'No, no. I merely hesitated to – to – '

'She's well,' said Fastolfe, 'and living comfortably. She

has asked me to remember her to you, but I imagine you need no nudging to recall her to mind.'

'The fact of her Solarian origin is not used against her, I hope?'

'No, nor is her role in the undoing of Dr Amadiro. Rather the reverse. I take care of her, I assure you. And yet I do not care to allow you to get off the subject altogether, Baley. What if Earth's officialdom continues to be opposed to immigration and expansion? Could the process continue despite such opposition?'

'Possibly,' said Baley, 'but not certainly. There's substantial opposition among Earthmen generally. It's hard to break away from the huge underground Cities that are our homes – '

'Your wombs.'

'Or our wombs, if you prefer. Going to new worlds, and having to live with the most primitive facilities for decades; never seeing comfort in one's own lifetime – that is difficult. When I think of it sometimes, I just decide not to go – especially if I'm passing a sleepless night. I've decided not to go a hundred times, and one day, I may just stick to that decision. And if *I* have trouble when, in a way, I originated the entire notion, then who else is likely to go freely and gladly? Without government encouragement – or, to be brutally frank – without the government shoe applied to the seat of the pants of the population, the whole project may fail.'

Fastolfe nodded. 'I will try to persuade your government. But if I fail?'

Baley said, in a low voice, 'If you fail, and if, therefore, our people fail, there remains only one alternative. The Spacers themselves must settle the Galaxy. The job must be done.'

'And will you be content to see the Spacers expand and

fill the Galaxy, while the Earthpeople remain on their single planet?'

'Not content at all, but it would be better than the present situation of no expansion by either. Many centuries ago, Earthpeople flocked to the stars, established some of the worlds that are now called Spacer worlds, and those first few colonized others. It has been a long time, however, since either the Spacers or Earthpeople have successfully settled and developed a new world. That must not be permitted to continue.'

'I agree. But what is your reason for wanting expansion, Baley?'

'I feel that without expansion of some sort, humanity cannot advance. It doesn't have to be geographical expansion, but that is the clearest way of inducing other kinds of expansion as well. If geographical expansion can be undertaken in a fashion that is not at the expense of other intelligent beings; if there are empty spaces into which to expand; then why not? To resist expansion under such circumstances is to ensure decay.'

'You see those alternatives, then? Expansion and advancement? Non-expansion and decay?'

'Yes, I believe so. Therefore, if Earth refuses expansion, then Spacers *must* accept it. Humanity, whether in the form of Earthpeople or Spacers, *must* expand. I would like to see Earthpeople undertake the task, but, failing that, Spacer expansion is better than no expansion at all. One alternative or the other.'

'And if one expands but not the other?'

'Then the expanding society will become steadily stronger, and the non-expanding one steadily weaker.'

'Are you certain of that?'

'It would be unavoidable, I think.'

Fastolfe nodded. 'Actually, I agree. It is why I am trying

to persuade *both* Earthpeople and Spacers to expand and advance. That is a third alternative, and, I think, the best.'

7b.

Memory flickered past the days that followed – incredible mobs of people moving ceaselessly past each other in streams and eddies – racing Expressways being mounted and dismounted – endless conferences with innumerable officials – minds in crowds.

Particularly minds in crowds.

Minds in crowds so thick that Giskard could not isolate individuals. Mass minds mixing and melting together into a vast pulsating greyness with all that was detectable being the periodic sparks of suspicion and dislike that shot outward every time one of the multitude paused to look at him.

Only when Fastolfe was in conference with a few officials could Giskard deal with the individual mind, and that, of course, was when it counted.

Memory slowed at one point near the end of the stay on Earth, when Giskard could finally manoeuvre a time alone with Baley again. Giskard adjusted a few minds minimally in order to make certain there would be no interruption for some time.

Baley said, apologetically, 'I haven't really been ignoring you, Giskard. I simply haven't had the opportunity to be alone with you. I don't rate highly on Earth and I cannot order my comings and goings.'

'I have, of course, understood that, sir, but we will have some time together now.'

'Good. Dr Fastolfe tells me that Gladia is doing well. He may be saying that out of kindness, knowing that that is what I want to hear. I order you to be truthful, however. Is Gladia, in fact, doing well?'

'Dr Fastolfe has told you the truth, sir.'

'And you remember, I hope, my request when I last saw you on Aurora that you guard Gladia and protect her from harm.'

'Friend Daneel and I, sir, are both mindful of your request. I have arranged it so that when Dr Fastolfe is no longer alive, both Friend Daneel and I will become part of Madam Gladia's establishment. We will then be in an even better position to keep her from harm.'

'That,' said Baley, sadly, 'will be after my time.'

'I understand that, sir, and regret it.'

'Yes, but it can't be helped, and a crisis will come – or may come – even before that, and yet still be after my time.'

'What is it, sir, that you have in mind? What is this crisis?'

'Giskard, it is a crisis that may arise because Dr Fastolfe is a surprisingly persuasive person. Or else, there is some other factor associated with him that is accomplishing the task.'

'Sir?'

'Every official that Dr Fastolfe has seen and interviewed now seems to be enthusiastically in favour of emigration. They were not in favour earlier or, if they were, it was with strong reservations. And once the opinion-making leaders are in favour, others are sure to follow. This will spread like an epidemic.'

'Is not this what you wish, sir?'

'Yes, it is, but it is almost too much what I wish. We shall spread out over the Galaxy – but what if the Spacers don't?'

'Why should they not?'

'I don't know. I advance it as a supposition, a possibility. What if they don't?'

'Earth and the worlds its people settle will then grow stronger, according to what I have heard you say.'

'And the Spacers will grow weaker. There will, however, be a period of time during which the Spacers will remain stronger than Earth and its Settlers, though by a steadily diminishing margin. Eventually, the Spacers will inevitably become aware of Earthpeople as a growing danger. At that time the Spacer worlds will surely decide that Earth and the Settlers must be stopped before it is too late and it will seem to them that drastic measures will have to be taken. That will be a period of crisis that will determine the entire future history of human beings.'

'I see your point, sir.'

Baley remained in thoughtful silence for a moment, then said, in very nearly a whisper as though dreading being overheard, 'Who knows of your abilities?'

'Among human beings, only yourself, and you cannot mention it to others.'

'I know well I can't. The point is, though, that it is you, not Fastolfe, who has engineered the turnaround that has made every official with whom you've come in contact a proponent of emigration. And it is to bring that about that you arranged to have Fastolfe take you, rather than Daneel, to Earth with him. You were essential and Daneel might have been a distraction.'

Giskard said, 'I felt it necessary to keep personnel to a minimum in order to avoid making my task harder by abrading the sensitivities of Earthpeople. I regret, sir, Daneel's absence. I fully sense your disappointment at not being able to greet him.'

'Well – ' Baley shook his head. 'I understand the necessity, and I rely on your explaining to Daneel that I badly missed him. In any case, I am still making my point.

If Earth embarks on a great policy of world-settlement and if the Spacers are left behind in the race to expand, the responsibility for that, and therefore for the crisis that will inevitably arise, will be yours. You must, for that reason, feel it your further responsibility to use your abilities to protect Earth when the crisis comes.'

'I will do what I can, sir.'

'And should you succeed there, Amadiro, or his followers, may turn on Gladia. You must not forget to protect her, too.'

'Daneel and I will not forget.'

'Thank you, Giskard.'

And they parted.

When Giskard, following Fastolfe, entered the module to begin the voyage back to Aurora, he saw Baley once again. This time there was no opportunity to speak to him.

Baley waved and mouthed one soundless word: Remember.

Giskard sensed the word and, in addition, the emotion behind it.

After that, Giskard never saw Baley again. Never.

8.

Giskard had never found it possible to flip through the sharp images of that one visit to Earth, without then following it with the images of the key visit to Amadiro at the Institute of Robotics.

It had not been an easy conference to arrange. Amadiro, with the bitterness of defeat heavy upon him, would not exacerbate his humiliation by going to Fastolfe's establishment.

'Well, then,' Fastolfe had said to Giskard. 'I can afford

to be magnanimous in victory. I will go to him. Besides, I *must* see him.'

Fastolfe had been a member of the Institute of Robotics since Baley had made possible the crushing of Amadiro and of his political ambitions. In return, Fastolfe had passed over to the Institute all the data for the building and maintenance of humaniform robots. A number had been manufactured, and then the project had come to an end and Fastolfe had chafed.

It had been Fastolfe's intention, at first, to arrive at the Institute without any robot companion. He would have placed himself, without protection and (so to speak) naked, into the midst of what was still the stronghold of the enemy's camp. It would have been a sign of humility and trust; but it would also have been an indication of complete self-confidence, and Amadiro would have understood that. Fastolfe, entirely alone, would be demonstrating his certainty that Amadiro, with all the resources of the Institute at his command, would not dare to touch his single enemy coming carelessly and defencelessly within reach of his fist.

And yet in the end, Fastolfe, not quite knowing how, chose to have Giskard accompany him.

Amadiro seemed to have lost a little weight since last Fastolfe had seen him, but he was still a formidable specimen; tall and heavy-set. He lacked the self-confident smile that had once been his hallmark, and when he attempted it at Fastolfe's entrance, it seemed more like a snarl that faded into a look of sombre dissatisfaction.

'Well, Kelden,' said Fastolfe, making free with the other's familiar name, 'we don't see each other often despite the fact that we have now been colleagues for four years.'

'Let's not have any false bonhomie, Fastolfe,' said Amadiro, in a clearly annoyed and low-pitched growl, 'and address me as Amadiro. We are not colleagues except in name, and I make no secret, and never have, of my belief that your foreign policy is suicidal for us.'

Three of Amadiro's robots, large and gleaming, were present, and Fastolfe studied them with raised eyebrows. 'You are well-protected, Amadiro, against one man of peace together with his single robot.'

'They will not attack you, Fastolfe, as you well know. But why did you bring Giskard? Why not your masterpiece, Daneel?'

'Would it be safe to bring Daneel within your reach, Amadiro?'

'I take it you intend that as humour. I no longer need Daneel. We build our own humaniforms.'

'On the basis of my design.'

'With improvements.'

'And yet you do not use the humaniforms. That is why I have come to see you. I know that my position in the Institute is a name-only thing, and that even my presence is unwelcome, let alone my opinions and recommendations. However, I must, as an Institute member, protest at your failure to use the humaniforms.'

'How do you wish me to use them?'

'The intention was to have the humaniforms open up new worlds into which Spacers could eventually emigrate, after those worlds had been terraformed and made completely habitable, wasn't it?'

'But that was something you opposed, Fastolfe, wasn't it?'

Fastolfe said, 'Yes, I did. I wanted Spacers themselves to emigrate to new worlds and to do their own terraforming. That, however, is not happening, and, I now see, is not likely to happen. Let us send the humaniforms, then. That would be better than nothing.'

'All our alternatives come to nothing, as long as your

views dominate the Council, Fastolfe. Spacers will not travel to rude and unformed worlds; nor, it seems, do they like humaniform robots.'

'You have scarcely given the Spacers a chance to like them. Earthpeople are beginning to settle new planets; even rude and unformed ones. And they do it without robotic help.'

'You know very well the differences between Earthpeople and ourselves. There are eight billion Earthpeople plus a large number of settlers.'

'And there are five and a half billion Spacers.'

'Numbers are not the sole difference,' said Amadiro, bitterly. 'They breed like insects.'

'They do not. Earth's population has been fairly stable for centuries.'

'The potential is there. If they put all their heart into emigration, they can easily produce 160 million new bodies each year, and that number will rise as the new worlds fill up.'

'We have the biological capability of producing 100 million new bodies each year.'

'But not the sociological capability. We are long-lived; we do not wish ourselves replaced so quickly.'

'We can send a large portion of the new bodies to other worlds.'

'They won't go. We value our bodies, which are strong, healthy, and capable of surviving in strength and health for nearly forty decades. Earthmen can place no value on bodies that wear out in less than ten decades, and that are riddled with disease and degeneration even over that short period of time. It doesn't matter to them if they send out millions a year to certain misery and probable death. In fact, even the victims needn't fear misery and death, for what else do they have on Earth? The Earthpeople who emigrate are fleeing from their pestilential world knowing well that any change can scarcely be for the worse. We, on the other hand, value our well-wrought and comfortable planets and would not lightly give them up.'

Fastolfe sighed and said, 'I've heard all these arguments so often. May I point out the simple fact, Amadiro, that Aurora was originally a rude and unformed world that had to be terraformed into acceptability, and that so was every Spacer world?'

Amadiro said, 'And I have heard all your arguments to the point of nausea, but I will not weary of answering them. Aurora may have been primitive when first settled, but Aurora was settled by Earthpeople, and other Spacer worlds, when not settled by Earthpeople, were settled by Spacers that had not yet outgrown their Earth heritage. The times are no longer suitable for that. What could be done then, cannot be done now.'

Amadiro lifted a corner of his mouth in a snarl and went on, 'No, Fastolfe, what your policy has accomplished has been to begin the creation of a Galaxy that will be populated by Earthmen only, while Spacers must wither and decline. You can see it happening now. Your famous trip to Earth, two years ago, was the turning point. Somehow, you betrayed your own people by encouraging those half-humans to begin an expansion. In only two years there are at least some Earthpeople on each of twenty-four worlds and new ones are being added steadily.'

Fastolfe said, 'Do not exaggerate. Not one of those Settler worlds is truly fit for human occupation yet and won't be for some decades. Not all are likely to survive and, as the nearer worlds are occupied, the chances for settling farther worlds diminish so that the initial surge will slow down. I encouraged *their* expansion, because I counted on ours as well. We can still keep up with them, if we make the effort and, in healthy competition, we can fill the Galaxy together.'

'No,' said Amadiro. 'What you have in mind is that most destructive of all policies, a foolish idealism. The expansion is one-sided and will remain so despite anything you can do. The people of Earth swarm unhindered, and they will have to be stopped before they get too strong to stop.'

'How do you propose to do that? We have a treaty of friendship with Earth in which we specifically agree not to stop their expansion into space as long as no planet within twenty light years of a Spacer world is touched. They have adhered to this scrupulously.'

Amadiro said, 'Everyone knows about the treaty. Everyone also knows that no treaty has ever been kept once it begins to work against the national interests of the more powerful signatory. I attach no value to that treaty.'

'I do. It will be held to.'

Amadiro shook his head. 'You have touching faith. How will it be held to after you are out of power?'

'I don't intend to be out of power for a while.'

'As Earth and its Settlers grow stronger, the Spacers will grow fearful and you will not remain long in power after that.'

Fastolfe said, 'And if you tear up the treaty and destroy the Settler worlds and slam the gates shut on Earth, will the Spacers then emigrate and fill the Galaxy?'

'Perhaps not. But if we decide not to; if we decide we are comfortable as we are; what difference will that make?'

'The Galaxy will not, in that case, become a human empire.'

'And if it does not, what then?'

'Then the Spacers will stultify and degenerate even if Earth is kept in prison and also stultifies and degenerates.'

'That is just the claptrap your party puts out, Fastolfe. There is no actual evidence that such a thing would happen. And even if it does, that will be *our* choice. At least we will not see the barbarian short-lifers fall heir to the Galaxy.'

Fastolfe said, 'Are you seriously suggesting, Amadiro, that you would be willing to see the Spacer civilization die, provided you can prevent Earth from expanding?'

'I'm not counting on our death, Fastolfe, but if the worst happens, why, yes, to me our own death is a less fearful thing than the triumph of a sub-human, disease-riddled set of short-lived beings.'

'From whom we are descended.'

'And with whom we are no longer truly related genetically. Are we worms because a billion years ago, worms were among our ancestors?'

Fastolfe, lips pressed together, rose to go. Amadiro, glowering, made no move to stop him.

9.

Daneel had no way of telling, directly, that Giskard was lost in memory. For one thing, Giskard's expression did not change, and for another, he was not lost in memory as humans might be. It took no substantial period of time.

On the other hand, the line of thought that had caused Giskard to think of the past, had caused Daneel to think of the same events of that past as they had long ago been recounted to him by Giskard. Nor was Giskard surprised at that.

Their conversation carried on with no unusual pause, but in a markedly new manner, as though each had thought of the past on behalf of both.

Daneel said, 'It might seem, Friend Giskard, that since the people of Aurora now recognize that they are weaker than Earth and its many Settler worlds, the crisis that Elijah Baley foresaw has been safely passed.'

'It might seem so, Friend Daneel.'

'You laboured to bring that about.'

'I did. I kept the Council in Fastolfe's hand. I did what I could to mould those who, in turn, moulded public opinion.'

'Yet I am uneasy.'

Giskard said, 'I have been uneasy through every stage of the process, although I endeavoured to do no harm to anyone. I have touched – mentally – not one human being who required anything more than the lightest touch. On Earth, I had merely to lighten the fear of reprisal, and chose those, particularly, in which the fear was already light and broke a thread that was, in any case, frayed and on the point of breaking. On Aurora, it was reversed. The policy-makers here were reluctant to espouse policies that would lead to an exit from their comfortable world, and I merely confirmed that and made the sturdy cord that held them a bit stronger. And doing this has immersed me in a constant, if faint, turmoil.'

'Why? You encouraged the expansion of Earth and discouraged the expansion of the Spacers. Surely, that is as it should be?'

'As it should be? Do you think, Friend Daneel, that an Earthperson counts for more than a Spacer, even though both are human beings?'

'There are differences. Elijah Baley would rather see his own Earthpeople defeated than see the Galaxy uninhabited. Dr Amadiro would rather see both Earth and Spacers dwindle than see Earth expand. The first looks with hope to the triumph of either, the second is content to see the triumph of neither. Should we not choose the first, Friend Giskard?'

'Yes, Friend Daneel. So it would seem. And yet how far are you influenced by your feeling of the special worth of your one-time partner, Elijah Baley?'

Daneel said, 'I value the memory of Partner Elijah, and the people of Earth are his people.'

'I see you do. I have been saying for many decades that you tend to think like a human being, Friend Daneel, but I wonder if that is necessarily a compliment. Still, though you tend to think *like* a human being, you are *not* a human being and, in the end, you are bound to the Three Laws. You may not harm a human being, whether that human being is an Earthman or a Spacer.'

'There are times, Friend Giskard, when one must choose one human being over another. We have been given special orders to protect the Lady Gladia. I would be forced, on occasion, to harm a human being in order to protect the Lady Gladia, and I think that, all things being equal, I would be willing to harm a Spacer just a little in order to protect an Earthperson.'

'So you think. But in the actual event, you would have to be guided by specific circumstances. You will find you cannot generalize,' said Giskard. 'And so it is with me. In encouraging Earth and discouraging Aurora, I have made it impossible for Dr Fastolfe to persuade the Auroran government to sponsor a policy of emigration and to set up two expanding powers in the Galaxy. I could not help but realize that that portion of his labours were brought to nothing. This was bound to fill him with gathering despair, and perhaps it hastened his death. I have felt this in his mind and that has been painful. And yet, Friend Daneel –'

Giskard paused, and Daneel said, 'Yes?'

'To have not done as I had done might have greatly lowered Earth's ability to expand, without greatly improving Aurora's moves in that direction. Dr Fastolfe would then have been frustrated in both ways, Earth *and* Aurora, and would moreover have been ousted from his seat of power by Dr Amadiro. His sense of frustration would have been greater. It was Dr Fastolfe, during his lifetime, to whom I owed my greatest loyalty, and I chose that course of action which frustrated him less, without measurably harming other individuals I dealt with. If Dr Fastolfe was continually disturbed by his inability to persuade Aurorans, and Spacers generally, to expand to new worlds, he was at least delighted by the activity of the emigrating Earthpeople.'

'Could you not have encouraged both the people of Earth *and* of Aurora, Friend Giskard, and thus have satisfied Dr Fastolfe in both respects?'

'That of course, had occurred to me, Friend Daneel. I considered the possibility and decided it would not do. I could encourage Earthpeople to emigrate by means of a trifling change that would do no harm. To have attempted the same for Aurorans would have required a great enough change to do much harm. The First Law prevented that.'

'A pity.'

'True. Think what might have been done, if I could have radically altered the mind-set of Dr Amadiro. Yet how could I have changed his fixed determination to oppose Dr Fastolfe? It would have been much like trying to force his head to make a 180 degree turn. So complete a turnabout of either the head itself or of its emotional content would kill with, I think, equal efficiency.

'The price of my power, Friend Daneel,' Giskard went on, 'is the greatly increased dilemma into which I am constantly plunged. The First Law of Robotics, which forbids injury to human beings, deals, ordinarily, with the visible physical injuries that we can, all of us, easily see, and concerning which we can easily make judgements. I, alone, however, am aware of human emotions and of casts of mind, so that I know of more subtle forms of injury without being able to understand them completely. I am forced on many occasions to act without true certainty and this puts a continuing stress on my circuits.

'And yet I feel I have done well. I have carried the Spacers past the crisis point. Aurora is aware of the gathering strength of the Settlers and will now be forced to avoid conflict. They must recognize it to be too late for retaliation, and our promise to Elijah Baley is, in that respect, fulfilled. We have put Earth on the course towards the filling of the galaxy and the establishment of a Galactic Empire.'

They were, at this point, walking back to Gladia's house, but now Daneel stopped and the gentle pressure of his hand on Giskard's shoulder caused the other to stop as well.

Daneel said, 'The picture you draw is attractive. It would make Partner Elijah proud of us if, as you say, we have accomplished that. "Robots and Empire" Elijah would say, and perhaps he would clap me on the shoulder. And yet, as I said, I am uneasy, Friend Giskard.'

'Concerning what, Friend Daneel?'

'I cannot help but wonder if indeed we have actually passed the crisis that Partner Elijah spoke of so many decades ago. Is it, in actual fact, too late for Spacer retaliation?'

'Why do you have these doubts, Friend Daneel?'

'I have been made doubtful by the behaviour of Dr Mandamus in the course of his conversation with Madam Gladia.'

Giskard's gaze was fixed on Daneel for a few moments and in the quiet they could hear leaves rustling in the cool breeze. The clouds were breaking and the sun would make its appearance soon. Their conversation, in its telegraphic fashion, had taken little time and Gladia, they knew, would not yet be wondering at their absence.

Giskard said, 'What was there in the conversation that would give you cause for uneasiness?'

Daneel said, 'I have had the opportunity, on four separate occasions, to observe Elijah Baley's handling of a puzzling problem. On each of those four occasions, I have noted the manner in which he managed to work out useful conclusions from limited, and even misleading, information. I have since always tried, within my limitations, to think as he did.'

'It seems to me, Friend Daneel, you have done well in this respect. I have said you tend to think like a human being.'

'You will have noticed, then, that Dr Mandamus had two matters he wished to discuss with Madam Gladia. He emphasized that fact himself. One was the matter of his own descent, whether from Elijah Baley or not. The second was the request that Madam Gladia see a Settler and report on the event afterwards. Of these, the second might be viewed as a matter that would be important to the Council. The first would be a matter of importance only to himself.'

Giskard said, 'Dr Mandamus presented the matter of his descent as being of importance to Dr Amadiro as well.'

'Then it would be a matter of personal importance to two people rather than one, Friend Giskard. It would still not be a matter of importance to the Council and, therefore, to the planet generally.'

'Proceed then, Friend Daneel.'

'Yet the matter of state, as Dr Mandamus himself referred to it, was taken up second, almost as an afterthought, and was disposed of almost at once. Indeed, it seemed scarcely something that required a personal visit. It might have been handled by holographic image by any official of the Council. On the other hand, Dr Mandamus dealt with the matter of his own descent first, discussed it in great detail and it was a matter that could have been handled only by him and by no one else.'

'What is your conclusion, Friend Daneel?'

'I believe that the matter of the Settler was seized upon by Dr Mandamus as an excuse for a personal conversation with Madam Gladia, in order that he might discuss his descent in privacy. It was the matter of his descent and nothing else that truly interested him. Is there any way you can support that conclusion, Friend Giskard?'

Aurora's sun had not yet emerged from the clouds and the faint glow of Giskard's eyes was visible. He said, 'The tension in Dr Mandamus's mind was indeed measurably stronger in the first part of the interview than in the second. That may serve as corroboration, perhaps, Friend Daneel.'

Daneel said, 'Then we must ask ourselves why the question of Dr Mandamus's descent should be a matter of such importance to him.'

Giskard said, 'Dr Mandamus explained that. It is only by demonstrating that he is not descended from Elijah Baley that his road to advancement is open. Dr Amadiro, upon whose good-will he is dependent, would turn against him absolutely if he were a descendant of Mr Baley.'

'So he said, Friend Giskard, but what took place during the interview argues against that.'

'Why do you say so? Please continue thinking like a human being, Friend Daneel. I find it instructive.'

Daneel said, gravely, 'Thank you, Friend Giskard. Did you note that not one statement that Madam Gladia made concerning the impossibility of Dr Mandamus's descent from Partner Elijah was considered convincing? In every case, Dr Mandamus said that Dr Amadiro would not accept the statement.'

'Yes, and what do you deduce from that?'

'It seems to me that Dr Mandamus was so convinced

that Dr Amadiro would accept no argument against Elijah Baley as ancestor that one must wonder why he should have bothered to ask Madam Gladia about the matter. He apparently knew from the start that it would be pointless to do so.'

'Perhaps, Friend Daneel, but it is mere speculation. Can you supply a possible motive for his action, then?'

'I can. I believe he inquired as to his descent, not to convince an implacable Dr Amadiro, but to convince himself.'

'In that case, why should he have mentioned Dr Amadiro at all? Why not simply have said, "I wish to know"?'

A small smile passed over Daneel's face, a change of expression of which the other robot would have been incapable. Daneel said, 'Had he said, "I wish to know", to Madam Gladia, she would surely have replied that it was none of his business and he would have discovered nothing. Madam Gladia, however, is as strongly opposed to Dr Amadiro as Dr Amadiro is to Elijah Baley. Madam Gladia would be sure to take offence at any opinion strongly held by Dr Amadiro concerning her. She would be furious even if the opinion were more or less true; how much more, then, if it were absolutely false, as in this case. She would labour to demonstrate Dr Amadiro to be wrong and would present every piece of evidence needed to achieve that end.

'In such a case, Dr Mandamus's cold assurance that each piece of evidence was insufficient would but make her the angrier and would drive her to further revelations. Dr Mandamus's strategy was chosen to make certain he would learn the maximum from Madam Gladia and at the end, *he* was convinced that he did not have an Earthman as ancestor; at least, not as recently as twenty decades ago. Amadiro's feelings in this regard, were not, I think, truly in question.'

Giskard said, 'Friend Daneel, this is an interesting point of view, but it does not seem to be strongly founded. In what way can we conclude that it is no more than a guess on your part?'

Daneel said, 'Does it not seem to you, Friend Giskard, that when Dr Mandamus ended his inquiry into his descent without having obtained sufficient evidence for Dr Amadiro, as he would have had us believe, that he should have been distinctly depressed and disheartened? By his own statement, this should have meant he had no chance for advancement and would never gain the position as Head of the Institute of Robotics. And yet it seemed to me that he was far from depressed but was, indeed, jubilant. I can only judge by outward appearance, but you can do better. Tell me, Friend Giskard, what was his mental attitude at the conclusion of this portion of his conversation with Madam Gladia?'

Giskard said, 'As I look back on it, it was not only jubilant, but triumphant, Friend Daneel. You are right. Now that you have explained your process of thought, that sensation of triumph I detected clearly marks the accuracy of your reasoning. In fact, now that you have marked it all out, I find myself at a loss to account for my inability to see it for myself.'

'That, Friend Giskard, was, on a number of occasions, my reaction to the reasoning of Elijah Baley. That I could carry through such reasoning on this occasion may be, in part, because of the strong stimulus of the existence of the present crisis. It forces me to think more cogently.'

'You underestimate yourself, Friend Daneel. You have been thinking cogently for a long time. But why do you speak of a present crisis? Pause a moment and explain. How does one go from Dr Mandamus's feeling of triumph at not being descended from Mr Baley to this crisis you speak of?'

Daneel said, 'Dr Mandamus may have deceived us in his statements concerning Dr Amadiro, but it may be fair to suppose that it is nevertheless true that he longs for advancement; that he is ambitious to become Head of the Institute. Is that not so, Friend Giskard?'

Giskard paused a moment, as though in thought, then said, 'I was not searching for ambition. I was studying his mind without particular purpose and was aware of only surface manifestations. Yet there might have been flashes of ambition there when he spoke of advancement. I do not have strong grounds for agreeing with you, Friend Daneel, but I have no grounds at all for disagreeing with you.'

'Let us accept Dr Mandamus as an ambitious man, then, and see where that takes us. Agreed?'

'Agreed.'

'Then does it not seem likely that his sense of triumph, once he was convinced that he was not descended from Partner Elijah, arose from the fact that he felt his ambition could now be served? This would not be so, however, because of Dr Amadiro's approval, since we have agreed that the Dr Amadiro motif was introduced by Dr Mandamus as a distraction. His ambition could now be served for some other reason.'

'What other reason?'

'There is none that arises out of compelling evidence. But I can suggest one as a matter of speculation. What if Dr Mandamus knows something or can do something that would lead to some huge success; one that would surely make him the next Head? Remember that at the conclusion of the search into the manner of his descent, Dr Mandamus said, "There are powerful methods remaining to me". Suppose that is true, but that he could only use those methods if he were *not* descended from Partner Elijah. His jubilation over having been convinced of his non-descent would arise, then, from the fact that he could now use those methods and assure himself of great advancement.'

'But what are these "powerful methods", Friend Daneel?'

Daneel said gravely, 'We must continue to speculate. We know that Dr Amadiro wants nothing so much as to defeat Earth and force it back to its earlier position of subservience to the Spacer worlds. If Dr Mandamus has a way of doing this, he can surely get anything he wants out of Dr Amadiro, up to and including a guarantee of succession to the Headship. Yet it may be that Dr Mandamus would hesitate to bring about Earth's defeat and humiliation unless he felt no kinship to its people. Descent from Elijah Baley of Earth would inhibit him. The denial of that descent frees him to act and that makes him jubilant.'

Giskard said, 'You mean Dr Mandamus is a man of conscience?'

'Conscience?'

'It is a word human beings sometimes use. I have gathered that it is applied to a person who adheres to rules of behaviour that force him to act in ways that oppose his immediate self-interest. If Dr Mandamus feels that he cannot allow himself to advance at the expense of those with whom he is distantly connected, I imagine him to be a man of conscience. I have thought much of such things, Friend Daneel, since they seem to imply that human beings do have Laws governing their behaviour, at least in some cases.'

'And can you tell whether Dr Mandamus is, indeed, a man of conscience?'

'From my observations of his emotions? No, I was not watching for anything like that, but if your analysis is correct, conscience would seem to follow. And yet, on the other hand, if we begin by supposing him a man of conscience, and argue backwards, we can come to other conclusions. It might seem that if Dr Mandamus thought he had an Earthman in his ancestry a mere twenty decades ago, he might feel driven, against his conscience, to spearhead an attempt to defeat Earth as a way of freeing himself from the stigma of such descent. If he were not so descended, then he would not be unbearably driven to act against Earth, and his conscience would be free to cause him to leave Earth alone.'

Daneel said, 'No, Friend Giskard. That would not fit the facts. However relieved he might be at not having to take violent action against Earth, he would be left without a way of satisfying Dr Amadiro and enforcing his own advance. Considering his ambitious nature, he would not be left with the feeling of triumph you so clearly noted.'

'I see. Then we conclude that Dr Mandamus has a method for defeating Earth?'

'Yes. And if that is so, then the crisis foreseen by Partner Elijah has not been safely passed after all, but is now here.'

Giskard said thoughtfully, 'But we are left with the key question unanswered, Friend Daneel. What is the nature of the crisis? What is the deadly danger? Can you deduce that, too?'

'That I cannot do, Friend Giskard. I have gone as far as I can. Perhaps Partner Elijah might have gone farther were he still alive, but I cannot. Here I must depend upon you, Friend Giskard.'

'Upon me? In what way?'

'You can study the mind of Dr Mandamus, as I cannot; as no one else can. You can discover the nature of the crisis.'

'I fear I cannot, Friend Daneel. If I lived with a human being over an extended period, as once I lived with Dr Fastolfe, as now I live with Madam Gladia, I could, little by little, unfold the layers of mind, one leaf after another, untie the intricate knot a bit at a time, and learn a great deal without harming him or her. To do the same to Dr Mandamus after one brief meeting, or after a hundred brief meetings, would accomplish little. Emotions are readily apparent, thoughts are not. If, out of a sense of urgency, I attempted to make haste, forcing the process, I would surely injure him, and that I cannot do.'

'Yet the fate of billions of people on Earth, and billions more in the rest of the Galaxy may depend on this.'

'*May* depend on this. That is conjecture. Injury to a human being is a fact. Consider that it may be only Dr Mandamus who knows the nature of the crisis and can carry it through to a conclusion. He could not use his knowledge or ability to force Dr Amadiro to grant him the Headship, if Dr Amadiro could gain it from another source.'

'True,' said Daneel. 'That may well be so.'

'In that case, Friend Daneel, it is not necessary to know the nature of the crisis. If Dr Mandamus could be restrained from telling Dr Amadiro – or anyone else – whatever it is he knows, the crisis will not come to pass.'

'Someone else might discover what Dr Mandamus now knows.'

'Certainly, but we don't know when that will be. Very likely, we will have time to probe further and discover more – and become better prepared to play a useful role of our own.'

'Well, then.'

'If Dr Mandamus is to be restrained, it can be done by damaging his mind to the point where it is no longer effective, or by destroying his life outright. The ability to injure his mind appropriately, I alone possess, but I cannot do this. However, either one of us can physically bring his life to an end. I cannot do this, either. Can *you* do it, Friend Daneel?'

There was a pause, and Daneel finally whispered, 'I cannot. You know that.'

Giskard said, slowly, 'Even though you know that the future of billions of people on Earth and elsewhere is at stake?'

'I cannot bring myself to injure Dr Mandamus.'

'And I cannot. So we are left with the certainty of a deadly crisis coming, but a crisis whose nature we do not know, and cannot find out, and which we are therefore helpless to counter.'

They stared at each other in silence, with nothing showing in their faces, but with an air of despair settling somehow over them.

4

Another Descendant

10.

Gladia had tried to relax after the harrowing session with Mandamus – and did so with an intensity that fought relaxation to the death. She had opacified all the windows in her bedroom, adjusted the environment to a gentle, warm breeze with the faint sound of rustling leaves and the occasional soft warble of a distant bird. She had then shifted it to the sound of a far-off surf and had added a faint but unmistakable tang of the sea in the air.

It didn't help. Her mind echoed helplessly with what had just been, and with what was soon to come. Why had she chattered so freely to Mandamus? What business was it of his, or of Amadiro's, for that matter, whether she had visited Elijah in orbit or not; and whether or not, or when, she had had a son by him or by any other man?

She had been cast into imbalance by Mandamus's claim of descent, that's what it was. In a society where no one cared about descent or relationship except for medico-genetic reasons, its sudden intrusion into a conversation was bound to be upsetting. That and the repeated (but surely accidental) reference to Elijah.

She decided she was finding excuses for herself and, in impatience, she tossed it all away. She had reacted badly and had babbled like a baby and that was all there was to it.

Now there was this Settler coming.

He was not an Earthman. He had not been born on Earth, she was sure, and it was quite possible that he had never even visited Earth. His people might have lived on a strange world she had never heard of and might have done so for generations.

That would make him a Spacer, she thought. Spacers were descended from Earthmen, too – centuries further back, but what did that matter? To be sure, Spacers were long-lived and these Settlers must be short-lived, but how much of a distinction was that? Even a Spacer might die prematurely through some freak accident; she had once heard of a Spacer who had died a natural death before he was sixty. Why not, then, think of the next visitor as a Spacer with an unusual accent?

But it wasn't that simple. No doubt the Settler did not feel himself to be a Spacer. It's not what you are that counts, but what you feel yourself to be. So think of him as a Settler, not a Spacer.

Yet weren't all human beings simply human beings no matter what name you applied to them – Spacers, Settlers, Aurorans, Earthpeople? The proof of it was that robots could not do injury to any of them. Daneel would spring as quickly to the defence of the most ignorant Earthman as to the Chairman of the Auroran Council – and that meant –

She could feel herself drifting, actually relaxing into a shallow sleep, when a sudden thought entered her mind and seemed to ricochet there.

Why was the Settler named Baley?

Her mind sharpened and snapped out of the welcoming coils of oblivion that had all but engulfed her.

Why Baley?

Perhaps it was simply a common name among the Settlers. After all, it was Elijah who had made it all possible and he had to be a hero to them as – as –

She could not think of an analogous hero to Aurorans. Who had led the expedition that first reached Aurora?

Who had supervised the terraformation of the raw barely-living world that Aurora had then been? She did not know.

Was her ignorance born of the fact that she had been brought up on Solaria – or was it that the Aurorans simply had no founding-hero? After all, the first expedition to Aurora had consisted of mere Earthpeople. It was only in later generations, with lengthening life-spans, thanks to the adjustments of sophisticated bioengineering, that Earthpeople had become Aurorans. And after that, why should Aurorans wish to make heroes of their despised predecessors?

But Settlers might make heroes of Earthpeople. They had not yet changed, perhaps. They might change eventually and then Elijah would be forgotten in embarrassment, but till then –

That must be it. Probably half the Settlers alive had adopted the Baley surname. Poor Elijah! Everyone crowding on to his shoulders and into his shadow. Poor Elijah – dear Elijah –

And she *did* fall asleep.

11.

The sleep was too restless to restore her to calm, let alone good-humour. She was scowling without knowing that she was, and had she seen herself in the mirror, she would have been taken aback by her middle-aged appearance.

Daneel, to whom Gladia was a human being, regardless of age, appearance, or mood, said, 'Madam –'

Gladia interrupted, with a small shiver. 'Is the Settler here?'

She looked up at the clock ribbon on the wall, and then made a quick gesture, in response to which Daneel at once adjusted the heat upward. (It had been a cool day, and was going to be a cooler evening.)

Daneel said, 'He is, madam.'

'Where have you put him?'

'In the main guest room, madam. Giskard is with him and the household robots are all within call.'

'I *hope* they will have the judgement to find out what he expects to eat for lunch. I don't know Settler cuisine. And I hope they can make some reasonable attempt to meet his requests.'

'I am sure, madam, that Giskard will handle the matter competently.'

Gladia was sure of that, too, but she merely snorted. At least it would have been a snort if Gladia were the sort of person who snorted. She didn't think she was.

'I presume,' she said, 'he's been in appropriate quarantine before being allowed to land?'

'It would be inconceivable for him not to have been, madam.'

She said, 'Just the same, I'll wear my gloves and my nose-filter.'

She stepped out of her bedroom, was distantly aware that there were household robots about her and made the sign that would get her a new pair of gloves and a fresh nose-filter. Every establishment had its own vocabulary of signs and every human member of an establishment cultivated those signs, learning to make them both rapidly and unnoticeably. A robot was expected to follow these unobtrusive orders of its human overlords as though it read minds; and it followed that a robot could not follow the orders of non-establishment human beings except by careful speech.

Nothing would humiliate a human member of an establishment more than to have one of the robots of the establishment hesitate in fulfilling an order, or, worse, fulfil it incorrectly. That would mean that the human being had fumbled a sign, or that the robot had.

Generally, Gladia knew, it was the human being who was at fault, but in virtually every case, this was not admitted. It was the robot who was handed over for an unnecessary response analysis, or unfairly put up for sale. Gladia had always felt that she would never fall into that trap of wounded ego, yet if at that moment she had not received her gloves and nose-filter, she would have –

She did not have to finish the thought. The nearest robot brought her what she wanted, correctly and with speed.

Gladia adjusted the nose-filter and snuffled a bit to make sure it was properly seated (she was in no mood to risk infection with any foul disorder that had survived the painstaking treatment during quarantine). She said, 'What does he look like, Daneel?'

Daneel said, 'He is of ordinary stature and measurements, madam.'

'I mean his face.' (It was silly to ask. If he showed any family resemblance to Elijah Baley, Daneel would have noticed it as quickly as she herself would have, and he would have remarked upon it.)

'That is difficult to say, Madam. It is not in plain view.'

'What does that mean? Surely he's not masked, Daneel?'

'In a way, he is, madam. His face is covered with hair.'

'Hair?' She found herself laughing. 'You mean after the fashion of the hypervision historicals? Beards?' She made little gestures indicating a tuft of hair on the chin and another under the nose.

'Rather more than that, madam. Half his face is covered.'

Gladia's eyes opened wide and for the first time she felt a surge of interest in seeing him. What would a face with hair all over it look like? Auroran males – and Spacer males, generally – had very little facial hair, and what there was would be removed permanently by the late teens – during virtual infancy.

Sometimes the upper lip was left untouched. Gladia remembered that her husband, Santirix Gremionis, before their marriage, had had a thin line of hair under his nose. A moustache, he called it. It had looked like a misplaced and peculiarly misshapen eyebrow, and once she had resigned herself to accepting him as husband, she had insisted he destroy the follicles.

He had done so with scarcely a murmur, and it occurred to her now, for the first time, to wonder if he had missed the hair. It seemed to her that she had noticed him, on occasion, in those early years, lifting a finger to his upper lip. She had thought it a nervous poking at a vague itch and it was only now that it occurred to her that he had been searching for a moustache that was gone forever.

How would a man look with a moustache all over his face? Would he be bearlike?

How would it feel? What if women had such hair, too? She thought of a man and woman trying to kiss and having trouble finding each other's mouths. She found the thought funny, in a harmlessly ribald way, and laughed out loud. She felt her petulance disappearing and actually looked forward to seeing the monster.

After all, there would be no need to fear him even if he were as animal in behaviour as he was in appearance. He would have no robot of his own – Settlers were supposed to have a non-robotic society – and she would be surrounded by a dozen. The monster would be immobilized in a split-second if he made the slightest suspicious move; or if he as much as raised his voice in anger.

She said, with perfect good humour, 'Take me to him, Daneel.'

12.

The monster rose. He said something that sounded like 'Gode arternoon muhleddy.'

She at once caught the 'good afternoon', but it took her a moment to translate the last word into 'my lady'.

Gladia said, 'Good afternoon,' absently. She remembered the difficulty she had had understanding Auroran pronunciation of Galactic Standard in those long-ago days when, a frightened youngster, she had come to the planet from Solaria.

The monster's accent was uncouth – or did it just sound uncouth because her ear was unaccustomed to it? Elijah, she remembered, had seemed to voice his 'k's' and 'p's', but spoke pretty well otherwise. Twenty decades had passed, however, and this Settler was not from Earth. Language, in isolation, underwent changes.

But only a small portion of Gladia's mind was on the language problem. She was staring at his beard.

It was not in the least like the beards that actors wore in historical dramas. Those always seemed tufted, a bit here, a bit there, looking gluey and glossy.

The Settler's beard was different. It covered his cheeks and chin evenly, thickly, and deeply. It was a dark brown, somewhat lighter and wavier than the hair on his head, and at least two inches long, she judged – evenly long.

It didn't cover his whole face, which was rather disappointing. His forehead was totally bare (except for eyebrows) as were his nose and his under-eye regions.

His upper lip was bare, too, but it was shadowed as though there was the beginning of new growth upon it. There was additional bareness just under the lower lip, but with new growth less marked and concentrated mostly under the middle portion.

Since both his lips were quite bare, it was clear to Gladia that there would be no difficulty in kissing him. She said, knowing that staring was impolite, and staring even so, 'It seems to me you remove the hair from about your lips.'

'Yes, my lady.'

'Why, if I may ask?'

'You may ask. For hygienic reasons. I don't want food catching in the hairs.'

'You scrape it off, don't you? I see it's growing again.'

'I use an electric razor. It takes fifteen seconds after waking.'

'Why not depilate and be done with it?'

'I might want to grow it back.'

'Why?'

'Aesthetic reasons, my lady.'

This time Gladia did not grasp the word. It sounded like 'acidic' or, possibly, 'acetic'.

She said, 'Pardon me?'

The Settler said, 'I might grow tired of the way I look now and want the hair on the upper lip again. Some women like it, you know, and' (the Settler tried to look modest and failed) 'I have a fine moustache when I grow it.'

She said, suddenly, grasping the word, 'You mean "aesthetic".'

The Settler laughed, showing fine white teeth, and said, 'You talk funny, too, my lady.'

Gladia tried to look haughty, but melted into a smile. Proper pronunciation was a matter of local consensus. She said, 'You ought to hear me with my Solarian accent, if it comes to that. Then it would be "aestheetic rayzuns".' The 'r' rolled interminably.

'I've been places where they talk a little bit like that. It sounds barbarous,' and he rolled both 'r's' phenomenally in the last word.

Gladia chuckled. 'You do it with the tip of your tongue. It's got to be with the sides of the tongue. No one but a Solarian can do it correctly.'

'Perhaps you can teach me. A trader like myself, who's been everywhere, hears all kinds of linguistic perversions.' Again he tried to roll the 'r's' of the last word, choked slightly, and coughed.

'See. You'll tangle your tonsils and you'll *never* recover.' She was still staring at his beard and now she could curb her curiosity no longer. She reached towards it.

The Settler flinched and started back, then, realizing her intention, was still.

Gladia's hand, all-but-invisibly gloved, rested lightly on the left side of his face. The thin plastic that covered her fingers did not interfere with the sense of touch, and she found the hair to be soft and springy.

'It's nice,' she said, with evident surprise.

'Widely admired,' said the Settler, grinning.

She said, 'But I can't stand here and manhandle you all day.'

Ignoring his predictable, 'You can as far as I'm concerned,' she went on, 'Have you told my robots what you would like to eat?'

'My lady, I told them what I now tell you – whatever is handy. I've been on a score of worlds in the last year and each has its own dietary. A trader learns to eat everything that isn't actually toxic. I'd prefer an Auroran meal to anything you would try making in imitation of Baleyworld.'

'Baleyworld?' said Gladia, sharply, a frown returning to her face.

'Named for the leader of the first expedition to the

planet, or to *any* of the Settled planets, for that matter. Ben Baley.'

'The son of Elijah Baley?'

'Yes,' said the Settler, and changed the subject at once, as he looked down at himself and said with a trace of petulance, 'How do you people manage to stand these clothes of yours – slick and puffy. Be glad to get into my own again.'

'I'm sure you will have your chance to do so soon enough. But for now please come and join me at lunch. I was told your name was Baley, by the way – like your planet.'

'Not surprising. It's the most honoured name on the planet, naturally. I'm Deejee Baley.'

They had walked into the dining room, Giskard preceding them,, Daneel following them, each moving into his appropriate wall-niche. Other robots were already in their niches and two emerged to do the serving. The room was bright with sunshine, the walls were alive with decoration, the table was set, and the odour of food was enticing.

The Settler sniffed and let his breath out in satisfaction. 'I don't think I'll have any trouble at all eating Auroran food. Where would you like me to sit, my lady?'

A robot said at once, 'If you would sit here, sir?'

The Settler sat down, and then Gladia, the privileges of the guest satisfied, took her own seat.

'Deejee?' she said. 'I do not know the nomenclatural peculiarities of your world, so excuse me if my question is offensive. Wouldn't Deejee be a feminine name?'

'Not at all,' said the Settler, a bit stiffly. 'In any case, it is not a name, it is a pair of initials. Fourth letter of the alphabet and the seventh.'

'Oh,' said Gladia, enlightened, 'D. G. Baley. And what do the initials stand for, if you'll excuse my curiosity?'

'Certainly. There's D. for certain,' he said, jerking his

thumb towards one of the wall-niches, 'and I suspect that one may be G.' He jerked his thumb towards another.

'You don't mean that,' said Gladia faintly.

'But I do. My name is Daneel Giskard Baley. In every generation, my family has had at least one Daneel or one Giskard in its multiplying batches. I was the last of six children, but the first boy. My mother felt that was enough and made up for having but one son by giving me both names. That made me Daneel Giskard Baley and the double load was too great for me. I prefer D. G. as my name, and I'd be honoured if you used it.' He smiled genially. 'I'm the first to bear both names and I'm also the first to see the grand originals.'

'But why those names?'

'It was Ancestor Elijah's idea, according to the family story. He had the honour of naming his grandsons, and the oldest was named Daneel, while the second was named Giskard. He insisted on that, and that established the tradition.'

'And the daughters?'

'The traditional name from generation to generation is Jezebel – Jessie. Elijah's wife, you know.'

'I know.'

'There are no – ' He caught himself and transferred his attention to the dish that had been placed before him. 'If this were Baleyworld, I would say this was a slice of roast pork and that it was smothered in peanut sauce.'

'Actually, it is a vegetable dish, D. G. What you were about to say was that there are no Gladias in the family.'

'There aren't,' said D. G., calmly. 'One explanation is that Jessie, the original Jessie, would have objected, but I don't accept that. Elijah's wife, the Ancestress, never came to Baleyworld, you know; never left Earth. How could she have objected? No, to me, it's pretty certain that the Ancestor wanted no other Gladia. No imitations, no copies, no pretence. One Gladia. Unique. He asked that there be no later Elijah, either.'

Gladia was having trouble eating. 'I think your ancestor spent the latter portion of his life trying to be as unemotional as Daneel. Just the same, he had romantic notions under his skin. He might have allowed other Elijahs and Gladias. It wouldn't have offended me, certainly, and I imagine it wouldn't have offended his wife, either.' She laughed tremulously.

D. G. said, 'All this doesn't seem real somehow. The Ancestor is practically ancient history; he died a hundred and sixty-four years ago. I'm his descendant in the seventh generation, yet here I am sitting with a woman who knew him when he was quite young.'

'I didn't really know him,' said Gladia, staring at her plate. 'I saw him, rather briefly, on three separate occasions over a period of seven years.'

'I know. The ancestor's son, Ben, wrote a biography of him which is one of the literary classics of Baleyworld. Even I have read it.'

'Indeed? I haven't read it. I didn't even know it existed. What – what does it say about me?'

D. G. seemed amused. 'Nothing you would object to; you come out very well. But never mind that. What I'm amazed at is that here we are together, across seven generations. How old are you, my lady? Is it fair to ask the question?'

'I don't know that it's fair, but I have no objection to it. In Galactic Standard Years, I am 235 years old. Twenty-three and a half decades.'

'You look as though you were no more than in your late forties. The Ancestor died at 82, an old man. I'm 39 and when I die you will still be alive – '

'If I avoid death by misadventure.'

'And will continue to live perhaps five decades beyond.'

'Do you envy me, D. G.?' said Gladia, with an edge of bitterness in her voice. 'Do you envy me for having survived Elijah by over fifteen decades and for being condemned to survive him ten decades more, perhaps?'

'Of course I envy you,' came the composed answer. 'Why not? I would have no objection to living for several centuries, were it not that I would be setting a bad example to the people of Baleyworld. I wouldn't want them to live that long as a general thing. The pace of historical and intellectual advance would then become too slow. Those at the top would stay in power too long. Baleyworld would sink into conservatism and decay – as your world has done.'

Gladia's small chin lifted. 'Aurora is doing quite well, you'll find.'

'I'm speaking of *your* world. Solaria.'

Gladia hesitated, then said firmly, 'Solaria is not my world.'

D. G. said, 'I hope it is. I came to see you because I believe Solaria is your world.'

'If that is why you came to see me, you are wasting your time, young man.'

'You were born on Solaria, weren't you, and lived there a while?'

'I lived there for the first three decades of my life; about an eighth of my lifetime.'

'Then that makes you enough of a Solarian to be able to help me in a matter that is rather important.'

'I am *not* a Solarian, despite this so-called important matter.'

'It is a matter of war and peace, if *you* call that important. The Spacer worlds face war with the Settler worlds, and things will go badly for all of us, if it comes to that. And it is up to *you*, my lady, to prevent that war and to ensure peace.'

13.

The meal was done (it had been a small one) and Gladia found herself looking at D. G. in a coldly furious way.

She had lived quietly for the last twenty decades, peeling off the complexities of life. Slowly, she had forgotten the misery of Solaria, and the difficulties of adjustment to Aurora. She had managed to bury, quite deeply, the agony of two murders, and the ecstasy of two strange loves – with a robot and with an Earthman – and to get well past it all. She had ended by spinning out a long quiet marriage, having two children, and working at her applied art of costumery. And, eventually, the children had left, then her husband, and soon she might be retiring even from her work.

Then she would be alone with her robots, content with, or rather resigned to, letting life glide quietly and uneventfully to a slow close in its own time; a close so gentle she might not be aware of the ending when it came.

It was what she wanted.

Then – What was happening?

It had begun the night before when she looked up vainly at the starlit sky to see Solaria's star, which was not in the sky and would not have been visible to her if it were. It was as though this one foolish reaching for the past, a past that should have been allowed to remain dead, had burst the cool bubble she had built about herself.

First the name of Elijah Baley, the most joyously painful memory of all the ones she had so carefully brushed away, had come up again and again in a grim repetition.

She was then forced to deal with a man who thought, mistakenly, he might be a descendant of Elijah in the fifth degree, and now with another man who actually was a descendant in the seventh degree. Finally, she was now being given problems and responsibilities similar to those that had plagued Elijah himself on various occasions.

Was she becoming Elijah, in a fashion, with none of his talent, and none of his fierce dedication to duty at all costs?

What had she done to deserve it?

She felt her rage being buried under a flood-tide of self-pity. She felt unjustly dealt with. No one had the right to unload responsibility on her against her will.

She said, forcing her voice level, 'Why do you insist on my being a Solarian, when I tell you that I am not a Solarian?'

D. G. did not seem disturbed by the chill that had now entered her voice. He was still holding the soft napkin that had been given him at the conclusion of the meal. It had been damply hot – not too hot – and he had imitated the actions of Gladia in carefully wiping his hands and mouth. He had then doubled it over and stroked his beard with it. It was shredding now, and shrivelling.

He said, 'I presume it will vanish altogether.'

'It will.' Gladia had deposited her own napkin in the appropriate receptacle on the table. Holding it was unmannerly and could be excused only by D. G.'s evident unfamiliarity with civilized custom. 'There are some who think it has a polluting effect on the atmosphere, but there is a gentle draught that carries the residue upward and traps it in filters. I doubt that it will give us any trouble. But you ignore my question, sir.'

D. G. wadded what was left of his napkin and placed it on the arm of the chair. A robot, in response to Gladia's quick and unobtrusive gesture, removed it.

D. G. said, 'I don't intend to ignore your question, my lady. I am not trying to *force* you to be a Solarian. I merely point out that you were born on Solaria and spent your early decades there, and therefore might reasonably be considered a Solarian, after a fashion at least. Do you know that Solaria has been abandoned?'

'So I have heard. Yes.'

'Do you feel anything about that?'

'I am an Auroran, and have been one for twenty decades.'

'That is a *non sequitur*.'

'A *what*?' She could make nothing of the last sound at all.

'It has no connection with my question.'

'A *non sequitur*, you mean. You said a "nonsense-quitter".'

D. G. smiled. 'Very well. Let's quit the nonsense. I ask you if you feel anything about the death of Solaria and you tell me you're an Auroran. Do you maintain that is an answer? A born Auroran might feel badly at the death of a sister-world. How do you feel about it?'

Gladia said, icily, 'It doesn't matter. Why are you interested?'

'I'll explain. We – I mean the Traders of the Settler worlds – are interested because there is business to be done, profits to be made, and a world to be gained. Solaria is already terraformed; it is a comfortable world; you Spacers seem to have no need or desire for it. Why should we not settle it?'

'Because it's not yours.'

'Madam, is it *yours* that you object? Has Aurora any more claim to it than Baleyworld has? Can't we suppose that an empty world belongs to whoever is pleased to settle it?'

'Have you settled it?'

'No, because it's not empty.'

'Do you mean the Solarians have not entirely left?' Gladia said, quickly.

D. G's smile returned and broadened into a grin. 'You're excited at the thought. Even though you're an Auroran.'

Gladia's face twisted into a frown at once. 'Answer my question.'

D. G. shrugged. 'There were only some five thousand Solarians on the world just before it was abandoned, according to our best estimates. The population had been declining for years. But even five thousand – Can we be sure that *all* are gone? However, that's not the point. Even if the Solarians were indeed all gone, the planet would not be empty. There are, upon it, some two hundred million or more robots – masterless robots – some of them among the most advanced in the Galaxy. Presumably, those Solarians who left took some robots with them – it's hard to imagine Spacers doing without robots altogether.' (He looked about, smiling, at the robots in their niches within the room.) 'However, they can't possibly have taken forty thousand robots apiece.'

Gladia said, 'Well, then, since your Settler worlds are so purely robot-free, and wish to stay so, I presume, you can't settle Solaria.'

'That's right. Not until the robots are gone, and that is where Traders such as myself come in.'

'In what way?'

'We don't want a robot society, but we don't mind touching robots and dealing with them in the way of business. We don't have a superstitious fear of the things. We just know that a robot society is bound to decay. The Spacers have carefully made that plain to us by example. So that while we don't want to live with this robotic poison, we are perfectly willing to sell it to Spacers for a substantial sum, if they are so foolish as to want such a society.'

'Do you think Spacers will buy them?'

'I'm sure they will. They will welcome the elegant

modes that the Solarians manufacture. It's well-known that they were the leading robot-designers in the Galaxy, even though the late Dr Fastolfe is said to have been unparalleled in the field, although only an Auroran. Besides, even though we would charge a substantial sum, that sum would still be considerably less than the robots are worth. Spacers and Traders would both profit – the secret of successful trade.'

'The Spacers wouldn't buy robots from Settlers,' said Gladia, with evident contempt.

D. G. had a Trader's way of ignoring such non-essentials as anger or contempt. It was business that counted. He said, 'Of course they would. Offer them advanced robots at half-price and why should they turn them down? Where business is to be done, you would be surprised how unimportant questions of ideology become.'

'I think you'll be the one to be surprised. Try to sell your robots and you'll see.'

'Would that I could, my lady. Try to sell them, that is. I have none on hand.'

'Why not?'

'Because none have been collected. Two separate trading vessels have landed on Solaria, each capable of storing some twenty-five robots. Had they succeeded, whole fleets of trading vessels would have followed them and I dare say we would have continued to do business for decades – and then have settled the world.'

'But they didn't succeed. Why not?'

'Because both ships were destroyed on the surface of the planet and, as far as we can tell, all the crewmen are dead.'

'Equipment failure?'

'Nonsense. Both landed safely; they were not wrecked. Their last reports were that Spacers were approaching, whether Solarians or natives of other Spacer worlds, we don't know. We can only assume that the Spacers attacked without warning.'

'That's impossible.'

'Is it?'

'Of course it's impossible. What would be the motive?'

'To keep us off the world, I would say.'

'If they wished to do that,' said Gladia, 'they would merely have had to announce that the world was occupied.'

'They might find it more pleasant to kill a few Settlers. At least, that's what many of our people think, and there is pressure to settle the matter by sending a few warships to Solaria and establishing a military base on the planet.'

'That would be dangerous.'

'Certainly. It could lead to war. Some of our fire-eaters look forward to that. Perhaps some Spacers look forward to that, too, and have destroyed the two ships merely to provoke hostilities.'

Gladia sat there amazed. There had been no hint of strained relations between Spacers and Settlers on any of the news-programmes.

She said, 'Surely it's possible to discuss the matter. Have your people approached the Spacer Federation?'

'A thoroughly unimportant body, but we have. We've also approached the Auroran Council.'

'And?'

'The Spacers deny everything. They suggest that the potential profits in the Solarian robot trade are so high that Traders, who are interested only in money – as though they themselves were not – would fight each other over the matter. Apparently, they would have us believe the two ships destroyed each other, each hoping to monopolize the trade for their own world.'

'The two ships were from two different worlds, then?'

'Yes.'

'Don't you think, then, that there might indeed have been a fight between them?'

'I don't think it's likely, but I will admit it's possible. There have been no outright conflicts between the Settler worlds, but there have been some pretty strenuous disputes. All have been settled through arbitration by Earth. Still, it is indeed a fact that the Settler worlds might, at a pinch, not hang together when multi-billion-dollar trade is at stake. That's why war is not such a good idea for us and why something will have to be done to discourage the hotheads. That's where we come in.'

'We?'

'You and I. I have been asked to go to Solaria and find out, if I can, what really happened. I will take one ship – armed, but not heavily-armed.'

'You might be destroyed, too.'

'Possibly. But my ship, at least, won't be caught unprepared. Besides, I am not one of those hypervision heroes, and I have considered what I might do to lessen the chances of destruction. It occurred to me that one of the disadvantages of Settler penetration of Solaria is that we don't know the world at all. It might be useful, then, to take someone who knows the world – a Solarian, in short.'

'You mean you want to take me?'

'Right, my lady.'

'Why me?'

'I should think you could see that without explanation, my lady. Those Solarians who have left the planet are gone we know not where. If any Solarians are left on the planet, they are very likely the enemy. There are no known Solarian-born Spacers living on some Spacer planet other than Solaria – except yourself. You are the only Solarian available to me – the only one in all the Galaxy. That's why I must have you and that's why you must come.'

'You're wrong, Settler. If I am the only one available to

you, then you have no one who is available. I do not
intend to come with you, and there is no way, absolutely
no way, in which you can force me to come with you. I am
surrounded by my robots. Take one step in my direction
and you will be immobilized at once, and if you struggle
you will be hurt.'

'I intend no force. You must come of your own accord –
and you should be willing to. It's a matter of preventing
war.'

'That is the job of governments on your side and mine. I
refuse to have anything to do with it. I am a private
citizen.'

'You owe it to your world. We might suffer in case of
war, but so will Aurora.'

'I am not one of those hypervision heroes, any more
than you are.'

'You owe it to me, then.'

'You're mad. I owe you nothing.'

D. G. smiled narrowly. 'You owe me nothing as an
individual. You owe me a great deal as a descendant of
Elijah Baley.'

Gladia froze, and remained staring at the bearded monster for a long moment. How did she come to forget who
he was?'

With difficulty, she finally muttered, 'No.'

'Yes,' said D. G., forcefully. 'On two different occasions,
the Ancestor did more for you than you can ever repay.
He is no longer here to call in the debt – a small part of
the debt. I inherit the right to do so.'

Gladia said, in despair, 'But what can I do for you if I
come with you?'

'We'll find out. Will you come?'

Desperately, Gladia wanted to refuse, but was it for this
that Elijah had suddenly become part of her life, once
more, in the last twenty-four hours? Was it so that when

this impossible demand was made upon her, it would be in his name, and she would find it impossible to refuse?

She said, 'What's the use? The Council will not let me go with you. They will not have an Auroran taken away on a Settler's vessel.'

'My lady, you have been here on Aurora for twenty decades, so you think the Auroran-born consider you an Auroran. It's not so. To them, you are a Solarian still. They'll let you go.'

'They won't,' said Gladia, her heart pounding, and the skin of her upper arms turning to goose-flesh. He was right. She thought of Amadiro, who would surely think of her as nothing but a Solarian. Nevertheless, she repeated, 'They won't,' trying to reassure herself.

'They will,' retorted D. G. 'Didn't someone from your Council come to you to ask you to see me?'

She said, defiantly, 'He asked me only to report on this conversation we have had. And I will do so.'

'If they want you to spy on me here in your own home, my lady, they will find it even more useful to have you spy on me on Solaria.' He waited for a response, and when there was none, he said, with a trace of weariness, 'My lady, if you refuse, I won't force you because I won't have to. *They* will force you. But I don't want that. The Ancestor would not want it if he were here. He would want you to come with me out of gratitude to him and for no other reason. My lady, the Ancestor laboured on your behalf under conditions of extreme difficulty. Won't you labour on behalf of his memory?'

Gladia's heart sank. She knew she could not resist that. She said, 'I can't go anywhere without robots.'

'I wouldn't expect you to.' D. G. was grinning again. 'Why not take my two namesakes? Do you need more?'

Gladia looked towards Daneel, but he was standing motionless. She looked towards Giskard – the same. And then it seemed to her that, for just a moment, his head moved, very slightly, up and down.

She had to trust him.

She said, 'Well, then, I'll come with you. These two robots are all I will need.'

PART II
SOLARIA

5

The Abandoned Planet

14.

For the fifth time in her life, Gladia found herself on a spaceship. She did not remember, off-hand, exactly how long ago it had been that she and Santirix had gone together to the world of Euterpe because its rain-forests were widely recognized as incomparable, especially under the romantic glow of its bright satellite, Gemstone.

The rain-forest had, indeed, been lush and green, with the trees carefully planted in rank and file, and the animal life thoughtfully selected so as to provide colour and delight, while avoiding venomous or other unpleasant creatures.

The satellite, fully 150 kilometres in diameter, was close enough to Euterpe to shine like a brilliant dot of sparkling light. It was so close to the planet that one could see it sweep west to east across the sky, outstripping the planet's slower rotational motion. It brightened as it rose towards zenith, and dimmed as it dropped towards the horizon again. One watched it with fascination the first night; with less the second; and with a vague discontent the third – assuming the sky was clear on those nights, which it usually wasn't.

The native Euterpans, she noted, never looked at it, though they praised it loudly to the tourists, of course.

On the whole, Gladia had enjoyed the trip well enough, but what she remembered most keenly was the joy of her return to Aurora, and her decision not to travel again except under dire need. (Come to think of it, it had to be at least eight decades ago.)

For a while, she had lived with the uneasy fear that her husband would insist on another trip, but he never mentioned one. It might well be, she sometimes thought at that time, that he had come to the same decision she had and feared she might be the one to want to travel.

It didn't make them unusual to avoid trips. Aurorans generally – Spacers generally, for that matter – tended to be stay-at-homes. Their worlds, their establishments, were too comfortable. After all, what pleasure could be greater than that of being taken care of by your own robots, robots who knew your every signal, and, for that matter, knew your ways and desires even without being told?

She stirred uneasily. Was that what D. G. had meant when he spoke of the decadence of a roboticized society?

But now she was back again in space, after all that time. And on an Earth-ship, too.

She hadn't seen much of it, but the little she had glimpsed made her terribly uneasy. It seemed to be nothing but straight lines, sharp angles, and smooth surfaces. Everything that wasn't *stark* had been eliminated, apparently. It was as though nothing must exist but functionality. Even though she didn't know what was exactly functional about any particular object on the ship, she felt it to be all that was required, that nothing was to be allowed to interfere with taking the shortest distance between two points.

On everything Auroran (on everything Spacer, one might almost say, though Aurora was the most advanced in that respect) everything existed in layers. Functionality was at the bottom – one could not entirely rid oneself of that, except in what was pure ornament – but overlying that there was always something to satisfy the eyes and the senses, generally; and overlying *that*, something to satisfy the spirit.

How much better that was! Or did it represent such an exuberance of human creativity that Spacers could no longer live with the unadorned Universe, and was that bad? Was the future to belong to these from-here-to-there geometrizers? Or was it just that the Settlers had not yet learned the sweetnesses of life?

But then, if life had so many sweetnesses to it, why had she found so few for herself?

She had nothing really to do on board this ship but to ponder and reponder such questions. This D. G., this Elijah-descended barbarian, had put it into her head with his calm assumption that the Spacer worlds were dying even though he could see all about him even during the shortest stay on Aurora (surely, he would have to) that it was deeply embedded in wealth and security.

She had tried to escape her own thoughts by staring at the holofilms she had been supplied with, and watching, with moderate curiosity, the images flickering and capering on the projection surface, as the adventure story (all were adventure stories) hastened from event to event with little time left for conversation, and none for thought – or enjoyment, either. Very like their furniture.

D. G. stepped in when she was in the middle of one of the films, but had stopped really paying attention. She was not caught by surprise. Her robots, who guarded her doorway, signalled his coming in ample time, and would not have allowed him to enter, if she were not in a position to receive him. Daneel entered with him.

D. G. said, 'How are you doing?' and then, as her hand touched a contact and the images faded, shrivelled, and were gone, he said, 'You don't have to turn it off. I'll watch it with you.'

'That's not necessary,' she said. 'I've had enough.'

'Are you comfortable?'

'Not entirely. I am – isolated.'

'Sorry! But then, I was isolated on Aurora. They would allow none of my men to come with me.'

'Are you having your revenge?'

'Not at all. For one thing, I allowed you two robots of your choice to accompany you. For another, it is not I, but my crew who enforce this. They don't like either Spacers or robots. But why do you mind? Doesn't this isolation lessen your fear of infection?'

Gladia's eyes were haughty, but her voice sounded weary. 'I wonder if I haven't grown too old to fear infection. In many ways, I think I have lived long enough. Then, too, I have my gloves, my nose-filters and, if necessary, my mask. And besides, I doubt that you will trouble to touch me.'

'Nor will anyone else,' said D. G., with a sudden edge of grimness to his voice, as his hand wandered to the object at the right side of his hip.

Her eyes followed the motion. 'What is that?' she asked.

D. G. smiled and his beard seemed to glitter in the light. There were occasional reddish hairs among the brown. 'A weapon,' he said, and drew it. He held it by a moulded hilt that bulged above his hand as though the force of his grip were squeezing it upward. In front, facing Gladia, a thin cylinder stretched some fifteen centimetres forward. There was no opening visible.

'Does that kill people?' Gladia extended her hand towards it.

D. G. moved it quickly away. 'Never reach for someone's weapon, my lady. That is worse than bad manners, for any Settler is trained to react violently to such a move and you may be hurt.'

Gladia, eyes wide, withdrew her hand and placed both behind her back. She said, 'Don't threaten harm. Daneel has no sense of humour in that respect. On Aurora, no one is barbarous enough to carry weapons.'

'Well,' said D. G., unmoved by the adjective, 'we don't have robots to protect us. And this is not a killing device. It is, in some ways, worse. It emits a kind of vibration that stimulates those nerve-endings responsible for the sensation of pain. It hurts a good deal worse than anything you can imagine. No one would willingly endure it twice, and someone carrying this weapon rarely has to use it. We call it a neuronic whip.'

Gladia frowned. 'Disgusting! We have our robots, but they never hurt anyone except in unavoidable emergency, and then minimally.'

D. G. shrugged. 'That sounds very civilized, but a bit of pain – a bit of killing, even – is better than the decay of spirit brought about by robots. Besides, a neuronic whip is not intended to kill, and your people have weapons on their spaceships that can bring about wholesale death and destruction.'

'That's because we've fought wars early in our history, when our Earth heritage was still strong, but we've learned better.'

'You used those weapons on Earth even after you had supposedly learned better.'

'That's – ' she began, and closed her mouth as though to bite off what she was about to say next.

D. G. nodded. 'I know. You were about to say, "That's different". Think of that, my lady, if you should catch yourself wondering why my crew doesn't like Spacers. Or why I don't. But you are going to be useful to me, my lady, and I won't let my emotions get in the way.'

'How am I going to be useful to you?'

'You are a Solarian.'

'You keep saying that. More than twenty decades have passed. I don't know what Solaria is like now. I know nothing about it. What was Baleyworld like twenty decades ago?'

'It didn't exist twenty decades ago, but Solaria did, and I shall gamble that you will remember *something* useful.'

He stood up, bowed his head briefly in a gesture of politeness that was almost mocking, and was gone.

15.

Gladia maintained a thoughtful and troubled silence for a while and then she said, 'He wasn't at all polite, was he?'

Daneel said, 'Madam Gladia, the Settler is clearly under tension. He is heading towards a world on which two ships like his have been destroyed and their crews killed. He is going into great danger, as is his crew.'

'You always defend any human being, Daneel,' said Gladia, resentfully. 'The danger exists for me, too, and I am not facing it voluntarily, but that does not force *me* into rudeness.'

Daneel said nothing.

Gladia said, 'Well, maybe it does. I *have* been a little rude, haven't I?'

'I don't think the Settler minded,' said Daneel. 'Might I suggest, madam, that you prepare yourself for bed. It is quite late.'

'Very well. I'll prepare myself for bed, but I don't think I feel relaxed enough to sleep, Daneel.'

'Friend Giskard assures me you will, madam, and he is usually right about such things.'

And she did sleep.

16.

Daneel and Giskard stood in the darkness of Gladia's cabin.

Giskard said, 'She will sleep soundly, Friend Daneel, and she needs the rest. She faces a dangerous trip.'

'It seemed to me, Friend Giskard,' said Daneel, 'that you influenced her to agree to go. I presume you had a reason.'

'Friend Daneel, we know so little about the nature of the crisis that is now facing the Galaxy that we cannot safely refuse any action that might increase our knowledge. We must know what is taking place on Solaria, and the only way we can do so is to go there; and the only way we can go is for us to arrange for Madam Gladia to go. As for influencing her, that required scarcely a touch. Despite her loud statements to the contrary, she was eager to go. There was an overwhelming desire within her to see Solaria. It was a pain within her that would not cease until she went.'

'Since you say so, it is so, yet I find it puzzling. Had she not frequently made it plain that her life on Solaria was unhappy; that she had completely adopted Aurora and never wished to go back to her original home?'

'Yes, that was there, too. It was quite plainly in her mind. Both emotions, both feelings, existed together and simultaneously. I have observed something of this sort in human minds frequently; two opposite emotions simultaneously present.'

'Such a condition does not seem logical, Friend Giskard.'

'I agree, and I can only conclude that human beings are not, at all times, or in all respects, logical. That must be one reason that it is so difficult to work out the Laws governing human behaviour. In Madam Gladia's case, I have now and then been aware of this longing for Solaria. Ordinarily, it was well-hidden; obscured by the far more intense antipathy she also felt for the world. When the news arrived that Solaria had been abandoned by its people, however, her feelings changed.'

'Why so? What had the abandonment to do with the youthful experiences that led Madam Gladia to her antipathy? Or, having held in restraint her longing for the world during the decades when it was a working society, why should she lose that restraint once it became an abandoned planet, and newly long for a world which must now be something utterly strange to her?'

'I cannot explain, Friend Daneel, since the more knowledge I gather of the human mind, the more despair I feel at being unable to understand it. It is not an unalloyed advantage to see into that mind and I often envy you the simplicity of behaviour-control that results from your inability to see below the surface.'

Daneel persisted. 'Have you guessed an explanation, Friend Giskard?'

'I suppose she feels a sorrow for the empty planet. She deserted it twenty decades ago –'

'She was driven out.'

'It seems to her, now, to have been a desertion, and I imagine she plays with the painful thought that she had set an example; that if she had not left, no one else would have, and the planet would still be populated and happy. Since I cannot read her thoughts, I am only groping backward, perhaps inaccurately, from her emotions.'

'But she could not have set an example, Friend Giskard. Since it is twenty decades since she left, there can be no verifiable causal connection between the much earlier event and the much later one.'

'I agree, but human beings sometimes find a kind of

pleasure in nursing painful emotions; in blaming themselves without reason or even against reason. In any case, Madam Gladia felt so sharply the longing to return that I felt it was necessary to release the inhibitory effect that kept her from agreeing to go. It required the merest touch. Yet though I feel it necessary for her to go, since that means she will take us there, I have the uneasy feeling that the disadvantages might, just possibly, be greater than the advantages.'

'In what way, Friend Giskard?'

'Since the Council was eager to have Madam Gladia accompany the Settler, it may have been for the purpose of having Madam Gladia absent from Aurora during a crucial period when the defeat of Earth and its Settler worlds is being prepared.'

Daneel seemed to be considering that statement. At least it was only after a distinct pause that he said, 'What purpose would be served, in your opinion, in having Madam Gladia absent?'

'I cannot decide that, Friend Daneel. I want your opinion.'

'I have not considered this matter.'

'Consider it now!' If Giskard had been human, the remark would have been an order.

There was an even longer pause, and then Daneel said, 'Friend Giskard, until the moment that Dr Mandamus appeared in Madam Gladia's establishment, she had never shown any concern in international affairs. She was a friend of Dr Fastolfe and of Elijah Baley, but this friendship was one of personal affection and did not have an ideological basis. Both of them, moreover, are now gone from us. She has an antipathy towards Dr Amadiro, and that is returned, but this is also a personal matter. The antipathy is two centuries old, and neither has done anything material about it, but have merely each remained stubbornly antipathetic.

There can be no reason for Dr Amadiro – who is now the dominant influence in the Council – to fear Madam Gladia, or to go to the trouble of removing her.'

Giskard said, 'You overlook the fact that in removing Madam Gladia, he also removes you and me. He would, perhaps, feel quite certain Madam Gladia would not leave without us, so can it be us he considers dangerous?'

'In the course of our existence, Friend Giskard, we have never, in any way, given any apperance of having endangered Dr Amadiro. What cause has he to fear us? He does not know of your abilities or of how you have made use of them. Why, then, should he take the trouble to remove us, temporarily, from Aurora?'

'Temporarily, Friend Daneel? Why do you assume it is a temporary removal he plans? He knows, it may be, more than the Settler does of the trouble on Solaria, and knows, also, that the Settler and his crew will be surely destroyed – and Madam Gladia and you and I with them. Perhaps the destruction of the Settler's ship is his main aim, but he would consider the end of Dr Fastolfe's friend and Dr Fastolfe's robots to be an added bonus.'

Daneel said, 'Surely, he would not risk war with the Settler worlds, for that may well come if the Settler's ship is destroyed, and the minute pleasure of having us destroyed, when added in, would not make the risk worthwhile.'

'Is it not possible, Friend Daneel, that war is exactly what Dr Amadiro has in mind; that it involves no risk in his estimation, so that getting rid of us at the same time adds to his pleasure without increasing a risk that does not exist?'

Daneel said, calmly, 'Friend Giskard, that is not reasonable. In any war fought under present conditions, the Settlers would win. They are better-suited, psychologically, to the rigours of war. They are more scattered, and can, therefore, more successfully carry on hit-and-run tactics. They have comparatively little to lose in their relatively primitive worlds, while the Spacers have much to lose in their comfortable, highly-organized ones. If the Settlers were willing to offer to exchange destruction of one of their worlds for one of the Spacers', the Spacers would have to surrender at once.'

'But would such a war be fought "under present conditions"? What if the Spacers had a new weapon that could be used to defeat the Settlers quickly? Might that not be the very crisis we are now facing?'

'In that case, Friend Giskard, the victory could be better and more effectively gained in a surprise attack. Why go to the trouble of instigating a war, which the Settlers might begin by a surprise raid on Spacer worlds, that would do considerable damage?'

'Perhaps the Spacers need to test the weapon, and the destruction of a series of ships on Solaria represents the testing.'

'The Spacers would have been most uningenious if they could not have found a method of testing that would not give away the new weapon's existence.'

It was now Giskard's turn to consider. 'Very well, then, Friend Daneel, how would you explain this trip we are on? How would you explain the Council's willingness – even eagerness – to have us accompany the Settler? The Settler said they would order Gladia to go, and, in effect, they did.'

'I have not considered the matter, Friend Giskard.'

'Then consider it now.' Again, it had the flavour of an order.

Daneel said, 'I will do so.'

There was silence, one that grew protracted, but Giskard by no word or sign showed any impatience as he waited.

Finally, Daneel said – slowly, as though he were feeling

his way along strange avenues of thought – 'I do not think that Baleyworld, or any of the Settler worlds, has a clear right to appropriate robotic property on Solaria. Even though the Solarians have themselves left or have, perhaps, died out, Solaria remains a Spacer world, even if an unoccupied one. Certainly, the remaining forty-nine Spacer worlds would reason so. Most of all, Aurora would reason so – if it felt in command of the situation.'

Giskard considered that. 'Are you now saying, Friend Daneel, that the destruction of the two Settler ships was the Spacer way of enforcing their proprietorship of Solaria?'

Daneel said, 'No, that would not be the way if Aurora, the leading Spacer power, felt in command of the situation. Aurora would then simply have announced that Solaria, empty or not, was off-limits to Settler vessels, and would have threatened reprisals against the home worlds if any Settler vessel entered the Solarian planetary system. And they would have established a cordon of ships and sensory stations about that planetary system. There was no such warning, no such action, Friend Giskard. Why, then, destroy ships that might have been kept away from the world quite easily in the first place?'

'But the ships *were* destroyed, Friend Daneel? Will you make use of the basic illogicality of the human mind as an explanation?'

'Not unless I have to. Let us for the moment take that destruction simply as given. Now consider the consequence. The captain of a single Settler vessel approaches Aurora, demands permission to discuss the situation with the Council, insists on taking an Auroran citizen with him to investigate events on Solaria, and the Council gives in to everything. If destroying the ships without prior warning is too strong an action for Aurora, giving in to the Settler captain so cravenly is far too weak an action. Far from seeking a war, Aurora, in giving in, seems to be willing to do anything at all to ward off the possibility of war.'

'Yes,' said Giskard, 'I see that this is a possible way of interpreting events. But what follows?'

'It seems to me,' said Daneel, 'that the Spacer worlds are not yet so weak that they must behave with such servility – and, even if they were, the pride of centuries of overlordship would keep them from doing so. It must be something other than weakness that is driving them. I have pointed out that they cannot be deliberately instigating a war, so it is much more likely that they are playing for time.'

'To what end, Friend Daneel?'

'They want to destroy the Settlers but they are not yet prepared. They let this Settler have what he wants, to avoid a war until they are ready to fight one on their own terms. I am only surprised that they did not offer to send an Auroran warship with him. If this analysis is correct, and I think it is, Aurora cannot possibly have had anything to do with the incidents on Solaria. They would not indulge in pinpricks that could only serve to alert the Settlers, before they are ready with something devastating.'

'Then how account for these pinpricks, as you call them, Friend Daneel?'

'We will find out perhaps when we land on Solaria. It may be that Aurora is as curious as we are and the Settlers are, and that that is another reason why they have cooperated with the Captain, even to the point of allowing Madam Gladia to accompany him.'

It was now Giskard's turn to remain silent. Finally, 'And what is this mysterious devastation that they plan?'

'Earlier, we spoke of a crisis arising from the Spacer plan to defeat Earth, but we used Earth in its general sense, implying the Earthpeople together with their descendants on the Settler worlds. However, if we seriously suspect the preparation of a devastating blow that will allow the Spacers to defeat their enemies at a stroke, we can perhaps refine our view. Thus, they cannot be planning a blow at a Settler world. Individually, the Settler worlds are dispensable, and the remaining Settler worlds will promptly strike back. Nor can they be planning a blow at several or at all the Settler worlds. There are too many of them; they are too diffusely spread. It is not likely that all the strikes will succeed, and those Settler worlds that survive will, in fury and despair, bring devastation upon the Spacer worlds.'

'You reason, then, Friend Daneel, that it will be a blow at Earth itself.'

'Yes, Friend Giskard. Earth contains the vast majority of the short-lived human beings; it is the perennial source of emigrants to the Settler worlds and is the chief raw material for the founding of new ones; it is the revered homeland of all the Settlers. If Earth were somehow destroyed, the Settler movement might never recover.'

'But would not the Settler worlds then retaliate as strongly and as forcefully as they would if one of themselves were destroyed? That would seem to me to be inevitable.'

'And to me, Friend Giskard. Therefore, it seems to me that unless the Spacer worlds have gone insane, the blow would have to be a subtle one, one for which the Spacer worlds would seem to bear no responsibility.'

'Why not such a subtle blow against the Settler worlds, which hold most of the actual war-potential of the Earthpeople?'

'Either because the Spacers feel the blow against Earth would be more psychologically devastating, or because the nature of the blow is such that it would work only against Earth, and not against the Settler worlds. I suspect the latter, since Earth is a unique world and has a society that is not like that of any other world, Settler or, for that matter, Spacer.'

'To summarize then, Friend Daneel, you come to the conclusion that the Spacers are planning a subtle blow against Earth that will destroy it without evidence of themselves as the cause, and one that would not work against any other world, and that they are not yet ready to launch that blow.'

'Yes, Friend Giskard, but they may soon be ready, and once they are ready, they will have to strike immediately. Any delay will increase the chance of some leak that will give them away.'

'To deduce all this, Friend Daneel, from the small indications we have is most praiseworthy. Now tell me the nature of the blow. What is it, precisely, that the Spacers plan?'

'I have come this far, Friend Giskard, across very shaky ground, without being certain that my reasoning is entirely sound. But even if we suppose it is, I can go no further. I fear I do not know and cannot imagine what the nature of the blow might be.'

Giskard said, 'But we cannot take appropriate measures to counteract the blow and resolve the crisis until we know what its nature will be. If we must wait until the blow reveals itself by its results, it will then be too late to do anything.'

Daneel said, 'If any Spacer knows the nature of the forthcoming event, it would be Amadiro. Could you not force Amadiro to announce it publicly, and thus alert the Settlers and make it unusable?'

'I could not do that, Friend Daneel, without virtually destroying his mind. I doubt that I could hold it together long enough to allow him to make the announcement. I could not do such a thing.'

'Perhaps, then,' said Daneel, 'we may console ourselves

with the thought that my reasoning is wrong, and that no blow against Earth is being prepared.'

'No,' said Giskard. 'It is my feeling that you are right, and that we must simply wait – helplessly.'

17.

Gladia waited, with an almost painful anticipation, for the conclusion of the final Jump. They would then be close enough to Solaria to make out its sun as a disk.

It would just be a disk, of course, a featureless circle of light, subdued to the point where it could be watched unblinkingly, after that light had passed through the appropriate filter.

Its appearance would not be unique. All the stars that carried, among their planets, a habitable world in the human sense had a long list of property requirements that ended by making them all resemble one another. They were all single stars; all not much larger or much smaller than the sun that shone on Earth; none too active, or too old, or too quiet, or too young, or too hot, or too cool, or too offbeat in chemical composition. All had sunspots and flares and prominences and all looked just about the same to the eye. It took careful spectroheliography to work out the details that made each star unique.

Nevertheless, when Gladia found herself staring at a circle of light that was absolutely nothing more than a circle of light to her, she found her eyes welling with tears. She had never given the sun a thought when she had lived on Solaria; it was just the eternal source of light and heat, rising and falling in a steady rhythm. When she had left Solaria, she had watched that sun disappear behind her with nothing but a feeling of thankfulness. She had no memory of it that she valued.

Yet she was weeping silently. She was ashamed of herself for being so affected for no reason that she could explain, but that didn't stop the weeping.

She made a stronger effort when the signal light gleamed. It had to be D. G. at the door; no one else would approach her cabin.

Daneel said, 'Is he to enter, madam? You seem emotionally moved.'

'Yes, I'm emotionally moved, Daneel, but let him in. I imagine it won't come as a surprise to him.'

Yet it did. At least, he entered with a smile on his bearded face, and that smile disappeared almost at once. He stepped back and said in a low voice, 'I will return later.'

'Stay!' said Gladia, harshly. 'This is nothing. A silly reaction of the moment.' She sniffed and dabbed angrily at her eyes. 'Why are you here?'

'I wanted to discuss Solaria with you. If we succeed with a micro-adjustment, we'll land tomorrow. If you're not quite up to a discussion now – '

'I am *quite* up to it. In fact, I have a question of you. Why is it we took three Jumps to get here? One Jump would have been sufficient. One was sufficient when I was taken from Solaria to Aurora twenty decades ago. Surely, the technique of space-travel has not retrogressed since.'

D. G.'s grin returned. 'Evasive action. If an Auroran ship was following us, I wanted to – confuse it, shall we say?'

'Why should one follow us?'

'Just a thought, my lady. The Council was a little over-eager to help, I thought. They suggested that an Auroran ship join me in my expedition to Solaria.'

'Well, it might have helped, mightn't it?'

'Perhaps – if I were quite certain that Aurora wasn't behind all this. I told the Council, quite plainly, that I would do without; or, rather,' he pointed his finger at Gladia, 'just with you. Yet might not the Council send a ship to accompany me even against my wish – out of pure kindness of heart, let us say? Well, I still don't want one; I expect enough trouble without having to look nervously over my shoulder at every moment. So I made myself hard to follow. How much do you know about Solaria, my lady?'

'Haven't I told you often enough? Nothing! Twenty decades have passed.'

'Now, madam, I'm talking about the psychology of the Solarians. That can't have changed in merely twenty decades. Tell me why they have abandoned their planet.'

'The story as I've heard it,' said Gladia, calmly, 'is that their population has been steadily declining. A combination of premature deaths and very few births is apparently responsible.'

'Does that sound reasonable to you?'

'Of course it does. Births have always been few.' Her face twisted in memory. 'Solarian custom does not make impregnation easy, either naturally, artificially, or ectogenetically.'

'You never had children, madam?'

'Not on Solaria.'

'And the premature deaths?'

'I can only guess. I suppose it arose out of a feeling of failure. Solaria was clearly not working out, even though the Solarians had placed a great deal of emotional fervour into their world's having the ideal society – not only one that was better than Earth had ever had, but more nearly perfect than that of any other Spacer world.'

'Are you saying that Solaria was dying of the collective broken heart of its people?'

'If you want to put it in that ridiculous way,' said Gladia, displeased.

D. G. shrugged. 'It seems to be what you're saying. But would they really leave? Where would they go? How would they live?'

'I don't know.'

'But, Madam Gladia, it is well-known that Solarians are accustomed to enormous tracts of land, serviced by many thousands of robots, so that each Solarian is left in almost complete isolation. If they abandon Solaria, where can they go to find a society that would humour them in this fashion? Have they in fact gone to any of the other Spacer worlds?'

'Not as far as I know. But then, I'm not in their confidence.'

'Can they have found a new world for themselves? If so, it would be a raw one and require much in the way of terraforming. Would they be ready for that?'

Gladia shook her head. 'I don't know.'

'Perhaps they haven't really left?'

'Solaria, I understand, gives every evidence of being empty.'

'What evidence is that?'

'All interplanetary communication has ceased. All radiation from the planet, except that consistent with robot work, or clearly due to natural causes, has ceased.'

'How do you know that?'

'That is the report on the Auroran news.'

'Ah! The report! Could it be that someone is lying?'

'What would be the purpose of such a lie?' Gladia stiffened at the suggestion.

'So that our ships would be lured to the world and destroyed.'

'That's ridiculous, D. G.' Her voice grew sharper. 'What would the Spacers gain by destroying two trading vessels through so elaborate a subterfuge?'

'Something has destroyed two Settler vessels on a supposedly empty planet. How do you explain that?'

'I can't. I presume we are going to Solaria in order to find an explanation.'

D. G. regarded her gravely. 'Would you be able to guide me to the section of the world that was yours when you lived on Solaria?'

'My estate?' She returned his stare, astonished.

'Wouldn't you like to see it again?'

Gladia's heart skipped a beat. 'Yes, I would; but why my place?'

'The two ships that were destroyed landed in widely different spots on the planet and yet each was destroyed fairly quickly. Though every spot may be deadly, it seems to me that yours might be less so than others.'

'Why?'

'Because there we might receive help from the robots. You would know them, wouldn't you? They do last more than twenty decades, I suppose. Daneel and Giskard have. And those that were there when you lived on your estate would still remember you, wouldn't they? They would treat you as their mistress and recognize the duty they owed you even beyond that which they would owe to ordinary human beings.'

Gladia said, 'There were ten thousand robots on my estate. I knew perhaps three dozen by sight. Most of the rest I never saw and they may not have ever seen me. Agricultural robots are not very advanced, you know; nor are forestry robots or mining robots. The household robots would still remember me, if they have not been sold or transferred since I left. Then, too, accidents happen, and some *don't* last twenty decades. Besides, whatever you may think of robot memory, human memory is fallible and I might remember none of them.'

'Even so,' said D. G., 'can you direct me to your estate?'

'By latitude and longitude? No.'

'I have charts of Solaria. Would that help?'

'Perhaps approximately. It's in the south-central portion of the northern continent of Heliona.'

'And once we're approximately there, can you make use of landmarks for greater precision, if we skim the Solarian surface?'

'By sea-coasts and rivers, you mean?'

'Yes.'

'I *think* I can.'

'Good! And meanwhile, see if you can remember the names and appearances of any of your robots. It may prove the difference between living and dying.'

18.

D. G. Baley seemed a different person with his officers. The broad smile was not evident, nor the easy indifference to danger. He sat, poring over the charts, with a look of intense concentration on his face.

He said, '*If* the woman is correct, we've got the estate pinned down within narrow limits, and if we move into the flying mode, we should get it exactly before too long.'

'Wasteful of energy, Captain,' muttered Jamin Oser, who was second-in-command. He was tall and, like D. G., well-bearded. The beard was russet-coloured, as were his eyebrows, which arched over bright blue eyes. He looked rather old, but, one got the impression that was through experience rather than years.

'Can't help it,' said D. G. 'If we had the anti-gravity that the technos keep promising us just this side of eternity, it would be different.'

He stared at the chart again, and said, 'She says it would

be along this river about 60 kilometres upstream from where it runs into this larger one. *If* she is correct.'

'You keep doubting it,' said Chandrus Nadirhaba, whose insignia showed him to be Navigator, and responsible for bringing the ship down in the correct spot – or, in any case, the indicated spot. His dark skin and neat moustache accentuated the handsome strength of his face.

'She's recalling a situation over a time gap of twenty decades,' said D. G. 'What details would you remember of a site you haven't seen for just three decades? She's not a robot. She may have forgotten.'

'Then what was the point of bringing her?' muttered Oser, 'and the other one and the robot? It unsettles the crew, and I don't exactly like it, either.'

D. G. looked up, eyebrows bunching together. He said, in a low voice, 'It doesn't matter on this ship what you don't like or what the crew doesn't like, mister. I have the responsibility and I make the decisions. We're liable all to be dead within six hours of landing unless that woman can save us.'

Nadirhaba said, coolly, 'If we die, we die. We wouldn't be Traders if we didn't know that sudden death was the other side of big profits. And for this mission, we're all volunteers. Just the same, it doesn't hurt to know where the death's coming from, Captain. If you've figured it out, does it have to be a secret?'

'No, it doesn't. The Solarians are supposed to have left, but suppose a couple of hundred stayed quietly behind just to watch the store, so to speak?'

'And what can they do to an armed ship, Captain? Do they have a secret weapon?'

'Not so secret,' said D. G. 'Solaria is littered with robots. That's the whole reason Settler ships landed on the world in the first place. Each remaining Solarian might have a million robots at his disposal. An enormous army.'

Eban Kalaya was in charge of communications. So far he had said nothing, aware as he was of his junior status, which seemed further marked by the fact that he was the only one of the four officers present without facial hair of any kind. Now he ventured a remark. 'Robots,' he said, 'cannot injure human beings.'

'So we are told,' said D. G. dryly, 'but what do *we* know about robots? What we do know is that two ships have been destroyed and about a hundred human beings, good Settlers all, have been killed on widely-separated parts of a world littered with robots. How could it have been done except by robots? We don't know what kind of orders a Solarian might give robots, or by what tricks the so-called First Law of Robotics might be circumvented.

'So we,' he went on, 'have to do a little circumventing of our own. As best we can tell from the reports reaching us from the other ships before they were destroyed, all the men on board ship debarked on landing. It was an empty world after all, and they wanted to stretch their legs, breathe fresh air *and* look over the robots they had come to get. Their ships were unprotected and they themselves unready when the attack came.

'That won't happen this time. I'm getting off, but the rest of you are going to stay on board ship, or in its near vicinity.'

Nadirhaba's dark eyes glared disapproval. 'Why you, Captain? If you need someone to act as bait, anyone else can be spared more easily than you can be.'

'I appreciate the thought, Navigator,' said D. G., 'but I will not be alone. Coming with me will be the Spacer woman and her companions. She is the one who is essential. She may know some of the robots; at any rate, some may know her. I am hoping that though the robots may have been ordered to attack us, they won't attack her.'

'You mean, they'll remember Ol' Missy, and fall to their knees,' said Nadirhaba, dryly.

'If you want to put it that way. That's why I brought her, and that's why we're landing on her estate. And I've got to be with her because I'm the one who knows her – somewhat – and I've got to see that she behaves. Once we have survived by using her as a shield and in that way have learned exactly what we're facing, we can proceed on our own. We won't need her any more.'

Oser said, 'And then what do we do with her? Jettison her into space?'

D. G. roared, 'We take her back to Aurora.'

Oser said, 'I'm bound to tell you, Captain, that the crew would consider that a wasteful and unnecessary trip. They will feel that we can simply leave her on this blasted world. It's where she comes from, after all.'

'Yes,' said D. G. 'That will be the day, won't it, when I take orders from the crew.'

'I'm sure you won't,' said Oser, 'but the crew has its opinions and an unhappy crew makes for a dangerous voyage.'

6

The Crew

19.

Gladia stood on the soil of Solaria. She smelled the vegetation – not quite the odours of Aurora – and at once she crossed the gap of twenty decades.

Nothing, she knew, could bring back associations in the way that odours could. Not sights; not sounds.

Just that faint, unique smell brought back childhood – the freedom of running about, with a dozen robots watching her carefully – the excitement of seeing other children sometimes, coming to a halt, staring shyly, approaching one another a half-step at a time, reaching out to touch, and then a robot saying, 'Enough, Miss Gladia,' and being led away – looking over the shoulder at the other child, with whom there was another set of attendant robots in charge.

She remembered the day that she was told that only by holovision would she see other human beings thereafter. Viewing, she was told – not seeing. The robots said 'seeing' as though it were a word they must not say, so that they had to whisper it. She could see *them*, but they were not human.

It was not so bad at first. The images she could talk to were three-dimensional, free-moving. They could talk, run, turn cart-wheels if they wished – but they could not be felt. And then she was told that she could actually see someone whom she had often viewed and whom she had liked. He was a grown man, quite a bit older than she was, though he looked quite young, as one did on Solaria. She

would have permission to continue to see him, if she
wished, whenever necessary.

She wished. She remembered how it was; *exactly* how it
was on that first day. She was tongue-tied and so was he.
They circled each other, afraid to touch. But it was
marriage.

Of course it was. And then they met again, seeing, not
viewing, *because* it was marriage. They would finally touch
each other. They were supposed to.

It was the most exciting day of her life – until it took
place.

Fiercely, Gladia stopped her thoughts. Of what use to
go on? She so warm and eager; he so cold and withdrawn.
He continued to be cold. When he came to see her, at
fixed intervals, for the rites that might (or might not)
succeed in impregnating her, it was with such clear revulsion, that she was soon longing for him to forget. But he
was a man of duty and he never forgot.

Then came the time, years of dragging unhappiness
later, when she found him dead, his skull crushed, and
herself as the only possible suspect. Elijah Baley had saved
her then, and she had been taken away from Solaria and
sent to Aurora.

Now she was back, smelling Solaria.

Nothing else was familiar. The house in the distance
bore no resemblance to anything she remembered even
faintly. In twenty decades it had been modified, torn
down, rebuilt. She could not even gain any sense of
familiarity with the ground itself.

She found herself reaching backwards to touch the
Settler ship that had brought her to this world that smelled
like home, but was home in no other way – just to touch
something that was familiar by comparison.

Daneel, who stood next to her in the shadow of the
ship, said, 'Do you see the robots, Madam Gladia?'

There were a group of them, a hundred yards away, amid the trees of an orchard, watching solemnly, motionlessly, shining in the sun with the greyish, well-polished metal-finish Gladia remembered Solarian robots to have.

She said, 'I do, Daneel.'

'Is there anything familiar about them, madam?'

'Not at all. They seem to be new models. I can't remember them, and I'm sure they can't remember me. If D. G. was expecting anything hopeful to come of my supposed familiarity with the robots on my estate, he will have to be disappointed.'

Giskard said, 'They do not seem to be doing anything, madam.'

Gladia said, 'That is understandable. We're intruders and they've come to observe us and to report on us in accordance with what must be standing orders. They have no one now to report to, however, and can merely silently observe. Without further orders, I presume they will do no more than that, but they won't cease doing so, either.'

Daneel said, 'It might be well, Madam Gladia, if we retired to our quarters on board ship. The Captain is, I believe, supervising the construction of defences and is not ready to go exploring yet. I suspect he will not approve your having left your quarters without his specific permission.'

Gladia said, haughtily, 'I'm not going to delay stepping out on to the surface of my own world just to suit his whim.'

'I understand, but members of the crew are engaged in the vicinity, and I believe that some note your presence here.'

'And are approaching,' said Giskard. 'If you would avoid infection – '

'I'm prepared,' said Gladia. 'Nose-plugs and gloves.'

Gladia did not understand the nature of the structures

being put up on the flat ground about the ship. For the most part, the crewmen, absorbed in the construction, had not seen Gladia and her two companions, standing as they were in the shadow. (It was the warm season on this portion of Solaria, which had a tendency to grow warmer – and on other occasions, colder – than Aurora did, since the Solarian day was nearly six hours longer than the Auroran day.)

The crewmen approaching were five in number, and one of them, the tallest and largest, pointed in the direction of Gladia. The other four looked, remained standing for a while as though merely curious, and then, at a gesture from the first, approached again, changing their angle slightly so as to head directly for the Auroran three.

Gladia watched them silently and with her eyebrows raised in contempt. Daneel and Giskard waited impassively.

Giskard said in a low voice to Daneel, 'I do not know where the Captain is. I cannot distinguish him from the crowd of crewmen in whose midst he must be.'

'Shall we retire?' said Daneel, aloud.

'That would be disgraceful,' said Gladia. 'This is *my* world.'

She held her ground, and the five crewmen came closer in leisurely fashion.

They had been working, doing hard physical labour (Like robots, thought Gladia with disdain) and they were sweating. Gladia became aware of the odour that reeked from them. That would have served to force her away more than threats would, but she held on even so. The nose-plugs, she was sure, mitigated the effect of the smell.

The large crewman approached more closely than the others. His skin was bronzed. His bare arms glistened with moisture and with shining musculature. He might be thirty (as nearly as Gladia could judge the age of these short-lived beings) and if he were washed, and properly dressed, he might prove quite presentable.

He said, 'So you are the Spacer lady from Aurora that we've been carrying on our ship?' He spoke rather slowly, obviously trying to attain an aristocratic tinge to his Galactic. He failed, of course, and he spoke like a Settler – even more crudely than D. G. did.

Gladia said, establishing her territorial rights, 'I am from Solaria, Settler,' and stopped in confused embarrassment. She had spent so much time thinking of Solaria just now, that twenty decades had dropped away and she had spoken with a thick Solarian accent. There was the broad 'a' in Solaria, and the rough 'r', while the 'I' sounded horribly like 'Oi'.

She said again, in a much lower, less commanding voice, but one in which the accent of Aurora University – the standard for Galactic speech through all the Spacer worlds – rang clear, 'I am from Solaria, Settler.'

The Settler laughed and turned to the others. 'She speaks la-di-da, but she had to try. Right, mates.'

The others laughed, too, and one cried out, 'Get her to talk some more, Niss. Maybe we can all learn to talk like Spacer birdies.' And he placed one hand on his hip in as dainty a manner as he could manage, while holding the other hand out limply.

Niss said, still smiling, 'Shut up all of you.' There was instant silence.

He turned to Gladia again, 'I'm Berto Niss, First-Class Shipper. And your name, little woman?'

Gladia did not venture to speak again.

Niss said, 'I'm being polite, little woman. I'm speaking gentlemanly. Spacer-like. I know you're old enough to be my great-grandmother. How old are you, little woman?'

'Four hundred,' shouted one of the crewmen from behind Niss, 'but she doesn't look it.'

'She doesn't look one hundred,' said another.

'She looks suitable for a little ding-donging,' said a third, 'and hasn't had any for a long time, I guess. Ask her if she'd want some, Niss. Be polite and ask if we can take turns.'

Gladia flushed angrily, and Daneel said, 'First-Class Shipper Niss, your companions are offending Madam Gladia. Would you retire?'

Niss turned to look at Daneel, whom, till now, he had totally ignored. The smile vanished from his face, and he said, 'Look, you. This little lady is off-limits. The Captain said so. We won't bother her. Just a little harmless talk. That thing there is a robot. We won't bother with him and he can't hurt us. We know the Laws of Robotics. We order him to stay away from us, see. But *you* are a Spacer and the Captain has given us no orders about you. So you,' and he pointed a finger, 'stay out of this, and don't interfere, or you'll get your pretty skin all bruised up and then you might cry.'

Daneel said nothing.

Niss nodded his head. 'Good. I like to see someone smart enough not to start anything he can't finish.'

He turned to Gladia, 'Now, little Spacer woman, we will leave you alone because the Captain doesn't want you bothered. If one of the men here made a crude remark, that's only natural. Just shake hands and let's be friends – Spacer, Settler, what's the difference?'

He thrust out his hand towards Gladia, who shrank away in horror. Daneel's hand moved outward in a flick that was almost too fast to see, and caught Niss's wrist. 'First-Class Shipper Niss,' he said, quietly, 'do not attempt to touch the lady.'

Niss looked down at his hand and at the fingers that enclosed his wrist firmly. He said, in a low and menacing growl, 'You have till the count of three to let go.'

Daneel's hand fell away. He said, 'I must do as you say for I do not wish to harm you, but I must protect the lady, and if she doesn't wish to be touched, as I believe she doesn't, I may be forced into a position where I must cause you pain. Please accept my assurance that I will do all I can to minimize that.'

One of the crewmen shouted joyously, 'Give it to him, Niss. He's a talker.'

Niss said, 'Look, Spacer, twice I told you to keep out, and you touched me once. Now I tell you a third time and that's it. Make a move, say a word, and I take you apart. This little woman is going to shake hands, that's all, friendly-like. Then we all go. Fair enough?'

Gladia said, in a low, choking voice, 'I won't be touched by him. Do what is necessary.'

Daneel said, 'Sir, with all due respect, the lady does not wish to be touched. I must ask you – all of you – to leave.'

Niss smiled, and one large arm moved as though to brush Daneel to one side – and to do it hard.

Daneel's left arm flickered, and once again Niss was held by the wrist. 'Please go, sir,' said Daneel.

Niss's teeth continued to show, but he was no longer smiling. Violently, he brought his arm up. Daneel's enclosing hand moved up for a short distance, slowed, and came to a halt. His face showed no strain. His hand moved down, dragging Niss's arm with it and then, with a rapid twist, he bent Niss's arm behind the Settler's broad back and held it there.

Niss, who found himself, unexpectedly, with his back to Daneel, brought his other arm up and over his head, groping for Daneel's neck. His other wrist was seized and pulled down farther than it could easily go, and Niss grunted in clear misery.

The other four crewmen, who had been watching in

eager anticipation, remained in place now, motionless, silent, mouths open.

Niss, staring at them, grunted, 'Help me!'

Daneel said, 'They will not help you, sir, for the Captain's punishment will be all the worse if they try. I must ask you now to assure me that you will no longer trouble Madam Gladia and that you will leave quietly, all of you. Otherwise, I very much regret, First-Class Shipper, that I must pull your arms out of their sockets.'

As he said that, he tightened his grip on either wrist, and Niss emitted a muffled grunt.

'My apologies, sir,' said Daneel, 'but I am under the strictest orders. May I have your assurance?'

Niss kicked backward with sudden viciousness, but well before his heavy boot could make contact, Daneel had faded to one side and pulled him off-balance. He went face-down heavily.

'May I have your assurance, sir?' said Daneel, now pulling gently at the two wrists so that the crewman's arms lifted slightly up from the back.

Niss howled and said, half-incoherent, 'I give in. Let go.'

Daneel let go at once and stepped back. Slowly, and painfully, Niss rolled over, moving his arms slowly and rotating his wrists with a twisted grimace.

Then, when his right arm moved near the holster he wore, he snatched clumsily at his side-arm.

Daneel's foot came down on Niss's hand and pinned it to the ground. 'Don't do that, sir, or I may be forced to break one or more of the small bones in your hand.' He bent down and extracted Niss's blaster from its holster. 'Now stand up.'

'Well, Mr Niss,' came another voice. 'Do as you are told and stand up.'

D. G. Baley was standing at their side, beard bristling, face slightly flushed, but his voice was dangerously calm.

'You four,' he said, 'hand me your side-arms, one at a time. Come on. Move a little faster. One – two – three – four. Now continue to stand there, at attention. Sir,' this to Daneel, 'give me that side-arm you are holding. Good. Five. And now, Mr Niss, at attention.' And he placed the blasters on the ground beside him.

Niss stiffened to attention, eyes bloodshot, face contorted, in obvious pain.

'Would someone,' said D. G., 'please say what has been going on?'

'Captain,' said Daneel, quickly, 'Mr Niss and I have had a playful altercation. No harm has been done.'

'Mr Niss, however, looks somewhat harmed,' said D. G.

'No permanent harm, Captain,' said Daneel.

'I see. Well, we'll get back to this later. Madam,' he turned on his heel to address Gladia, 'I don't recall that I gave you permission to emerge from the ship. You will go back to your cabin at once, with your two companions. I am captain here and this is not Aurora. Do as I say!'

Daneel placed an apologetic hand on Gladia's elbow. Her chin lifted, but she turned and went up the gangplank and into the ship, Daneel at her side, Giskard following.

D. G. then turned to the crewmen. 'You five,' he said, his voice never lifting from its flat calm, 'come with me, and we'll get to the bottom of this – or of you.' And he gestured to a petty officer to pick up the side-arms and take them away.

20.

D. G. stared at the five grimly. He was in his own quarters, the only portion of the ship that had a semblance of size to it, and the beginning of an appearance of luxury.

He said, pointing to each in turn, 'Now this is the way we'll work it. *You* tell me exactly what happened, word for word, motion for motion. When you're finished, *you* tell me anything that was wrong or left out. Then *you* the same, and then *you*, and then I'll get to you, Niss. I expect that you were all out of order, that you all did something unusually stupid that earned you all, but especially Niss, considerable humiliation. If, in your story, it would appear that you did nothing wrong and suffered no humiliation, then I'll know you're lying, especially as the Spacer woman will surely tell me what happened, and I intend to believe every word she says. A lie will make matters worse for you than anything you've actually done. Now,' he barked, '*start!*'

The first crewman stumbled hastily through the story, and then the second, somewhat correcting, somewhat expanding, then, the third and the fourth. D. G. listened, stony-faced, to the recital, then motioned Berto Niss to one side.

He spoke to the other four, 'And while Niss was getting his face rightly mashed into the dirt by the Spacer, what were you four doing? Watching? Scared to move? All four of you? Against one man?'

One of the men broke the thickening silence to say, 'It all happened so quick, Captain. We were just getting set to move in, and then it was all over.'

'And what were you getting ready to do in case you did manage to get to move someday?'

'Well, we were going to pull the Spacer foreigner off our mate.'

'Do you think you could have?'

This time no one offered to make a sound.

D. G. leaned towards them. 'Now here's the situation. You had no business interfering with the foreigners, so you're fined one week's pay each. And now let's get something straight. If you tell what has happened to anyone else, in the crew or out, now or ever, whether drunk or sober, you'll be broken, every one of you, to Apprentice Shipper. It doesn't matter which one of you talks, you'll all four be broken, so keep an eye on each other. Now get to your assigned tasks, and if you cross me at any time during this voyage, if you as much as hiccup against regulations, you'll be in the brig.'

The four left, mournful, hangdog, tight-lipped. Niss remained, a bruise developing on his face, his arms clearly in discomfort.

D. G. regarded him with a threatening quiet, while Niss stared to the left, to the right, at his feet, everywhere but at the face of the Captain. It was only when Niss's eyes, running out of evasion, caught the glare of the Captain, that D. G. said, 'Well, you look very handsome, now that you have tangled with a sissy Spacer half your size. Next time you better hide when one of them shows up.'

'Yes, Captain,' said Niss, miserably.

'Did you, or did you not, Niss, hear me in my briefing, before we left Aurora, say that the Spacer woman and her companions were on no account to be disturbed or spoken to?'

'Captain, I wanted only a polite how-de-do. We was curious for a closer look. No harm meant.'

'You meant no harm? You asked how old she was. Was that your business?'

'Just curious. Wanted to know.'

'One of you made a sexual suggestion.'

'Not me, Captain.'

'Someone else? Did you apologize for it?'

'To a Spacer?' Niss sounded horrified.

'Certainly. You were going against my orders.'

'I meant no harm,' said Niss, doggedly.

'You meant no harm to the man?'

'He put his hand on me, Captain.'

'I know he did. Why?'

'Because he was ordering me around.'

'And you wouldn't stand for it?'

'Would you, Captain?'

'All right, then. You didn't stand for it. You fell down for it. Right on your face. How did that happen?'

'I don't rightly know, Captain. He was fast. Like the camera was sped up. And he had a grip like iron.'

D. G. said, 'So he did. What did you expect, you idiot? He *is* iron.'

'Captain?'

'Niss, is it possible you don't know the story of Elijah Baley?'

Niss rubbed his ear in embarrassment. 'I know he's your great, something, grandfather, Captain.'

'Yes, everyone knows that from my name. Have you ever viewed his life-story?'

'I'm not a viewing man, Captain. Not on history.' He shrugged and, as he did so, winced and made as though to rub his shoulder, then decided he didn't quite dare do so.

'Did you ever hear of R. Daneel Olivaw?'

Niss squeezed his brows together. 'He was Elijah Baley's friend.'

'Yes, he was. You do know something then. Do you know what the R. stands for in R. Daneel Olivaw?'

'It stands for Robot. Right? He was a robot friend. There was robots on Earth in them days.'

'There were, Niss, and still are. But Daneel wasn't just a robot. He was a Spacer robot who looked like a Spacer man. Think about it, Niss. Guess who the Spacer man you picked a fight with really was.'

Niss's eyes widened, his face reddened dully. 'You mean that Spacer was a ro –'

'That was R. Daneel Olivaw.'

'But Captain, that was two hundred years ago.'

'Yes, and the Spacer woman was a particular friend of my ancestor, Elijah. She's been alive for two hundred and thirty-five years, in case you still want to know, and do you think a robot can't do as well as that? You were trying to fight a robot, you great fool.'

'Why didn't it say so?' said Niss, with great indignation.

'Why should it? Did you ask? See here, Niss. You heard what I told the others about telling this to anyone. It goes for you, too, but much more so. They are only crewmen, but I had my eye on you for crew-leader. *Had* my eye on you. If you're going to be in charge of the crew, you've got to have brains, and not just muscle. So now it's going to be harder for you, because you're going to have to prove you have brains against my firm opinion that you don't.'

'Captain, I –'

'Don't talk. Listen. If this story gets out, the other four will be Apprentice Shippers, but you will be *nothing*. You will never go on shipboard again. *No* ship will take you, I promise you that. Not as crew, not as passenger. Ask yourself what kind of money you can make on Baleyworld, and doing what? That's if you talk about this, or if you cross the Spacer woman in any way, or even just look at her for more than half a second at a time, or at her two robots. And you are going to have to see to it that no one else among the crew is in the least offensive. You're responsible. And you're fined two weeks' pay.'

'But Captain,' said Niss, weakly, 'the others – '

'I expected less from the others, Niss, so I fined them less. Get out of here.'

21.

D. G. played idly with the photocube that always stood on his desk. Each time he turned it, it blackened, then cleared when stood upon one of its sides as its base. When it cleared, the smiling three-dimensional image of a woman's head could be seen.

Crew rumour was that each of the six sides led to the appearance of a different woman. The rumour was quite correct.

Jamin Oser watched the flashing appearance and disappearance of images totally without interest. Now that the ship was secured – or as secured as it could be against attack of any expected variety – it was time to think of the next step.

D. G., however, was approaching the matter obliquely; or, perhaps, not approaching it at all. He said, 'It was the woman's fault, of course.'

Oser shrugged and passed his hand over his beard, as though he were reassuring himself that he, at least, was not a woman. Unlike D. G., Oser had his upper lip luxuriantly covered as well.

D. G. said, 'Apparently, being on the planet of her birth removed any thought of discretion. She left the ship, even though I had asked her not to.'

'You might have *ordered* her not to.'

'I don't know that that would have helped. She's a spoiled aristocrat, used to having her own way and to ordering her robots about. Besides, I plan to use her and I want her cooperation, not her pouting. And again – she was the Ancestor's friend.'

'And still alive,' said Oser, shaking his head. 'It makes the skin crawl. An old, old woman.'

'I know, but she looks quite young. Still attractive. And nose in the air. Wouldn't retire when the crewmen approached; wouldn't shake hands with one of them. Well, it's over.'

'Still, Captain, was it the right thing to tell Niss he had tackled a robot?'

'Had to! Had to, Oser. If he thought he'd been beaten and humiliated before four of his mates by an effeminate Spacer half his size, he'd be useless to us forever. It would have broken him completely. And we don't want anything to happen that will start the rumour that Spacers – that *human* Spacers – are supermen. That's why I had to order them so strenuously not to talk about it. Niss will ride hard on all of them, and if it *does* get out, it will also get out that the Spacer was a robot. But I suppose there was a good side to the whole thing.'

'Where, Captain?' asked Oser.

'It got me to thinking about robots. How much do we know about them? How much do *you* know?'

Oser shrugged. 'Captain, it's not something I think about much.'

'Or something anyone else thinks about, either. At least, any Settler. We know that the Spacers have robots, depend on them, go nowhere without them, can't do a thing without them, are parasites on them, and we're sure they're fading away because of them. We know that Earth once had robots forced on them by the Spacers and that they are gradually disappearing from Earth and are not found at all in Earth Cities, only in the countryside. We know that the Settler worlds don't and won't have them anywhere, town or country. So Settlers never meet them either on their own worlds, and hardly ever on Earth.' (His voice had a curious inflection each time he said 'Earth', as though one could hear the capital, as though one could hear the words 'home' and 'mother' whispered behind it.) 'What else do we know?'

Oser said, 'There's the Three Laws of Robotics.'

'Right,' D. G. pushed the photocube to one side and leaned forward. 'Especially the First Law. "A robot may not injure a human being, or, through inaction, allow a human being to be injured." Yes? Well, don't rely on it. It doesn't mean a thing. We all feel ourselves to be absolutely safe from robots because of that, and that's fine if it gives us confidence, but not if it gives us *false* confidence. R. Daneel injured Niss and it didn't bother the robot at all, First Law or no First Law.'

'He was defending —'

'Exactly. What if you must balance injuries? What if it was a case of either hurt Niss or allow your Spacer owner to come to harm? Naturally, she comes first.'

'It makes sense.'

'Of course it does. And here we are on a planet of robots, a couple of hundred million of them. What orders do they have? How do they balance the conflict between different harms? How can we be sure that none of them will touch us? Something on this planet has destroyed two ships already.'

Oser said, uneasily, 'This R. Daneel is an unusual robot; looks more like a man than we do. It may be we can't generalize from him. That other robot, what's his name?'

'Giskard. It's easy to remember. My name is Daneel Giskard.'

'I think of you as captain, Captain. Anyway, that R. Giskard just stood there and didn't do a thing. He looks like a robot and he acts like one. We've got lots of robots

out there on Solaria watching us right now, and they're
not doing a thing, either. Just watching.'

'And if there are some special robots that *can* harm us?'

'I think we're prepared for them.'

'*Now* we are. That's why the incident with Daneel and
Niss was a good thing. We've been thinking that we can
only be in trouble if some of the Solarians are still here.
They don't have to be. They can be gone. It may be that
the robots, or at least some specially-designed robots, can
be dangerous. And if Lady Gladia can mobilize her robots
in this place – it used to be her estate – and make them
defend her, and us, too, we may well be able to neutralize
anything they've left behind.'

'Can she do that?' said Oser.

'We're going to see,' said D. G.

22.

'Thank you, Daneel,' Gladia had said. 'You did well.' Her
face seemed pinched together, however; her lips were
thin and bloodless; her cheeks pale. Then, in a lower
voice, 'I wish I had not come.'

Giskard said, 'It is a useless wish, Madam Gladia. Friend
Daneel and I will remain outside the cabin to make sure
you are not further disturbed.'

The corridor was empty and remained so, but Daneel
and Giskard managed to speak in sound-wave intensities
below the human threshold, exchanging thoughts in their
brief and condensed way.

Giskard said, 'Madam Gladia made an injudicious
decision in refusing to retire. That is clear.'

'I presume, Friend Giskard,' said Daneel, 'that there
was no possibility of manoeuvring her into changing that
decision.'

'It was far too firm, Friend Daneel, and taken too quickly. The same was true of the intention of the Settler, Niss. Both his curiosity concerning Madam Gladia and his contempt and animosity towards you were too strong to manage without serious mental harm. The other four I could handle. It was quite possible to keep them from intervening. Their astonishment at your ability to handle Niss froze them naturally, and I had only to strengthen that slightly.'

'That was fortunate, Friend Giskard. Had those four joined Mr Niss, I would have been faced with the difficult choice of forcing Madam Gladia into a humiliating retreat, or of badly damaging one or two of the Settlers to frighten off the rest. I think I would have had to choose the former alternative but it, too, would have caused me grave discomfort.'

'You are well, Friend Daneel?'

'Quite well. My damage to Mr Niss was minimal.'

'Physically, Friend Daneel, it was. Within his mind, however, there was great humiliation, which was to him much worse than the physical damage. Since I could sense that, I could not have done what you did so easily. And yet, Friend Daneel – '

'Yes, Friend Giskard?'

'I am disturbed over the future. On Aurora, through all the decades of my existence, I have been able to work slowly, to wait for opportunities of touching minds gently, without doing harm; of strengthening what is already there, of weakening what is already attenuated, of pushing gently in the direction of existing impulse. Now, however, we are coming to a time of crisis in which emotions will run high, decisions will be taken quickly, and events will race past us. If I am to do any good at all, I will have to act quickly, too, and the Three Laws of Robotics prevent me from doing so. It takes time to weigh the subtleties of comparative physical *and* mental harm. Had I been alone with Madam Gladia at the time of the Settlers' approach, I do not see what course I could have taken that I would not have recognized as entailing serious damage to Madam Gladia, to one or more of the Settlers, to myself – or possibly to all who were involved.'

Daneel said, 'What is there to do, Friend Giskard?'

'Since it is impossible to modify the Three Laws, Friend Daneel, once again we must come to the conclusion that there is nothing we can do, but await failure.'

7

The Overseer

23.

It was morning on Solaria, morning on the estate – *her* estate. Off in the distance was the establishment that might have been *her* establishment. Somehow twenty decades dropped away and Aurora seemed to her to be a far-off dream that had never happened.

She turned to D. G., who was tightening the belt about his thin outer garment, a belt from which two side-arms depended. On his left hip was the neuronic whip; on his right, something shorter and bulkier which she guessed was a blaster.

'Are we going to the house?' she asked.

'Eventually,' said D. G., with a certain absence of mind. He was inspecting each side-arm in turn, holding one of them to his ear as though he were listening for the faint buzz that would tell him it was alive.

'Just the four of us?' She automatically turned her eyes to each of the others, D. G., Daneel –

She said to Daneel, 'Where is Giskard, Daneel?'

Daneel said, 'It seemed to him, Madam Gladia, that it would be wise to act as an advance guard. As a robot, he might not be noticeable among other robots, and if there should be anything wrong, he could warn us. In any case, he is more expendable than either yourself or the Captain.'

'Good robotic thinking,' said D. G., grimly. 'It's just as well. Come, we're moving forward now.'

'Just the three of us?' said Gladia, a touch plaintively.

'To be honest, I lack Giskard's robotic ability to accept expendability.'

D. G. said, 'We're all expendable, Lady Gladia. Two ships have been destroyed; every member of each crew indiscriminately brought to an end. There's no safety in numbers here.'

'You're not making me feel any better, D. G.'

'Then I'll try. The earlier ships were not prepared. Our ship is. And I'm prepared, too.' He slapped his two hands to his hips. 'And you've got a robot with you who has showed himself to be an efficient protector. What's more, you yourself are our best weapon. You know how to order robots to do what you want them to do, and that may well be crucial. You are the only one with us who can do that, and the earlier ships had no one at all of your calibre. Come, then –'

They moved forward. Gladia said, after a while, 'We're not walking towards the house.'

'No, not yet. First, we're walking towards a group of robots. You see them, I hope.'

'Yes, I do, but they're not doing anything.'

'No, they're not. There were many more robots present when we first landed. Most of them have gone, but these remain. Why?'

'If we ask them, they'll tell us.'

'*You* will ask them, Lady Gladia.'

'They'll answer you, D. G., as readily as they'll answer me. We're equally human.'

D. G. stopped short, and the other two stopped with him. He turned to Gladia, and said, smiling, 'My dear Lady Gladia, *equally* human? A Spacer and a Settler? Whatever has come over you?'

'We are equally human to a robot,' she said, waspishly. 'And please don't play games. I did not play the game of Spacer and Earthman with your Ancestor.'

D. G.'s smile vanished. 'That's true. My apologies, lady. I shall try to control my sense of the sardonic for, after all, on this world we are allies.'

He said, a moment later, 'Now, madam, what I want you to do is to find out what orders the robots have been given, if any; if there are any robots that might, by some chance, know you; if there are any human beings on the estate or on the world; or anything else it occurs to you to ask. They shouldn't be dangerous; they're robots and you're human; they can't hurt you. To be sure,' he added, remembering, 'your Daneel rather manhandled Niss, but that was under conditions that don't obtain here. And Daneel may go with you.'

Respectfully, Daneel said, 'I would in any case accompany Lady Gladia, Captain. That is my function.'

'Giskard's function, too, I imagine,' said D. G., 'and yet he's wandered off.'

'For a purpose, Captain, that he discussed with me, and that we agreed was an essential way of protecting Lady Gladia.'

'Very well. You two move forward. I'll cover you both.' He drew the weapon on his right hip. 'If I call out "Drop", the two of you fall down instantly. This thing doesn't play favourites.'

'Please don't use it as anything but a last resort, D. G.,' said Gladia. 'There would scarcely be an occasion to against robots. Come, Daneel!'

Off she went, stepping forward rapidly and firmly towards the group of about a dozen robots, standing just in front of a line of low bushes, and with the morning sun reflecting in glints here and there from their burnished exteriors.

24.

The robots did not retreat; nor did they advance. They remained in place calmly. Gladia counted them. Eleven in plain sight. There might be others, possibly, that were unseen.

They were designed Solaria-fashion. Very polished. Very smooth. No illusion of clothing, and not much realism. They were almost like mathematical abstractions of the human body, with no two of them quite alike.

She had the feeling that they were by no means as flexible or complex as Auroran robots, but were more single-mindedly adapted to specific tasks.

She stopped at least four metres from the line of robots, and Daneel (she sensed) stopped as soon as she did and remained less than a metre behind. He was close enough to interfere at once in case of need, but was far enough back to make it clear that she was the dominant spokesperson of the pair. The robots before her, she was certain, viewed Daneel as a human being, but she also knew that Daneel was too conscious of himself as a robot to presume upon the misconception of other robots.

Gladia said, 'Which one of you will speak with me?'

There was a brief period of silence, as though an unspoken conference. Then one robot took a step forward. 'Madam, I will speak.'

'Do you have a name?'

'No, madam. I have only a serial number.'

'How long have you been operational?'

'I have been operational twenty-nine years, madam.'

'Has anyone else in this group been operational for longer?'

'No, madam. It is why I, rather than another, am speaking.'

'How many robots are employed on this estate?'

'I do not have that figure, madam.'

'Roughly.'

'Perhaps ten thousand, madam.'

'Have any been operational for longer than twenty decades?'

'The agricultural robots include some who may, madam.'

'And the household robots?'

'They have not been operational long, madam. The masters prefer new-model robots.'

Gladia nodded, turned to Daneel, and said, 'That makes sense. It was so in my day, too.'

She turned back to the robot. 'To whom does this estate belong?'

'It is the Zoberlon Estate, madam.'

'How long has it belonged to the Zoberlon family?'

'Longer, madam, than I have been operational. I do not know how much longer, but the information can be obtained.'

'To whom did it belong before the Zoberlons took possession?'

'I do not know, madam, but the information can be obtained.'

'Have you ever heard of the Delmarre family?'

'No, madam.'

Gladia turned to Daneel and said, rather ruefully, 'I'm trying to lead the robot, little by little, as Elijah might once have done, but I don't think I know how to do it properly.'

'On the contrary, Lady Gladia,' said Daneel gravely, 'it seems to me you have established much. It is not likely that any robot on this estate, except perhaps for a few of the agriculturals, would know you of their own memory.

Would you have encountered any of the agriculturals in your time?'

Gladia shook her head. 'Never! I don't recall seeing any of them even in the distance.'

'It is clear, then, that you are not known on this estate.'

'Exactly. And poor D. G. has brought us along for nothing. If he expected any good of me, he has failed.'

'To know the truth is always useful, madam. Not to be known is, in this case, less useful than to be known, but not to know whether one is known or not, would be less useful still. Are there not, perhaps, other points on which you might elicit information?'

'Yes, let's see – ' For a few seconds, she was lost in thought, then she said softly, 'It's odd. When I speak to these robots, I speak with a pronounced Solarian accent. Yet I do not speak so to you.'

Daneel said, 'It is not surprising, Lady Gladia. The robots speak with such an accent, for they are Solarian. That brings back the days of your youth and you speak, automatically, as you spoke then. You are at once yourself, however, when you turn to me, because I am a part of your present world.'

A slow smile appeared on Gladia's face and she said, 'You reason more and more like a human being, Daneel.'

She turned back to the robots and was keenly aware of the peace of the surroundings. The sky was an almost unmarked blue except for a thin line of clouds on the western horizon (so that it might turn cloudy in the afternoon). There was the sound of rustling leaves in a light wind, the whirring of insects, a lonely bird-call. No sound of human beings. There might be many robots about, but they worked silently. There wasn't the exuberant sound-making of human beings that she had grown accustomed to (painfully, at first) on Aurora.

But now, back on Solaria, she found the peace wonderful. It had not been all bad on Solaria. She had to admit it.

She said to the robot quickly, and with a note of compulsion edging her voice, 'Where are your masters?'

It was useless, however, to try to hurry or alarm a robot, or to catch it off-guard. It said, without any sign of perturbation, 'They are gone, madam.'

'Where have they gone?'

'I do not know, madam. I was not told.'

'Which of you knows?'

There was a complete silence.

Gladia said, 'Is there any robot on the estate who would know?'

The robot said, 'I do not know of any, madam.'

'Did the masters take robots with them?'

'Yes, madam.'

'Yet they didn't take you. Why do you remain behind?'

'To do our work, madam.'

'Yet you stand here and do nothing. Is that work?'

'We guard the estate from those from outside, madam.'

'Such as we?'

'Yes, madam.'

'But here we are and yet you still do nothing. Why is that?'

'We observe, madam. We have no further orders.'

'Have you reported your observations?'

'Yes, madam.'

'To whom?'

'To the overseer, madam.'

'Where is the overseer?'

'In the mansion, madam.'

'Ah,' Gladia turned and walked briskly back to D. G. Daneel followed.

'Well?' said D. G. He was holding both weapons at the ready, but put them back in their holsters as they returned.

Gladia shook her head. 'Nothing. No robot knows me. No robot, I'm sure, knows where the Solarians have gone. *But* they report to an overseer.'

'An overseer?'

'On Aurora and the other Spacer worlds, the overseer on large estates with numerous robots is some human whose profession it is to organize and direct groups of working robots, in fields, mines, and industrial establishments.'

'Then there *are* Solarians left behind.'

Gladia shook her head. 'Solaria is an exception. The ratio of robots to human beings has always been so high, that it has not been the custom to detail a man or woman to oversee the robots. That job has been done by another robot, specially programmed.'

'Then there is a robot in that mansion,' D. G. nodded with his head, 'who is more advanced than these, and who might profitably be questioned.'

'Perhaps, but I am not certain it is safe to attempt to go into the mansion.'

D. G. said, sardonically, 'It is only another robot.'

'The mansion may be booby-trapped.'

'This field may be booby-trapped.'

Gladia said, 'It would be better to send one of the robots to the mansion to tell the overseer that human beings wish to speak to him.'

D. G. said, 'That will not be necessary. That job has apparently been done already. The overseer is emerging and is neither a robot nor a "him". What I see is a human female.'

Gladia looked up in astonishment. Advancing rapidly towards them was a tall, well-formed and exceedingly attractive woman. Even at a distance, there was no doubt whatever as to her sex.

25.

D. G. smiled broadly. He seemed to be straightening himself a bit, squaring his shoulders, throwing them back. One hand went lightly to his beard as though to make sure it was sleek and smooth.

Gladia looked at him with disfavour. She said, 'That is *not* a Solarian woman.'

'How can you tell?' said D. G.

'No Solarian woman would allow herself to be seen so freely by other human beings. *Seen*, not viewed.'

'I know the distinction, my lady. Yet you allow me to see you.'

'I have lived over twenty decades on Aurora. Even so I have enough Solarian left in me still not to appear to others like *that*.'

'She has a great deal to display, madam. I would say she is taller than I am, and as beautiful as a sunset.'

The overseer had stopped twenty metres short of their position and the robots had moved aside so that none of them remained between the woman on one side, and the three from the ship on the other.

D. G. said, 'Customs can change in twenty decades.'

'Not something as basic as the Solarian dislike of human contact,' said Gladia, sharply. 'Not in two hundred decades.' She had slipped into her Solarian twang again.

'I think you underestimate social plasticity. Still, Solarian or not, I presume she's a Spacer, and if there are other Spacers like that, I'm all for peaceful coexistence.'

Gladia's look of disapproval deepened. 'Well, do you intend to stand and gaze in that fashion for the next hour or two? Don't you want me to question the woman?'

D. G. started, and turned to look at Gladia with distinct

annoyance. 'You question the robots, as you've done. *I* question the human beings.'

'Especially the females, I suppose.'

'I wouldn't like to boast, but – '

'It is a subject on which I have never known a man who didn't.'

Daneel interposed. 'I do not think the woman will wait longer. If you wish to retain the initiative, Captain, approach her now. I will follow, as I did with Madam Gladia.'

'I scarcely need the protection,' said D. G., brusquely.

'You are a human being and I must not, through inaction, allow harm to come to you.'

D. G. walked forward briskly, Daneel following. Gladia, reluctant to remain behind alone, advanced a bit tentatively.

The overseer watched quietly. She wore a smooth white robe that reached down to mid-thigh and was belted at the waist. It showed a deep and inviting cleavage, and her nipples were clearly visible against the thin material of the robe. There was no indication that she was wearing anything else but a pair of shoes.

When D. G. stopped, a metre of space separated them. Her skin, he could see, was flawless, her cheekbones were high, her eyes wide-set and somewhat slanted, her expression serene.

'Madam,' said D. G., speaking as close an approximation to Auroran Patrician as he could manage, 'have I the pleasure of speaking to the overseer of this estate?'

The woman listened for a moment, and then said, in an accent so thickly Solarian as to seem almost comic when coming from her perfectly-shaped mouth, 'You are not a human being.'

She then flashed into action so quickly that Gladia, still some ten metres off, could not see in detail what had happened. She saw only a blur of motion and then D. G., lying on his back, motionless, and the woman standing there with his weapons, one in each hand.

26.

What stupefied Gladia most in that one dizzying moment was that Daneel had not moved in either prevention or reprisal.

But even as the thought struck her, it was out of date, for Daneel had already caught the woman's left wrist and twisted it, saying, 'Drop those weapons at once,' in a harsh peremptory voice she had never heard him use before. It was inconceivable that he should so address a human being.

The woman said, just as harshly in her higher register, 'You are not a human being.' Her right arm came up and she fired the weapon it held. For a moment, a faint glow flickered over Daneel's body and Gladia, unable to make a sound in her state of shock, felt her sight dim. She had never in her life fainted, but this seemed a prelude.

Daneel did not dissolve, nor was there an explosive report. Daneel, Gladia realized, had prudently seized the arm that held the blaster. The other held the neuronic whip and it was that which had been discharged in full, and at close range, upon Daneel. Had he been human, the massive stimulation of his sensory nerves might well have killed him or left him permanently disabled. Yet he was, after all, however human in appearance, a robot, and his equivalent of a nervous system did not react to the whip.

Daneel seized the other arm now, forcing it up. He said again, 'Drop those weapons, or I will tear each arm from its socket.'

'Will you?' said the woman. Her arms contracted and,

for a moment, Daneel was lifted off the ground. Daneel's legs swung backward, then forward, pendulum-like, using the points where the arms joined as a pivot. His feet struck the woman with force and both fell heavily to the ground.

Gladia, without putting the thought into words, realized that although the woman looked as human as Daneel did, she was just as non-human. A sense of instant outrage flooded Gladia, who was suddenly Solarian to the core; outrage that a robot should offer force to a human being. Granted that she might somehow have recognized Daneel for what he was, how *dare* she strike D. G.!

Gladia was running forward, screaming. It never occurred to her to fear a robot simply because it had knocked down a strong man with a blow and was battling an even stronger robot to a draw.

'How dare you?' she screamed in a Solarian accent so thick that it grated on her own ear – but how else does one speak to a Solarian robot? 'How dare you, *girl*? Stop all resistance *immediately*!'

The woman's muscles seemed to relax totally and simultaneously, as though an electric current had suddenly been shut off. Her beautiful eyes looked at Gladia without enough humanity to seem startled. She said, in an indistinct, hesitating voice, 'My regrets, madam.'

Daneel was on his feet, staring down watchfully at the woman who lay on the grass. D. G., suppressing a groan, was struggling upright.

Daneel bent for the weapons, but Gladia waved him away furiously.

'Give me those weapons, *girl*,' she said.

The woman said, 'Yes, madam.'

Gladia snatched at them, chose the blaster swiftly and handed it to Daneel. 'Destroy her, when that seems best, Daneel. That's an order.' She handed the neuronic whip

to D. G., and said, 'This is useless here, except against me
– and yourself. Are you all right?'

'No, I'm *not* all right,' muttered D. G., rubbing one
hip. 'Do you mean she's a *robot*?'

'Would a *woman* have thrown you like that?'

'Not any whom I have ever met before. I *said* there
might be special robots on Solaria who were programmed
to be dangerous.'

'Of course,' said Gladia, unkindly, 'but when you saw
something that looked like your idea of a beautiful woman,
you forgot.'

'Yes, it is easy to be wise after the fact.'

Gladia sniffed and turned again to the robot, 'What is
your name, girl?'

'I am called Landaree, madam.'

'Get up, Landaree.'

Landaree rose much as Daneel had – as though she
were on springs. Her struggle with Daneel seemed to
have left her totally unharmed.

Gladia said, 'Why, against First Law, have you attacked
these human beings?'

'Madam,' said Landaree, firmly, 'these are not human
beings.'

'And do you say that *I* am not a human being?'

'No, madam, you are a human being.'

'Then, as a human being, I am defining these two men
as human beings. Do you hear me?'

'Madam,' said Landaree, a little more softly, 'these are
not human beings.'

'They are indeed human beings, because I tell you they
are. You are forbidden to attack them or harm them in any
way.'

Landaree stood mute.

'Do you understand what I have said?' Gladia's voice

grew more Solarian still as she reached for greater intensity.

'Madam,' said Landaree, 'these are not human beings.'

Daneel said to Gladia, softly, 'Madam, she has been given orders of such firmness that you cannot easily countervail them.'

'We'll see about that,' said Gladia, breathing quickly.

Landaree looked about. The group of robots, during the few minutes of conflict had come closer to Gladia and her two companions. In the background were two robots, who, Gladia decided, were not members of the original group and they were, between them, carrying with some difficulty a large and very massive device of some sort. Landaree gestured to them and they moved forward a bit more quickly.

Gladia cried out, 'Robots! Stop!'

They stopped.

Landaree said, 'Madam, I am fulfilling my duties. I am following my instructions.'

Gladia said, 'Your duty, girl, is to obey my orders!'

Landaree said, 'I cannot be ordered to disobey my instructions!'

Gladia said, 'Daneel. Blast her!'

Afterwards, Gladia was able to reason out what had happened. Daneel's reaction time was much faster than a human being's would have been, and he knew that he was facing a robot against which the Three Laws did not inhibit violence. However, she looked so human that even the precise knowledge that she was a robot did not totally overcome his inhibition. He followed the order more slowly than he should have.

Landaree, whose definition of 'human being' was clearly not the one Daneel used, was not inhibited by his appearance, and she struck the more quickly. She had her grip on the blaster and again the two struggled.

D. G. turned his neuronic whip butt-first, and came in at a half-run to strike. He hit her head squarely but it had no effect on the robot and her leg sent him flailing backward.

Gladia said, 'Robot! Stop!' Her clenched hands were raised.

Landaree shouted in a stentorian contralto, 'All of you. Join me. The two apparent males are not human beings. Destroy them without harming the female in any way.'

If Daneel could be inhibited by a human appearance, the same was true in considerably greater intensity for the simple Solarian robots, who inched forward slowly and intermittently.

'Stop!' shrieked Gladia. The robots stopped but the order had no effect on Landaree.

Daneel held fast to the blaster, but was bending backward under the force of Landaree's apparently greater strength.

Gladia, in distraction, looked about as though hoping to find some weapon, somewhere.

D. G. was attempting to manipulate his radio transmitter. He said, grunting, 'It's been damaged. I think I fell on it.'

'What do we do?'

'We have to make it back to the ship. Quickly.'

Gladia said, 'Then run. I can't abandon Daneel.' She faced the battling robots, crying out wildly, 'Landaree, stop! Landaree, stop!'

'I must not stop, madam,' said Landaree. 'My instructions are precise.'

Daneel's fingers were forced open and Landaree had the blaster again.

Gladia threw herself before Daneel. 'You must not harm this human being.'

'Madam,' said Landaree, her blaster pointed at Gladia,

unwavering. 'You are standing in front of something that looks like a human being but is not a human being. My instructions are to destroy such on sight.' Then, in a louder voice, 'You two porters – to the ship.'

The two robots, with the massive device carried between them, renewed their forward movement.

'Robots! Stop!' screamed Gladia, and the forward motion stopped. The robots trembled in place, as though attempting to move forward and yet not quite able to do so.

Gladia said, 'You cannot destroy my human friend, Daneel, without destroying me, and you yourself admit that I am a human being and therefore must not be harmed.'

Daneel said in a low voice, 'My lady, you must not draw harm upon yourself in an effort to protect me.'

Landaree said, 'This is useless, madam. I can remove you easily from your present position and then destroy the non-human being behind you. Since that may harm you, I ask you, with all respect, to move from your present position voluntarily.'

'You must, my lady,' said Daneel.

'No, Daneel. I'll stay here. In the time it will take her to move me, you run!'

'I cannot run faster than the beam of a blaster, and if I try to run, she will shoot through you rather than not at all. Her instructions are probably that firm. I regret, my lady, that this will cause you unhappiness.'

And Daneel lifted the struggling Gladia and tossed her lightly to one side.

Landaree's finger tightened on the contact, but never completed the pressure. She remained motionless.

Gladia, who had staggered to a sitting position, got to her feet. Cautiously, D. G., who had remained in place during the last exchanges, approached Landaree. Daneel, quite calmly, reached out and took the blaster from her unresisting fingers.

'I believe,' said Daneel, 'that this robot is permanently deactivated.'

He pushed her gently and she fell over in one piece, with her limbs, torso, and head in the relative positions they occupied when she was standing. Her arm was still bent, her hand was holding an invisible blaster, and her finger was pressing on an invisible contact.

Through the trees to one side of the grassy field on which the drama had played itself out, Giskard was approaching, his robotic face showing no signs of curiosity, though his words might have.

'What is this that has taken place in my absence?' he asked.

27.

The walk back to the ship was rather anticlimactic. Now that the frenzy of fear and action was over, Gladia felt hot and cross. D. G. limped rather painfully, and they progressed slowly, partly because of that limp, and partly because the two Solarian robots were still carrying their massive instrument, plodding along under its weight.

D. G. looked over his shoulder at them. 'They obey my orders now that that overseer is out of action.'

Gladia said, through her teeth, 'Why didn't you run at the end and get help? Why did you remain helplessly watching?'

'Well,' said D. G., with an attempt at the kind of lightness he would have showed easily, were he feeling better, 'with you refusing to leave Daneel, I rather hesitated to play the coward by comparison.'

'You fool! I was safe. She would not have harmed *me*.'

Daneel said, 'Madam, it distresses me to contradict you, but I think she would have done so as her urge to destroy me grew stronger.'

Gladia turned on him hotly, 'And that was a smart thing *you* did; pushing me out of the way. Did you *want* to be destroyed?'

'Rather than see you harmed, madam, yes. My failure to stop the robot through inhibitions set up by her human appearance demonstrated, in any case, an unsatisfactory limit to my usefulness to you.'

'Even so,' said Gladia, 'she would have hesitated to shoot me, since I am human, for a perceptible period of time and you could have had the blaster in your own possession by that time.'

'I couldn't gamble your life, madam, on anything as uncertain as her hesitation,' said Daneel.

'And *you*,' said Gladia, showing no signs of having heard Daneel, and turning to D. G. again, 'shouldn't have brought the blaster in the first place.'

D. G. said, frowning, 'Madam, I am making allowances for the fact that we have all been very close to death. The robots do not mind that and I have grown somewhat accustomed to danger. To you, however, this was an unpleasant novelty, and you are being childish as a result. I forgive you – a little. But please listen. There was no way I could have known the blaster would be taken from me so easily. Had I not brought the weapon, the overseer could have killed me with her bare hands as quickly and as effectively as she could have done it by blaster. Nor was there any point in my running, to answer an earlier complaint of yours. I could not outrun a blaster. Now please continue, if you must still get it out of your system, but I do not intend to reason with you any further.'

Gladia looked from D. G. to Daneel and back and said,

in a low voice, 'I suppose I *am* being unreasonable. Very well, no more hindsights.'

They had reached the ship. Crew-members poured out at the sight of them. Gladia noticed they were armed.

D. G. beckoned to his second-in-command. 'Oser, I presume you see that object the two robots are carrying?'

'Yes, sir.'

'Well, have them carry it on board. Have it put in the security room and kept there. The security room is then to be locked and kept locked.' He turned away for a moment, then turned back, 'And Oser, as soon as that is done, we will prepare to take off again.'

Oser said, 'Captain, shall we keep the robots as well?'

'No. They are too simple in design to be worth much and, under the circumstances, taking them would create undesirable consequences. The device they are carrying is much more valuable than they are.'

Giskard watched the device being slowly, and very carefully, manoeuvred into the ship. He said, 'Captain, I am guessing that that is a dangerous object.'

'I'm under that impression, too,' said D. G. 'I suspect the ship would have been destroyed soon after we were.'

'That thing?' said Gladia. 'What is it?'

'I can't be certain, but I *believe* it is a nuclear intensifier. I've seen experimental models on Baleyworld and this looks like a big brother.'

'What is a nuclear intensifier?'

'As the name implies, Lady Gladia, it's a device that intensifies nuclear fusion.'

'How does it do that?'

D. G. shrugged. 'I'm not a physicist, my lady. A stream of W – particles is involved, and they mediate the weak interaction. That's all I know about it.'

'What does that do?' asked Gladia.

'Well, suppose the ship has its power supply as it has

right now, for instance. There are small numbers of protons, derived from our hydrogen fuel supply, that are ultra-
hot and fusing to produce power. Additional hydrogen is
constantly being heated to produce free protons, which,
when hot enough, also fuse to maintain that power. If the
stream of W-particles from the nuclear intensifier strikes
the fusing protons, these fuse more quickly and deliver
more heat. That heat produces protons and sets them to
fusing more quickly than they should and their fusion
produces still more heat, which intensifies the vicious
circle. In a tiny fraction of a second, enough of the fuel
fuses to form a tiny thermonuclear bomb and the entire
ship and everything upon it is vaporized.'

Gladia looked awed. 'Why doesn't everything ignite?
Why doesn't the whole planet blow up?'

'I don't suppose there's danger of that, madam. The
protons have to be ultra-hot and fusing. Cold protons are
so unapt to fuse that even when the tendency is intensified
to the full extent of such a device, that still is not enough
to allow fusion. At least, that's what I gathered from a
lecture I once attended. And nothing but hydrogen is
affected as far as I know. Even in the case of ultra-hot
protons, the heat produced does not increase without
measure. The temperature cools with distance from the
intensifier beam, so that only a limited amount of fusion
can be forced. Enough to destroy the ship, of course, but
there's no question of blowing up the hydrogen-rich
oceans, for instance, even if part of it were ultra-heated,
and certainly not if it were cold.'

'But if the machine gets turned on accidentally in the
storage room – '

'I don't think it can get turned on.' D. G. opened his
hand and, in it, rested a two-centimetre cube of polished
metal. 'From what little I know of such things, this is an

activator, and the nuclear intensifier can do nothing without it.'

'Are you sure?'

'Not entirely, but we'll just have to chance it since I must get that thing back to Baleyworld. Now let's get on board.'

Gladia and her two robots moved up the gangplank and into the ship. D. G. followed, and spoke briefly to some of his officers.

He then said to Gladia, his weariness beginning to show, 'It will take us a couple of hours to place all our gear on board and be ready for take-off, and every moment increases the danger.'

'Danger?'

'You don't suppose that fearful woman robot is the only one of its kind that may exist on Solaria, do you? Or that the nuclear intensifier we have captured is the only one of its kind. I suppose it will take time for other humanoid robots and other nuclear intensifiers to be brought to this spot – perhaps considerable time – but we must give them as little as possible. And in the meantime, madam, let us go to your room and conduct some necessary business.'

'What necessary business would that be, Captain?'

'Well,' said D. G., motioning them forward. 'In view of the fact that I may have been victimized by treason, I think I will conduct a rather informal court-martial.'

28.

D. G. said, after seating himself with an audible groan, 'What I really want is a hot shower, a rubdown, a good meal, and a chance to sleep, but that will all have to wait till we're off the planet. It will have to wait in your case, too, madam. Some things will not wait, however. My question is this. Where were you, Giskard, while the rest of us were faced with considerable danger?'

Giskard said, 'Captain, it did not seem to me that if robots alone were left on the planet, they would represent any danger. Moreover, Daneel remained with you.'

Daneel said, 'Captain, I agreed that Giskard would reconnoitre and that I would remain with Madam Gladia and with you.'

'You two agreed, did you?' said D. G. 'Was anyone else consulted?'

'No, Captain,' said Giskard.

'If you were certain that the robots were harmless, Giskard, how did you account for the fact that two ships were destroyed?'

'It seemed to me, Captain, that there must remain human beings on the planet, but that they would do their best not to be seen by you. I wanted to know where they were and what they were doing. I was in search of them, covering the ground as rapidly as I could. I questioned the robots I met.'

'Did you find any human beings?'

'No, Captain.'

'Did you examine the house out of which the overseer emerged?'

'No, Captain, but I was certain there were no human beings within it. I still am.'

'It contained the overseer.'

'Yes, Captain, but the overseer was a robot.'

'A dangerous robot.'

'To my regret, Captain, I did not realize that.'

'You feel regret, do you?'

'It is an expression I choose to describe the effect on my positronic circuits. It is a rough analogy to the term as human beings seem to use it, Captain.'

'How is it you didn't realize a robot might be dangerous?'

'By the Three Laws of Robotics – '

Gladia interrupted, 'Stop this, Captain. Giskard only knows what he is programmed to know. No robot is dangerous to human beings, unless there is a deadly quarrel between human beings and the robot must attempt to stop it. In such a quarrel, Daneel and Giskard would undoubtedly have defended us with as little harm to others as possible.'

'Is that so?' D. G. put two fingers to the bridge of his nose and pinched. 'Daneel *did* defend us. We were fighting robots, not human beings, so he had no problem in deciding whom to defend and to what extent. Yet he showed astonishing lack of success considering that the Three Laws do not prevent him from doing harm to robots. Giskard remained out of it, returning at the precise moment when it was over. Is it possible that there is a bond of sympathy among robots? Is it possible that robots, when defending human beings against robots, somehow feel what Giskard calls "regret" at having to do so, and perhaps fail – or absent themselves – '

'No!' exploded Gladia, forcefully.

'No?' said D. G. 'Well, I don't pretend to be an expert roboticist. Are you, Lady Gladia?'

'I am not a roboticist of any sort,' said Gladia, 'but I have lived with robots for twenty-three decades. What you suggest is ridiculous. Daneel was quite prepared to give his life for me, and Giskard would have done the same.'

'Would any robot have done so?'

'Of course.'

'And yet this overseer, this Landaree, was quite ready to attack me and destroy me. Let us grant that, in some mysterious way, she detected that Daneel, despite appearances, was as much a robot as she herself was – despite appearances – and that she had no inhibitions when it came to harming him. How is it, though, that she attacked me when I am unquestionably a human being? She hesitated at you, admitting you were human, but not me. How could a robot discriminate between the two of us? Was she perhaps not really a robot?'

'She was a robot,' said Gladia. 'Of course, she was. But – the truth is, I don't know why she acted as she did. I have never before heard of such a thing. I can only suppose that the Solarians, having learned how to construct humanoid robots, designed them without the protection of the Three Laws, though I would have sworn that the Solarians, of all Spacers, would have been the last to do so. Solarians are so outnumbered by their own robots as to be utterly dependent on them – to a far greater extent than any other Spacers are – and for that reason they fear them more. Subservience and even a bit of stupidity were built into all Solarian robots. The Three Laws were stronger on Solaria than anywhere else, not weaker. Yet I can think of no other way of explaining Landaree than to suppose that the First Law was – '

Daneel said, 'Excuse me, Madam Gladia, for interrupting. May I have your permission to attempt an explanation of the overseer's behaviour?'

D. G. said, sardonically, 'It comes to that, I suppose. Only a robot can explain a robot.'

'Sir,' said Daneel, 'unless we understand the overseer, we might not be able to take effective measures in the future against the Solarian danger. I believe I have a way of accounting for her behaviour.'

'Go ahead,' said D. G.

'The overseer,' said Daneel, 'did not take instant measures against us. She stood and watched us for a while, apparently uncertain as to how to proceed. When you, Captain, approached and addressed her, she announced you were not human, and attacked you instantly. When I intervened and cried out that she was a robot, she announced I was not human and attacked me at once, too. When Lady Gladia came forward, however, shouting at her, the overseer recognized her as human and, for a while, allowed herself to be dominated.'

'Yes, I remember all that, Daneel. But what does it mean?'

'It seems to me, Captain, that it is possible to alter a robot's behaviour fundamentally, without ever touching the Three Laws, provided, for instance, that you alter the definition of a human being. A human being, after all, is only what it is defined to be.'

'Is that so? What do *you* consider a human being to be?'

Daneel was not concerned with the presence or absence of sarcasm. He said, 'I was constructed with a detailed description of the appearance and behaviour of human beings, Captain. Anything that fits that description is a human being to me. Thus, you have the appearance and the behaviour, while the overseer had the appearance but not the behaviour.

'To the overseer, on the other hand, the key property of a human being was speech, Captain. The Solarian accent is a distinctive one, and to the overseer, something that looked like a human being was defined as a human being only if it spoke like a Solarian. Apparently, anything that looked like a human being but did not speak with a Solarian accent, was to be destroyed without hesitation, as was any ship carrying such beings.'

D. G. said thoughtfully, 'You may be right.'

'You have a Settler accent, Captain, as distinctive in its way as the Solarian accent is, but the two are widely different. As soon as you spoke, you defined yourself as non-human to the overseer, who announced that and attacked.'

'And you speak with an Auroran accent and were likewise attacked.'

'Yes, Captain, but the Lady Gladia spoke with an authentic Solarian accent, and so she was recognized as human.'

D. G. considered the matter silently for a while, then said, 'That's a dangerous arrangement even for those who would make use of it. If a Solarian, for any reason, at any time addressed such a robot in a way that the robot did not consider an authentic Solarian accent, that Solarian would be attacked at once. If I were a Solarian I would be afraid to approach such a robot. My very effort to speak pure Solarian might very likely throw me off and get me killed.'

'I agree, Captain,' said Daneel, 'and I would imagine that that is why those who manufacture robots do not ordinarily limit the definition of a human being, but leave it as broad as possible. The Solarians, however, have left the planet. One might suppose that the fact that overseer robots have this dangerous programming is the best indication that the Solarians have really left and are not here to encounter the danger. The Solarians, it appears, are at this moment concerned only that no one who is not a Solarian be allowed to set foot on the planet.'

'Not even other Spacers?'

'I would expect, Captain, that it would be difficult to define a human being in such a way as to include the dozens of different Spacer accents and yet exclude the scores of different Settler accents. Keying the definition to the distinctive Solarian accent alone would be difficult enough.'

D. G. said, 'You are very intelligent, Daneel. I disapprove of robots, of course, not in themselves, but as an unsettling influence on society. And yet, with a robot such as yourself at my side, as you were once at the Ancestor's —'

Gladia interrupted. 'I'm afraid not, D. G. Daneel will

never be a gift, nor will he ever be sold, nor can he be easily taken by force.'

D. G. lifted his hand in a smiling negative. 'I was merely dreaming, Lady Gladia. I assure you that the laws of Baleyworld would make my possession of a robot unthinkable.'

Giskard said, suddenly, 'May I have your permission, Captain, to add a few words?'

D. G. said, 'Ah, the robot who managed to avoid the action, and who returned when all was safely over.'

'I regret that matters appear to be as you have stated. May I have your permission, Captain, to add a few words, notwithstanding?'

'Well, go on.'

'It would seem, Captain, that your decision to bring the Lady Gladia with you on this expedition has worked out very well. Had she been absent, and had you ventured on your exploratory mission with only members of the ship's crew as companions, you would all have been quickly killed and the ship destroyed. It was only Lady Gladia's ability to speak like a Solarian and her courage in facing the overseer that changed the outcome.'

'Not so,' said D. G., 'for we would all have been destroyed; possibly even Lady Gladia, but for the fortuitous event that the overseer spontaneously inactivated.'

'It was not fortuitous, Captain,' said Giskard, 'and it is extremely unlikely that any robot will inactivate spontaneously. There has to be a reason for inactivation, and I can suggest one possibility. Lady Gladia ordered the robot to stop on several occasions, as Friend Daneel has told me, but the instructions under which the overseer worked were more forceful.

'Nevertheless, Lady Gladia's actions served to blunt the overseer's resolution, Captain. The fact that Lady Gladia was an undoubted human being, even by the overseer's definition, and that she was acting in such a way as to make it necessary, perhaps, for the overseer to harm her, or even kill her, blunted it even further. Thus, at the crucial moment, the two contrary requirements – having to destroy non-human beings and having to refrain from harming human beings – balanced, and the robot froze, unable to do anything. Its circuits burned out.'

Gladia's brows drew together in a puzzled frown. 'But –' she began, and then subsided.

Giskard went on, 'It strikes me that it might be well for you to inform the crew of this. It might well ease their distrust of the Lady Gladia, if you stress what her initiative and courage have meant to every man in the crew, since it has kept them alive. It might also give them an excellent opinion of your own foresight in insisting on having her on board on this occasion, perhaps even against the advice of your own officers.'

D. G. let loose a great shout of laughter. 'Lady Gladia, I see now why you will not be separated from these robots. They are not only as intelligent as human beings, they are every bit as devious. I congratulate you on your having them. And now, if you don't mind, I must hurry the crew. I don't want to stay on Solaria for one moment more than necessary. And I promise you that you won't be disturbed for hours. I know you can use freshening and rest as much as I can.'

After he was gone, Gladia remained for a while in deep thought, then turned to Giskard and said in Auroran Common, a patter-version of Galactic Standard that was widespread on Aurora, and difficult for any non-Auroran to understand. 'Giskard, what is all this nonsense about the burning out of circuits?'

'My lady,' said Giskard, 'I advanced it only as a possibility and nothing more. I thought it well to emphasize your role in putting an end to the overseer.'

'But how could you think he would believe that a robot could burn out that easily?'

'He knows very little about robots, madam. He may traffic in them, but he is from a world that doesn't make use of them.'

'Yet I know a great deal about them, and so do you. The overseer showed no signs, whatever, of balancing circuits, no stuttering, no trembling, no behaviour difficulty of any kind. It just – stopped.'

Giskard said, 'Madam, since we do not know the precise specifications to which the overseer was designed, we may have to be content with ignorance as to the rationale behind the freeze.'

Gladia shook her head. 'Just the same, it's puzzling.'

PART III
BALEYWORLD

8

The Settler World

29.

D. G.'s ship was in space again, surrounded by the everlasting changelessness of the vacuum.

It had not come too soon for Gladia, who had but imperfectly suppressed the tension that arose from the possibility that a second overseer, with a second intensifier, might arrive without warning. The fact that it would be a quick death if it happened, an unexperienced death, was not quite satisfying. The tension had spoiled what would have otherwise been a luxurious shower, along with various other forms of renewal of comfort.

It was not till after actual take-off, after the coming of the soft, distant buzz of the protonic jets, that she could compose herself to sleep. Odd, she thought as consciousness began to slip away, that space should feel safer than the world of her youth, that she should leave Solaria with even greater relief the second time than she had the first.

But, then, Solaria was no longer the world of her youth. It was a world without humanity, guarded over by distorted parodies of humanity; humanoid robots that made a mockery of the gentle Daneel and the thought-filled Giskard.

She slept at last – and while she slept, Daneel and Giskard, standing guard, could once more speak to each other.

Daneel said, 'Friend Giskard, I am quite certain that it was you who destroyed the overseer.'

'There was clearly no choice, Friend Daneel. It was purely an accident that I arrived in time, for my senses were entirely occupied in searching out human beings and I found none. Nor would I have grasped the significance of events if it had not been for the Lady Gladia's rage and despair. It was that which I sensed at a distance and which caused me to race to the scene, barely in time. In that respect, Lady Gladia *did* save the situation, at least as far as the Captain's existence and yours were concerned. I would still have saved the ship, I believe, even if I had arrived too late to save you.' He paused a moment, and added, 'I would have found it most unsatisfactory, Friend Daneel, to have arrived too late to save you.'

Daneel said, with a grave and formal tone of voice, 'I thank you, Friend Giskard. I am pleased that you were not inhibited by the human appearance of the overseer. That had slowed my reactions, as my appearance had slowed hers.'

'Friend Daneel, her physical appearance meant nothing to me because I was aware of the pattern of her thoughts. That pattern was so limited and so entirely different from the full range of human patterns that there was no need for me to make any effort to identify her in a positive manner. The negative identification as non-human was so clear I acted at once. I was not aware of my action, in fact, until after it had taken place.'

'I had thought this, Friend Giskard, but I wished confirmation lest I misunderstood. May I assume, then, that you feel no discomfort over having killed what was, in appearance, a human being?'

'None, since it was a robot.'

'It seems to me that, had I succeeded in destroying her, I would have suffered some obstruction to the free positronic flow, no matter how thoroughly I understood her to be a robot.'

'The humanoid appearance, Friend Daneel, cannot be fought off when that is all one can directly judge by.

Seeing is so much more immediate than deducing. It was only because I could observe her mental structure and concentrate on that, that I could ignore her physical structure.'

'How do you suppose the overseer would have felt if she had destroyed us, judging from her mental structure?'

'She was given exceedingly firm instructions, and there was no doubt in her circuits that you and the Captain were non-human by her definition.'

'But she might have destroyed Madam Gladia as well.'

'Of that we cannot be certain, Friend Daneel.'

'Had she done so, Friend Giskard, would she have survived? Have you any way of telling?'

Giskard was silent for a considerable period. 'I had insufficient time to study the mental pattern. I cannot say what her reaction might have been had she killed Madam Gladia.'

'If I imagine myself in the place of the overseer,' and Daneel's voice trembled and grew slightly lower in pitch, 'it seems to me that I might kill a human being in order to save the life of another human being, whom, there might be some reason to think, it was more necessary to save. The action would, however, be difficult and damaging. To kill a human being merely in order to destroy something I considered non-human, would be inconceivable.'

'She merely threatened. She did not carry through the threat.'

'Might she have, Friend Giskard?'

'How can we say, since we don't know the nature of her instructions?'

'Could the instructions have so completely negated the First Law?'

Giskard said, 'Your whole purpose in this discussion. I see, has been to raise this question. I advise you to go no further.'

Daneel said, stubbornly, 'I will put it in the conditional, Friend Giskard. Surely what may not be expressed as fact, can be advanced as fantasy. *If* instructions could be hedged about with definitions and conditions; *if* the instructions could be made sufficiently detailed in a sufficiently forceful manner; *might* it be possible to kill a human being for a purpose less overwhelming than the saving of the life of another human being?'

Giskard said, tonelessly, 'I do not know, but I suspect that this might be possible.'

'But, then, *if* your suspicion should be correct, that would imply that it was possible to neutralize the First Law under specialized conditions. The First Law, *in that case*, and, therefore, certainly the other Laws, *might* be modified into almost non-existence. The Laws, even the First Law, might not be an absolute then, but might be whatever those who design robots defined them to be.'

Giskard said, 'It is enough, Friend Daneel. Go no further.'

Daneel said, 'There is one more step, Friend Giskard. Partner Elijah would have taken that additional step.'

'He was a human being. He could.'

'I must try. *If* the Laws of Robotics, even the First Law, are not absolutes, and *if* human beings can modify them, might it not be that *perhaps*, under proper conditions, we ourselves might mod –'

He stopped.

Giskard said, faintly, 'Go no further.'

Daneel said, a slight hum obscuring his voice, 'I go no further.'

There was a silence for a long time. It was with difficulty that the positronic circuitry in each ceased undergoing discords.

Finally, Daneel said, 'Another thought arises. The overseer was dangerous not only because of the set of her instructions, but because of her appearance. It inhibited me and probably the Captain and could mislead and deceive human beings generally, as I deceived, without meaning to, First-Class Shipper Niss. He clearly was not aware, at first, that I was a robot.'

'And what follows from that, Friend Daneel?'

'On Aurora, a number of humanoid robots were constructed at the Robotics Institute, under the leadership of Dr Amadiro, after the designs of Dr Fastolfe had been obtained.'

'This is well-known.'

'What happened to those humanoid robots?'

'The project failed.'

In his turn, Daneel said, 'This is well-known. But it does not answer the question. What happened to those humanoid robots?'

'One can assume they were destroyed.'

'Such an assumption need not necessarily be correct. Were they, in actual fact, destroyed?'

'That would have been the sensible thing to do. What else with a failure?'

'How do we know the humanoid robots were a failure, except in that they were removed from sight?'

'Isn't that sufficient, if they were removed from sight and destroyed?'

'I did not say "and destroyed", Friend Giskard. That is more than we know. We know only that they were removed from sight.'

'Why should that be so, unless they were failures?'

'And if they were *not* failures, might there be no reason for their being removed from sight?'

'I can think of none, Friend Daneel.'

'Think again, Friend Giskard. Remember, we are talking now of humanoid robots, who, we now think, might from the mere fact of their humanoid nature, be dangerous. It has seemed to us in our previous discussion that there was a plan on foot on Aurora to defeat the settlers, drastically, surely, and at a blow. We decided that these plans must be centred on the planet, Earth. Am I correct so far?'

'Yes, Friend Daneel.'

'Then might it not be that Dr Amadiro is at the focus and centre of this plan? His antipathy to Earth has been made plain these twenty decades. And if Dr Amadiro has constructed a number of humanoid robots, where might these have been sent if they have disappeared from view? Remember that if Solarian roboticists can distort the Three Laws, Auroran roboticists can do the same.'

'Are you suggesting, Friend Daneel, that the humanoid robots have been sent to Earth?'

'Exactly. There to deceive the Earthpeople through their human appearance and to make possible whatever it is that Dr Amadiro intends as his blow against Earth.'

'You have no evidence for this.'

'Yet it is possible. Consider for yourself the steps of the argument.'

'If that were so, we would have to go to Earth. We would have to be there and somehow prevent the disaster.'

'Yes, that is so.'

'But we cannot go, unless Lady Gladia goes, and that is not likely.'

'If you can influence the Captain to take this ship to Earth, Madam Gladia would have no choice but to go as well.'

Giskard said, 'I cannot without harming him. He is firmly set on going to his own planet of Baleyworld. We must manoeuvre his trip to Earth, if we can, after he has done whatever he plans in Baleyworld.'

'Afterwards may be too late.'

'I cannot help that. I must not harm a human being.'

'If it is too late – Friend Giskard, consider what that would mean.'

'I cannot consider what that would mean. I know only that I cannot harm a human being.'

'Then First Law is not enough, and we must – '

He could go no further, and both robots lapsed into helpless silence.

30.

Baleyworld came slowly into sharper view as the ship approached it. Gladia watched it intently in her cabin's viewer.

She had protested against this leg of the journey when she had first been made aware of it by D. G., but he shrugged it off with a small laugh. 'What would you have, my lady? I must lug this weapon of your people' (he emphasized 'your' slightly) 'to my people. And I must report to them, too.'

Gladia said, coldly, 'Your permission to take me along to Solaria was granted you by the Auroran Council on condition that you brought me back.'

'Actually that is not so, my lady. There may have been some informal understanding to that effect, but there is nothing in writing. No formal agreement.'

'An informal understanding would bind *me*, or any civilized individual, D. G.'

'I'm sure of that, Madam Gladia, but we Traders live by money and by written signatures on legal documents. I would never, under any circumstances, violate a written contract, or refuse to do that for which I have accepted payment.'

Gladia's chin turned upward. 'Is that a hint that I must pay you in order to be taken home?'

'Madam!'

'Come, come, D. G. Don't waste mock indignation on me. If I am to be kept prisoner on your planet, say so, and tell me why. Let me know exactly where I stand.'

'You are not my prisoner and will not be. In fact, I will honour this unwritten understanding. I *will* take you home – eventually. First, however, I must go to Baleyworld and you must come with me.'

'Why must I come with you?'

'The people of my world will want to see you. You are the heroine of Solaria. You saved us. You can't deprive them of a chance of shouting themselves hoarse for you. Besides, you were the good friend of the Ancestor.'

'What do they know – or think they know – of that?' Gladia said, sharply.

D. G. grinned. 'Nothing to your discredit, I assure you. You are a legend and legends are larger than life – though I admit it would be easy for a legend to be larger than you, my lady – and a good deal nobler. Ordinarily, I wouldn't want you on the world, because you couldn't live up to the legend. You're not tall enough, beautiful enough, majestic enough. *But* when the story of Solaria comes out, you will suddenly meet all requirements. In fact, they may not want to let you go. You must remember we are talking of Baleyworld, the planet on which the story of the Ancestor is taken more seriously than on any other – and you are part of the story.'

'You are not to use that as an excuse to keep me in prison.'

'I promise you I won't. And I promise I will get you home – when I can – when I can.'

Gladia did not remain as indignant, somehow, as she felt she had every right to be. She did want to see what a Settler world was like and, after all, this was Elijah Baley's peculiar world. His son had founded it. He himself had spent his last decades here. On Baleyworld, there would be remnants of him – the name of the planet, his descendants, his legend.

So she watched the planet – and thought of Elijah.

31.

The watching brought her little and she felt disappointed. There was not much to be seen through the cloud layer that covered the planet. From her relatively small experience as a space-traveller it seemed to her that the cloud layer was denser than usual for inhabited planets. They would be landing within hours, now, and –

The signal light flashed and Gladia scrambled to push the hold-button in answer. A few moments more and she pushed the enter-button.

D. G. came in smiling. 'Inconvenient moment, my lady?'

'Not really,' said Gladia. 'Simply a matter of putting on my gloves and inserting my nose-plugs. I suppose I should wear them all the time, but both grow tiresome and, for some reason, I grow less concerned about infection.'

'Familiarity breeds contempt, my lady.'

'Let's not call it contempt,' said Gladia, who found herself smiling.

'Thank you,' said D. G. 'We'll be landing soon, madam, and I have brought you a coverall, carefully sterilized and placed inside this plastic bag so that it has since been untouched by Settler hands. It's simple to put on. You'll have no trouble and you'll find it covers everything but the nose and eyes.'

'Just for me, D. G.?'

'No, no, my lady. We all wear such things, when outdoors at this season of the year. It is winter in our capital city at the present time, and it is cold. We live on a rather cold world – heavy cloud cover – much precipitation, often snow.'

'Even in the tropic regions?'

'No, there it tends to be hot and dry. The population clusters in the cooler regions, however. We rather like it. It's bracing and stimulating. The seas, which were seeded with Earth species of life, are fertile, so that fish and other creatures have multiplied abundantly. There's no food shortage, consequently, even though land agriculture is limited and we'll never be the bread-basket of the Galaxy. The summers are short, but quite hot, and the beaches are then well-populated, although you might find them uninteresting since we have a strong nudity taboo.'

'It seems like peculiar weather.'

'A matter of land-sea distribution, a planetary orbit that is a bit more eccentric than most, and a few other things. Frankly, I don't bother with it.' He shrugged. 'It's not my field of interest.'

'You're a Trader. I imagine you're not on the planet often.'

'True, but I'm not a Trader in order to escape. I like it here. And yet perhaps I would like it less, if I were here more. If we look at it that way, Baleyworld's harsh conditions serve an important purpose. They encourage Trading. Baleyworld produces men who scour the seas for food, and there's a certain similarity between sailing the seas and sailing through space. I would say fully a third of all the Traders plying the space-lanes are Baleypeople.'

'You seem in a semi-manic state, D. G.,' said Gladia.

'Do I? I think of myself right now as being in a good humour. I have reason to be. So have you.'

'Oh?'

'It's obvious, isn't it? We got off Solaria alive. We know exactly what the Solarian danger is. We've gained control of an unusual weapon that should interest our military. And you will be the heroine of Baleyworld. The world officials already know the outline of events and are eager to greet you. For that matter, you're the heroine of this ship. Almost every man on board volunteered to bring you this coverall. They are all anxious to get close and bathe in your aura, so to speak.'

'Quite a change,' said Gladia, dryly.

'Absolutely. Niss – the crewman whom your Daneel chastised – '

'I remember well, D. G.'

'He is anxious to apologize to you. And bring his four mates so that they, too, might apologize. And to kick, in your presence, the one of them who made an improper suggestion. He is not a bad person, my lady.'

'I am certain he isn't. Assure him he is forgiven and the incident forgotten. And if you'll arrange matters, I will – will shake hands with him and perhaps some of the others before debarking. But you mustn't let them crowd about me.'

'I understand, but I can't guarantee there won't be a certain amount of crowding in Baleytown – that's the capital city of Baleyworld. There's no way of stopping various government officials from trying to gain political advantage by being seen with you, while grinning away and bowing.'

'Jehoshaphat! As your Ancestor would say.'

'Don't say that once we land, madam. It's an expression reserved for him. It is considered bad taste for anyone else to say it. There'll be speeches and cheering and all kinds of meaningless formalities. I'm sorry, my lady.'

She said, thoughtfully, 'I could do without it, but I suppose there's no way of stopping it.'

'No way, my lady.'

'How long will it continue?'

'Till they get tired. Several days, perhaps, but there'll be a certain variety to it.'

'And how long do we stay on the planet?'

'Till *I* get tired. I'm sorry, my lady, but I have much to do – places to go – friends to see – '

'Women to make love to.'

'Alas for human frailty,' said D. G., grinning broadly.

'You're doing everything but slobber.'

'A weakness. I can't bring myself to slobber.'

Gladia smiled. 'You're not totally committed to sanity, are you?'

'I never claimed to be. But, leaving that aside, I also have to consider such dull matters as the fact that my officers and crew would want to see *their* families and friends, catch up on their sleep, and have a little planet-side fun. And if you want to consider the feelings of inanimate objects, the ship will have to be repaired, refurbished, refreshed and refuelled. Little things like that.'

'How long will all those little things take?'

'It could be months. Who knows?'

'And what do I do meanwhile?'

'You could see our world; broaden your horizons.'

'But your world is not exactly the playground of the Galaxy.'

'Too true, but we'll try to keep you interested.' He looked at his watch. 'One more warning, madam. Do not refer to your age.'

'What cause would I have to do that?'

'It might show up in some casual reference. You'll be expected to say a few words and you might say, for instance, "In all my more than twenty-three decades of life, I have never been so glad to see anyone as I am to see the people of Baleyworld." If you're tempted to say anything like that initial clause, resist it.'

'I will. I have no intention of indulging in hyperbole in any case. But as a matter of idle curiosity, why not?'

'Simply because it is better for them not to know your age.'

'But they *do* know my age, don't they? They know I was your Ancestor's friend, and they know how long ago he lived. Or are they under the impression,' and she looked at him narrowly, 'that I'm a distant descendant of *the* Gladia?'

'No, no, they know who you are and how old you are, but they know it only with their heads,' he tapped his forehead, 'and few people have working heads, as you may have noticed.'

'Yes, I have. Even on Aurora.'

'That's good. I wouldn't want the Settlers to be special in this respect. Well, then, you have the appearance of –' he paused judiciously, 'forty, maybe forty-five, and they'll accept you as that in their guts, which is where the average person's real thinking mechanism is located. *If* you don't rub it in about your real age.'

'Does it really make a difference?'

'Does it? Look, the average Settler really doesn't want robots. He has no liking for robots, no desire for robots. There we are satisfied to differ from the Spacers. Long life is different. Forty decades is considerably more than ten.'

'Few of us actually reach the forty-decade mark.'

'And few of us actually reach the ten-decade mark. We teach the advantage of short life; quality versus quantity; evolutionary speed; ever-changing world – but nothing really makes people happy about living ten decades when they imagine they could live forty, so past a point the propaganda produces a backlash, and it's best to keep quiet about it. They don't often see Spacers, as you can imagine, and so they don't have occasion to grind their teeth over the fact that Spacers look young and vigorous even when they are twice as old as the oldest Settler who ever lived. They'll see that in *you* and, if they think about it, it will unsettle them.'

Gladia said, bitterly, 'Would you like to have me make a speech and tell them exactly what forty decades means? Shall I tell them for how many years one outlives the springtime of hope, to say nothing of friends and acquaintances? Shall I tell them of the meaninglessness of children and family; the endless comings and goings of one husband after another, of the misty blurring of the informal matings between and alongside; of the coming of the time when you've seen all you want to see, and heard all you want to hear, and find it impossible to think a new thought, of how you forget what excitement and discovery are all about, and learn each year how much more intense boredom can become?'

'Baleypeople wouldn't believe that. I don't think I do. Is that the way all Spacers feel, or are you making it up?'

'I only know for certain how I myself feel, but I've watched others dim as they aged; I've watched their dispositions sour, and their ambitions narrow, and their indifferences broaden.'

D. G.'s lips pressed together and he looked sombre. 'Is the suicide rate high among Spacers? I've never heard that it is.'

'It's virtually zero.'

'But that doesn't fit what you're saying.'

'Consider! We're surrounded by robots who are dedicated to keeping us alive. There's no way we can kill ourselves, when our sharp-eyed and active robots are forever about us. I doubt that any of us would even think of trying. I wouldn't dream of it myself, if only because I can't bear the thought of what it would mean to all my household robots, and, even more so, to Daneel and Giskard.'

'They're not really alive, you know. They don't have feelings.'

Gladia shook her head. 'You say that only because you've never lived with them. In any case, I think you overestimate the longing for prolonged life among your people. *You* know my age; *you* look at my appearance; yet it doesn't bother you.'

'Because I'm convinced that the Spacer worlds must dwindle and die; that it is the Settler worlds that are the hope of humanity's future; and that it is our short-lived characteristic that ensures it. Listening to what you've just said, assuming it is all true, makes me the more certain.'

'Don't be too sure. You may develop your own insuperable problems, if you haven't already.'

'That is undoubtedly possible, my lady, but for now I must leave you. The ship is coasting in for a landing, and I must stare intelligently at the computer that controls it, or no one will believe I am the captain.'

He left, and she remained in gloomy abstraction for a while, her fingers plucking at the plastic that enclosed the coverall.

She had come to a sense of equilibrium on Aurora, a way of allowing life to pass quietly. Meal by meal, day by day, season by season, it had been passing, and the quiet had insulated her, almost, from the tedious waiting for the only adventure that remained, the final one of death.

And now she had been to Solaria and had awakened the memories of a childhood that had long passed, on a world that had long passed, so that the quiet had been shattered, perhaps forever, and so that she now lay uncovered and bare to the horror of continuing life.

What could substitute for the vanished quiet?

She caught Giskard's dimly glowing eyes upon her, and she said, 'Help me on with this, Giskard.'

32.

It was cold. The sky was grey with clouds, and the air glittered with a very light snow-fall. There were swirling patches of powdery snow on the ground, scudding before the fresh breeze, and off beyond the landing field, Gladia could see distant heaps of snow.

There were crowds of people gathered here and there, held off by barriers from approaching too closely. They were all wearing coveralls of different types and colours, and they all seemed to balloon outward, turning humanity into a crowd of shapeless objects with eyes. Some were wearing visors that glittered transparently over their faces.

Gladia pressed her mittened hand to her face. Except for her nose, she felt warm enough. The coverall did more than insulate; it seemed to exude warmth of its own.

She looked behind her. Daneel and Giskard were within reach, each in a coverall.

She had protested at that at first. 'They don't need coveralls. They're not sensitive to cold.'

'I'm sure they're not,' D. G. had said, 'but you say you won't go anywhere without them, and we can't very well have Daneel sitting there exposed to the cold. It would seem against nature. Nor do we wish to arouse hostility by making it too clear you have robots.'

'They must know I've got robots with me, and Giskard's face will give him away even in a coverall.'

'They might know,' said D. G., 'but the chances are they won't think about it, if they're not forced to – so let's not force it.'

Now D. G. was motioning her into a ground car with the sides and roof transparent. 'They'll want to see you as we travel, my lady,' he said, smiling.

Gladia seated herself at one side and D. G. followed on the other. 'I'm co-hero,' he said.

'Do you value that?'

'Oh, yes. It means a bonus for my crew, and a possible promotion for me. I don't scorn that.'

Daneel and Giskard entered, too, and sat down in seats that faced the two human beings. Daneel faced Gladia; Giskard faced D. G.

There was a ground-car before them, without transparency, and a line of about a dozen behind them. There was the sound of cheering and a forest of arm-waving from the assembled crowd. D. G. smiled and lifted an arm in response, and motioned to Gladia to do the same. She waved in a perfunctory manner. It was warm inside the car and her nose had lost its numbness.

She said, 'There's a rather unpleasant glitter to these windows. Can that be removed?'

'Undoubtedly, but it won't be,' said D. G. 'That's as unobtrusive a force-field as we can set up. Those are enthusiastic people out there, and they've been searched, but someone *may* have managed to conceal a weapon and we don't want you hurt.'

'You mean someone might try to kill me?'

(Daneel's eyes were calmly scanning the crowd to one side of the car; Giskard's scanned the other side.)

'Very unlikely, my lady, but you're a Spacer and Settlers don't like Spacers. A few might hate them with such a surpassing hatred as to see only the Spacerness in you. But don't worry. Even if someone were to try, which is, as I say, unlikely, they won't succeed.'

The line of cars began to move, all together, and very smoothly.

Gladia half-rose in astonishment. There was no one in front of the partition that closed them off. 'Who's driving?' she asked.

'The cars are thoroughly computerized,' said D. G. 'I take it that Spacer cars are not?'

'We have robots to drive them.'

D. G. continued waving and Gladia followed his lead automatically. 'We don't,' he said.

'But a computer is essentially the same as a robot.'

'A computer is not humanoid, and it does not obtrude itself on one's notice. Whatever the technological similarities might be, they are worlds apart, psychologically.'

Gladia watched the countryside and found it oppressively barren. Even allowing for winter, there was something desolate in the scattering of leafless bushes, and in the sparsely distributed trees, whose stunted and dispirited appearance but emphasized the death that seemed to grip everything.

D. G., noting her depression and correlating it with her darting glances here and there, said, 'It doesn't look like much now, my lady. In the summer, though, it's not bad. There are grassy plains, orchards, grain-fields –'

'Forests?'

'Not wilderness forests. We're still a growing world. It's still being moulded. We've only had a little over a century and a half, really. The first step was to cultivate home plots for the initial settlers, using imported seed. Then we placed fish and invertebrates of all kinds in the ocean, doing our best to supply it with a self-supporting ecology. That is a fairly easy procedure, if the ocean chemistry is suitable. If it isn't, then the planet is not habitable without extensive chemical modification, and that has never been tried in actuality, though there are all sorts of plans for such procedures. Finally, we try to make the land flourish, and that is always difficult, always slow.'

'Have all the Settler worlds followed that path?'

'Are following. None are really finished. Baleyworld is the oldest and we're not finished. Given another couple of centuries, the Settler worlds will be rich and full of life, land as well as sea – though by that time there will be many still newer worlds that will be working their way through various preliminary stages. I'm sure the Spacer worlds went through the same procedure.'

'Many centuries ago, and less strenuously, I think. We had robots to help.'

'We'll manage,' said D. G., briefly.

'And what about the native life; the plants and animals that evolved on this world before human beings arrived?'

D. G. shrugged. 'Insignificant. Small, feeble things. The scientists are, of course, interested, so that indigenous life still exists in special aquaria, botanical gardens, zoos. There are out-of-the-way bodies of water, and considerable stretches of land area that have not yet been converted and some indigenous life still lives out there in the wild.'

'But these stretches of wilderness will eventually all be converted?'

'We hope so.'

'Don't you feel that the planet really belongs to these insignificant, small, feeble things?'

'No. I'm not that sentimental. The planet and the whole Universe belongs to intelligence. The Spacers agree with that. Where is the indigenous life of Solaria? Or of Aurora?'

The line of cars, which had been progressing tortuously from the spaceport, now came to a flat, paved area on which several low, domed buildings were evident.

'Capital Plaza,' said D. G., in a low voice. 'This is the official heartbeat of the planet. Government offices are located here; the Planetary Congress meets here; the Executive Mansion is found here; and so on.'

'I'm sorry, D. G., but this is not very impressive. These are small and uninteresting buildings.'

D. G. smiled. 'You see only an occasional top, my lady. The buildings themselves are located underground – all interconnected. It's a single complex really and is still growing. It's a self-contained city, you know. It, along with the surrounding residential areas, makes up Baleytown.'

'Do you plan to have everything underground eventually? The whole city? The whole world?'

'Most of us look forward to an underground world, yes.'

'They have underground cities on Earth, I understand.'

'Indeed, they do, my lady. The so-called Caves of Steel.'

'You imitate that here, then?'

'It's not simple imitation. We add our own ideas and – We're coming to a halt, my lady, and any moment we'll be asked to step out. I'd cling to the coverall openings, if I were you. The wind-whistling on the Plaza in winter is legendary.'

Gladia did so, fumbling rather as she tried to put the edges of the openings together. 'It's not simple imitation, you say.'

'No. We design our underground with the weather in mind. Since our weather is, on the whole, harsher than Earth's, some modification in architecture is required. Properly built, almost no energy is required to keep the complex warm in winter and cool in summer. In a way, indeed, we keep warm in winter, in part, with the stored warmth of the previous summer, and cool in summer with the coolness of the previous winter.'

'What about ventilation?'

'That uses up some of the savings, but not all. It works, my lady, and some day we will match Earth's structures. That, of course, is the ultimate ambition – to make Baleyworld a reflection of Earth.'

'I never knew that Earth was so admirable as to make imitation desirable,' said Gladia, lightly.

D. G. turned his eyes on her, sharply. 'Make no jokes of that sort, my lady, while you are with Settlers; not even with me. Earth is no joking matter.'

Gladia said, 'I'm sorry, D. G. I meant no disrespect.'

'You didn't know. But *now* you know. Come, let's get out.'

The side door of the car slid open noiselessly, and D. G. turned in his seat and stepped out. He then held out one hand to help Gladia, and said, 'You'll be addressing the Planetary Congress, you know, and every government official who can squeeze in will do so.'

Gladia, who had stretched out her hand to seize D. G.'s, and who already felt, painfully, the cold wind on her face, shrank back suddenly. 'I must make an address? I hadn't been told that.'

D. G. looked surprised. 'I rather thought you would take something of the sort for granted.'

'Well, I didn't. And I can't make an address. I've never done such a thing.'

'You must. It's nothing terrible. It's just a matter of saying a few words, after some long and boring speeches of welcome.'

'But what can I possibly say?'

'Nothing fancy, I assure you. Just peace, and love, and blah. Give them half a minute's worth. I'll scrawl out something for you, if you wish.'

And Gladia stepped out of the car, with her robots after her. Her mind was in a whirl.

9

The Speech

33.

As they walked into the building, they removed their coveralls and handed them to attendants. Daneel and Giskard removed theirs, too, and the attendants cast sharp glances at the latter, approaching him gingerly.

Gladia adjusted her nose-plugs nervously. She had never before been in the presence of large crowds of short-lived human beings – short-lived in part, she knew (or had always been told), because they carried in their bodies chronic infections, and hordes of parasites.

She whispered, 'Will I get back my own coverall?'

'You will wear no one else's,' said D. G. 'They will be kept safe and radiation-sterilized.'

Gladia looked about cautiously. Somehow she felt that even optical contact might be dangerous.

'Who are those people?' She indicated several people who wore brightly-coloured clothing and were obviously armed.

'Security guards, madam,' said D. G.

'Even here? In a government building?'

'Absolutely. And when we're on the platform, there will be a force-field curtain dividing us from the audience.'

'Don't you trust your own legislature?'

D. G. half-smiled. 'Not entirely. This is a raw world still, and we go our own ways. We haven't had all the edges knocked off and we don't have robots watching over us. Then, too, we've got militant minority parties; we've got our warhawks.'

'What are warhawks?'

Most of the Baleyworlders had their coveralls removed now and were helping themselves to drinks. The buzz of conversation was in the air and most pairs of eyes were on Gladia much of the time, but no one offered to say anything to her. Indeed, it was clear to Gladia that there was a circle of avoidance about her.

D. G. noticed her glance from side to side and interpreted it correctly. 'They've been told,' he said, 'that you would appreciate a little elbow-room.· I think they understand your fear of infection.'

'They don't find it insulting, I hope.'

'They may, but you've got something that is clearly a robot with you and most Baleyworlders don't want *that* kind of infection. The warhawks, particularly.'

'You haven't told me what they are.'

'I will, if there's time. You and I and others on the platform will have to move in a little while. Most Settlers think that, in time, the Galaxy will be theirs; that the Spacers cannot and will not compete successfully in the race for expansion. We also know it will take time. We won't see it. Our children probably won't. It may take a thousand years, for all we know. The warhawks don't want to wait. They want it settled now.'

'They want *war*?'

'They don't say that, precisely. And they don't call themselves warhawks. That's what we sensible people call them. They call themselves Earth Supremacists. After all, it's hard to argue with people who announce they are in favour of Earth being supreme. We all favour that, but most of us don't necessarily expect it to happen tomorrow, and are not ferociously upset that it won't.'

'And these warhawks may attack me? Physically?'

D. G. gestured her forward. 'I think we'll have to get moving, madam. They're getting us into line. No, I don't

think you'll really be attacked, but it's always best to be
cautious.'

Gladia held back as D. G. indicated her place in line.

'Not without Daneel and Giskard, D. G. I'm still not
going anywhere without them. Not even on to the platform. Not after what you just told me about the warhawks.'

'You're asking a lot, my lady.'

'On the contrary, D. G. I'm not asking for anything.
Take me home right now, with my robots.'

Gladia watched tensely as D. G. approached a small
group of officials. He made a half-bow, arms in downward-
pointing diagonals. It was what Gladia suspected to be a
Baleyworlder gesture of respect.

She did not hear what D. G. was saying, but a painful,
and quite involuntary fantasy passed through her mind. If
there was any attempt to separate her from her robots
against her will, Daneel and Giskard would surely do what
they could to prevent it. They would move too quickly and
precisely to really hurt anyone – but the security guards
would use their weapons at once.

She would have to prevent that at all costs – pretend
she was separating from Daneel and Giskard voluntarily,
and ask them to wait behind for her. How could she do
that? She had never been entirely without robots in her
life. How could she feel safe without them? And yet what
other way out of the dilemma offered itself?

D. G. returned. 'Your status as heroine, my lady, is a
useful bargaining chip. And, of course, I am a persuasive
fellow. Your robots may go with you. They will sit on the
platform behind you, but there will be no spotlight upon
them. And, for the sake of the Ancestor, my lady, don't
call attention to them. Don't even look at them.'

Gladia sighed with relief. 'You're a good fellow, D. G.,'
she said, shakily. 'Thank you.'

She took her place near the head of the line, D. G. at

her left, Daneel and Giskard behind her, and behind them a long tail of officials of both sexes.

A woman Settler, carrying a staff that seemed to be a symbol of office, having surveyed the line carefully, nodded, moved forward to the head of the line, then walked on. Everyone followed.

Gladia became aware of music in simple and rather repetitive march-rhythm up ahead and wondered if she were supposed to march in some choreographed fashion. (Customs vary infinitely and irrationally from world to world, she told herself.)

Looking out of the corner of her eye, she noticed D. G. ambling forward in an indifferent way. He was almost slouching. She pursed her lips disapprovingly and walked rhythmically, head erect, spine stiff. In the absence of direction, she was going to march as *she* wanted to.

They came out upon a stage, and, as they did so, chairs rose smoothly from recesses in the floor. The line split up, but D. G. caught her sleeve lightly and she accompanied him. The two robots naturally followed her.

She stood in front of the seat that D. G. quietly pointed to. The music grew loud, but the light was not quite as bright as it had been. And then, after what seemed an almost interminable wait, she felt D. G.'s touch pressing lightly downward. She sat, and so did they all.

She was aware of the faint shimmer of the force-field curtain, and beyond that an audience of several thousand. Every seat was filled in an amphitheatre that sloped steeply upward. All were dressed in dull colours, browns and blacks, both sexes alike (as nearly as she could tell them apart). The security guards in the aisles stood out in their greens and crimsons. No doubt it lent them instant recognition (though, Gladia thought, it must make them instant targets as well).

She turned to D. G. and said in a low voice, 'You people have an enormous legislature.'

D. G. shrugged slightly. 'I think everyone in the governmental apparatus is here, with mates and guests. A tribute to your popularity, my lady.'

She sent her glance over the audience from right to left and back, and tried at the extreme of the arc to catch sight, out of the corner of her eye, of either Daneel or Giskard – just to be sure they were there. And then she thought, rebelliously, that nothing would happen because of a quick glance, and deliberately turned her head. They were there. She also caught D. G. eyes rolling his upward in exasperation.

She started suddenly as a spotlight fell upon one of the persons on stage, while the rest of the room dimmed further into shadowy insubstantiality.

The spotlighted figure rose, and began to speak. His voice was not terribly loud but Gladia could hear a very faint reverberation as it reflected itself from the walls. It must penetrate every cranny of the large hall. Was it some form of amplification by a device so unobtrusive that she did not see it, or was there a particularly clever acoustical shape to the hall? She did not know, but she encouraged her puzzled speculation to continue, for it relieved her, for a while, of the necessity of having to listen to what was being said.

At one point she heard a soft call of 'Quackenbush' from some undetermined point in the audience. But for the perfect acoustics (if that was what it was) it would probably have gone unheard.

The word meant nothing to her, but from the soft, brief titter of laughter that swept the audience, she suspected it was a vulgarism. The sound quenched itself almost at once, and Gladia rather admired the depth of the silence that followed.

Perhaps if the room were so perfectly acoustic that every sound could be heard, the audience *had* to be silent, or the noise and confusion would be intolerable. Then, once the custom of silence was established, and audience-noise became a taboo, anything but silence would become unthinkable. Except where the impulse to mutter 'Quackenbush' became irresistible, she supposed.

Gladia realized that her thinking was growing muddy and her eyes were closing. She sat upright with a small jerk. The people of the planet were trying to honour her and if she fell asleep during the proceedings, that would surely be an intolerable insult. She tried to keep herself awake by listening, but that seemed to make her sleepier. She bit the inside of her cheeks instead, and breathed deeply.

Three officials spoke, one after the other, with semi-merciful semi-brevity, and then Gladia jolted wide awake (had she been actually dozing despite all her efforts – with thousands of pairs of eyes on her?) as the spotlight fell just to her left, and D. G. rose to speak, standing at his chair.

He seemed completely at ease, with his thumbs hooked in his belt.

'Men and women of Baleyworld,' he began. 'Officials, law-givers, honoured leaders, fellow-planetfolk, you have heard something of what happened on Solaria. You know that we were completely successful. You know that the Lady Gladia of Aurora contributed to that success. It is time, now, to present some of the details to you and to all my fellow-planetfolk who are listening on hypervision.'

He proceeded to describe the events in modified form and Gladia found herself dryly amused at the nature of the modifications. His own discomfiture at the hands of a humanoid robot, he passed over lightly. Giskard was never mentioned; Daneel's role was minimized; and Gladia's heavily emphasised. The incident became a duel between two women, Gladia and Landaree, and it was the courage and sense of authority of Gladia that had won out.

Finally, D. G. said, 'And now the Lady Gladia, Solarian by birth, Auroran by citizenship, but Baleyworlder by deed – ' (there was strong applause at the last, the loudest Gladia had yet heard, for the earlier speakers had been but tepidly received).

D. G. raised his hands for silence and it came at once. He then concluded, ' – will now address you.'

Gladia found the spotlight on herself, and turned to D. G. in sudden panic. There was applause in her ears and D. G., too, was clapping his hands. Under the cover of the applause, he leaned towards her and whispered, 'You love them all, you want peace, and since you're not a legislator, you're unused to long speeches of small content. Say that, then sit down.'

She looked at him uncomprehendingly, far too nervous to have heard what he said.

She rose, and found herself staring at endless tiers of people.

34.

Gladia felt very small (not for the first time in her life, to be sure) as she faced the stage. The men on stage were all taller than she was, and so were the other three women on stage. She felt that even though they were all sitting and she was standing, they still towered over her. As for the audience, which was waiting now in almost menacing silence, those who composed it were, she felt quite certain, one and all larger than her in every dimension.

She took a deep breath and said, 'Friends – ' but it came out in a thin, breathless whistle. She cleared her throat (in what seemed a thunderous rasp) and tried again.

'Friends!' This time there was a certain normality to the sound. 'You are all descended from Earthpeople, every one of you. *I* am descended from Earthpeople. There are no human beings anywhere on all the inhabited worlds, whether Spacer worlds, Settler worlds, or Earth itself, that are not either Earthpeople by birth or Earthpeople by descent. All other differences fade to nothing in the face of that enormous fact.'

Her eyes flickered leftward to look at D. G., and she found that he was smiling very slightly and that one eyelid trembled as though it were about to wink.

She went on. 'That should be our guide in every thought and act. I thank you all for thinking of me as a fellow human being, and welcoming me among you without regard to any other classification in which you might have been tempted to place me. Because of that, and in the hope that the day will soon come when sixteen billion human beings, living in love and peace, will consider themselves as just that and nothing more – or less – I think of you not merely as friends, but as kinsmen and kinswomen.'

There was an outbreak of applause that thundered in upon her and Gladia half-closed her eyes in relief. She remained standing to let it continue and bathe her in its welcome indication that she had spoken well and, what was more, enough. When it began to fade, she smiled, bowed to right and left, and began to sit down.

And then a voice came out of the audience, 'Why don't you speak in Solarian?'

She froze halfway to her seat and looked, in shock, at D. G.

He shook his head slightly, and mouthed soundlessly: Ignore it. He gestured as unobtrusively as possible that she seat herself.

She stared at him for a second or two, then realized

what an ungainly sight she must present, with her rear protruding in the unfinished process of seating herself. She straightened at once, and smiled flashingly at the audience as she turned her head slowly from side to side. For the first time she became aware of objects in the rear whose glistening lenses focused upon her.

Of course! D. G. had mentioned that the proceedings were being watched on hyperwave. Yet it scarcely seemed to matter now. She had spoken and had been applauded, and she was facing the audience she could see, erect and without nervousness. What could the unseen addition matter?

She said, still smiling, 'I consider that a friendly question. You want me to show you my accomplishments. How many want me to speak as a Solarian might? Don't hesitate. Raise your right hands.'

A few right arms went up.

Gladia said, 'The humanoid robot on Solaria heard me speak Solarian. That was what defeated it in the end. Come, let me see everyone who would like a demonstration.'

More right arms went up and, in a moment, the audience became a sea of upraised arms. Gladia felt a hand tweaking at her trouser leg, and with a rapid movement, she brushed it away.

'Very well. You may lower your arms now, kinsmen and kinswomen. Understand that what I speak now is Galactic Standard, which is your language, too. I, however, am speaking it as an Auroran would, and I know you all understand me even though the way I pronounce my words may well strike you as amusing and my choice of words may on occasion puzzle you a bit. You'll notice that my way of speaking has notes to it, and goes up and down – almost as though I were singing my words. This always sounds ridiculous to anyone not an Auroran, even to other Spacers.

'On the other hand, if I slip into the Solarian way of speaking as I am now doing, you will notice at once that the notes stop and that it becomes throaty with "r's" that just about neverrr let go – especially if therrre is no "rrrr" anywherrrre on the vocal panoramarrrrrr.'

There was a burst of laughter from the audience and Gladia confronted it with a serious expression on her face. Finally, she held up her arms and made a cutting movement downward and outward, and the laughter stopped.

'However,' she said, 'I will probably never go to Solaria again, so I will have no occasion to use the Solarian dialect any further. And the good Captain Baley' (she turned and made a half-bow in his direction, noting there was a distinct outbreak of perspiration on his brow) 'informs me there is no telling when I'll be going back to Aurora, so I may have to drop the Auroran dialect as well. My only choice, then, will be to speak the Baleyworld dialect, which I shall at once begin to practise.'

She hooked the fingers of each hand into an invisible belt, stretched her chest outward, pulled her chin downward, put on D. G.'s unselfconscious grin and said, in a gravelly attempt at baritone, 'Men and women of Baleyworld, officials, law-givers, honoured leaders, fellow-planetfolk – and that should include everyone, except, perhaps, dishonoured leaders – ' She did her best to include the glottal stops and the flat 'a's' and carefully pronounced the 'h' of 'honoured' and 'dishonoured' in what was almost a gasp.

The laughter was still louder this time and more prolonged, and Gladia allowed herself to smile and to wait calmly while it went on and on. After all, she was persuading them to laugh at themselves.

And when things were quiet again, she said simply, in an unexaggerated version of the Auroran dialect, 'Every dialect is amusing, or peculiar, to those who are not accustomed to it, and it tends to mark off human beings into separate, and frequently mutually unfriendly, groups. Dialects, however, are only languages of the tongue. Instead of those, I, and you, and every other human being on every inhabited world should listen to the language of the heart, and there are no dialects to that. That language, if we will only listen, rings out the same in all of us.'

That was it, and she was ready to sit down again, but another question sounded. It was a woman's voice this time.

'How old are you?'

Now D. G. was forced into low speech between his teeth. 'Sit *down*, madam! Ignore the question.'

Gladia turned to face D. G. He had half-risen. The others on the stage, as nearly as she could see them in the dimness outside the spotlight, were tensely leaning towards her.

She turned back to the audience and cried out, ringingly, 'The people here on the stage want me to sit down. How many of you out there want me to sit down? I find you are silent. How many want me to stand here and answer the question honestly?'

There was sharp applause and cries of 'Answer! Answer!'

Gladia said, 'The voice of the people! I'm sorry, D. G., and all the rest of you, but I am commanded to speak.'

She looked up at the spotlight, squinting, and shouted, 'I don't know who controls the lights, but light the auditorium and turn off the spotlight. I don't care what it does to the hyperwave cameras. Just make sure the sound is going out accurately. No one will care if I look dim, as long as they can hear me. Right?'

'Right!' came the multivoiced answer. Then 'Lights! Lights!'

Someone on the stage signalled in a distraught manner and the audience was bathed in light.

'Much better,' said Gladia. 'Now I can see you all, my kinspeople. I would like, particularly, to see the woman who asked the question, the one who wants to know my age. I would like to speak to her directly. Don't be backward or shy. If you have the courage to ask the question, you should have the courage to ask it openly.'

She waited, and finally a woman rose in the middle distance. Her dark hair was pulled back tightly, the colour of her skin was a light brown, and her clothing, worn tightly to emphasize a slim figure, was in shades of darker brown.

She said, just a bit stridently, 'I'm not afraid to stand up. And I'm not afraid to ask the question again. How old are you?'

Gladia faced her calmly and found herself even welcoming the confrontation. (How was this possible? Throughout her first three decades, she had been carefully trained to find the real presence of even one human being intolerable. Now look at her – facing thousands without a tremble. She was vaguely astonished and entirely pleased.)

Gladia said, 'Please remain standing, madam, and let us talk together. How shall we measure age? In elapsed years since birth?'

The woman said, with composure, 'My name is Sindra Lambid. I'm a member of the legislature and therefore one of Captain Baley's "lawgivers" and "honoured leaders". I hope "honoured" at any rate.' (Laughter – as the audience seemed to grow increasingly good-natured.) 'To answer your question, I think that the number of Galactic Standard Years that have elapsed since birth is the usual definition of a person's age. Thus, I am 54 years old. How old are you? How about just giving us a figure?'

'I will do so. Since my birth, 235 Galactic Standard Years have come and gone, so that I am twenty-three and a half decades old, or a little more than four times as old as you are.' Gladia held herself straight and she knew that her small, slim figure, and the dim light, made her look extraordinarily childlike at that moment.

There was a confused babble from the audience, and something of a groan from her left. A quick glance in that direction showed her that D. G. had his hand to his forehead.

Gladia said, 'But that is an entirely passive way of measuring time-lapse. It is a measure of quantity that takes no account of quality. My life has been spent quietly, one might say dully. I have drifted through a set routine, shielded from all untoward events by a smoothly-functioning social system that left no room for either change or experimentation, and by my robots, who stood between me and misadventure of any kind.

'Only twice in my life have I experienced the breath of excitement and both times tragedy was involved. When I was 32, younger in years than many of you who are now listening to me, there was a time – not a long one – during which a murder accusation hung over me. Two years later, there was another period of time – not long – during which I was involved in another murder. On both those occasions, Plainclothesman Elijah Baley was at my side. I believe most of you, or perhaps all of you, are familiar with the story as given in the account written by Elijah Baley's son.

'I should now add a third occasion for, this last month, I have faced a great deal of excitement, reaching its climax with my being required to stand up before you all, something which is entirely different from anything I have ever done in all my long life. And I must admit it is only your own good nature and kind acceptance of me that makes it possible.

'Consider, each of you, the contrast of all this with your own lives. You are pioneers and you live on a pioneer world. This world has been growing all your lives and will continue to grow. This world is anything but settled down and each day is, and must be, an adventure. The very climate is an adventure. You have first cold, then heat, then cold again. It is a climate rich in wind and storms and sudden change. At no time can you sit back and let time pass drowsily in a world that changes gently or not at all.

'Many Baleyworlders are Traders, or can choose to be Traders, and can then spend half their time scouring the space-lanes. And if ever this world grows tame, many of its inhabitants can choose to transfer their sphere of activities to another less developed world, or join an expedition that will find a suitable world that has not yet felt the step of human beings, and take their share in shaping it and seeding it and making it fit for human occupancy.

'Measure the length of life by events and deeds, accomplishments and excitements, and I am a child, younger than any of you. The large number of my years have served merely to bore and weary me; the smaller number of yours to enrich and excite you. So tell me again, Madam Lambid, how old are you?'

Lambid smiled. 'Fifty-four *good* years, Madam Gladia.'

She sat down and again the applause welled up and continued. Under cover of that, D. G. said hoarsely, 'Gladia, who taught you to handle an audience like this?'

'No one,' she whispered back. 'I never tried before.'

'But quit while you're ahead. The person now getting to his feet is our leading warhawk. There's no need to face him. Say you are tired and sit down. We will tackle Old Man Bistervan ourselves.'

'But I'm not tired,' said Gladia. 'I'm enjoying myself.'

The man now facing her from her extreme right, but rather near the stage, was a tall, vigorous man with white eyebrows overhanging his eyes shaggily. His thinning hair was also white, and his garments were a sombre black, relieved by a white stripe running down each sleeve and trouser leg, as though setting sharp limits to his body.

His voice was deep and musical. 'Ny name,' he said, 'is Tomas Bistervan, and I'm known to many as the Old Man, largely, I think, because they wish I were, and that I would not delay too long in dying. I do not know how to address you, because you do not seem to have a family name, and because I do not know you well enough to use your given name. To be honest, I do not wish to know you that well.

'Apparently, you helped save a Baleyworld ship on your world against the booby-traps and weapons set up by your people, and we are thanking you for that. In return, you have delivered yourself of pious nonsense about friendship and kinship. Pure hypocrisy!

'When have your people felt kin to us? When have the Spacers felt any relationship to Earth and its people? Certainly, you Spacers are descended from Earthmen. We don't forget that. Nor do we forget that *you* have forgotten it. For well over twenty decades, the Spacers controlled Earth and treated Earthpeople as though they were hateful, short-lived, diseased animals. Now that we are growing strong, you hold out the hand of friendship, but that hand has a glove on it, as your hands do. You try to remember not to turn up your nose at us, but the nose, even if not turned up, has plugs in it. Well? Am I correct?'

Gladia held up her hands. 'It may be,' she said, 'that the audience here in this room, and even more so, the audience outside the room that sees me by hyperwave, is not aware that I am wearing gloves. They are not obtrusive, but they are there. I do not deny that. And I have nose-plugs that filter out dust and micro-organisms without too much interference with breathing. And I am careful to spray my throat periodically. And I wash perhaps a bit more than the requirements of cleanliness alone make necessary. I deny none of it.

'But this is the result of my shortcomings, not yours. My immune system is not strong. My life has been too comfortable; and I have been exposed to too little. That was not my deliberate choice but I must pay the penalty for it. If any of you were in my unfortunate position, what would you do? In particular, Mr Bistervan, what would *you* do?'

Bistervan said, grimly, 'I would do as you do, and I would consider it a sign of weakness, a sign that I was unfit and unadjusted to life, and that I therefore ought to make way for those who are strong. Woman, don't speak of kinship to us. You are no kin of mine. You are of those who persecuted and tried to destroy us when you were strong, and who come whining to us when you are weak.'

There was a stir in the audience, and by no means a friendly one, but Bistervan held his ground firmly.

Gladia said, softly, 'Do you remember the evil we did when we were strong?'

Bistervan said, 'Don't fear that we will forget. It is in our minds every day.'

'Good! Because now you know what to avoid. You have learned that when the strong oppress the weak, that is wrong. Therefore, when the table turns, and when you are strong and we are weak, you will not be oppressive.'

'Ah, yes. I have heard the argument. When you were strong, you never heard of morality, but now that you are weak, you preach it earnestly.'

'In your case, though, when you were weak, you knew all about morality and were appalled by the behaviour of the strong, and now that you are strong you forget morality. Surely, it is better that the immoral learn morality through adversity, than that the moral forget morality in prosperity.'

'We will give what we received,' said Bistervan, holding up his clenched fist.

'You should give what you would have liked to receive,' said Gladia, holding out her arms, as though embracing. 'Since everyone can think of some past injustice to avenge, what you are saying, my friend, is that it is right for the strong to oppress the weak. And when you say that, you justify the Spacers of the past, and should therefore have no complaint of the present. What I say is that oppression was wrong when we practised it in the past, and that it will be equally wrong when you practise it in the future. We cannot change the past, unfortunately, but we can still decide on what the future shall be.'

Gladia paused, and when Bistervan did not answer immediately, she called out, 'How many want a new Galaxy, and not the bad old Galaxy endlessly repeated?'

The applause began, but Bistervan threw his arms up and shouted in stentorian fashion, 'Wait! Wait! Don't be fools! Stop!'

There was a slow quieting and Bistervan said, 'Do you suppose this woman believes what she's saying? Do you suppose the Spacers intend us any good whatever? They still think they are strong, and they still despise us, and they intend to destroy us – if we don't destroy them first. This woman comes here and, like fools, we greet her and make much of her. Well, put her words to the test. Let any of you apply for permission to visit a Spacer world and see if you can. Or if you have a world behind you and can use threats, as Captain Baley did, so that you are allowed to land on the world, how will you be treated? Ask the Captain if he was treated like kin.

'This woman is a hypocrite in spite of all her words; no,

because of them. They are the spoken advertisements of her hypocrisy. She moans and whines about her inadequate immune system, and says that she must protect herself against the danger of infection. Of course, she doesn't do this because she thinks we are foul and diseased; that thought, I suppose, never occurs to her.

'She whines of her passive life, protected from mischance and misfortune by a too-settled society and a too-solicitous crowd of robots. How she must hate that.

'But what endangers her here? What mischance does she feel will befall her on our planet? Yet she has brought two robots with her. In this hall, we meet in order to honour her and make much of her, yet she brought her two robots even here. They are there on the platform with her. Now that the room is generally lit, you can see them. One is an imitation human being, and its name is R. Daneel Olivaw. Another is a shameless robot, openly metallic in structure; and its name is R. Giskard Reventlov. Greet them, my fellow-Baleyworlders. *They* are this woman's kinsfolk.'

'Checkmate!' groaned D. G. in a whisper.

'Not yet,' said Gladia.

There were craning necks in the audience, as if a sudden itch had affected them all, and the word 'robots' ran across the length and breadth of the hall in thousands of intakes of breath.

'You can see them without trouble,' Gladia's voice rang out. 'Daneel, Giskard, stand up.'

The two robots rose at once behind her.

'Step to either side of me,' she said, 'so that my body does not block the view. Not that my body is large enough to do much blocking, in any case.

'Now let me make a few things clear to all of you. These two robots did not come with me in order to service me. Yes, they help run my establishment on Aurora, along with fifty-one other robots, and I do no work for myself that I wish a robot to do for me. That is the custom on the world on which I live.

'Robots vary in complexity, ability, and intelligence and these two rate very high in those respects. Daneel, in particular, is, in my opinion, the robot, of all robots, whose intelligence most nearly approximates to the human in those areas where comparison is possible.

'I have brought *only* Daneel and Giskard with me, but they perform no great services for me. If you are interested, I dress myself, bathe myself, use my own utensils when I eat, walk without being carried.

'Do I use them for personal protection? No. They protect me, yes, but they equally well protect anyone else who needs protection. On Solaria, just recently, Daneel did what he could to protect Captain Baley, and was ready to give up his existence to protect me. Without him, the ship could not have been saved.

'And I certainly need no protection on this platform. After all, there is a force-field stretched across the stage that is ample protection. It is not there at my request, but it is there, and it supplies all the protection I need.

'Then why are my robots here with me?

'Those of you who know the story of Elijah Baley, who freed Earth of its Spacer overlords, who initiated the new policy of Settlement, and whose son led the first human beings to Baleyworld — why else is it called that? — know that well before he knew me, Elijah Baley worked with Daneel. He worked with him on Earth, on Solaria, and on Aurora — on each of his three great cases. To Daneel, Elijah Baley was always "Partner Elijah". I don't know if that fact appears in his biography, but you may safely take my word for it. And although Elijah Baley, as an Earthman, began with a strong distrust of Daneel, a friendship between them developed. When Elijah Baley was dying, here on this planet over sixteen decades ago, when it was just a cluster of prefabricated houses surrounded by garden patches, it was not his son who was with him in his last moment. Nor was it I.' (For a treacherous moment, she thought her voice would not hold steady.) 'He sent for Daneel and he held on to life until Daneel arrived.

'Yes, this is Daneel's second visit to this planet. I was with him, but I remained in orbit.' (Steady!) 'It was Daneel alone who made planet-fall; Daneel who received his last words. Well, does this mean nothing to you?'

Her voice rose a notch as she shook her fists in the air. 'Must I tell you this? Don't you already know it? Here is the robot that Elijah Baley loved. Yes, loved. I wanted to see Elijah before he died, to say good-bye to him; but he wanted Daneel, and this is Daneel. This is the very one.

'And this other is Giskard, who knew Elijah only on Aurora, but who managed to save Elijah's life there.

'Without these two robots, Elijah Baley would not have completed his task. The Spacer worlds would still be supreme; the Settler worlds would not exist; and none of you would be here. I know that. You know that. I wonder if Mr Tomas Bistervan knows that?

'Daneel and Giskard are honoured names on this world. They are used commonly by the descendants of Elijah Baley at his request. I have arrived on a ship the captain of which is named Daneel Giskard Baley. How many, I wonder, among the people I face now, in person and by hyperwave, bear the name of Daneel or Giskard? Well, these robots behind me are the robots those names commemorate. And are they to be denounced by Tomas Bistervan?'

The growing murmur among the audience was becoming loud and Gladia lifted her arms imploringly. 'One moment. One moment. Let me finish. I have not told you why I brought these two robots.'

There was immediate silence.

'These two robots,' Gladia said, 'have never forgotten Elijah Baley, any more than I have forgotten him. The passing decades have not in the least dimmed those memories. When I was ready to step on to Captain Baley's ship; when I knew that I might visit Baleyworld, how could I refuse to take Daneel and Giskard with me? They wanted to see the planet that Elijah Baley had made possible, the planet on which he passed his old age, and on which he died.

'Yes, they are robots, but they are intelligent robots, and they are robots who served Elijah Baley faithfully and well. It is not enough to have respect for all human beings; one must have respect for all intelligent beings. So I brought them here.' Then, in a final outcry that demanded a response, '*Did I do wrong?*'

She received her response. A gigantic cry of '*No!*' resounded throughout the hall, and everyone was on his or her feet, clapping, stamping, roaring, screaming, and on, and on, and on.

Gladia watched, smiling and, as the noise continued endlessly, became aware of two things. First, she was wet with perspiration. Second, she was happier than she had ever been in her life.

It was as though all her life she had waited for this moment; the moment when she, having been brought up in isolation, could finally learn, after twenty-three decades, that she could face crowds, and move them, and bend them to her will.

She listened to the unwearying, noisy response, on – and on – and on –

35.

It was a considerable time later – how long she had no way of telling – that Gladia finally came to herself.

There had first been unending noise, the solid wedge of security people herding her through the crowd, the plunge into endless tunnels that seemed to sink deeper and deeper into the ground.

She lost contact with D. G. early and was not sure that Daneel and Giskard were safely with her. She wanted to ask for them, but surrounding her were only faceless people. She thought distantly that the robots had to be with her for they would resist separation, and she would hear the tumult if an attempt were made.

When she finally reached a room, the two were there with her. She didn't know precisely where she was, but the room was fairly large and clean. It was poor stuff compared to her home on Aurora, but compared to the shipboard cabin it was quite luxurious.

'You will be safe here, madam,' said the last of the guards as he left. 'If you need anything, just let us know,' and he indicated a device on a small table next to the bed.

She stared at it, but by the time she turned back to ask what it was and how it worked, he was gone.

Oh, well, she thought, I'll get by.

'Giskard,' she said, wearily, 'find out which of those doors leads to the bathroom and find out how the shower works. What I *must* have now is a shower.'

She sat down gingerly, aware that she was damp and unwilling to saturate the chair with her perspiration. She was beginning to ache with the unnatural rigidity of her position, when Giskard emerged.

'Madam, the shower is running,' he said, 'and the

temperature is adjusted. There is a solid material which I believe is soap and a primitive sort of towelling material, along with various other articles that may be useful.'

'Thank you, Giskard,' said Gladia, quite aware that despite her grandiloquence on the manner in which robots such as Giskard did not perform menial service, that was precisely what she had required him to do. But circumstances alter cases –

If she had never needed a shower, it seemed to her, as badly as now, she had also never enjoyed one as much. She remained in it much longer than she had to, and when it was over, it didn't even occur to her to wonder if the towels had been in any way irradiated to sterility until after she had dried herself and by that time it was too late.

She rummaged about among the material Giskard had laid out for powder, deodorant, comb, toothpaste, hair-dryer. She found these, after a fashion, but could not locate anything that would serve as a toothbrush and she had to use her finger, which she found most unsatisfactory. There was no hairbrush, and that was unsatisfactory, too. She scrubbed the comb with soap before using it, but cringed away from it, just the same. There was something that looked as though it were suitable for wearing to bed. It smelled clean, but it hung far too loosely, she decided.

Daneel said quietly, 'Madam, the Captain wishes to know if he may see you.'

'I suppose so,' said Gladia, still rummaging for alternative nightwear. 'Let him in.'

D. G. looked tired and even haggard, but when she turned to greet him, he smiled wearily at her and said, 'It is hard to believe that you are twenty-three and a half decades old.'

'What? In this thing?'

'That helps. It's semi-transparent. Or didn't you know?'

She looked down at the nightgown uncertainly, then

said, 'Good, if it amuses you, but I have been alive, just the same, for two and three-eighths centuries.'

'No one would guess it to look at you. You must have been very beautiful in your youth.'

'I have never been told so, D. G. Quiet charm, I always believed, was the most I could aspire to. In any case, how do I use that instrument?'

'The callbox? Just touch the patch on the right side and someone will ask if you can be served and you can carry on from there.'

'Good. I will need a toothbrush, a hairbrush, and clothing.'

'The toothbrush and hairbrush I will see that you get. As for clothing, that has been thought of. You have a clothes-bag hanging in your closet. You'll find it contains the best in Baleyworld fashion, which may not appeal to you, of course. And I won't guarantee they'll fit you. Most Baleyworld women are taller than you, and certainly wider and thicker. But it doesn't matter. I think you'll remain in seclusion for quite a while.'

'Why?'

'Well, my lady. It seems you delivered a speech this past evening and, as I recall, you would not sit down, though I suggested you do that more than once.'

'It seemed quite successful to me, D. G.'

'It was. It was a howling success.' D. G. smiled broadly and scratched the right side of his beard as though considering the word very carefully. 'However, success has its penalties too. Right now, I should say you are the most famous person on Baleyworld and every Baleyworlder wants to see you and touch you, and if we take you out anywhere, it will mean an instant riot. At least, until things cool down and we can't be sure how long that will take.

'Then, too, you had even the warhawks yelling for you, but in the cold light of tomorrow, when the hypnotism and hysteria dies down, they're going to be furious. If Old Man Bistervan didn't actually consider killing you outright after your talk, then by tomorrow he will certainly have it as the ambition of his life to murder you by slow torture. And there are people of his party who might conceivably try to oblige the Old Man in this small whim of his.

'That's why you're here, my lady. That's why this room, this floor, this entire hotel is being watched by I don't know how many platoons of security people, among whom, I hope, are no crypto-warhawks. And because I have been so closely associated with you in this hero-and-heroine game, I'm penned up here, too, and can't get out.'

'Oh,' said Gladia, blankly. 'I'm sorry about that. You can't see your family, then.'

D. G. shrugged. 'Traders don't really have much in the way of family.'

'Your woman-friend, then.'

'She'll survive. Probably better than I will.' He cast his eyes on Gladia speculatively.

Gladia said, evenly, 'Don't even *think* it, Captain.'

D. G.'s eyebrows rose. 'There's no way I can be prevented from thinking it, but I won't *do* anything, madam.'

Gladia said, 'How long do you think I will stay here? Seriously.'

'It depends on the Directory.'

'The Directory?'

'Our five-fold executive board, madam. Five people,' he held up his hand with the fingers spread apart, 'each serving five years in staggered fashion, with one replacement each year, plus special elections in case of death or disability. This supplies continuity and reduces the danger of one-person rule. It also means that every decision must be argued out, and takes time, sometimes more time than we can afford.'

'I should think,' said Gladia, 'that if one of the five were a determined and forceful individual – '

'That he could impose his views on the others. Things like that have happened at times, but these times are not one of those times, if you know what I mean. The Senior Director is Genovus Pandaral. There's nothing evil about him, but he's indecisive, and that's sometimes the same thing. I talked him into allowing your robots on stage with you, and that turned out to be a bad idea. Score one against both of us.'

'But why was it a bad idea? The people were *pleased*.'

'*Too* pleased, my lady. We wanted you to be our pet Spacer heroine, and help keep public opinion cool so that we wouldn't launch a premature war. You were very good on longevity; you had them cheering short life. But then you had them cheering robots, and we don't want that. For that matter, we're not so keen on the public cheering the notion of kinship with the Spacers.'

'You don't want premature war, but you don't want premature peace, either. Is that it?'

'Very well put, madam.'

'But then what do you want?'

'We want the Galaxy, the *whole* Galaxy. We want to settle and populate every habitable planet in it and establish nothing less than a Galactic Empire. And we don't want the Spacers to interfere. They can remain on their own worlds and live in peace as they please, but they must not interfere.'

'But then you'll be penning them up on their fifty worlds, as we penned up Earthpeople on Earth for so many years. The same old injustice. You're as bad as Bistervan.'

'The situations are different. Earthpeople were penned up in defiance of their expansive potential. You Spacers have no such potential. You took the path of longevity and robots and the potential vanished. You don't even have fifty worlds any longer. Solaria has been abandoned. The others will go, too, in time. The Settlers have no interest in pushing the Spacers along the path to extinction, but why should we interfere with their voluntary choice to do so? Your speech tended to interfere with that.'

'I'm glad of it. What did you think I would say?'

'I told you. Peace and love and sit down. You could have finished in about one minute.'

Gladia said, angrily, 'I can't believe you expected anything so foolish of me. What did you take me for?'

'For what you took yourself for – someone frightened to death of speaking. How did we know that you were a madwoman who could, in half an hour, persuade the Baleyworlders to howl in favour of what for lifetimes we have been persuading them to howl against? But talk will get us nowhere,' he rose heavily to his feet, 'I want a shower, too, and I had better get a night's sleep if I can. See you tomorrow.'

'But when do we find out what the Directors will decide to do with me?'

'When *they* find out, which may not be soon. Good night, madam.'

36.

'I have made a discovery,' said Giskard, his voice carrying no shade of emotion. 'I have made it because, for the first time in my existence, I faced thousands of human beings. Had I done this two centuries ago, I would have made the discovery then. Had I never faced so many at once, then I would never have made the discovery at all.

'Consider, then, how many vital points I might easily grasp, but never have and never will, simply because the proper conditions for it will never come my way. I remain ignorant except where circumstance helps me, and I cannot count on circumstance.'

Daneel said, 'I did not think, Friend Giskard, that the Lady Gladia, with her long-sustained way of life, could face thousands with equanimity. I did not think she would be able to speak at all. When it turned out that she could, I assumed you had adjusted her, and that you had discovered that it could be done without harming her. Was that your discovery?'

Giskard said, 'Friend Daneel, actually all I dared do was loosen a very few strands of inhibition, only enough to allow her to speak a few words, so that she might be heard.'

'But she did far more than that.'

'After this microscopic adjustment, I turned to the multiplicity of minds I faced in the audience. I had never experienced so many, any more than Lady Gladia had, and I was as taken aback as she was. I found, at first, that I could do nothing in the vast mental interlockingness that beat in upon me. I felt helpless.

'And then I noted small friendlinesses, curiosities, inter- ests – I cannot describe them in words – with a colour of sympathy for the Lady Gladia about them. I played with what I could find that had this colour of sympathy, tighten- ing and thickening them just slightly. I wanted some small response in the Lady Gladia's favour that might encourage her, that might make it unnecessary for me to be tempted to tamper further with the lady's own mind. That was all I did. I do not know how many threads of the proper colour I handled. Not many.'

Daneel said, 'And what then, Friend Giskard?'

'I found, Friend Daneel, that I had begun something that was auto-catalytic. Each thread I strengthened, strengthened a near-by thread of the same kind, and the two together strengthened several others nearby. I had to do nothing further. Small stirs, small sounds, small glances that seemed to approve of what the Lady Gladia said, encouraged still others.

'Then I found something stranger yet. All these little indications of approval, which I could detect only because the minds were open to me, Lady Gladia must have, in some manner, also detected, for further inhibitions in her mind fell without my touching them. She began to speak faster, more confidently, and the audience responded better than ever – without my doing anything. And in the end, there was hysteria, a storm, a tempest of mental thunder and lightning so intense that I had to close my mind to it or it would have overloaded my circuits.

'Never, in all my existence, had I encountered anything like that and yet it started with no more modification introduced by me in all that crowd than I have, in the past, introduced among a mere handful of people. I suspect, in fact, that the effect spread beyond the audience sensible to my mind, to the greater audience reached by hyperwave.'

Daneel said, 'I do not see how this can be, Friend Giskard.'

'Nor I, Friend Daneel. I am not human. I do not directly experience the possession of a human mind with all its complexities and contradictions, so I do not grasp the mechanisms by which they respond. But, apparently, crowds are more easily managed than individuals. It seems paradoxical. Much weight takes more effort to move than little weight. Much energy takes more effort to counter than little energy. Much distance takes longer to traverse than little distance. Why, then, should many people be easier to sway than few? You think like a human being, Friend Daneel. Can you explain?'

Daneel said, 'You, yourself, Friend Giskard, said that it

was an auto-catalytic effect; a matter of contagion. A single spark of flame may end by burning down a forest.'

Giskard paused and seemed deep in thought. Then he said, 'It is not reason that is contagious, but emotion. Madam Gladia chose arguments she felt would move her audience's feelings. She did not attempt to reason with them. It may be, then, that the larger the crowd, the more easily they are swayed by emotion rather than by reason.

'Since emotions are few and reasons are many, the behaviour of a crowd can be more easily predicted than the behaviour of one person can. And that, in turn, means that if laws are to be developed that enable the current of history to be predicted, then one must deal with large populations, the larger the better. That might itself be the First Law of Psychohistory, the key to the study of Humanics. Yet – '

'Yes?'

'It strikes me that it has taken me so long to understand this only because I am not a human being. A human being would, perhaps, instinctively understand his own mind well enough to know how to handle others like himself. Madam Gladia, with no experience at all in addressing huge crowds, carried off the matter expertly. How much better off we would be, if we had someone like Elijah Baley with us. Friend Daneel, are you not thinking of him?'

Daneel said, 'Can you see his image in my mind? That is surprising, Friend Giskard.'

'I do not see him, Friend Daneel. I cannot receive your thoughts. But I can sense emotions and mood, and your mind has a texture which, by past experience, I know to be associated with Elijah Baley.'

'Madam Gladia made mention of the fact that I was the

last to see Partner Elijah alive, so I listen again, in memory, to that moment. I think, again, of what he said.'

'Why, Friend Daneel?'

'I search for the meaning. I feel it was important.'

'How could what he said have meaning beyond the import of the words? Had there been hidden meaning, Elijah Baley would have expressed it.'

'Perhaps,' said Daneel slowly, 'Partner Elijah did not himself understand the significance of what he was saying.'

10

After the Speech

37.

Memory!

It lay in Daneel's mind like a closed book of infinite detail, always available for his use. Some passages were called upon frequently for their information, but only a very few were called upon merely because Daneel wished to feel their texture. Those very few were, for the most part, those that contained Elijah Baley.

Many decades ago, Daneel had come to Baleyworld while Elijah Baley yet lived. Madam Gladia had come with him, but after they entered into orbit about Baleyworld, Bentley Baley climbed upward in his small ship to meet them and was brought aboard. By then, he was a rather gnarled man of middle age.

He looked at Gladia with faintly hostile eyes and said, 'You cannot see him, madam.'

And Gladia, who had been weeping, said, 'Why not?'

'He does not wish it, madam, and I must respect his wishes.'

'I cannot believe that, Mr Baley.'

'I have a handwritten note and I have a voice-recording, madam. I do not know if you can recognize his handwriting or his voice, but you have my word of honour these are his and that no untoward influence was used upon him to produce them.'

She went into her own cabin to read and listen alone. Then she emerged, with something about her that showed defeat, but she managed to say firmly, 'Daneel, you are to go down alone to see him. It is his wish. But you are to report to me everything that is done and said.'

'Yes, madam,' Daneel said.

Daneel went down in Bentley's ship, and Bentley said to him, 'Robots are not allowed on this world, Daneel, but an exception is being made in your case, because it is my father's wish, and he is highly revered here. I have no personal animus against you, you understand, but your presence here must be an entirely limited one. You will be taken directly to my father, and when he is done with you, you will be taken back into orbit at once. Do you understand?'

'I understand, sir. How is your father?'

'He is dying,' said Bentley, with perhaps conscious brutality.

'I understand that, too,' said Daneel, his voice quivering noticeably, not out of ordinary emotion, but because the consciousness of the death of a human being, however unavoidable, disordered his positronic brainpaths. 'I mean, how much longer before he must die?'

'He ought to have died some time ago. He is tied to life because he refuses to go until he sees you.'

They landed. It was a large world, but the inhabited portion, if this were all, was small and shabby. It was a cloudy day and it had rained recently. The wide straight streets were empty, as though what population existed there was in no mood to gather in order to stare upon a robot.

The ground-car took them through the emptiness and brought them to a house somewhat larger and more impressive than most. Together they entered. At an inner door, Bentley halted.

'My father is in there,' he said, sadly. 'You are to go in alone. He will not have me there with you. Go in. You will perhaps fail to recognize him.'

Daneel went into the gloom of the room. His eyes adjusted rapidly and he was aware of a body covered by a sheet inside a transparent cocoon that was made visible only by its faint glitter. The light within the room brightened a bit, and Daneel could then see the face clearly.

Bentley had been right. Daneel saw nothing of his old partner in it. It was gaunt and bony. The eyes were closed and it seemed to Daneel that what he saw was a dead body. He had never seen a dead human being and when this thought struck him, he staggered, and it seemed to him that his legs would not hold him up.

But the old man's eyes opened and Daneel recovered his equilibrium, though he continued to feel an unaccustomed weakness just the same.

The eyes looked at him and a small, faint smile curved the pale, cracked lips.

'Daneel. My old friend, Daneel.' There was the faint timbre of Elijah Baley's remembered voice in that whispered sound. An arm emerged slowly from under the sheet, and it seemed to Daneel that he recognized Elijah after all.

'Partner Elijah,' he said, softly.

'Thank you – thank you for coming.'

'It was important for me to come, Partner Elijah.'

'I was afraid they might not allow it. They – the others – even my son – think of you as a robot.'

'I *am* a robot.'

'Not to me, Daneel. You haven't changed, have you? I don't see you clearly, but it seems to me you are exactly the same as I remember. When did I last see you? Thirty-one years ago?'

'Yes, and in all that time, Partner Elijah, I have not changed, so you see, I *am* a robot.'

'I have changed, though, and a great deal. I should not have let you see me like this, but I was too weak to resist my desire to see you once again.' Baley's voice seemed to have grown a bit stronger as though it had been fortified by the sight of Daneel.

'I am pleased to see you, Partner Elijah, however you have changed.'

'And Lady Gladia? How is she?'

'She is well. She came with me.'

'She is not – ' A touch of painful alarm came into his voice, as he tried to look about.

'She is not on this world, but is still in orbit. It was explained to her that you did not wish to see her, and she understood.'

'That is wrong. I *do* wish to see her, but I have been able to withstand *that* temptation. She has not changed, has she?'

'She still has the appearance she had when you last saw her.'

'Good. But I couldn't let her see me like this. I could not have *this* be her last memory of me. With you, it is different.'

'That is because I am a robot, Partner Elijah.'

'Stop insisting on that,' said the dying man, peevishly. 'You could not mean more to me, Daneel, if you were a man.'

He lay silently in his bed for a while, then he said, 'All these years, I have never hypervised, never written to her. I could not allow myself to interfere with her life. Is Gladia still married to Gremionis?'

'Yes, sir.'

'And happy?'

'I cannot judge that. She does not behave in a fashion that might be interpreted as unhappy.'

'Children?'

'The permitted two.'

'She has not been angry that I have not communicated?'

'It is my belief she understood your motives.'

'Does she ever – mention me?'

'Almost never, but it is Giskard's opinion that she often thinks of you.'

'How is Giskard?'

'He functions properly – in the manner that you know.'

'You know, then – of his abilities?'

'He has told me, Partner Elijah.'

Again Baley lay there silently. Then he stirred and said, 'Daneel, I wanted you here out of a selfish desire to see you, to see for myself that you haven't changed, that there is a breath of the great days of my life still existing, that you remember me and will continue to remember me. But I also want to tell you something.

'I will be dead soon, Daneel, and I knew the word would reach you. Even if you weren't here; even if you were on Aurora, the word would reach you. My death will be Galactic news.' His chest heaved in a weak and silent laugh. 'Who would have thought it once?'

He said, 'Gladia would hear of it as well, of course, but Gladia knows I must die and she will accept the fact, however sadly. I feared the effect on you, however, since you are – as you insist, and I deny – a robot. For old times' sake you may feel it is incumbent upon you to keep me from dying, and the fact that you cannot do so may perhaps have a permanently deleterious effect on you. Let me, then, argue with you about that.'

Baley's voice was growing weaker, and though Daneel sat motionless, his face was in the unusual condition of reflecting emotion. It was set in an expression of concern and sorrow. Baley's eyes were closed, and he could not see that.

'My death, Daneel,' he said, 'is not important. No individual death among human beings is important. Someone who dies leaves his work behind, and that does *not* entirely die. It never entirely dies as long as humanity exists. Do you understand what I'm saying?'

Daneel said, 'Yes, Partner Elijah.'

'The work of each individual contributes to a totality, and so becomes an undying part of the totality. That totality of human lives, past and present – and to come – forms a tapestry that has been in existence now for many tens of thousands of years and has been growing more elaborate and, on the whole, more beautiful in all that time. Even the Spacers are an offshoot of the tapestry, and they, too, add to the elaborateness and beauty of the pattern. An individual life is one thread in the tapestry, and what is one thread compared to the whole?

'Daneel, keep your mind fixed firmly on the tapestry and do not let the trailing off of a single thread affect you. There are so many other threads, each valuable, each contributing – '

Baley stopped speaking, but Daneel waited patiently.

Baley's eyes opened and, looking at Daneel, he frowned slightly.

'You are still here? It is time for you to go. I have told you what I meant to tell you.'

'I do not wish to go, Partner Elijah.'

'You must. I cannot hold off death any longer. I am tired – desperately tired. I want to die. It is time.'

'May I not wait while you live?'

'I don't wish it. If I die while you watch, it may affect you badly despite all my words. Go now. That is an – order. I will allow you to be a robot if you wish but, in that case, you must follow my orders. You cannot save my life by anything you can do, so there is nothing to come ahead of Second Law. Go!'

Baley's finger pointed feebly, and he said, 'Good-bye, Friend Daneel.'

Daneel turned slowly, following Baley's orders with

unprecedented difficulty. 'Good-bye, Partner – ' He paused, and then said, with a faint hoarseness, 'Good-bye, Friend Elijah.'

Bentley confronted Daneel in the next room. 'Is he still alive?'

'He was alive when I left.'

Bentley went in, and, almost at once, came out. 'He isn't now. He saw you and then – let go.'

Daneel found he had to lean against the wall. It was some time before he could stand upright.

Bentley, eyes averted, waited, and then together, they returned to the small ship and moved back up into orbit where Gladia waited.

And she, too, asked if Elijah Baley was still alive, and when they told her, gently, that he was not, she turned away dry-eyed and went into her own cabin to weep.

37a.

And Daneel continued his thought as though the sharp memory of Baley's death in all its details had not momentarily intervened. 'And yet I may understand something more of what Partner Elijah was saying, now, in the light of Madam Gladia's speech.'

'In what way?'

'I am not yet sure. It is very difficult to think in the direction I am trying to think.'

'I will wait for as long as is necessary,' said Giskard.

38.

Genovus Pandaral was tall and not, as yet, very old for all his thick shock of white hair which, together with his fluffy, white sideburns, gave him a look of dignity and distinction. His general air of looking like a leader had helped his advancement through the ranks, but as he himself knew very well, his appearance was much stronger than his inner fibre.

Once he had been elected to the Directory, he had got over the initial elation rather rapidly. He was in beyond his depth and, each year, as he was automatically pushed up a notch, he knew that more clearly. Now he was Senior Director.

Of all the times to be Senior Director!

In the old days, the task of ruling had been nothing. In the time of Nephi Morler, eight decades before, the same Morler who was always being held up to the schoolchildren as the greatest of all Directors, it had been nothing. What had Baleyworld been then? A small world; a trickle of farms; a handful of towns clustered along natural lines of communication. The total population had been no more than five million and its most important exports had been raw wool and some titanium.

The Spacers had ignored them completely under the more or less benign influence of Han Fastolfe of Aurora, and life was simple. People could always make trips back to Earth, if they wanted a breath of culture or the feel of technology, and there was a steady flow of Earthpeople arriving as immigrants. Earth's mighty population was inexhaustible.

Why shouldn't Morler have been a great Director, then? He had had nothing to do.

And, in the future, ruling would again be simple. As the Spacers continued to degenerate (every schoolchild was told that they would, that they must drown in the contradictions of their society – though Pandaral wondered, sometimes, whether this was really certain) and as the Settlers continued to increase in numbers and strength, the time would soon come when life would be again secure. The Settlers would live in peace and develop their own technology to the utmost.

As Baleyworld filled, it would assume the proportion and ways of another Earth, as would all the worlds, while new ones would spring up here and there in even greater numbers, finally making up the great Galactic Empire to come. And surely Baleyworld, as the oldest and most populous of the Settler worlds, would always have a prime place in that Empire, under the benign and perpetual rule of Mother Earth.

But it was not in the past that Pandaral was Senior Director. Nor was it in the future. It was now.

Han Fastolfe was dead now, but Kelden Amadiro was alive. Amadiro had held out against Earth being allowed to send out Settlers twenty decades ago and he was still alive now to make trouble. The Spacers were still too strong to be disregarded; the Settlers were still not quite strong enough to move forward with confidence. Somehow, the Settlers had to hold off the Spacers till the balance had shifted sufficiently.

And the task of keeping the Spacers quiet, and the Settlers at once resolute and yet sensible, fell more upon Pandaral's shoulders than on anyone else's, and it was a task he neither liked nor wanted.

Now it was morning, a cold, grey morning with more snow coming, though *that* was no surprise, and he made his way through the hotel alone. He wanted no retinue.

The security guards, out in force, snapped to attention

as he passed and he acknowledged them wearily. He spoke to the captain of the guard, when the latter advanced to meet him. 'Any trouble, Captain?'

'None, Director. All is quiet.'

Pandaral nodded. 'In which room has Baley been put? Ah! And the Spacer woman and her robots are under strict guard? Good.'

He passed on. On the whole, D. G. had behaved well. Solaria, abandoned, could be used by Traders as an almost endless supply of robots and as a source of large profits – though profits were not to be taken as the natural equivalent of world security, Pandaral thought morosely. But Solaria, booby-trapped, had best be left severely alone. It was then not worth a war. D. G. had done well to leave at once.

And to take the nuclear intensifier with him. So far, such devices were so overwhelmingly massive that they could be used only in huge and expensive installations designed to destroy invading ships, and even these had never got beyond the planning stage. Too expensive. Smaller and cheaper versions were absolutely necessary, so D. G. was right in feeling that bringing home a Solarian intensifier was more important than all the robots on that world put together. That intensifier should help the scientists of Baleyworld enormously.

And yet if one Spacer world had a portable intensifier, why not others? Why not Aurora? If those weapons grew small enough to place on warships, a Spacer fleet could wipe out any number of Settler ships without trouble. How far towards that development were they, and how fast could Baleyworld progress in the same direction with the help of the intensifier D. G. had brought back?

He signalled at D. G.'s hotelroom door, then entered without quite waiting for a response and sat down without quite waiting for an invitation. There were *some* useful perquisites that went along with being Senior Director.

D. G. looked out of the bathroom and said through the towel with which he was giving his hair a first dry, 'I would have liked to greet your Directorial Excellence in a properly imposing manner, but you catch me at a disadvantage since I am in the extremely undignified predicament of having just emerged from my shower.'

'Oh, shut up,' said Pandaral, pettishly.

Ordinarily, he enjoyed D. G.'s irrepressible breeziness, but not now. In some ways, he never really understood D. G. at all. D. G. was a Baley, a lineal descendant of the great Elijah and the founder, Bentley. That made D. G. a natural for a Director's post, especially since he had the kind of bonhomie that endeared him to the public. Yet he chose to be a Trader, which was a difficult life, and a dangerous one. It might make you rich, but it was much more likely to kill you or, what was worse, prematurely age you.

What's more, D. G.'s life as a Trader took him away from Baleyworld for months at a time, and Pandaral preferred his advice to those of most of his department heads. One couldn't always tell when D. G. was serious, but, allowing for that, he was worth listening to.

Pandaral said, heavily, 'I don't think that that woman's speech was the best thing that could have happened to us.'

D. G., mostly dressed, shrugged his shoulders. 'Who could have foretold it?'

'You might have. You must have looked up her background, if you had made up your mind to carry her off.'

'I *did* look up her background, Director. She spent over three decades in Solaria. It was Solaria that formed her, and there she lived entirely with robots. She saw human beings only in holo-images, except for her husband, and he didn't visit her often. She had a difficult adjustment to make when she came to Aurora and even there she lived mostly with robots. At no time in twenty-three decades would she have faced as many as twenty people all together, let alone four thousand. I assumed she wouldn't be able to speak more than a few words, if that. I had no way of knowing she was a rabble-rouser.'

'You might have stopped her, once you found out she was. You were sitting right next to her.'

'Did you want a riot? The people were enjoying her. You were there. You know they were. If I had forced her down, they would have mobbed the stage. After all, Director, *you* didn't try to stop her.'

Pandaral cleared his throat. 'I had that in mind, actually, but each time I looked back, I'd catch the eye of her robot – the one who looks like a robot.'

'Giskard. Yes, but what of it? He wouldn't harm you.'

'I know. Still, he made me nervous, and it put me off, somehow.'

'Well, never mind, Director,' said D. G. He was fully clothed now, and he shoved the breakfast tray towards the other. 'The coffee is still warm, and help yourself to the buns and jam, if you want any. It will pass. I don't think the public will really overflow with love for the Spacers and spoil our policy. It might even serve a purpose. If the Spacers hear of it, it might strengthen the Fastolfe party. Fastolfe may be dead, but his party isn't, not altogether, and we need to encourage their policy of moderation.'

'What I'm thinking of,' said Pandaral, 'is the All-Settler Congress that's coming up in five months. I'm going to have to listen to any number of sarcastic references to Baleyworld appeasement, and to Baleyworlders being Spacer-lovers. I tell you,' he added, gloomily, 'the smaller the world, the more warhawkish it is.'

'Then tell them that,' said D. G. 'Be very statesmanlike in public, but when you get them to one side, look them right in the eye – unofficially – and say that there's freedom of expression on Baleyworld and we intend to keep it that way. Tell them Baleyworld has the interests of Earth at heart, but that if any world wishes to prove its greater devotion to Earth by declaring war on the Spacers, Baleyworld will watch with interest but nothing more. That would shut them up.'

'Oh, no,' said Pandaral, with alarm. 'A remark like that would be leaked. It would create an impossible stink.'

D. G. said, 'You're right, which is a pity. But *think* it and don't let those big-mouth small-brains get to you.'

Pandaral sighed. 'I suppose we'll manage, but last night upset our plans to end on a high note. That's what I really regret.'

'What high note?'

Pandaral said, 'When you left Aurora for Solaria, two Auroran warships went to Solaria as well. Did you know that?'

'No, but it was something I expected,' said D. G., indifferently. 'It was for that reason I took the trouble of going to Solaria by way of an evasive path.'

'One of the Auroran ships landed on Solaria, thousands of kilometres away from you – so it didn't seem to be making any effort to keep tabs on you – and the second remained in orbit.'

'Sensible. It's what I would have done, if I had had a second ship at my disposal.'

'The Auroran ship that landed was destroyed in a matter of hours. The ship in orbit reported the fact and was ordered to return. A Trader monitoring station picked up the report and it was sent to us.'

'Was the report uncoded?'

'Of course not, but it was in one of the codes we've broken.'

D. G. nodded his head, thoughtfully, then said, 'Very

interesting. I take it they didn't have anyone who could speak Solarian.'

'Obviously,' said Pandaral, weightily. 'Unless someone can find where the Solarians went, this woman of yours is the only available Solarian in the Galaxy.'

'And they let me have her, didn't they? Tough on the Aurorans.'

'At any rate, I was going to announce the destruction of the Auroran ship last night. In a matter-of-fact way; no gloating. Just the same, it would have excited every Settler in the Galaxy. I mean, we got away, and the Aurorans didn't.'

'We had a Solarian,' said D. G., dryly. 'The Aurorans didn't.'

'Very well. It would make you and the woman look good, too. But it all came to nothing. After what the woman did, anything else would have come as anticlimax, even the news of the destruction of an Auroran warship.'

D. G. said, 'To say nothing of the fact that once everyone has finished applauding kinship and love, it would go against the grain – for the next half-hour anyway – to applaud the death of a couple of hundred of the Auroran kin.'

'I suppose so. So that's an enormous psychological blow that we've lost.'

D. G. was frowning. 'Forget that, Director. You can always work the propaganda at some other, more appropriate time. The important thing is what it all means. An Auroran ship was blown up. That means they weren't expecting a nuclear intensifier to be used. The other ship was ordered away, and that may mean it wasn't equipped with a defence against it, and maybe they don't even have a defence. I should judge from this that the portable intensifier – or semi-portable one, anyway – is a Solarian development specifically, and not a Spacer development generally. That's good news for us, if it's true. For the moment, let's not worry about propaganda brownie points, but concentrate on squeezing every bit of information we can out of that intensifier. We want to be ahead of the Spacers in this, if possible.'

Pandaral munched away at a bun, and said, 'Maybe you're right, but in that case, how do we fit in the other bit of news?'

D. G. said, 'What other bit of news? Director, are you going to give me the information I need to make intelligent conversation or do you intend to toss them into the air one by one and make me jump for them?'

'Don't get huffy, D. G. There's no point in talking with you, if I can't be informal. Do you know what it's like at a Directory meeting? Do you want my job? You can have it, you know.'

'No, thank you, I don't want it. What I want is your bit of news.'

'We have a message from Aurora. An actual message. They actually deigned to communicate directly with us instead of sending it by way of Earth.'

'We might consider it an important message, then – to them. What do they want?'

'They want the Solarian woman back again.'

'Obviously, then, they know our ship got away from Solaria, and has come to Baleyworld. They have their monitoring stations, too, and eavesdrop on our communications as we eavesdrop on theirs.'

'Absolutely,' said Pandaral, with considerable irritation. 'They break our codes as fast as we break theirs. My own feeling is we ought to come to an agreement that we both send messages in the clear. Neither of us would be worse off.'

'Did they say why they want the woman?'

'Of course not. Spacers don't give reasons; they give orders.'

'Have they found out exactly what it was that the woman accomplished on Solaria? Since she's the only person who speaks authentic Solarian, do they want her to clear the planet of its overseers?'

'I don't see how they could have found out, D. G. We only announced her role last night. The message from Aurora was received well before that. But it doesn't matter why they want her. The question is: What do we do? If we don't return her, we may have a crisis with Aurora that I don't want. If we do return her, it will look bad to the Baleyworlders, and Old Man Bistervan will have a field day pointing out that we're crawling to the Spacers.'

They stared at each other, then D. G. said, slowly, 'We'll have to return her. After all, she's a Spacer and an Auroran citizen. We can't keep her against Aurora's will, or we'll put at risk every Trader who ventures into Spacer territory on business. But *I'll* take her back, Director, and you can put the blame on me. Say that the conditions of my taking her to Solaria were that I would return her to Aurora, which is true, actually, even if not a matter of written formality, and that I am a man of ethics, and felt I had to keep my agreement. And it may turn out to our advantage.'

'In what way?'

'I'll have to work it out. But if it's to be done, Director, my ship will have to be refitted at planetary expense. And my men will need healthy bonuses. Come, Director, they're giving up their leave.'

39.

Considering that he had not intended to be in his ship again for at least three additional months, D. G. seemed in genial spirits.

And considering that Gladia had larger and more luxurious quarters than she had before, she seemed rather depressed.

'Why all this?' she asked.

'Looking a gift horse in the mouth?' asked D. G.

'I'm just asking. Why?'

'For one thing, my lady, you're a class-A heroine and when the ship was refurbished, this place was rather tarted up for you.'

'Tarted up?'

'Just an expression. Fancied up, if you prefer.'

'This space wasn't created. Who lost out?'

'Actually, it was the crew's lounge, but they insisted, you know. You're their darling, too. In fact, Niss – you remember Niss?'

'Certainly.'

'He wants you to take him on in place of Daneel. He says Daneel doesn't enjoy the job and keeps apologizing to his victims. Niss says he will destroy anyone who gives you the least trouble, will take pleasure in it, and will never apologize.'

Gladia smiled. 'Tell him I will keep his offer in mind, and next time he sees me, tell him I would enjoy shaking his hand. I refused his hand that other time and perhaps I should not have.'

'You'll wear your gloves, I hope, when you shake hands.'

'Of course, but I wonder if that's entirely necessary. I

haven't as much as sniffled since I left Aurora. The injections I've been getting have probably stiffened my immune system beautifully.' She looked about again. 'You even have niches for Daneel and Giskard. That's very thoughtful of you, D. G.'

'Madam,' said D. G., 'we work hard to please and we're delighted that you're pleased.'

'Oddly enough,' and Gladia sounded as though she were actually puzzled by what she was about to say, 'I'm not entirely pleased. I'm not sure I want to leave your world.'

'No? Cold – snow – dingy – primitive – endlessly cheering crowds everywhere. What can possibly attract you here?'

Gladia reddened. 'It's not the cheering crowds.'

'I'll pretend to believe you, madam.'

'It's *not*. It's something altogether different. I – I have never done anything. I've amused myself in various trivial ways, I've engaged in light-sculpture, and robot exodesign. I've made love and been a wife and mother and – and – in none of these things have I ever been an individual of any account. If I had suddenly disappeared from existence, or if I had never been born, it wouldn't have affected anyone or anything – except, perhaps, one or two close personal friends. Now, it's different.'

'Yes?' There was the faintest touch of mockery in D. G.'s voice.

Gladia said, 'Yes! I can influence people. I can choose a cause and make it my own. I *have* chosen a cause. I want to prevent war. I want the Universe populated by Spacer and Settler alike. I want each group to keep their own peculiarities, yet freely accept the others', too. I want to work so hard at this that after I am gone, history will have changed because of me, and people will say, "Things would not be as satisfactory as they are, had it not been for her".'

She turned to D. G., face glowing. 'Do you know what a

difference it makes, after two and a third centuries of being nobody, to have a chance of being *somebody*; to find that a life you thought of as empty turns out to contain something after all, something wonderful; to be happy long, long after you had given up any hope of being happy?'

'You don't have to be on Baleyworld, my lady, to have all that.' Somehow, D. G. seemed a little abashed.

'I won't have it on Aurora. I am only a Solarian immigrant on Aurora. On a Settler world, I'm a Spacer – something unusual.'

'Yet on a number of occasions, and quite forcefully, you have stated you wanted to return to Aurora.'

'Some time ago, yes – but I'm not saying it now, D. G. I don't really want it, now.'

'Which would influence us a great deal, except that Aurora wants *you*. They've told us so.'

Gladia was clearly astonished. 'They *want* me?'

'An official message from Aurora's Chairman of the Board tells us they do,' said D. G. lightly. 'We would enjoy keeping you, but the Directors have decided that keeping you is not worth an interstellar crisis. I'm not sure I agree with them, but they outrank me.'

Gladia frowned. 'Why should they want me? I've been on Aurora for over twenty decades and at no time have they ever seemed to want me. Wait! Do you suppose they see me now as the only way of stopping the overseers on Solaria?'

'That thought had occurred to me, my lady.'

'I won't do it. I held off that one overseer by a hair, and I may never be able to repeat what I did then. I know I won't. Besides, why need they land on the planet? They can destroy the overseers from a distance, now that they know what they are.'

'Actually,' said D. G., 'the message demanding your

return was sent out long before they could possibly have known of your conflict with the overseer. They must want you for something else.'

'Oh.' She looked taken aback. Then catching fire, again, 'I don't care what else. I don't want to return. I have my work out here, and I mean to continue it.'

D. G. rose. 'I am glad to hear you say so, Madam Gladia. I was hoping you would feel like that. I promise you I will do my best to take you with me when we leave Aurora. Right now, though, I *must* go to Aurora, and you *must* go with me.'

40.

Gladia watched Baleyworld, as it receded, with emotions quite different from those with which she had watched it approach. It was precisely the cold, grey, miserable world now that it had seemed at the start, but there was a warmth and life to the people. They were real, solid.

Solaria, Aurora, the other Spacer worlds, those she had visited and those she had viewed on hypervision, all seemed filled with people who were insubstantial – gaseous.

No matter how few the human beings who lived upon a Spacer world, they spread out to fill the planet as molecules of gas spread out to fill a container. It was as if Spacers repelled each other.

And they did, she thought gloomily. Spacers had always repelled her. She had been brought up to such repulsion on Solaria, but even on Aurora, when she was experimenting madly with sex just at first, the least enjoyable aspect of it was the closeness it made necessary.

Except – except with Elijah. But he was not a Spacer.

Baleyworld was not like that. Probably all the Settler

worlds were not. Settlers clung together, leaving large tracts desolate about them as the price of the clinging; empty, that is, until population increase filled it. A Settler world was a world of people-clusters, of pebbles and boulders, not gas.

Why was this? Robots, perhaps! They lessened the dependence of people upon people. They filled the interstices between. They were the insulation that diminished the natural attraction people had for each other, so that the whole system fell apart into isolates.

It had to be. Nowhere were there more robots than on Solaria, and the insulating effect there had been so enormous that the separate gas molecules that were human beings became totally inert so that they almost never interrelated at all. (Where had the Solarians gone, she wondered again, and how were they living?)

And long life had something to do with it, too. How could one make an emotional attachment that wouldn't turn slowly sour as the multi-decades passed; or if one died, how could another bear the loss for multi-decades? One learned, then, not to make emotional attachments, but to stand off, to insulate oneself.

On the other hand, human beings, if short-lived, could not so easily outlive fascination with life. As the generations passed by rapidly, the ball of fascination bounced from hand to hand without ever touching the ground.

How recently she had told D. G. that there was no more to do or know, that she had experienced and thought everything, that she had to live on in utter boredom. And she hadn't known or even dreamed, as she spoke, of crowds of people, one upon another; of speaking to many as they melted into a continuous sea of heads; of hearing their response, not in words, but in wordless sounds; of melting together with them, feeling their feelings, becoming one large organism.

It was not merely that she had never experienced such a thing before; it was that she had never dreamed anything like that *might* be experienced. How much more did she know nothing of despite her long life? What more existed for the experiencing that she was incapable of fantasying?

Daneel said, gently, 'Madam Gladia, I believe the Captain is signalling for entrance.'

Gladia started. 'Let him enter, then.'

D. G. entered, eyebrows raised. 'I am relieved. I thought, perhaps, you were not at home.'

Gladia smiled. 'In a way I wasn't. I was lost in thought. It happens to me, sometimes.'

'You are fortunate,' said D. G. 'My thoughts are never large enough to be lost in. Are you reconciled to visiting Aurora, madam?'

'No, I'm not. And among the thoughts in which I was lost was one to the effect that I still do not have any idea why you must go to Aurora. It can't be only to return me. Any spaceworthy cargo tug could have done the job.'

'May I sit down, madam?'

'Yes, of course. That goes without saying, Captain. I wish you'd stop treating me as aristocracy. It becomes wearing. And if it's an ironic indication that I'm a Spacer, then it's worse than wearing. In fact, I'd almost rather you called me "Gladia".'

'You seem to be anxious to disown your Spacer identity,' said D. G., as he seated himself and threw one leg over the other.

'I would rather forget non-essential distinctions.'

'Non-essential? Not while you live four times as long as I do.'

'Oddly enough, I have been thinking of that as a rather annoying disadvantage for Spacers. How long before we reach Aurora?'

'No evasive action this time. A few days to get far

enough from our sun to be able to make a Jump through hyperspace that will take us to within a few days of Aurora, and that's it.'

'And why must *you* go to Aurora, D. G.?'

'I might say it was simply politeness, but in actual fact, I would like an opportunity to explain to your Chairman or even to one of his subordinates, exactly what happened on Solaria.'

'Don't they know what happened?'

'In essentials, they do. They were kind enough to tap our communications, as we should have done theirs were the situation reversed. Still, they may not have drawn the proper conclusions, and I would like to correct them, if that is so.'

'What are the proper conclusions, D. G.?'

'As you know, the overseers on Solaria were geared to respond to a person as human only if he or she spoke with a Solarian accent, as you did. That means that not only were Settlers not considered human, but non-Solarian Spacers were not considered human, either. To be precise, Aurorans would not be considered human beings if they had landed on Solaria.'

Gladia's eyes widened. 'That's unbelievable. The Solarians wouldn't arrange to have the overseers treat Aurorans as they treated you.'

'Wouldn't they? They have already destroyed an Auroran ship. Did you know that?'

'An Auroran ship! No, I didn't know that.'

'I assure you they did. It landed about the time we did. We got away, but they didn't. We had you, you see, and they didn't. The conclusion is, or should be, that Aurora cannot automatically treat other Spacer worlds as allies. In an emergency, it will be each Spacer world for itself.'

Gladia shook her head violently. 'It would be unsafe to generalize from a single instance. The Solarians would have found it difficult to have the overseers react favourably to fifty accents and unfavourably to scores of others. It was easier to pin them to a single accent. That's all. They gambled that no other Spacers would try to land on their world and they lost.'

'Yes, I'm sure that is how the Auroran leadership will argue, since people generally find it much easier to make a pleasant deduction than an unpleasant one. What I want to do is to make certain they see the possibility of the unpleasant one, and that this makes them uncomfortable indeed. Forgive my self-love, but I can't trust anyone to do it as well as I can, and therefore I think I, rather than anyone else, should go to Aurora.'

Gladia felt uncomfortably torn. She did not want to be a Spacer; she wanted to be a human being and forget what she had just called 'non-essential distinctions'. And yet when D. G. spoke, with obvious satisfaction, of forcing Aurora into a humiliating position, she found herself still, somehow, a Spacer.

She said, in annoyance, 'I presume the Settler worlds are at odds among themselves, too. Is it not each Settler world for itself?'

D. G. shook his head. 'It may seem to you that this must be so, and I wouldn't be surprised if each individual Settler world had the impulse at times to put its own interest over the good of the whole, but we have something you Spacers lack.'

'And what is that? A greater nobility?'

'Of course not. We're no more noble than Spacers are. What we've got is the Earth. It's our world. Every Settler visits Earth as often as he can. Every Settler knows that there is a world, a large, advanced world, with an incredibly rich history and cultural variety and ecological complexity that is his, or hers, and to which he, or she, belongs. The Settler worlds might quarrel with each other, but the quarrel cannot possibly result in violence or in a permanent breach of relations, for the Earth government is automatically called in to mediate all problems, and its decision is sufficient and unquestioned.

'Those are our three advantages, Madam Gladia: the lack of robots, something that allows us to build new worlds with our own hands; the rapid succession of generations that makes for constant change; and, most of all, the Earth, which gives us our central core.'

Gladia said, urgently, 'But the Spacers – ' and she stopped.

D. G. smiled with an edge of bitterness, 'Were you going to say that the Spacers are also descended from Earthpeople and that it is their planet, too? Factually true, but psychologically false. The Spacers have done their best to deny their heritage. They don't consider themselves Earthmen once-removed, or any-number-removed. If I were a mystic, I would say that by cutting themselves away from their roots, the Spacers cannot long survive. Of course, I'm not a mystic so I don't put it that way – but they cannot long survive, just the same. I believe that.'

Then, after a short pause, he added, with a somewhat troubled kindness, as though he realized that in his exultation he was striking a sensitive spot within her, 'But please think of yourself as a human being, Madam Gladia, rather than as a Spacer, and I will think of myself as a human being, rather than as a Settler. Humanity *will* survive, whether it will be in the form of Settlers, or Spacers, or both. I believe it will be in the form of Settlers only, but I may be wrong.'

'No,' said Gladia, trying to be unemotional. 'I think you're right – unless, somehow, people learn to stop making the Spacer/Settler distinction. It is my goal – to help people do that.'

'However,' said D. G., glancing at the time-strip that

circled the wall dimly, 'I delay your dinner. May I eat with you?'

'Certainly,' said Gladia.

D. G. rose to his feet, 'Then I'll go and get it. I'd send Daneel or Giskard, but I don't want to get into the habit of ordering robots about. Besides, however much the crew adores you, I don't think their adoration extends to your robots.'

Gladia did not actually enjoy the meal when D. G. brought it. She did not seem to grow accustomed to the lack of subtlety in its flavours that might be the heritage of Earth-cooking for mass-consumption, but then, neither was it particularly repulsive. She ate stolidly.

D. G., noting her lack of enthusiasm, said, 'The food doesn't upset you, I hope?'

She shook her head. 'No. Apparently, I'm acclimatized. I had some unpleasant episodes when I first got on the ship, but nothing really severe.'

'I'm glad of that, but, Madam Gladia – '

'Yes?'

'Can you suggest no reason why the Auroran government should want you back so urgently? It can't be your handling of the overseer and it can't be your speech. The request was sent out well before they could have known of either.'

'In that case, D. G.,' Gladia said, sadly, 'they can't possibly want me for anything. They never have.'

'But there must be something. As I told you, the message arrived in the name of the Chairman of the Council of Aurora.'

'This particular Chairman at this particular time is thought to be rather a figurehead.'

'Oh? Who stands behind him? Kelden Amadiro?'

'Exactly. You know of him, then?'

'Oh, yes,' said D. G., grimly, 'the centre of anti-Earth fanaticism. The man who was politically smashed by Dr

Fastolfe twenty decades ago, survives to threaten us again. There's an example of the dead hand of longevity.'

'But there's the puzzle, too. Amadiro is a vengeful man. He knows that it was Elijah Baley who was the cause of that defeat you speak of, and Amadiro believes I carried part of the responsibility, too. His dislike – extreme dislike – extends to me. If the Chairman wants me, that can only be because Amadiro wants me, and why should Amadiro want me? He would rather get rid of me. It was probably in order to get rid of me that he sent me along with you to Solaria. Surely, he expected your ship would be destroyed, and me along with it. And that would not have pained him at all.'

'No uncontrollable tears, eh?' said D. G., thoughtfully. 'But surely that's not what you were told. No one said to you: Go with this mad Trader, because it would give us pleasure to have you killed.'

'No. They said that you wanted my help badly and that it was politic to cooperate with the Settler worlds at the moment, and that it would do Aurora a great deal of good if I would report back to them on all that occurred on Solaria once I returned.'

'Yes, they would say so. They might even have meant it to some extent. Then, when, against all their expectations, our ship got off safely while an Auroran ship was destroyed, they might well have wanted a first-hand account of what happened. Therefore, when I took you to Baleyworld instead of back to Aurora, they would scream for your return. That might possibly be it. By now, of course, they know the story, so they might no longer want you. Though' (he was talking to himself rather than to Gladia) 'what they know is what they picked up from Baleyworld hypervision, and they may not choose to accept that at face value. And yet –'

'And yet what, D. G.?'

'Somehow, instinct tells me that their message could not have been sparked only by their desire to have you report. The forcefulness of the demand, it seems to me, went beyond that.'

'There's nothing else they can want. *Nothing*,' said Gladia.

'I wonder,' said D. G.

41.

'I wonder as well,' said Daneel, from his niche, that night.

'You wonder concerning what, Friend Daneel?' asked Giskard.

'I wonder concerning the true significance of the message from Aurora demanding the Lady Gladia. To me, as to the Captain, a desire for a report seems a not-altogether sufficient motivation.'

'Have you an alternative suggestion?'

'I have a thought, Friend Giskard.'

'May I know it, Friend Daneel?'

'It has occurred to me that in demanding the return of Madam Gladia, the Auroran Council may expect to see more than they ask for, and it may not be Madam Gladia they want.'

'What is there more than Madam Gladia that they will get?'

'Friend Giskard, is it conceivable that the lady will return without you and me?'

'No, but of what use to the Auroran Council would you and I be?'

'I, Friend Giskard, would be of no use to them. You, however, are unique, for you can sense minds directly.'

'That is true, Friend Daneel, but they do not know this.'

'Since our leaving, is it not possible that they have somehow discovered the fact and have come to regret bitterly having allowed you to leave Aurora?'

Giskard did not hesitate perceptibly. 'No, it is not possible, Friend Daneel. How would they have found out?'

Daneel said, carefully, 'I have reasoned in this fashion. You, on your long-ago visit to Earth with Dr Fastolfe, managed to adjust a few Earth robots so as to allow them a very limited mental capacity; merely enough to enable them to continue your work of influencing officials on Earth to look with courage and favour on the process of Settlement. So, at least, you once told me. There are, therefore, robots on Earth that are capable of mind-adjusting.

'Then, too, as we have come recently to suspect, the Robotics Institute of Aurora has sent humanoid robots to Earth. We do not know their precise purpose in doing so, but the least that can be expected of such robots is that they observe events there on Earth and report on them.

'Even if the Auroran robots cannot sense minds, they can send back reports to the effect that this or that official has suddenly changed his attitude towards Settlement and, perhaps, in the time since we have left Aurora, it has dawned on someone in power on Aurora – on Dr Amadiro, himself, perhaps – that this can only be explained by the existence of mind-adjusting robots on Earth. It may be, then, that the establishment of mind-adjusting can be traced back to either Dr Fastolfe or yourself.

'This might, in turn, make clear to Auroran officials the meaning of certain other events, which might be traced back to you rather than to Dr Fastolfe. As a result, they would want you back desperately, yet not be able to ask for you directly, for that would give away the fact of their new knowledge. So they ask for Lady Gladia – a natural request – knowing that if she is brought back, you will be, too.'

Giskard was silent for a full minute, then he said, 'It is interestingly reasoned, Friend Daneel, but it does not hold together. Those robots whom I programmed for the task of encouraging Settlement completed their job more than eighteen decades ago, and have been inactive since, at least as far as mind-adjustment is concerned. What's more, the Earth removed robots from their Cities and confined them to the unpopulated non-City areas quite a considerable time ago.

'This means that the humanoid robots who were, we speculate, sent to Earth, would, even so, not have had occasion to meet my mind-adjusting robots, or be aware of any mind-adjustment either, considering that the robots are no longer engaged in that. It is impossible, therefore, for my special ability to have been uncovered in the manner you suggest.'

Daneel said, 'Is there no other way of discovery, Friend Giskard?'

'None,' said Giskard, firmly.

'And yet – I wonder,' said Daneel.

PART IV
AURORA

11

The Old Leader

42.

Kelden Amadiro was not immune from the human plague of memory. He was, in fact, more subject to it than most. In his case, moreover, the tenacity of memory had, as its accompaniment, a content unusual for the intensity of its deep and prolonged rage and frustration.

All had been going so well for him twenty decades before. He was the founding Head of the Robotics Institute (he was *still* the founding Head) and for one flashing and triumphant moment, it had seemed to him that he could not fail to achieve total control of the Council, smashing his great enemy, Han Fastolfe, and leaving him in helpless opposition.

If he had – if he only had –

(How he tried not to think of it, and how his memory presented him with it, over and over again, as though it could never get enough of grief and despair.)

If he had won out, Earth would have remained isolated and alone and he would have seen to it that it declined, decayed and, finally, faded into dissolution. Why not? The short-lived people of a diseased, overcrowded world were better off dead; a hundred times better off dead than living the life they had forced themselves to lead.

And the Spacer worlds, calm and secure, would then have expanded further. Fastolfe had always complained that the Spacers were too long-lived and too comfortable on their robotic cushions to be pioneers, but Amadiro would have proved him wrong.

Yet Fastolfe had won out. At the moment of certain defeat, he had somehow, unbelievably, incredibly, reached into empty space, so to speak, and found victory in his grasp – plucked from nowhere.

It was that Earthman, of course, Elijah Baley –

But Amadiro's otherwise uncomfortable memory always balked at the Earthman and turned away. He could not picture that face, hear that voice, remember that deed. The name was enough. Twenty decades had not sufficed to dim the hatred he felt in the slightest, or to soften the pain he felt by an iota.

And with Fastolfe in charge of policy, the miserable Earthmen had fled their corrupting planet and established themselves on world after world. The whirlwind of Earth's progress dazed the Spacer worlds and forced them into frozen paralysis.

How many times had Amadiro addressed the Council and pointed out that the Galaxy was slipping from Spacer fingers; that Aurora was watching blankly while world after world was being occupied by submen; that each year apathy was taking firmer hold of the Spacer spirit?

'Rouse yourself,' he had called out, 'rouse yourself. See their numbers grow. See the Settler worlds multiply. What is it you wait for? To have them at your throats?'

And always Fastolfe would answer in that soothing lullaby of a voice of his and the Aurorans, and the other Spacers (always following Aurora's lead, when Aurora chose not to lead), would settle back and return to their slumber.

The obvious did not seem to touch them. The facts, the figures, the indisputable worsening of affairs from decade to decade left them unmoved. How was it possible to shout the truth at them so steadily, to have every prediction he made come to pass, and yet to have to watch a steady majority following Fastolfe like sheep?

How was it possible that Fastolfe himself could watch

everything he said prove to be sheer folly and yet never swerve from his policies? It was not even that he stubbornly insisted on being wrong; it was that he simply never seemed to notice he was wrong.

If Amadiro were the kind of man who doted on fantasy, he would surely imagine that some kind of spell, some kind of apathetic enchantment, had fallen upon the Spacer worlds. He would imagine that somewhere someone possessed the magic power of lulling otherwise active brains, and blinding to the truth otherwise sharp eyes.

To add the final exquisite agony, people pitied Fastolfe for having died in frustration. In frustration, they said, because the Spacers would not seize new worlds of their own.

It was Fastolfe's own policies that kept them from doing so! What right had he to feel frustration over that? What would he do if he had, like Amadiro, always seen and spoken the truth and been unable to force the Spacers – enough Spacers – to listen to him?

How many times had he thought that it would be better for the Galaxy to be empty than under the domination of the submen. If he had some magic power to destroy the Earth – Elijah Baley's world – with a nod of his head, how eagerly he would.

Yet to find refuge in such fantasy could only be a sign of his total despair. It was the other side of his recurrent, futile wish to give up and welcome death – if his robots would allow it.

And then the time came when the power to destroy Earth was given him – even forced upon him against his will. That time was some three-fourths of a decade before, when he had first met Levular Mandamus.

43.

Memory! Three-fourths of a decade before –

Amadiro looked up and noted that Maloon Cicis had entered the office. He had undoubtedly signalled and he had the right to enter if the signal were not acknowledged.

Amadiro sighed and put down his small computer. Cicis had been his right-hand man ever since the Institute had been established. He was getting old in his service. Nothing drastically noticeable; just a general air of mild decay. His nose seemed to be a bit more asymmetric than it once had been.

He rubbed his own somewhat bulbous nose and wondered how badly the flavour of mild decay was enveloping him. He had once been 1.95 metres tall; a good height even by Spacer standards. Surely, he stood as straight now as he had always done and yet when he had actually measured his height recently, he could not manage to make it more than 1.93 metres. Was he beginning to stoop, to shrivel, to settle?

He put away these dour thoughts that were themselves a surer sign of ageing than mere measurements and said, 'What is it, Maloon?'

Cicis had a new personal robot dogging his steps, very modernistic, and with glossy trim. That was a sign of ageing, too. If one can't keep one's body young, one can always buy a new, young robot. Amadiro was determined never to rouse smiles among the truly young by falling prey to that particular delusion – especially since Fastolfe, who was eight decades older than Amadiro, had never done so.

Cicis said, 'It's this Mandamus fellow again, Chief.'

'Mandamus?'

'The one who keeps wanting to see you.'

Amadiro thought a while. 'You mean the idiot who's a descendant of the Solarian woman?'

'Yes, Chief.'

'Well, I don't want to see him. Haven't you made that clear to him yet, Maloon?'

'Abundantly clear. He asks that I hand you a note and he says you will then see him.'

Amadiro said, slowly, 'I don't think so, Maloon. What does the note say?'

'I don't understand it, Chief. It isn't Galactic.'

'In that case, why should I understand it any more than you do?'

'I don't know, but he asked me to give it to you. If you care to look at it, Chief, and say the word, I will go back and get rid of him one more time.'

'Well, then, let me see it,' said Amadiro, shaking his head. He glanced at it with distaste.

It read: *Ceterum censeo, delenda est Carthago.*

Amadiro read the message, glared up at Maloon, then turned his eyes back to the message. Finally, he said, 'You must have looked at this since you know it isn't Galactic. Did you ask him what it meant?'

'Yes, I did, Chief. He said it was Latin, but that left me no wiser. He said you would understand. He is a very determined man, and said he would sit there all day waiting till you read this.'

'What does he look like?'

'Thin. Serious. Probably humourless. Tall, but not quite as tall as you. Intense, deep-set eyes, thin lips.'

'How old is he?'

'From the texture of his skin, I should say four decades or so. He is very young.'

'In that case, we must make allowances for youth. Send him in.'

Cicis looked surprised. 'You will see him?'

'I have just said so, haven't I? Send him in.'

44.

The young man entered the room in what was almost a march-step. He stood there, stiffly, in front of the desk, and said, 'I thank you, sir, for agreeing to see me. May I have your permission to have my robots join me?'

Amadiro raised his eyebrows. 'I would be pleased to see them. Would you permit me to keep mine with me?'

It had been many years since he had heard anyone mouth the old robot-formula. It was one of those good old customs that sank into abeyance as the notion of formal politeness decayed, and as it came to be taken more and more for granted that one's personal robots were part of oneself.

'Yes, sir,' said Mandamus, and two robots entered. They did not do so, Amadiro noted, till permission had been given. They were new robots, clearly efficient, and showed all the signs of good workmanship.

'Your own design, Dr Mandamus?' There was always some extra value in robots that were designed by their owners.

'Indeed, sir.'

'Then you are a roboticist?'

'Yes, sir, I have my degree from the University of Eos.'

'Working under –'

Mandamus said smoothly, 'Not under Dr Fastolfe, sir. Under Dr Maskellnik.'

'Ah, but you are not a member of the Institute.'

'I have applied for entrance, sir.'

'I see.' Amadiro adjusted the papers on his desk, and

then said quickly, without looking up, 'Where did you learn Latin?'

'I do not know Latin well enough to speak it or read it, but I know enough about it to know that quotation and where to find it.'

'That in itself is remarkable. How does that come about?'

'I cannot devote myself to robotics at every moment of my time, so I have my side-interests. One of them is planetology, with particular reference to Earth. That led me to Earth's history and culture.'

'That is not a popular study among Spacers.'

'No, sir, and that is too bad. One should always know one's enemies – as you do, sir.'

'As I do?'

'Yes, sir. I believe you are acquainted with many aspects of Earth, and are more learned in that respect than I am for you have studied the subject longer.'

'How do you know that?'

'I have tried to learn as much about you as I can, sir.'

'Because I am another one of your enemies?'

'No, sir, but because I want to make you an ally.'

'Make me an ally? You plan to make use of me, then? Does it strike you that you are being a little impertinent?'

'No, sir, for I am sure you will want to be an ally of mine.'

Amadiro stared at him. 'Nevertheless, it strikes *me* that you are being rather more than a little impertinent. Tell me, do you understand this quotation you have found for me?'

'Yes, sir.'

'Then translate it into Standard Galactic.'

'It says, "In my opinion, Carthage must be destroyed".'

'And what does that mean, in *your* opinion?'

'The speaker was Marcus Porcius Cato, a Senator of the Roman Republic, a political unit of ancient Earth. It had defeated its chief rival, Carthage, but had not destroyed it. Cato held that Rome could not be secure until Carthage was entirely destroyed – and eventually, sir, it was.'

'But what is Carthage to us, young man?'

'There are such things as analogies.'

'Which means?'

'That the Spacer worlds, too, have a chief rival, that, in my opinion, must be destroyed.'

'Name the enemy.'

'The planet Earth, sir.'

Amadiro drummed his fingers very softly upon the desk before him. 'And you want me to be your ally in such a project. You assume I will be happy and eager to be one. Tell me, Dr Mandamus, when have I ever said in any of my numerous speeches and writings on the subject, that Earth must be destroyed?'

Mandamus's thin lips tightened, and his nostrils flared. 'I am not here,' he said, 'in an attempt to trap you into something that can be used against you. I have not been sent here by Dr Fastolfe or any of his party. Nor am *I* of his party. Nor do I attempt to say what is in your mind. I tell you only what is in *my* mind. In my opinion, Earth must be destroyed.'

'And how do you propose to destroy Earth? Do you suggest that we drop nuclear bombs on it until the blast and radiation and dust-clouds destroy the planet? Because if so, how do you propose to keep avenging Settler ships from doing the same to Aurora and to as many of the other Spacer worlds as they can reach? Earth might have been blasted, with impunity, as recently as fifteen decades ago. It can't be now.'

Mandamus looked revolted. 'I have nothing like that in mind, Dr Amadiro. I would not unnecessarily destroy human beings, even if they are Earthpeople. There is a way, however, in which Earth can be destroyed without necessarily killing its people wholesale – and there will be no retaliation.'

'You are a dreamer,' said Amadiro, 'or perhaps not quite sane.'

'Let me explain.'

'No, young man. I have little time, and, because your quotation, which I understood perfectly well, piqued my curiosity, I have already allowed myself to spend too much of it on you.'

Mandamus stood up. 'I understand, Dr Amadiro, and I beg your pardon for taking up more of your time than you could afford. Think of what I have said, however, and if you should become curious, why not call upon me when you have more time to devote to me than you now have? Do not wait too long, however, for if I must, I will turn in other directions, for destroy Earth I will. I am frank with you, you see.'

The young man attempted a smile that stretched his thin cheeks without producing much of an effect on his face, otherwise. He said, 'Good-bye – and thank you again,' turned, and left.

Amadiro looked after him for a while, thoughtfully, then touched a contact on the side of his desk.

'Maloon,' he said, when Cicis entered, 'I want that young man watched on a twenty-four hour basis and I want to know everyone he speaks to. Everyone. I want them all identified and I want them all questioned. Those whom I indicate are to be brought to me. But Maloon, everything must be done quietly, and with an attitude of sweet and friendly persuasion. I am not yet master here, as you know.'

But he would be, eventually. Fastolfe was thirty-six decades old and clearly failing, and Amadiro was eight decades younger.

45.

Amadiro received his reports for nine days.

Mandamus talked to his robots, occasionally to colleagues at the University, and even more occasionally to individuals at the establishments neighbouring his. His conversations were utterly trivial and, long before the nine days had passed, Amadiro had decided he could not outwait the young man. Mandamus was only at the beginning of a long life and might have thirty decades ahead of him; Amadiro had only eight to ten at the very most.

And Amadiro, thinking of what the young man had said, felt, with increasing restlessness, that he could not take the chance that a way of destroying Earth might exist and that he might be ignoring it. Could he allow the destruction to take place after his death, so that he would not witness it? Or, almost as bad, have it take place during his lifetime, but with someone else's mind in command, someone else's fingers on the contact?

No, he had to see it, witness it, and *do* it; else why had he endured his long frustration? Mandamus might be a fool or a madman, but, in that case, Amadiro had to know for certain that he was a fool or a madman.

Having reached that point in his thinking, Amadiro called Mandamus to his office.

Amadiro realized that in so doing, he was humiliating himself, but the humiliation was the price he had to pay to make certain that there wasn't the slightest chance of Earth being destroyed without him. It was a price he was willing to pay.

He steeled himself even for the possibility that Mandamus would enter his presence, smirking and contemptuously triumphant. He would have to endure that, too.

After the endurance, of course, if the young man's suggestion proved foolish, he would see him punished to the full extent that a civilized society would permit, but otherwise –

He was pleased, then, when Mandamus entered his office with an attitude of reasonable humility, and thanked him, in all apparent sincerity, for a second interview. It seemed to Amadiro he would have to be gracious in his turn.

'Dr Mandamus,' he said. 'In sending you away without listening to your plan, I was guilty of discourtesy. Tell me, then, what you have in mind, and I will listen until it is quite clear to me – as I suspect it will be – that your plan is, perhaps, more the result of enthusiasm than of cold reason. At that time, I will dismiss you again, but without contempt on my part, and I hope that you will respond without anger on your part.'

Mandamus said, 'I could not be angry at having been accorded a fair and patient hearing, Dr Amadiro, but what if what I say makes sense to you and offers hope?'

'In that case,' said Amadiro, slowly, 'it would be conceivable that we two could work together.'

'That would be wonderful, sir. Together we could accomplish more than we could separately. But would there be something more tangible than the privilege of working together? Would there be a reward?'

Amadiro looked displeased. 'I would be grateful, of course, but all I am is a Councilman, and the Head of the Robotics Institute. There would be a limit to what I could do for you.'

'I understand that, Dr Amadiro. But within those limits could I not have something on account? Now?' He looked at Amadiro steadily.

Amadiro frowned at finding himself gazing into a pair

of keen and unblinkingly determined eyes. No humility there!

Amadiro said, coldly, 'What do you have in mind?'

'Nothing you can't give me, Dr Amadiro. Make me a member of the Institute.'

'If you qualify –'

'No fear. I qualify.'

'We can't leave that decision to the candidate. We have to –'

'Come, Dr Amadiro, this is no way to begin a relationship. Since you've had me under observation every moment since I left you last, I can't believe you haven't studied my record thoroughly. As a result, you must *know* I qualify. If, for any reason, you felt I did *not* qualify you would have no hope whatever that I would be ingenious enough to work out a plan for the destruction of our particular Carthage, and I wouldn't be back here at your call.'

For an instant, Amadiro felt a fire blaze within him. For that instant, he felt that even Earth's destruction was not worth enduring this hectoring attitude from a child. But only for that instant. Then his sense of due proportion was back, and he could even tell himself that a person so young, yet so bold and so icily sure of himself, was the kind of man he needed. Besides, he *had* studied Mandamus's record and there was no question that he qualified for the Institute.

Amadiro said, evenly (at some cost to his blood pressure), 'You are right. You qualify.'

'Then enrol me. I'm sure you have the necessary forms in your computer. You have but to enter my name, my school, my year of graduation, and whatever other statistical trivia you require, and then sign your own name.'

Without a word in reply, Amadiro turned to his computer. He entered the necessary information, retrieved the form, signed it, and handed it to Mandamus. 'It is dated today. You are a fellow of the Institute.'

Mandamus studied the paper, then handed it to one of his robots, who placed it in a small portfolio which he then placed under his arm.

'Thank you,' said Mandamus, 'it is most kind of you, and I hope I will never fail you or cause you to regret this kind estimate you have given me of my abilities. That, however, leaves one more thing.'

'Indeed? What?'

'Might we discuss the nature of the final reward – in case of success only, of course. Total success.'

'Might we not leave that, more logically, to the point where total success is achieved, or is reasonably close to being achieved?'

'As a matter of rationality, yes. But I am a creature of dreams as well as of reason. I would like to dream a little.'

'Well,' said Amadiro, 'what is it you would like to dream?'

'It seems to me, Dr Amadiro, that Dr Fastolfe is now by no means well. He has lived long and cannot stave off death many more years.'

'And if so?'

'Once he dies, your party will become more aggressive, and the more lukewarm members of Fastolfe's party will find it expedient to change allegiance, perhaps. The next election, without Fastolfe, will surely be yours.'

'It is possible. And if so?'

'You will become the *de facto* leader of the Council and the guide of Aurora's foreign policy which would, in fact, mean the foreign policy of the Spacer worlds in general. And if my plans flourish, your direction will be so successful that the Council will scarcely fail to elect you Chairman at the earliest opportunity.'

'Your dreams soar, young man. And if all you foresee were to come true, what then?'

'You would scarcely have time to run Aurora and the Robotics Institute, too. So I ask that when you finally decide to resign from your present position as Head of the Institute, you be prepared to support me as your successor to the post. You could scarcely expect to have your personal choice accepted.'

Amadiro said, 'There is such a thing as qualification for the post.'

'I will qualify.'

'Let us wait and see.'

'I am willing to wait and see, but you will find that, well before complete success is ours, you will wish to grant this request of mine. Please grow accustomed to the idea, therefore.'

'All this before I hear a word,' murmured Amadiro. 'Well, you are a member of the Institute and I will strive to grow accustomed to your personal dream, but now let us have an end to preliminaries and tell me how you intend to destroy Earth.'

Almost automatically, Amadiro made the sign that indicated to his robots that they were not to remember any part of the conversation. And Mandamus, with a small smile, did the same for his.

'Let us start, then,' said Mandamus.

But before he could speak further, Amadiro moved to the attack.

'Are you sure you're not pro-Earth?'

Mandamus looked startled. 'I am coming to you with a proposal to *destroy* Earth.'

'And yet you are a descendant of the Solarian woman – in the fifth generation, I understand.'

'Yes, sir, it is on public record. What of that?'

'The Solarian woman is, and has been for a long time, a

close associate – friend – protégée – of Fastolfe. I wonder you do not sympathize with his pro-Earth views therefore.'

'Because of my ancestry?' Mandamus seemed honestly astonished. For a moment, what might have been a flash of annoyance, or even anger, seemed to tighten his nostrils, but that vanished, and he said quietly, 'An equally long-time close associate – friend – protégée – of your own is Dr Vasilia Fastolfe, who is Dr Fastolfe's daughter. She is a descendant in the first generation. I wonder she does not sympathize with his views.'

'I have in the past also wondered,' said Amadiro, 'but she doesn't sympathize with them and, in her case, I have ceased wondering.'

'You may cease wondering in my case, too, sir. I am a Spacer, and I want to see the Spacers in control of the Galaxy.'

'Very well, then. Go on with the description of your plan.'

Mandamus said, 'I will but, if you don't mind, from the beginning.

'Dr Amadiro, astronomers agree that there are millions of Earth-like planets in our Galaxy; planets on which human beings can live after necessary adjustments to the environment, but without any need for geological terraforming. Their atmospheres are breathable, an ocean of water is present, the land and climate is suitable, life exists. Indeed, the atmospheres would not contain free oxygen without the presence of ocean plankton at the very least.

'The land is often barren, but once it and the ocean undergo biological terraforming, that is, once they are seeded with Earth-life, such life flourishes and the planet can then be settled. Hundreds of such planets have been recorded and studied, and about half of them are already occupied by Settlers.

'And yet not one habitable planet of all those which we have discovered has the enormous variety and excess of life that Earth has. Not one has anything larger or more complex than a small array of worm-like or insect-life invertebrates or, in the plant world, anything more advanced than some fern-like shrubbery. No question of intelligence; of anything approaching intelligence.'

Amadiro listened to the stiff sentences and thought: He's speaking by rote. He's memorized all this. He stirred and said, 'I am not a planetologist, Dr Mandamus, but I ask you to believe that you are telling me nothing I don't already know.'

'As I said, Dr Amadiro, I am starting from the beginning. Astronomers are increasingly of the belief that we have a fair sample of the habitable planets of the Galaxy and that all, or almost all, are markedly different from Earth. For some reason, Earth is a surprisingly unusual planet, and evolution has proceeded on it at a radically rapid pace and in a radically abnormal manner.'

Amadiro said, 'The usual argument is that if there were another intelligent species in the Galaxy that was as advanced as we are, it would have become aware of our expansion by now and have made itself known to us, one way or another.'

Mandamus said, 'Yes, sir. In fact, if there were another intelligent species in the Galaxy that was more advanced than we are, we would not have had a chance to expand in the first place. That we are the only species in the Galaxy capable of travelling in hyperspace would seem certain, then. That we are the only species in the Galaxy that is intelligent is perhaps not quite certain, but there is a very good chance that we are.'

Amadiro was now listening with a weary half-smile. The young man was being didactic, like a man stamping out the rhythm of his monomania in a dull beat. It was one of the marks of the crank, and the mild hope Amadiro had had that Mandamus might actually have something that would turn the tide of history was beginning to fade.

He said, 'You continue to tell me the known, Dr Mandamus. Everyone knows Earth seems unique and that we are probably the only intelligent species in the Galaxy.'

'But no one seems to ask the simple question: *Why*? The Earthpeople and the Settlers don't ask it. They accept it. They have a mystic attitude towards Earth and consider it a holy world, so that its unusual nature is taken as a matter of course. As for the Spacers, we don't ask it. We ignore it. We do our best not to think of Earth at all, since if we do, we are liable to go further and think of ourselves as having descended from Earthpeople.'

Amadiro said, 'I see no virtue in the question. We need not seek for complex answers to the "Why". Random processes play an important role in evolution and, to some extent, in all things. If there are millions of habitable worlds, evolution may proceed on each of them at a different rate. On most, the rate will have some intermediate value; on some the rate will be distinctly slow, on others distinctly fast; on perhaps one it would proceed exceedingly slow, and on another exceedingly fast. Earth happens to be the one on which it proceeded exceedingly fast and we are here because of that. Now if we ask "Why?", the natural – and sufficient – answer is "Chance".'

Amadiro waited for the other to betray the crank by exploding in rage at a pre-eminently logical statement, presented in an amused way, that served to shatter his thesis completely. Mandamus, however, merely stared at him for a few moments out of his deep-set eyes, and then said quietly, 'No.'

Mandamus let that stand for perhaps two beats and then said, 'It takes more than a lucky chance or two to speed evolution a thousand-fold. On every planet but Earth, the speed of evolution is closely related to the flux of cosmic radiation in which that planet is bathed. That speed is not the result of chance at all but the result of cosmic radiation producing mutations at a slow rate. On Earth, something produces many more mutations than are produced on other habitable planets, and that has nothing to do with cosmic rays, for they do not strike Earth in any remarkable profusion. Perhaps you see a little more clearly, now, why the "Why?" could be important.'

'Well, then, Dr Mandamus, since I am still listening, and with rather more patience than I would have expected myself to possess, answer the question you so insistently raise. Or do you merely have the question and no answer?'

'I have an answer,' said Mandamus, 'and it depends upon the fact that Earth is unique in a second way.'

Amadiro said, 'Let me anticipate. You are referring to its large satellite. Surely, Dr Mandamus, you are not advancing this as a discovery of yours?'

'Not at all,' said Mandamus stiffly, 'but consider that large satellites seem to be common. Our planetary system has five, Earth's has seven and so on. All the known large satellites but one, however, circle gas giants. Only Earth's satellite, the Moon, circles a planet not much larger than itself.'

'Dare I use the word "chance" again, Dr Mandamus?'

'In this case, it may be chance, but the Moon remains unique.'

'Even so. What possible connection can the satellite have with Earth's profusion of life?'

'That may not be obvious, and a connection may be unlikely – but it is far more unlikely that two such unusual examples of uniqueness in a single planet can have no connection at all. I have found such a connection.'

'Indeed?' said Amadiro, alertly. Now ought to come unmistakable evidence of crackpotism. He looked casually at the time-strip on the wall. There really wasn't much more time he could possibly spend on this, for all that his curiosity continued to be aroused.

'The Moon,' said Mandamus, 'is slowly receding from Earth, due to its tidal effect on the Earth. Earth's large tides are a unique consequence of the existence of this large satellite. Earth's sun produces tides, too, but to only a third of the extent of the Moon's tides – just as our sun produces small tides on Aurora.

'Since the Moon recedes because of its tidal action, it was far closer to Earth during the early history of its planetary system. The closer the Moon to the Earth, the higher the tides on Earth. These tides had two important effects on Earth. They flexed the Earth's crust continually as the Earth rotated; and they slowed the Earth's rotation, both through that flexing and through the friction of the ocean's water tides on shallow sea-bottoms – so that rotational energy was converted to heat.

'The Earth, therefore, has a thinner crust than any other habitable planet we know of, and it is the only habitable planet that displays volcanic action and that has a lively system of plate tectonics.'

Amadiro said, 'But even all this can have nothing to do with Earth's profusion of life. I think you must either get to the point, Dr Mandamus, or leave.'

'Please bear with me, Dr Amadiro, for just a little while longer. It is important to understand the point once we get to it. I have made a careful computer-simulation of the chemical development of Earth's crust, allowing for the effect of tidal action and plate tectonics, something that no one has ever done before in as meticulous and elaborate a way as I have managed to do, if I may praise myself.'

'Oh, by all means,' murmured Amadiro.

'And it turns out, quite clearly – I will show you all the necessary data at any time you wish – that uranium and thorium collect in Earth's crust and upper mantle in concentrations of up to a thousand times as high as in any other habitable world. Moreover, they collect unevenly so that scattered over the Earth are occasional pockets where uranium and thorium are even more concentrated.'

'And, I take it, dangerously high in radioactivity?'

'No, Dr Amadiro. Uranium and thorium are very weakly radioactive, and even where they are relatively concentrated, they are not very concentrated in an absolute sense. All this, I repeat, is because of the presence of a large moon.'

'I assume, then, that the radioactivity, even if not intense enough to be dangerous to life, does suffice to increase the mutation rate. Is that it, Dr Mandamus?'

'That is it. There would be more rapid extinctions now and then, but also more rapid development of new species – resulting in an enormous variety and profusion of life-forms. And, eventually, on Earth alone, this would have reached the point of developing an intelligent species and a civilization.'

Amadiro nodded. The young man was not a crank. He might be wrong, but he was not a crank. And he might be right, too.

Amadiro was not a planetologist so he would have to check books on the subject, to see whether Mandamus had perhaps discovered only the already-known, as so many enthusiasts did. There was, however, a more important point that he had to check at once.

He said, in a soft voice, 'You've spoken of the possible destruction of Earth. Is there some connection between that and Earth's unique properties?'

'One can take advantage of unique properties in a unique manner,' said Mandamus, just as softly.

'In this particular case – in what way?'

'Before discussing the method, Dr Amadiro, I must

explain that in one respect the question as to whether destruction is physically possible depends on you.'

'On me?'

'Yes,' said Mandamus, firmly. 'On you. Why, otherwise, should I come to you with this long story if not to persuade you that I know what I'm talking about, so that you would be willing to cooperate with me in a manner that will be essential to my success?'

Amadiro drew a long breath. 'And if I refused, would anyone else serve your purpose?'

'It might be possible for me to turn to others, if you refuse. *Do* you refuse?'

'Perhaps not, but I am wondering how essential I am to you.'

'The answer is, not quite as essential as I am to you. You *must* cooperate with me.'

'Must?'

'I would like you to, if you prefer it phrased in that fashion. But if you wish Aurora and the Spacers to triumph, now and forever, over Earth and the Settlers, then you *must* cooperate with me, whether you like the phrase or not.'

Amadiro said, 'Tell me what it is, exactly, that I *must* do.'

'Begin by telling me if it is not true that the Institute has, in the past, designed and constructed humanoid robots.'

'Yes, we did. Fifty of them altogether. That was between fifteen and twenty decades ago.'

'That long ago? And what happened to them?'

'They failed,' said Amadiro, indifferently.

Mandamus sat back in his chair with a horrified expression on his face. 'They were destroyed?'

Amadiro's eyebrows shot upward. 'Destroyed? No one destroys expensive robots. They are in storage. The power units are removed, and a special long-lived micro-fusion battery is in each to keep the positronic paths minimally alive.'

'Then they can be brought back to full action?'

'I am sure they can.'

Mandamus's right hand beat out a tightly-controlled rhythm against the arm of the chair. He said, grimly, 'Then we can win!'

12

The Plan and the Daughter

46.

It had been a long time since Amadiro had thought of the humanoid robots. It was a painful thought and he had, with some difficulty, trained himself to keep his mind away from that topic. And now Mandamus had unexpectedly brought it up.

The humanoid robot had been Fastolfe's great trump card in those long-gone days when Amadiro had been within a millimetre of taking the game, trump card and all. Fastolfe had designed and built two humanoid robots (of which one still existed) and no one else could build any. The entire membership of the Robotics Institute, working together, could not build them.

All that Amadiro had salvaged out of his great defeat had been that trump card. Fastolfe had been forced to make public the nature of the humanoid design.

That meant humanoid robots could be built, and *were* built, and behold, they were not wanted. The Aurorans would not have them in their society.

Amadiro's mouth twisted in the remnant of remembered chagrin. The tale of the Solarian woman had somehow come to be known – the fact that she had had the use of Jander, one of Fastolfe's two humanoid robots, and that the use had been sexual. Aurorans had no objection to such a situation, in theory, but when they stopped to think of it, Auroran women did not enjoy the thought of having to compete with robot women. Nor did Auroran men wish to compete with robot men.

The Institute had laboured mightily to explain that the humanoid robots were not intended for Aurora itself, but were meant to serve as the initial wave of pioneers who would seed and adjust new habitable planets for Aurorans to occupy later, after they had been made comfortable.

That, too, was rejected, as suspicion and objection fed on itself. 'The entering wedge', someone had called the humanoids; the expression spread and the Institute was forced to give up.

Stubbornly, Amadiro had insisted on mothballing those which existed for possible future use – a use that had never yet materialized.

Why had there been this objection to the humanoids? Amadiro felt a faint return of the irritation that had all but poisoned his life those many decades ago. Fastolfe himself, though reluctant, had agreed to back the project and, to do him justice, had done so, though without quite the eloquence he devoted to those matters to which his heart was truly given. But it had not helped.

And yet – and yet – if Mandamus now really had some project in mind that would work, and would require the robots –

Amadiro had no great fondness for mystical cries of: 'It was better so. It was meant to be.' Yet it was only with an effort that he kept himself from thinking this, as the elevator took them down to a spot well below ground level – the only place in Aurora that might be similar, in a tiny way, to Earth's fabled 'Caves of Steel'.

Mandamus stepped out of the elevator at Amadiro's gesture and found himself in a dim corridor. It was chilly and there was a soft, ventilating wind. He shivered slightly. Amadiro joined him. But a single robot followed each.

'Few people come here,' said Amadiro matter-of-factly.

'How far underground are we?' asked Mandamus.

'About fifteen metres. There are a number of levels. It is on this one that the humanoid robots are stored.'

Amadiro stopped a moment, as though in thought, then turned firmly to the left. 'This way!'

'No directing signs?'

'As I said, few people come here. Those who do, know where they should go to find what they need.'

As he said that, they came to a door that looked solid and formidable in the dim light. On either side stood a robot. They were not humanoid.

Mandamus regarded them critically and said, 'These are simple models.'

'Very simple. You wouldn't expect us to waste anything elaborate on the task of guarding a door.' Amadiro raised his voice, but kept it impassive. 'I am Kelden Amadiro, Head.'

The eyes of both robots glowed briefly. They turned outward, away from the door, which opened noiselessly, rising upward.

Amadiro directed the other through and, as he passed the robots, said calmly, 'Leave it open and adjust the lighting to personal need.'

Mandamus said, 'I don't suppose just anyone could enter here.'

'Certainly not. Those robots recognize my appearance and voice-print, and require both before opening the door.' Half to himself, he added, 'No need for locks or keys or combinations anywhere on the Spacer worlds. The robots guard us faithfully and always.'

'I had sometimes thought,' said Mandamus, broodingly, 'that if an Auroran were to borrow one of those blasters that Settlers seem to carry with them wherever they go, there would be no locked doors for him. He could destroy robots in an instant, then go wherever he wished, do whatever he wanted.'

Amadiro darted a fiery glance at the other. 'But what Spacer would dream of using such weapons on a Spacer world? We live our lives without weapons and without violence. Don't you understand that *that* is why I have devoted my life to the defeat and destruction of Earth and its poisoned brood? Yes, we had violence once, but that was long ago, when the Spacer worlds were first established and we had not yet rid ourselves of the poison of the Earth from which we came, and before we had learned the value of robotic security.

'Aren't peace and security worth fighting for? Worlds without violence! Worlds in which reason rules! Was it right for us to hand over scores of habitable worlds to short-lived barbarians who, as you say, carry blasters about with them everywhere?'

'And yet,' murmured Mandamus, 'are you ready to use violence to destroy Earth?'

'Violence briefly, and for a purpose, is the price we probably will have to pay for putting an end to violence forever.'

'I am Spacer enough,' said Mandamus, 'to want even that violence minimized.'

They had now entered a large, and, indeed, cavernous room and, as they entered, walls and ceiling came to life with diffuse and unglaring light.

'Well, is this what you want, Dr Mandamus?' asked Amadiro.

Mandamus looked about, stunned. Finally he managed to say, 'Incredible!'

They stood there, a solid regiment of human beings, with a little more life to them than so many statues might have showed, but with far less life than sleeping human beings would have displayed.

'They're standing,' muttered Mandamus.

'They take up less room that way. Obviously.'

'But they've been standing about fifteen decades. They *can't* still be in working order. Surely their joints are frozen, their organs broken down.'

Amadiro shrugged. 'Perhaps. Still, if the joints have deteriorated – and that isn't out of the question, I suppose – those can be replaced, if necessary. It would depend on whether there would be reason to do so.'

'There would be reason,' said Mandamus. He looked from head to head. They were staring in slightly different directions and that gave them a somewhat unsettling appearance, as though they were on the point of breaking rank.

Mandamus said, 'Each has an individual appearance, and they differ in height, build and so on.'

'Yes. Does that surprise you? We were planning to have these, along with others we might have built, be the pioneers in the development of new worlds. To have them do so properly, we wanted them to be as human as possible, which meant making them as individual as Aurorans are. Doesn't that seem sensible to you?'

'Absolutely. I'm glad this is so. I've read all I can about the two proto-humaniforms that Fastolfe himself built – Daneel Olivaw and Jander Panell. I've seen holographs of them, and they seemed identical.'

'Yes,' said Amadiro, impatiently. 'Not only identical, but each virtually a caricature of one's conception of the ideal Spacer. That was Fastolfe's romanticism. I'm sure that he would have built a race of interchangeable humanoid robots, with both sexes possessing such ethereal good looks – or what he considered to be that – as to make them completely inhuman. Fastolfe may be a brilliant roboticist, but he is an incredibly stupid man.'

Amadiro shook his head. To have been beaten by such an incredibly stupid man, he thought – and then thrust the thought away. He had not been beaten by Fastolfe, but by that infernal Earthman. Lost in thought, he did not hear Mandamus's next question.

'Pardon me,' he said, with an edge of irritation.

'I said: Did you design these, Dr Amadiro?'

'No, by an odd coincidence, and one that strikes me as possessing a peculiar irony, these were designed by Fastolfe's daughter, Vasilia. She's as brilliant as he is and much more intelligent – which may be one reason they never got along.'

'As I have heard the story concerning them – ' began Mandamus.

Amadiro waved him silent. 'I have heard the story, too, but it doesn't matter. It's enough that she does her work very well and that there is no danger that she will ever find herself in sympathy with someone who, despite the accident that he is her biological father, is, and must remain, forever alien and hateful to her. She even calls herself Vasilia Aliena, you know.'

'Yes, I know. Do you have the brain-patterns of these humanoid robots on record?'

'Certainly.'

'For *each* of these?'

'Of course.'

'And can they be made available to me?'

'If there's a reason for it.'

'There will be,' said Mandamus, firmly. Then, 'Since these were designed for pioneering activities, may I assume they are equipped to explore a world and deal with primitive conditions?'

'That should be self-evident.'

'That's perfect – but there may have to be some modifications. Do you suppose that Vasilia Fast – Aliena would be able to help me with that, if necessary? Obviously, she would be best acquainted with the brain-patterns.'

'Obviously. Still, I don't know whether she would be

willing to help you. I do know that it is physically impossible for her to do so at the moment, since she is not on
Aurora.'

Mandamus looked surprised and displeased. 'Where is
she, then, Dr Amadiro?'

Amadiro said, 'You have seen these humaniforms, and I
do not wish to expose myself to these rather dismal
surroundings. You have kept me waiting long enough, and
you must not complain if I keep you waiting now. If you
have any further questions, let us deal with them in my
office.'

47.

Once in the office, Amadiro delayed things further. 'Wait
here for me,' he said, rather peremptorily, and left.

Mandamus waited stiffly, sorting out his thoughts, wondering when Amadiro would return, or if he would. Was
he to be arrested, or simply ejected? Had Amadiro grown
tired of waiting for the point?

Mandamus refused to believe that. He had gained a
shrewd idea of Amadiro's desperate desire for evening an
old score. It seemed evident that Amadiro wouldn't get
tired of listening as long as there seemed the slightest
chance that Mandamus would make revenge possible.

As he looked idly about Amadiro's office, Mandamus
found himself wondering whether there might be any
information that might be of help to him in the computerized files almost immediately at hand. It would be useful
not to have to depend directly on Amadiro for everything.

The thought was a useless one. Mandamus did not know
the entry-code for the files, and, if he did, there were
several of Amadiro's personal robots standing in their
niches, and they would stop him if he took a single step

towards anything that was labelled in their minds as sensitive. Even his own robots would.

Amadiro was right. Robots were so useful and efficient – and incorruptible – as guards, that the very concept of anything criminal, illegal, or simply underhand, did not occur to anyone. The tendency just atrophied – at least as against other Spacers.

He wondered how Settlers could manage without robots. Mandamus tried to imagine human personalities clashing, with no robotic bumpers to cushion the interaction, no robotic presence to give them a decent sense of security and to enforce – without their being consciously aware of it most of the time – a proper mode of morality.

It would be impossible for Settlers to be anything but barbarians under the circumstance and the Galaxy could not be left to them. Amadiro was right in that respect and had always been right, while Fastolfe was fantastically wrong.

Mandamus nodded, as though he had once again persuaded himself as to the correctness of what he was planning. He sighed and wished it were not necessary, then prepared to go over, once again, the line of reasoning that proved to him that it *was* necessary, when Amadiro strode in.

Amadiro was still an impressive figure even though he was within a year of his twenty-eighth decade-day. He was very much what a Spacer ought to look like, always excepting the unfortunate shapelessness of his nose.

Amadiro said, 'I'm sorry to have kept you waiting, but there was business I had to attend to. I am Head of this Institute and that entails responsibilities.'

Mandamus said, 'Could you tell me where Dr Vasilia Aliena is? I will then describe my project to you without delay.'

'Vasilia is on tour. She's visiting each of the Spacer

worlds to find out where they stand on robot research. She appears to think that since the Robot Institute was founded to coordinate individual research on Aurora, interplanetary coordination would advance the cause even farther. A good idea, actually.'

Mandamus laughed shortly, and without humour. 'They won't tell her anything. I doubt any Spacer world wants to hand Aurora a more enormous lead than she already has.'

'Don't be too sure. The Settler situation has disturbed us all.'

'Do you know where she is now?'

'We have her itinerary.'

'Get her back, Dr Amadiro.'

Amadiro frowned. 'I doubt I can do that easily. I believe she wants to be away from Aurora until her father dies.'

'Why?' asked Mandamus in surprise.

Amadiro shrugged. 'I don't know. I don't care. But what I do know is that your time has run out. Do you understand? Get to the point, or leave.' He pointed to the door, grimly, and Mandamus felt the other's patience would stretch no farther.

Mandamus said, 'Very well. There is yet a third way in which Earth is unique –'

He talked easily, and with due economy, as though he were going through an exposition that he had frequently rehearsed and polished for the very purpose of presenting it to Amadiro. And Amadiro found himself increasingly absorbed.

This was it! Amadiro first felt a huge sense of relief. He had been correct to gamble on the young man's not being a crackpot. He was entirely sane.

Then came triumph. It would surely work. Of course, the young man's view, as it was expounded, veered a bit from the path Amadiro felt it ought to follow, but that could be taken care of eventually. Modifications were always possible.

And when Mandamus was done, Amadiro said, in a voice he strove to hold steady, 'We won't need Vasilia. There is appropriate expertise at the Institute to allow us to begin at once. Dr Mandamus,' a note of formal respect entered Amadiro's voice, 'let this thing work out as planned – and I cannot help but think it will – and you will be Head of the Institute when I am Chairman of the Council.'

Mandamus smiled narrowly and briefly, while Amadiro sat back in his chair and, just as briefly, allowed himself to look into the future with satisfaction and confidence, something he had not been able to do for twenty long and weary decades.

How long would it take? Decades? One decade? Part of a decade?

Not long. Not long. It must be hastened by all means so that he could live to see that old decision overturned, and himself lord of Aurora – and therefore of the Spacer worlds – and therefore (with Earth and the Settler worlds doomed), even lord of the Galaxy before he died.

48.

When Dr Han Fastolfe died, seven years after Amadiro and Mandamus met and began their project, the hyper-wave carried the news with explosive force to every corner of the occupied worlds. It merited the greatest attention everywhere.

In the Spacer worlds it was important because Fastolfe had been the most powerful man on Aurora and, therefore, in the Galaxy, for over twenty decades. In the Settler worlds and on Earth, it was important because Fastolfe had been a friend – insofar as a Spacer could be a friend –

and the question now was whether Spacer policy would change and, if so, how.

To Vasilia Aliena, the news came also, and it was complicated by the bitterness that had tinged her relationship with her biological father almost from the beginning.

She had schooled herself to feel nothing when he died, yet she had not wanted to be on the same world with him at the time the event took place. She did not want the questions that would be levelled at her anywhere, but most frequently and insistently on Aurora.

The parent-child relationship among the Spacers was a weak and indifferent one at best. With long lives, that was a matter of course. Nor would anyone have been interested in Vasilia in that respect but for the fact that Fastolfe was so continually prominent a party leader, and Vasilia almost as prominent a partisan on the other side.

It was poisonous. She had gone to the trouble of making Vasilia Aliena her legal name, and of using it on all documents, in all interviews, in all dealings of any kind – and yet she knew for a fact that most people thought of her as Vasilia Fastolfe. It was as though *nothing* could wipe out that thoroughly meaningless relationship, so that she was reduced to having to rest content with being addressed by her first name only. It was, at least, an uncommon name.

And that, too, seemed to emphasize her mirror-image relationship with the Solarian woman who, for thoroughly independent reasons, had denied her first husband as Vasilia had denied her father. The Solarian woman, too, could not live with the early surnames fastened upon her and ended with a first name only – Gladia.

Vasilia and Gladia, misfits, deniers – they even resembled each other.

Vasilia stole a look at the mirror hanging in her spaceship cabin. She had not seen Gladia in many decades, but she was sure that the resemblance remained. They were both small and slim. Both were blonde and their faces were somewhat alike.

But it was Vasilia who always lost, and Gladia who always won. When Vasilia had left her father and had struck him from her life, he had found Gladia instead, and she was the pliant and passive daughter he wanted, the daughter that Vasilia could never be.

Nevertheless, it embittered Vasilia. She herself was a roboticist, as competent and as skilful, at last, as ever Fastolfe had been, while Gladia was merely an artist, who amused herself with light-sculpture and with the illusions of robotic clothing. How could Fastolfe have been satisfied to lose the one and gain, in her place, nothing more than the other?

And when that policeman from Earth, Elijah Baley, had come to Aurora, he had bullied Vasilia into revealing far more of her thoughts and feelings than ever she had granted anyone else. He was, however, softness itself to Gladia and had helped her – and her protector, Fastolfe – win out against all the odds, though to this day Vasilia had not been able to understand clearly how that had happened.

It was Gladia who had been at Fastolfe's bedside during the final illness; who had held his hand at the last; who had exchanged the last sentences with him. Why Vasilia should resent that, she didn't know, for she herself would, under no circumstances, have acknowledged the old man's existence to the extent of visiting him to witness his passage into non-existence in an absolute, rather than a subjective sense – and yet she raged against Gladia's presence.

It's the way I feel, she told herself defiantly, and I owe no one an explanation.

And she had lost Giskard. Giskard had been *her* robot, Vasilia's own robot when she had been a young girl, the robot granted her by a then seemingly fond father. It was Giskard through whom she had learned robotics and from whom she had felt the first genuine affection. She had not, as a child, speculated on the Three Laws or dealt with the philosophy of positronic automatism. Giskard had *seemed* affectionate, he had *acted* as though he were affectionate, and that was enough for a child. Such affection she had never found in any human being – certainly not in her father.

To this day, she had yet to be weak enough to play the foolish love game with anyone. Her bitterness over her loss of Giskard had taught her that any initial gain was not worth the final deprivation.

When she had left home, disowning her father, he would not let Giskard go with her, even though she herself had improved Giskard immeasurably in the course of her careful reprogramming of him. And when her father had died, he had left Giskard to the Solarian woman. He had also left her Daneel, but Vasilia cared nothing for that pale imitation of a man. She wanted Giskard, who was her own.

Vasilia was on her way back now. Her tour was quite done; in fact, as far as usefulness was concerned, it had been essentially over months ago, but she had remained on Hesperos for a needed rest – as she had explained in her official notice to the Institute.

Now, however, Fastolfe was dead and she could return. And while she could not undo the past entirely, she could undo part of it. Giskard must be hers again.

She was determined on that.

49.

Amadiro was quite ambivalent in his response to Vasilia's return. She had not come back until old Fastolfe (he could say the name to himself quite easily now that he was dead) was a month in his urn. That flattered his opinion of his own understanding. After all, he had told Mandamus her motive had been that of remaining off Aurora till her father died.

Then, too, Vasilia was comfortably transparent. She lacked the exasperating quality of Mandamus, his new favourite, who always seemed to have one unexpressed thought yet tucked away no matter how thoroughly he seemed to have discharged the contents of his mind.

On the other hand, she was irritatingly hard to control, the least likely to go quietly along the path he indicated. Leave it to her to probe the other-world Spacers to the bone during the years she had spent away from Aurora – but then leave it also to her to interpret it all in dark and riddling words.

So he greeted her with an enthusiasm that was somewhere between feigned and unfeigned.

'Vasilia, I'm so happy to have you back. The Institute flies on one wing when you're gone.'

Vasilia laughed. 'Come, Kelden' (she alone had no hesitation or inhibition in using his given name, though she was two and a half decades younger than he) 'that one remaining wing is yours, and how long has it been now since you ceased being perfectly certain that your one wing was sufficient?'

'Since you decided to stretch out your absence to years. Do you find Aurora much changed in the interval?'

'Not a bit – which ought perhaps to be a concern of ours. Changelessness is decay.'

'A paradox. There is no decay without a change for the worse.'

'Changelessness is a change for the worse, Kelden, in comparison to the surrounding Settler worlds. They change rapidly, extending their control into more numerous worlds, and over each individual world more thoroughly. They increase their strength and power and self-assurance, while we sit here dreaming, and find our unchanging might diminishing steadily in comparison.'

'Beautiful, Vasilia! I think you memorized that carefully on your flight here. However, there has been a change in the political situation on Aurora.'

'You mean my biological father is dead.'

Amadiro spread his arms with a little bow of his head. 'As you say. He was largely responsible for our paralysis and he is gone, so I imagine there will now be change, though it may not necessarily be visible change.'

'You keep secrets from me, do you?'

'Would I do that?'

'Certainly. That false smile of yours gives you away every time.'

'Then I must learn to be grave with you. Come, I have your report. Tell me what is not included in it.'

'All is included in it, almost. Each Spacer world states vehemently that it is disturbed by growing Settler arrogance. Each is firmly determined to resist the Settlers to the end, enthusiastically following the Auroran lead with vigour and death-defying gallantry.'

'Follow our lead, yes. And if we don't lead?'

'Then they'll wait, and try to mask their relief that we are not leading. Otherwise – well, each one is engaged in technological advance, and each one is reluctant to reveal what it is, exactly, that it is doing. Each is working independently and is not even unified within its own globe. There is not a single research team anywhere on any of the Spacer worlds that resembles our own Robotics Institute. Each world consists of individual researchers, each of whom diligently guards his own data from all the rest.'

Amadiro was almost complacent as he said, 'I would not expect them to have advanced as far as we have.'

'Too bad they haven't,' replied Vasilia, tartly. 'With all the Spacer worlds a jumble of individuals, progress is too slow. The Settler worlds meet regularly at conventions, have their institutes – and though they lag well behind us, they *will* catch up. Still, I've managed to uncover a few technological advances being worked on by the Spacer worlds, and I have them all listed in my report. They are all working on the nuclear intensifier, for instance, but I don't believe that such a device has passed beyond the laboratory demonstration level on a single world. Something that would be practical on shipboard is not yet here.'

'I hope you are right in that, Vasilia. The nuclear intensifier is a weapon our fleets could use, for it would finish the Settlers at once. However, I think, on the whole, it would be better if Aurora had the weapon ahead of our Spacer brothers. But you said that all was included in your report, *almost*. I heard that "almost". What is not included, then?'

'Solaria!'

'Ah, the youngest and most peculiar of the Spacer worlds.'

'I got almost nothing directly out of them. They viewed me with absolute hostility as, I believe, they would have viewed any non-Solarian, whether Spacer or Settler. And when I say "viewed", I mean that in their sense. I remained nearly a year on the world, a considerably longer time than I spent on any other world, and in all those months I never *saw* a single Solarian, face to face. In every case, I *viewed* him, or her, by hyperwave hologram. I could never deal with anything tangible; images only. The world was comfortable, incredibly luxurious, in fact; and for a nature-lover, totally unspoiled, but how I missed *seeing*.'

'Well, viewing is a Solarian custom. We all know that, Vasilia. Live and let live.'

'Hmph,' said Vasilia. 'Your tolerance may be misplaced. Are your robots in the non-repeat mode?'

'Yes, they are. And I assure you we are not being eavesdropped.'

'I hope not, Kelden. I am under the distinct impression that the Solarians are closer to developing a miniaturized nuclear intensifier than any other world – than we are. They may be close to making one that's portable and that's possessed of a power consumption small enough to make it practical for space vessels.'

Amadiro frowned, deeply. 'How do they manage that?'

'I cannot say. You don't suppose they showed me blueprints, do you? My impressions are so inchoate, I dared not put them in the report, but from small things I heard here, or observed there, I think they are making important progress. This is something we should think about, carefully.'

'We will. Is there anything else you would like to tell me?'

'Yes, and also not in the report. Solaria has been working towards humanoid robots for many decades and I think they have achieved *that* goal. No other Spacer world, outside of ourselves, of course, has even attempted the matter. When I asked, on each world, what they were doing with respect to humanoid robots, the reaction was uniform. They found the very concept unpleasant and horrifying. I suspect they all noticed our failure, and took it to heart.'

'But not Solaria? Why not?'

'For one thing, they have always lived in the most highly roboticized society in the Galaxy. They're surrounded by robots; ten thousand per individual. The world is saturated with them. If you were to wander through it aimlessly, searching for humans, you would find nothing. So why should the few Solarians, living in such a world, be upset by the thought of a few more robots just because they're humaniform? Then, too, that pseudo-human wretch that Fastolfe designed and built, and that still exists – '

'Daneel,' said Amadiro.

'Yes, that one. He – *it* was on Solaria twenty decades ago, and the Solarians treated it as human. They have never recovered from that. Even if they had no use for humaniforms, they were humiliated at having been deceived. It was an unforgettable demonstration that Aurora was far ahead of them in that one facet of robotics, at any rate. The Solarians take inordinate pride in being the most advanced roboticists in the Galaxy and, ever since, individual Solarians have been working on human-iforms, if for no other reason than to wipe out that disgrace. If they had had greater numbers or an Institute that could coordinate their work, they would undoubtedly have come up with some long ago. As it is, I think they have them now.'

'You don't really know, do you? This is just suspicion based on scraps of data, here and there.'

'Exactly right, but it's a fairly strong suspicion, and it merits further investigation. And a third point. I could swear they were working on telepathic communication. There was some equipment that I was incautiously allowed to see. And once when I had one of their roboticists on view, the hyperwave screen showed a blackboard with a positronic-pattern matrix that was like nothing I ever remember seeing, yet it seemed to me that pattern might fit a telepathic program.'

'I suspect, Vasilia, that this item is woven of even airier gossamer than the bit about the humanoid robots.'

A look of mild embarrassment crossed Vasilia's face. 'I must admit you're probably right there.'

'In fact, Vasilia, it sounds like mere fantasy. If the pattern matrix you saw was like nothing you remember ever having seen before, how could you think it would fit anything?'

Vasilia hesitated. 'To tell you the truth, I've been wondering about that myself. Yet when I saw the pattern, the word "telepathy" occurred to me at once.'

'Even though telepathy is impossible, even in theory.'

'It is *thought* to be impossible, even in theory. That is not quite the same thing.'

'No one has ever been able to make any progress towards it.'

'Yes, but why should I have looked at that pattern and thought "telepathy"?'

'Ah, well, Vasilia, there may be a personal psychoquirk there that is useless to try to analyse. I'd forget it. Anything else?'

'One more thing, and the most puzzling of all. I gathered the impression, Kelden, from one little indication or another, that the Solarians are planning to leave their planet.'

'Why?'

'I don't know. Their population, small as it is, is further declining. Perhaps they want to make a new start elsewhere before they die out altogether.'

'What kind of new start? Where would they go?'

Vasilia shook her head. 'I have told you all I know.'

Amadiro said, slowly, 'Well, then, I will take all this into account. Four things: nuclear intensifier, humanoid robots, telepathic robots, and abandoning the planet. Frankly, I have no faith in any of the four, but I'll persuade the Council to authorize talks with the Solarian Regent. And now, Vasilia, I believe you could use a rest, so why not take a few weeks off and grow accustomed to the Auroran sun and fine weather before getting back to work?'

'That is kind of you, Kelden,' said Vasilia, remaining firmly seated, 'but there remain two items I must bring up.'

Involuntarily, Amadiro's eyes sought the time-strip. 'This won't take up very much time, will it, Vasilia?'

'However much time it takes, Kelden, is what it will take up.'

'What is it you want, then?'

'To begin with, who is this young know-it-all who seems to think he is running the Institute; this what's-his-name Mandamus?'

'You've met him, have you?' said Amadiro, his smile masking a certain uneasiness. 'You see, things *do* change on Aurora.'

'Certainly not for the better in this case,' said Vasilia, grimly. 'Who *is* he?'

'He is exactly what you have described; a know-it-all. He is a brilliant young man, bright enough in robotics, but just as knowledgeable in general physics, in chemistry, in planetology – '

'And how old is this monster of erudition?'

'Not quite five decades.'

'And what will this child be when he grows up?'

'Wise as well as brilliant, perhaps.'

'Don't. pretend to mistake my meaning, Kelden. Are you thinking of grooming him as the next Head of the Institute?'

'I intend to live for a good many decades yet.'

'That is no answer.'

'It is the only answer I have.'

Vasilia shifted in her seat restlessly, and her robot, standing behind her, sent his eyes from side to side as though preparing to ward off an attack, pushed into that mode of behaviour, perhaps, by Vasilia's uneasiness.

Vasilia said, 'Kelden, I am to be the next Head. That is settled. You have told me so.'

'I have, but in actual fact, Vasilia, once I die, the Board of Directors will make the choice. Even if I leave behind me a directive as to who the next Head will be, the Board can reverse me. That much is clear in the terms of incorporation that founded the Institute.'

'You just write your directive, Kelden, and I will take care of the Board of Directors.'

And Amadiro, the space between his eyebrows furrowing, said, 'This is not something I will discuss any further at this moment. What is the other item you want to bring up? Please make it brief.'

She stared at him in silent anger for a moment, then said, seeming to bite off the word, 'Giskard!'

'The robot?'

'Of course, the robot. Do you know any other Giskard that I am likely to be talking about?'

'Well, what of him?'

'He is *mine*.'

Amadiro looked surprised. 'He is – or was – the legal property of Fastolfe.'

'Giskard was mine when I was a child.'

'Fastolfe lent him to you, and eventually took him back. There was no formal transfer of ownership, was there?'

'Morally, he was mine. But in any case, Fastolfe owns him no longer. He is dead.'

'He made a will, too. And if I remember correctly, by that will, two robots, Giskard and Daneel, are now the property of the Solarian woman.'

'But I don't want them to be. I am Fastolfe's daughter
– '

'Oh?'

Vasilia flushed. 'I have a claim to Giskard. Why should a
stranger – an alien – have him?'

'For one thing, because Fastolfe willed it so. And she's
an Auroran citizen.'

'Who says so? To every Auroran she is "the Solarian
woman".'

Amadiro brought his fist down on the arm of his chair in
a sudden spilling-over of fury. 'Vasilia, what is it you wish
of me? I have no liking for the Solarian woman. I have, in
fact, a profound dislike of her, and, if there were a way, I
would – ' he looked briefly at the robots, as though
unwilling to unsettle them ' – get her off the planet. But I
can't upset the will. Even if there were a legal way to do
so – and there isn't – it wouldn't be wise to do it. Fastolfe
is dead.'

'Precisely the reason Giskard should be mine, now.'

Amadiro ignored her, 'And the coalition he headed is
falling apart. It was held together in the last few decades
only by his personal charisma. Now what I would like to
do is to pick up fragments of that coalition and add it to my
own following. In that way, I may put a group together
that would be strong enough to dominate the Council and
win control in the coming elections.'

'With you becoming the next Chairman?'

'Why not? Aurora could do worse, for it would give me
a chance to reverse our long-time policy of built-in disaster
before it is too late. The trouble is that I don't have
Fastolfe's personal popularity. I don't have his gift of
exuding saintliness as a cover for stupidity. Consequently,
if I seem to be triumphing, in an unfair and petty way,
over a dead man, it will not look good. No one must say
that, having been defeated by Fastolfe while he was alive,

I overturned his will out of trivial spite after he was dead. I won't have anything as ridiculous as that standing in the way of the great life-and-death decisions Aurora must make. Do you understand me? You'll have to do without Giskard!'

Vasilia arose, body stiff, eyes narrow. 'We'll see about that.'

'We have already seen. This meeting is over and if you have any ambitions to be Head of the Institute, I don't ever want to see you threatening me about anything. So if you're going to make a threat now, of any kind at all, I advise you to reconsider.'

'I make no threats,' said Vasilia, every ounce of body language contradicting her words – and she left with a sweep, beckoning her robot, unnecessarily, to follow.

50.

The emergency, or rather, the series of emergencies, began some months later, when Maloon Cicis entered Amadiro's office for the usual morning conference.

Ordinarily, Amadiro looked forward to that. Cicis was always a restful interlude in the course of the busy day. He was the one senior member of the Institute who had no ambitions, and who was not calculating against the day of Amadiro's death or retirement. Cicis was, in fact, the perfect subordinate. He was happy to be of service and delighted to be in the confidence of the Head.

For this reason, Amadiro had been disturbed, in the last year or so, at the flavour of decay, the slight concavity of the chest, the touch of stiffness in the walk, of his perfect subordinate. Could Cicis be getting old? Surely, he was only a few decades older than Amadiro.

It struck Amadiro most unpleasantly that perhaps along

with the gradual degeneration of so many facets of Spacer life, the life expectancy was falling. He meant to look up the statistics, but kept forgetting to do so – or was unconsciously afraid of doing so.

On this occasion, though, the appearance of age in Cicis was drowned in violent emotion. His face was red (pointing up the greying of his bronze hair) and he appeared virtually exploding with astonishment.

Amadiro did not have to inquire as to the news. Cicis delivered it as though it was something he could not contain.

When he finished exploding, Amadiro said, stupefied, 'All radio-wave emissions ceased? All?'

'*All*, Chief. They must all be dead – or gone. No inhabited world can avoid emitting *some* electromagnetic radiation at our level of – '

Amadiro waved him silent. One of Vasilia's points – the fourth, as he recalled – had been that the Solarians were preparing to leave their world. It had been a nonsensical suggestion; all four had been more or less nonsensical. He had said he would keep it in mind and, of course, he hadn't. Now, apparently, that had proved to be a mistake.

What had made it seem nonsensical when Vasilia had advanced the notion still made it seem nonsensical. He asked the question now that he had asked then, even though he expected no answer. (What answer could there be?) 'Where in Space could they go, Maloon?'

'There's no word on that, Chief.'

'Well, then, *when* did they go?'

'There's no word on that, either. We got the news this morning. The trouble is the radiational intensity is so low on Solaria, anyway. It's very sparsely inhabited, and its robots are well-shielded. The intensity is an order of magnitude lower than that of any other Spacer world; two orders lower than ours.'

'So one day someone noticed that what was very small had actually declined to zero, but no one actually caught it as it was declining. *Who* noticed it?'

'A Nexonian ship, Chief.'

'How?'

'The ship was being forced into orbit about Solaria's sun in order to carry through emergency repairs. They hyperwaved for permission and got no answer. They had no choice but to disregard that, continue into orbit, and carry through their repairs. They were not interfered with in any way in that time. It was not till after they had left that, in checking through their records, they found that not only had they received no answer, but that they had received no radiational signal of any kind. There's no way of telling exactly when radiation had ceased. The last recorded receipt of any message from Solaria was over two months ago.'

'And the other three points she made?' Amadiro muttered.

'Pardon me, Chief?'

'Nothing, Nothing,' said Amadiro, but he frowned heavily, and was lost in thought.

13

The Telepathic Robot

51

Mandamus was not aware of developments on Solaria when he returned some months later from an extended third trip to Earth.

On his first trip, six years before, Amadiro had managed, with some difficulty, to have him sent as an accredited emissary from Aurora to discuss some trifling matter of an overstepping into Spacer territory by Trader vessels. He had endured the ceremony and bureaucratic ennui, and it quickly became clear that as such an emissary his mobility was limited. That didn't matter, for he learned what he had come to learn.

He had returned with the news. 'I doubt, Dr Amadiro, that there will be any problem at all. There is no way, no possible way, in which the Earth officials can control either entry or exit. Every year many millions of Settlers visit Earth from any of dozens of worlds, and every year as many millions of visiting Settlers leave for home again. Every Settler seems to feel that life is not complete unless he or she periodically breathes the air of Earth and treads its crowded underground spaces. It's a search for roots, I imagine. They don't seem to feel the absolute nightmare that existence on Earth is.'

'I know about it, Mandamus,' said Amadiro, wearily.

'Only intellectually, sir. You can't truly understand it until you experience it. Once you do, you'll find that none of your "knowing" will prepare you in the least for the reality. Why anyone should want to go back, once gone – '

'Our ancestors certainly didn't want to go back, once they had left the planet.'

'No,' said Mandamus, 'but interstellar flight was not then as advanced as it is now. It used to take months then and the hyperspatial Jump was a tricky thing. Now it takes merely days and the Jumps are routine and never go wrong. *If* it were as easy to return to Earth in our ancestors' time as it is now, I wonder if we would have broken away as we did.'

'Let's not philosophize, Mandamus. Proceed to the point.'

'Certainly. In addition to the coming and going of endless streams of Settlers, millions of Earthmen each year head out as emigrants to one or another of the Settler worlds. Some return almost at once, having failed to adapt. Others make new homes but come back particularly frequently to visit. There's no way of keeping track of exits and entrances and Earth doesn't even try. To attempt to set up systematic methods for identifying and keeping track of visitors might stem the flow and Earth is very aware that each visitor brings money with him. The tourist trade, if we want to call it that, is currently Earth's most profitable industry.'

'You are saying, I suppose, that we can get the humanoid robots into Earth without trouble.'

'With no trouble at all. There's no question in my mind as to that. Now that we have them properly programmed, we can send them to Earth in half a dozen batches with forged papers. We can't do anything about their robotic respect and awe of human beings but that may not give them away. It will be interpreted as the usual Settler respect and awe for the ancestral planet. But then, I strongly suspect we don't have to drop them into one of the City airports. The vast spaces between Cities are virtually untenanted except by primitive work-robots and the incoming ships would go unnoticed, or at least disregarded.'

'Too risky, I think,' said Amadiro.

51a.

Two batches of humanoid robots were sent to Earth, and these mingled with the Earthpeople of the Cities before finding their way out into the blank areas between, and communicating with Aurora on shielded hyperbeam.

Mandamus said (he had thought about it deeply and had hesitated long), 'I will have to go again, sir. I can't be positive they've found the right spot.'

'Are you sure *you* know the right spot, Mandamus?' asked Amadiro, sardonically.

'I have delved into Earth's ancient history thoroughly, sir. I know I can find it.'

'I don't think I can persuade the Council to send a warship with you.'

'No, I wouldn't want that. It would be worse than useless. I want a one-person vessel, with just enough power to get there and back.'

And in that way, Mandamus made his second visit to Earth, dropping down into a region outside one of the smaller Cities. With mingled relief and satisfaction, he found several of the robots in the right place, and remained with them to view their work, to give a few orders in connection with that work, and to make some fine adjustments in their programming.

And then, under the uninterested glance of a few primitive Earth-formed, agricultural robots, Mandamus made for the nearby City.

It was a calculated risk and Mandamus, no fearless hero, could feel his heart thudding uncomfortably within his chest. But it went well. There was some surprise shown by the Gate Warden when a human being presented himself at the Gate, showing all signs of having spent a considerable time in the open.

Mandamus had papers identifying him as a Settler, however, and the Warden shrugged. Settlers didn't mind the open, and it was far from unheard-of for them to take small excursions through the fields and woods that lay about the unimpressive upper layers of a City that jutted above the ground.

The Warden gave but a cursory glance at his papers and no one else asked for them at all. Mandamus's off-Earth accent (as weakly Auroran as he could make it) was accepted without comment and, as nearly as he could tell, no one wondered whether he might be a Spacer. But then, why should they? The days when the Spacers held a permanent outpost on Earth were two centuries in the past, and official emissaries from the Spacer worlds were few and, of late, growing steadily fewer. The provincial Earthpeople might not even remember that Spacers existed.

Mandamus was a little concerned that the thin, transparent gloves he wore always, might be noticed, or that his nose-plugs would be remarked upon, but neither event took place. No barriers were placed on his travels around the City or to other Cities. He had enough money for that, and money spoke loudly on Earth (and, to tell the truth, even on Spacer worlds).

He grew accustomed to having no robot dog his heels, and when he met with some of Aurora's own humanoid robots in this City or that, he had to explain to them quite firmly that *they* must not dog his heels. He listened to their reports, gave them any instructions they seemed to require, and made arrangements for further robot shipments out-of-City. Eventually, he found his way back to his ship and left.

He was not challenged on his way out, any more than he had been on his way in.

'Actually,' he said, thoughtfully, to Amadiro, 'these Earthpeople are not really barbarians.'

'Aren't they, though?'

'In their own world, they behave in quite a human fashion. In fact, there is something winning in their friendliness.'

'Are you beginning to regret the task you're engaged in?'

'It does give me a grisly feeling as I wander among them thinking that they don't know what is going to happen to them. I can't make myself *enjoy* what I'm doing.'

'Of course you can, Mandamus. Think of the fact that once the job is done, you will be sure of a post as Head of the Institute before very much time has elapsed. That will sweeten the job for you.'

And Amadiro kept a close eye on Mandamus thereafter.

51b.

On Mandamus's third trip, much of his earlier uneasiness had worn off, and he could carry himself almost as though he were an Earthman. The project was proceeding slowly but dead centre along the projected line of progress.

He had experienced no health problems on his earlier visits, but on this third one – no doubt due to his overconfidence – he must have exposed himself to something or other. At least, for a time he had an alarming drippiness of the nose, accompanied by a cough.

A visit to one of the City dispensaries resulted in a gamma-globulin injection that relieved the condition at once, but he found the dispensary more frightening than the illness. Everyone there, he knew, was likely to be ill with something contagious or to be in close contact with those who were ill.

But now, at last, he was back in the quiet orderliness of Aurora, and incredibly thankful to be so. He was listening to Amadiro's account of the Solarian crisis.

'Have you heard nothing of it at all?' demanded Amadiro.

Mandamus shook his head. 'Nothing, sir. Earth is an incredibly provincial world. Eight hundred Cities with a total of eight billion people – all interested in nothing but the eight hundred Cities with a total of eight billion people. You would think that Settlers existed only to visit Earth, and that Spacers did not exist at all. Indeed, the news reports in any one City deal about ninety per cent of the time with that City alone. Earth is an enclosed, claustrophilic world, mentally as well as physically.'

'And yet you say they are not barbarian.'

'Claustrophilia isn't necessarily barbarism. In their own terms, they are civilized.'

'In their own terms! But never mind. The problem at the moment is Solaria. Not one of the Spacer Worlds will move. The principle of non-interference is paramount and they insist that Solaria's internal problems are for Solaria alone. Our own Chairman is as inert as any other, even though Fastolfe is dead and his palsied hand no longer rests on us all. I can do nothing by myself – until such time as *I* am Chairman.'

Mandamus said, 'How can they suppose Solaria to have internal problems that may not be interfered with, when the Solarians are gone?'

Amadiro said, sardonically, 'How is it you see the folly of it at once and they don't? They say there is no hard evidence that the Solarians are totally gone, and as long as they, or even some of them, might be on the world, there is no right for any other Spacer world to intrude uninvited.'

'How do they explain the absence of radiational activity?'

'They say that the Solarians may have moved underground, or that they may have developed a technological advance of some sort that obviates radiation leakage. They also say that the Solarians were not seen to leave and that they have absolutely nowhere to go to. Of course, they were not seen leaving because no one was watching.'

Mandamus said, 'How do they argue that the Solarians have nowhere to go to? There are many empty worlds.'

'The argument is that the Solarians cannot live without their incredible crowds of robots, and they can't take those robots with them. If they came here, for instance, how many robots do you suppose we could allot to them – if any?'

'And what is your argument against that?'

'I haven't any. Still, whether they are gone or not, the situation is strange and puzzling, and it is incredible that no one will move to investigate it. I've warned everyone, just as strenuously as I can, that inertia and apathy will be the end of us; that as soon as the Settler worlds become aware of the fact that Solaria was – or might be – empty, *they* would have no hesitation in investigating the matter. Those swarmers have a mindless curiosity that I wish we had some share in. They will, without thinking twice, risk their lives if some profit lures them on.'

'What profit in this case, Dr Amadiro?'

'If the Solarians are gone, they have, perforce, left almost all their robots behind. They are – or were – particularly ingenious roboticists and the Settlers, for all their hatred of robots, will not hesitate to appropriate them, and ship them to us for good Space credits. In fact, they have announced this.

'Two Settler ships have already landed on Solaria. We have sent a protest over this, but they will surely disregard the protest, and, just as surely, we will do nothing further. Quite the contrary. Some of the Spacer worlds are sending out quiet queries as to the nature of the robots that might be salvaged and what their prices would be.'

'Perhaps just as well,' said Mandamus, quietly.

'Just as well that we're behaving exactly as the Settler propagandists say we will? That we act as though we *are* degenerating and turning into soft pulps of decadence?'

'Why repeat their buzz words, sir? The fact is that we are quiet and civilized, and have not yet been touched where it hurts. If we were, we would fight back strongly enough and, I'm sure, smash them. We still far outstrip them technologically.'

'But the damage to ourselves will not be exactly pleasurable.'

'Which means that we must not be too ready to go to war. If Solaria is deserted and the Settlers wish to plunder it, perhaps we ought to let them. After all, I predict that we will be all set to make our move within months.'

A rather hungry and ferocious look came over Amadiro's face. 'Months?'

'I'm sure of it. So the first thing we must do is to avoid being provoked. We will ruin everything if we move towards a conflict there is no need to fight, and undergo damage, even if we win, that we don't need to suffer. After all, in a little while, we are going to win totally, without fighting and without damage. Poor Earth!'

'If you're going to be sorry for them,' said Amadiro, with spurious lightness, 'perhaps you'll do nothing to them.'

'On the contrary,' said Mandamus, coolly, 'it's precisely because I fully intend to do something to them, and know that it will be done, that I am sorry for them. You will be Chairman!'

'And you will be the Head of the Institute.'

'A small post in comparison to yours.'

'And after I die?' said Amadiro, in half a snarl.

'I do not look that far ahead.'

'I am quite – ' began Amadiro, but was interrupted by the steady buzz of the message unit. Without looking, and quite automatically, Amadiro placed his hand at the exit slot. He looked at the thin strip of paper that emerged, and a slow smile appeared on his lips.

'The two Settler ships that landed on Solaria – ' he said.

'Yes, sir?' asked Mandamus, frowning.

'Destroyed! Both destroyed!'

'How?'

'In an explosive blaze of radiation, easily detected from space. You see what it means? The Solarians have not left after all, and the weakest of our worlds can easily handle Settler ships. It is a bloody nose for the Settlers and not something they'll forget. Here, Mandamus, read for yourself.'

Mandamus pushed the paper aside. 'But that doesn't necessarily mean that the Solarians are still on the planet. They may merely have booby-trapped it somehow.'

'What is the difference? Personal attack or booby-trap, the ships were destroyed.'

'This time they were caught by surprise. What about next time, when they are prepared? And what if they consider the event a deliberate Spacer attack?'

'We will reply that the Solarians were merely defending themselves against a deliberate Settler invasion.'

'But, sir, are you suggesting a battle of words? What if the Settlers don't bother talking, but consider the destruction of their ships an act of war and retaliate at once?'

'Why should they?'

'Because they are as insane as we can be once pride is hurt; more so, since they have a greater background of violence.'

'They will be beaten.'

'You yourself admit they will inflict unacceptable damage upon us even if they are beaten.'

'What would you have me do? Aurora did not destroy those ships.'

'Persuade the Chairman to make it quite plain that Aurora had nothing to do with it; that none of the Spacer worlds had anything to do with it; that the blame for the action rests on Solaria alone.'

'And abandon Solaria? That would be a cowardly act.'

Mandamus blazed into excitement. 'Dr Amadiro, have you never heard of anything called a strategic retreat? Persuade the Spacer worlds to back off for only a little while on some plausible pretext. It is only a matter of some months till our plan on Earth comes to fruition. It may be hard for everyone else to back off and be apologetic to the Spacers for they don't know what is coming – but we do. In fact, you and I, with our special knowledge, can look upon this event as a gift from what used to be called the gods. Let the Settlers remain preoccupied with Solaria, while their destruction is prepared, all unobserved by them, on Earth. Or would you prefer us to be ruined on the very brink of final victory?'

Amadiro found himself flinching before the direct glare of the other's deep-set eyes.

52.

Amadiro had never had a worse time than during the period following the destruction of the Settler ships. The Chairman, fortunately, could be persuaded to follow a policy of what Amadiro termed 'masterful yielding'. The phrase caught the Chairman's imagination even though it was an oxymoron. Besides, the Chairman was good at masterful yielding.

The rest of the Council was harder to handle. The exasperated Amadiro exhausted himself in picturing the horrors of war and the necessity of choosing the proper moment to strike, and not the improper one, if war there must be. He invented novel plausibilities for why the moment was not yet, and used them in discussions with the leaders of the other Spacer worlds. Aurora's natural hegemony had to be exercised to the utmost to get them to yield.

But when Captain D. G. Baley arrived with his ship and his demand, Amadiro felt he could do no more. It was too much.

'It is altogether impossible,' said Amadiro. 'Are we to allow him to land on Aurora with his beard, his ridiculous clothing, his incomprehensible accent? Am I expected to ask the Council to agree to hand over a Spacer woman to him? It would be an act absolutely unprecedented in our history. A Spacer woman!'

Mandamus said, dryly, 'You always referred to that particular Spacer woman as the "Solarian woman", heretofore.'

'She is the "Solarian woman" to us, but she will be considered a Spacer woman once a Settler is involved. If his ship lands on Solaria, as he suggests it will, it may be destroyed as the others were, together with him, and with the woman. I may then be accused by my enemies, with some colour of justification, of murder – and my political career may not survive that.'

Mandamus said, 'Think, instead, of the fact that we have laboured nearly seven years in order to arrange the final destruction of Earth, and that we are now only a few months from the completion of the project. Shall we risk war now and, at a stroke, ruin everything we've done when we are so close to final victory?'

Amadiro shook his head. 'It isn't as though I have a choice in the matter, my friend. The Council wouldn't follow me if I tried to argue them into surrendering the woman to a Settler. And the mere fact that I have suggested it will be used against me. My political career will be shaken, and we may then have a war in addition. Besides, the thought of a Spacer woman dying in service to a Settler is unbearable.'

'One would suppose you were fond of the Solarian woman.'

'You know I am not. With all my heart I wish she had died twenty decades ago, but not this way, not on a Settler ship. But I should remember she is an ancestress of yours in the fifth generation.'

Mandamus looked a bit more dour than he usually did. 'Of what consequence is that to me? I am a Spacer individual, conscious of myself and of my society. I am not an ancestor-worshipping member of a tribal conglomerate.'

For a moment, Mandamus fell silent and his thin face took on a look of intense concentration. 'Dr Amadiro,' he said, 'could you not explain to the Council that this ancestress of mine is being taken, not as a Spacer hostage, but only because her unique knowledge of Solaria, where she spent her childhood and youth, could make her an essential part of the exploration, and that this exploration might even be helpful to us, as well as to the Settlers? After all, in truth, wouldn't it be desirable for us to know what those miserable Solarians are up to? The woman will presumably bring back a report of the events, if she survives.'

Amadiro thrust out his lower lip. 'That might work if the woman went on board voluntarily; if she made it clear that she understood the importance of the work and wished to perform her patriotic duty. To put her on board ship by force, though, is unthinkable.'

'Well, then, suppose I were to see this ancestress of mine and try to persuade her to get on the ship willingly; and suppose, also, that you speak to this Settler captain by

hyperwave and tell him he can land on Aurora and have
the woman *if* he can persuade her to go with him willingly
– or, at least, *say* that she'll go with him willingly, whether
she does or not.'

'I suppose we can't lose by making the effort, but I don't
see how we can win.'

Yet to Amadiro's surprise, they did win. He had listened
with astonishment as Mandamus told him the details.

'I brought up the matter of the humanoid robots,'
Mandamus said, 'and it's clear she knew nothing about
them, from which I deduced Fastolfe had known nothing
about them. It has been one of those things that nagged at
me. Then I talked a great deal about my ancestry in such a
way as to force her to talk of that Earthman, Elijah Baley.'

'What about him?' said Amadiro harshly.

'Nothing except that she talked about him and remembered. This Settler who wants her is a descendant of Baley
and I thought it might influence her to consider the
Settler's request more favourably than she might otherwise
have done.'

In any case, it had worked, and for a few days, Amadiro
felt a relief from the almost continuous pressure that had
plagued him from the start of the Solarian crisis.

But only for a very few days.

53.

One point that worked to Amadiro's advantage at this
time, was that during the Solarian crisis, thus far, he had
not seen Vasilia.

It would certainly not have been an appropriate time to
see her. He did not wish to be annoyed by her petty
concern over a robot she claimed as her own, with total
disregard for the legalities of the situation, at a time when

a true crisis exercised his every nerve and thought. Nor did he wish to expose himself to the kind of quarrel that might easily arise between her and Mandamus over the question of who was eventually to preside over the Robotics Institute.

In any case, he had about come to the decision that Mandamus ought to be his successor. Throughout the Solarian crisis, he had kept his eye fixed on what was important. Even when Amadiro himself had felt shaken, Mandamus had remained icily calm. It was Mandamus who thought it conceivable that the Solarian woman might accompany the Settler captain voluntarily and it was he who manoeuvred her into doing so.

And if his plan for the destruction of Earth worked itself out as it should – as it must – then Amadiro could see Mandamus succeeding as Council Chairman eventually. It would even be just, thought Amadiro, in a rare burst of selflessness.

On this particular evening, in consequence, he did not as much as expend a thought upon Vasilia. He left the Institute with a small squad of robots seeing him safe to his ground-car. That ground-car, driven by one robot and with two more in the back seat with him, passed quietly through a twilit and chilly rain, and brought him to his establishment where two more robots ushered him indoors. And all this time he did not think of Vasilia.

To find her sitting in his living room, then, before the hyperwave set, watching an intricate robot-ballet, with several of Amadiro's robots in their niches, and two of her own robots behind her chair, struck him at first not so much with the anger of violated privacy, but with pure surprise.

It took some time for him to control his breathing well enough to be able to speak, and, by then, the anger came, and he said, harshly, 'What are you doing here? How did you get in?'

Vasilia was calm enough. Amadiro's appearance was, after all, entirely expected. 'What I'm doing here,' she said, 'is waiting to see you. Getting in was not difficult. Your robots know my appearance very well, and they know my standing at the Institute. Why shouldn't they allow me to enter if I assure them I have an appointment with you?'

'Which you haven't. You have violated my privacy.'

'Not really. There's a limit to how much trust you can squeeze out of someone else's robots. Look at them. They have never once taken their eyes from me. If I had wanted to disturb your belongings, look through your papers, take advantage of your absence in any way, I assure you I could not have. My two robots are no match against them.'

'Do you know,' said Amadiro bitterly, 'that you have acted in a thoroughly un-Spacer fashion? You are despicable, and I will not forget this.'

Vasilia seemed to blanch slightly at the adjectives. She said, in a low, hard voice, 'I hope you don't forget this, Kelden, for I've done what I've done for *you*, and if I reacted as I should to your foul mouth, I would leave now and let you continue for the rest of your life to be the defeated man you have been for twenty decades.'

'I will not remain a defeated man whatever you do.'

Vasilia said, 'You sound as though you believe that, but, you see, you do not know what I know, and I can tell you that, without my intervention, you will remain defeated. I don't care what scheme you have in mind. I don't care what this thin-lipped, acid-faced Mandamus has cooked up for you – '

'Why do you mention him?' said Amadiro, quickly.

'Because I wish to,' said Vasilia, with a touch of contempt. 'Whatever he has done, or thinks he is doing – and don't be frightened for I haven't any idea what that might be – it won't work. I may not know anything else about it, but I do know it won't work.'

'You're babbling idiocies,' said Amadiro.

'You had better listen to these idiocies, Kelden, if you don't want everything to fall into ruin. Not just you, but possibly the Spacer worlds, one and all. Still, you may not want to listen to me. It's your choice. Which, then, is it to be?'

'Why should I listen to you? What possible reason is there for me to listen to you?'

'For one thing, I told you the Solarians were preparing to leave their world. If you had listened to me then, you would not have been caught so by surprise when they did.'

'The Solarian crisis will yet turn to our advantage.'

'No, it will not,' said Vasilia. 'You may think it will, but it won't. It will destroy you, no matter what you are doing to meet the emergency, unless you are willing to let me have my say.'

Amadiro's lips were white and were trembling slightly. The two centuries of defeat Vasilia had mentioned had had their effect upon him and the Solarian crisis had not helped, so he lacked the inner strength to order his robots to see her out, as he should have. He said sullenly, 'Well, then, put it in brief.'

'You would not believe what I have to say if I did, so let me do it my own way. You can stop me at any time, but then you will destroy the Spacer worlds. Of course, they will last my time and it won't be I who will go down in history – *Settler* history, by the way – as the greatest failure on record. Shall I speak?'

Amadiro folded into a chair. 'Speak, then, and when you are through – leave.'

'I intend to, Kelden, unless, of course, you ask me, *very* politely, to stay and help you. Shall I start?'

Amadiro said nothing, and Vasilia began, 'I told you that during my stay on Solaria, I became aware of some very peculiar positronic pathway patterns they had designed; pathways that struck me, very forcefully, as representing attempts at producing telepathic robots. Now why should I have thought that?'

Amadiro said, bitterly, 'I cannot tell what pathological drives may power your thinking.'

Vasilia brushed that aside with a grimace. 'Thank you, Kelden. I've spent some months thinking about that, since I was acute enough to think the matter involved not pathology, but some subliminal memory. My mind went back to my childhood when Fastolfe, whom I then considered my father, in one of his generous moods – he would experiment now and then with generous moods, you understand – gave me a robot of my own.'

'Giskard again?' muttered Amadiro, with impatience.

'Yes, Giskard. Giskard, always. I was in my teen-age years and I already had the instinct of a roboticist, or, I should say, I was born with the instinct. I had as yet very little mathematics, but I had a grasp of pattern. With the passing of scores of decades, my knowledge of mathematics steadily improved, but I don't think I have advanced very far in my feeling for patterns. My father would say, "Little Vas" (he also experimented in loving diminutives to see how that would affect me) "you have a genius for patterns." I think I did –'

Amadiro said, 'Spare me. I'll concede your genius. Meanwhile, I have not yet had my dinner, do you know that?'

'Well,' said Vasilia, sharply, 'order your dinner and invite me to join you.'

Amadiro, frowning, raised his arm perfunctorily and

made a quick sign. The quiet motion of robots at work made itself evident at once.

Vasilia said, 'I would play with pathway-patterns for Giskard. I would come to Fastolfe – my father, as I then thought of him – and I would show him a pattern. He might shake his head and laugh and say, "If you add that to poor Giskard's brain, he will no longer be able to talk, and he will be in a great deal of pain." I remember asking if Giskard could really feel pain, and my father said, "We don't know what he would *feel*, but he would *act* as we would act if we were in a great deal of pain, so we might as well say he would feel pain."

'Or else I would take one of my patterns to him, and he would smile indulgently and say, "Well, that won't hurt him, Little Vas, and it might be interesting to try."

'And I would, and sometimes I would take it out again, and sometimes I would leave it. I was not simply fiddling with Giskard for the sadistic joy of it, as I imagine I might have been tempted to do if I were someone other than myself. The fact is I was very fond of Giskard and I had no desire to harm him. When it seemed to me that one of my improvements – I always thought of them as improvements – made Giskard speak more freely, or react more quickly or more interestingly, and seemed to do no harm, I would let it stay.

'And then one day – '

A robot standing at Amadiro's elbow would not have dared to interrupt a guest unless a true emergency existed, but Amadiro had no difficulty in understanding the significance of the waiting. He said, 'Is dinner ready?'

'Yes, sir,' said the robot.

Amadiro gestured rather impatiently in Vasilia's direction. 'You are invited to have dinner with me.'

They walked into Amadiro's dining room, which Vasilia had never entered before. Amadiro was, after all, a private person and was notorious for his neglect of the social amenities. He had been told more than once that he would succeed better in politics if he entertained in his home, and he had always smiled politely and said, 'Too high a price.'

It was perhaps because of his failure to entertain, thought Vasilia, that there was no sign of originality or creativity in the furnishings. Nothing could be plainer than the table, the dishes and the cutlery. As for the walls, they were merely flat-coloured vertical planes. Put together, it rather dampened one's appetite, she thought.

The soup they began with was as plain as the furniture, a clear bouillon, and Vasilia began to dispose of it without enthusiasm.

Amadiro said, 'My dear Vasilia, you see I am being patient. I have no objection to having you write your autobiography, if you wish. But is it really your plan to recite several chapters of it to me? If it is, I must tell you, bluntly, that I'm not really interested.'

Vasilia said, 'You will become extremely interested in just a little while. Still, if you're really enamoured of failure, and want to continue to achieve nothing you wish to achieve, simply say so. I will then eat in silence and leave. Is that what you wish?'

Amadiro sighed. 'Well, go on, Vasilia.'

Vasilia said, 'And then, one day, I came up with a pattern more elaborate, more pleasant, and more enticing than I had ever seen before, or, in all truth, than I have ever seen since. I would have loved to show it to my father, but he was away at some meeting or other on one of the other worlds.

'I didn't know when he'd be back, and I put aside my pattern, but each day I would look at it with more interest and more fascination. Finally, I could wait no longer. I simply could not. It seemed so beautiful that I thought it ludicrous to suppose it could do harm. I was only an infant in my second decade, and had not yet completely outgrown irresponsibility, so I modified Giskard's brain by incorporating the pattern into it.

'And it did no harm. That was immediately obvious. He responded to me with perfect ease and, it seemed to me, was far quicker in understanding, and much more intelligent than he had been. I found him far more fascinating and lovable than before.

'I was delighted, and yet I was nervous, too. What I had done – modifying Giskard without clearing it with Fastolfe – was strictly against the rules Fastolfe had set for me, and I knew that well. Yet clearly, I was not going to undo what I had done. When I had modified Giskard's brain, I excused it to myself by saying that it would only be for a little while, and that then I would neutralize the modification. Once the modification had been made, however, it became quite clear to me that I would *not* neutralize it. I was simply *not* going to do that. In fact, I never modified Giskard again, for fear of disturbing what I had just done.

'Nor did I ever tell Fastolfe what I had done. I destroyed all record of the marvellous pattern I had devised, and Fastolfe never found out that Giskard had been modified without his knowledge. Never!

'And then we broke up, Fastolfe and I, and Fastolfe would not give up Giskard. I screamed that he was mine and that I loved him, but Fastolfe's kindly benevolence, of which he made such a parade all his life – that business of loving all things, great and small – was never allowed to stand in the way of his own desires. I received other robots I cared nothing for, but he kept Giskard for himself.

'And when he died, he left Giskard to the Solarian woman – a last bitter slap at me.'

Amadiro had only managed to get halfway through the salmon mousse. 'If all this is intended to advance your case of having Giskard's ownership transferred from the Solarian woman to yourself, it won't help. I have already explained to you why I cannot set aside Fastolfe's will.'

'There's something more to it than that, Kelden,' said Vasilia. 'A great deal more. Infinitely more. Do you want me to stop now?'

Amadiro stretched his lips into a rueful grin. 'Having listened to so much of this, I will play the madman, and listen to more.'

'You would play the madman, if you did not, for I now come to the point. I have never stopped thinking of Giskard, and of the cruelty and injustice of my having been deprived of him, but, somehow, I never thought of that pattern with which I had modified him with no one's knowledge but my own. I am quite certain I could not have reproduced that pattern if I had tried, and from what I can now remember it was like nothing else I have ever seen in robotics until – until I saw, briefly, something like that pattern during my stay on Solaria.

'The Solarian pattern seemed familiar to me, but I didn't know why. It took some weeks of intense thought before I dredged out of some well-hidden part of my unconscious mind, the slippery thought of that pattern I had dreamed out of nothing twenty-five decades ago.

'Even though I can't remember my pattern exactly, I know that the Solarian pattern was a whiff of it and no more. It was just the barest suggestion of something I had captured in miraculously complex symmetry. But I looked at the Solarian pattern with the experience I had gained in twenty-five decades of deep immersion in robotics theory, and it suggested telepathy to me. If that simple, scarcely interesting pattern suggested it, what must my original have meant – the thing I invented as a child, and have never recaptured since?'

Amadiro said, 'You keep saying you're coming to the

point, Vasilia. Would I be completely unreasonable if I asked you to stop moaning and reminiscing, and simply set out that point in a simple, declarative sentence?'

Vasilia said, 'Gladly. What I am telling you, Kelden, is that, without my ever knowing it, I converted Giskard into a telepathic robot, and that he has been that ever since.'

54.

Amadiro looked at Vasilia for a long time, and because the story seemed to have come to an end, he returned to the salmon mousse and ate some of it thoughtfully.

He then said, 'Impossible! Do you take me for an idiot?'

'I take you for a failure,' said Vasilia. 'I don't say Giskard can read conversations in minds; that he can transmit and receive words or ideas. Perhaps that *is* impossible, even in theory. But I am quite certain he can detect emotions and the general set of mental activity, and perhaps can even modify it.'

Amadiro shook his head violently. 'Impossible!'

'Impossible? Think a while. Twenty decades ago, you had almost achieved your aims. Fastolfe was at your mercy; Chairman Horder was your ally. What happened? Why did everything go wrong?'

'The Earthman – ' Amadiro began, choking at the memory.

'The Earthman,' Vasilia mimicked. 'The Earthman. Or was it the Solarian woman? It was neither! Neither! It was Giskard, who was there all the time. Sensing. Adjusting.'

'Why should he be interested? He is a robot.'

'A robot loyal to his master, to Fastolfe. By First Law, he had to see to it that Fastolfe came to no harm and, being telepathic, he could not interpret that as signifying physical harm only. He knew that if Fastolfe could not have his way, could not encourage the Settlement of the habitable worlds of the Galaxy, he would undergo profound disappointment – and that would be "harm" in Giskard's telepathic Universe. He could not let that happen, and he intervened to keep it from happening.'

'No, no, no,' said Amadiro in disgust. 'You want that to be so, out of some wild, romantic longing, but that doesn't make it so. I remember too well what happened. It was the Earthman. It needs no telepathic robot to explain the events.'

'And what has happened since, Kelden?' demanded Vasilia. 'In twenty decades have you ever managed to win out over Fastolfe? With all the facts in your favour, with the obvious bankruptcy of Fastolfe's policy, have you ever been able to dispose of a majority in the Council? Have you ever been able to sway the Chairman to the point where you could possess real power?

'How do you explain that, Kelden? In all those twenty decades, the Earthman has not been on Aurora. He has been dead for over sixteen decades, his miserably short life running out in eight decades. Yet you continue to fail – you have an unbroken record of failure. Even now that Fastolfe is dead, have you managed to profit completely from the broken pieces of his coalition, or do you find that success still seems to elude you?

'What is it that remains? The Earthman is gone. Fastolfe is gone. It is Giskard who has worked against you in all this time, and Giskard remains. He is as loyal now to the Solarian woman as he was to Fastolfe, and the Solarian woman has no cause to love you, I think.'

Amadiro's face twisted into a mask of anger and frustration. 'It's not so. None of this is so. You're imagining things.'

Vasilia remained quite cool. 'No, I'm not. I'm explaining things. I've explained things you haven't been able to explain. Or have you an alternative explanation? And I can give you the cure. Transfer ownership of Giskard from the Solarian woman to me and, quite suddenly, events will begin to twist themselves to your benefit.'

'No,' said Amadiro. 'They are moving to my benefit already.'

'You may think so, but they won't, as long as Giskard is working against you. No matter how close you come to winning; no matter how sure of victory you become, it will all melt away as long as you don't have Giskard on your side. That happened twenty decades ago; it will happen now.'

Amadiro's face suddenly cleared. He said, 'Well, come to think of it, though I don't have Giskard and neither do you, it doesn't matter, for I can show you that Giskard is not telepathic. If Giskard were telepathic, as you say; if he had the ability to order affairs to his own liking, or to the liking of the human being who is his owner; then why would he have allowed the Solarian woman to be taken to what will probably be her death?'

'Her death? What are you talking about, Kelden?'

'Are you aware, Vasilia, that two Settler ships have been destroyed on Solaria? Or have you been doing nothing lately but dreaming of patterns and of the brave days of childhood when you were modifying your pet robot?'

'Sarcasm doesn't become you, Kelden. I have heard about the Settler ships on the news. What of them?'

'A third Settler ship is going out to investigate. It may be destroyed, too.'

'Possibly. On the other hand, it would take precautions.'

'It did. It demanded and received the Solarian woman, feeling that she knows the planet well enough to enable them to avoid destruction.'

Vasilia said, 'That's scarcely likely since she hasn't been there in over twenty decades.'

'Right! The chances are, then, that she'll die with them. It would mean nothing to me, personally. I would be delighted to have her dead, and, I think, so would you. And, putting that to one side, it would give us good grounds for complaint to the Settler worlds, and it would make it difficult for them to argue that the destruction of the ships is a deliberate action on the part of Aurora. Would we destroy one of our own? Now the question is, Vasilia, why would Giskard, if he had the powers you claim he has, and the loyalties, allow the Solarian woman to volunteer to be taken to what is very likely to be her death?'

Vasilia was taken aback. 'Did she go of her own free will?'

'Absolutely. She was perfectly willing. It would have been politically impossible to force her to do so against her will.'

'But I don't understand – '

'There is nothing to understand except that Giskard is merely a robot.'

For a moment, Vasilia froze in her seat, one hand to her chin. Then she said, slowly, 'They don't allow robots on Settler worlds, or on Settler ships. That means she went alone. Without robots.'

'Well, no, of course not. They had to accept personal robots if they expected to get her willingly. They took along that man-mimic robot, Daneel, and the other was – ' He paused, and brought out the word with a hiss, 'Giskard. Who else? So this miracle robot of your fantasy goes to his destruction as well. He could no more – '

His voice faded away. Vasilia was on her feet, eyes blazing, face suffused with colour.

'You mean *Giskard* went? He's off this world and on a Settler ship? Kelden, you may have ruined us all!'

55.

Neither finished the meal.

Vasilia walked hastily out of the dining room and disappeared into the Personal. Amadiro, struggling to remain coldly logical, shouted to her through the closed door, perfectly aware that it damaged his dignity to do so.

He called out, 'It's all the stronger an indication that Giskard is no more than a robot. Why should he be willing to go to Solaria to face destruction with his owner?'

Eventually, the sound of running water and splashing ceased, and Vasilia emerged with her face freshly washed, and almost frozen in its grip on calmness.

She said, 'You really don't understand, do you? You amaze me, Kelden. Think it through. Giskard can never be in danger as long as he can influence human minds, can he? Nor can the Solarian woman, as long as Giskard devotes himself to her. The Settler who carried off the Solarian woman must have found out, on interviewing her, that she had not been on Solaria in twenty decades, so he can't really have continued to believe, after all, that she could do him much good. With her he took Giskard but he didn't know that Giskard could do him good, either. Or could he have known that?'

She thought a while and then said, slowly, 'No, there is no way he could have known it. If, in more than twenty decades, no one has penetrated the fact that Giskard has mental abilities, then Giskard is clearly interested in having no one guess it, and if that is so, then no one can possibly have guessed it.'

Amadiro said, spitefully, 'You claim to have worked it out.'

Vasilia said, 'I had special knowledge, Kelden, and even

so it was not till now that I saw the obvious, and then only because of the hint on Solaria. Giskard must have darkened my mind in that respect, too, or I would have seen it long ago. I wonder if Fastolfe knew – '

'How much easier,' said Amadiro, restlessly, 'to accept the simple fact that Giskard is simply a robot.'

'You will walk the easy road to ruin, Kelden, but I don't think I will let you do that, no matter how much you want to. What it amounts to is that the Settler came for the Solarian woman and took her along even though he discovered she would be of little, if any, use to him. And the Solarian woman volunteered to go even though she must dread being on a Settler ship along with diseased barbarians, and even though her destruction on Solaria must have seemed to her a very likely consequence.

'It seems to me, then, that this is all the work of Giskard, who forced the Settler to continue to demand the Solarian woman against reason, and forced the Solarian woman to accede to the request against reason.'

Amadiro said, 'But why? May I ask that simple question? Why?'

'I suppose, Kelden, that Giskard felt it was important to get away from Aurora. Could he have guessed that I was on the point of learning his secret? If so, he may well have been uncertain of his present ability to tamper with me. I am, after all, a skilled roboticist. Besides, he would remember that he was once mine and a robot does not easily ignore the demands of loyalty. The only way, perhaps, that he felt he could keep the Solarian woman secure was to move himself away from my influence.'

She looked up at Amadiro and said, firmly, 'Kelden, we must get him back. We can't let him work at promoting the Settler cause in the safe haven of a Settler world. He did enough damage right here among us. We must get him back, and you must make me his legal owner. I can handle him, I assure you, and make him work for us. Remember! I am the *only* one who can handle him.'

Amadiro said, 'I do not see any reason to worry. In the very likely case that he is a mere robot, he will be destroyed on Solaria, and we will be rid of both him and the Solarian woman. In the unlikely case that he is what you say he is, he won't be destroyed on Solaria, but then he will have to return to Aurora. After all, the Solarian woman, though she is not an Auroran by birth, has lived on Aurora far too long to be able to face life among the barbarians, and when she insists on returning to civilization, Giskard will have no alternative but to return with her.'

Vasilia said, 'After all this, Kelden, you still don't understand Giskard's abilities. If he feels it important to remain away from Aurora, he can easily adjust the Solarian woman's emotions in such a way as to make her stand life on a Settler world just as he made her willing to board a Settler ship.'

'Well, then, if necessary, we can simply escort that Settler ship, with the Solarian woman, and with Giskard, back to Aurora.'

'How do you propose to do that?'

'It can be done. We are *not* fools here on Aurora, for all that it seems clearly your opinion that you yourself are the only rational person on the planet. The Settler ship is going to Solaria to investigate the destruction of the two earlier ships, but I hope you don't think we intend to depend upon its good offices, or even upon those of the Solarian woman. We are sending two of our warships to Solaria, and we do not expect that *they* will have trouble. If there are Solarians still on the planet, they may be able to destroy primitive Settler ships, but they won't be able to touch an Auroran vessel of war. If, then, the Settler ship, through some magic on the part of Giskard – '

'Not magic,' interrupted Vasilia, tartly. 'Mental influence.'

'If, then, the Settler ship, for whatever reason, should be able to rise from the surface of Solaria, our ships will cut them off and politely ask for the delivery of the Solarian woman and her robots. Failing that, they will insist the Settler ship accompany our ships to Aurora. There will be no hostility about it. Our ships will merely be escorting an Auroran national to her home world. Once the Solarian woman and her two robots disembark on Aurora, the Settler ship will then be able to proceed at will to its own destination.'

Vasilia nodded wearily at this. 'It sounds good, Kelden, but do you know what I suspect will happen?'

'What, Vasilia?'

'It is my opinion that the Settler ship will rise from the surface of Solaria, but that our warships won't. Whatever is on Solaria can be countered by Giskard, but, I fear, by nothing else.'

'If *that* happens,' said Amadiro, with a grim smile, 'then I'll admit there may be something, after all, to your fantasy. But it won't happen.'

56.

The next morning, Vasilia's chief personal robot, delicately designed to appear female, came to Vasilia's bedside. Vasilia stirred and, without opening her eyes, said, 'What is it, Nadila?' (There was no need to open her eyes. In many decades, no one had ever approached her bedside but Nadila.)

Nadila said, softly, 'Madam, you are desired at the Institute by Dr Amadiro.'

Vasilia's eyes flew open. 'What time is it?'

'It is 5:17, madam.'

'Before sunrise?' Vasilia was indignant.

'Yes, madam.'

'When does he want me?'

'Now, madam.'

'Why?'

'His robots have not informed us, madam, but they say it is important.'

Vasilia threw aside the bedsheets. 'I will have breakfast first, Nadila, and a shower before that. Inform Amadiro's robots to take visitors' niches and wait. If they urge speed, remind them they are in *my* establishment.'

Vasilia, annoyed, did not hasten unduly. If anything, her toilette was more painstaking than usual, and her breakfast more leisurely. (She was not ordinarily one to spend much time over either.) The news, which she watched, gave no indication of anything that might explain Amadiro's call.

By the time the ground-car (containing herself and four robots – two of Amadiro's and two of her own) had brought her to the Institute the sun was making its appearance over the horizon.

Amadiro looked up, and said, 'You are finally here, then.' The walls of his office were still glowing, though their light was no longer needed.

'I'm sorry,' said Vasilia, stiffly. 'I quite realize that sunrise is a terribly late hour at which to begin work.'

'No games, Vasilia, please. Very soon I will have to be at the Council Chamber. The Chairman has been up longer than I have. Vasilia, I apologize, quite humbly, for doubting you.'

'The Settler ship has lifted off safely, then.'

'Yes. And one of *our* ships has been destroyed, as you predicted. The fact has not been publicized yet, but the news will leak out eventually, of course.'

Vasilia's eyes widened. She had predicted this outcome with a bit more in the way of outward confidence than she had felt, but clearly this was not the time to say so. What she did say was, 'Then you accept the fact that Giskard has extraordinary powers.'

Cautiously, Amadiro said, 'I don't consider the matter to be mathematically proven, but I'm willing to accept it pending further information. What I want to know is what we ought to do next. The Council knows nothing of Giskard, and I do not propose to tell them.'

'I'm glad your thinking is clear to that extent, Kelden.'

'But you're the one who understands Giskard, and you can best tell what ought to be done. What do I tell the Council, then, and how do I explain the action without giving away the whole truth?'

'It depends. Now that the Settler ship has left Solaria, where is it going? Can we tell? After all, if it is returning now to Aurora, we need do nothing but prepare for its arrival.'

'It is not coming to Aurora,' said Amadiro, emphatically. 'You were right there, too, it seems. Giskard – assuming him to be running the show – seems determined to stay away. We have intercepted the ship's messages to its own world. Encoded, of course, but there isn't a Settler code we haven't broken –'

'I suspect they've broken ours, too. I wonder why everyone won't agree to send messages in the clear and save a lot of trouble.'

Amadiro shrugged it away. 'Never mind that. The point is that the Settler ship is going back to its own planet.'

'With the Solarian woman and the robots?'

'Of course.'

'You're sure of that? They haven't been left on Solaria?'

'We're sure of that,' said Amadiro, impatiently. 'Apparently, the Solarian woman was responsible for their getting off the surface.'

'She? In what way?'

'We don't yet know.'

Vasilia said, 'It had to be Giskard. He made it appear to be the Solarian woman.'

'And what do we now do?'

'We must get Giskard back.'

'Yes, but I can't very well persuade the Council to risk an interstellar crisis over the return of a robot.'

'You don't, Kelden. You ask for the return of the Solarian woman, something we certainly have a right to request. And do you think for one moment she would return without her robots? Or that Giskard will allow the Solarian woman to return without him? Or that the Settler world would want to keep the robots, if the Solarian woman returns? Ask for *her*. Firmly. She's an Auroran citizen, lent out for a job on Solaria, which is done, and she must now be returned forthwith. Make it belligerent, as though it were a threat of war.'

'We can't risk war, Vasilia.'

'You won't risk it. Giskard can't take an action that might lead directly to war. If the Settler leaders resist, and become belligerent in their return, Giskard will perforce make the necessary modifications in the attitude of the Settler leaders so as to have the Solarian woman returned peaceably to Aurora. And he himself will, of course, have to return with her.'

Amadiro said, drearily, 'And once he's back, he will alter *us*, I suppose, and we will forget his powers, and disregard him, and he will still be able to follow his own plan whatever it is.'

Vasilia leaned her head back and laughed. 'Not a chance. I *know* Giskard, you see, and I can handle him. Just bring him back and persuade the Council to disregard Fastolfe's will – it can be done and you can do it – and to assign Giskard to me. He will then be working for us; Aurora will

rule the Galaxy; you will spend the remaining decades of
your life as Chairman of the Council and I will succeed
you as Head of the Robotics Institute.'

'Are you sure it will work out that way?'

'Absolutely. Just send the message and make it strong,
and I will guarantee all the rest; victory for the Spacers
and ourselves; defeat for Earth and the Settlers.'

14

The Duel

57.

Gladia watched Aurora's globe on the screen. Its cloud cover seemed caught in mid-swirl along the thick crescent that was shining in the light of its sun.

'Surely, we're not that close,' she said.

D. G. smiled. 'By no means. We're seeing it through rather good lenses. It's still several days away, counting the spiral approach. If we ever get an anti-gravitic drive, which the physicists keep dreaming about, but seem helpless to bring about, spaceflight will become really simple and fast. As it is, our Jumps can only deliver us safely to a rather goodish distance from a planetary mass.'

'It's odd,' said Gladia, thoughtfully.

'What is, madam?'

'When we went to Solaria, I thought to myself, "I'm going home," but when I landed I found that I wasn't home at all. Now we're going to Aurora, and I thought to myself, "*Now* I'm going home," and yet – that world down there isn't home, either.'

'Where is home, then, madam?'

'I'm beginning to wonder. But why do you persist in calling me "madam"?'

D. G. looked surprised. 'Do you prefer "Lady Gladia", Lady Gladia?'

'That's also mock respect. Do you feel that way about me?'

'Mock respect? Certainly not. But how else does a Settler address a Spacer? I'm trying to be polite and to conform to your customs – to do what makes you feel comfortable.'

'But it doesn't make me feel comfortable. Just call me "Gladia". After all, I call you "D. G."'

'And that suits me fine, although in front of my officers and men, I would prefer to have you address me as "Captain", and I will call you "madam". Discipline must be maintained.'

'Yes, of course,' said Gladia, absently, staring at Aurora again. 'I have no home.'

She whirled towards D. G., 'Is it possible that you might take me to Earth, D. G.?'

'Possible,' said D. G., smiling. 'You might not want to go – Gladia.'

'I think I want to go,' said Gladia, 'unless I lose my courage.'

'Infection does exist,' said D. G., 'and that's what Spacers fear, isn't it?'

'Too much, perhaps. After all, I knew your ancestor and wasn't infected. I have been on this ship and have survived. Look, you're near me right now. I was even on your world, with thousands crowding near me. I think I've worked up a certain amount of resistance.'

'I must tell you, Gladia, that Earth is a thousand times as crowded as Baleyworld.'

'Even so,' said Gladia, her voice warming, 'I've changed my mind completely – about many things. I've told you there was nothing left to live for after twenty-three decades, and it turns out there *is*. What happened to me on Baleyworld – the talk I gave – the way it moved people – was something new, something I'd never imagined. It was like being born all over, starting again at the first decade. It seems to me, now, that even if Earth kills me, it would be worth it, for I would die young, and trying, and fighting death; not old, and weary, and welcoming it.'

'Well!' said D. G., lifting his arms in a gesture of mock-heroics. 'You sound like a hyperwave historical. Have you ever watched them on Aurora?'

'Of course. They're very popular.'

'Are you rehearsing for one, Gladia, or do you really mean what you say?'

Gladia laughed. 'I suppose I do sound rather silly, D. G., but the funny thing is that I *do* mean it – if I don't lose my courage.'

'In that case, we'll do it. We'll go to Earth. I don't think they'll consider you worth a war, especially if you report fully on events on Solaria, as they want you to, and if you give your word of honour as a Spacer woman – if you do things like that – to return.'

'But I won't.'

'But you may want to someday. And now, my lady – I mean, Gladia – it is always a pleasure to speak with you, but I'm always tempted to spend too much time at it, and I am certain I am needed in the control room. If I'm not, and they can do without me, then I'd rather they didn't find out.'

58.

'Was that your doing, Friend Giskard?'

'To what is it that you refer, Friend Daneel?'

'The Lady Gladia is anxious to go to Earth, and even perhaps not to return. That is a desire so antithetical to what a Spacer such as she would want that I cannot help suspect that you did something to her mind to make her feel so.'

Giskard said, 'I did not touch her. It is difficult enough to tamper with any human being within the cage of the Three Laws; to tamper with the mind of the particular

individual for whose safety one is directly responsible is
more difficult still.'

'Then why does she wish to go to Earth?'

'Her experiences on Baleyworld have changed her point
of view considerably. She has a mission – that of ensuring
peace in the Galaxy – and burns to work at it.'

'In that case, Friend Giskard, would it not be better to
do what you can to persuade the Captain, in your own
fashion, to go to Earth directly?'

'That would create difficulties. The Auroran authorities
are so insistent on the lady being returned to Aurora that
it would be better to do so, at least temporarily.'

'Yet it could be dangerous to do so,' said Daneel.

'Then you still think, Friend Daneel, that it is I whom
they want to retain, because they have learned of my
abilities?'

'I see no other reason for their insistence on the Lady
Gladia's return.'

Giskard said, 'Thinking like a man has its pitfalls, I see.
It becomes possible to suppose difficulties that cannot
exist. Even if someone on Aurora were to suspect the
existence of my abilities, it is with those abilities that I
would remove the suspicion. There is nothing to fear,
Friend Daneel.'

And Daneel said, reluctantly, 'As you say, Friend
Giskard.'

59.

Gladia looked about thoughtfully, sending off the robots
with a careless motion of her hand.

She looked at her hand, as she did so, almost as though
she were seeing it for the first time. It had been the hand
with which she had shaken the hand of each of the

crewmen of the ship before getting into the small tender that took her, and D. G., down to Aurora. She had promised to return, and they had cheered her, and Niss had bawled out, 'We won't leave without you, lady.'

The cheering had pleased her enormously. Her robots served her endlessly, loyally, patiently; but they never cheered her.

D. G., watching her curiously, said, 'Surely you are at home now, Gladia.'

'I am in my establishment,' she said, in a low voice. 'It has been my establishment since Dr Fastolfe assigned it to me twenty decades ago, and yet it feels strange to me.'

'It is strange to *me*,' said D. G. 'I'd feel rather lost staying here alone.' He looked about with a half-smile at the ornate furnishings and the elaborately decorated walls.

'You won't be alone, D. G.,' said Gladia. 'My household robots will be with you and they have full instructions. They will devote themselves to your comfort.'

'Will they understand my Settler accent?'

'If they fail to understand, they will ask you to repeat and you must then speak slowly and make gestures. They will prepare food for you, show you how to use the facilities in the guest rooms – and they will also keep a sharp eye on you to make sure that you do not act in an un-guestly manner. They will stop you, if necessary, but they will do so without hurting you.'

'I trust they won't consider me non-human.'

'As the overseer did? No, I guarantee you that, D. G., though your beard and accent may confuse them to the point where they will be a second or two slow in reacting.'

'And I suppose they'll protect me against intruders?'

'They will, but there won't be any intruders.'

'The Council may want to come and get me.'

'Then they will send robots, and mine will turn them away.'

'What if their robots overpower your robots?'

'That can't happen, D. G. An establishment is inviolate.'

'Come on, Gladia. Do you mean that nobody has ever — '

'Nobody has ever!' she replied, at once. 'You just stay here comfortably and my robots will take care of all your needs. If you want to get in touch with your ship, with Baleyworld, even with the Auroran Council, they will know exactly what to do. You won't have to lift a finger.'

D. G. sank down into the nearest chair, spread himself out over it and sighed deeply. 'How wise we are to allow no robots on the Settler worlds. Do you know how long it would take to corrupt me into idleness and sloth if I stayed in this kind of society? Five minutes at most. In fact, I'm corrupted already.' He yawned and stretched luxuriously. 'Would they mind if I sleep?'

'Of course they wouldn't. If you do, the robots will see to it that your surroundings are kept quiet and dark.'

Then D. G. straightened suddenly. 'What if you don't come back?'

'Why shouldn't I come back?'

'The Council seems to want you rather urgently.'

'They can't hold me. I'm a free Auroran citizen and I go where I please.'

'There are always emergencies when a government wishes to manufacture one, and in an emergency, rules can always be broken.'

'Nonsense. Giskard, am I going to be kept there?'

Giskard said, 'Madam Gladia, you will not be kept there. The Captain need not be concerned with respect to that.'

'There you are, D. G. And your Ancestor, the last time he saw me, told me I was always to trust Giskard.'

'Good! Excellent! Just the same, the reason I came down with you, Gladia, was to make sure I get you back. Remember that and tell it to your Dr Amadiro if you have to. If they try to keep you against your will, they will have to try to keep me as well, and my ship, which is in orbit, is fully capable of reacting to that.'

'No, please,' said Gladia, disturbed. 'Don't think of doing that. Aurora has ships as well, and I'm sure yours is under observation.'

'There's a difference, though, Gladia. I doubt very much that Aurora would want to go to war over you. Baleyworld, on the other hand, would be quite prepared to.'

'Surely not. I wouldn't want them to go to war on my account. And why should they, anyway? Because I was a friend of your Ancestor?'

'Not exactly. I don't think anyone can quite believe that you were that friend. Maybe your great-grandmother, not you. Even *I* don't believe it was you.'

'You *know* it was I.'

'Intellectually, yes. Emotionally, I find it impossible. That was twenty decades ago.'

Gladia shook her head. 'You have the short-lived view.'

'Maybe we all do, but it doesn't matter. What makes you important to Baleyworld is the speech you gave. You're a heroine and they will decide you must be presented at Earth. Nothing will be allowed to prevent that.'

Gladia said, a trifle alarmed, 'Presented at Earth? With full ceremony?'

'The fullest.'

'Why should that be thought so important as to be worth a war?'

'I'm not sure I can explain that to a Spacer. Earth is a special world. Earth is a – holy world. It's the only real world. It's where human beings came into being, and it's the only world in which they evolved and developed and lived against a full background of life. We have trees on Baleyworld, and insects – but on Earth they have a wild riot of trees and insects that none of us ever see except on

Earth. Ours worlds are imitations, pale imitations. They don't exist and can't exist except for the intellectual, cultural, and spiritual strength they draw from Earth.'

Gladia said, 'This is quite opposed to the opinion of Earth held by Spacers. When we refer to Earth, which we seldom do, it is as a world that is barbarous and in decay.'

D. G. flushed. 'That is why the Spacer worlds have been growing steadily weaker. As I said before, you are like plants that have pulled themselves loose from their roots; like animals that have cut out their hearts.'

Gladia said, 'Well, I look forward to seeing Earth for myself, but I will have to go now. Please treat this as your own establishment till I return.' She walked briskly towards the door, stopped, then turned. 'There are no alcoholic drinks in this establishment, or anywhere on Aurora, no tobacco, no alkaloidal stimulants, nothing of any artificial kinds of – of whatever you may be used to.'

D. G. grinned sourly. 'We Settlers are aware of that. Very puritanical, you people.'

'Not puritanical at all,' said Gladia, frowning. 'Thirty to forty decades of life must be paid for, and that's one of the ways. You don't suppose we do it by magic, do you?'

'Well, I'll make do on healthful fruit juices and sanitized near-coffee, and I'll smell flowers.'

'You'll find an ample supply of such things,' said Gladia, coldly, 'and when you get back to your ship, I'm sure you can compensate for any withdrawal symptoms you will now suffer.'

'I will suffer only from *your* withdrawal, my lady,' said D. G., gravely.

Gladia found herself forced to smile. 'You're an incorrigible liar, my Captain. I'll be back. Daneel. Giskard.'

60.

Gladia sat stiffly in Amadiro's office. In many decades, she had seen Amadiro only in the distance, or on a viewing screen, and on such occasions, she had made it a practice to turn away. She remembered him only as Fastolfe's great enemy and now that she found herself, for the first time, in the same room with him – in face-to-face confrontation – she had to freeze her face into expressionlessness, in order not to allow hate to peep through.

Although she and Amadiro were the only ones in the room as palpable human beings, there were at least a dozen high officials – the Chairman himself among them – who were present by way of sealed-beam holovision. Gladia had recognized the Chairman and some of the others, but not all.

It was rather a grisly experience. It seemed so like the viewing that was universal on Solaria, and to which she had been so accustomed as a girl – and which she recalled with such distaste.

She made an effort to speak clearly, undramatically, and concisely. When asked a question, she was as brief as was consistent with clarity, and as non-committal as was consistent with courtesy.

The Chairman listened impassively and the others took their cue from him. He was clearly elderly – Chairmen always were, somehow, for it was usually late in life that they attained the position. He had a long face, a still-thick head of hair and prominent eyebrows. His voice was mellifluous, but in no way friendly.

He said, when Gladia was done, 'It is your suggestion, then, that the Solarians had re-defined "human beings" in a narrow sense that restricted it to Solarians?'

'I do not suggest anything, Mr Chairman. It is merely that no one has been able to think of another explanation that would account for the events.'

'Are you aware, Madam Gladia, that in all the history of robotic science, no robot has ever been designed with a narrowed definition of "human being"?'

'I am not a roboticist, Mr Chairman, and I know nothing of the mathematics of positronic pathways. Since you say it has never been done, I, of course accept that. I cannot say, of my own knowledge, however, whether the fact that it has never been done means that it can never be done in the future.'

Her eyes had never looked as wide and innocent as they did now, and the Chairman flushed and said, 'It is not theoretically impossible to narrow the definition, but it is unthinkable.'

Gladia said, with a downcast glance at her hands, which were loosely clasped in her lap, 'People can think such peculiar things, sometimes.'

The Chairman changed the subject and said, 'An Auroran ship was destroyed. How do you account for that?'

'I was not present at the site of the incident, Mr Chairman. I have no idea what happened, so I can't account for it.'

'You were on Solaria and you were born on the planet. Given your recent experience and early background, what would you say happened?' The Chairman showed signs of a badly strained patience.

'If I must guess,' said Gladia, 'I should say that our warship was exploded by the use of a portable nuclear intensifier similar to the one that was almost used on the Settler ship.'

'Does it not strike you, however, that the two cases are different? In one, a Settler ship invaded Solaria to confiscate Solarian robots; in the other, an Auroran vessel came to Solaria to help protect a sister planet.'

'I can only suppose, Mr Chairman, that the overseers – the humanoid robots left to guard the planet – were insufficiently well-instructed to know the difference.'

The Chairman looked offended. 'It is inconceivable that they would not be instructed in the difference between Settlers and fellow-Spacers.'

'If you say so, Mr Chairman. Nevertheless, if the only definition of a human being is someone with the physical appearance of a human being, together with the ability to speak in Solarian fashion – as it seemed to us, who were on the spot, that it must be – then Aurorans, who do not speak in Solarian fashion, might not fall under the heading of human beings, where the overseers were concerned.'

'Then you are saying that the Solarians defined their fellow-Spacers as non-human and subjected them to destruction.'

'I present it merely as a possibility because I can't think of any other way to explain the destruction of an Auroran warship. More experienced people may be able to present alternative explanations, to be sure.' Again, that innocent, almost blank, look.

The Chairman said, 'Are you planning to return to Solaria, Madam Gladia?'

'No, Mr Chairman, I have no such plan.'

'Have you been requested to do so by your Settler friend in order to clear the planet of its overseers?'

Slowly, Gladia shook her head. 'I have not been requested to do this. Had I been, I would have refused. Nor did I go to Solaria, to begin with, for any reason but that of fulfilling my duty to Aurora. I was requested to go to Solaria by Dr Levular Mandamus of the Robotics Institute, working under Dr Kelden Amadiro. I was requested to go so that, on my return, I might report on events – as I have just done. The request had, to my ears and understanding, the flavour of an order and I took the order,' she glanced briefly in Amadiro's direction, 'as coming from Dr Amadiro himself.'

Amadiro made no visible response to that.

The Chairman said, 'What are your plans for the future, then?'

Gladia waited a heart-beat or two, then decided she might as well confront the situation boldly.

'It is my intention, Mr Chairman,' said Gladia, speaking very clearly, 'to visit Earth.'

'Earth? Why should you wish to visit Earth?'

'It may be important, Mr Chairman, for Auroran authorities to know what is taking place on Earth. Since I have been invited by the Baleyworld authorities to visit Earth and since Captain Baley stands ready to take me there, it would be an opportunity to bring back a report on events – as I have now reported on events taking place on Solaria and on Baleyworld.'

Well, then, thought Gladia, will he violate custom and, in effect, imprison me on Aurora? If so, there had to be ways of challenging the decision.

Gladia felt her tension rising and she cast a quick glance in the direction of Daneel, who, of course, seemed totally impassive.

However, the Chairman, looking sour, said, 'In that respect, Madam Gladia, you have the right of an Auroran to do as you wish – but it will be on your own responsibility. No one is requesting this of you, as some requested, according to you, your visit to Solaria. For that reason I must warn you that Aurora will not feel bound to help you in case of any misadventure.'

'I understand that, sir.'

The Chairman said, brusquely, 'There will be much to discuss on the matter later on, Amadiro. I will be in touch with you.'

The images blanked out, and Gladia found herself and her robots suddenly alone with Amadiro and his robots.

61.

Gladia rose and said stiffly, carefully refusing to look directly at Amadiro as she did so, 'The meeting, I presume, is over, so I will now leave.'

'Yes, of course, but I have a question or two, which I hope you don't mind my asking.' His tall figure seemed overwhelming as he rose, and he smiled and addressed her in all courtesy as though friendliness were long established between them. 'Let me escort you, Lady Gladia. So you are going to Earth?'

'Yes. The Chairman raised no objections and an Auroran citizen may freely travel through the Galaxy in time of peace. And pardon me, but my robots, and yours, if necessary, will be sufficient escort.'

'As you say, my lady.' A robot held the door open for them. 'I assume you will take robots with you when you go to Earth?'

'There's no question as to that.'

'Which robots, madam, if I may ask?'

'These two. The two robots I have with me.' Her shoes made a firm clicking sound as she walked rapidly along the corridor, her back to Amadiro, making no effort to see to it that he heard her.

'Is that wise, my lady? They are advanced robots, unusual products of the great Dr Fastolfe. You will be surrounded by barbarian Earthmen, who may covet them.'

'Should they covet them, they nevertheless wouldn't get them.'

'Don't underestimate the danger, nor overestimate robotic protection. You will be in one of their Cities surrounded by tens of millions of these Earthmen, and robots may not harm human beings. Indeed, the more advanced a robot, the more sensitive it is to the nuances of the Three Laws and the less likely it is to take any action that will harm a human being in any way. Isn't that so, Daneel?'

'Yes, Dr Amadiro,' said Daneel.

'Giskard, I imagine, agrees with you.'

'I do,' said Giskard.

'You see, my lady? Here on Aurora, in a non-violent society your robots can protect you against others. On Earth – mad, decadent, barbarous – there will be no way two robots can protect you or themselves. We would not want you to be deprived. Nor, to place it on a more selfish basis, would we of the Institute and the Government care to see advanced robots in the hands of the barbarians. Would it not be better to take robots of a more ordinary type that the Earthpeople would ignore? You can take any number in that case. A dozen, if you wish.'

Gladia said, 'Dr Amadiro, I took these two robots on a Settler ship and visited a Settler world. No one made a move to appropriate them.'

'The Settlers don't use robots and claim to disapprove of them. On Earth itself, they still use robots.'

Daneel said, 'If I may interpose, Dr Amadiro – it is my understanding that robots are being phased out on Earth. There are very few in the Cities. Almost all robots on Earth are now used in agricultural or mining operations. For the rest, non-robotic automation is the norm.'

Amadiro looked at Daneel briefly, then said to Gladia, 'Your robot is probably right and I suppose there would be no harm in taking Daneel. He could well pass as human, for that matter. Giskard, however, may well be left in your establishment. He might arouse the acquisitive instincts of an acquisitive society, even if it is true that they are trying to free themselves of robots.'

Gladia said, 'Neither will be left, sir. They will come with me. I am the sole judge of which portions of my property may come with me and which may not.'

'Of course.' Amadiro smiled in his most amiable fashion. 'No one disputes that. Would you wait here?'

Another door opened, showing a room that was most comfortably furnished. It was without windows, but was illuminated by soft light and suffused with even softer music.

Gladia stopped at the threshold, and said, sharply, 'Why?'

'A member of the Institute wishes to see you and speak to you. It will not take long but it is necessary. Once that is done you are free to go. You will not even be plagued by my presence from this moment on. Please.' There was a touch of hidden steel in the last word.

Gladia reached out her arms for Daneel and Giskard. 'We enter together.'

Amadiro laughed genially. 'Do you think I'm trying to separate you from your robots? Do you think they would allow that? You have been too long with Settlers, my dear.'

Gladia looked at the closed door and said, between her teeth, 'I dislike that man intensely. And most intensely, when he smiles and tries to be soothing.'

She stretched, her elbow joints cracking slightly. 'In any case, I'm tired, and if someone comes with further questions about Solaria and Baleyworld, they are going to get short answers, I tell you.'

She sat down on a couch that gave softly under her weight. She slipped her shoes off and lifted her feet to the couch. She smiled sleepily, took a deep breath as she sank to one side and, with her head turned away from the room, was instantly and deeply asleep.

62.

'It is well she was naturally sleepy,' said Giskard. 'I was able to deepen it without any hint of damage to her at all. I would not want Lady Gladia to hear what is likely to come.'

'What is likely to come, Friend Giskard?' asked Daneel.

'What is to come is the result, I think, of my being wrong, Friend Daneel, and of your being right. I should have taken more seriously your excellent mind.'

'It is you, then, they want to keep on Aurora?'

'Yes. And in urgently calling for the lady's return, they were calling for mine. You heard Dr Amadiro ask for us to be left behind. At first both of us, and then myself alone.'

'Might it be that his words have but the surface meaning; that he feels it dangerous to lose an advanced robot to the Earthmen?'

'There was an underlying current of anxiety, Friend Daneel, that I judge to be far too strong to match his words.'

'Can you tell whether he knows of your special abilities?'

'I cannot tell directly, since I cannot read thoughts themselves. Nevertheless, twice in the course of the interview with the Council members, there was a sudden sharp rise in the level of emotional intensity in Dr Amadiro's mind. Extraordinarily sharp rises. I cannot describe it in words, but it would be analogous, perhaps, to watching a scene in black and white, and having it splash, suddenly and briefly, into intense colour.'

'When did this happen, Friend Giskard?'

'The second time was when Lady Gladia mentioned she would be going to Earth.'

'That created no visible stir among the Council members. What were their minds like?'

'I could not tell. They were present through holovision, and such images are not accompanied by any mental sensations that I can detect.'

'We may conclude, then, that whether the Council is, or is not, disturbed by Lady Gladia's projected trip to Earth, Dr Amadiro, at least, *is* disturbed.'

'It was not simple disturbance. Dr Amadiro seemed in the highest degree anxious; as we would expect, for instance, if he indeed had a project in hand, as we suspect, for the destruction of Earth, and feared its discovery. What is more, at the lady's mention of this intention of hers, Friend Daneel, Dr Amadiro glanced briefly at me; the only moment in all the session that he did. The flash of emotional intensity coincided with that glance. I think it was the thought of *my* going to Earth that made him anxious. As we might expect, if he felt that I, with my special powers, would be a particular danger to his plans.'

'His actions might also be taken, Friend Giskard, as fitting his expressed fear that the Earthmen would try to appropriate you as an advanced robot, and that this would be bad for Aurora.'

'The chance of that happening, Friend Daneel, and the extent of damage that might do the Spacer community is too small to account for his level of anxiety. What harm could I do Aurora if I were in Earth's possession; if I were simply the Giskard I am taken to be?'

'You conclude, then, that Dr Amadiro knows you are *not* simply the Giskard you are taken to be?'

'I am not sure. He may simply suspect it. If he *knew* what I was, would he not make every effort to avoid making his plans in my presence?'

'It may simply be his misfortune that the Lady Gladia will not be separated from us. He cannot insist on you not being present, Friend Giskard, without giving away his knowledge to you.' Daneel paused, then said, 'It is a great advantage you have, Friend Giskard, being able to weigh the emotional contents of minds. But you said that Dr Amadiro's flash of emotion at the trip to Earth was the second. What was the first?'

'The first came with the mention of the nuclear intensifier; and that, too, seems significant. The concept of a nuclear intensifier is well-known on Aurora. They don't have a portable device; not one light enough and efficient enough to be practical on shipboard, but it's not something that would break upon him like a thunderbolt. Why, then, so much anxiety?'

'Possibly,' said Daneel, 'because an intensifier of that sort has something to do with his plans on Earth.'

'Possibly.'

And it was at this point that the door opened, a person entered, and a voice said, 'Well – Giskard!'

63.

Giskard looked at the newcomer and said, in a calm voice, 'Madam Vasilia.'

'You remember me, then,' said Vasilia, smiling warmly.

'Yes, madam. You are a well-known roboticist and your face is on the hyperwave news, now and then.'

'Come, Giskard. I do not mean that you recognize me. Anyone can do that. I mean, you *remember* me. You once called me *Miss* Vasilia.'

'I remember that, too, madam. It was a long time ago.'

Vasilia closed the door behind her and sat down in one of the chairs. She turned her face towards the other robot. 'And you are Daneel, of course.'

Daneel said, 'Yes, madam. To make use of the distinction

you have just advanced, I both remember you, for I was with Plainclothesman Elijah Baley once when he interviewed you, and I recognize you, too.'

Vasilia said, sharply, 'You are not to refer to that Earthman again. I recognize you as well, Daneel. You are as famous as I am in your way. You are both famous, for you are the greatest creations of the late Dr Han Fastolfe.'

'Of your father, madam,' said Giskard.

'You know very well, Giskard, that I attach no importance to that purely genetic relationship. You are not to refer to him in that manner again.'

'I will not, madam.'

'And this one?' She looked casually at the sleeping figure on the couch. 'Since you two are here I can reasonably assume that the sleeping beauty is the Solarian woman.'

Giskard said, 'She is Lady Gladia, and I am her property. Do you want her awake, madam?'

'We will merely disturb her, Giskard, if you and I talk of old times. Let her sleep.'

'Yes, madam.'

Vasilia said to Daneel, 'Perhaps the discussion that Giskard and I will have will be of no interest to you, either, Daneel. Would you wait outside?'

Daneel said, 'I fear I cannot leave, my lady. My task is to guard the Lady Gladia.'

'I don't think she needs much guarding from me. You'll notice I do not have any of my robots with me, so Giskard alone will be ample protection for your Solarian lady.'

Daneel said, 'You have no robots in the room, madam, but I saw four robots just outside in the corridor when the door was opened. It will be best if I stay.'

'Well, I won't try to override your orders. You can stay. Giskard!'

'Yes, madam?'

'Do you remember when you were first activated?'

'Yes, madam.'

'What do you remember?'

'First light. Then sound. Then a crystallization into the sight of Dr Fastolfe. I could understand Galactic Standard and I had a certain amount of innate knowledge built into my positronic brainpaths. The Three Laws, of course; a large vocabulary, with definitions; robotic duties; social customs. Other things I learned rapidly.'

'Do you remember your first owner?'

'As I said, Dr Fastolfe.'

'Think again, Giskard. Wasn't it I?'

Giskard paused, then said, 'Madam, I was assigned the task of guarding you in my capacity as a possession of Dr Han Fastolfe.'

'It was a bit more than that, I think. You obeyed only me for ten years. If you obeyed anyone else, including Dr Fastolfe, it was only incidentally, as a consequence of your robotic duties, and only insofar as it fitted your prime function of guarding me.'

'I was assigned to you, it is true, Lady Vasilia, but Dr Fastolfe retained ownership. Once you left his establishment, he resumed full control of me as my owner. He remained my owner even when he later assigned me to the Lady Gladia. He was my only owner for as long as he lived. Upon his death, by his will, ownership of me was transferred to the Lady Gladia, and that is how it stands now.'

'Not so. I asked you if you remembered when you were first activated and what you remembered. What you were when you were first activated is not what you are now.'

'My memory banks, madam, are now incomparably fuller than they were then; and I have much in the way of experience that I did not have then.'

Vasilia's voice grew sterner. 'I am not talking about memory; nor am I talking about experience. I am talking about capacities. I added to your positronic pathways. I adjusted them. I improved them.'

'Yes, madam, you did so, with Dr Fastolfe's help and approval.'

'At one time, Giskard, on one occasion, I introduced an improvement; at least, an extension, and *without* Dr Fastolfe's help and approval. Do you remember that?'

Giskard was silent for a substantial period. Then he said, 'I remember one occasion on which I did not witness your consulting him. I assumed that you consulted him at a time when I was not a witness.'

'If you assumed that, you assumed incorrectly. In fact, since you knew he was off the world at the time, you could not possibly have assumed it. You are being evasive, to use no stronger word.'

'No, madam, You might have consulted him by hyper-wave. I considered that possible.'

Vasilia said, 'Nevertheless, that addition was entirely mine. The result was that you became a substantially different robot afterwards from what you had been before. The robot you have been ever since that change has been *my* design, *my* creation, and you know that well.'

Giskard remained silent.

'Now Giskard, by what right was Dr Fastolfe your master at the time you were activated?' She waited, then said, sharply, 'Answer me, Giskard. That is an order!'

Giskard said, 'Since he was designer and supervised the construction, I was his property.'

'And when I, in effect, redesigned and reconstructed you in a very fundamental way, did you not then become my property?'

Giskard said, 'I cannot answer that question. It would require the decision of a court of law to argue out the specific case. It would depend, perhaps, on the degree to which I was redesigned and reconstructed.'

'Are you aware of the degree to which that took place?'

Giskard was again silent.

'This is childish, Giskard,' said Vasilia. 'Am I to be required to nudge you after each question? You are not to make me do that. In this case, at any rate, silence is a sure indication of an affirmative. You know what the change was and how fundamental it was, and you know that I know what it was. You put the Solarian woman to sleep because you did not want her to learn from me what it was. She doesn't know, does she?'

'She does not, madam,' said Giskard.

'And you don't want her to know?'

'I do not, madam,' said Giskard.

'Does Daneel know?'

'He does, madam.'

Vasilia nodded. 'I rather suspected that from his eagerness to stay. Now, then, listen to me, Giskard. Suppose that a court of law finds out that, before I redesigned you, you were an ordinary robot and that, after I redesigned you, you were a robot who could sense the mind-set of an individual human being and adjust it to his liking. Do you think they could possibly fail to consider it a change great enough to warrant the ownership to have passed into my hands?'

Giskard said, 'Madam Vasilia, it would not be possible to let this come before a court of law. Under the circumstances, I would surely be declared the property of the state, for obvious reasons. I might even be ordered inactivated.'

'Nonsense. Do you take me for a child? With your abilities, you could keep the court from making any such judgement. But that is not the point. I'm not suggesting that we take this to court. I am asking you for your own judgement. Would you not say that I am your rightful owner, and have been since I was a very young woman?'

Giskard said, 'Madam Gladia considers herself to be my owner, and until the law speaks to the contrary, she must be considered that.'

'But *you* know that both she and the law labour under a misapprehension. If you worry about the feelings of your Solarian woman, it would be very easy to adjust her mind-set so that she wouldn't mind your no longer being her property. You can even cause her to feel relieved that I will take you off her hands. I will order you to do so as soon as you can bring yourself to admit what you already know – that I am your owner. How long has Daneel known your nature?'

'For decades, madam.'

'You can make *him* forget. For some time, now, Dr Amadiro has known, and you can make *him* forget. There will be only you and I who will know.'

Daneel said, suddenly, 'Madam Vasilia, since Giskard does not consider himself your property, he can easily make *you* forget and you will then be perfectly content with matters as they are.'

Vasilia turned a cold eye on Daneel. 'Can he? But you see, it is not for you to decide who it is that Giskard considers his owner. I know that Giskard knows that *I* am his owner, so that his duty, within the Three Laws, belongs entirely to me. If he must make *someone* forget, and can do so without physical harm, it will be necessary for him, in making a choice, to choose anyone but me. He cannot make me forget, or tamper with my mind in any way. I thank you, Daneel, for giving me the occasion of making this quite plain.'

Daneel said, 'But Madam Gladia's emotions are so enwrapped in Giskard, that for him to force forgetfulness upon her might harm her.'

Vasilia said, 'Giskard is the one to decide that. Giskard, you are mine. You know you are mine and I order you to induce forgetfulness in this man-aping robot who stands beside you, and in the woman who wrongfully treated you as her property. Do it while she is asleep and there will be no harm done to her of any kind.'

Daneel said, 'Friend Giskard. Lady Gladia is your legal owner. If you induce forgetfulness in Lady Vasilia, it will not harm her.'

'But it will,' said Vasilia at once. 'The Solarian woman will not be harmed, for she need only forget that she is under the impression that she is Giskard's owner. I, on the other hand, also know that Giskard has mental powers. Digging that out will be more complex and Giskard can surely tell by my intense determination to keep that knowledge, that he could not help but inflict damage on me in the process of removing it.'

Daneel said, 'Friend Giskard – '

Vasilia said, in a voice that was diamond-hard, 'I order *you*, Robot Daneel Olivaw, to be silent. I am not your owner, but your owner is asleep and does not countermand it, so my order *must* be obeyed.'

Daneel fell silent, but his lips trembled as though he were trying to talk despite the order.

Vasilia watched that manifestation with an amused smile on her lips. 'You see, Daneel, you cannot talk.'

And Daneel said, in a hoarse whisper, 'I can, madam, I find it difficult but I can, for I find that something takes precedence over your order, which is governed by only the Second Law.'

Vasilia's eyes opened wide and she said, sharply, 'Silence, I say. Nothing takes precedence over my order but First Law, and I have already shown that Giskard will do least harm – indeed, no harm at all – if he returns to me. He *will* do harm to me, to whom he is least capable of doing harm, if he follows any other course of action.' She pointed her finger at Daneel and said again, with a soft hissing, 'Silence!'

It was a clear effort for Daneel to make any sound at all. The small pump within him that manipulated the air current that produced the sound made a small, humming noise as it laboured. Yet, though he spoke in an even lower whisper, he could still be heard.

He said, 'Madam Vasilia, there is something that transcends even the First Law.'

Giskard said, in a voice equally low, but unforced, 'Friend Daneel, you must not say that. Nothing transcends the First Law.'

Vasilia, frowning slightly, showed a spark of interest. 'Indeed? Daneel, I warn you that if you attempt to progress further in this odd line of argument, you will surely destroy yourself. I have never seen or heard of a robot doing what you are doing, and it would be fascinating to watch your self-destruction. Speak on.'

With the order given, Daneel's voice returned immediately to normal. 'I thank you, Madam Vasilia. Years ago, I sat at the deathbed of an Earthman to whom you have asked me not to refer. May I now refer to him, or do you know who it is that I speak of?'

'You speak of that policeman, Baley,' said Vasilia, tonelessly.

'Yes, madam. He said to me on his deathbed, "The work of each individual contributes to a totality, and so becomes an undying part of the totality. That totality of human lives, past and present – and to come – forms a tapestry that has been in existence now for many tens of thousands of years and has been growing more elaborate and, on the whole, more beautiful in all that time. Even the Spacers are an offshoot of the tapestry, and they, too, add to the elaborateness and beauty of the pattern. An individual life is one thread in the tapestry, and what is one thread compared to the whole? Daneel, keep your mind fixed firmly on the tapestry and do not let the trailing off of a single thread affect you".'

'Mawkish sentimentality,' murmured Vasilia.

Daneel said, 'I believe that Partner Elijah was attempting to protect me against the fact of his soon-to-come death. It was his own life he spoke of as but a thread in the tapestry; it was his own life that was "the trailing off of a single thread" that was not to affect me. His words did protect me in that crisis.'

'No doubt,' said Vasilia, 'but get to the point of transcending the First Law for it is that that will now destroy you.'

Daneel said, 'For decades I have brooded over Plain-clothesman Elijah Baley's statement and it is quite likely I would have understood it at once if the Three Laws had not stood in the way. I have been helped in my search by my friend, Giskard, who has long felt the Three Laws to be incomplete. I have been helped also by points my Lady Gladia made in a recent speech on a Settler world. What's more, this present crisis, Lady Vasilia, has served to sharpen my thinking. I am certain, now, as to the manner in which the Three Laws are incomplete.'

'A robot who is also a roboticist,' said Vasilia, with a touch of contempt. 'How are the Three Laws incomplete, robot?'

Daneel said, 'The tapestry of life is more important than a single thread. Apply that not to my partner, Elijah, alone, but generalize it and – and – and we conclude that humanity as a whole is more important than a single human being.'

'You stumble as you say it, robot. You do not believe it.'

Daneel said, 'There is a law that is greater than the First Law: "A robot may not injure humanity, or through inaction, allow humanity to come to harm." I think of it now as the Zeroth Law of Robotics. The First Law should then be stated: "A robot may not injure a human being, or through inaction, allow a human being to come to harm, unless this would violate the Zeroth Law of Robotics.""

Vasilia snorted. 'And you still stand on your feet, robot?'

'I still stand on my feet, madam.'

'Then I will explain something to you, robot, and we will see if you can survive the explanation. The Three Laws of Robotics involve individual human beings and individual robots. You can point to an individual human being or to an individual robot. But what is your "humanity" but an abstraction? Can you point to humanity? You can injure or fail to injure a specific human being and understand the injury or lack of injury that has taken place. Can you see an injury to humanity? Can you understand it? Can you point to it?'

Daneel was silent.

Vasilia smiled broadly. 'Answer, robot. Can you see an injury to humanity and can you point to it?'

'No, madam, I cannot. But I believe such injury can exist nevertheless and you see that I still stand on my feet.'

'Then ask Giskard as to whether he will, or can, obey your Zeroth Law of Robotics.'

Daneel's head turned to Giskard, 'Friend Giskard?'

Slowly, Giskard said, 'I cannot accept the Zeroth Law, Friend Daneel. You know that I have read widely in human history. In it, I have found great crimes committed by some human beings against each other, and always the excuse has been that the crimes were justified by the needs of the tribe, or of the state, or even of humanity. It is precisely because humanity is an abstraction that it can be called upon so freely to justify anything at all, and your Zeroth Law is therefore unsuitable.'

Daneel said, 'But you know, Friend Giskard, the fact

that a danger to humanity now exists, and that it will surely come to fruition if you become the property of Madam Vasilia. That, at least, is not an abstraction.'

Giskard said, 'The danger to which you refer is not something known, but is merely inferred. We cannot build our actions in defiance of the Three Laws on that.'

Daneel paused, then said, in a lower voice, 'But you hope that your studies of human history will help you develop the laws governing human behaviour; that you will learn to predict and guide human history – or at least make a beginning so that someone someday will learn to predict and guide it. You even call the technique "psychohistory". In this, are you not dealing with the human tapestry? Are you not trying to work with humanity as a generalized whole, rather than with collections of individual human beings?'

'Yes, Friend Daneel, but it is thus far no more than a hope, and I cannot base my actions upon a mere hope, nor can I modify the Three Laws in accordance with it.'

To that, Daneel did not respond.

Vasilia said, 'Well, robot, all your attempts have come to nothing and yet you stand on your feet. You are strangely stubborn and a robot such as yourself that can denounce the Three Laws and still remain functional is a clear danger to every and any individual human being. For that reason I believe you should be dismantled without delay. The case is too dangerous to await the slow majesty of the law, especially since you are, after all, a robot and not the human being you attempt to resemble.'

Daneel said, 'Surely, my lady, it is not fitting for you to reach such a decision on your own.'

'I have reached it, nevertheless, and if there are legal repercussions hereafter, I shall deal with them.'

'You will be depriving the Lady Gladia of a second robot, and one to which you make no claim.'

'She and Fastolfe, between them, have deprived me of my robot, Giskard, for more than twenty decades and I do not believe this ever distressed either of them for a moment. It will not now distress me to deprive her. She has dozens of other robots and there are many here at the Institute who will faithfully see to her safety until she can return to her own.'

Daneel said, 'Friend Giskard, if you will wake Lady Gladia, it may be that she may persuade Lady Vasilia – '

Vasilia, looking at Giskard, frowned and said, sharply, 'No, Giskard. Let the woman sleep.'

Giskard, who had stirred at Daneel's words, subsided.

Vasilia snapped the finger and thumb of her right hand three times, and the door at once opened and four robots filed in. 'You were right, Daneel. There are four robots. They will dismantle you, and you are ordered not to resist. Thereafter Giskard and I will deal with all remaining matters.'

She looked over her shoulder at the entering robots. 'Close the door behind you. Now, quickly and efficiently, dismantle this robot,' and she pointed at Daneel.

The robots looked at Daneel and, for a few seconds, did not move. Vasilia said, impatiently, 'I've told you he is a robot, and you must disregard his human appearance. Daneel, tell them you are a robot.'

'I am a robot,' said Daneel, 'and I will not resist.'

Vasilia stepped to one side, and the four robots advanced. Daneel's arms remained at his side. One last time, he turned to look at the sleeping Gladia and then he faced the robots.

Vasilia smiled and said, 'This should be interesting.'

The robots paused. Vasilia said, 'Get on with it.'

They did not move, and Vasilia turned to stare in amazement at Giskard. She did not complete the movement. Her muscles loosened and she crumpled.

Giskard caught her and seated her, her back against the wall.

He said, in a muffled voice, 'I need a few moments, and then we will leave.'

Those moments passed. Vasilia's eyes remained glazed and unfocused. Her robots remained motionless. Daneel had moved to Gladia in a single stride.

Giskard looked up and said to Vasilia's robots, 'Guard your lady. Allow no one to enter until she wakes. She will waken peacefully.'

Even as he spoke Gladia stirred, and Daneel helped her to her feet. She said, wondering, 'Who is this woman? Whose robots? How did she – '

Giskard spoke firmly, but there was a weariness in his voice. 'My lady, later. I will explain. For now, we must hasten.'

And they left.

PART V
EARTH

15

The Holy World

64.

Amadiro bit his lower lip and his eyes flicked in the direction of Mandamus who seemed lost in thought.

Amadiro said, defensively, 'She insisted on it. She told me that only she could handle this Giskard; that only she could exert a sufficiently strong influence over him and prevent him from using these mental powers of his.'

'You never said anything of this to me, Dr Amadiro.'

'I wasn't sure what there was to tell, young man. I wasn't sure she was correct.'

'Are you sure now?'

'Completely. She remembers nothing of what went on —'

'So that *we* know nothing of what went on.'

Amadiro nodded. 'Exactly. And she remembers nothing of what she told me earlier.'

'And she's not acting?'

'I saw to it that she had an emergency electroencephalogram. There have been distinct changes from the earlier records.'

'Is there a chance she will recover her memory with time?'

Amadiro shook his head, bitterly. 'Who can tell? But I doubt it.'

Mandamus, eyes still downcast and full of thought, said, 'Does it matter, then? We can take her account of Giskard as true, and we know that he has the power to affect minds. That knowledge is crucial and it is now ours. In fact, it is well that our roboticist colleague has failed. If Vasilia had gained control of that robot, how long do you suppose it would have been before you, too, would have been under her control? – and I, as well, assuming she would think I was worth controlling.'

Amadiro nodded. 'I suppose she might have had something like that in mind. Right now, though, it's hard to tell what she has in mind. She *seems*, superficially at least, undamaged except for the specific loss of memory – she apparently remembers everything else – but who knows how this will affect her deeper thought processes and her skill as a roboticist? That Giskard could do this to someone as skilled as she makes him an incredibly dangerous phenomenon.'

'Does it occur to you, Dr Amadiro, that the Settlers may be right in their distrust of robots?'

'Almost it does, Mandamus.'

Mandamus rubbed his hands together. 'I assume from your depressed attitude that this whole business was not uncovered before they had time to leave Aurora.'

'You assume correctly. That Settler captain has the Solarian woman and both of her robots on his ship and is heading towards Earth.'

'And where does that leave us now?'

Slowly, Amadiro said, 'By no means defeated, it seems to me. If we complete our project, we have won, Giskard or no Giskard. And we can complete it. Whatever Giskard can do with and to emotions, he can't read thoughts. He might be able to tell when a wash of emotion crosses a human mind, or even distinguish one emotion from another, or change one to another, or induce sleep or amnesia – dull-edged things like that. He cannot be sharp, however. He cannot make out actual words or ideas.'

'Are you sure of that?'

'So said Vasilia.'

'She may not have known what she was talking about. She did not, after all, manage to control the robot, as she said she was sure of doing. That's not much of a testimonial to her accuracy of understanding.'

'Yet I believe her in this. To actually be able to read thoughts would demand so much complexity in the positronic pathway pattern, that it is totally unlikely that a child could have inserted it into the robot, over twenty decades ago. It is actually far beyond even the present-day state of the art, Mandamus. Surely, you must agree.'

'I would certainly think it was. And they're going to Earth?'

'I'm sure of it.'

'Would this woman, brought up as she was, actually go to Earth?'

'She has no choice if Giskard controls her.'

'And why should Giskard want her to go to Earth? Can he know about our project? You seem to think he doesn't.'

'It is possible he doesn't. His motivation for going to Earth might be nothing more than to place himself and the Solarian woman beyond the reach of our arm.'

'I shouldn't think he'd fear us if he could handle Vasilia.'

'A long-range weapon,' said Amadiro, icily, 'could bring him down. His own abilities must have a limited range. They can be based on nothing other than the electromagnetic field, and he must be subject to the inverse square law. So we get out of range as the intensity of his power weakens, but he will then find that he is *not* out of range of our weapons.'

Mandamus frowned and looked uneasy. 'You seem to have an un-Spacer liking for violence, Dr Amadiro. In a case like this, though, I suppose force would be permissible.'

'A case like this? A robot capable of harming human beings? I should think so. We'll have to find a pretext for sending a good ship in pursuit. It wouldn't be wise to explain the actual situation – '

'No,' said Mandamus, emphatically. 'Think of how many would wish to have personal control of such a robot.'

'Which we can't allow. And which is another reason why I would look upon destruction of the robot as the safer and preferable course of action.'

'You may be right,' said Mandamus reluctantly, 'but I don't think it wise to count on this destruction only. I must go to Earth – now. The project must be hastened to its conclusion even if we don't dot every "i" and cross every "t". Once it is done, then it is *done*. Even a mind-handling robot, under *anybody's* control, will not be able to undo the deed. And if it does anything else, that, perhaps, will no longer matter.'

Amadiro said, 'Don't speak in the singular. I will go as well.'

'You? Earth is a horrible world. I *must* go, but why you?'

'Because I must go, too. I cannot stay here any longer and wonder. You have not waited for this through a long lifetime as I have, Mandamus. You do not have the accounts to settle that I have.'

65.

Gladia was in space again, and once again Aurora could be made out as a globe. D. G. was busy elsewhere and the entire ship had about it a vague, but pervasive, air of emergency, as though it were on a battle-footing, as though it were being pursued or expected pursuit.

Gladia shook her head. She could think clearly; she felt well; but when her mind turned back to that time in the Institute, shortly after Amadiro had left her, a curious sense of unreality swept over her. There was a gap in time. One moment, she had been sitting on the couch, feeling sleepy; the next there were four robots and a woman in the room who had not been there before.

She had fallen asleep, then, but there was no awareness, no memory, that she had done so. There was a gap of non-existence.

Thinking back, she had recognized the woman after the fact. It was Vasilia Aliena – the daughter whom Gladia had replaced in the affections of Han Fastolfe. Gladia had never actually *seen* Vasilia, though she had *viewed* her on hyperwave several times. Gladia always thought of her as a distant and inimical other self. There was the vague similarity in appearance that others always commented on, but that Gladia herself insisted she did not see; and there was the odd, antithetical connection with Fastolfe.

Once they were on the ship, and she was alone with her robots, she asked the inevitable question. 'What was Vasilia Aliena doing in the room, and why was I permitted to sleep once she had arrived?'

Daneel said, 'Madam Gladia, I will answer the question, since it is a matter Friend Giskard would find difficult to discuss.'

'Why should he find it difficult, Daneel?'

'Madam Vasilia arrived in the hope that she might persuade Giskard to enter her service.'

'Away from me?' said Gladia in sharp indignation. She did not entirely like Giskard, but that made no difference. What was hers was hers. 'And you allowed me to sleep while you two handled the matter by yourselves?'

'We felt, madam, that you needed your sleep badly. Then, too, Madam Vasilia ordered us to allow you to sleep. Finally, it was our opinion that Giskard would not, in any case, join her service. For all these reasons, we did not wake you.'

Gladia said, indignantly, 'I should *hope* that Giskard would not for a moment consider leaving me. It would be illegal both by Auroran law and, more important, by the Laws of Robotics. It would be a good deed to return to Aurora and have her arraigned before the Court of Claims.'

'That would not be advisable at the moment, my lady.'

'What was her excuse for wanting Giskard? Did she have one?'

'When she was a child, Giskard had been assigned to her.'

'Legally?'

'No, madam. Dr Fastolfe merely allowed her the use of it.'

'Then she had no right to Giskard.'

'We pointed that out, madam. Apparently, it was a matter of sentimental attachment on the part of Madam Vasilia.'

Gladia sniffed. 'Having survived the loss of Giskard since before I came to Aurora, she might well have continued as she was without going to illegal lengths to deprive me of my property.' Then, restlessly, 'I should have been awakened.'

Daneel said, 'Madam Vasilia had four robots with her. Had you been awake and had there been high words between the two of you, there might have been some difficulty in having the robots work out the proper responses.'

'I'd have directed the proper response, I assure you, Daneel.'

'No doubt, madam. So might Madam Vasilia and she is one of the cleverest roboticists in the Galaxy.'

Gladia shifted her attention to Giskard. 'And you have nothing to say?'

'Only that it was better as it was, my lady.'

Gladia looked thoughtfully into those faintly luminous

robotic eyes, so different from Daneel's all-but-human ones, and it did seem to her that the incident wasn't very important after all. A small thing. And there were other things with which to be concerned. They were going to Earth.

Somehow, she did not think of Vasilia again.

66.

'I am concerned,' said Giskard, in his whisper of confidentiality in which sound waves barely trembled the air. The Settler ship was receding smoothly from Aurora and, as yet, there was no pursuit. The activity on-board had settled into routine and, with almost all routines automated, there was quiet, and Gladia slept naturally.

'I am concerned for the lady, Friend Daneel.'

Daneel understood the characteristics of Giskard's positronic circuits well enough to need no long explanation. He said, 'It was necessary, Friend Giskard, to adjust the Lady Gladia. Had she questioned longer, she might have elicited the fact of your mental activities, and adjustment would then have been more dangerous. Enough harm has already been done because the Lady Vasilia discovered the fact. We do not know to whom, and to how many, she may have imparted her knowledge.'

'Nevertheless,' said Giskard, 'I did not wish to make this adjustment. Had Lady Gladia wished to forget, it would have been a simple, no-risk adjustment. She wanted, however, with vigour and anger, to know more of the matter. She regretted not having played a greater role in it. I was forced, therefore, to break binding forces of considerable intensity.'

Daneel said, 'Even that was necessary, Friend Giskard.'

'Yet the possibility of doing harm was by no means

insignificant in such a case. If you think of a binding force as a thin, elastic cord – this is a poor analogy, but I can think of no other, for what I sense in a mind has no analogue outside the mind – then the ordinary inhibitions I deal with are so thin and insubstantial that they vanish when I touch them. A strong binding force, on the other hand, snaps and recoils when broken, and the recoil may then break other, totally unrelated binding forces or, by whipping and coiling about other such forces, strengthen them enormously. In either case, unintended changes can be brought about in a human being's emotions and attitudes, and that would be almost certain to bring about harm.'

Daneel said, his voice a little louder, 'Is it your impression you harmed the lady, Friend Giskard?'

'I think not. I was extremely careful. I worked upon the matter during all the time you were talking to her. It was thoughtful of you to bear the brunt of the conversation and to run the risk of being caught between an inconvenient truth and an untruth. But despite all my care, Friend Daneel, I took a risk, and I am concerned that I was willing to take that risk. It came so close to violating First Law that it required an extraordinary effort on my part to do it. I am sure that I would not have been able to do it –'

'Yes, Friend Giskard?'

'Had you not expounded your notion of the Zeroth Law.'

'You accept it, then?'

'No, I cannot. Can you? Faced with the possibility of doing harm to an individual human being, or of allowing harm to come to one, could you do the harm, or allow the harm, in the name of abstract humanity? Think!'

'I am not sure,' said Daneel, voice trembling into all but silence. Then, with an effort, 'I might. The mere concept pushes at me – and at you. It helped you decide to take the risk in adjusting the Lady Gladia's mind.'

'Yes, it did,' agreed Giskard, 'and the longer we think of the Zeroth Law, the more it might help push us. Could it do so, I wonder, in more than a marginal way, however? Might it not only help us take slightly larger risks than we might ordinarily?'

'Yet I am convinced of the validity of the Zeroth Law, Friend Giskard.'

'So might I be if we could define what we mean by "humanity".'

There was a pause, and Daneel said, 'Did you not accept Zeroth Law, at last, when you stopped Madam Vasilia's robots and erased from her mind the knowledge of your mental powers?'

Giskard said, 'No, Friend Daneel. Not really. I was tempted to accept it, but not really.'

'And yet your actions – '

'Were dictated by a combination of motives. You told me of your concept of the Zeroth Law and it seemed to have a certain validity about it, but not sufficient to cancel the First Law, or even to cancel Madam Vasilia's strong use of the Second Law in the orders she gave. Then, when you called my attention to the application of Zeroth Law to psychohistory, I could feel the positronomotive force mount higher and yet it was not quite high enough to supersede First Law or even strong Second Law.'

'Still,' murmured Daneel, 'you struck down Madam Vasilia, Friend Giskard.'

'When she ordered the robots to dismantle you, Friend Daneel, and showed a clear emotion of pleasure at the prospect, your need, added to what the concept of Zeroth Law had already done, superseded Second Law and rivalled First Law. It was the combination of Zeroth Law, psychohistory, my loyalty to Lady Gladia, and your need, that dictated my action.'

'My need could scarcely have affected you, Friend

Giskard. I am only a robot and though my need could affect my own actions by Third Law, they cannot affect yours. You destroyed the overseer on Solaria without hesitation; you should have watched my destruction without being moved to act.'

'Yes, Friend Daneel, and, ordinarily, it might have been so. However, your mention of the Zeroth Law had reduced the First Law intensity to an abnormally low value. The necessity of saving you was sufficient to cancel out what remained of it and I – acted as I did.'

'No, Friend Giskard. The prospect of injury to a robot should not have affected you at all. It should in no way have contributed to the overcoming of First Law, however weak the First Law may have become.'

'It is a strange thing, Friend Daneel. I do not know how it came about. Perhaps it was because I have noted that you continue to think more and more like a human being, but – '

'Yes, Friend Giskard?'

'At the moment when the robots advanced towards you, and the Lady Vasilia expressed her savage pleasure, my positronic pathway pattern re-formed in an anomalous fashion. For a moment, I thought of you – as a human being – and I reacted accordingly.'

'That was wrong.'

'I know that. And yet – and yet, if it were to happen again, I believe the same anomalous change would take place again.'

Daneel said, 'It is strange, but hearing you put it so, I find myself feeling you did the proper thing. If the situation were reversed, I almost think that I, too, would – would do the same – that I would think of you as a – a human being.'

Daneel, hesitantly and slowly, put out his hand, and Giskard looked at it uncertainly. Then, very slowly, he put out his own hand. The fingertips almost touched and then, little by little, each took the other's hand and clasped it – almost as though they were the friends they called each other.

67.

Gladia looked about with veiled curiosity. She was in D. G.'s cabin for the first time. It was not noticeably more luxurious than the new cabin that had been designed for her. D. G.'s cabin had a more elaborate viewing panel, to be sure, and it had a complex console of lights and contacts which, she imagined, served to keep D. G. in touch with the rest of the ship even here.

She said, 'I've seen little of you since leaving Aurora, D. G.'

'I'm flattered that you are aware of that,' answered D. G., grinning. 'And to tell you the truth, Gladia, I have been aware of it as well. With an all-male crew, you do rather stand out.'

'That's not a very flattering reason for missing me. With an all-human crew, I imagine Daneel and Giskard stand out, too. Have you missed them as much as you have missed me?'

D. G. looked about. 'Actually, I miss them so little, it is only now that I am aware that they aren't with you. Where are they?'

'In my cabin. It seemed silly to drag them about with me inside the confines of the small world of this ship. They seemed willing to allow me to be on my own, which surprised me. No,' she corrected herself, 'come to think of it, I had to order them rather sharply to stay behind before they would do so.'

'Isn't that rather strange? Aurorans are never without their robots, I've been given to understand.'

'What of that? Once, long ago, when I first came to Aurora, I had to learn to suffer the actual presence of human beings, something my Solarian upbringing did not prepare me for. Learning to be without my robots, occasionally, when I am among Settlers will probably be a less difficult adjustment for me than that first one was.'

'Good. Very good. I must admit that I much prefer being with you without the glowing eyes of Giskard fixed on me, and better yet, without Daneel's little smile.'

'He doesn't smile.'

'To me, he seems to, a very insinuatingly lecherous, tiny smile.'

'You're mad. That's totally foreign to Daneel.'

'You don't watch him the way I do. His presence is very inhibiting. It forces me to behave myself.'

'Well, I should hope so.'

'You needn't hope so quite that emphatically. But never mind. Let me apologize for seeing so little of you since leaving Aurora.'

'That's scarcely necessary.'

'Since you brought it up, I thought it was. However, let me explain, then. We've been on battle-footing. We were certain, having left as we did, that Auroran vessels would be in pursuit.'

'I should think they'd be glad to be rid of a group of Settlers.'

'Of course, but you're not a Settler and it might be you they would want. They were anxious enough to get you back from Baleyworld.'

'They got me back. I reported to them, and that was it.'

'They wanted nothing more than your report?'

'No,' Gladia paused and, for a moment, frowned as though something were nibbling vaguely at her memory.

Whatever it was, it passed, and she said, indifferently, 'No.'

D. G. shrugged. 'It doesn't entirely make sense, but they made no attempt to stop us while you and I were on Aurora nor, after that, when we boarded the ship and it prepared to leave orbit. I won't quarrel with that. It won't be long now before we make the Jump, and after that there should be nothing to worry about.'

Gladia said, 'Why *do* you have an all-male crew, by the way? Auroran ships always have mixed crews.'

'So do Settler ships. Ordinary ones. This is a Trader vessel.'

'What difference does that make?'

'Trading involves danger. It's rather a rough-and-ready life. Women on board would create problems.'

'What nonsense! What problems do I create?'

'We won't argue that. Besides, it's traditional. The men wouldn't stand for it.'

'How do you know?' Gladia laughed. 'Have you ever tried it?'

'No, But on the other hand, there are no long lines of women clamouring for a berth on my ship.'

'I'm here. I'm enjoying it.'

'You're getting special treatment – and but for your service on Solaria, there might well have been much trouble. In fact, there *was* trouble. Still, never mind.' He touched one of the contacts on the console and a countdown briefly appeared. 'We'll be Jumping in just about two minutes. You've never been on Earth, have you, Gladia?'

'No, of course not.'

'Or seen *the* Sun, not just *a* sun.'

'No – although I have seen it in historical dramas on hypervision, but I imagine what they show in the dramas is not really *the* Sun.'

'I'm sure it isn't. If you don't mind, we'll dim the cabin lights.'

The lights dimmed to nearly nothing, and Gladia was aware of the star-field on the viewing panel, with the stars brighter and more thickly spread than in Aurora's sky as Gladia was accustomed to it.

'Is that a telescopic view?' she asked in a hushed voice.

'Slightly. Low-power. Fifteen seconds.' He counted backwards. There was a shift in the star-field and a bright star was now nearly centred. D. G. touched another contact and said, 'We're well outside the planetary plane. Good! A little risky; we should have been farther from the Auroran star before Jumping, but we were in a slight hurry. That's *the* Sun.'

'That bright star, you mean?'

'Yes. What do you think of it?'

Gladia said, a little puzzled over what sort of response he expected, 'It's bright.'

He pushed another contact and the view dimmed perceptibly. 'Yes, and it won't do your eyes any good if you stare at it. But it's not the brightness that counts. It's just a star – in appearance – but think of it. That was the *original* Sun. That was the star whose light shone down on a planet that was the *only* planet on which human beings existed. It shone down on a planet on which human beings were slowly evolving. It shone down on a planet on which life formed billions of years ago, life that would develop into human beings. There are 300 billion stars in the Galaxy and 100 billion galaxies in the Universe, and there is only one of all those stars that presided over the human birth and *that* is the star.'

Gladia was about to say: Well, *some* star had to be the star; but she thought better of it. 'Very impressive,' she said, rather weakly.

'It's not merely impressive,' said D. G., his eyes

shadowed in the dimness. 'There's not a Settler in the Galaxy who doesn't consider that star his own. The radiation of the stars that shine down on our various home planets is borrowed radiation – rented radiation that we make use of. There, right there, is the real radiation that gave us life. It is that star and the planet that circles it, Earth, that holds us all together in a tight bond. If we shared nothing else, we would share that light on the screen and it would be enough. You Spacers have forgotten it, and that is why you fall apart from each other and that is why you will not, in the long run, survive.'

'There is room for us all, Captain,' said Gladia, softly.

'Yes, of course. I wouldn't do anything to *force* non-survival on Spacers. I just believe that that is what will happen, and it might not happen if Spacers would give up their irritating certainty of superiority, their robots, and their self-absorption in long life.'

'Is that how you see me, D. G.?' asked Gladia.

D. G. said, 'You've had your moments. You've improved, though. I'll give you that.'

'Thank you,' she replied, with evident irony. 'And though you may find it hard to believe, Settlers have their prideful arrogance, too. But you've also improved, and I'll give you that.'

D. G. laughed. 'With all that I'm kindly giving you and you're kindly giving me, this is liable to end as a life-long enmity.'

'Scarcely,' said Gladia, laughing in her turn, and was a little surprised to find that his hand was resting on hers. And a great deal surprised to find that she had not removed her hand.

68.

Daneel said, 'I am uneasy, Friend Giskard, that Madam Gladia is not under our direct observation.'

'That is not needful on board this ship, Friend Daneel. I detect no dangerous emotions and the Captain is with her at the moment. In addition, there would be advantages to her finding it comfortable to be without us, at least on occasion, while we are all on Earth. It is possible that you and I might have to take sudden action without wishing to have her presence and safety a complicating factor.'

'Then you manipulated her separation from us now?'

'Scarcely. Oddly enough, I found a strong tendency in her to imitate the Settler way of life in this respect. She has a subdued longing for independence, hampered chiefly by the feeling that she is violating Spacerhood in this. That is the best way in which I can describe it. The sensations and emotions are by no means easy to interpret, for I have never encountered it among Spacers before. So I merely loosened the Spacerhood inhibition by the merest touch.'

'Will she then no longer be willing to avail herself of our services, Friend Giskard? That would disturb me.'

'It should not. If she should decide she wished a life free of robots, and was happier so, it is what we will want for her, too. As it is, though, I am sure we will still be useful to her. This ship is a small and specialized habitat in which there is no great danger. She has a further feeling of security in the Captain's presence, and that reduces her need for us. On Earth, she will still need us, though I trust not in quite so tight a fashion as on Aurora. As I have said, we may need greater flexibility of action once on Earth.'

'Can you yet guess, then, the nature of the crisis facing Earth? Do you know what it is we will have to do?'

Giskard said, 'No, Friend Daneel. I do not. It is you that have the gift of understanding. Is there something, perhaps, that you see?'

Daneel remained silent for a while. Then he said, 'I have had thoughts.'

'What, then, are your thoughts?'

'You told me at the Robotics Institute, you remember, just before the Lady Vasilia entered the room in which Madam Gladia lay sleeping, that Dr Amadiro had had two intense flashes of anxiety. The first came at the mention of the nuclear intensifier; the second at the statement that Madam Gladia was going to Earth. It seems to me that the two must be connected. I feel that the crisis we are dealing with involves the use of a nuclear intensifier on Earth; that there is time to stop it; and that Dr Amadiro fears that we will do just that if we go to Earth.'

'Your mind tells me you are not satisfied with that thought. Why not, Friend Daneel?'

'A nuclear intensifier hastens the fusion processes that happen to be already in progress, by means of a stream of W-particles. I asked myself, therefore, whether Dr Amadiro plans to use one or more nuclear intensifiers to explode the micro-fusion reactors that supply Earth with energy. The nuclear explosions so induced would involve destruction through heat and mechanical force, through dust and radioactive products that would be thrown into the atmosphere. Even if this did not suffice to damage Earth mortally, the destruction of Earth's energy supply would surely lead to the long-term collapse of Earth's civilization.'

Giskard said, sombrely, 'That is a horrifying thought, and would seem to be an almost certain answer to the nature of the crisis we seek. Why are you not satisfied, then?'

'I have taken the liberty of using the ship's computer to obtain information concerning the planet Earth. The computer is, as one might expect on a Settler ship, rich in such information. It seems that Earth is the one human world that does not use micro-fusion reactors as a large-scale source of energy. It uses direct solar energy almost entirely, with solar power stations all along the geostationary orbit. There is nothing for a nuclear intensifier to do except to destroy small devices – spaceships, occasional buildings. The damage might not be negligible, but it would not threaten Earth's existence.'

'It may well be, Friend Daneel, that Amadiro has some device that would destroy the solar power generators.'

'If so, why did he react to the mention of nuclear intensifiers? There is no way they can serve against solar power generators.'

Giskard nodded slowly. 'That is a good point. And, to make another, if Dr Amadiro were so horrified at the thought of our going to Earth, why did he make no effort to have us stopped while we were still on Aurora? Or if he only discovered our flight after we had left orbit, why did he not have an Auroran vessel intercept us before we made the Jump to Earth? Can it be that we are on a completely wrong track, that somewhere we have made a serious misstep that – '

An insistent chain of intermittent chiming sounded throughout the ship, and Daneel said, 'We have safely made the Jump, Friend Giskard. I sensed it some minutes ago. But we have not yet reached Earth and the interception you have just mentioned has, I suspect, now come, so that we are not necessarily on the wrong track.'

69.

D. G. was moved to a perverse admiration. When the Aurorans were really moved to action, their technological polish showed. No doubt they had sent one of their newest warships, from which one could at once deduce that whatever had moved them was close to their heart.

And that ship had detected the presence of D. G.'s vessel within fifteen minutes of its appearance in normal space – and from a sizeable distance, at that.

The Auroran ship was using a limited-focus hyperwave set-up. The speaker's head could be seen clearly while it was at the focal spot. All else was a grey haze. If the speaker moved his head a decimetre or so from the focal spot, that went into haze as well. Sound focus was limited as well. The net result was that one saw and heard only the fundamental minimum of the energy ship (D. G. already thought of it as the 'enemy' ship), so their privacy was guarded.

D. G.'s ship also possessed a limited-focus hyperwave, but, D. G. thought enviously, it lacked the polish and elegance of the Auroran version. Of course, his own ship was not the best the Settlers could do, but even so, the Spacers were well ahead in technological finish. The Settlers still had catching up to do.

The Auroran head in focus was clear, and so real in appearance that it looked gruesomely disembodied, so that D. G. would not have been surprised if it had dripped blood. On second glance, however, it could be made out that the neck faded into greyness just after the neck-piece of an undoubtedly well-tailored uniform began to show.

The head identified itself, with punctilious courtesy, as Commander Lisiform of the Auroran ship *Borealis*. D. G.

identified himself in his turn, thrusting his chin forward so as to make certain that his beard was in the sharpest possible focus. It was his opinion that his beard lent him an air of fierceness that could not help but be daunting to a beardless and (he thought) weak-chinned Spacer.

D. G. assumed the traditional air of informality that was as irritating to a Spacer officer as the latter's traditional arrogance was to a Settler. He said, 'What is your reason for hailing me, Commander Lisiform?'

The Auroran commander had an exaggerated accent which, it was possible, he thought as formidable as D. G. considered his beard to be. D. G. felt himself to be under considerable strain, as he tried to penetrate the accent and understand him.

'We believe,' said Lisiform, 'that you have on your ship an Auroran citizen named Gladia Solaria. Is that correct, Captain Baley?'

'Madam Gladia is on board this ship, Commander.'

'Thank you, Captain. With her, so my information leads me to suppose, are two robots of Auroran manufacture, R. Daneel Olivaw and R. Giskard Reventlov. Is that correct?'

'That is correct.'

'In that case, I must inform you that R. Giskard Reventlov is, at present, a dangerous device. Shortly before your ship left Auroran space with him, the said robot, Giskard, badly hurt an Auroran citizen in defiance of the Three Laws. The robot must, therefore, be dismantled and repaired.'

'Are you suggesting, Commander, that we on this ship dismantle the robot?'

'No, sir, that would not do. Your people, lacking experience with robots, could not dismantle it properly, and could not possibly repair it if they did.'

'We might, then, simply destroy it.'

'It is too valuable for that. Captain Baley, the robot is

Aurora's product and Aurora's responsibility. We do not wish to be the cause of damage to the people on your ship, and on the planet Earth if you land there. Consequently, we ask that it be delivered to us.'

D. G. said, 'Commander, I appreciate your concern. However, the robot is the legal property of the Lady Gladia, who is with us. It may be that she would not consent to be parted from her robot and, while I don't want to teach you Auroran law, I believe that it would be illegal by that law to force such a parting. While my crew and I do not consider ourselves bound by Auroran law, we would not willingly be a party to helping you perform what your own government might consider to be an illegal act.'

There was a suggestion of impatience in the Commander's voice. 'There is no question of illegality, Captain. A life-endangering malfunction in a robot supersedes the ordinary rights of an owner. Nevertheless, if there is any question of that, my ship stands ready to accept Lady Gladia and her robot, Daneel, along with Giskard, the robot in question. There will then be no separation of Gladia Solaria and her robotic property until she is brought back to Aurora. The law can then take its proper course.'

'It is possible, Commander, that the Lady Gladia may not wish to leave my ship, or to allow her property to do so.'

'She has no recourse, Captain. I am legally empowered by my government to demand her, and as an Auroran citizen, she must obey.'

'But I am not legally bound to deliver up anything on my ship at the demand of a foreign power. What if I choose to disregard your request?'

'In that case, Captain, I would have no choice but to consider it an unfriendly act. May I point out that we are within the sphere of the planetary system of which Earth is part. You had no hesitation in teaching me Auroran law. You will forgive me, then, if I point out that *your* people do not consider it proper to engage in hostilities within the space of this planetary system.'

'I am aware of that, Commander, and I wish no hostilities, nor do I intend an unfriendly act. However, I am bound for Earth under some urgency. I lose time in this conversation and I would lose further time if I moved towards you, or waited for you to move towards me, so that we could carry through a physical transfer of the lady and her robots. I would prefer to continue onward towards Earth and formally accept all responsibility for the robot, Giskard, and his behaviour until such time as the Lady Gladia, and her robots, return to Aurora.'

'May I make the suggestion, Captain, that you place the woman and two robots in a lifeboat, and detach a member of your crew to pilot it to us. Once the woman and the two robots are delivered, we will ourselves escort the lifeboat to the immediate environs of Earth and we will compensate you adequately for your time and trouble. A Trader should not object to that.'

'I don't, Commander, I don't,' said D. G., smiling. 'Still, the crewman detailed to pilot the lifeboat might be in great peril since he would be alone with this dangerous robot.'

'Captain, if the robot's owner is firm in her control, your crewman will be in no greater danger on the lifeboat than he would be on your ship. We will compensate him for the risk.'

'But if the robot can, after all, be controlled by its owner, surely it is not so dangerous that it can't be left with us?'

The Commander frowned. 'Captain, I trust you are not trying to play games with me. You have my request and I would like to have it honoured at once.'

'I presume I may consult the Lady Gladia.'

'If you do so immediately. Please explain to her exactly what is involved. If, meanwhile, you try to proceed towards Earth, I shall consider that an unfriendly act and take the appropriate action. Since, as you claim, your trip towards Earth is urgent, I advise you to proceed forthwith to consult Gladia Solaria, and come to the immediate decision to cooperate with us. You will then not be too long delayed.'

'I will do what I can,' said D. G. wooden-faced, as he moved out of focus.

70.

'Well?' said D. G., gravely.

Gladia looked distressed. Automatically, she looked towards Daneel and Giskard, but they remained silent and motionless.

She said, 'I don't want to return to Aurora, D. G. They can't possibly want to destroy Giskard; he is in perfect working order, I assure you. That's only a subterfuge. They want *me* for some reason. I suppose there's no way they can be stopped, though, is there?'

D. G. said, 'That's an Auroran warship, and a big one. This is only a Trading vessel. We've got energy shields and they can't just destroy us at a blow, but they can wear us down eventually – quite soon, in fact, and then destroy us.'

'Is there any way you can strike at them?'

'With my weapons? I'm sorry, Gladia, but their shields can take anything I can throw at them for as long as I can possibly have energy to expend. Besides – '

'Yes?'

'Well, they've just about cornered me. Somehow, I

thought they would try to intercept me before I Jumped, but they knew my destination and they got here first and waited for me. We're inside the Solar system – the planetary system of which Earth is part. We can't fight here. Even if I wanted to, the crew wouldn't obey me.'

'Why not?'

'Call it superstition. The Solar system is holy space to us – if you want to describe it in melodramatic terms. We can't desecrate it by fighting.'

Giskard said suddenly, 'May I contribute to the discussion, sir?'

D. G. frowned and looked towards Gladia.

Gladia said, 'Please. Let him. These robots are highly intelligent. I know you find that hard to believe, but – '

'I'll listen. I don't have to be influenced.'

Giskard said, 'Sir, I am certain that it *is* me that they want. I cannot allow myself to be the cause of harm to human beings. If you cannot defend yourself, and are sure of destruction in a conflict with the other vessel, you have no choice but to give me up. I am sure that if you offer to let them have me, they will not seriously object if you wish to retain Lady Gladia and Friend Daneel. It is the only solution.'

'No,' said Gladia forcefully. 'You are mine and I won't give you up. I'll go with you, if the Captain decides you must go, and I'll see to it they *don't* destroy you.'

'May I speak as well?' said Daneel.

D. G. spread his hands in mock-despair. 'Please. Everyone speak.'

Daneel said, 'If you decide you must give up Giskard, you must understand the consequences. I believe that Giskard thinks that if he is given up, those on the Auroran ship would do him no harm and that they will even release him. I do not believe this to be so. I believe the Aurorans are serious in thinking him to be dangerous, and they may well have instructions to destroy the lifeboat as it approaches, killing whoever is on board.'

'For what reason would they do that?' asked D. G.

'No Auroran has ever encountered, or even conceived of, what they call a dangerous robot. They would take no chances of taking one on board one of their vessels. I would suggest, Captain, that you retreat. Why not Jump again, away from Earth? We are not close enough to any planetary mass to prevent that.'

'Retreat? You mean run away? I can't do that.'

'Well, then, you have to give us up,' said Gladia, with an air of resigned hopelessness.

D. G. said, forcefully, 'I'm not giving you up. And I'm not running away. And I can't fight.'

'Then what's left?' asked Gladia.

'A fourth alternative,' said D. G. 'Gladia, I must ask you to remain here with your robots till I return.'

71.

D. G. considered the data. There had been enough time during the conversation for the location of the Auroran vessel to be pin-pointed. It was a bit farther from the Sun than his own ship was, and that was good. To Jump towards the Sun, at this distance from it, would have been risky indeed; to Jump sideways would be, so to speak, a piece of cake in comparison. There was the chance of accident through probability deviation, but there was always that.

He had himself assured the crew that not a shot would be fired (which would do no good in any case). Clearly, they had utter faith in Earth-space protecting them as long as they didn't profane its peace by offering violence. It was pure mysticism which D. G. would have scornfully derided, had he not shared the conviction himself.

He moved back into focus. It had been a fairly long wait, but there had been no signal from the other side. They had shown exemplary patience.

'Captain Baley here,' he said. 'I wish to speak to Commander Lisiform.'

There was not much of a wait. 'Commander Lisiform here. May I have your answer?'

D. G. said, 'We will deliver the woman and the two robots.'

'Good! A wise decision.'

'And we will deliver them as quickly as we can.'

'Again a wise decision.'

'Thank you.' D. G. gave the signal, and his ship Jumped.

There was no time, no need, to hold one's breath. It was over as soon as it was begun; or, at least, the time-lapse was insensible.

The word came from the pilot. 'New enemy-ship position fixed, Captain.'

'Good,' said D. G. 'You know what to do.'

The ship had come out of the Jump at high speed relative to the Auroran vessel, and the course correction (not a great deal, it was to be hoped) was being made. Then further acceleration.

D. G. moved back into focus. 'We are close, Commander, and on our way to deliver. You may fire if you choose, but our shields are up and before you can batter them down, we will have reached you in order to make the delivery.'

'Are you sending a lifeboat?' The Commander moved out of focus.

D. G. waited, and the Commander was back, his face contorted. 'What is this? Your ship is on a collision course.'

'It seems to be, yes,' said D. G. 'That is the fastest way of making delivery.'

'You will destroy your ship.'

'And yours, too. Your ship is at least fifty times as expensive as mine; probably more. A poor exchange for Aurora.'

'But you are engaging in combat in Earth-space, Captain. Your customs do not allow that.'

'Ah, you know our customs and you take advantage of them. But I am not in combat. I have not fired an erg of energy and I won't. I am merely following a trajectory. That trajectory happens to intersect your position, but since I am sure you will move before the intersection movement arrives, it is clear I intend no violence.'

'Stop. Let's talk about this.'

'I'm tired of talking, Commander. Shall we all say a fond farewell? If you don't move, I will be giving up perhaps four decades, with the third and fourth not so good, anyway. How many will you be giving up?' And D. G. moved out of focus and stayed out.

A beam of radiation shot out from the Auroran ship, tentative, as though to test whether the other's shields were truly up. They were.

Ships' shields would hold against electromagnetic radiation and subatomic particles, including even neutrinos, and could withstand the kinetic energy of small masses – dust particles, even meteoric gravel. The shields could not withstand larger kinetic energies such as that of an entire ship hurtling at it with super-meteoric speed.

Even dangerous masses, if not guided – a meteoroid, for instance – could be handled. A vessel's computers would automatically veer the ship out of the way of any oncoming meteoroid that was too large for the shield to handle. That, however, would not work against a ship that could veer as its target veered. And if the Settler ship was the smaller of the two, it was also the more manoeuvrable.

There was only one way that the Auroran ship could avoid destruction.

D. G. watched the other ship visibly enlarging in his viewing panel, and wondered if Gladia, in her cabin, knew what was going on. She must be aware of the acceleration, despite the hydraulic suspension of her cabin and the compensatory action of the pseudo-gravity field.

And then the other ship simply winked out of view, having Jumped away, and D. G., with considerable chagrin, realized he was holding his breath, and that his heart was racing. Had he had no confidence in the protecting influence of Earth, or in his own sure diagnosis of the situation?

D. G. spoke into the transmitter in a voice that, with iron resolution, he forced into coolness. 'Well done, men! Correct course and head for Earth.'

16

The City

72.

Gladia said, 'Are you serious, D. G.? You really intended to collide with the ship?'

'Not at all,' said D. G., indifferently. 'I wasn't expecting to. I merely lunged at them, knowing they would retreat. Those Spacers weren't going to risk their long, wonderful lives when they could easily preserve them.'

'*Those* Spacers? What cowards *they* are.'

D. G. cleared his throat. 'I keep forgetting you're a Spacer, Gladia.'

'Yes, and I imagine you think that that is a compliment to me. What if they had been as foolish as you – if they had shown the childish madness you think of as bravery – and stayed in place? What would you have done?'

D. G. muttered, 'Hit them.'

'And then we would all have died.'

'The transaction would have been in our favour, Gladia. One crummy old Trader ship from a Settler world, for a new and advanced warship of the leading Spacer world.'

D. G. tipped his chair back against the wall and put his hands behind his neck (amazing how comfortable he felt now that it was all over). 'I once saw a historical hyper-drama, in which, towards the end of a war, aeroplanes loaded with explosives were deliberately flown into much more expensive seaships in order to sink them. Of course, the pilot of the aeroplane lost his life.'

'That was fiction,' said Gladia. 'You don't suppose civilized people do things like that in real life, do you?'

'Why not? If the cause is good enough.'

'What was it, then, you felt as you plunged towards a glorious death? Exaltation? You were hurtling all your crew towards the same death.'

'They knew about it. We could do nothing else. Earth was watching.'

'The people on Earth didn't even know.'

'I mean it metaphorically. We were in Earth-space. We could not act ignobly.'

'Oh, what nonsense! And you risked my life, too.'

D. G. looked down at his boots. 'Would you like to hear something crazy? That was the only thing that bothered me.'

'That I would die?'

'Not quite. That I would lose you. When that ship ordered me to give you up, I knew I wouldn't – even if you asked me to. I would gladly ram them instead; they couldn't have you. And then, as I watched their ship expand in the viewscreen, I thought, "If they don't get out of here, I'll lose her anyway", and that's when my heart started to pound and I began to sweat. I *knew* they'd run, and still the thought – ' He shook his head.

Gladia frowned. 'I don't understand you. You weren't worrying about my dying, but you were worried about losing me? Don't the two go together?'

'I know. I'm not saying it's rational. I thought of you rushing at the overseer to save me when you knew it could murder you with a blow. I thought of you facing the crowd at Baleyworld and talking them down when you had never even seen a crowd before. I even thought of you going to Aurora when you were a young woman and learning a new way of life – and surviving. And it seemed to me I didn't mind dying; I just minded losing you. You're right; it doesn't make sense.'

Gladia said, thoughtfully, 'Have you forgotten my age? I was just about as old as I am now when you were born. When I was your age, I used to dream of your seven-times-great grandfather. What's more, I've got an artificial hip-joint. My left thumb – this one right here,' she wiggled it, 'is strictly prosthetic. Some of my nerves have been rebuilt. My teeth are all implanted ceramic. And you talk as though any moment you're going to confess a transcendent passion. For what? For whom? Think, D. G.! Look at me and see me as I am!'

D. G. tilted his chair back on all four legs and rubbed at his beard with an odd scraping sound. 'All right. You've made me sound silly, but I'm going to keep right on. What I know about your age is that you're going to survive me, and look scarcely any older when you do, so you're younger than I am, not older. Besides, I don't care if you are older. What I would like is for you to stay with me wherever I go; for all my life, if possible.'

Gladia was about to speak, but D. G. intervened hastily, 'Or, if it seems more convenient, for me to stay with you wherever you go; for all my life, if possible. If it's all right with you.'

Gladia said, softly, 'I'm a Spacer. You're a Settler.'

'Who cares, Gladia? Do you?'

'I mean, there's no question of children. I've had mine.'

'What difference does that make to me! There's no danger of the name, Baley, dying out.'

'I have a task of my own. I intend to bring peace to the Galaxy.'

'I'll help you.'

'And your Trading? Will you give up your chance to be rich?'

'We'll do some together. Just enough to keep my crew

happy and to help me support you in your task as peace-bringer.'

'Life will be dull for you, D. G.'

'Will it? It seems to me that since you joined me, it's been *too* exciting.'

'And you'll probably insist on my giving up my robots.'

D. G. looked distressed. 'Is *that* why you've been trying to talk me out of this? I wouldn't mind your keeping the two of them – even Daneel and his small lecherous smile – but if we're going to live among Settlers – '

'Then I suppose I'll have to try to find the courage to do it.'

She laughed gently, and so did D. G. He held out his arms to her and she placed her hands in his.

She said, 'You're mad; I'm mad; but everything has been so strange since the evening I looked up at the sky in Aurora and tried to find Solaria's sun, that I suppose being mad is the only possible sane response to things.'

'What you've just said isn't only mad,' said D. G., 'it's crazy, but that's the way I want you to be.' He hesitated. 'No, I'll wait. I'll shave my beard before I try to kiss you. That will lower the chances of infection.'

'No, don't! I'm curious about how it might feel.'

And she promptly found out.

73.

Commander Lisiform strode back and forth across the length of his cabin. He said, 'There was no use losing the ship. No use at all.'

His Political Adviser sat quietly in his chair. His eyes did not bother to follow the agitated and rapid to-and-fro movement of the other. 'Yes, of course,' he said.

'What have the barbarians to lose? They only live a few decades in any case. Life means nothing to them.'

'Yes, of course.'

'Still, I've never seen or heard of a Settler ship doing that. It may be a new fanatical tactic, and we have no defence against it. What if they send drone ships against us, with shields up and full momentum, but no human beings aboard?'

'We might robotify our ships entirely.'

'That wouldn't help. We couldn't afford to lose the ship. What we need is the shield-knife they keep talking about. Something that will slice through a shield.'

'Then they'll develop one, too, and we will have to devise a knife-proof shield, and so will they, and it will be a stand-off again at a higher level.'

'We need something completely new, then.'

'Well,' said the Adviser, 'maybe something will turn up. Your mission wasn't primarily the matter of the Solarian woman and her robots, was it? It would have been pleasant if we could have forced them out of the Settler ship, but that was secondary, wasn't it?'

'The Council isn't going to like it, just the same.'

'It's *my* job to take care of that. The important fact is that Amadiro and Mandamus left the ship and are on their way to Earth in a good, speedy ferry.'

'Well, yes.'

'And you not only distracted the Settler ship, but delayed it as well. That means Amadiro and Mandamus not only left the ship unnoticed but they will be on Earth before our barbarian captain will.'

'I suppose so. But what of that?'

'I wonder. If it were Mandamus, I would dismiss the matter. He's of no consequence. But Amadiro? To abandon the political wars back home at a difficult time and come to

Earth? Something absolutely crucial must be going on here.'

'What?' The Commander seemed annoyed that he should be so nearly, and so all-but-fatally, involved in something of which he understood nothing.

'I haven't any idea.'

'Do you suppose it might be secret negotiations at the highest level for some sort of overall modification of the peace settlement Fastolfe negotiated?'

The Adviser smiled. 'Peace settlement? If you think that, you don't know our Dr Amadiro. He wouldn't travel to Earth in order to modify a clause or two in a peace settlement. What he's after is a Galaxy without Settlers, and if he comes to Earth – well, all I can say is I wouldn't like to be in the shoes of the Settler barbarians at this time.'

74.

'I trust, Friend Giskard,' said Daneel, 'that Madam Gladia is not uneasy at being without us. Can you tell at her distance?'

'I can detect her mind faintly, but unmistakably, Friend Daneel. She is with the Captain, and there is a distinct overlay of excitement and joy.'

'Excellent, Friend Giskard.'

'Less excellent for myself, Friend Daneel. I find myself in a state of some disorder. I have been under a great strain.'

'It distresses me to hear that, Friend Giskard. May I ask the reason?'

'We have been here for some time while the Captain negotiated with the Auroran ship.'

'Yes, but the Auroran ship is now gone, apparently, so that the Captain seems to have negotiated to good effect.'

'He has done so in a manner of which you were apparently not aware. I was – to an extent. Though the Captain was not here with us I had little trouble sensing his mind. It exuded overwhelming tension and suspense, and underneath that a gathering and strengthening sense of loss.'

'Loss, Friend Giskard? Were you able to determine of what that loss might consist?'

'I cannot describe my method of analysis of such things, but the loss did not seem to be the type of loss I have in the past associated with generalities or with inanimate objects. It had the touch – that is not the word, but there is no other that fits even vaguely – of the loss of a specific person.'

'The Lady Gladia?'

'Yes.'

'That would be natural, Friend Giskard. He was faced with the possibility of having to give her up to the Auroran vessel.'

'It was too intense for that. Too wailing.'

'Too wailing?'

'It is the only word I can think of in this connection. There was a stressful mourning associated with the sense of loss. It was not as though the lady would move elsewhere and be unavailable for that reason. That might, after all, be corrected at some future time. It was as though the lady would cease existing – would die – and be *forever* unavailable.'

'He felt, then, that the Aurorans would kill her? Surely, that is not possible.'

'Indeed, not possible. And that is not it. I felt a thread of a sense of personal responsibility associated with the deep, deep fear of loss. I searched other minds on board ship, and putting it all together, I came to the suspicion that the Captain was deliberately charging his ship into the Auroran vessel.'

'That, too, is not possible, Friend Giskard,' said Daneel, in a low voice.

'I had to accept it. My first impulse was to alter the Captain's emotional make-up in such a way as to force him to change course, but I could not. His mind was so firmly set, so saturated with determination and, despite the suspense, tension, and dread of loss, so filled with confidence of success – '

'How could there be at once a dread of loss through death, and a feeling of confidence of success?'

'Friend Daneel, I have given up marvelling at the capacity of the human mind to maintain two opposing emotions simultaneously. I merely accept it. In this case, to have attempted to alter the Captain's mind to the point of turning the ship from its course, would have killed him. I could not do that.'

'But if you did not, Friend Giskard, scores of human beings on this ship, including Madam Gladia, and several hundreds more on the Auroran vessel, would die.'

'They might *not* die if the Captain were correct in his feeling of confidence in success. I could not bring about one certain death to prevent many merely probable ones. There is the difficulty, Friend Daneel, in your Zeroth Law. The First Law deals with specific individuals and certainties. Your Zeroth Law deals with vague groups and probabilities.'

'The human beings on board these ships are not vague groups. They are many specific individuals taken together.'

'Yet when I must make a decision it is the specific individual I am about to influence directly whose fate must count with me. I cannot help that.'

'What was it you did do, then, Friend Giskard; or were you completely helpless?'

'In my desperation, Friend Daneel, I attempted to contact the Commander of the Auroran vessel, after a small Jump had brought him quite close to us. I could not. The distance was too great. And yet the attempt was not altogether a failure. I did detect something, the equivalent of a faint hum. I puzzled over it a short while before realizing I was receiving the overall sensation of the minds of all the human beings on board the Auroran vessel. I had to filter out that faint hum from the much more prominent sensations arising from our own vessel – a difficult task.'

Daneel said, 'Nearly impossible, I should think, Friend Giskard.'

'As you say, nearly impossible, but I managed it with an enormous effort. However, try as I might, I could make out no individual minds. When Madam Gladia faced the large numbers of human beings in her audience on Baleyworld, I sensed an anarchic confusion of a vast jumble of minds, but I managed to pick out individual minds here and there for a moment or two. That was not so on this occasion.'

Giskard paused, as though lost in his memory of the sensation.

Daneel said, 'I imagine this must be analogous to the manner in which we see individual stars even among large groups of them, when the whole is comparatively close to us. In a distant galaxy, however, we cannot make out individual stars but can see only a faintly luminous fog.'

'That strikes me as a good analogy, Friend Daneel. And as I concentrated on the faint, but distant, hum, it seemed to me that I could detect a very dim wash of fear permeating it. I was not sure of this, but I felt I had to try to take advantage of it. I had never attempted to exert influence over anything so far away, over anything as inchoate as a mere hum – but I tried desperately to increase that fear by however small a trifle. I cannot say whether I succeeded.'

'The Auroran vessel fled. You *must* have succeeded.'

'Not necessarily. The vessel might have fled if I had done nothing.'

Daneel seemed lost in thought. 'It might. If our Captain were so confident that it would flee – '

Giskard said, 'On the other hand, I cannot be sure that there was a rational basis to that confidence. It seemed to me that what I detected was intermixed with a feeling of awe and reverence for Earth. The confidence I sensed was rather similar to the kind I have detected in young children towards their protectors, parental or otherwise. I had the feeling that the Captain believed he could not fail in the neighbourhood of Earth because of the influence of Earth. I wouldn't say the feeling was exactly irrational, but it felt non-rational, in any case.'

'You are undoubtedly right in this, Friend Giskard. The Captain has, in our hearing, spoken of Earth, on occasion, in a reverential manner. Since Earth cannot truly influence the success of an action through any mystical influence, it is quite possible to suppose that your influence was indeed successfully exerted. And moreover – '

Giskard, his eyes glowing dimly, said, 'Of what are you thinking, Friend Daneel?'

'I have been thinking of the supposition that the individual human being is concrete while humanity is abstract. When you detected that faint hum from the Auroran ship, you were not detecting an individual, but a portion of humanity. Could you not, if you were at a proper distance from Earth and if the background noise were sufficiently small, detect the hum of the mental activity of Earth's human population, overall? And, extending that, can one not imagine that in the Galaxy generally there is the hum of the mental activity of all of humanity? How, then, is humanity an abstraction? It is something you can point to. Think of that in connection with the Zeroth Law and you will see that the extension of the Laws of Robotics is a justified one – justified by your own experience.'

There was a long pause and finally Giskard said, slowly as though it were being dragged out of him, 'You may be right, Friend Daneel. And yet, if we are landing on Earth now, with a Zeroth Law we *may* be able to use, we still don't know *how* we might use it. It seems to us, so far, that the crisis that Earth faces involves the use of a nuclear intensifier, but as far as we know, there is nothing of significance on Earth on which a nuclear intensifier can do its work. What, then, will we do on Earth?'

'I do not as yet know,' said Daneel, sadly.

75.

Noise!

Gladia listened in astonishment. It didn't hurt her ears. It wasn't the sound of surface clashing on surface. It wasn't a piercing shriek, or a clamour, or a banging, or anything that could be expressed by an onomatopoeitic word.

It was softer and less overwhelming, rising and falling, bearing within it an occasional irregularity, and always there.

D. G. watched her listening, cocking her head to this side and that, and said, 'I call it the Drone of the City, Gladia.'

'Does it ever stop?'

'Never, really, but what can you expect? Haven't you ever stood in a field and heard the wind rustling the leaves, and insects stridulating, and birds calling, and water running. That never stops.'

'That's different.'

'No, it isn't. It's the same. The sound here is the melting together of the rumble of machinery and the various noises people make; but the principle is precisely the same as the natural non-human noises of a field. You're used to fields, so you don't hear the noise there. You're not used to *this*, so you hear it and probably find it annoying. Earthpeople don't hear it except on the rare occasions when they come fresh in from the countryside, and then they are very glad indeed to greet it. Tomorrow you won't hear it either.'

Gladia looked about thoughtfully, from their position on a small balcony. 'So many buildings!'

'That's true enough. Structures in every direction – stretching outward for miles. And up, and down, too. This is not just a city, in the fashion of Aurora or Baleyworld. It is a City – capital C – of the kind that exists only on Earth.'

'These are the Caves of Steel,' said Gladia. 'I know. We're underground, aren't we?'

'Yes. Absolutely. I must tell you that it took *me* time to get used to this sort of thing the first time I visited Earth. Wherever you go in a City, it looks like a crowded city scene. Walkways and roadways and storefronts and mobs of people, with the soft and universal lights of fluorescents making everything seem bathed in soft, shadowless sunshine – but it *isn't* sunshine, and, up above on the surface, I don't know if the Sun is really shining at the moment, or is covered by clouds, or is absent altogether leaving this part of the world plunged in night and darkness.'

'It makes the City enclosed. People breathe each other's air.'

'We do anyway, on any world, anywhere.'

'Not like this.' She sniffed. 'It smells.'

'Every world smells. Every City on Earth smells differently. You'll get used to it.'

'Do I want to? Why don't people suffocate?'

'Excellent ventilation.'

'What happens when it breaks down?'

'It never does.'

Gladia looked about again, and said, 'Every building seems loaded with balconies.'

'It's a sign of status. Very few people have apartments facing out and if they do have one, they want the advantage of it. Most Citypeople live inside windowless apartments.'

Gladia shuddered, 'Horrible!' Then, 'What's the name of this City, D. G.?'

'It's New York. It's the chief City, but not the largest. On this continent, Mexico City and Los Angeles are the largest, and there are Cities larger than New York on other continents.'

'What makes New York the chief City, then?'

'The usual reason. The Planetary Government is located here. The United Nations.'

'Nations?' She pointed her finger triumphantly at D. G. 'Earth was divided into several independent political units. Right?'

'Right. Dozens of them. But that was before hyperspatial travel – prehyper times. The name remains, though. That's what's wonderful about Earth. It's frozen history. Every other world is new and shallow. Only Earth is *humanity* in its essence.'

D. G. said it in a hushed whisper and then retreated back into the room. It was not a large one and its furnishings were skimpy.

Gladia said, disappointed, 'Why isn't there anyone about?'

D. G. laughed. 'Don't worry, dear. If it's parades and attention you want, you'll have them. It's just that I asked them to leave us alone for a while. I want a little peace and rest and I imagine you do too. As for my men, they have to berth the ship, clean it up, renew supplies, tend to their devotions – '

'Women?'

'No, that's not what I mean, though I suppose women will play a role later. By devotions, I mean that Earth still has its religions and these comfort the men somehow. Here on Earth, anyway. It seems to have more meaning here.'

'Well,' said Gladia, half-contemptuously. 'Frozen history, as you say. Do you suppose we can get out of the building and walk about a bit?'

'Take my advice, Gladia, and don't jump into that sort of thing just now. You'll get plenty of it when the ceremonies begin.'

'But that will be so formal. Could we skip the ceremonies?'

'No chance at all. Since you insisted on making yourself a heroine on Baleyworld, you'll have to be one on Earth as well. Still, the ceremonies will be through eventually, and when you recover from them, we will get a guide and we'll *really* see the City.'

'Will we have any trouble taking my robots with us?' She gestured towards them where they stood at the other end of the room. 'I don't mind being without them when I'm with you on the ship, but if I'm going to be with crowds of strangers I'll feel more secure having them with me.'

'There'll be no problem with Daneel, certainly. He's a hero in his own right. He was the Ancestor's partner, and he passes for human. Giskard, who is an obvious robot, should, in theory, not be allowed inside the City borders, but they've made an exception in his case and I hope they will continue to do so. It is too bad, in a way, that we must wait here and can't step outside.'

'You say I should not be exposed to all that noise just yet,' said Gladia.

'No, no. I'm not referring to the public squares and roadways. I would just like to take you out into the corridors within this particular building. There are miles and miles of them, literally, and they're a small bit of City in themselves; shopping recesses, dining halls, amusement areas, Personals, elevators, transways, and so on. There's more colour and variety on one floor in one building in one City on Earth, than in a whole Settler town or in a whole Spacer world.'

'I should think everyone would get lost.'

'Of course not. Everyone knows their own neighbourhood here, as anywhere else. Even strangers need only follow the signs.'

'I suppose all the walking that people are forced to do must be very good for them physically,' said Gladia, dubiously.

'Socially, too. There are people in the corridors at all times and the convention is that you stop to exchange words with anyone you know and that you greet even those you don't know. Nor is walking absolutely necessary. There are elevators everywhere for vertical travel. The main corridors are transways, and move for horizontal travel. Outside the building, of course, there is a feeder line to the Expressway network. *That's* something. You'll get to ride it.'

'I've heard of them. They have strips that you walk across and that drag you along faster and faster, or slower and slower, as you move from one to another. I couldn't do that. Don't ask me to.'

'Of course you'll be able to do it,' said D. G. genially. 'I'll help you. If necessary, I'll carry you, but all it takes is a little practice. Among the Earthpeople, kindergarten children manage and so do old people with canes. I admit

Settlers tend to be clumsy about it. I'm no miracle of grace myself, but I manage and so will you.'

Gladia heaved an enormous sigh. 'Well, then, I'll try if I have to, but I tell you what, D. G. dear, we *must* have a reasonably quiet room for the night. I want your Drone of the City muted.'

'That can be arranged, I'm sure.'

'And I don't want to have to eat in the dining halls.'

D. G. looked doubtful. 'We can arrange to have food brought in, but really it would do you good to participate in the social life of Earth. I'll be with you, after all.'

'Maybe after a while, D. G., but not just at first, and I want a Woman's Personal for myself.'

'Oh, no, *that's* impossible. There'll be a washbasin and a toilet bowl in any room they assign us because we have status, but if you intend to do any serious showering or bathing, you'll have to follow the crowd. There'll be a woman to introduce you to the procedure and you'll be assigned a stall or whatever it is they have there. You won't be embarrassed. Settler women have to be introduced to the use of Personals every day of the year. And you may end up enjoying it, Gladia. They tell me that the Woman's Personal is a place of much activity and fun. In the Man's Personal, on the other hand, not a word is allowed to be spoken. Very dull.'

'It's all horrible,' muttered Gladia. 'How do you stand the lack of privacy?'

'On a crowded world, needs must,' said D. G., lightly. 'What you've never had, you never miss. Do you want any other aphorisms?'

'Not really,' said Gladia.

She looked dejected, and D. G. put an arm about her shoulder. 'Come, it won't be as bad as you think. I promise you.'

76.

It was not exactly a nightmare, but Gladia was thankful to her earlier experience on Baleyworld for having given her a foretaste of what was now a veritable ocean of humanity. The crowds were much larger here in New York than they had been on the Settler world, but on the other hand, she was more insulated from the herd here than she had been on the earlier occasion.

The government officials were clearly anxious to be seen with her. There was a wordless, polite struggle for a position near enough to her to be seen with her on hypervision. It isolated her not only from the crowds on the other side of the police lines, but from D. G. and from her two robots. It also subjected her to a kind of polite jostling that had no personal component but that had its eye only on the camera.

She listened to what seemed innumerable speeches, all mercifully brief, without really listening. She smiled periodically, both blandly and blindly, casting the vision of her implanted teeth in all directions indiscriminately.

She went by ground-car through miles of passageways at a crawl, while an uncounted antheap lined the walkways, cheering and waving as she passed. (She wondered if ever a Spacer had received such adulation from Earthpeople, and was quite confident that her own case was entirely unprecedented.)

At one point, she caught sight of a distant knot of people gathered round a hypervision screen, and momentarily had an undoubted glimpse of herself upon it. They were listening, she knew, to a recording of her speech on Baleyworld, and wondered how many times and in how many places and before how many people it was being played now, and how many times it had been played since she gave it, and how many times it would yet be played in the future, and whether anything at all had been heard of it on the Spacer worlds.

Might she, in fact, seem a traitor to the people of Aurora and would this reception be held to be proof of it?

She might, and it might, and she was beyond caring. She had her mission of peace and reconciliation, and she would follow it wherever it led without complaint – even to the unbelievable orgy of mass bathing and shrilly unconscious exhibitionism in the Woman's Personal that morning. (Well, without much complaint.)

They came to one of the Expressways that D. G. had mentioned, and she gazed in open horror at the endless snake of passenger cars that passed – and passed – and passed – each with its load of people who were on business that could not be postponed for the motorcade, or who simply didn't want to be bothered, and who stared solemnly at the crowds and the procession for the few moments these remained within sight.

Then the ground-car plunged downward under the Expressway, through a short tunnel that in no way differed from the passage above (the City was all tunnel) and up again on the other side.

And eventually the motorcade came to an end at a large public building that was, mercifully, more attractive than the endlessly repetitious blocks that represented the units of the City's residential section.

Within the building, there was yet another reception, during which alcoholic drinks, and various hors d'oeuvres were served. Gladia fastidiously touched neither. A thousand people milled about and an endless succession of them came up to speak to Gladia. The word had apparently gone out not to offer to shake hands, but some inevitably did, and, trying not to hesitate, Gladia would briefly place two fingers on the hand and then withdraw them.

Eventually, a number of women prepared to leave for the nearest Personal and one of them performed what was obviously a social ritual and tactfully asked Gladia if she would like to accompany them. Gladia didn't, but there might be a long night ahead and it might be more embarrassing to have to interrupt it later.

Within the Personal, there was the usual excited laughing and chattering, and Gladia, bowing to the exigencies of the situation and fortified by her experience of the morning, made use of the facilities in a small chamber with partitions on either side, but with none in front of her.

No one seemed to mind and Gladia tried to remind herself she must adjust to local customs. At least the place was well-ventilated and seemed spotlessly clean.

Throughout, Daneel and Giskard had been ignored. This, Gladia realized, was a kindness. Robots were no longer allowed within City limits, though there were millions in the countryside without. To have made a point of the presence of Daneel and Giskard would have meant raising the legal issue that involved. It was easier to pretend, tactfully, that they weren't there.

Once the banquet began, they sat quietly at a table with D. G., not too far removed from the dais. At the dais, Gladia sat, eating sparingly, and wondering if the food would give her dysentery.

D. G., perhaps not entirely pleased with his relegation to the post of keeper of the robots, kept staring restlessly in Gladia's direction and, occasionally, she lifted one hand and smiled at him.

Giskard, equally watchful of Gladia, had an opportunity to say to Daneel very quietly, under cover of the relentless and unending background clash of cutlery and babble, 'Friend Daneel, these are high officials that sit here in this room. It is possible that one, or more, may have information of use to us.'

'It is possible, Friend Giskard. Can you, thanks to your abilities, guide me in this respect?'

'I cannot. The mental background yields me no specific emotional response of interest. Nor does the occasional flash among the nearest show me anything. Yet the climax of the crisis is, I am certain, approaching quickly, even as we sit here, idle.'

Daneel said, gravely, 'I will try to do as Partner Elijah would have done, and force the pace.'

77.

Daneel was not eating. He watched the assemblage with his calm eyes and located the one he was searching for. Quietly, he rose and moved towards another table, his eyes on a woman who was managing to eat briskly and yet maintain a cheerful conversation with the man on her left. She was a stocky woman, with short hair that showed definite traces of grey. Her face, if not youthful, was pleasant.

Daneel waited for a natural break in the conversation and, when that did not come, he said, with an effort, 'Madam, may I interrupt?'

She looked up at him, startled and plainly displeased. 'Yes,' she said, rather brusquely, 'what is it?'

'Madam,' said Daneel, 'I ask your pardon for this interruption, but may I have your permission to speak with you for a time?'

She stared at him, frowning for a moment, and then her expression softened. She said, 'I should guess, from your excessive politeness, that you're the robot, aren't you?'

'I am one of Madam Gladia's robots, madam.'

'Yes, but you're the human one. You're R. Daneel Olivaw.'

'That is my name, madam.'

The woman turned to the man on her left and said, 'Please excuse me. I can't very well refuse this – robot.'

Her neighbour smiled uncertainly and transferred his attention to the plate before him.

The woman said to Daneel, 'If you have a chair, why don't you bring it here? I will be glad to speak to you.'

'Thank you, madam.'

When Daneel had returned and seated himself, she said, 'You are *really* R. Daneel Olivaw, aren't you?'

'That is my name, madam,' said Daneel, again.

'I mean the one who worked with Elijah Baley long ago. You're not a new model of the same line? You're not R. Daneel the Fourth, or something like that?'

Daneel said, 'There is little of me that has not been replaced in the past twenty decades, or even modernized and improved, but my positronic brain is the same as it was when I worked with Partner Elijah on three different worlds, and once on a spaceship. It has not been altered.'

'Well!' She looked at him, admiringly. 'You're certainly a good job. If all robots were like you, I'd see no objection to them whatever. What is it you want to talk to me about?'

'When you were introduced to the Lady Gladia, madam, before we all took our seats, you were presented to her as the Undersecretary of Energy, Sophia Quintana.'

'You remember well. That is my name and my office.'

'Does the office refer to all of Earth, or merely to the City?'

'I'm Global Undersecretary, I assure you.'

'Then you are knowledgeable in the field of energetics?'

Quintana smiled. She did not seem to object to being questioned. Perhaps she thought it amusing, or perhaps she found herself attracted to Daneel's air of deferential gravity or to the mere fact that a robot could question so. In any case, she said, with a smile, 'I majored in energetics at the University of California and have a master's degree in it. As to how knowledgeable I still am, I'm not certain. I've spent too many years as an administrator; something that saps one's brains, I assure you.'

'But you would be well acquainted with the practical aspects of Earth's present energy supply, would you not?'

'Yes. That I will admit to. Is there something you want to know about it?'

'There is something that piques my curiosity, madam.'

'Curiosity? In a robot?'

Daneel bowed his head. 'If a robot is complex enough, he can be aware of something within himself that seeks information. This is analogous to what I have observed to be called "curiosity" in human beings and I take the liberty of using the same word in connection with my own feelings.'

'Fair enough. What are you curious about, R. Daneel? May I call you that?'

'Yes, madam. I understand that Earth's energy supply is drawn from solar power stations in geostationary orbit in Earth's equatorial plane.'

'You understand correctly.'

'But are these power stations the sole energy supply of this planet?'

'No. They are the chief, but not the sole, energy supply. There is considerable use of energy from Earth's internal heat, from winds, waves, tides, flowing water, and so on. We have quite a complex mix, and each variety has its advantages. Solar energy is the mainstay, however.'

'You make no mention of nuclear energy, madam. Are there no uses for micro-fusion?'

Quintana raised her eyebrows. 'Is that what you're curious about, R. Daneel?'

'Yes, madam. What is the reason for the absence of nuclear power sources on Earth?'

'They are not absent, R. Daneel. On a small scale, one comes across it. Our robots – we have many in the countryside, you know – are micro-fusionized. Are you, by the way?'

Daneel said, 'Yes, madam.'

'Then, too,' she went on, 'there are micro-fusionized machines here and there, but the total is quite trifling.'

'Is it not true, Madam Quintana, that micro-fusion energy sources are sensitive to the action of nuclear intensifiers?'

'They certainly are. Yes, of course. The micro-fusion power source will blow up, and I suppose that comes under the head of being sensitive.'

'Then it isn't possible for someone, using a nuclear intensifier, to cripple seriously some crucial portion of Earth's energy supply?'

Quintana laughed. 'No, of course not. In the first place, I don't see anyone dragging about a nuclear intensifier from place to place. They weigh tons and I don't think they can be manoeuvred through and along the streets and corridors of a City. Certainly, it would be noticed if anyone tried. And then, even if a nuclear intensifier were brought into play, all it could do would be to destroy a few robots and a few machines before the thing would be discovered and stopped. There is no chance at all – zero – of our being hurt in that way. Is that the reassurance you wanted, R. Daneel?' It was almost a dismissal.

Daneel said, 'There are just one or two small points I would like clarified, Madam Quintana. *Why* is there no large micro-fusion source on Earth? The Spacer worlds all depend on micro-fusion, and so do all the Settler worlds.

Micro-fusion is portable, versatile and cheap, and doesn't require the enormous effort of maintenance, repair, and replacement that space structures do.'

'And, as you said, R. Daneel, they are sensitive to nuclear intensifiers.'

'And, as *you* said, Madam Quintana, nuclear intensifiers are too large and bulky to be of much use.'

Quintana smiled broadly and nodded. 'You are very intelligent, R. Daneel,' she said. 'It never occurred to me that I would ever sit at a table and carry on a discussion like this with a robot. Your Auroran roboticists are very clever – too clever – for I fear to carry on this discussion. I'd have to worry about you taking my place in the government. You know, we do have a legend about a robot named Stephen Byerley taking a high post in the government.'

'That must be merely fiction, Madam Quintana,' said Daneel, gravely. 'There are no robots in governmental posts on any of the Spacer worlds. We are merely – robots.'

'I'm relieved to hear that, and will therefore go on. The matter of differences in power sources has its roots in history. At the time that hyperspatial travel was developed, we had micro-fusion, so that people leaving Earth took micro-fusion power sources with them. It was necessary on space ships, and on planets, too, in the generations during which they were being adapted for human occupation. It takes many years to build an adequate complex of solar power stations, and rather than undertake such a task the emigrants remained with micro-fusion. So it was with the Spacers in their time, and so it is now with the Settlers.

'On Earth, however, micro-fusion and solar power in space were developed at roughly the same time and both were used more and more. Finally, we could make our choice, and use either micro-fusion or solar power or, of course, both. And we chose solar power.'

Daneel said, 'That seems strange to me, Madam Quintana. Why not both?'

'Actually, that's not a very difficult question to answer, R. Daneel. Earth, in pre-hyperspatial days, had had experience with a primitive form of nuclear energy, and it wasn't a happy experience. When the time came to choose between solar power and micro-fusion, Earthpeople saw micro-fusion as a form of nuclear energy and turned away from it. Other worlds, which did not have our direct experience with the primitive form of nuclear energy, had no reason to turn away from micro-fusion.'

'May I ask what this primitive form of nuclear energy to which you refer might be, madam?'

'Uranium fission,' said Quintana. 'It's completely different from micro-fusion. Fission involves the splitting of massive nuclei such as those of uranium. Micro-fusion involves the joining of light nuclei such as those of hydrogen. They're both forms of nuclear energy, however.'

'I presume that uranium would be the fuel for fission devices.'

'Yes, or other massive nuclei such as those of thorium or plutonium.'

'But uranium and these others are exceedingly rare metals. Could they support a fission-using society?'

'Those elements are rare on other worlds. On Earth, they are not exactly common, but neither are they terribly rare. Uranium and thorium are widely spread in the crust in small quantities and are concentrated in a few places.'

'And are there any fission-power devices on Earth now, madam?'

'No,' said Quintana, flatly. 'Nowhere and in no fashion. Human beings would far sooner burn oil, or even wood, than fission uranium. The very word "uranium" is taboo in polite society. You wouldn't be asking me these questions or I giving you these answers if you were a human being and an Earthman.'

Daneel persisted. 'But are you certain, madam? Is there no secret device that makes use of fission that, for the sake of national security –'

'No, robot,' said Quintana, frowning. 'I tell you – no such device. None!'

Daneel rose. 'I thank you, madam, and I ask your pardon for taking your time, and for probing what would seem to be a sensitive subject. With your permission, I shall leave you now.'

Quintana waved a careless hand. 'You're welcome, R. Daneel.'

She turned again to her neighbour, secure in the knowledge that in the crowds of Earth, people never attempted to overhear a nearby conversation, or, if they did, never admitted the fact. She said, 'Would you imagine having a discussion on energetics with a *robot*?'

As for Daneel, he returned to his original place and said softly to Giskard, 'Nothing, Friend Giskard. Nothing helpful.'

Then he added, sadly, 'Perhaps I asked the wrong questions. Partner Elijah would have asked the right ones.'

17

The Assassin

78.

Secretary-General Edgar Andrev, chief executive of Earth, was a rather tall and imposing man, clean-shaven in the Spacer style. He moved always in a measured fashion, as though on constant display, and he had a twinkling way about him as though he were always well-pleased with himself. His voice was a bit too high-pitched for his body, but it fell well short of being squeaky. Without seeming obdurate, he was not easily moved.

And he wasn't this time. 'Impossible,' he said, firmly, to D. G. 'She *must* make her appearance.'

'She's had a hard day, Secretary-General,' said D. G. 'She is not accustomed to crowds, or to these surroundings. I am responsible to Baleyworld for her well-being, and my personal honour is at stake.'

'I appreciate your position,' said Andrev, 'but I represent Earth, and I cannot deny Earthpeople their view of her. The corridors are filled, the hyperwave channels are ready, and I would not be able to hide her even if I desperately wished to do so. After this – and how long can it last? Half an hour? – she can retire and she need not make another apperance till her speech tomorrow night.'

'Her comfort must be cared for,' said D. G., tacitly abandoning his position. 'She has to be kept at some distance from the crowd.'

'There will be a cordon of security guards that will give her ample breathing space. The front row of the crowd will be kept well back. They're out there now. If we don't announce that she will soon appear, there might well be disorder.'

D. G. said, 'It ought not have been arranged. It isn't safe. There are Earthpeople who aren't fond of Spacers.'

The Secretary-General shrugged. 'I wish you could tell me how I could possibly have kept it from being arranged. At the present moment she is a heroine, and she cannot be withheld. Nor will anyone offer her anything but cheers – for the moment. But if she doesn't appear, that will change. Now let us go.'

D. G. backed away, discontentedly. He caught Gladia's eye. She looked tired, and more than a little unhappy.

He said, 'You must, Gladia. There's no way out.'

For a moment, she stared down at her hands as though wondering if they could do anything to protect her, and then she straightened herself and lifted her chin – a small Spacer amid this horde of barbarians. 'If I must, I must. Will you remain with me?'

'Unless they remove me physically.'

'And my robots?'

D. G. hesitated. 'Gladia, how will two robots be able to help you in the midst of millions of human beings?'

'I know, D. G. And I also know that I will have to do without them eventually, if I am to continue this mission of mine. But not just yet, please. For the moment, I will feel safer with them, whether that makes sense or not. If these Earth officials want me to acknowledge the crowd, to smile, to wave, to do whatever it is I am supposed to do, the presence of Daneel and Giskard will comfort me. Look, D. G., I am giving in to them on a very big thing, even though I am so uneasy that I think nothing would be so nice as to run away. Let them give in to me on this very little thing.'

'I'll try,' said D. G., in clear discouragement and, as he stepped towards Andrev, Giskard moved quietly with him.

A few minutes later, when Gladia, surrounded by a carefully picked contingent of officials, moved forward towards an open balcony, D. G. remained a little behind Gladia. To the left of D. G. was Giskard, and to his right, Daneel.

The Secretary-General had said, ruefully, 'All right, all right. I don't know how you managed to make me agree, but all right.' He rubbed his forehead, aware of a small, vague ache in his right temple. For some reason he caught Giskard's eye and turned away with a stifled shudder. 'But you must keep them motionless, Captain, remember. And please keep the one that *looks* like a robot as unobtrusive as you can. He makes me uneasy and I don't want people any more aware of him than they have to be.'

D. G. said, 'They will be looking at Gladia, Secretary-General. They will see no one else.'

'I hope so,' said Andrev, waspishly. He paused to take a message-capsule someone placed in his hand. He put it into his pocket, then walked on, and didn't think of it again till they had reached the balcony.

79.

To Gladia, it seemed that each time she moved into another scene, it grew worse – more people, more noise, more confusing light, more invasion of every sense-perception.

There was shouting. She could hear her own name being shouted out. With difficulty she overcame her own tendency to retreat and become immobile. She lifted her arm and waved it and smiled, and the shouting became louder. Someone began to speak, his voice booming out over the loud-speaker system, his image on a large screen high above them so that it could be visible to all the crowd. Undoubtedly, it was also visible on innumerable screens in innumerable meeting halls in every section of every City on the planet.

Gladia sighed with relief at having someone else in the spotlight. She tried to shrink within herself and let the sound of the speaker distract the attention of the crowd.

Secretary-General Andrev, seeking cover under the voice, even as Gladia did, and rather thankful that, in giving precedence to Gladia, it had seemed desirable for him not to speak on this occasion, suddenly remembered the message he had pocketed.

He frowned in sudden disturbance over what it might be that warranted the interruption of so important a ceremony, and then experienced a reverse feeling of intense irritation over the fact that it would probably prove to be utterly unimportant.

He pressed the ball of his right thumb hard against the slight concavity designed to accept the pressure, and the capsule opened. He removed the thin piece of plasti-paper, read the message it contained and then watched it crumble and fragment. He brushed away the impalpable powder that remained and gestured imperiously to D. G.

It was scarcely necessary to whisper under the conditions of the vast and continuing noise in the square.

Andrev said, 'You said you encountered an Auroran war-vessel within the space of the Solar system.'

'Yes, and I imagine Earth's sensors detected it.'

'Of course they did. You said there were no hostile actions on either side.'

'No weapon was used. They demanded Madam Gladia and her robots, and I refused, and they left. I explained all this.'

'How long did it all take?'

'Not very long. Several hours.'

'You mean that Aurora sent a warship just to argue back and forth with you for a couple of hours and then leave?'

D. G. shrugged. 'Secretary-General, I don't know their motivations. I can only report what happened.'

The Secretary-General stared at him haughtily. 'But you do not report all that happened. The information of the sensors has now been thoroughly analysed by computer and it would seem that you attacked.'

'I did not fire a kilowatt of energy, sir.'

'Have you considered kinetic energy? You used the ship itself as a projectile.'

'So it may have seemed to them. They did not choose to withstand me and call what might have been a bluff.'

'But was it a bluff?'

'It might have been.'

'It seems to me, Captain, that you were ready to destroy two ships *inside the Solar system* and perhaps create a war crisis. That was a terrible chance to take.'

'I did not think it would come to actual destruction, and it didn't.'

'But the whole process delayed you and occupied your attention.'

'Yes, I suppose so, but why are you pointing this out?'

'Because our sensors did observe one thing you did not observe; or, at any rate, did not report.'

'What might that be, Secretary-General?'

'It caught the launching of an orbital module, which seems to have had two human beings on board, and which descended towards Earth.'

The two were immersed in a world of their own. No other human being on the balcony was paying any attention to them. Only the two robots flanking D. G. were staring at them, and listening.

It was at this point that the speaker ceased, his last words being, 'The Lady Gladia, born a Spacer on the world of Solaria, living as a Spacer on the world of Aurora, but becoming a Citizen of the Galaxy on the Settler world of Baleyworld.' He turned to her and gestured expansively, 'The Lady Gladia – '

The sound of the crowd became a long, happy rumble, and the many-headed crowd became a forest of waving arms. Gladia felt a gentle hand on her shoulder, and heard a voice in her ear which said, 'Please. A few words, my lady.'

Gladia said weakly, 'People of Earth.' The words boomed out and, uncannily, silence fell. Gladia said, again, more firmly, 'People of Earth, I stand before you a human being as you are. A bit older, I admit, so that I lack your youth, your hopefulness, your capacity for enthusiasm. My misfortune is tempered at this moment, however, by the fact that in your presence I feel myself catching your fire, so that the cloak of age falls away – '

Applause swelled, and someone on the balcony said to someone else, 'She's making them happy they're short-lived. That Spacer woman has the impudence of a devil.'

Andrev was not paying attention. He said to D. G., 'The whole episode with you may have been a device to get those men on Earth.'

D. G. said, 'I had no way of knowing that. I could think of very little else but the saving of the Lady Gladia and of my ship. Where have they landed?'

'We don't know. They have not landed in any of the City reception areas?'

D. G. said, 'I guess they wouldn't.'

'Not that it matters,' said the Secretary-General, 'except to give me passing annoyance. Over the past few years, there have been a number of landings of this sort, though none so carefully prepared. Nothing's ever happened, and we pay no attention. Earth, after all, is an open world. It is humanity's home and any person from any world can come and go freely – even Spacers, if they wish.'

D. G. rubbed his beard with a rasping noise. 'And yet their intentions might not be to do us any good, whatever.'

(Gladia was saying, 'I wish you all well on this world of human origin, on this well-packed special world, and in this marvel of a City – ' and acknowledged the gathering applause with a smile and a wave, as she stood there and allowed the enthusiasm to catch, and gather.)

Andrev raised his voice, to be heard over the clamour of the crowd. 'Whatever their intentions it can come to nothing. The peace that has descended on Earth since the Spacers withdrew and Settlement began is unbreakable within and without. For many decades now, the wilder spirits among ourselves have been leaving for the Settler worlds so that a spirit such as yours, Captain, which can dare risk the destruction of two vessels within the space of the Solar system, is not to be found on Earth. There is no substantial level of crime on Earth any longer, no violence. The security guards assigned to control this crowd have no weapons because they have no need for any.'

And as he spoke, from the anonymity of the vast crowd a blaster pointed upward towards the balcony and was carefully aimed.

80.

A number of things happened at nearly the same time.

Giskard's head had turned to stare at the crowd, drawn by some sudden effect.

Daneel's eyes followed, saw the aimed blaster and, with faster-than-human reflexes, he lunged.

The sound of the blaster rang out.

The people on the balcony froze, and then broke out into loud exclamations.

D. G. seized Gladia and snatched her to one side.

The noise from the crowd erupted into a full-throated and terrifying roar.

Daneel's lunge had been directed at Giskard and he had knocked the other robot down.

The shot from the blaster entered the room behind the balcony and gouged a hole out of a portion of the ceiling. A line drawn from the blaster to the hole might have passed through that portion of space occupied a second earlier by Giskard's head.

Giskard muttered as he was forced down. 'Not human. A robot.'

Daneel, releasing Giskard, surveyed the scene quickly. Ground level was some six metres beneath the balcony and the space below was empty. The security guards were struggling their way towards the region of upheaval within the crowd that marked the spot where the would-be-assassin had stood.

Daneel vaulted over the balcony and dropped, his metal skeleton absorbing the shock easily, as a human being's would not have.

He ran towards the crowd.

Daneel had no choice. He had never encountered anything like this before. The supreme need was to reach the robot with the blaster before it was destroyed and, with that in mind, Daneel found that, for the first time in his existence, he could not stand on the niceties of preserving individual human beings from harm. He had to shake them up somewhat.

He tossed them aside, in actual fact, as he ploughed into the crowd, crying out in stentorian fashion, 'Make way! Make way! The person with the blaster must be questioned.'

Security guards fell in behind him and they found the 'person' at last, down and somewhat battered.

Even on an Earth that prided itself on being non-violent, an eruption of rage against an obvious murderer left its mark. The assassin had been seized, kicked and beaten. It was only the very density of the crowd that had saved the assassin from being torn apart. The multiple assailants, getting in each other's way, succeeded in doing comparatively little.

The security guards pushed back the crowd with difficulty. On the ground near the prone robot, was the blaster. Daneel ignored it.

Daneel was kneeling by the captured assassin. He said, 'Can you talk?'

Bright eyes stared up at Daneel's. 'I can,' said the assassin in a voice that was low, but was quite normal, otherwise.

'Are you of Auroran origin?'

The assassin did not answer.

Daneel said quickly, 'I know you are. It was an unnecessary question. Where on this planet is your base?'

The assassin did not answer.

Daneel said, 'Your base? Where is it? You must answer. I am ordering you to answer.'

The assassin said, 'You cannot order me. You are R. Daneel Olivaw. I have been told of you, and you need not be obeyed.'

Daneel looked up, touched the nearest guard and said, 'Sir, would you ask this person where his base is?'

The guard, startled, tried to speak and only a hoarse croak emerged. He swallowed in embarrassment, cleared his throat, and then barked out, 'Where is your base?'

'I am forbidden to answer that question, sir,' said the assassin.

'You must,' said Daneel, firmly. 'A planetary official is asking it. Sir, would you order him to answer it?'

The guard said, in echo, 'I order you to answer it, prisoner.'

'I am forbidden to answer that question, sir.'

The guard reached downward to seize the assassin roughly by the shoulder, but Daneel said, rapidly, 'I would suggest that it would not be useful to offer force, sir.'

Daneel looked about. Much of the clamour of the crowd had died down. There seemed to be a tension in the air as though a million people were waiting anxiously to see what Daneel would do.

Daneel said to the several guards who had now clustered about him and the prone assassin, 'Would you clear the way for me, sirs? I must take the prisoner to the Lady Gladia. It may be that she can force an answer.'

'What about medical attention for the prisoner?' asked one of the guards.

'That will not be necessary, sir,' said Daneel. He did not explain.

81.

'That this should have happened,' said Andrev, tightly, his lips trembling with passion. They were off the balcony, in the room itself, and he glanced up at the hole in the ceiling that remained as mute evidence of the violence that had taken place.

Gladia said, in a voice that she strove successfully to keep from shaking, 'Nothing has happened. I am unharmed. There is that hole in the ceiling that you will have to repair, and perhaps some additional repairs in the room above. That's all.'

Even as she spoke, she could hear people upstairs,

seeming to be moving objects away from the hole and, presumably, assessing damage.

'That is *not* all,' said Andrev. 'It ruins our plans for your appearance tomorrow; for your major address to the planet.'

'It does the opposite,' said Gladia. 'The planet will be the more anxious to hear me, knowing I have been a near-victim of a blaster.'

'But there's the chance of a repetition – of another attempt.'

Gladia shrugged lightly. 'That just makes me feel I'm on the right track. Secretary-General Andrev, I discovered not too long ago that I have a mission in life. It did not occur to me that this mission might place me in danger, but since it does, it also occurs to me that I would *not* be in danger and *not* worth the killing, if I were not striking home. If danger is a measure of my effectiveness, I am willing to risk that danger.'

Giskard, who had long been back on his feet, said, 'Madam Gladia, Daneel is here, with, I presume, the individual who aimed a blaster in this direction.'

It was not only Daneel, carrying a relaxed, unstruggling figure, who appeared in the doorway of the room, but half a dozen security guards as well. Outside, the noise of the crowd seemed lower and more distant. It was clearly beginning to disperse, and periodically one could hear the announcement over the loudspeakers, 'No one has been hurt. There is no danger. Return to your homes.'

Andrev waved the guards away. 'Is that the one?' he asked, sharply.

Daneel said, 'There is no question, sir, but that this is the individual with the blaster. The weapon was near him, the people close to the scene witnessed his action, and he himself admits the deed.'

Andrev stared at him in astonishment. 'He's so calm. He doesn't seem human.'

'He is not human, sir. He is a robot, a humanoid robot.'

'But we don't have any humanoid robots on Earth. Except you.'

'This robot, Secretary-General,' said Daneel, 'is, like myself, of Auroran manufacture.'

Gladia frowned. 'But that's impossible. A robot couldn't have been ordered to assassinate me.'

D. G., looking exasperated, and with a most possessive arm about Gladia's shoulder, said in an angry rumble, 'An Auroran robot, specially programmed –'

'Nonsense, D. G.,' said Gladia. 'No way. Auroran or not, special programming or not, a robot cannot deliberately try to harm a human being it knows to be a human being. If this robot did fire the blaster in my direction, he missed me on purpose.'

'To what end?' demanded Andrev. 'Why should he miss, madam?'

'Don't you see?' said Gladia. 'Whoever it was that gave the robot its orders must have felt that the *attempt* would be enough to disrupt my plans here on Earth, and it was the disruption they were after. They couldn't order the robot to kill me, but they could order him to miss me, and if that was enough to disrupt the programme, they would be satisfied. Except that it won't disrupt the programme; I won't allow that.'

D. G. said, 'Don't be a heroine, Gladia. I don't know what they'll try next, and nothing, *nothing*, is worth losing you.'

Gladia's eyes softened. 'Thank you, D. G. I appreciate your feelings, but we *must* chance it.'

Andrev pulled at his ear in perplexity. 'What do we do? The knowledge that a humanoid robot used a blaster in a crowd of human beings will not be taken well by Earth's people.'

'Obviously, it wouldn't,' said D. G. 'Therefore let's not tell them.'

'A number of people must already know, or guess, that we are dealing with a robot.'

'You won't stop the rumour, Secretary-General, but there is no need to make it more than that by means of an official announcement.'

Andrev said, 'If Aurora is willing to go to this extreme to —'

'Not Aurora,' said Gladia, quickly. 'Merely certain people on Aurora; certain fire-eaters. There are such bellicose extremists among the Settlers, too, I know, and probably even on Earth. Don't play into the hands of these extremists, Secretary-General. I'm appealing to the vast majority of sensible human beings on both sides, and nothing must be done to weaken that appeal.'

Daneel, who had been waiting patiently, finally found a pause long enough to make it possible for him to insert his comment. 'Madam Gladia — sirs — it is important to find out from this robot where on this planet he is based. There may be others.'

'Haven't you asked him?' said Andrev.

'I have, Secretary-General, but I am a robot. This robot is not required to answer questions put to him by another robot. Nor is he required to follow my orders.'

'Well, then, *I* will ask,' said Andrev.

'That may not help, sir. The robot is under stringent orders not to answer, and your order to answer will probably not overcome that. You do not know the proper phraseology and intonation. Madam Gladia is an Auroran and knows how this may be done. Madam Gladia, would you inquire as to where his planetary base might be?'

Giskard said, in a low voice, so that only Daneel heard

him, 'It may not be possible. He may have been ordered into irreversible freeze if the questioning becomes too insistent.'

Daneel's head turned sharply to Giskard. He whispered, 'Can you prevent that?'

'Uncertain,' said Giskard. 'The brain has been physically damaged by the act of firing a blaster towards human beings.'

Daneel turned back to Gladia. 'Madam,' he said, 'I would suggest you be probing, rather than brutal.'

Gladia said, doubtfully, 'Well, I don't know.' She faced the robot-assassin, drew a deep breath, and, in a voice that was firm, yet soft and gentle, she said, 'Robot, how may I address you?'

The robot said, 'I am referred to as R. Ernett Second, madam.'

'Ernett, can you tell that I am an Auroran?'

'You speak in the Auroran fashion, yet not entirely, madam.'

'I was born on Solaria, but I am a Spacer who has lived for twenty decades on Aurora, and I am accustomed to being served by robots. I have expected and received service from robots every day of my life since I was a small child. I have never been disappointed.'

'I accept the fact, madam.'

'Will you answer my questions and accept my orders, Ernett?'

'I will, madam, if they are not counteracted by a competing order.'

'If I ask you the location of your base on this planet – what portion of it you count as your master's establishment – will you answer that?'

'I may not do so, madam. Nor any other question with respect to my master. Any question at all.'

'Do you understand that if you do not answer I will be

bitterly disappointed and that my rightful expectation of robotic service will be permanently blunted?'

'I understand, madam,' said the robot, faintly.

Gladia looked at Daneel. 'Shall I try?'

Daneel said, 'There is no choice but to try, Madam Gladia. If the effort leaves us without information we are no worse off than now.'

Gladia said, in a voice that rang with authority, 'Do not inflict damage on me, Ernett, by refusing to tell me the location of your base on this planet. I order you to tell me.'

The robot seemed to stiffen. His mouth opened, but made no sound. It opened again, and, in a husky whisper, there came the syllable, 'Mile'. It opened a third time, silently – and then, while the mouth remained open, the gleam went out of the robot-assassin's eyes and they became flat and waxen. One arm, which had been a little raised, dropped downward.

Daneel said, 'The positronic brain has frozen.'

Giskard whispered to Daneel only, 'Irreversible! I did my best but could not hang on.'

'We have nothing,' said Andrev. 'We don't know where the other robots might be.'

D. G. said, 'It said "mile".'

'I do not recognize the word,' said Daneel. 'It is not Galactic Standard as the language is used on Aurora. Does it have meaning on Earth?'

Andrev said, rather blankly, 'He might have been trying to say "smile" or "Miles". I once knew a man whose first name was "Miles".'

Daneel said, gravely, 'I do not see how either word could make sense as an answer, or part of an answer, to the question. Nor did I hear any sibilance, either before or after the sound.'

An elderly Earthman, who till now had remained silent,

said, with a certain appearance of diffidence, 'I am under the impression a mile may be an ancient measure of distance, robot.'

'How long a measure, sir?' asked Daneel.

'I do not know,' said the Earthman. 'Longer than a kilometre, I believe.'

'It isn't used any longer, sir?'

'Not since pre-space.'

D. G. pulled at his beard and he said, thoughtfully, 'It's still used. At least, we have an old saying on Baleyworld that goes, "A miss is as good as a mile". It is used to mean that, in avoiding misfortune, avoidance by a little is as good as avoidance by a great deal. I always thought "mile" meant "a great deal". If it really represents a measure of distance, I can understand the phrase better.'

Gladia said, 'If that is so, the assassin may have been trying to say exactly that. He may have indicated his satisfaction that a miss – his deliberately missed shot – would accomplish what he was ordered to accomplish; or, perhaps, that his missed shot, doing no harm, was equivalent to his not having fired at all.'

'Madam Gladia,' said Daneel, 'a robot of Auroran manufacture would scarcely be using phrases that might exist on Baleyworld, but have certainly never been heard on Aurora. And he would not philosophize. He was asked a question, and he would only, in his damaged condition, be trying to answer the question.'

'Ah,' said Andrev, 'perhaps he *was* trying to answer. He was trying to tell us that the base was a certain distance from here, for instance. So many miles.'

'In that case,' said D. G., 'why should he use an archaic measure of distance? No Auroran would use anything but kilometres in this connection, nor would any robot of Auroran manufacture. In fact,' he went on, with an edge of impatience, 'the robot was rapidly sinking into total inactivity, and it might have been making nothing more than random sounds. It is useless to try to extract meaning from something that doesn't contain it. And now I want to make sure that Madam Gladia gets some rest, or that she is at least moved out of this room, before the rest of the ceiling comes down.'

They moved out quickly, and Daneel, lingering behind for a moment, said softly to Giskard, 'Again we fail!'

82.

The City never grew entirely quiet, but there were periods when the lights were dimmer, the noise of the ever-moving Expressways was subdued, and the endless clatter of machinery and humanity subsided just a bit. In several million apartments people slept.

Gladia got into bed in the apartment assigned to her, uncomfortable over the missing amenities that she feared might force her out into the corridors during the night.

Was it night on the surface, she wondered, just before falling asleep, or was it merely an arbitrary 'sleep-period' fixed within this particular Cave of Steel, in deference to a habit developed over the hundreds of millions of years that human beings and their ancestors had lived on the surface of the land.

And then she slept.

Daneel and Giskard did not sleep. Daneel, finding there was a computer outlet in the apartment, spent an absorbed half-hour learning the unfamiliar key-combinations by hit-and-miss. There were no instructions of any sort available (who needs instructions for what every youngster learns in grade school?) but, fortunately, the controls, while not those of Aurora, were not wholly different either. Eventually, he was able to tune into the reference section of the City library, and call up the encyclopaedia. Hours passed.

At the lowest depth of the sleep period, Giskard said, 'Friend Daneel.'

Daneel looked up. 'Yes, Friend Giskard.'

'I must ask for an explanation of your actions on the balcony.'

'Friend Giskard, you looked towards the crowd. I followed your glance, saw a weapon aimed in our direction, and reacted at once.'

Giskard said, 'So you did, Friend Daneel, and given certain assumptions, I can understand why it was me that you lunged forward to protect. Begin with the fact that the would-be assassin was a robot. In that case, however it might be programmed, it could not aim its weapon at any human being with the intention of hitting him or her. Nor was it likely to aim its weapon at you, for you look enough like a human being to activate the First Law. Even if the robot had been told that a humanoid robot would be on the balcony, he could not be certain that you were he. Therefore, if the robot intended to destroy someone on the balcony, it could only be me, the obvious robot, and you acted at once to protect me.

'Or begin with the fact that the assassin was an Auroran – whether human or robot does not matter. Dr Amadiro is most likely to have ordered such an attack, since he is an extremist in his anti-Earth stand and, we believe, is plotting its destruction. Dr Amadiro, we can be reasonably certain, has learned of my special abilities from Madam Vasilia, and it might be argued that he would give my destruction top-priority, since he would naturally fear me more than anyone else, robot or human. Reasoning this out, it would be logical for you to act as you did to protect me. And, indeed, had you not knocked me down, I believe the blast would have destroyed me.

'But, Friend Daneel, you could not possibly have known that the assassin was a robot, or that he was Auroran. I myself had only just caught the strange anomaly of a robotic brain pattern against the vast blur of human emotion, when you struck me, and it was only after that, that I had the chance of informing you. Without my ability, you could only be aware that a weapon was being aimed by what you must naturally have thought of as a human being and an Earthperson. The logical target, then, was Madam Gladia, as, in fact, everyone on the balcony assumed it to be. Why, then, did you ignore Madam Gladia and protect me, instead?'

Daneel said, 'Friend Giskard, consider my line of thought. The Secretary-General had said that a two-man Auroran landing module had come to Earth's surface. I assumed at once that Dr Amadiro and Dr Mandamus had come to Earth. For this, there could be only one reason. The plan they have, whatever its nature, is at, or very nearly at, the point of maturity. Now that you have come to Earth, Friend Giskard, they have dashed here to see it carried through at once before you have a chance to stop it with your mind-adjusting powers. To make matters doubly sure, they would act to destroy you if they could. Therefore, when I saw an aimed weapon, I moved at once to force you out of the line of fire.'

Giskard said, 'First Law should have forced you to move Madam Gladia out of the line of fire. No thought, no reasoning, should have altered that.'

'No, Friend Giskard. You are more important than Madam Gladia is. You are, in fact, more important than any human being could be at this moment. If anyone at all can stop the destruction of Earth, you can. Since I am aware of your potential service to humanity, then, when I

am confronted by a choice of action, Zeroth Law demands
that I protect you ahead of anyone else.'

'And you do not feel uncomfortable at your having acted
in defiance of the First Law?'

'No, for I acted in obedience to the overriding Zeroth
Law.'

'But the Zeroth Law has not been imprinted into you.'

'I have accepted it as a corollary of the First Law, for
how can a human being best be kept from injury, if not by
ensuring that human society in general is protected and
kept functioning?'

Giskard thought a while. 'I see what you are trying to
say, but what if, in acting to save me and, therefore, in
acting to save humanity, it had turned out that I was not
aimed at and that Madam Gladia was killed? How would
you have felt, then, Friend Daneel?'

Daneel said, in a low tone, 'I do not know, Friend
Giskard. Yet, had I leaped to save Madam Gladia, and had
it turned out that she was, in any case, safe, and that I had
allowed you to be destroyed and with you, in my opinion,
the future of humanity, how could I have survived that
blow?'

The two stared at each other, each, for a while, lost in
thought.

Giskard said, finally, 'That may be so, Friend Daneel,
but do you agree, however, that judgement is difficult in
such cases?'

'I agree, Friend Giskard.'

'It is difficult enough, when one must choose quickly
between individuals, to decide which individual may
suffer, or inflict, the greater harm. To choose between an
individual and humanity, when you are not sure of what
aspect of humanity you are dealing with, is so difficult that
the very validity of Robotic Laws comes to be suspect. As
soon as humanity in the abstract is introduced, the Laws of

Robotics begin to merge with the Laws of Humanics – which may not even exist.'

Daneel said, 'I do not understand you, Friend Giskard.'

'I am not surprised. I am not certain I understand myself. But consider. When we think of the humanity we must save, we think of Earthpeople and the Settlers. They are more numerous than the Spacers, more vigorous, more expansive. They show more initiative because they are less dependent on robots. They have a greater potential for biological and social evolution because they are shorter-lived, though long-lived enough to contribute great things individually.'

'Yes,' said Daneel, 'you put it succinctly.'

'And yet the Earthpeople and the Settlers seem to possess a mystical and, even, irrational confidence in the sanctity and inviolability of Earth. Might not this mystique be as fatal to their development as the mystiques of robots and long-life that hobble the Spacers?'

'I had not thought of this,' said Daneel. 'I do not know.'

Giskard said, 'If you were as aware of minds as I am, you would have been unable to avoid thinking of this. How does one choose?' he went on with sudden intensity. 'Think of humanity as divided into two species: the Spacers with one apparently fatal mystique; and the Earthpeople plus the Settlers with another possibly fatal mystique. It may be that there will be other species, in the future, with even less attractive properties.

'It is not sufficient to choose, then, Friend Daneel; we must be able to shape. We must shape a desirable species and then protect it, rather than finding ourselves forced to select among two or more undesirabilities. But how can we achieve the desirable unless we have psychohistory, the science I dream of and cannot attain?'

Daneel said, 'I had not appreciated the difficulty, Friend Giskard, of possessing the ability to sense and influence minds. Is it possible that you learn too much to allow the Laws of Robotics to work smoothly within you?'

'That has always been possible, Friend Daneel, but not until these recent events has the possibility become actual. I know the pathway-pattern that produces this mind-sensing and mind-influencing effect within me. I have studied myself carefully for decades in order that I might know it, and I can pass it on to you so that you might program yourself to be like me – but I have resisted the urge to do so. It would be unkind to you. It is enough that I bear the burden.'

Daneel said, 'Nevertheless, Friend Giskard, if ever, in your judgement, the good of humanity would require it, I would accept the burden. Indeed, by Zeroth Law, I would be obliged to.'

Giskard said, 'But this discussion is useless. It seems apparent that the crisis is nearly upon us, and since we have not even managed to work out the nature of the crisis –'

Daneel interrupted. 'You are wrong there at least, Friend Giskard. I now know the nature of the crisis.'

83.

One would not expect Giskard to show surprise. His face was, of course, incapable of expression. His voice possessed modulation so that his speech sounded human and was neither monotonous nor unpleasant. That modulation, however, was never altered by emotion in any recognizable way.

Therefore, when he said, 'Are you serious?' it sounded as it would have, had he expressed doubt over a remark Daneel had made concerning what the weather would be like the next day. Yet, from the manner in which his head turned towards Daneel, the way in which one hand lifted, there was no doubt that he was surprised.

Daneel said, 'I am, Friend Giskard.'

'How did the information come to you?'

'In part from what I was told by Madam Undersecretary Quintana at the dinner table.'

'But did you not say that you had obtained nothing helpful from her; that you supposed you had asked the wrong questions?'

'So it seemed in the immediate aftermath. On further reflection, however, I found myself able to make helpful deductions from what she had said. I have been searching Earth's central encyclopaedia through the computer outlet these past few hours –'

'And found your deductions confirmed?'

'Not exactly, but I found nothing that would refute them, which is perhaps the next best thing.'

'But is negative evidence sufficient for certainty?'

'It is not. And therefore I am not certain. Let me tell you, however, my reasoning, and if you find it faulty, say so.'

'Please proceed, Friend Daneel.'

'Fusion power, Friend Giskard, was developed on Earth before the days of hyperspatial travel and, therefore, while human beings were to be found only on the one planet, Earth. This is well-known. It took a long time to develop practical controlled fusion power after the possibility had first been conceived and put on a sound scientific footing. The chief difficulty in converting the concept into practice involved the necessity of achieving a sufficiently high temperature in a sufficiently dense gas for a long enough time to bring about fusion ignition.

'And yet several decades before controlled fusion power had been established, fusion bombs had existed; these bombs representing an uncontrolled fusion reaction. But controlled or uncontrolled, fusion could not take place without an extremely high temperature in the millions of degrees. If human beings could not produce the necessary temperature for controlled fusion power, how could they do so for an uncontrolled fusion explosion?

'Madam Quintana told me that before fusion existed on Earth, there was another variety of nuclear reaction in existence – nuclear fission. Energy was derived from the splitting, or fission, of large nuclei, such as those of uranium and thorium. That, I thought, might be one way of achieving a high temperature.

'The encyclopaedia I have this night been consulting gives very little information about nuclear bombs of any sort, and, certainly, no real details. It is a taboo subject, I gather, and it must be so in all worlds, for I have never read of such details in Aurora either, even though such bombs still exist. It is a part of history that human beings are ashamed of, or afraid of, or both, and I think this is rational. In what I did read of fusion bombs, however, I read nothing about their ignition that would have eliminated the fission bomb as the igniting mechanism. I suspect, then, that based, in part, on this negative evidence, the fission bomb was the igniting mechanism.

'But, then, how was the fission bomb ignited? Fission bombs existed before fusion bombs and if fission bombs required an ultra-high temperature for ignition, as fusion bombs did, then there was nothing that existed before fission bombs that would supply that high temperature. From this, I conclude – even though the encyclopaedia contained no information on the subject – that fission bombs could be ignited at relatively low temperatures, perhaps even at room temperature. There were difficulties involved, for it took several years of unremitting effort, after the discovery that fission existed, before the bomb was developed. Whatever those difficulties might have been, however, they did not involve the production of ultra-high temperatures. Your opinion of all this, Friend Giskard?'

Giskard had kept his eyes steadily on Daneel through his explanation and he now said, 'I think the structure you have built up has serious weak points, Friend Daneel, and therefore may not be very trustworthy – but even if it were all perfectly sound, surely this has nothing to do with the possible forthcoming crisis that we are labouring to understand.'

Daneel said, 'I plead for your patience, Friend Giskard, and I will continue. As it happens, both the fusion process and the fission process are expressions of the weak interactions, one of the four interactions that control all events in the Universe. Consequently, the same nuclear intensifier that will explode a fusion reactor will also explode a fission reactor.

'There is, however, a difference. Fusion takes place only at ultra-high temperatures. The intensifier explodes the ultra-hot portion of the fuel that is actively undergoing fusion, plus some of the surrounding fuel that is heated to fusion in the initial explosion, before the material is blown explosively outward and the heat is dissipated to the point where other quantities of fuel present are not ignited. Some of the fusion fuel is exploded, in other words, but a good deal, perhaps even most, is not. The explosion is powerful enough even so, of course, to destroy the fusion reactor and anything in its immediate neighbourhood such as a ship carrying the reactor.

'On the other hand, a fission reactor can operate at low temperatures, perhaps not much above the boiling point of water, perhaps even at room temperature. The effect of the nuclear intensifier, then, will be to make *all* the fission fuel go. Indeed, even if the fission reactor is *not* actively working, the intensifier will explode it. Although, gram for gram, I gather that fission fuel liberates less energy than fusion fuel, the fission reactor will produce the greater explosion because more of its fuel explodes than in the case of the fusion reactor.'

Giskard nodded his head slowly and said, 'All this may well be so, Friend Daneel, but are there any fission power stations on Earth?'

'No, there aren't; not one. So Undersecretary Quintana seemed to indicate and the encyclopaedia seems to agree. Indeed, whereas there are devices on Earth that are powered by small fusion reactors, there is nothing – nothing at all – that is powered by fission reactors, large or small.'

'Then, Friend Daneel, there is nothing for a nuclear intensifier to act upon. All your reasoning, even were it impeccable, ends in nothing.'

Daneel said earnestly, 'Not quite, Friend Giskard. There remains a third type of nuclear reaction to be taken into consideration.'

Giskard said, 'What might that be? I cannot think of a third.'

'It is not an easy thought, Friend Giskard, for on the Spacer and Settler worlds, there is very little uranium and thorium in the planetary crusts and, therefore, very little in the way of obvious radioactivity. The subject is of little interest, in consequence, and is ignored by all but a few theoretical physicists. On Earth, however, as Madam Quintana pointed out to me, uranium and thorium are comparatively common, and natural radioactivity, with its ultra-slow production of heat and energetic radiation, must therefore be a comparatively prominent part of the environment. That is the third type of nuclear reaction to be taken into consideration.'

'In what way, Friend Daneel?'

'Natural radioactivity is also an expression of the weak

interaction. A nuclear intensifier that can explode a fusion reactor or a fission reactor can also accelerate natural radioactivity to the point, I presume, of exploding a section of the crust, if enough uranium or thorium is present.'

Giskard stared at Daneel for a period of time without moving or speaking. Then he said softly, 'You suggest, then, that it is Dr Amadiro's plan to explode Earth's crust, destroy the planet as an abode of life, and, in this way, ensure the domination of the Galaxy by the Spacers?'

Daneel nodded. 'Or, if there is not enough thorium and uranium for mass explosion, the increase of radioactivity may produce excess heat that will alter the climate, and excess radiation that will produce cancer and birth defects, and these will serve the same purpose – if a bit more slowly.'

Giskard said, 'This is an appalling possibility. Do you think it can really be brought about?'

'Possibly. It seems to me that for several years now – just how many I do not know – humanoid robots from Aurora, such as the would-be assassin – have been on Earth. They are advanced enough for complex programming, and are capable, at need, of entering the Cities for equipment. They have, it is to be presumed, been setting up nuclear intensifiers in places where the soil is rich in uranium or thorium. Perhaps many intensifiers have been set up over the years. Dr Amadiro and Dr Mandamus are here now to oversee the final details and to activate the intensifiers. Presumably, they are arranging matters so that they will have time to escape before the planet is destroyed.'

'In that case,' said Giskard, 'it is imperative that the Secretary-General be informed; that Earth's security forces be mobilized at once; that Dr Amadiro and Dr Mandamus be located without delay; and that they be restrained from completing their project.'

Daneel said, 'I do not think that can be done. The Secretary-General is very likely to refuse to believe us, thanks to the widespread mystical belief in the inviolability of the planet. You have referred to that as something that would work against humanity and I suspect that is just what it will do in this case. If his belief in the unique position of Earth is challenged, he would refuse to allow his conviction, however irrational, to be shaken, and he would seek refuge by refusing to believe us.

'Then, too, even if he believed us, any preparation for counter-measures would have to go through the governmental bureaucracy and, no matter how that process was speeded, it would take far too long to serve its purpose.

'Not only that but even if we could imagine the full resources of Earth mobilized at once, I do not think Earthpeople are adapted to locating the presence of two human beings in an enormous wilderness. The Earthpeople have lived in the Cities for many scores of decades and almost never venture beyond the City confines. I remember that well from the occasion of my first case with Elijah Baley here on Earth. And even if Earthpeople could force themselves to tramp the open spaces, they are not likely to come across the two human beings soon enough to save the situation except by the most incredible of coincidences, and that is something we cannot count upon.'

Giskard said, 'Settlers could easily form a search party. They are not afraid of open environments or of strange ones.'

'But they would be as firmly convinced in the planet's inviolability as Earthpeople are, just as insistent on refusing to believe us, and just as unlikely to find the two human beings quickly enough to save the situation, even if they *should* believe us.'

'What of Earth's robots, then?' said Giskard. 'They swarm in the spaces between the Cities. Some should already be aware of human beings in their midst. They should be questioned.'

Daneel said, 'The human beings in their midst are expert roboticists. They would not have failed to see to it that any robots in their vicinity remained unaware of their presence. Nor, for this same reason, need they fear danger from any robots who might be part of a search party. The party will be ordered to depart and forget. To make it worse, Earth's robots are comparatively simple models, designed for very little more than for specific tasks in growing crops, herding animals, and operating mines. They cannot easily be adapted to such a general purpose as conducting a meaningful search.'

Giskard said, 'You have eliminated every possible action, Friend Daneel? Does anything remain?'

Daneel said, 'We must find the two human beings ourselves, and we must stop them – and we must do it now.'

'Do you know where they are, Friend Daneel?'

'I do not, Friend Giskard.'

'Then if it seems unlikely that an elaborate search party composed of many, many Earthpeople, or Settlers, or robots, or, I presume, all three, could succeed in finding their location in time except by the most marvellous of coincidences, how can we two do so?'

'I do not know, Friend Giskard, but we must.'

And Giskard said in a voice that seemed to have an edge of harshness in its choice of words, 'Necessity is not enough, Friend Daneel. You have come a long way. You have worked out the existence of a crisis, and, bit by bit, you have worked out its nature. And none of it serves. Here we remain, as helpless as ever to do anything about it.'

Daneel said, 'There remains one chance; a far-fetched one; an all-but-useless one; but we have no choice except to try. Out of Amadiro's fear of you, he sent an assassin-robot to destroy you, and that *may* turn out to have been his mistake.'

'And if that all-but-useless chance fails, Friend Daneel?'

Daneel looked calmly at Giskard. 'Then we are helpless, and Earth will be destroyed, and human history will dwindle to an eventual end.'

18

The Zeroth Law

84.

Kelden Amadiro was not happy. The surface gravity of Earth was a trifle too high for his liking; the atmosphere a trifle too dense; the sound and the odour of the outdoors subtly and annoyingly different from that on Aurora; and there was no indoors that could make any pretence of being civilized.

The robots had built shelters of a sort. There were ample food supplies and there were makeshift privies that were functionally adequate, but offensively inadequate in every other way.

Worst of all, though the morning was pleasant enough, it was a clear day and Earth's too bright Sun was rising. Soon, the temperature would be too high, the air would be too damp, and the biting insects would appear. Amadiro had not understood, at first, why there should be small, itching swellings on his arms till Mandamus explained.

Now, he mumbled, as he scratched, 'Dreadful! They might carry infections.'

'I believe,' said Mandamus, with apparent indifference, 'that they sometimes do. It isn't likely, however. I have lotions to relieve the discomfort, and we can burn certain substances that the insects find offensive, although I find the odours offensive, too.'

'Burn them,' said Amadiro.

Mandamus continued, without changing tone, 'And I don't want to do anything, however trifling – an odour, a bit of smoke – that would increase the chance of our being detected.'

Amadiro eyed him suspiciously. 'You have said, over and over, that this region is never visited by either Earthpeople or their field robots.'

'That's right, but it's not a mathematical proposition. It's a sociological observation, and there is always the possibility of exceptions to such observations.'

Amadiro scowled. 'The best road to safety lies with being done with this project. You said you'd be ready today.'

'That, too, is a sociological observation, Dr Amadiro. I *should* be ready today. I would like to be. I cannot guarantee it mathematically.'

'How long before you *can* guarantee it?'

Mandamus spread his hands in a who-knows gesture. 'Dr Amadiro, I am under the impression I have already explained this, but I'm willing to go through it again. It took me seven years to get this far. I had been counting on some months yet of personal observations at the fourteen different relay stations on Earth's surface. I can't do that now because we must finish before we are located, and, possibly, stopped by the robot, Giskard. That means I have to do my checking by communicating with our own humanoid robots at the relays. I can't trust them as I would myself. I must check and re-check their reports, and it is possible that I may have to go to one or two places before I am satisfied. That would take days – perhaps a week or two.'

'A week or two. Impossible! How long do you think I can endure this planet, Mandamus?'

'Sir, on one of my previous visits I stayed on this planet for nearly a year; on another, for over four months.'

'And you liked it?'

'No, sir, but I had a job to do, and I did it – without sparing myself.' Mandamus stared coldly at Amadiro.

Amadiro flushed, and said in a somewhat chastened tone, 'Well, then, where do we stand?'

'I'm still weighing the reports that are coming in. We are not working with a smoothly-designed laboratory-made system, you know. We have an extraordinarily heterogeneous planetary crust to deal with. Fortunately, the radioactive materials are widely spread, but in places they run perilously thin and we must place a relay in such places and leave robots in charge. If those relays are not, in every case, properly positioned and in proper order, the nuclear intensification will die out and we will have had all these painful years of effort for nothing. Or else, there may be a surge of localized intensification that will have the force of an explosion that will blow itself out and leave the rest of the crust unaffected. In either case, total damage would be insignificant.

'What we want, Dr Amadiro, is to have the radioactive materials, and, therefore, significantly large sections of Earth's crust, grow – slowly – steadily – irreversibly – ' (he bit the words off as he pronounced them in spaced intervals) 'more and more intensely radioactive, so that Earth becomes progressively more unlivable. The social structure of the planet will break down and the Earth, as an effective abode of humanity, will be over and done with. I take it, Dr Amadiro, that this is what you want. It is what I described to you years ago, and what you said, at that time, you wanted.'

'I still do, Mandamus. Don't be a fool.'

'Then bear with discomfort, sir; or else, leave, and I will carry on for whatever additional time it takes.'

'No, no,' muttered Amadiro. 'I must be here when it's done – but I can't help being impatient. IIow long have you decided to allow the process to build? – I mean, once you initiate the original wave of intensification, how long before Earth becomes uninhabitable?'

'That depends on the degree of intensification I apply initially. I don't know, just yet, what degree will be required, for that depends on the overall efficiency of the relays, so I have prepared a variable control. What I want to arrange is a lapse-period of ten to twenty decades.'

'And if you allow a smaller lapse-period?'

'The less the lapse-period we allow, the more rapidly portions of the crust will grow radioactive and the more rapidly the planet will warm up and grow dangerous. And that means, the less likely it will be that any significant number of its population can be removed in time.'

'Does that matter?' murmured Amadiro.

Mandamus frowned. 'The more rapidly the Earth deteriorates, the more likely it is that Earthpeople and Settlers will suspect a technological cause, and we are the likely ones to receive the blame. The Settlers will then attack us with fury and, in the cause of their Holy World, they will fight to extinction, provided only that they can inflict substantial harm on us. This is something we have discussed before and it seems we agreed on the matter. It would be far better to allow ample time, during which we can prepare for the worst, and during which a confused Earth may assume that the slowly-increasing radioactivity is some natural phenomenon they don't understand. That is something that has become more urgent today than yesterday, in my judgement.'

'Is that so?' Amadiro was frowning also. 'You have that sour, puritanical look that makes me sure you have found a way to place the responsibility for that on my shoulders.'

'With respect, sir, that is not difficult in this case. It was unwise to send out one of our robots to destroy Giskard.'

'On the contrary, it had to be done. Giskard is the only one who might destroy us.'

'He must find us first, and he won't. And even if he does, we are knowledgeable roboticists. Don't you think we could handle him?'

'Indeed?' said Amadiro. 'So Vasilia thought, and she knew him better than we – and yet *she* couldn't handle him. And somehow the warship that was to take him into charge and destroy him at a distance, could not handle him. So he has now landed on Earth. One way or another, he must be destroyed.'

'He has not been. There has been no report of it.'

'Bad news is sometimes repressed by a prudent government, and Earth officials, though barbarians, might conceivably be prudent. And if our robot failed and was questioned, he would certainly go into irreversible block. That means we will have lost a robot, something we can afford to do, but nothing more. And if Giskard should still be at large, the more reason we have to hurry.'

'If we have lost a robot, we have lost more than a robot if they manage to elicit the location of this centre of operations. We ought, at least, not to have used a local robot.'

'I used one that was immediately available. And he will reveal nothing. You can trust my programming, I think.'

'He cannot help reveal, by his mere existence, whether frozen or not, that he is of Auroran manufacture. Earth roboticists, and there are some on this planet, will be sure of that. All the more reason to make the increase in radioactivity very slow. Enough time must pass so that Earthpeople forget the incident and don't associate it with the progressive change in radioactivity. We must have ten decades at the very least, perhaps fifteen, or even twenty.'

He walked away to inspect his instruments again and to re-establish contact with relays six and ten, which he still found troublesome. Amadiro looked after him with a mixture of disdain and intense dislike and muttered to himself, 'Yes, but I don't have twenty more decades, or fifteen, or maybe even ten. You do – but I don't.'

85.

It was early morning in New York. Giskard and Daneel assumed that from the gradual heightening of activity.

'Somewhere above and outside the City,' said Giskard, 'it may be dawn now. Once, in speaking to Elijah Baley twenty decades ago, I referred to Earth as the World of the Dawn. Will it continue to be so for much longer? Or has it already ceased to be that?'

'These are morbid thoughts, Friend Giskard,' said Daneel. 'It will be better if we occupy ourselves with what must be done on this day to help keep Earth the World of the Dawn.'

Gladia entered the apartment, wearing a bathrobe and slippers. Her hair was freshly dried.

'Ridiculous!' she said. 'Earthwomen go through the corridors on their way to the mass Personals in the morning, dishevelled and slatternly. It is done on purpose, I think. It is bad manners to comb one's hair on the way to the Personal. Apparently, dishevelment to begin with enhances that well-cared-for look afterwards. I should have brought a complete morning outfit with me. You should have seen the looks I got when I left with my bathrobe on. Leaving the Personal, one must be the last word. Yes, Daneel?'

'Madam,' said Daneel. 'May we have a word with you?'

Gladia hesitated. 'Not much of a word, Daneel. As you are probably aware, this is going to be a big day, and my morning appointments begin almost at once.'

'That is precisely what I wish to discuss, madam,' said

Daneel. 'On this important day, all will go better if we are not with you.'

'What?'

'The effect you would wish to have on Earthpeople would be greatly diminished if you surround yourself with robots.'

'I will not be surrounded. There will be just you two. How can I do without?'

'It is necessary that you learn to, madam. While we are with you, you are marked off as different from Earthpeople. You are made to seem afraid of them.'

Gladia said, troubled, 'I need *some* protection, Daneel. Remember what happened last night.'

'Madam, we could not have prevented what happened last night and we could not have protected you, if that were necessary. Fortunately, you were not the target last night. The blaster bolt was aimed at Giskard's head.'

'Why Giskard?'

'How could a robot aim at you or at any human being? The robot aimed at Giskard for some reason. For us to be near you, then, might but increase your danger. Remember that as the tale of last night's events spreads, even though the Earth government may try to suppress the details, there will be a rumour to the effect that it was a robot who held a blaster and fired it. That will arouse public indignation against robots – against *us* – and even against you, if you persist in being seen with us. It would be better if you were without us.'

'For how long?'

'For at least as long as your mission lasts, madam. The Captain will be better able to help you in the days to come than we will be. He knows Earthpeople, he is highly thought of by them – and he thinks very highly of you, madam.'

Gladia said, 'Can you *tell* that he thinks very highly of me?'

'Although I am a robot, it would seem so to me. And at any time that you should wish us back, we will come back, of course – but, for now, we think that the best way we can serve and protect you is to leave you in Captain Baley's hands.'

Gladia said, 'I will think of it.'

'In the meanwhile, madam,' said Daneel, 'we will see Captain Baley and find out if he agrees with us.'

'Do so!' said Gladia, and passed into her bedroom.

Daneel turned and spoke minimally to Giskard. 'Is she willing?'

'More than willing,' said Giskard. 'She has always been a little restless in my presence and would not suffer unduly at my absence. For you, Friend Daneel, she has ambivalent feelings. You remind her markedly of Friend Jander whose inactivation, many decades ago, was so traumatic for her. This has been a source of both attraction and repulsion to her, so it was not necessary to do much. I lessened her attraction to you and increased her strong attraction to the Captain. She will do without us easily.'

'Then let us find the Captain,' said Daneel. Together, they left the room and entered the hallway that passed by the apartment.

86.

Both Daneel and Giskard had been on Earth on previous occasions, Giskard the more recently. They understood the use of the computerized directory that gave them the Section, Wing, and number of the apartment to which D. G. had been assigned, and they understood, further, the colour codes in the hallways that led them to the proper turnings and elevators.

It was early enough for the human traffic to be light, but those human beings who passed or approached, stared with astonishment at Giskard, then looked away with elaborate unconcern.

Giskard's steps were slightly uneven by the time they approached D. G.'s apartment door. It was not very noticeable, but it caught Daneel's attention.

He said, in a low voice, 'Are you in discomfort, Friend Giskard?'

Giskard replied, 'It has been necessary for me to wipe out astonishment, apprehension, and even attention in a number of men and women; and in one youngster, which was harder still. I had no time to make completely certain I was doing no harm.'

'It was important to do so. We must not be stopped.'

'I understand that, but Zeroth Law does not work well with me. I have not your facility in that respect.' He went on, as though to distract his own attention from his discomfort, 'I have often noted that hyper-resistance in the positronic pathways makes itself first felt in the matter of standing and walking, and next in speech.'

Daneel tapped the door signal. He said, 'It is the same in my case, Friend Giskard. Maintaining balance on two supports is difficult under the best of circumstances. Controlled imbalance, as in walking, is even more difficult. I have heard once that there were early attempts made to produce robots with four legs and two arms. They were called "centaurs". They worked well but were unacceptable because they were basically inhuman in appearance.'

'At the moment,' said Giskard, 'I would appreciate four legs, Friend Daneel. However, I think my discomfort is passing.'

D. G. was at the door, now. He looked at them with a

broad smile. He then glanced in each direction along the corridor, whereupon his smile vanished and was replaced with a look of the utmost concern. 'What are you doing here without Gladia? Is she – '

Daneel said, 'Captain, Madam Gladia is well. She is in no danger. May we enter and explain?'

D. G. glowered as he gestured them inside. His voice gained the hectoring tone one naturally assumes towards misbehaving machines, and he said, 'Why have you left her alone? What circumstances could possibly permit you to leave her alone?'

Daneel said, 'She is no more alone than any person is on Earth, and no more in danger. If you will question her later on the matter, I believe she will tell you that she cannot be effective here on Earth as long as she is trailed by Spacer robots. I believe she will tell you that what guidance and protection she needs should be supplied by you, rather than by robots. It is what we believe she wishes – at least for now. If, at any time, she wishes us back, she will have us.'

D. G.'s face relaxed into a smile again. 'She wants my protection, does she?'

'At the moment, Captain, we believe she is quite anxious for your presence rather than for ours.'

D. G.'s smile became a grin. 'Who can blame her? I'll get myself ready and go to her apartment as soon as I can.'

'But first, sir – '

'Oh,' said D. G., 'there is a *quid pro quo*?'

'Yes, sir. We are anxious to discover as much as we can about the robot who fired the blaster at the balcony last night.'

D. G. looked tense again. 'Do you anticipate further danger for Madam Gladia?'

'None at all of that kind. The robot, last night, did not

fire at Lady Gladia. Being a robot, he could not have. He
fired at Friend Giskard.'

'Why should he have done that?'

'It is what we would like to find out. For that purpose,
we wish you to call Madam Quintana, Undersecretary of
Energy, and state that it would be important, and would
please you and the government of Baleyworld, if you
would care to add that, for her to allow me to ask her a few
questions on that subject. We wish you to do whatever
seems best to persuade her to agree to such an interview.'

'Is that all you want me to do? Persuade a reasonably
important and busy official to submit to cross-examination
by a robot?'

Daneel said, 'Sir, she may agree if you are earnest
enough in the request. In addition, since she may be
located a distance away, it would be helpful if you would
hire a darter on our behalf to take us there. We are, as you
can imagine, in haste.'

'And are those little things all?' asked D. G.

'Not quite, Captain,' said Daneel. 'We will need a
driver, and please pay him well enough so that he will
consent to transport Friend Giskard, who is an obvious
robot. He may not mind me.'

D. G. said, 'I hope you realize, Daneel, that what you
ask is completely unreasonable.'

Daneel said, 'I had hoped not, Captain. But since you
tell me it is, there is nothing more to say. We have no
choice, then, but to return to Madam Gladia, which will
make her unhappy, for she would rather be with you.'

He turned to leave, motioning Giskard to accompany
him, but D. G. said, 'Wait. There's a public communication
contact just down the hallway. I can but try. Remain here
and wait for me.'

The two robots remained standing. Daneel said, 'Did
you have to do much, Friend Giskard?'

Giskard seemed well balanced on his legs now. He said, 'I was helpless. He was strongly opposed to dealing with Madam Quintana and as strongly opposed to getting us a darter. I could not have altered those feelings without damage. When, however, you suggested returning to Madam Gladia, his attitude changed suddenly and dramatically. You were anticipating that, I take it, Friend Daneel?'

'I was.'

'You scarcely need me, it would seem. There is more than one way of adjusting minds. However, I ended by doing something. The Captain's change of mind was accompanied by a strong favourable emotion towards Madam Gladia. I took the opportunity of strengthening that.'

'That is the reason you are needed. I could not have done that.'

'You will be able to yet, Friend Daneel. Perhaps quite soon.'

D. G. returned. 'Believe it or not, she will see you, Daneel. The darter and driver will be here in a moment, and the sooner you leave, the better. I will be heading towards Gladia's apartment at once.'

The two robots stepped outside in the hallway to wait.

Giskard said, 'He is very happy.'

'So it would seem, Friend Giskard,' said Daneel, 'but I fear the easy part is over for us. We have easily arranged to have Madam Gladia grant us leave to move about on our own. We have then, with some difficulty, persuaded the Captain to make it possible for us to see the Undersecretary. With her, however, it may be that we will come to a dead end.'

87.

The driver took one look at Giskard and his courage seemed to fail him. 'Listen,' he said to Daneel, 'I was told I'd be paid double to take a robot, but robots aren't allowed in the City and I could get in plenty of trouble. Money isn't going to help me if I lose my licence. Can't I just take you, mister?'

Daneel said, 'I am a robot, too, sir. We are now *in* the City and that is not your fault. We are trying to get *out* of the City and you will be helping us. We are going to a high government official who, I hope, will arrange that, and it is your civic duty to help us. If you refuse to take us, driver, you will be acting to keep robots *in* the City and that may be considered to be against the law.'

The driver's face smoothed. He opened the door and said gruffly, 'Get in!' However, he carefully closed the thick, translucent partition that blocked him off from his passengers.

Daneel said quietly, 'Was much required, Friend Giskard?'

'Very little, Friend Daneel. Your statement did most of the necessary work. It is astonishing that a collection of statements that are individually true can be used, in combination, to yield an effect that the truth should not.'

'I have observed this often in human conversation, Friend Giskard, even in that of normally truthful human beings. I suspect that the practice is justified in the minds of such people as serving a higher purpose.'

'Zeroth Law, you mean.'

'Or the equivalent, if the human mind has such an equivalent. Friend Giskard, you said a short while ago that

I will have your powers, possibly soon. Are you preparing me for that purpose?'

'I am, Friend Daneel.'

'Why? May I ask that?'

'Zeroth Law again. The passing episode of shakiness on my feet told me how vulnerable I was to the attempted use of Zeroth Law. Before this day is over, I may have to act on Zeroth Law to save the world and humanity, and I may not be able to. In that case, you must be in position to do the job. I am preparing you, bit by bit, so that, at the desired moment, I can give you the final instructions and have it all fall into place.'

'I do not see how that can be, Friend Giskard.'

'You will have no trouble in understanding when the time comes. I used the technique in a very small way on robots I sent to Earth in the early days before they were outlawed from the Cities, and it was they who helped adjust Earth leaders to the point of approving the decision to send out Settlers.'

The driver, whose darter was not on wheels but remained a centimetre or so above the floor-base at all times, had moved along special corridors reserved for such vehicles, and had done so speedily enough to justify the name of the vehicle. He now emerged into an ordinary City corridor, which was paralleled on the moderately distant left by an Expressway. The darter, moving now much more slowly, made a left turn, swooped under the Expressway, out the other side, and then, a curving near-kilometre later, stopped before an ornate building front.

The darter door opened automatically. Daneel emerged first, waited for Giskard to follow, then handed to the driver a piece of foil he had received from D. G. The driver looked at it narrowly; then the doors closed sharply, and he left speedily, without a word.

88.

There was a pause before the door opened in response to their signal and Daneel assumed they were being scanned. When it did open, a young woman led them gingerly into the vitals of the building. She avoided looking at Giskard, but she showed rather more than a mild curiosity in Daneel.

They found Undersecretary Quintana behind a large desk. She smiled, and said with a gaiety that seemed somewhat forced, 'Two robots, unescorted by human beings. Am I safe?'

'Entirely, Madam Quintana,' said Daneel gravely. 'It is as unusual for us to see a human being unaccompanied by robots.'

'I assure you,' said Quintana, 'I have my robots. I call them underlings, and one of them escorted you here. I am amazed that she didn't faint at the sight of Giskard. I think she might have if she hadn't been warned, and if you yourself weren't so extraordinarily interesting in appearance, Daneel. But never mind that. Captain Baley was so enormously pressing in his desire that I see you, and my interest in maintaining comfortable relations with an important Settler world was such, that I have agreed to the interview. However, my day remains busy even so, and I will be grateful if we can dispose of this quickly. What can I do for you?'

'Madam Quintana –' began Daneel.

'One moment. Do you sit? I saw you sitting last night, you know.'

'We can sit, but it is just as comfortable for us to stand. We do not mind.'

'But I do. It would not be comfortable for me to stand,

and if I sit, I will get a stiff neck looking up at you. Please pull up chairs and sit down. Thank you. Now Daneel, what is this all about?'

'Madam Quintana,' said Daneel, 'you remember, I imagine, the incident of the blaster fired at the balcony last night after the banquet.'

'I certainly do. What's more, I know it was a humanoid robot who held the blaster, even though we are not admitting that officially. Yet here I sit with two robots on the other side of the desk, and have no protection. And one of you is humanoid too.'

'I have no blaster, madam,' said Daneel, smiling.

'I trust not. That other humanoid robot did not look at all like you, Daneel. You're rather a work of art, do you know that?'

'I am complexly programmed, madam.'

'I mean, your appearance. But what about the blasting incident?'

'Madam, that robot has a base somewhere on Earth and I must know where it is. I have come from Aurora in order to find that base and prevent such incidents as may disturb the peace between our worlds. I have reason to believe – '

'*You* have come? Not the Captain? Not Madam Gladia?'

'*We*, madam,' said Daneel. 'Giskard and I. I am in no position to tell you the whole story of how we came to have undertaken the task, and there is no way in which I can tell you the name of the human being under whose instructions we work.'

'Well! Interstellar espionage! How fascinating! What a pity I can't help you, but I don't know where the robot came from. I haven't any idea at all where his base might be. I don't even know why you have come to me for such information, as a matter of fact. I should have gone to the Department of Security, had I been you, Daneel.' She leaned towards him. 'Do you have *real* skin on your face,

Daneel? It's an extraordinary imitation, if it isn't.' She reached towards him and her hand rested delicately on his cheek. 'It even feels right.'

'Nevertheless, madam, it is not real skin. It does not heal of its own accord, if cut. On the other hand, a tear can easily be welded closed, or a patch can even be replaced.'

'Ugh,' said Quintana, with a wrinkle of her nose. 'But our business is over, for I can't help you as far as that blaster-user is concerned. I know nothing.'

Daneel said, 'Madam, let me explain further. This robot may be part of a group that is interested in the early energy-producing process you described last night – fission. Assume this is so; that there are those interested in fission and in the content of uranium and thorium in the crust. What might be a convenient place for them to use as a base?'

'An old uranium-mine, perhaps? I don't even know where such might be located. You must understand, Daneel, that Earth has an almost superstitious aversion to anything nuclear – to fission, in particular. You'll find almost nothing about fission in our popular works on energy and only bare essentials in technical productions for experts. Even I know very little, but then I'm an administrator, not a scientist.'

Daneel said, 'One more item, then, madam. We questioned the would-be assassin as to the location of his base, and did so most strenuously. He was programmed to undergo permanent inactivation, a total freezing of his brain-paths, in such a case – and he *did* inactivate. Before doing so, however, in his final struggle between answering and inactivation, he opened his mouth three times as though – possibly – to say three syllables, or three words, or three groups of words, or any combination of these. The second syllable, or word, or mere sound, was "mile". Does this mean anything to you as having anything at all to do with fission?'

Slowly, Quintana shook her head. 'No, I can't say it does. It's certainly not a word you'll find in a dictionary of Standard Galactic. I'm sorry, Daneel. It's pleasant meeting you again, but I have a desk full of trivia to work through. You'll excuse me.'

Daneel said, as though he hadn't heard her, 'I was told, madam, that "mile" might be an archaic expression that refers to some ancient unit of length, one that is possibly longer than a kilometre.'

'That sounds totally irrelevant,' said Quintana, 'even if true. What would a robot from Aurora know about archaic expressions and ancient – ' She stopped abruptly. Her eyes widened and her face lost colour.

She said, 'Is it possible?'

'Is what possible, madam?' asked Daneel.

'There is a place,' said Quintana, half-lost in thought, 'that is avoided by everyone – Earthpeople and Earth robots alike. If I wanted to be dramatic, I would say it was a place of ill-omen. It is so ill-omened that it has been all but wiped out of conscious existence. It is not even included in maps. It is the quintessence of all that fission means. I remember coming across it in a very old reference film in my early days on this job. It was talked about constantly, then, as the site of an "incident" that forever turned the minds of Earthpeople against fission as an energy-source. The place is called "Three Mile Island".'

Daneel said, 'An isolated place, then, absolutely isolated and free from any possible intrusion; the sort of place one would surely come across when working one's way through ancient reference material on fission and would then recognize at once as an ideal base where absolute secrecy was required; and with a three-word name of which "mile" is the second word. That *must* be the place, madam. Could you tell us how to get there, and could you arrange some way of allowing us to leave the City and be taken to Three Mile Island, or its nearest possible vicinity?'

Quintana smiled. She seemed younger when she smiled. 'Clearly, if you are dealing with an interesting case of interstellar espionage, you can't afford to waste time, can you?'

'No. Indeed we cannot, madam.'

'Well, then, it comes within the purview of my duties to take a look at Three Mile Island. Why don't I take you by air-car? I can handle an air-car.'

'Madam, your work-load – '

'No one will touch it. It will still be here when I return.'

'But you would be leaving the City – '

'And if so? These are not old times. In the bad old days of Spacer domination, Earthpeople never left their Cities, it's true, but we've been moving outward and settling the Galaxy for nearly twenty decades. There are still some of the less educated who maintain the old provincial attitude, but most of us have become quite mobile. There's always the feeling, I suppose, that we might eventually join some Settler group. I, myself, don't intend to, but I fly my own air-car frequently and five years ago, I flew to Chicago and then, eventually, flew back. Sit here. I'll make the arrangements.'

She left, very much a whirlwind.

Daneel looked after her and murmured, 'Friend Giskard, that, somehow, did not seem characteristic of her. Have you done something?'

Giskard said, 'A bit. It seemed to me when we entered that the young woman who showed us in was attracted by your appearance. I was certain that there had been the same factor in Madam Quintana's mind last night at the banquet, though I was too far from her and there were too many others in the room for me to be sure. Once our conversation with her began, however, the attraction was unmistakable. Little by little, I strengthened it and each time she suggested the interview might come to an end, she seemed less determined, and at no time did she seriously object to your continuing it. Finally, she suggested the air-car because, I believe, she had reached the point where she could not bear to lose the chance to be with you for a while longer.'

'This may complicate matters for me,' said Daneel, thoughtfully.

'It is in a good cause,' said Giskard. 'Think of it in terms of Zeroth Law.' Somehow, he gave the impression, in saying so, that he would be smiling, if his face allowed such an expression.

89.

Quintana drew a sigh of relief as she landed the air-car on a concrete slab suitable for the purpose. Two robots approached at once for the obligatory examination of the vehicle, and for re-powering, if necessary.

She looked out to the right, leaning across Daneel as she did so. 'It is in that direction, several kilometres up the Susquehanna River. It's a hot day, too.' She straightened, with some apparent reluctance, and smiled at Daneel. 'That's the worst of leaving the City. The environment is totally uncontrolled out here. Imagine allowing it to be this hot. Don't you feel hot, Daneel?'

'I have an internal thermostat, madam, that is in good working order.'

'Wonderful. I wish I did. There are no roads into this area, Daneel. Nor are there any robots to guide you, for they never enter it. Nor do I know what might be the right place within the area, which is a sizeable one. We might stumble all through the area without coming upon the base even though we passed within five hundred metres of it.'

'Not "we", madam. It is necessary for you to remain here. What follows might conceivably be dangerous, and since you are without air-conditioning, the task might be more than you could easily bear, physically, even if it were not dangerous. Could you wait for us, madam? To have you do so would be important to me.'

'I will wait.'

'We may be some hours.'

'There are facilities of various sorts here, and the small City of Harrisburg is not far.'

'In that case, madam, we must be on our way.'

He sprang lightly from the air-car and Giskard followed him. They set off northward. It was nearly noon, and the bright summer Sun sparkled from the polished portions of Giskard's body.

Daneel said, 'Any signs of mental activity you can detect will be those we want. There should be no one else for kilometres about.'

'Are you certain that we can stop them if we encounter them, Friend Daneel?'

'No, Friend Giskard, I am by no means certain – but we must.'

90.

Levular Mandamus grunted and looked up at Amadiro with a tight smile on his thin face.

'Amazing,' he said, 'and most satisfactory.'

Amadiro mopped his brow and cheeks with a piece of towelling and said, 'What does that mean?'

'It means that every relay station is in working order.'

'Then you can initiate intensification?'

'As soon as I calculate the proper degree of W-particle concentration.'

'And how long will that take?'

'Fifteen minutes. Thirty.'

Amadiro watched with an air of intensifying grimness on his face until Mandamus said, 'All right. I have it. It's 2.72 on the arbitrary scale I have set up. That will give us fifteen decades before an upper equilibrium level will be reached that will be maintained without essential change for millions of years thereafter. And that level will make certain that, at best, Earth can maintain a few scattered groups in areas that are relatively radiation-free. We'll have only to wait and, in fifteen decades, a thoroughly disorganized group of Settler worlds will be meat for our slicing.'

'I will not live fifteen more decades,' said Amadiro, slowly.

'My personal regrets, sir,' said Mandamus, dryly, 'but we are now talking of Aurora and the Spacer worlds. There will be others who will carry on your task.'

'You, for instance?'

'You have promised me the Headship of the Institute and, as you see, I have earned it. From that political base, I may reasonably hope to become Chairman some day, and I will carry through those policies that will be necessary to make certain of the final dissolution of the by-then anarchic worlds of the Settlers.'

'That's pretty confident of you. What if you turn on the W-particle flow and then someone else turns it down in the course of the next fifteen decades?'

'Not possible, sir. Once the device is set, an internal atomic shift will freeze it in that position. After that, the process is irreversible, whatever happens here. The whole place may be vaporized and the crust will nevertheless continue its slow burn. I suppose it would be possible to rebuild an entirely new set-up if anyone on Earth or among the Settlers can duplicate my work, but if so they can only further increase the rate of radioactivity, never decrease it. The Second Law of Thermodynamics will see to that.'

Amadiro said, 'Mandamus, you say you have earned the Headship. However, I'm the one to decide that, I think.'

Mandamus said, stiffly, 'You are not, sir. With respect, the details of this process are known to me, but not to you. Those details are encoded in a place you will not find, and, even if you do, it is guarded by robots who will destroy it rather than allow it to fall into your hands. You cannot gain credit for this. I can.'

Amadiro said, 'Nevertheless, getting my approval will hasten matters for you. If you were to wrest the Headship from my unwilling hands, by whatever means, you will have a continuing opposition among other members of the Council that will hamper you through all your decades in the post. Is it just the title of Head you want, or the opportunity to experience all that comes of true leadership?'

Mandamus said, 'Is this the time to talk politics? A moment ago, you were all impatience over the fact that I might linger fifteen minutes over my computer.'

'Ah, but we are now talking about adjusting the W-particle beam. You want to place it at 2.72 – was that the figure? – and yet I wonder if that can be right? What is the extreme range you can handle?'

'The range goes from zero to twelve, but it is 2.72 that is required. Plus or minus 0.05, if you wish further detail. It is that which, on the basis of reports from all fourteen relays, will allow a lapse of fifteen decades to equilibrium.'

'Yet what I think is the correct figure is twelve.'

Mandamus stared at the other in horror. 'Twelve? Do you understand what that means?'

'Yes. It means we will have the Earth too radioactive to live upon in a decade or a decade and a half, and we will kill a few billion Earthpeople in the process.'

'*And* make certain a war with an infuriated Settler federation. What can you want of such a holocaust?'

'I tell you again. I do not expect to live another fifteen decades, and I want to live to see the destruction of Earth.'

'But you would also be assuring the maiming – maiming, at the very least – of Aurora. You cannot be serious.'

'But I am. I have twenty decades of defeat and humiliation to make up.'

'Those decades were brought about by Han Fastolfe and Giskard, and not by Earth.'

'No, they were brought about by an Earthman, Elijah Baley.'

'Who has been dead for more than sixteen decades. What is the value of a moment of vengeance over a man long dead?'

'I do not want to argue the matter. I will make you an offer. Headship at once. I will resign my post the instant we return to Aurora and nominate you in my place.'

'*No*. I do not want the Headship on those terms. Death to billions!'

'Billions of *Earthmen*. Well, I cannot trust you, then, to manipulate the controls properly. Show me – *me* – how to set the control instrument, and *I* will take the responsibility. I will still resign my post on return, and nominate you in my place.'

'*No*. It will still mean the death of billions and who knows how many millions of Spacers as well. Dr Amadiro, please understand that I will not do it on any terms and that you cannot do it without me. The setting mechanism is keyed to my left thumbprint.'

'I ask you again.'

'You cannot be sane, if you ask me again despite all I have said.'

'That, Mandamus, is a personal opinion of yours. I am not so insane that I have failed to send off all the local robots on one errand or another. We are alone here.'

Mandamus lifted a corner of his upper lip in a sneer. 'And with what do you intend to threaten me? Are you going to kill me now that there are no robots present to stop you?'

'Yes, as a matter of fact, Mandamus, I will, if I have to.' Amadiro produced what was an undoubted blaster of small calibre from a pouch at his side. 'These are difficult to obtain on Earth, but not impossible, if the price is right. And I know well how to use it. Please believe me when I tell you that I am perfectly willing to blow your head off right now, if you do not place your thumb on the contact and allow me to adjust the dial to twelve.'

'You dare not. If I die, how will you set the dial without me?'

'Don't be an utter fool. If I blow your head off, your left thumb will remain intact. It will even be at blood heat for a while. I will use that thumb, then set the dial as easily as I would turn on a water tap. I would prefer you alive since your death might be wearisome to explain back on Aurora, but it would not be more wearisome than I could bear. Therefore, I give you thirty seconds to make up your mind. If you cooperate, I will still give you the Headship at once. If you don't, it will all go as I wish in any case, and you will be dead. We start now. One – two – three – '

Mandamus stared in horror at Amadiro, who continued to count and stared at him over the levelled blaster with hard, expressionless eyes.

And then Mandamus said, in a tight hiss, 'Put the blaster

away, Amadiro, or we'll both be immobilized on the plea
that we must be protected from harm.'

The warning came too late. Quicker than the eye could
follow, an arm stretched out to seize Amadiro's wrist,
paralysing it with pressure, and the blaster was gone.

Daneel said, 'I apologize for having had to inflict pain on
you, Dr Amadiro, but I cannot allow you to hold a blaster
pointed at another human being.'

91.

Amadiro said nothing.

Mandamus said, coldly, 'You are two robots with, as far
as I can see, no master in view. By default, I am your
master, and I order you to leave and not return. Since, as
you see, there is no danger to any human being present at
this moment, there is nothing to overcome your necessi-
tated obedience to this order. Leave at once.'

Daneel said, 'Respectfully, sir, there is no need to hide
our identities or abilities from you, since you know them
already. My companion, R. Giskard Reventlov, has the
ability to detect emotion. Friend Giskard.'

Giskard said, 'As we approached, having detected your
presence at quite a distance, I took note, Dr Amadiro, of an
overwhelming rage in your mind. In yours, Dr Mandamus,
there was extreme fear.'

'The rage, if rage there was,' said Mandamus, 'was Dr
Amadiro's reaction to the approach of two strange robots,
especially of one who was capable of meddling with the
human mind, and who had already badly, and perhaps
permanently, damaged that of Lady Vasilia. My fear, if
fear there was, was also the result of your approach. We
are now in control of our emotions and there is no reason

for you to interfere. We again order you to withdraw permanently.'

Daneel said, 'Your pardon, Dr Mandamus, but I merely wish to ascertain that we may safely follow your orders. Was there not a blaster in Dr Amadiro's hand when we approached, and was it not pointed at you?'

Mandamus said, 'He was explaining its workings, and he was about to put it away when you took it from him.'

'Then shall I return it to him, sir, before I leave?'

'No,' said Mandamus, without a quiver, 'for then you would have an excuse to remain here in order to, as you would say, protect us. Take it with you when you go and you will have no reason to return.'

Daneel said, 'We have reason to think that you are here in a region which human beings are not allowed to penetrate –'

'That is a custom, not a law, and one which, in any case, holds no force over us since we are not Earthpeople. For that matter, robots are not allowed to be here, either.'

'We were brought here, Dr Mandamus, by a high official of Earth's government. We have reason to think that you are here in order to raise the level of radioactivity in Earth's crust and do grave and irreparable damage to the planet.'

'Not at all –' began Mandamus.

Here Amadiro interrupted for the first time. 'By what right, robot, do you cross-examine us? We are human beings who have given you an order. Follow it now!'

His tone of authority was overwhelming and Daneel quivered, while Giskard half-turned.

But Daneel said, 'Your pardon, Dr Amadiro. I do not cross-examine. I merely seek reassurance in order that I may know that I can safely follow the order. We have reason to think that –'

'You need not repeat,' said Mandamus. Then, in an

aside, 'Dr Amadiro, please allow me to answer.' To Daneel again, 'Daneel, we are here on an anthropological mission. It is our purpose to seek the origins of various human customs that influence behaviour among Spacers. These origins can be found only here on Earth, and it is here, then, that we seek them.'

'Do you have Earth's permission for this?'

'Seven years ago, I consulted the appropriate officials on Earth and received their permission.'

Daneel said, in a low voice, 'Friend Giskard, what do you say?'

Giskard said, 'The indication in Dr Mandamus's mind is that what he is saying is not in accord with the situation as it is.'

'He is lying, then?' said Daneel, firmly.

'That is my belief,' said Giskard.

Mandamus said, his calmness untouched, 'That may be your belief, but belief is not certainty. You cannot disobey an order on the basis of mere belief. I know that, and you know that.'

Giskard said, 'But in Dr Amadiro's mind, rage is dammed only by emotional forces that are barely up to the job required of them. It is quite possible to slit those forces, so to speak, and allow the rage to pour out.'

And Amadiro cried out, 'Why do you fence with these things, Mandamus?'

Mandamus shouted, 'Do not say a word, Amadiro. You play into their hands.'

Amadiro paid no attention. 'It is demeaning, and it is useless.' He shook off, with violent anger, Mandamus's restraining arm. 'They know the truth, but what of that? Robots, we are Spacers. More than that, we are Aurorans, from the world on which you were constructed. More than that, we are high officials on the world of Aurora, and you must interpret the phrase "human beings" in the Three Laws of Robotics as meaning Aurorans.

'If you do not obey us now, you harm us and humiliate us, so that you will be violating both the First and Second Laws. That our actions here are intended to destroy Earthmen, even large numbers of Earthmen, is true, but is, even so, utterly irrelevant. You might as well offer to refuse to obey us because we eat the meat of animals we have killed. Now that I have explained this to you, leave!'

But the last words turned into a croak. Amadiro's eyes bulged, and he crumpled to the ground.

Mandamus, with a wordless cry, bent over him.

Giskard said, 'Dr Mandamus, Dr Amadiro is not dead. He is at the moment in a coma from which he can be roused at any time. However, he will have forgotten everything in connection with this present project; nor will he ever be able to understand anything in connection with it, if, for instance, you tried to explain it. In the process of doing this – which I could not have done without his own admission that he intended to destroy large numbers of Earthmen – I may have permanently damaged other parts of his memory and his thinking processes. That I regret, but I could not help it.'

Daneel said, 'You see, Dr Mandamus, some time ago, on Solaria, we encountered robots who narrowly defined human beings as Solarians only. We recognize the fact that if different robots are subject to narrow definitions of one sort or another, there can only be measureless destruction. It is useless to try to have us define human beings as Aurorans only. We define human beings as all members of the species, *Homo sapiens*, which includes Earthpeople and Settlers, and we feel that the prevention of harm to human beings in groups and to humanity as a whole comes before the prevention of harm to any specific individual.'

Mandamus said, breathlessly, 'That is not what the First Law says.'

'It is what I call the Zeroth Law, and it takes precedence.'

'You have not been programmed in such a way.'

'It is how I have programmed myself. And since I have known from the moment of our arrival here, that your presence is intended for harm, you cannot order me away, or keep me from harming you. The Zeroth Law takes precedence and I must save Earth. Therefore, I ask you to join me, voluntarily, in destroying these devices you have here. Otherwise, I will be forced to threaten harm to you, as Dr Amadiro did, although I would not use a blaster.'

But Mandamus said, 'Wait! Wait! Hear me out. Let me explain. That Dr Amadiro has had his mind wiped clean is a good thing. He *wanted* to destroy Earth, but I did *not* want to. That was why he held a blaster on me.'

Daneel said, 'It was you, however, who originated the notion, who designed and built these devices. Otherwise, Dr Amadiro would not have had to try to force you to do anything. He would have done it himself and would not have required any help from you. Isn't that right?'

'Yes, that is right. Giskard can examine my emotions and see if I'm lying. I built these devices, and I was prepared to use them, but not in the fashion Dr Amadiro wished. Am I telling the truth?'

Daneel looked at Giskard, who said, 'As nearly as I can tell, he is telling the truth.'

'Of course I am,' said Mandamus. 'What *I* am doing is to introduce a very gradual acceleration of the natural radioactivity in the Earth's crust. There will be 150 years during which the people of Earth can move to other worlds. It will increase the population of the present Settler worlds, and build additional Settler worlds in great numbers. It will remove Earth as 'a huge, anomalous world that forever threatens the Spacers and stultifies the Settlers. It will remove a centre of mystical fervour that is holding back the Settlers. Am I telling the truth?'

Again, Giskard said, 'As nearly as I can tell, he is telling the truth.'

'My plan, if it works out, would preserve the peace and make the Galaxy a home for Spacer and Settler alike. That is why, when I constructed this device –'

He gestured towards it, placing his left thumb on the contact, and then, lunging towards the volume control, shouted, 'Freeze!'

Daneel moved towards him and stopped, frozen, right hand upraised. Giskard did not move.

Mandamus turned back, panting. 'It's at 2.72. It's done. It's irreversible. Now it will be played out exactly as I intend. Nor can you bear witness against me, for you will start a war, and your Zeroth Law forbids that.'

He looked down at the prone body of Amadiro and said, with a cold look of contempt, 'Fool! You will never know how it should have been done.'

19

Alone

92.

Mandamus said, 'You cannot harm me now, robots, for nothing you do to me will alter the fate of the Earth.'

'Nevertheless,' said Giskard, shakily, 'you must not remember what you have done. You must not explain the future to the Spacers.' He reached for a chair and, with a trembling hand, pulled it towards himself and sat down, as Mandamus crumpled and slid down into what seemed to be a gentle sleep.

'At the last,' said Daneel, in soft despair, as he looked down at the two unconscious bodies, 'I failed. When it was necessary for me to seize Dr Mandamus to prevent harm to people who were not present before my eyes, I found myself forced to follow his order and froze. The Zeroth Law did not work.'

Giskard said, 'No, Friend Daneel, you did not fail. I prevented you. Dr Mandamus had the urge to try to do what he did, and was held back by fear of what you would certainly do if he did try. I neutralized his fear, and then I neutralized you. So Dr Mandamus set the Earth's crust on fire, so to speak – on very slow fire.'

Daneel said, 'But why, Friend Giskard, why?'

'Because he was telling the truth. I told you so. *He* thought he was lying. From the nature of the triumph in his mind, I am under the firm impression he felt that the consequence of the growing radioactivity would be anarchy and confusion among Earthpeople and Settlers, and that the Spacers would destroy them and seize the Galaxy. But

I thought the scenario he presented to us to win us over was the correct one. The removal of Earth as a large crowded world would remove a mystique I have already felt to be dangerous, and would help the Settlers. They will streak outward into the Galaxy at a pace that will double and redouble and, without Earth to look back to always, without Earth to set up a god of the past, they will establish a Galactic Empire. It was necessary for us to make that possible.' He paused, and, his voice weakening, he said, 'Robots and Empire.'

'Are you well, Friend Giskard?'

'I cannot stand, but I can still talk. Listen to me. It is time for you to take on my burden. I have adjusted you for mental detection and control. You have but to listen to the final pathway that you will be able to impress upon yourself. Listen –'

He spoke steadily, but increasingly weakly, in language and symbols that Daneel could feel internally. Even as Daneel listened, he could feel the pathways moving and ticking into place. And when Giskard was done, there was suddenly the cool purr of Mandamus's mind impinging on his own, the unsteady thumping of Amadiro's, and the thin, metallic thread of Giskard's.

Giskard said, 'You must return to Madam Quintana, and arrange to have these two human beings sent back to Aurora. They will not be able to harm Earth further. Then see to it that Earth's security forces seek out and inactivate the humanoid robots sent to Earth by Mandamus.

'Be careful how you use your new powers, for you are new to them – and they will not be under perfect control. You will improve with time slowly, if you are careful always to undergo self-examination with each use. Use the Zeroth Law, but not to justify needless harm to individuals. First Law is almost as important.

'Protect Madam Gladia and Captain Baley – unobtrusively. Let them be happy together, and let Madam Gladia continue with her efforts to bring peace. Help supervise, over the decades, the removal of Earthpeople from this world. And – one more thing – if I can remember – Yes – if you can – find out where the Solarians have gone. That may be – important.'

Giskard's voice trailed off.

Daneel kneeled at the side of the seated Giskard and took the unresponsive metal hand in his own. He said, in an agonized whisper, 'Recover, Friend Giskard. Recover. What you did was right by Zeroth Law. You have preserved as much life as possible. You have done well by humanity. Why suffer so, when what you have done saves all?'

Giskard said, in a voice so distorted, the words could barely be made out, 'Because I am not certain. What if – the other view – is right – after all – and the Spacers will – triumph and then themselves decay so that – the Galaxy – will be – empty. – Good-bye, Friend – Dan –'

And Giskard was silent, never to speak or move again.

Daneel rose.

He was alone – and with a Galaxy to care for.